THE CAMBRIDGE EDITION OF THE WORKS OF
F. SCOTT FITZGERALD

(TO BE SAVED)

DATA ON NEW FITZGERALD BOOK.

Title

ALL THE SAD YOUNG MEN

(9 short stories)

Print list of previous books as before with addition of this
title under "Stories". Binding uniform with others
Jacket plain (as you suggest,) with text instead of picture
Dedication: To Ring and Ellis Lardner

The Stories (now under revision) will reach you by
July 15th. No proofs need be sent over here!
It will be fully up to the other collections, and will contain
only one of those Post stories that people were so
snooty about (you have read only one of the stories
("Absolution") — all the others were so good that I
had difficulty in selling them, except two.

To be used in book:

They are, in approximate ~~publishing~~ order ~~to be used~~

1. The Rich Boy (Just finished. Serious story and very good)	13,000	wds.
2. Absolution ("from Mercury)	6,500	"
3. Winter Dreams (A sort of 1st draft of the Gatsby idea from Metropolitan 1923)	9,000	"
4. Rags Martin-Jones and the Prince of Wales (Fantastic Jazz, so good that Lorimer & Long refused it. from McCalls)	6,000 5,000	" "
5. The Baby Party (from Hearsts. A fine story)		
6. Dice, Brass Knuckles and Guitar (from Hearsts. Exuberant Jazz in my early manner)	8,000	"
7. The Sensible Thing (Story about Zelda + me. All True. from Liberty)	5,000	"
8. Hot & Cold Blood (Good story, from Hearsts)	6,000	"
9. Gretchen's Forty Winks (From Post. Farrar, Christian Gauss and Jesse Williams thought it my best. It isn't)	7,000	"

Total — about - - - - - - - - - - - - - - - 64,500

(And possibly one other short one)

ALL THE SAD
YOUNG MEN

* * *

F. SCOTT FITZGERALD

Edited by
JAMES L. W. WEST III

CAMBRIDGE
UNIVERSITY PRESS

CAMBRIDGE UNIVERSITY PRESS
Cambridge, New York, Melbourne, Madrid, Cape Town, Singapore, São Paulo

Cambridge University Press
The Edinburgh Building, Cambridge CB2 2RU, UK

Published in the United States of America by Cambridge University Press, New York

www.cambridge.org
Information on this title: www.cambridge.org/9780521402408

First published 2007

Printed in the United Kingdom at the University Press, Cambridge

A catalogue record for this publication is available from the British Library

ISBN-13 978-0-521-40240-8 hardback
ISBN-10 0-521-40240-9 hardback

CONTENTS

ALL THE SAD YOUNG MEN

ADDITIONAL STORIES, April 1925–April 1928

ACKNOWLEDGMENTS

I thank Eleanor Lanahan, Thomas P. Roche, Jr., and Chris Byrne, the Trustees of the F. Scott Fitzgerald Estate, for their interest and support. I am grateful to Phyllis Westberg of Harold Ober Associates, Inc., for helping with permissions and for other advice and assistance. Special thanks to Cecilia Ross for access to the Fitzgerald manuscripts that are held by his grandchildren.

Illustrations for this volume are reproduced from the F. Scott Fitzgerald Papers and the Charles Scribner's Sons Archives, Manuscript Division, Department of Rare Books and Special Collections, Princeton University Library. The cover of the transcript for the Daddy Browning–Peaches Heenan divorce trial is reproduced, with permission, from the copy in the University of Minnesota Law Library. Page 16 from the typescript of "Magnetism" is reproduced from the F. Scott Fitzgerald Collection, Clifton Waller Barrett Library, Special Collections, University of Virginia Library.

Don C. Skemer, AnnaLee Pauls, and Margaret Sherry Rich at Princeton were unfailingly cheerful and helpful. For assistance in solving two problems of emendation and annotation, I thank Marissa Ain of the Yale Club, New York City, and Scott Surrency of the Department of Italian at Pennsylvania State University. Bryant Mangum and Benita A. Moore, colleagues in the Fitzgerald field, generously made the results of their own research available to me. Richard Buller and Tim Young helped me to acquire the photograph of Lois Moran.

At Penn State I am grateful to Susan Welch, Dean of the College of the Liberal Arts; to Ray Lombra, Associate Dean for Research; and to Robert L. Caserio, Head of the Department of English, for their continuing support. Research assistance was provided by LaVerne Kennevan Maginnis, Jeanne Alexander, Robert R. Bleil, and Gregg Baptista.

J. L. W. W. III

ILLUSTRATIONS

(Beginning on page 495)

Frontispiece. F. Scott Fitzgerald to Maxwell Perkins, ca. 1 June 1925.

INTRODUCTION

I. BACKGROUND

The first edition of F. Scott Fitzgerald's short-fiction collection *All the Sad Young Men* (1926) contains nine stories, including three of his best—"The Rich Boy," "Winter Dreams," and "Absolution." The entire collection is strong: its themes are consistent from story to story, its characters are memorable, and its language is pitch-perfect and luminous. Fitzgerald began to assemble and revise the material for the collection in May 1925, a few weeks after formal publication of *The Great Gatsby*. He was in Paris and had recently settled into an apartment at 14 rue de Tilsitt with his wife and daughter. Fitzgerald believed that *Gatsby* would demonstrate to reviewers and readers that he had achieved new maturity and control in his writing. He wanted *All the Sad Young Men* to reinforce this impression.

Early in June, Fitzgerald wrote to Maxwell Perkins, his editor at Charles Scribner's Sons, giving this tentative table of contents:

ALL THE SAD YOUNG MEN
(9 short stories)
...

1.	The Rich Boy (Just finished. Serious story and very good)	13,000	wds.
2.	Absolution (From *Mercury*)	6,500	"
3.	Winter Dreams (A sort of 1st draft of the Gatsby idea from *Metropolitan* 1923)	9,000	"
4.	Rags Martin-Jones and the Pr-nce of Wales (Fantastic Jazz, so good that Lorimer + Long refused it. From *McCalls*)	6,000	"
5.	The Baby Party (From *Hearsts*. A fine story)	5,000	"
6.	Dice, Brass Knuckles and Guitar (From *Hearsts*. Exuberant Jazz in my early manner)	8,000	"

7. The Sensible Thing (Story about Zelda + me. All   5,000   "
   True. From *Liberty*)
8. Hot + Cold Blood (Good Story, from *Hearsts*)   6,000   "
9. Gretchen's Forty Winks (From Post. Farrar, Christian   7,000   "
   Gauss and Jesse Williams thought it my best. It isn't.)

   Total – about --- 64,500
   (And possibly one other short one)[1]

Perkins was enthusiastic. He cleared the way for *All the Sad Young Men* to pass quickly through production and into print for the fall season—a fairly simple task, since Scribners maintained its own manufacturing plant on West 43rd Street, and the printers there could move the occasional book through on an accelerated schedule. By 9 July, Perkins was having the dust-jacket art prepared; on 27 July he sent the royalty agreement to Fitzgerald, noting in his accompanying letter, however, that the promised manuscript had not yet arrived.[2] It took Fitzgerald another month to send the manuscript.

---

[1] *Dear Scott/Dear Max: The Fitzgerald–Perkins Correspondence*, ed. John Kuehl and Jackson R. Bryer (New York: Scribners, 1971): 112–13. Misspellings and other irregularities in Fitzgerald's letters are reproduced without correction in this introduction. George Horace Lorimer was the editor of the *Saturday Evening Post*; Ray Long edited *Hearst's International*. John Farrar, then the editor of *The Bookman*, had reviewed *Tales of the Jazz Age* for the *New York Herald* (8 October 1922), and *The Vegetable* for *The Bookman* (September 1923). Christian Gauss, a professor of modern languages at Princeton, was Fitzgerald's mentor during his undergraduate years at the university. Jesse Lynch Williams, who had co-founded the Triangle Club at Princeton with Booth Tarkington in 1891, was a fiction-writer and playwright whose 1917 drama *Why Marry?* won a Pulitzer Prize.

[2] In a 9 May letter, Perkins asked Fitzgerald whether he would send typescripts to be used as setting copies by the compositors or whether he, Perkins, should have someone locate the texts in back issues of the magazines in which they had first appeared. Fitzgerald did not answer the question in any letter that has survived, but he revised the stories so heavily for their appearances in *All the Sad Young Men* that he must necessarily have had fresh typescripts made and sent these to Perkins. Whether Fitzgerald began his revising on his own sets of tearsheets or on carbon typescripts is not known, except in the case of "The Rich Boy," which had not yet appeared in *Red Book*, and for which Fitzgerald began revising on a carbon. (Tearsheets are copies of the published serial texts, torn from the magazines in which they appeared.)

In his cover letter to Perkins, dated 28 August, he explained the delay: "Here's the stuff," he wrote. "I've been working over it for a month—especially this version of *The Rich Boy*. The Red Book hasn't yet published it but I have asked them to hurry + they should by November."[3]

The problem with the publication date for "The Rich Boy" in *Red Book* ended up delaying the release of *All the Sad Young Men*. Fitzgerald had begun the story in March 1925 and had worked on it during the spring and summer months that followed, sending a version to his literary agent, Harold Ober, in early August. Ober had sold that version to *Red Book* for a high price—$3,500. The magazine wanted to publish "The Rich Boy" as a two-part story but could not clear the necessary space until January and February 1926. The *Red Book* editors therefore told Perkins and Fitzgerald, with apologies, that Scribners would have to wait until late February to release *All the Sad Young Men*. The magazine wanted to publish the story first, before Fitzgerald put it between hard covers.

Author and editor now relaxed. Fitzgerald had not asked initially to see galleys of the collection, but now there was time for him to do so, even with the proofs passing back and forth across the Atlantic. Galleys were mailed to him in mid-October; he marked them and had them back to Perkins by 25 November. Bound copies of *All the Sad Young Men* were ready in early January, and Fitzgerald had a copy in his hands by the 19th. "It is beautiful," he wrote to Perkins. "Max, I'm enormously obliged" (*Dear Scott/Dear Max*, 130).

The nine stories that Fitzgerald chose for the Scribners edition of *All the Sad Young Men* had all been published in magazines: "The Rich Boy," *Red Book*, 46 (January–February 1926); "Winter Dreams," *Metropolitan Magazine*, 56 (December 1922); "The Baby

---

[3] *Dear Scott/Dear Max*, p. 119. Fitzgerald had withdrawn "Dice, Brassknuckles and Guitar" from the original table of contents, sent to Perkins early in June, and had substituted "The Adjuster." "Dice," an early presentation of the poor boy–rich girl theme found in *Gatsby*, has been reprinted in the Cambridge edition of *Tales of the Jazz Age* (2002), pp. 277–97. The version printed there derives from a set of tearsheets revised by Fitzgerald when he meant to include "Dice" in *All the Sad Young Men*. The tearsheets are among his papers at Princeton.

Party," *Hearst's International*, 47 (February 1925); "Absolution," *American Mercury*, 2 (June 1924); "Rags Martin-Jones and the Pr-nce of W-les," *McCall's*, 51 (July 1924); "The Adjuster," *Red Book*, 45 (September 1925); "Hot and Cold Blood," *Hearst's International*, 44 (August 1923); "'The Sensible Thing,'" *Liberty*, 1 (5 July 1924); and "Gretchen's Forty Winks," *Saturday Evening Post*, 196 (15 March 1924).

All the Sad Young Men was formally published on 26 February 1926 at a price of $2.00. It sold well: a first printing of 10,100 was quickly exhausted; two more printings followed, one in March of 3,020 copies and another in May of 3,050. This was an unusually strong sale for a collection of short fiction. *The Great Gatsby*, a novel, had only sold around 21,000 copies the previous spring.

The notices for *All the Sad Young Men* were nearly all laudatory. Many reviewers noted that Fitzgerald's writing had become more sophisticated and that a new artistry was apparent in his work. Several critics gave extra praise to "The Rich Boy," "Winter Dreams," and "Absolution." "Mr. Fitzgerald has graduated from the jazz age," wrote Henry F. Pringle in the *New York World* (28 February). "These are splendid pieces of work," said an anonymous reviewer for the *Cleveland Plain Dealer* (14 March); "they prove that Fitzgerald's is no mere flashy talent, but a deep and comprehensive one." "The level of achievement is high," wrote James Gray in the *St. Paul Dispatch* (2 March). "Fitzgerald has acquired maturity, a happy profundity," said the anonymous reviewer for the *Milwaukee Journal* (12 March). "It is a joy to read these tales," said Harry Hansen in the *Chicago Daily News* (3 March). A few reviewers hit sour notes: one found the majority of the stories to be "entirely lacking in any real distinction," and another felt that not one of the stories measured "up to standard."[4] In the main, however, the notices were positive. Fitzgerald must have been pleased.

---

[4] These and other reviews of *All the Sad Young Men* have been reprinted in *F. Scott Fitzgerald: The Critical Reception*, ed. Jackson R. Bryer (New York: Burt Franklin, 1978): 253–80. The two disapproving notices are by R. Ellsworth Larsson in the *New York Sun* (27 March) and John McClure in the *New Orleans Times-Picayune* (11 April).

2. ADDITIONAL STORIES

The eleven short stories added to this volume of the Cambridge edition were not collected by Fitzgerald during his lifetime. They are the uncollected stories that he published in magazines between 10 April 1925, the publication date of *The Great Gatsby*, and 28 April 1928, when the first installment of the Basil Duke Lee series, "The Scandal Detectives," appeared in the *Saturday Evening Post*. (The Basil stories will appear in an upcoming volume of the Cambridge edition.) Many of these additional narratives are excellent: "The Dance," "The Love Boat," "The Bowl," and "Magnetism" are as good as all but the best of Fitzgerald's short fiction; and "Jacob's Ladder" is one of the dozen or so best stories he ever wrote. If Fitzgerald had lived longer, he would surely have collected some of these stories, but he managed to publish only one more volume of short fiction— *Taps at Reveille* (1935)—before he died in 1940. And, too, some of these stories were so closely related to his novels that he might have hesitated to reprint them until late in his career. "The Love Boat," for example, echoes many of the themes in *The Great Gatsby*; and both "Jacob's Ladder" and "Magnetism" were mined for words and phrases that reappear in *Tender Is the Night*.[5]

The Cambridge edition is an *omnium gatherum*: these uncollected stories have been included so that readers can see the full range of Fitzgerald's production during this period. The eleven additional stories are as follows: "One of My Oldest Friends," *Woman's Home Companion*, 52 (September 1925); "A Penny Spent," *Saturday Evening Post*, 198 (10 October 1925); "'Not in the Guidebook,'" *Woman's Home Companion*, 52 (November 1925); "Presumption,"

---

[5] It was Fitzgerald's habit, especially in the middle and late years of his career, to use short stories as dress rehearsals for the characters, themes, and language that would appear in his novels. For the textual borrowing between "Jacob's Ladder" and *Tender Is the Night*, see George Anderson, "F. Scott Fitzgerald, Emile Zola, and the Stripping of 'Jacob's Ladder' for *Tender Is the Night*," in Richard Layman and Joel Myerson, eds., *The Professions of Authorship: Essays in Honor of Matthew J. Bruccoli* (Columbia: University of South Carolina Press, 1996): 169–83. See also Alan Margolies, "Climbing 'Jacob's Ladder,'" in *New Essays on F. Scott Fitzgerald's Neglected Stories*, ed. Jackson R. Bryer (Columbia: University of Missouri Press, 1996): 89–103.

Saturday Evening Post, 198 (9 January 1926); "The Adolescent Marriage," *Saturday Evening Post*, 198 (6 March 1926); "The Dance," *Red Book*, 47 (June 1926); "Your Way and Mine," *Woman's Home Companion*, 54 (May 1927); "Jacob's Ladder," *Saturday Evening Post*, 200 (20 August 1927); "The Love Boat," *Saturday Evening Post*, 200 (8 October 1927); "The Bowl," *Saturday Evening Post*, 200 (21 January 1928); and "Magnetism," *Saturday Evening Post*, 200 (3 March 1928).

3. EDITORIAL PRINCIPLES

No copy-texts have been declared for these stories. This editorial procedure has been described by G. Thomas Tanselle in "Editing without a Copy-Text," *Studies in Bibliography*, 47 (1994): 1–22. Equal authority is vested in serial and collected texts and, where appropriate, in the holographs and typescripts that precede them. Emending decisions are recorded in the apparatus.[6]

This is the first volume of short fiction in the Cambridge edition for which a significant amount of holograph and typescript evidence survives. For the original nine stories a holograph survives for "Rags Martin-Jones," and typescripts are extant for "The Rich Boy," "The Adjuster," "Hot and Cold Blood," and "Gretchen's Forty Winks." For the eleven added stories, typescripts survive for "A Penny Spent," "'Not in the Guidebook,'" "The Adolescent Marriage," "The Dance," "Your Way and Mine," "Jacob's Ladder," "The Love Boat," "The Bowl," and "Magnetism." The typescripts are quite helpful: most of them bear Fitzgerald's handwritten revisions, and three of them preserve passages that were expurgated before publication. A description of the evidence that survives for each story appears at the head of the emendations for that story in the apparatus. The authority of each document is commented on there, and the strategy for emendation is described. As in all

---

[6] For an elaboration of this approach, see "Editorial Principles" in *This Side of Paradise*, ed. James L. W. West III (Cambridge: Cambridge University Press, 1995): xl–xlii.

collections of this kind, each story represents a separate editorial problem.

For the nine stories chosen by Fitzgerald for the 1926 volume we also have magazine texts which, when collated against the Scribners versions, yield the revising (much of it quite heavy) that Fitzgerald did in the spring of 1925, plus any revisions in proof that he introduced that autumn. These variants can be attributed to Fitzgerald with confidence. The collations have revealed no evidence of unwarranted editorial intrusion at Scribners—no sophistications or expurgations or fancied improvements. The magazine texts, and the holographs and typescripts that precede them, when they survive, sometimes exhibit spelling, punctuation, word division, and capitalization that are more characteristic of Fitzgerald's known usages than are similar features of the Scribners texts. Several of the typescripts, however, were prepared by typists in France or Italy who automatically imposed British forms of spelling, punctuation, and word division on the texts—single instead of double quotation marks in dialogue, for example, or *-ise* and *-our* spellings. Revisions by Fitzgerald in the wording or punctuation of these typescripts carry considerable authority, but, because he could not type, the texture of *typed* accidentals in these same documents has been treated with some skepticism and has not been assigned unduly heavy weight.

Fitzgerald introduced no late revisions into any of the stories in this volume. He kept tearsheets of many of the stories but did not make revisions on them. No copy of the Scribners 1926 edition of *All the Sad Young Men*, with revisions marked by Fitzgerald, is known to survive. Machine collation discloses no plate variants in the second and third impressions. No British edition of the collection was published. Several of the stories were reprinted during Fitzgerald's lifetime in Canadian or British magazines; five were syndicated; three were reprinted in short-fiction anthologies. None of these reprintings contains authoritative revisions.[7]

---

[7] See section C of Matthew J. Bruccoli, *F. Scott Fitzgerald: A Descriptive Bibliography*, revised edn. (Pittsburgh: University of Pittsburgh Press, 1987), entries 121, 135, 140, 148, 149, 158, 159, 161, 164, 165, 168, 169, 175, and 176.

When Fitzgerald made his initial selections for *Taps at Reveille* in 1934, he included "Jacob's Ladder" in the collection. Perkins had the story set up in type and mailed the galley proofs to Fitzgerald. So many passages in "Jacob's Ladder" had been transferred to *Tender Is the Night*, however, that Fitzgerald, when he reread the story in galleys, decided not to include it in *Taps*. The galley proofs survive among his papers at Princeton.

"The Rich Boy"

The history of composition for "The Rich Boy" had a significant effect on its published texts.[8] Fitzgerald began writing the story in March 1925 while he and his wife, Zelda, were vacationing in Capri. In April he told Ober that he was "stretching" the story "into a three parter called *The Rich Boy* which might bring $5000.00 or so from College Humor or the Red Book."[9] Fitzgerald promised to mail the story to Ober in a week, but illness (his and Zelda's) slowed his progress. By late May he had returned to Paris and had given the third version of the story to a typist, but that version did not entirely suit him, and he continued to revise the text into July. "*The Rich Boy* has been a scource of much trouble but its in shape at last," he told Ober; "I'm rewriting the 3d part this week" (*As Ever, Scott Fitz—*, 79). Finally in early August he sent Ober a complete ribbon typescript bearing heavy handwritten revisions. Ober had the story retyped and sold it to *Red Book*. "The Rich Boy" was published there in two parts, as noted earlier, in January and February 1926.

Fitzgerald, in Paris, had retained a carbon copy of the typescript he had mailed to Ober. Using this carbon he continued to revise "The Rich Boy" for *All the Sad Young Men*, putting the story through at least one more intermediate typescript and arriving at a version that pleased him by late August. This final version was mailed to Perkins

---

[8] The account that follows is drawn from James L. W. West III and J. Barclay Inge, "F. Scott Fitzgerald's Revision of 'The Rich Boy,'" *Proof*, 5 (1977): 127–46.

[9] Fitzgerald to Ober, ca. 6 April 1925, in *As Ever, Scott Fitz—Letters between F. Scott Fitzgerald and His Literary Agent, Harold Ober, 1919–1940*, ed. Matthew J. Bruccoli and Jennifer McCabe Atkinson (Philadelphia and New York: Lippincott, 1972): 77.

on the 28th, together with setting-copy typescripts for the other stories in the collection.

Four versions of "The Rich Boy" survive today, two of them embodied in a single document: (a) the typed text of the surviving typescript of the *Red Book* version, *before* Fitzgerald revised it by hand; (b) the text of this same typescript *after* Fitzgerald had revised it by hand; (c) the serial text from *Red Book*, and (d) the collected text from *All the Sad Young Men*. Collations among these four versions show that the carbon copy retained by Fitzgerald in Paris did not bear the same late handwritten revisions that he had made on the typescript sent to Ober. (That is to say, Fitzgerald did not transfer these revisions from the ribbon onto the carbon before putting the ribbon copy into the transatlantic mail.) As a consequence, three separate patterns of textual variation emerge:

1. Fitzgerald does not revise a reading on the Ober typescript but does revise it on the carbon, or on a subsequent typescript. The original reading therefore appears in *Red Book*; the revised reading is published in *All the Sad Young Men*.
2. Fitzgerald revises a reading on the Ober typescript but does not revise it on the carbon or on a later typescript. The revised reading therefore appears in *Red Book*; the original reading is printed in *All the Sad Young Men*.
3. Fitzgerald revises a reading on the Ober typescript, then revises it differently on the carbon, or on a subsequent typescript. The first revised reading is published in *Red Book*; the second revised reading appears in *All the Sad Young Men*.

In order to produce an eclectic text (here one might call it a portmanteau text), an editor might theoretically blend the revisions from categories 1 and 2. The readings in category 3, however, would present problems. Which readings should have precedence? Probably those from *All the Sad Young Men*, since that text falls later in the revising process—but should the surviving versions of "The Rich Boy" in fact be merged in this way? If Fitzgerald had wanted to preserve the revisions from the typescript mailed to Ober, he would presumably have done so. After studying the four texts and performing experiments in blending, the editor has decided that it would be a mistake to

-6-

he fell in love with a conservative and rather proper girl.

Her name was Paula Legendre, a dark, serious young beauty from California. Her family kept a winter residence just outside of town and she was enormously popular, for there is a large class of men whose egotism can't endure humor in a woman. But Anson wasn't like that and I couldn't understand the attraction of her "sincerity" (that was the thing to say about her) for his keen and somewhat sardonic mind.

Nevertheless they fell in love, and on her terms, for he no longer joined the twilight gathering at the De Sota bar, and whenever they were seen together they were engaged in a long, serious dialogue that must have gone on several weeks. Long afterwards he told me that it was not about anything in particular but was composed on both sides of immature and even meaningless statements — the emotional content that gradually came to fill it grew up not out of the words but out of its enormous seriousness. It was a sort of hypnosis. Often it was interrupted, giving way to that simple humor called fun; when they were alone it was resumed again, solemn, low-keyed, pitched so as to give each other a sense of one-ness in feelings and thoughts. They came to resent any interruptions of it, to be unresponsive to facetiousness about life, even to the mild cynicism of their contemporaries with which they had until recently agreed. They were only happy when the dialogue was going on and its seriousness enveloped them like the amber shadow of an open fire. Toward the end

Page 6 from the revised ribbon typescript of "The Rich Boy," which Fitzgerald mailed to Harold Ober for sale to *Red Book*. The passage that Fitzgerald has deleted does not appear in the magazine text, but because he did not cut it from the carbon copy, it is printed in *All the Sad Young Men*. Fitzgerald Papers, Princeton University Libraries.

attempt an eclectic text. The two published texts, for *Red Book* and *All the Sad Young Men*, were produced for different appearances in print. Blending these texts produces an unsatisfactory hybrid, especially in sentences that conflate the revising done in different stints of work. The text published in this edition is that of *All the Sad Young Men*.[10]

A by-product of this collating has been the discovery that "The Rich Boy" was expurgated before it appeared in *Red Book*. Predictably a "God damned" from the typescript becomes "damned" in the serial text (Cambridge text, 29), but more noteworthy is the removal of references to Paula Legendre's swollen shape during pregnancy. Readers of "The Rich Boy" will remember that, near the end of the story, on a hot Friday afternoon in May, Anson Hunter (the protagonist) runs into Paula, his earliest love, in the lobby of the Plaza Hotel. She is now Mrs. Peter Hagerty and is expecting her fourth child. The text of the typescript reads: "Near the revolving door the figure of a woman, obviously with child, stood sideways to the light" (Cambridge text, 37). The words "obviously with child" were edited out before the story appeared in *Red Book*.

Paula invites Anson to spend the weekend with her and her husband at their country home, and he accepts. When they arrive at Paula's house, her three children welcome her by hugging her. The typescript reads: "Abstractedly and with difficulty Paula took each one into her arms, a caress which they accepted stiffly, as they had evidently been told not to bump into Mummy" (Cambridge text, 38). Again the reference to Paula's shape seems to have been judged improper for *Red Book* readers; the sentence appears in the magazine in truncated form, with a full stop after "arms." The alteration makes Paula appear cool toward her children, or perhaps clumsy, and the reader has still not been told that she is pregnant.

These editorial excisions make for difficulties when Anson learns, a month later, that Paula has died in childbirth. A copy-editor at *Red*

---

[10] The surviving typescript of "The Rich Boy" (essentially, the *Red Book* version) is available for comparison and study. It has been facsimiled in *F. Scott Fitzgerald Manuscripts*, vol. 6, part 1, ed. Matthew J. Bruccoli (New York and London: Garland, 1991): 173–233.

Book must have recognized the problem and tried to make a quick repair by changing "This baby" to "The baby that's coming," but the remedy is inadequate. Readers of the *Red Book* text must have been puzzled: Paula dies in childbirth without its having been made clear that she is pregnant. Fortunately the version published in *All the Sad Young Men* was not similarly meddled with. The references to Paula's pregnancy are published there without alteration, and the reader is not wrong-footed.

Another type of change was requested by Ludlow Fowler, the model for Anson Hunter. Fowler, a classmate of Fitzgerald's at Princeton, had served as best man when Fitzgerald married Zelda in 1920, and the two men had remained on friendly terms. (Fowler was one of the few people present at Fitzgerald's funeral in 1940.) While composing "The Rich Boy," Fitzgerald wrote to Fowler as follows:

I have written a fifteen thousand word story about you called *The Rich Boy*—it is so disguised that no one except you and me and maybe two of the girls concerned would recognize, unless you give it away, but it is in a large measure the story of your life, toned down here and there and symplified. Also many gaps had to come out of my imagination. It is frank, unsparing but sympathetic and I think you will like it—it is one of the best things I have ever [d]one. Where it will appear and when, I don't as yet know.[11]

Fitzgerald sent a version of "The Rich Boy" to Fowler in September 1925—likely a carbon copy of the typescript he had mailed to Perkins. After reading the story, Fowler contacted Fitzgerald, asking that two passages be cut before the story was published in *Red Book*. Fitzgerald agreed: on 1 October he wired Ober, "PLEASE CUT AS FOWLER REQUESTS" (*As Ever, Scott Fitz—*, 80). Later that month Fitzgerald wrote in a letter to Ober, "Too bad about the Fowler changes—still the Red Book shouldn't mind making them as they're both rather realistic, crude statements for a popular magazine. It is the story of his life—he's an old friend—we went to Princeton

---

[11] Fitzgerald to Fowler, n.d. [March 1925], in *Correspondence of F. Scott Fitzgerald*, ed. Matthew J. Bruccoli and Margaret M. Duggan (New York: Random House, 1980): 152.

together + he told me those things in confidence" (*As Ever, Scott Fitz—*, 81).

Fitzgerald could not make the cuts himself because he was in Paris. He seems to have assumed that Fowler would go to Ober's office and indicate which passages he wanted to have removed. Fowler, for his part, apparently believed that Fitzgerald would contact Ober and identify the passages. As it turned out no one made the cuts, and the two passages appeared in the *Red Book* text. Fitzgerald made sure that the cuts were made for *All the Sad Young Men*. When he asked Perkins in October to send him galley proofs, he explained, "The reason I want to get proof on *The Rich Boy* is that the original of the hero wants something changed—something that would identify him" (*Dear Scott/Dear Max*, 122). Fitzgerald made the cuts on the proofs, and the passages do not appear in *All the Sad Young Men*. They have not been reinstated to the Cambridge text but are printed in an appendix of this volume, together with another passage from the typescript (anti-semitic comments by Robert Hunter, Anson's uncle) that appears neither in *Red Book* nor in *All the Sad Young Men*.

"Winter Dreams"

The characters and themes of "Winter Dreams" are quite close to those of *The Great Gatsby*. Fitzgerald referred to the story as a "sort of 1st draft of the Gatsby idea" in the letter he wrote to Perkins in early June. Fitzgerald had taken several passages from the serial text in *Metropolitan* and had incorporated them, slightly revised, into *Gatsby*. This was a common practice for him, especially when he had produced, for a short story, some particularly good descriptive passages or some especially telling lines of dialogue. His rule in such cases was either not to reprint the story at all, if the borrowings were heavy, or to remove or rewrite the passages if he did reprint the story. He chose the second strategy with "Winter Dreams," carefully cutting or reworking the text that he had transferred to *Gatsby* and in the process thoroughly revising the rest of the story. Midway through the *Metropolitan* text, for example, one finds this passage:

But what gave it an air of breathless intensity was the sense that it was inhabited by Judy Jones—that it was as casual a thing to her as the little house in the village had once been to Dexter. There was a feeling of mystery in it, of bedrooms upstairs more beautiful and strange than other bedrooms, of gay and radiant activities taking place through these deep corridors and of romances that were not musty and laid already in lavender, but were fresh and breathing and set forth in rich motor cars and in great dances whose flowers were scarcely withered. They were more real because he could feel them all about him, pervading the air with the shades and echoes of still vibrant emotion.

An altered but still quite recognizable version of this paragraph appears on pages 177–78 of the Scribners first edition of *Gatsby*. Fitzgerald cut the passage entirely in revising "Winter Dreams" for *All the Sad Young Men*.

Several paragraphs along in the *Metropolitan* text, one discovers another passage that Fitzgerald reused in *Gatsby*, on page 179 of the first edition:

Suddenly she turned her dark eyes directly upon him and the corners of her mouth drooped until her face seemed to open like a flower. He dared scarcely to breathe; he had the sense that she was exerting some force upon him, making him overwhelmingly conscious of the youth and mystery that wealth imprisons and preserves, the freshness of many clothes, of cool rooms and gleaming things, safe and proud above the hot struggles of the poor.

The porch was bright with the bought luxury of starshine. The wicker of the settee squeaked fashionably when he put his arm around her, commanded by her eyes. He kissed her curious and lovely mouth and committed himself to the following of a grail.

Here Fitzgerald rewrote the two paragraphs entirely, producing this version for *All the Sad Young Men*:

Then she smiled and the corners of her mouth drooped and an almost imperceptible sway brought her closer to him, looking up into his eyes. A lump rose in Dexter's throat, and he waited breathless for the experiment, facing the unpredictable compound that would form mysteriously from the elements of their lips. Then he saw—she communicated her excitement to him, lavishly, deeply, with kisses that were not a promise but a fulfillment.

They aroused in him not hunger demanding renewal but surfeit that would demand more surfeit . . . kisses that were like charity, creating want by holding back nothing at all.

It did not take him many hours to decide that he had wanted Judy Jones ever since he was a proud, desirous little boy. (Cambridge text, 54)

The revision of "Winter Dreams," of which these passages offer typical examples, was heavy enough to produce two independent versions of the story. The differences cannot adequately be represented in a table of variants. The revised version, which appeared first in *All the Sad Young Men*, is published in this volume.[12] The magazine version has been reprinted twice recently and can be consulted as a full text for comparison.[13]

4. RESTORATIONS AND REGULARIZATIONS

For "The Love Boat," "Jacob's Ladder," and "Magnetism"— published in 1927 and 1928 in the *Saturday Evening Post*—the extant typescripts are unusually valuable. Collation of these typescripts against the serial texts has uncovered expurgations in all three stories, meant to scrub out any touch of sex or scandal, however faint. These verbal cleansings were designed to render the stories suitable for the broad, conventional, middle-class readership of the *Post*. No purpose will be served now by criticizing such editorial practices. The *Post* wished to avoid controversy, and Fitzgerald (who liked to know that his stories reached enormous audiences through the magazine and who wanted the top money that it paid to its authors) must have known that any objection from him would have

---

[12] Thomas E. Daniels has argued at length, but unconvincingly, that the *Metropolitan* version of "Winter Dreams" should function as copy-text for a scholarly edition of the story. See "The Texts of 'Winter Dreams,'" *Fitzgerald/Hemingway Annual 1977*: 77–100.

[13] For the *Metropolitan* version of "Winter Dreams," a text now in the public domain, see James L. W. West III, *The Perfect Hour: The Romance of F. Scott Fitzgerald and Ginevra King* (New York: Random House, 2005); and *The Best Early Stories of F. Scott Fitzgerald*, ed. Bryant Mangum (New York: Modern Library, 2005).

been futile. It is not certain that he saw magazine proofs or knew of these expurgations. No evidence survives to show that he compared the *Post* texts, after they were published, to typescripts that he might have saved. Fitzgerald used sex and scandal sparingly in his fiction, but he knew how to employ both with telling effect. The survival of his typescripts has made it possible to reinstate the excised words and sentences and to restore the passages to the form in which he originally created them.

"Jacob's Ladder"

The surviving typescript of "Jacob's Ladder," preserved by the Ober agency in its files, is now at Princeton. In that typescript (which bears Fitzgerald's final handwritten revisions) the sixteen-year-old Jenny Delehanty, soon to take the screen name Jenny Prince, offers herself sexually to Jacob Booth as a form of thanks to him for sponsoring her budding movie career. Jenny and Jacob are riding together in "the dark cave" of a taxi-cab. She kisses him and he reciprocates, but "without enjoying it." She is too young, and he senses that her offer of herself is insincere. Fitzgerald writes:

> . . . there was no shadow of passion in her eyes or on her mouth, there was a faint spray of champagne on her breath. She clung nearer, desperately. He took her hands and put them in her lap. *Her childish intention of giving herself to him shocked him.*
> "*You're young enough to be my daughter,*" he said.
> "*You're not so old.*"
> She leaned away from him resentfully.
> "What's the matter? Don't you like me?"   (Cambridge text, 340)

The italicized words above disappear between the typescript and the *Post* text, making Jenny's intentions unclear. Does she simply want more kisses? If that is all, then why does Jacob react as he does?

Later in the story, Jacob visits Jenny in Hollywood. She is older and has had several successes on the screen; Jacob decides that he now wants a full romantic involvement with her, but she has changed her mind. In the typescript he says to her: "If I didn't thrill you, as you call it, why were you so ready to make me a present of yourself last summer?" (Cambridge text, 351). In the *Post* text, the second part of the sentence has become bland: "why did you seem to care so much last summer?"

Apart from these bleachings, one also discovers a series of typographical effects in the final paragraphs of "Jacob's Ladder" that Fitzgerald wanted but that the *Post* was unable, or perhaps was disinclined, to provide. Jacob has now realized that he is never to have Jenny. By the end of the story she has become a woman, a professional cinema actress, and is no longer the girl he fell in love with earlier. And, she tells him, she has herself fallen for another man—a young actor in Hollywood. Jacob, crushed, says farewell to Jenny at the Plaza Hotel, where she is staying during a visit to New York. Then he walks west along 59th Street to Columbus Circle, where he turns south and walks down Broadway. At 51st Street he sees Jenny's name on the marquee of the Capitol Theatre—an enormous gilded movie palace, a cavernous shrine where viewers came during the 1920s to worship the images of film stars. The Capitol is showing one of Jenny's early movies. Jacob realizes that the Jenny he loves is still present in that film, captured by the camera, always young, impervious to change and to the passage of time. He created this woman: he invented her screen name, Jenny Prince, and bestowed it on her. Now that name hovers above his head. Here are the final few paragraphs of the story as Fitzgerald originally wrote them:

The name startled him, as if a passer-by had spoken it. He stopped and stared. Other eyes rose to that sign, people hurried by him and turned in.

Jenny Prince.

Now that she no longer belonged to him, the name assumed a significance entirely its own. It hung there, cool and impervious on the night, a challenge, a defiance.

Jenny Prince.

"Come and rest upon my loveliness," it said. "Fulfill your secret dreams in wedding me for an hour."

JENNY PRINCE.

It was untrue—she was back at the Plaza Hotel, in love with somebody. But the name, with its bright insistence, rode high upon the night.

"I love my dear public. They are all so sweet to me."

The wave appeared far off, sent up white-caps, rolled toward him with the might of pain, washed over him. Never any more. Never any more. Beautiful child who tried so hard one night to give herself to me. Never any more. Never any more. The wave beat upon him, drove him down, pounding with hammers of agony on his ears. Proud and impervious, the name on high challenged the night.

JENNY PRINCE

She was there! All of her, the best of her—the effort, the power, the triumph, the beauty. Jacob moved forward with a group and bought a ticket at the window. Confused, he stared around the great lobby. Then he saw an entrance and, walking in, found himself a place in the vast throbbing darkness. (Cambridge text, 357–58)

Fitzgerald marked his typescript to show the expansion of Jenny's name in Jacob's mind—from simple roman letters, to italics, to full capitals, to large centered caps (see the facsimile on page xxix). The *Post*, publishing this passage in narrow-gauge columns on a back page, did not reproduce the effects that Fitzgerald wanted. Because the typescript has survived, it has been possible to restore these effects in the Cambridge text.

Near the end of the story, Fitzgerald had also meant to touch one final time on Jacob's earlier refusal of Jenny's sexual advances. Jacob muses: "Beautiful child who tried so hard one night to give herself to me." These words were cut from the text, along with the repetitive chant that follows: "Never any more. Never any more." (Overtones of Keats are obvious in the story; the repetition of "Never any more" calls to mind "Nevermore" in "The Raven," Poe's lament for the lost Lenore.) And finally, a typist's left index finger appears to have erred, striking the "f" key instead of the "v" just below and producing "fast throbbing darkness" instead of "vast throbbing darkness" as the last three words of the story.[14] In the *Post* text a hyphen has been added to produce "fast-throbbing." All subsequently published texts of "Jacob's Ladder" have followed the *Post* version, printing the earlier passages in expurgated form, printing "Jenny

[14] The extant typescript of "Jacob's Ladder," bearing Fitzgerald's final handwritten revisions, was sent to Ober for retyping and sale to the *Post*. Probably the "vast/fast" typo occurred during this retyping.

him with the might of ~~sleepy~~ pain, washed over him. Never any more.
Never any more. ~~My~~ Beautiful child who tried so hard one night to
give herself to me. Never any more . Never any more. The wave
beat upon him, drove him down, pounding with hammers of agony on
his ears. Proud and impervious, the name on high challenged the
night.

JENNY PRINCE ← large letters

She was there! All of her the best of her — the effort,
the power, the triumph, the beauty. Jacob moved forward with a
group and bought a ticket at the window. Confused he stared around
the great lobby. Then he saw an entrance and walking in, found
himself a place in the vast throbbing darkness.

37

The final page of the surviving typescript of "Jacob's Ladder," with Fitzgerald's handwritten revisions and his instructions about type size and location. Fitzgerald Papers,
Princeton University Libraries.

Prince" with no typographical variation, and ending the story with "fast-throbbing darkness" instead of "vast throbbing darkness."[15] The correct readings from the surviving typescript have been restored in this edition. The text of "Jacob's Ladder" as Fitzgerald originally wrote it is published here for the first time.

"The Love Boat"

Between typescript and print, "The Love Boat" was deprived of a reference to a tabloid scandal of the 1920s that was tawdry but appropriate. In the first scene of the story Bill Frothington and two of his friends, all three of them recent graduates of Harvard, crash a high-school graduation party being given on a tourist paddlewheeler on the Thames River in southern Connecticut. Bill, a rich boy, meets a pretty lower-class girl named Mae Purley at the party and pursues her that summer. They quarrel, however, and he breaks off the romance. After serving in the First World War, Bill comes home and marries a woman from his own social class. Eight years pass. Bill, now in his early thirties and weary of his marriage, returns to the same town at the same time of year and seeks out Mae. She too has married, and her beauty has faded.

Bill knows that he probably cannot recapture his lost youth, but fortified by a strong dose of brandy he makes a final attempt. He wanders down to the river and sees a paddlewheeler about to depart from the dock, again with a party of high-school seniors aboard for a graduation party. Bill goes onto the boat and insinuates himself into the festivities. Tipsy and fragrant from the brandy, he begins to cut in on the young dancers, particularly on a girl named May who resembles Mae Purley as she looked when she was young. Bill tries to persuade May to come with him to a private part of the boat, but she refuses. In Fitzgerald's original text, in both the surviving holograph and the typescript, the teenage boys begin to make fun of Bill:

> "I'm Daddy Browning," somebody was saying. "I got a swell love-nest up in the Bronx, Peaches."

---

[15] The *Post* text of "Jacob's Ladder" has been reprinted in *Bits of Paradise*, ed. Matthew J. Bruccoli (New York: Scribners, 1973); and in *The Short Stories of F. Scott Fitzgerald: A New Collection*, ed. Matthew J. Bruccoli (New York: Scribners, 1989).

(35)

~~evil-minded old school marm~~ "

When he danced with Mae again
he was cut in on almost immediately.
People were cutting in all over the
dancing floor, now — evidently he had
started something. He cut back, and again
he started ~~to~~ suggest ~~that~~ they go
outside but ~~he allen~~ he saw that
her attention was held by some ~~horsepla~~
horse-play going on across the room.

"I'm Daddy Browning," somebody
was saying, "I got a swell love-nest
up in the Bronx, ~~and~~ Peaches."

"Won't you come outside ~~with~~
me", said Bill, "There's the most
wonderful moon".

"I'd rather dance",

"We could dance out there."

She leaned away from him
and looked up with innocent scorn
into his eyes.

Page 35 from Fitzgerald's composite typescript/manuscript of "The Love Boat," with mention of Daddy Browning and Peaches Heenan. These references were cut before the story appeared in the *Saturday Evening Post* and have been restored to the Cambridge text. Fitzgerald Papers, Princeton University Libraries.

And several paragraphs along:

> "Just look at old Daddy Browning step."
> "Hey, Peaches."
> "Peaches, ask him if I can have some of this dance."
>
> (Cambridge text, 377–78)

Who was Daddy Browning? Who was Peaches? They were in fact the principals in a lurid divorce case covered by the tabloids during the fall and winter of 1926–27, less than a year before "The Love Boat" appeared in the *Post*. In 1925 Edward "Daddy" Browning, a millionaire in his early fifties, married Frances "Peaches" Heenan, a chubby fifteen-year-old girl he had met at a high-school dance. The marriage was short-lived. Peaches, egged on by her mother, sued Daddy for divorce in October 1926, alleging mental cruelty and sexual perversion and charging, among other things, that Daddy had kept a honking gander in their bedroom. The trial was given wide coverage by the press: the judge did not believe Peaches' story and suspected her and her mother of gold-digging; he awarded Peaches only a small settlement. Four days after the verdict, however, Peaches signed a $100,000 vaudeville contract and began to appear on stage, clad in a skimpy outfit and accompanied by a pet gander, which was itself decked out in a hat and bow tie. For several months, while public curiosity lasted, Peaches recounted to her audiences the tale of her marriage to Daddy.[16]

By mentioning Daddy Browning and Peaches, the boys in "The Love Boat" are saying that Bill has a sexual yen for May. There is nothing subtle about the taunt: to these boys Bill is foolish and lecherous. But in the *Post* text, and therefore in the only subsequent reprinting of the story, all mention of Daddy Browning and Peaches has been removed.[17] Bill is now only called "daddy"—once, in lower-case. He seems harmless, a man in early middle age who is nostalgic for his lost youth. Readers of 1927 would have known

---

[16] See *The New Encyclopedia of American Scandal*, ed. George Childs Kohn (New York: Facts on File, Inc., 2001).

[17] The *Post* text of "The Love Boat" has been reprinted in *The Price Was High: The Last Uncollected Stories of F. Scott Fitzgerald*, ed. Matthew J. Bruccoli (New York: Harcourt Brace Jovanovich, 1979).

immediately what was being implied by the reference to Daddy and Peaches, had it remained in the story. Fitzgerald must have wanted the ambiguity. Bill might only be making an innocent attempt to relive his past, but as a bored husband in his early thirties he might also have something else in mind. This ambiguity has been reintroduced in the Cambridge text of "The Love Boat," which follows the typescript and restores Daddy Browning and Peaches to the story.

"Magnetism"

Evidence of bowdlerization at the *Post* is also found in the prepublication materials that survive for "Magnetism." Here the setting-copy typescript itself is extant, not at Princeton but at the Barrett Library, University of Virginia. This typescript bears the markings of the *Post* editors and shows how the story was wiped clean of sexual innuendo.

"Magnetism," set in Hollywood, tells the story of George Hannaford, a popular movie star, and his wife, Kay Tompkins, a film actress. George and Kay are engaged in a simmering argument over Helen Avery, an ingénue with whom George is starring in a movie and with whom he has been having a mild flirtation. In retaliation Kay has rekindled an old romance with a man named Arthur Busch. She has attended a party, with Arthur and George as joint escorts, and has staged an affectionate scene with Arthur in such a way that George will be certain to see it. Now she and George are back home, preparing to go to bed. They sleep in separate bedrooms, but with a connecting bath. George wants to smooth over the quarrel; he understands that his wife does not really love Arthur Busch, and he is certain that he does not love Helen Avery.

Kay, however, wishes to prolong the hostilities. In the original typed text of the setting copy, she says: "I'm going upstairs. Please don't come in my room tonight" (Cambridge text, 417). A copy-editor at the *Post*, working in green ink, has flagged the second sentence, and another editor, using a red pencil, has struck the sentence out, substituting the single word "Goodnight"—which accordingly appears in the *Post*. A full collation of this setting copy against the *Post* text reveals that there was additional expurgation in proof. Later in the story, George (now on better terms with Kay) enters her

-16-

homeward through the clear California night.

He said nothing, Kay said nothing. He was incredulous.
He suspected that Kay had kissed a man here and there, but he had
never seen it happen or given it any thought; this was different.
There had been an element of tenderness in it and there was something veiled and remote in Kay's eyes that he had never seen there
before.

Without having spoken, they entered the house; Kay stopped
by the library door and looked in.

"There's someone there," she said, and she added without
interest; "I'm going upstairs. ~~Please don't come in my room tonight.~~" *Good night.*

As she ran up the stairs the person in the library stepped
out into the hall.

"Mr. Hannaford—"

He was a pale somewhat tough young man; his face was
vaguely familiar, but George didn't remember where he had seen it
before.

"Mr. Hannaford?" said the young man, "I recognize you from
your pictures." He looked at George, obviously a little awed.

"What can I do for you?"

"Well, will you come in here?"

"What is it? I don't know who you are."

"My name is Donavan. I'm Margaret Donavan's brother." His
face hardened a little.

"Is anything the matter?"

Donavan made a motion toward the door.

Page 16 of the setting copy for "Magnetism," showing expurgation by the editors at
the *Post*. "Please don't come in my room tonight" was flagged and queried in green
ink by a copy-editor. A second editor, working in red pencil, cut the sentence and
substituted "Goodnight." Barrett Library, University of Virginia.

bedroom where, in the typescript, he finds her "sitting up in bed in her nightgown" (Cambridge text, 427). In the *Post* this phrase has become "lying down." In the same scene, several paragraphs along, the typescript reads, "Kay sat forward in the bed" (Cambridge text, 427). This sentence was removed altogether in proof and does not appear in the *Post* or in any subsequent reprinting.[18]

Married couples often smooth over arguments by using sex as a palliative. Sometimes they fight to arouse themselves for sex. Perhaps George and Kay have moved through quarrels in this way before; perhaps George wants to try the remedy again. Probably this is what Fitzgerald means, ever so subtly, to suggest—but with the editing at the *Post*, the point is lost. The lines have been restored to the Cambridge text.

Regularized features

Fitzgerald employed American spellings for most words. He did favor some British forms—"grey" and "glamour," for example, and "theatre." These have been allowed to stand. He was inconsistent about word division; study of his holographs, however, has yielded his preferences for most words, such as "good-bye," "motorboat," "taxi-cab," and "wrist watch."

Fitzgerald used italics for emphasis and, usually, for words in languages other than English. His habit was to enclose the names of books and newspapers and the titles of literary works within quotation marks. These tendencies have been followed in this edition. Question marks and exclamation points that follow italicized words are italicized. The only narrative breaks retained from serial texts are those indicated by roman or Arabic numerals. Nonstructural breaks signaled by blank space followed by a display cap—inserted by magazines to break up the text visually—have been ignored. For the stories in this volume, typescript evidence usually survives to resolve such matters of spacing.

[18] The *Post* text of "Magnetism" has been reprinted in *The Stories of F. Scott Fitzgerald*, ed. Malcolm Cowley (New York: Scribners, 1951); in *The Bodley Head Scott Fitzgerald*, vol. 5 (London: Bodley Head, 1963); and in *The Stories of F. Scott Fitzgerald*, vol. 4 (Harmondsworth, Middlesex: Penguin, 1968).

"Mother" and "Father," as proper nouns, are capitalized. Seasons are given in lower-case; years are in Arabic numerals. The numbers of cross-streets in New York City are in Arabic numerals, and numbered avenues (Fifth Avenue) are spelled out. Dashes are one-em in length; three ellipsis points appear within sentences, four at the ends of sentences.

Fitzgerald sometimes punctuated lines of dialogue this way: "I called to apologize," she added, "please excuse me." Or, "I'll be glad to sign," he said, "do you have a pen?" The second comma in these readings has been emended to a period; when necessary the first word in the second sentence of dialogue has been capitalized. Fitzgerald sometimes left the comma out between two adjectives of equal weight and nearly always omitted the comma between the final two elements in a series. He sometimes did not put a comma before the conjunction in a compound sentence. All three practices are preserved in the Cambridge texts, so long as there is no possibility of confusion.

These emendation practices have introduced a measure of consistency to the accidentals in this volume. No effort, however, has been made to create a system of pointing and to impose it on Fitzgerald's texts. To do so would only subject them to yet another round of house styling. A record of the emendations is printed in the apparatus.

ALL THE SAD YOUNG MEN

TO
RING AND ELLIS LARDNER

THE RICH BOY

Begin with an individual and before you know it you find that you have created a type; begin with a type, and you find that you have created—nothing. That is because we are all queer fish, queerer behind our faces and voices than we want anyone to know or than we know ourselves. When I hear a man proclaiming himself an "average, honest, open fellow" I feel pretty sure that he has some definite and perhaps terrible abnormality which he has agreed to conceal—and his protestation of being average and honest and open is his way of reminding himself of his misprision.

There are no types, no plurals. There is a rich boy, and this is his and not his brothers' story. All my life I have lived among his brothers but this one has been my friend. Besides, if I wrote about his brothers I should have to begin by attacking all the lies that the poor have told about the rich and the rich have told about themselves—such a wild structure they have erected that when we pick up a book about the rich, some instinct prepares us for unreality. Even the intelligent and impassioned reporters of life have made the country of the rich as unreal as fairyland.

Let me tell you about the very rich. They are different from you and me. They possess and enjoy early, and it does something to them, makes them soft where we are hard and cynical where we are trustful, in a way that, unless you were born rich, it is very difficult to understand. They think, deep in their hearts, that they are better than we are because we had to discover the compensations and refuges of life for ourselves. Even when they enter deep into our world or sink below us, they still think that they are better than we are. They are different. The only way I can describe young Anson Hunter is to approach him as if he were a foreigner and cling stubbornly to my point of view. If I accept his for a moment I am lost—I have nothing to show but a preposterous movie.

II

Anson was the eldest of six children who would some day divide a fortune of fifteen million dollars, and he reached the age of reason—is it seven?—at the beginning of the century when daring young women were already gliding along Fifth Avenue in electric "mobiles." In those days he and his brother had an English governess who spoke the language very clearly and crisply and well, so that the two boys grew to speak as she did—their words and sentences were all crisp and clear and not run together as ours are. They didn't talk exactly like English children but acquired an accent that is peculiar to fashionable people in the city of New York.

In the summer the six children were moved from the house on 71st Street to a big estate in northern Connecticut. It was not a fashionable locality—Anson's father wanted to delay as long as possible his children's knowledge of that side of life. He was a man somewhat superior to his class, which composed New York society, and to his period, which was the snobbish and formalized vulgarity of the Gilded Age, and he wanted his sons to learn habits of concentration and have sound constitutions and grow up into right-living and successful men. He and his wife kept an eye on them as well as they were able until the two older boys went away to school, but in huge establishments this is difficult—it was much simpler in the series of small and medium-sized houses in which my own youth was spent—I was never far out of the reach of my mother's voice, of the sense of her presence, her approval or disapproval.

Anson's first sense of his superiority came to him when he realized the half-grudging American deference that was paid to him in the Connecticut village. The parents of the boys he played with always inquired after his father and mother, and were vaguely excited when their own children were asked to the Hunters' house. He accepted this as the natural state of things, and a sort of impatience with all groups of which he was not the center—in money, in position, in authority—remained with him for the rest of his life. He disdained to struggle with other boys for precedence—he expected it to be given him freely and when it wasn't he withdrew into his family. His family was sufficient, for in the East money is still a somewhat feudal thing, a clan-forming thing. In the snobbish West, money separates families to form "sets."

At eighteen, when he went to New Haven, Anson was tall and thick-set with a clear complexion and a healthy color from the ordered life he had led in school. His hair was yellow and grew in a funny way on his head, his nose was beaked—these two things kept him from being handsome—but he had a confident charm and a certain brusque style, and the upper-class men who passed him on the street knew without being told that he was a rich boy and had gone to one of the best schools. Nevertheless his very superiority kept him from being a success in college—the independence was mistaken for egotism, and the refusal to accept Yale standards with the proper awe seemed to belittle all those who had. So, long before he graduated, he began to shift the center of his life to New York.

He was at home in New York—there was his own house with "the kind of servants you can't get anymore"—and his own family, of which, because of his good humor and a certain ability to make things go, he was rapidly becoming the center, and the debutante parties, and the correct manly world of the men's clubs, and the occasional wild spree with the gallant girls whom New Haven only knew from the fifth row. His aspirations were conventional enough—they included even the irreproachable shadow he would someday marry, but they differed from the aspirations of the majority of young men in that there was no mist over them, none of that quality which is variously known as "idealism" or "illusion." Anson accepted without reservation the world of high finance and high extravagance, of divorce and dissipation, of snobbery and of privilege. Most of our lives end as a compromise—it was as a compromise that his life began.

He and I first met in the late summer of 1917 when he was just out of Yale, and, like the rest of us, was swept up into the systematized hysteria of the war. In the blue-green uniform of the naval aviation he came down to Pensacola, where the hotel orchestras played "I'm Sorry, Dear" and we young officers danced with the girls. Everyone liked him, and though he ran with the drinkers and wasn't an especially good pilot, even the instructors treated him with a certain respect. He was always having long talks with them in his confident, logical voice—talks which ended by his getting himself, or more frequently another officer, out of some impending trouble. He was convivial, bawdy, robustly avid for pleasure, and we were all surprised when he fell in love with a conservative and rather proper girl.

Her name was Paula Legendre, a dark, serious beauty from somewhere in California. Her family kept a winter residence just outside of town, and in spite of her primness she was enormously popular; there is a large class of men whose egotism can't endure humor in a woman. But Anson wasn't that sort, and I couldn't understand the attraction of her "sincerity"—that was the thing to say about her—for his keen and somewhat sardonic mind.

Nevertheless, they fell in love—and on her terms. He no longer joined the twilight gathering at the De Soto bar, and whenever they were seen together they were engaged in a long, serious dialogue, which must have gone on several weeks. Long afterward he told me that it was not about anything in particular but was composed on both sides of immature and even meaningless statements—the emotional content that gradually came to fill it grew up not out of the words but out of its enormous seriousness. It was a sort of hypnosis. Often it was interrupted, giving way to that emasculated humor we call fun; when they were alone it was resumed again—solemn, low-keyed, and pitched so as to give each other a sense of unity in feeling and thought. They came to resent any interruptions of it, to be unresponsive to facetiousness about life, even to the mild cynicism of their contemporaries. They were only happy when the dialogue was going on and its seriousness bathed them like the amber glow of an open fire. Toward the end there came an interruption they did not resent—it began to be interrupted by passion.

Oddly enough Anson was as engrossed in the dialogue as she was and as profoundly affected by it, yet at the same time aware that, on his side, much was insincere and, on hers, much was merely simple. At first, too, he despised her emotional simplicity as well, but with his love her nature deepened and blossomed and he could despise it no longer. He felt that if he could enter into Paula's warm safe life he would be happy. The long preparation of the dialogue removed any constraint—he taught her some of what he had learned from more adventurous women and she responded with a rapt holy intensity. One evening after a dance they agreed to marry and he wrote a long letter about her to his mother. The next day Paula told him that she was rich, that she had a personal fortune of nearly a million dollars.

III

It was exactly as if they could say "Neither of us has anything: we shall be poor together"—just as delightful that they should be rich instead. It gave them the same communion of adventure. Yet when Anson got leave in April and Paula and her mother accompanied him north, she was impressed with the standing of his family in New York and with the scale on which they lived. Alone with Anson for the first time in the rooms where he had played as a boy, she was filled with a comfortable emotion, as though she were preeminently safe and taken care of. The pictures of Anson in a skull cap at his first school, of Anson on horseback with the sweetheart of a mysterious forgotten summer, of Anson in a gay group of ushers and bridesmaids at a wedding, made her jealous of his life apart from her in the past, and so completely did his authoritative person seem to sum up and typify these possessions of his that she was inspired with the idea of being married immediately and returning to Pensacola as his wife.

But an immediate marriage wasn't discussed—even the engagement was to be secret until after the war. When she realized that only two days of his leave remained, her dissatisfaction crystallized in the intention of making him as unwilling to wait as she was. They were driving to the country for dinner and she determined to force the issue that night.

Now a cousin of Paula's was staying with them at the Ritz, a severe bitter girl who loved Paula but was somewhat jealous of her impressive engagement, and as Paula was late in dressing, the cousin, who wasn't going to the party, received Anson in the parlor of the suite.

Anson had met friends at five o'clock and drunk freely and indiscreetly with them for an hour. He left the Yale Club at a proper time, and his mother's chauffeur drove him to the Ritz, but his usual capacity was not in evidence, and the impact of the steam-heated sitting-room made him suddenly dizzy. He knew it, and he was both amused and sorry.

Paula's cousin was twenty-five, but she was exceptionally naive, and at first failed to realize what was up. She had never met Anson before, and she was surprised when he mumbled strange information and nearly fell off his chair, but until Paula appeared it didn't occur to her that what she had taken for the odor of a dry-cleaned uniform was really whiskey. But Paula understood as soon as she appeared; her only thought was to get Anson away before her mother saw him, and at the look in her eyes the cousin understood too.

When Paula and Anson descended to the limousine they found two men inside, both asleep; they were the men with whom he had been drinking at the Yale Club, and they were also going to the party. He had entirely forgotten their presence in the car. On the way to Hempstead they awoke and sang. Some of the songs were rough, and though Paula tried to reconcile herself to the fact that Anson had few verbal inhibitions, her lips tightened with shame and distaste.

Back at the hotel the cousin, confused and agitated, considered the incident, and then walked into Mrs. Legendre's bedroom saying: "Isn't he funny?"

"Who is funny?"

"Why—Mr. Hunter. He seemed so funny."

Mrs. Legendre looked at her sharply.

"How is he funny?"

"Why, he said he was French. I didn't know he was French."

"That's absurd. You must have misunderstood." She smiled: "It was a joke."

The cousin shook her head stubbornly.

"No. He said he was brought up in France. He said he couldn't speak any English and that's why he couldn't talk to me. And he couldn't!"

Mrs. Legendre looked away with impatience just as the cousin added thoughtfully, "Perhaps it was because he was so drunk," and walked out of the room.

This curious report was true. Anson, finding his voice thick and uncontrollable, had taken the unusual refuge of announcing that he spoke no English. Years afterward he used to tell that part of the story, and he invariably communicated the uproarious laughter which the memory aroused in him.

Five times in the next hour Mrs. Legendre tried to get Hempstead on the phone. When she succeeded there was a ten-minute delay before she heard Paula's voice on the wire.

"Cousin Jo told me Anson was intoxicated."

"Oh, no. . . ."

"Oh, yes. Cousin Jo says he was intoxicated. He told her he was French and fell off his chair and behaved as if he was very intoxicated. I don't want you to come home with him."

"Mother, he's all right! Please don't worry about—"

"But I do worry. I think it's dreadful. I want you to promise me not to come home with him."

"I'll take care of it, Mother. . . ."

"I don't want you to come home with him."

"All right, Mother. Good-bye."

"Be sure now, Paula. Ask someone to bring you."

Deliberately Paula took the receiver from her ear and hung it up. Her face was flushed with helpless annoyance. Anson was stretched asleep out in a bedroom upstairs, while the dinner party below was proceeding lamely toward conclusion.

The hour's drive had sobered him somewhat—his arrival was merely hilarious—and Paula hoped that the evening was not spoiled after all, but two imprudent cocktails before dinner completed the disaster. He talked boisterously and somewhat offensively to the party at large for fifteen minutes and then slid silently under the table, like a man in an old print—but, unlike an old print, it was rather horrible without being at all quaint. None of the young girls present remarked upon the incident—it seemed to merit only silence. His uncle and two other men carried him upstairs, and it was just after this that Paula was called to the phone.

An hour later Anson awoke in a fog of nervous agony, through which he perceived after a moment the figure of his Uncle Robert standing by the door.

"... I said are you better?"

"What?"

"Do you feel better, old man?"

"Terrible," said Anson.

"I'm going to try you on another bromo-seltzer. If you can hold it down, it'll do you good to sleep."

With an effort Anson slid his legs from the bed and stood up.

"I'm all right," he said dully.

"Take it easy."

"I thin' if you gave me a glassbrandy I could go downstairs."

"Oh, no—"

"Yes, that's the only thin'. I'm all right now. . . . I suppose I'm in Dutch dow' there."

"They know you're a little under the weather," said his uncle deprecatingly. "But don't worry about it. Schuyler didn't even get here. He passed away in the locker room over at the Links."

Indifferent to any opinion, except Paula's, Anson was nevertheless determined to save the debris of the evening, but when after a cold bath he made his appearance most of the party had already left. Paula got up immediately to go home.

In the limousine the old serious dialogue began. She had known that he drank, she admitted, but she had never expected anything like this—it seemed to her that perhaps they were not suited to each other, after all. Their ideas about life were too different, and so forth. When she finished speaking, Anson spoke in turn, very soberly. Then Paula said she'd have to think it over; she wouldn't decide tonight; she was not angry but she was terribly sorry. Nor would she let him come into the hotel with her, but just before she got out of the car she leaned and kissed him unhappily on the cheek.

The next afternoon Anson had a long talk with Mrs. Legendre while Paula sat listening in silence. It was agreed that Paula was to brood over the incident for a proper period and then, if mother and daughter thought it best, they would follow Anson to Pensacola. On his part he apologized with sincerity and dignity—that was all; with every card in her hand Mrs. Legendre was unable to establish any advantage over him. He made no promises, showed no humility, only delivered a few serious comments on life which brought him off with rather a moral superiority at the end. When they came south three weeks later, neither Anson in his satisfaction nor Paula in her relief at the reunion realized that the psychological moment had passed forever.

IV

He dominated and attracted her and at the same time filled her with anxiety. Confused by his mixture of solidity and self-indulgence, of sentiment and cynicism—incongruities which her gentle mind was unable to resolve—Paula grew to think of him as two alternating personalities. When she saw him alone, or at a formal party, or with his casual inferiors, she felt a tremendous pride in his strong attractive presence, the paternal, understanding stature of his mind. In other company she became uneasy when what had been a fine imperviousness to mere gentility showed its other face. The other face was gross, humorous, reckless of everything but pleasure. It startled her mind temporarily away from him, even led her into a short covert experiment with an old beau, but it was no use—after four months of Anson's enveloping vitality there was an anaemic pallor in all other men.

In July he was ordered abroad and their tenderness and desire reached a crescendo. Paula considered a last-minute marriage—decided against it only because there were always cocktails on his breath now, but the parting itself made her physically ill with grief. After his departure she wrote him long letters of regret for the days of love they had missed by waiting. In August Anson's plane slipped down into the North Sea. He was pulled onto a destroyer after a night in the water and sent to hospital with pneumonia; the armistice was signed before he was finally sent home.

Then, with every opportunity given back to them, with no material obstacle to overcome, the secret weavings of their temperaments came between them, drying up their kisses and their tears, making their voices less loud to one another, muffling the intimate chatter of their hearts until the old communication was only possible by letters from far away. One afternoon a society reporter waited for two hours in the Hunters' house for a confirmation of their engagement. Anson denied it; nevertheless an early issue carried the report as a leading paragraph—they were "constantly seen together at Southampton, Hot Springs, and Tuxedo Park." But the serious dialogue had turned a corner into a long, sustained quarrel, and the affair was almost played out. Anson got drunk flagrantly and missed an engagement with her, whereupon Paula made certain behavioristic demands. His despair was helpless before his pride and his knowledge of himself: the engagement was definitely broken.

"Dearest," said their letters now, "Dearest, Dearest, when I wake up in the middle of the night and realize that after all it was not to be, I feel that I want to die. I can't go on living anymore. Perhaps when we meet this summer we may talk things over and decide differently—we were so excited and sad that day and I don't feel that I can live all my life without you. You speak of other people. Don't you know there are no other people for me but only you. . . ."

But as Paula drifted here and there around the East she would sometimes mention her gaieties to make him wonder. Anson was too acute to wonder. When he saw a man's name in her letters he felt more sure of her and a little disdainful—he was always superior to such things. But he still hoped that they would someday marry.

Meanwhile he plunged vigorously into all the movement and glitter of post-bellum New York, entering a brokerage house, joining half a dozen clubs, dancing late, and moving in three worlds—his own world, the world of young Yale graduates, and that section of the half-world which rests one end on Broadway. But there was always a thorough and infractible eight hours devoted to his work in Wall Street, where the combination of his influential family connection, his sharp intelligence, and his abundance of sheer physical energy brought him almost immediately forward. He had one of those invaluable minds with partitions in it; sometimes he appeared at his office refreshed by less than an hour's sleep, but such occurrences were rare. So early as 1920 his income in salary and commissions exceeded twelve thousand dollars.

As the Yale tradition slipped into the past he became more and more of a popular figure among his classmates in New York, more popular than he had ever been in college. He lived in a great house and had the means of introducing young men into other great houses. Moreover, his life already seemed secure, while theirs, for the most part, had arrived again at precarious beginnings. They commenced to turn to him for amusement and escape, and Anson responded readily, taking pleasure in helping people and arranging their affairs.

There were no men in Paula's letters now but a note of tenderness ran through them that had not been there before. From several sources he heard that she had "a heavy beau," Lowell Thayer, a Bostonian of wealth and position, and though he was sure she still loved him, it made him uneasy to think that he might lose her after all. Save for one unsatisfactory day she had not been in New York for almost five months, and as the rumors multiplied he became increasingly anxious to see her. In February he took his vacation and went down to Florida.

Palm Beach sprawled plump and opulent between the sparkling sapphire of Lake Worth, flawed here and there by house-boats at anchor, and the great turquoise bar of the Atlantic Ocean. The huge bulks of the Breakers and the Royal Poinciana rose as twin paunches from the bright level of the sand and around them clustered the Dancing Glade, Bradley's House of Chance and a dozen modistes and milliners with goods at triple prices from New York. Upon the trellissed verandah of the Breakers two hundred women stepped right, stepped left, wheeled and slid in that then celebrated calisthenic known as the double-shuffle, while in half-time to the music two thousand bracelets clicked up and down on two hundred arms.

At the Everglades Club after dark Paula and Lowell Thayer and Anson and a casual fourth played bridge with hot cards. It seemed to Anson that her kind serious face was wan and tired—she had been around now for four, five years. He had known her for three.

"Two spades."

"Cigarette? . . . Oh, I beg your pardon. By me."

"By."

"I'll double three spades."

There were a dozen tables of bridge in the room, which was filling up with smoke. Anson's eyes met Paula's, held them persistently even when Thayer's glance fell between them. . . .

"What was bid?" he asked abstractedly.

"Rose of Washington Square"

sang the young people in the corners:

"I'm withering there
In basement air—"

The smoke banked like fog, and the opening of a door filled the room with blown swirls of ectoplasm. Little Bright Eyes streaked past the tables seeking Mr. Conan Doyle among the Englishmen who were posing as Englishmen about the lobby.

"You could cut it with a knife."

". . . cut it with a knife."

". . . a knife."

At the end of the rubber Paula suddenly got up and spoke to Anson in a tense, low voice. With scarcely a glance at Lowell Thayer, they walked out the door and descended a long flight of stone steps— in a moment they were walking hand in hand along the moonlit beach.

"Darling, darling. . . ." They embraced recklessly, passionately, in a shadow. . . . Then Paula drew back her face to let his lips say what she wanted to hear—she could feel the words forming as they kissed again. . . . Again she broke away, listening, but as he pulled her close once more she realized that he had said nothing—only *"Darling! Darling!"* in that deep, sad whisper that always made her cry. Humbly, obediently, her emotions yielded to him and the tears streamed down her face, but her heart kept on crying: "Ask me—Oh, Anson, dearest, ask me!"

"Paula. . . . *Paula!*"

The words wrung her heart like hands and Anson feeling her tremble knew that emotion was enough. He need say no more, commit their destinies to no practical enigma. Why should he, when he might hold her so, biding his own time, for another year— forever? He was considering them both, her more than himself. For a moment, when she said suddenly that she must go back to her hotel, he hesitated, thinking first, "This is the moment after all," and then: "No, let it wait—she is mine. . . ."

He had forgotten that Paula too was worn away inside with the strain of three years. Her mood passed forever in the night.

He went back to New York next morning filled with a certain restless dissatisfaction. Late in April, without warning, he received a telegram from Bar Harbor in which Paula told him that she was engaged to Lowell Thayer and that they would be married immediately in Boston. What he never really believed could happen had happened at last.

Anson filled himself with whiskey that morning, and going to the office, carried on his work without a break—rather with a fear of what would happen if he stopped. In the evening he went out as usual, saying nothing of what had occurred; he was cordial, humorous, unabstracted. But one thing he could not help—for three days, in any place, in any company, he would suddenly bend his head into his hands and cry like a child.

V

In 1922 when Anson went abroad with the junior partner to investigate some London loans, the journey intimated that he was to be taken into the firm. He was twenty-seven now, a little heavy without being definitely stout, and with a manner older than his years. Old people and young people liked him and trusted him, and mothers felt safe when their daughters were in his charge, for he had a way, when he came into a room, of putting himself on a footing with the oldest and most conservative people there. "You and I," he seemed to say, "we're solid. We understand."

He had an instinctive and rather charitable knowledge of the weaknesses of men and women, and, like a priest, it made him the more concerned for the maintenance of outward forms. It was typical of him that every Sunday morning he taught in a fashionable Episcopal Sunday school—even though a cold shower and a quick change into a cutaway coat were all that separated him from the wild night before.

After his father's death he was the practical head of his family, and, in effect, guided the destinies of the younger children. Through a complication his authority did not extend to his father's estate, which was administrated by his Uncle Robert, who was the horsey member of the family, a good-natured, hard-drinking member of that set which centers about Wheatley Hills.

Uncle Robert and his wife, Edna, had been great friends of Anson's youth, and the former was disappointed when his nephew's superiority failed to take a horsey form. He backed him for a city club which was the most difficult in America to enter—one could only join if one's family had "helped to build up New York" (or, in other words, were rich before 1880)—and when Anson, after his election, neglected it for the Yale Club, Uncle Robert gave him a little talk on the subject. But when on top of that Anson declined to enter Robert Hunter's own conservative and somewhat neglected brokerage house, his manner grew cooler. Like a primary teacher who has taught all he knew, he slipped out of Anson's life.

There were so many friends in Anson's life—scarcely one for whom he had not done some unusual kindness and scarcely one whom he did not occasionally embarrass by his bursts of rough conversation or his habit of getting drunk whenever and however he liked. It annoyed him when anyone else blundered in that regard—about his own lapses he was always humorous. Odd things happened to him and he told them with infectious laughter.

I was working in New York that spring, and I used to lunch with him at the Yale Club, which my university was sharing until the completion of our own. I had read of Paula's marriage, and one afternoon, when I asked him about her, something moved him to tell me the story. After that he frequently invited me to family dinners at his house and behaved as though there was a special relation between us, as though with his confidence a little of that consuming memory had passed into me.

I found that despite the trusting mothers, his attitude toward girls was not indiscriminately protective. It was up to the girl—if she showed an inclination toward looseness, she must take care of herself, even with him.

"Life," he would explain sometimes, "has made a cynic of me."
By life he meant Paula. Sometimes, especially when he was drinking, it became a little twisted in his mind, and he thought that she
had callously thrown him over.

This "cynicism," or rather his realization that naturally fast girls
were not worth sparing, led to his affair with Dolly Karger. It wasn't
his only affair in those years, but it came nearest to touching him
deeply, and it had a profound effect upon his attitude toward life.

Dolly was the daughter of a notorious "publicist" who had married into society. She herself grew up into the Junior League, came
out at the Plaza, and went to the Assembly; and only a few old families like the Hunters could question whether or not she "belonged,"
for her picture was often in the papers, and she had more enviable
attention than many girls who undoubtedly did. She was dark-haired
with carmine lips and a high lovely color which she concealed under
pinkish-grey powder all through the first year out, because high color
was unfashionable—Victorian-pale was the thing to be. She wore
black, severe suits and stood with her hands in her pockets, leaning
a little forward, with a humorous restraint on her face. She danced
exquisitely—better than anything she liked to dance—better than
anything except making love. Since she was ten she had always been
in love, and, usually, with some boy who didn't respond to her. Those
who did—and there were many—bored her after a brief encounter,
but for her failures she reserved the warmest spot in her heart. When
she met them she would always try once more—sometimes she succeeded, more often she failed.

It never occurred to this gypsy of the unattainable that there was
a certain resemblance in those who refused to love her—they shared
a hard intuition that saw through to her weakness, not a weakness
of emotion but a weakness of rudder. Anson perceived this when
he first met her, less than a month after Paula's marriage. He was
drinking rather heavily, and he pretended for a week that he was
falling in love with her. Then he dropped her abruptly and forgot—
immediately he took up the commanding position in her heart.

Like so many girls of that day Dolly was slackly and indiscreetly wild. The unconventionality of a slightly older generation
had been simply one facet of a post-war movement to discredit

obsolete manners—Dolly's was both older and shabbier, and she saw in Anson the two extremes which the emotionally shiftless woman seeks, an abandon to indulgence alternating with a protective strength. In his character she felt both the sybarite and the solid rock, and these two satisfied every need of her nature.

She felt that it was going to be difficult, but she mistook the reason—she thought that Anson and his family expected a more spectacular marriage, but she guessed immediately that her advantage lay in his tendency to drink.

They met at the large debutante dances, but as her infatuation increased they managed to be more and more together. Like most mothers Mrs. Karger believed that Anson was exceptionally reliable, so she allowed Dolly to go with him to distant country clubs and suburban houses without inquiring closely into their activities or questioning her explanations when they came in late. At first these explanations might have been accurate, but Dolly's worldly ideas of capturing Anson were soon engulfed in the rising sweep of her emotion. Kisses in the back of taxis and motor cars were no longer enough; they did a curious thing:

They dropped out of their world for awhile and made another world just beneath it where Anson's tippling and Dolly's irregular hours would be less noticed and commented on. It was composed, this world, of varying elements—several of Anson's Yale friends and their wives, two or three young brokers and bond salesmen and a handful of unattached men, fresh from college, with money and a propensity to dissipation. What this world lacked in spaciousness and scale it made up for by allowing them a liberty that it scarcely permitted itself. Moreover it centered around them and permitted Dolly the pleasure of a faint condescension—a pleasure which Anson, whose whole life was a condescension from the certitudes of his childhood, was unable to share.

He was not in love with her and in the long feverish winter of their affair he frequently told her so. In the spring he was weary—he wanted to renew his life at some other source—moreover, he saw that either he must break with her now or accept the responsibility of a definite seduction. Her family's encouraging attitude precipitated his decision—one evening when Mr. Karger knocked discreetly at the library door to announce that he had left a bottle of old brandy in the dining room, Anson felt that life was hemming him in. That night he wrote her a short letter in which he told her that he was going on his vacation and that in view of all the circumstances they had better meet no more.

It was June. His family had closed up the house and gone to the country, so he was living temporarily at the Yale Club. I had heard about his affair with Dolly as it developed—accounts salted with humor, for he despised unstable women, and granted them no place in the social edifice in which he believed—and when he told me that night that he was definitely breaking with her I was glad. I had seen Dolly here and there and each time with a feeling of pity at the hopelessness of her struggle, and of shame at knowing so much about her that I had no right to know. She was what is known as "a pretty little thing," but there was a certain recklessness which rather fascinated me. Her dedication to the goddess of waste would have been less obvious had she been less spirited—she would most certainly throw herself away, but I was glad when I heard that the sacrifice would not be consummated in my sight.

Anson was going to leave the letter of farewell at her house next morning. It was one of the few houses left open in the Fifth Avenue district, and he knew that the Kargers, acting upon erroneous information from Dolly, had foregone a trip abroad to give their daughter her chance. As he stepped out the door of the Yale Club into Vanderbilt Avenue the postman passed him, and he followed back inside. The first letter that caught his eye was in Dolly's hand.

He knew what it would be—a lonely and tragic monologue, full of the reproaches he knew, the invoked memories, the "I wonder if's"—all the immemorial intimacies that he had communicated to Paula Legendre in what seemed another age. Thumbing over some bills, he brought it on top again and opened it. To his surprise it was a short, somewhat formal note, which said that Dolly would be unable to go to the country with him for the week-end, because Perry Hull from Chicago had unexpectedly come to town. It added that Anson had brought this on himself: "—if I felt that you loved me as I love you I would go with you at any time any place, but Perry is *so* nice, and he so much wants me to marry him—"

Anson smiled contemptuously—he had had experience with such decoy epistles. Moreover, he knew how Dolly had labored over this plan, probably sent for the faithful Perry and calculated the time of his arrival—even labored over the note so that it would make him jealous without driving him away. Like most compromises it had neither force nor vitality but only a timorous despair.

Suddenly he was angry. He sat down in the lobby and read it again. Then he went to the phone, called Dolly and told her in his clear, compelling voice that he had received her note and would call for her at five o'clock as they had previously planned. Scarcely waiting for the pretended uncertainty of her "Perhaps I can see you for an hour," he hung up the receiver and went down to his office. On the way he tore his own letter into bits and dropped it in the street.

He was not jealous—she meant nothing to him—but at her pathetic ruse everything stubborn and self-indulgent in him came to the surface. It was a presumption from a mental inferior and it could not be overlooked. If she wanted to know to whom she belonged she would see.

He was on the doorstep at quarter past five. Dolly was dressed for the street, and he listened in silence to the paragraph of "I can only see you for an hour," which she had begun on the phone.

"Put on your hat, Dolly," he said, "we'll take a walk."

They strolled up Madison Avenue and over to Fifth while Anson's shirt dampened upon his portly body in the deep heat. He talked little, scolding her, making no love to her, but before they had walked six blocks she was his again, apologizing for the note, offering not to see Perry at all as an atonement, offering anything. She thought that he had come because he was beginning to love her.

"I'm hot," he said when they reached 71st Street. "This is a winter suit. If I stop by the house and change, would you mind waiting for me downstairs? I'll only be a minute."

She was happy; the intimacy of his being hot, of any physical fact about him, thrilled her. When they came to the iron-grated door and Anson took out his key she experienced a sort of delight.

Downstairs it was dark, and after he ascended in the lift Dolly raised a curtain and looked out through opaque lace at the houses over the way. She heard the lift machinery stop and, with the notion of teasing him, pressed the button that brought it down. Then on what was more than an impulse she got into it and sent it up to what she guessed was his floor.

"Anson," she called, laughing a little.

"Just a minute," he answered from his bedroom . . . then after a brief delay: "Now you can come in."

He had changed and was buttoning his vest.

"This is my room," he said lightly. "How do you like it?"

She caught sight of Paula's picture on the wall and stared at it in fascination, just as Paula had stared at the pictures of Anson's childish sweethearts five years before. She knew something about Paula—sometimes she tortured herself with fragments of the story.

Suddenly she came close to Anson, raising her arms. They embraced. Outside the area window a soft artificial twilight already hovered, though the sun was still bright on a back roof across the way. In half an hour the room would be quite dark. The uncalculated opportunity overwhelmed them, made them both breathless, and they clung more closely. It was imminent, inevitable. Still holding one another, they raised their heads—their eyes fell together upon Paula's picture, staring down at them from the wall.

Suddenly Anson dropped his arms, and sitting down at his desk tried the drawer with a bunch of keys.

"Like a drink?" he asked in a gruff voice.

"No, Anson."

He poured himself half a tumbler of whiskey, swallowed it and then opened the door into the hall.

"Come on," he said.

Dolly hesitated.

"Anson—I'm going to the country with you tonight, after all. You understand that, don't you?"

"Of course," he answered brusquely.

In Dolly's car they rode out to Long Island, closer in their emotions than they had ever been before. They knew what would happen—not with Paula's face to remind them that something was lacking, but when they were alone in the still hot Long Island night that did not care.

The estate in Port Washington where they were to spend the week-end belonged to a cousin of Anson's who had married a Montana copper operator. An interminable drive began at the lodge and twisted under imported poplar saplings toward a huge, pink, Spanish house. Anson had often visited there before.

After dinner they danced at the Linx Club. About midnight Anson assured himself that his cousins would not leave before two—then he explained that Dolly was tired; he would take her home and return to the dance later. Trembling a little with excitement they got into a borrowed car together and drove to Port Washington. As they reached the lodge he stopped and spoke to the night-watchman.

"When are you making a round, Carl?"

"Right away."

"Then you'll be here till everybody's in?"

"Yes, sir."

"All right. Listen: if any automobile, no matter whose it is, turns in at this gate, I want you to phone the house immediately." He put a five-dollar bill into Carl's hand. "Is that clear?"

"Yes, Mr. Anson." Being of the Old World, he neither winked nor smiled. Yet Dolly sat with her face turned slightly away.

Anson had a key. Once inside he poured a drink for both of them—Dolly left hers untouched—then he ascertained definitely the location of the phone, and found that it was within easy hearing distance of their rooms, both of which were on the first floor.

Five minutes later he knocked at the door of Dolly's room.

"Anson?" He went in, closing the door behind him. She was in bed, leaning up anxiously with elbows on the pillow; sitting beside her he took her in his arms.

"Anson, darling."

He didn't answer.

"Anson. . . . Anson! I love you. . . . Say you love me. Say it now—can't you say it now? Even if you don't mean it?"

He did not listen. Over her head he perceived that the picture of Paula was hanging here upon this wall.

He got up and went close to it. The frame gleamed faintly with thrice-reflected moonlight—within was a blurred shadow of a face that he saw he did not know. Almost sobbing, he turned around and stared with abomination at the little figure on the bed.

"This is all foolishness," he said thickly. "I don't know what I was thinking about. I don't love you and you'd better wait for somebody that loves you. I don't love you a bit, can't you understand?"

His voice broke and he went hurriedly out. Back in the salon he was pouring himself a drink with uneasy fingers, when the front door opened suddenly, and his cousin came in.

"Why, Anson, I hear Dolly's sick," she began solicitously. "I hear she's sick. . . ."

"It was nothing," he interrupted, raising his voice so that it would carry into Dolly's room. "She was a little tired. She went to bed."

For a long time afterwards Anson believed that a protective God sometimes interfered in human affairs. But Dolly Karger, lying awake and staring at the ceiling, never again believed in anything at all.

VI

When Dolly married during the following autumn, Anson was in London on business. Like Paula's marriage, it was sudden, but it affected him in a different way. At first he felt that it was funny and had an inclination to laugh when he thought of it. Later it depressed him—it made him feel old.

There was something repetitive about it—why, Paula and Dolly had belonged to different generations. He had a foretaste of the sensation of a man of forty who hears that the daughter of an old flame has married. He wired congratulations and, as was not the case with Paula, they were sincere—he had never really hoped that Paula would be happy.

When he returned to New York, he was made a partner in the firm, and as his responsibilities increased he had less time on his hands. The refusal of a life-insurance company to issue him a policy made such an impression on him that he stopped drinking for a year and claimed that he felt better physically, though I think he missed the convivial recounting of those Celliniesque adventures which, in his early twenties, had played such a part in his life. But he never abandoned the Yale Club. He was a figure there, a personality, and the tendency of his class, who were now seven years out of college, to drift away to more sober haunts was checked by his presence.

His day was never too full nor his mind too weary to give any sort of aid to anyone who asked it. What had been done at first through pride and superiority had become a habit and a passion. And there was always something—a younger brother in trouble at New Haven, a quarrel to be patched up between a friend and his wife, a position to be found for this man, an investment for that. But his specialty was the solving of problems for young married people. Young married people fascinated him and their apartments were almost sacred to him—he knew the story of their love affair, advised them where to live and how, and remembered their babies' names. Toward young wives his attitude was circumspect: he never abused the trust which their husbands—strangely enough in view of his unconcealed irregularities—invariably reposed in him.

He came to take a vicarious pleasure in happy marriages and to be inspired to an almost equally pleasant melancholy by those that went astray. Not a season passed that he did not witness the collapse of an affair that perhaps he himself had fathered. When Paula was divorced and almost immediately remarried to another Bostonian, he talked about her to me all one afternoon. He would never love anyone as he had loved Paula, but he insisted that he no longer cared.

"I'll never marry," he came to say; "I've seen too much of it, and I know a happy marriage is a very rare thing. Besides, I'm too old."

But he did believe in marriage. Like all men who spring from a happy and successful marriage, he believed in it passionately—nothing he had seen would change his belief, his cynicism dissolved upon it like air. But he did really believe he was too old. At twenty-eight he began to accept with equanimity the prospect of marrying without romantic love; he resolutely chose a New York girl of his own class, pretty, intelligent, congenial, above reproach—and set about falling in love with her. The things he had said to Paula with sincerity, to other girls with grace, he could no longer say at all without smiling, or with the force necessary to convince.

"When I'm forty," he told his friends, "I'll be ripe. I'll fall for some chorus girl like the rest."

Nevertheless he persisted in his attempt. His mother wanted to see him married, and he could now well afford it—he had a seat on the stock exchange, and his earned income came to twenty-five thousand a year. The idea was agreeable: when his friends—he spent most of his time with the set he and Dolly had evolved—closed themselves in behind domestic doors at night, he no longer rejoiced in his freedom. He even wondered if he should have married Dolly. Not even Paula had loved him more, and he was learning the rarity, in a single life, of encountering true emotion.

Just as this mood began to creep over him a disquieting story reached his ear. His Aunt Edna, a woman just this side of forty, was carrying on an open intrigue with a dissolute, hard-drinking young man named Cary Sloane. Everyone knew of it except Anson's Uncle Robert, who for fifteen years had talked long in clubs and taken his wife for granted.

Anson heard the story again and again with increasing annoyance. Something of his old feeling for his uncle came back to him, a feeling that was more than personal, a reversion toward that family solidarity on which he had based his pride. His intuition singled out the essential point of the affair, which was that his uncle shouldn't be hurt. It was his first experiment in unsolicited meddling, but with his knowledge of Edna's character he felt that he could handle the matter better than a district judge, or his uncle.

His uncle was in Hot Springs. Anson traced down the sources of the scandal so that there should be no possibility of mistake and then he called Edna and asked her to lunch with him at the Plaza next day. Something in his tone must have frightened her, for she was reluctant, but he insisted, putting off the date until she had no excuse for refusing.

She met him at the appointed time in the Plaza lobby, a lovely, faded, grey-eyed blonde in a coat of Russian sable. Five great rings, cold with diamonds and emeralds, sparkled on her slender hands. It occurred to Anson that it was his father's intelligence and not his uncle's that had earned the fur and the stones, the rich brilliance that buoyed up her passing beauty.

Though Edna scented his hostility, she was unprepared for the directness of his approach.

"Edna, I'm astonished at the way you've been acting," he said in a strong frank voice. "At first I couldn't believe it."

"Believe what?" she demanded sharply.

"You needn't pretend with me, Edna. I'm talking about Cary Sloane. Aside from any other consideration, I didn't think you could treat Uncle Robert—"

"Now look here, Anson—" she began angrily, but his peremptory voice broke through hers:

"—and your children in such a way. You've been married eighteen years, and you're old enough to know better."

"You can't talk to me like that! You—"

"Yes I can. Uncle Robert has always been my best friend." He was tremendously moved. He felt a real distress about his uncle, about his three young cousins.

Edna stood up, leaving her crab-flake cocktail untasted.

"This is the silliest thing—"

"Very well, if you won't listen to me I'll go to Uncle Robert and tell him the whole story—he's bound to hear it sooner or later. And afterwards I'll go to old Moses Sloane."

Edna faltered back into her chair.

"Don't talk so loud," she begged him. Her eyes blurred with tears. "You have no idea how your voice carries. You might have chosen a less public place to make all these crazy accusations."

He didn't answer.

"Oh, you never liked me, I know," she went on. "You're just taking advantage of some silly gossip to try and break up the only interesting friendship I've ever had. What did I ever do to make you hate me so?"

Still Anson waited. There would be the appeal to his chivalry, then to his pity, finally to his superior sophistication—when he had shouldered his way through all these there would be admissions, and he could come to grips with her. By being silent, by being impervious, by returning constantly to his main weapon, which was his own true emotion, he bullied her into frantic despair as the luncheon hour slipped away. At two o'clock she took out a mirror and a handkerchief, shined away the marks of her tears and powdered the slight hollows where they had lain. She had agreed to meet him at her own house at five.

When he arrived she was stretched on a chaise-longue which was covered with cretonne for the summer, and the tears he had called up at luncheon seemed still to be standing in her eyes. Then he was aware of Cary Sloane's dark anxious presence upon the cold hearth.

"What's this idea of yours?" broke out Sloane immediately. "I understand you invited Edna to lunch and then threatened her on the basis of some cheap scandal."

Anson sat down.

"I have no reason to think it's only scandal."

"I hear you're going to take it to Robert Hunter and to my father."

Anson nodded.

"Either you break it off—or I will," he said.

"What God damned business is it of yours, Hunter?"

"Don't lose your temper, Cary," said Edna nervously. "It's only a question of showing him how absurd—"

"For one thing, it's my name that's being handed around," interrupted Anson. "That's all that concerns you, Cary."

"Edna isn't a member of your family."

"She most certainly is!" His anger mounted. "Why—she owes this house and the rings on her fingers to my father's brains. When Uncle Robert married her she didn't have a penny."

They all looked at the rings as if they had a significant bearing on the situation. Edna made a gesture to take them from her hand.

"I guess they're not the only rings in the world," said Sloane.

"Oh, this is absurd," cried Edna. "Anson, will you listen to me? I've found out how the silly story started. It was a maid I discharged who went right to the Chilicheffs—all these Russians pump things out of their servants and then put a false meaning on them." She brought down her fist angrily on the table: "And after Tom lent them the limousine for a whole month when we were south last winter—"

"Do you see?" demanded Sloane eagerly. "This maid got hold of the wrong end of the thing. She knew that Edna and I were friends, and she carried it to the Chilicheffs. In Russia they assume that if a man and a woman—"

He enlarged the theme to a disquisition upon social relations in the Caucasus.

"If that's the case it better be explained to Uncle Robert," said Anson dryly, "so that when the rumors do reach him he'll know they're not true."

Adopting the method he had followed with Edna at luncheon he let them explain it all away. He knew that they were guilty and that presently they would cross the line from explanation into justification and convict themselves more definitely than he could ever do. By seven they had taken the desperate step of telling him the truth— Robert Hunter's neglect, Edna's empty life, the casual dalliance that had flamed up into passion—but like so many true stories it had the misfortune of being old, and its enfeebled body beat helplessly against the armor of Anson's will. The threat to go to Sloane's father sealed their helplessness, for the latter, a retired cotton broker out of Alabama, was a notorious fundamentalist who controlled his son by a rigid allowance and the promise that at his next vagary the allowance would stop forever.

They dined at a small French restaurant and the discussion continued—at one time Sloane resorted to physical threats, a little later they were both imploring him to give them time. But Anson was obdurate. He saw that Edna was breaking up and that her spirit must not be refreshed by any renewal of their passion.

At two o'clock in a small night-club on 53d Street, Edna's nerves suddenly collapsed and she cried to go home. Sloane had been drinking heavily all evening, and he was faintly maudlin, leaning on the table and weeping a little with his face in his hands. Quickly Anson gave them his terms. Sloane was to leave town for six months, and he must be gone within forty-eight hours. When he returned there was to be no resumption of the affair, but at the end of a year Edna might, if she wished, tell Robert Hunter that she wanted a divorce and go about it in the usual way.

He paused, gaining confidence from their faces for his final word.

"Or there's another thing you can do," he said slowly. "If Edna wants to leave her children, there's nothing I can do to prevent your running off together."

"I want to go home!" cried Edna again. "Oh, haven't you done enough to us for one day?"

Outside it was dark, save for a blurred glow from Sixth Avenue down the street. In that light those two who had been lovers looked for the last time into each other's tragic faces, realizing that between them there was not enough youth and strength to avert their eternal parting. Sloane walked suddenly off down the street and Anson tapped a dozing taxi-driver on the arm.

It was almost four: there was a patient flow of cleaning water along the ghostly pavement of Fifth Avenue, and the shadows of two night women flitted over the dark façade of St. Thomas's church. Then the desolate shrubbery of Central Park where Anson had often played as a child, and the mounting numbers, significant as names, of the marching streets. This was his city, he thought, where his name had flourished through five generations. No change could alter the permanence of its place here, for change itself was the essential substratum by which he and those of his name identified themselves with the spirit of New York. Resourcefulness and a powerful will—for his threats in weaker hands would have been less than nothing—had beaten the gathering dust from his uncle's name, from the name of his family, from even this shivering figure that sat beside him in the car.

Cary Sloane's body was found next morning on the lower shelf of a pillar of Queensboro Bridge. In the darkness and in his excitement he had thought that it was the water flowing black beneath him, but in less than a second it made no possible difference—unless he had planned to think one last thought of Edna, and call out her name as he struggled feebly in the water.

VII

Anson never blamed himself for his part in this affair—the situation which brought it about had not been of his making. But the just suffer with the unjust, and he found that his oldest and somehow his most precious friendship was over. He never knew what distorted story Edna told, but he was welcome in his uncle's house no longer.

Just before Christmas Mrs. Hunter retired to a select Episcopal heaven, and Anson became the responsible head of his family. An unmarried aunt who had lived with them for years ran the house and attempted with helpless inefficiency to chaperone the younger girls. All the children were less self-reliant than Anson, more conventional both in their virtues and in their shortcomings. Mrs. Hunter's death had postponed the debut of one daughter and the wedding of another. Also it had taken something deeply material from all of them, for with her passing the quiet, expensive superiority of the Hunters came to an end.

For one thing, the estate, considerably diminished by two inheritance taxes and soon to be divided among six children, was not a notable fortune anymore. Anson saw a tendency in his youngest sisters to speak rather respectfully of families that hadn't "existed" twenty years ago. His own feeling of precedence was not echoed in them—sometimes they were conventionally snobbish, that was all. For another thing, this was the last summer they would spend on the Connecticut estate; the clamor against it was too loud: "Who wants to waste the best months of the year shut up in that dead old town?" Reluctantly he yielded—the house would go into the market in the fall, and next summer they would rent a smaller place in Westchester County. It was a step down from the expensive simplicity of his father's idea, and, while he sympathized with the revolt, it also annoyed him; during his mother's lifetime he had gone up there at least every other week-end—even in the gayest summers.

Yet he himself was part of this change, and his strong instinct for life had turned him in his twenties from the hollow obsequies of that abortive leisure class. He did not see this clearly—he still felt that there was a norm, a standard of society. But there was no norm, it was doubtful if there had ever been a true norm in New York. The few who still paid and fought to enter a particular set succeeded only to find that as a society it scarcely functioned—or, what was more alarming, that the Bohemia from which they fled sat above them at table.

At twenty-nine Anson's chief concern was his own growing loneliness. He was sure now that he would never marry. The number of weddings at which he had officiated as best man or usher was past all counting—there was a drawer at home that bulged with the official neckties of this or that wedding-party, neckties standing for romances that had not endured a year, for couples who had passed completely from his life. Scarf-pins, gold pencils, cuff-buttons, presents from a generation of grooms had passed through his jewel-box and been lost—and with every ceremony he was less and less able to imagine himself in the groom's place. Under his hearty good-will toward all those marriages there was despair about his own.

And as he neared thirty he became not a little depressed at the inroads that marriage, especially lately, had made upon his friendships. Groups of people had a disconcerting tendency to dissolve and disappear. The men from his own college—and it was upon them he had expended the most time and affection—were the most elusive of all. Most of them were drawn deep into domesticity, two were dead, one lived abroad, one was in Hollywood writing continuities for pictures that Anson went faithfully to see.

Most of them, however, were permanent commuters with an intricate family life centering around some suburban country club, and it was from these that he felt his estrangement most keenly.

In the early days of their married life they had all needed him; he gave them advice about their slim finances, he exorcised their doubts about the advisability of bringing a baby into two rooms and a bath, especially he stood for the great world outside. But now their financial troubles were in the past and the fearfully expected child had evolved into an absorbing family. They were always glad to see old Anson, but they dressed up for him and tried to impress him with their present importance, and kept their troubles to themselves. They needed him no longer.

A few weeks before his thirtieth birthday the last of his early and intimate friends was married. Anson acted in his usual role of best man, gave his usual silver tea-service, and went down to the usual Homeric to say good-bye. It was a hot Friday afternoon in May, and as he walked from the pier he realized that Saturday closing had begun and he was free until Monday morning.

"Go where?" he asked himself.

The Yale Club, of course; bridge until dinner, then four or five raw cocktails in somebody's room and a pleasant confused evening. He regretted that this afternoon's groom wouldn't be along—they had always been able to cram so much into such nights: they knew how to attach women and how to get rid of them, how much consideration any girl deserved from their intelligent hedonism. A party was an adjusted thing—you took certain girls to certain places and spent just so much on their amusement; you drank a little, not much more than you ought to drink, and at a certain time in the morning you stood up and said you were going home. You avoided college boys, sponges, future engagements, fights, sentiment and indiscretions. That was the way it was done. All the rest was dissipation.

In the morning you were never violently sorry—you made no resolutions, but if you had overdone it and your heart was slightly out of order, you went on the wagon for a few days without saying anything about it, and waited until an accumulation of nervous boredom projected you into another party.

The lobby of the Yale Club was unpopulated. In the bar three very young alumni looked up at him, momentarily and without curiosity.

"Hello there, Oscar," he said to the bartender. "Mr. Cahill been around this afternoon?"

"Mr. Cahill's gone to New Haven."

"Oh . . . that so?"

"Gone to the ball game. Lot of men gone up."

Anson looked once again into the lobby, considered for a moment and then walked out and over to Fifth Avenue. From the broad window of one of his clubs—one that he had scarcely visited in five years—a grey man with watery eyes stared down at him. Anson looked quickly away—that figure sitting in vacant resignation, in supercilious solitude, depressed him. He stopped and, retracing his steps, started over 47th Street toward Teak Warden's apartment. Teak and his wife had once been his most familiar friends—it was a household where he and Dolly Karger had been used to go in the days of their affair. But Teak had taken to drink, and his wife had remarked publicly that Anson was a bad influence on him. The remark reached Anson in an exaggerated form—when it was finally cleared up, the delicate spell of intimacy was broken, never to be renewed.

"Is Mr. Warden at home?" he inquired.

"They've gone to the country."

The fact unexpectedly cut at him. They were gone to the country and he hadn't known. Two years before he would have known the date, the hour, come up at the last moment for a final drink and planned his first visit to them. Now they had gone without a word.

Anson looked at his watch and considered a week-end with his family, but the only train was a local that would jolt through the aggressive heat for three hours. And tomorrow in the country, and Sunday—he was in no mood for porch-bridge with polite undergraduates, and dancing after dinner at a rural road-house, a diminutive of gaiety which his father had estimated too well.

"Oh no," he said to himself. . . . "No."

He was a dignified, impressive young man, rather stout now, but otherwise unmarked by dissipation. He could have been cast for a pillar of something—at times you were sure it was not society, at others nothing else—for the law, for the church. He stood for a few minutes motionless on the sidewalk in front of a 47th Street apartment-house; for almost the first time in his life he had nothing whatever to do.

Then he began to walk briskly up Fifth Avenue, as if he had just been reminded of an important engagement there. The necessity of dissimulation is one of the few characteristics that we share with dogs, and I think of Anson on that day as some well-bred specimen who had been disappointed at a familiar back door. He was going to see Nick, once a fashionable bartender in demand at all private dances, and now employed in cooling non-alcoholic champagne among the labyrinthine cellars of the Plaza Hotel.

"Nick," he said, "what's happened to everything?"

"Dead," Nick said.

"Make me a whiskey sour." Anson handed a pint bottle over the counter. "Nick, the girls are different; I had a little girl in Brooklyn and she got married last week without letting me know."

"That a fact? Ha-ha-ha," responded Nick diplomatically. "Slipped it over on you."

"Absolutely," said Anson. "And I was out with her the night before."

"Ha-ha-ha," said Nick, "ha-ha-ha!"

"Do you remember the wedding, Nick, in Hot Springs where I had the waiters and the musicians singing 'God Save the King'?"

"Now where was that, Mr. Hunter?" Nick concentrated doubtfully. "Seems to me that was—"

"Next time they were back for more, and I began to wonder how much I'd paid them," continued Anson.

"—seems to me that was at Mr. Trenholm's wedding."

"Don't know him," said Anson decisively. He was offended that a strange name should intrude upon his reminiscences; Nick perceived this.

"Naw—aw—" he admitted, "I ought to know that. It was one of *your* crowd—Brakins . . . Baker—"

"Bicker Baker," said Anson responsively. "They put me in a hearse after it was over and covered me up with flowers and drove me away."

"Ha-ha-ha," said Nick. "Ha-ha-ha."

Nick's simulation of the old family servant paled presently and Anson went upstairs to the lobby. He looked around—his eyes met the glance of an unfamiliar clerk at the desk, then fell upon a flower from the morning's marriage hesitating in the mouth of a brass cuspidor. He went out and walked slowly toward the blood-red sun over Columbus Circle. Suddenly he turned around and, retracing his steps to the Plaza, immured himself in a telephone-booth.

Later he said that he tried to get me three times that afternoon, that he tried everyone who might be in New York—men and girls he had not seen for years, an artist's model of his college days whose faded number was still in his address book—Central told him that even the exchange existed no longer. At length his quest roved into the country, and he held brief disappointing conversations with emphatic butlers and maids. So-and-so was out, riding, swimming, playing golf, sailed to Europe last week. Who shall I say phoned?

It was intolerable that he should pass the evening alone—the private reckonings, which one plans for a moment of leisure, lose every charm when the solitude is enforced. There were always women of a sort, but the ones he knew had temporarily vanished, and to pass a New York evening in the hired company of a stranger never occurred to him—he would have considered that that was something shameful and secret, the diversion of a traveling salesman in a strange town.

Anson paid the telephone bill—the girl tried unsuccessfully to joke with him about its size—and for the second time that afternoon started to leave the Plaza and go he knew not where. Near the revolving door the figure of a woman, obviously with child, stood sideways to the light—a sheer beige cape fluttered at her shoulders when the door turned and, each time, she looked impatiently toward it as if she were weary of waiting. At the first sight of her a strong nervous thrill of familiarity went over him, but not until he was within five feet of her did he realize that it was Paula.

"Why, Anson Hunter!"

His heart turned over.

"Why, Paula—"

"Why, this is wonderful. I can't believe it, *Anson!*"

She took both his hands and he saw in the freedom of the gesture that the memory of him had lost poignancy to her. But not to him—he felt that old mood that she evoked in him stealing over his brain, that gentleness with which he had always met her optimism as if afraid to mar its surface.

"We're at Rye for the summer. Pete had to come east on business—you know of course I'm Mrs. Peter Hagerty now—so we brought the children and took a house. You've got to come out and see us."

"Can I?" he asked directly. "When?"

"When you like. Here's Pete." The revolving door functioned, giving up a fine tall man of thirty with a tanned face and a trim mustache. His immaculate fitness made a sharp contrast with Anson's increasing bulk, which was obvious under the faintly tight cutaway coat.

"You oughtn't to be standing," said Hagerty to his wife. "Let's sit down here." He indicated lobby chairs but Paula hesitated.

"I've got to go right home," she said. "Anson, why don't you—why don't you come out and have dinner with us tonight? We're just getting settled, but if you can stand that—"

Hagerty confirmed the invitation cordially.

"Come out for the night."

Their car waited in front of the hotel, and Paula with a tired gesture sank back against silk cushions in the corner.

"There's so much I want to talk to you about," she said. "It seems hopeless."

"I want to hear about you."

"Well"—she smiled at Hagerty—"that would take a long time too. I have three children—by my first marriage. The oldest is five, then four, then three." She smiled again. "I didn't waste much time having them, did I?"

"Boys?"

"A boy and two girls. Then—oh, a lot of things happened, and I got a divorce in Paris a year ago and married Pete. That's all—except that I'm awfully happy."

In Rye they drove up to a large house near the beach club, from which there issued presently three dark slim children who broke from an English governess and approached them with an esoteric cry. Abstractedly and with difficulty Paula took each one into her arms, a caress which they accepted stiffly, as they had evidently been told not to bump into Mummy. Even against their fresh faces Paula's skin showed scarcely any weariness—for all her physical languor she seemed younger than when he had last seen her at Palm Beach seven years ago.

At dinner she was preoccupied, and afterwards, during the homage to the radio, she lay with closed eyes on the sofa, until Anson wondered if his presence at this time were not an intrusion. But at nine o'clock, when Hagerty rose and said pleasantly that he was going to leave them by themselves for awhile, she began to talk slowly about herself and the past.

"My first baby," she said—"the one we call Darling, the biggest little girl—I wanted to die when I knew I was going to have her, because Lowell was like a stranger to me. It didn't seem as though she could be my own. I wrote you a letter and tore it up. Oh, you were *so* bad to me, Anson."

It was the dialogue again, rising and falling. Anson felt a sudden quickening of memory.

"Weren't you engaged once?" she asked—"a girl named Dolly something?"

"I wasn't ever engaged. I tried to be engaged, but I never loved anybody but you, Paula."

"Oh," she said. Then after a moment: "This baby is the first one I ever really wanted. You see, I'm in love now—at last."

He didn't answer, shocked at the treachery of her remembrance. She must have seen that the "at last" bruised him, for she continued:

"I was infatuated with you, Anson—you could make me do anything you liked. But we wouldn't have been happy. I'm not smart enough for you. I don't like things to be complicated like you do." She paused. "You'll never settle down," she said.

The phrase struck at him from behind—it was an accusation that of all accusations he had never merited.

"I could settle down if women were different," he said. "If I didn't understand so much about them, if women didn't spoil you for other women, if they had only a little pride. If I could go to sleep for awhile and wake up into a home that was really mine—why, that's what I'm made for, Paula, that's what women have seen in me and liked in me. It's only that I can't get through the preliminaries anymore."

Hagerty came in a little before eleven; after a whiskey Paula stood up and announced that she was going to bed. She went over and stood by her husband.

"Where did you go, dearest?" she demanded.

"I had a drink with Ed Saunders."

"I was worried. I thought maybe you'd run away."

She rested her head against his coat.

"He's sweet, isn't he, Anson?" she demanded.

"Absolutely," said Anson, laughing.

She raised her face to her husband.

"Well, I'm ready," she said. She turned to Anson: "Do you want to see our family gymnastic stunt?"

"Yes," he said in an interested voice.

"All right. Here we go!"

Hagerty picked her up easily in his arms.

"This is called the family acrobatic stunt," said Paula. "He carries me upstairs. Isn't it sweet of him?"

"Yes," said Anson.

Hagerty bent his head slightly until his face touched Paula's.

"And I love him," she said. "I've just been telling you, haven't I, Anson?"

"Yes," he said.

"He's the dearest thing that ever lived in this world, aren't you, darling? . . . Well, good-night. Here we go. Isn't he strong?"

"Yes," Anson said.

"You'll find a pair of Pete's pajamas laid out for you. Sweet dreams—see you at breakfast."

"Yes," Anson said.

VIII

The older members of the firm insisted that Anson should go abroad for the summer. He had scarcely had a vacation in seven years, they said. He was stale and needed a change. Anson resisted.

"If I go," he declared, "I won't come back anymore."

"That's absurd, old man. You'll be back in three months with all this depression gone. Fit as ever."

"No." He shook his head stubbornly. "If I stop, I won't go back to work. If I stop, that means I've given up—I'm through."

"We'll take a chance on that. Stay six months if you like—we're not afraid you'll leave us. Why, you'd be miserable if you didn't work."

They arranged his passage for him. They liked Anson—everyone liked Anson—and the change that had been coming over him cast a sort of pall over the office. The enthusiasm that had invariably signalled up business, the consideration toward his equals and his inferiors, the lift of his vital presence—within the past four months his intense nervousness had melted down these qualities into the fussy pessimism of a man of forty. On every transaction in which he was involved he acted as a drag and a strain.

"If I go I'll never come back," he said.

Three days before he sailed Paula Legendre Hagerty died in child-birth. I was with him a great deal then, for we were crossing together, but for the first time in our friendship he told me not a word of how he felt, nor did I see the slightest sign of emotion. His chief preoccupation was with the fact that he was thirty years old—he would turn the conversation to the point where he could remind you of it and then fall silent, as if he assumed that the statement would start a chain of thought sufficient to itself. Like his partners I was amazed at the change in him, and I was glad when the *Paris* moved off into the wet space between the worlds, leaving his principality behind.

"How about a drink?" he suggested.

We walked into the bar with that defiant feeling that characterizes the day of departure and ordered four martinis. After one cocktail a change came over him—he suddenly reached across and slapped my knee with the first joviality I had seen him exhibit for months.

"Did you see that girl in the red tam?" he demanded, "the one with the high color who had the two police dogs down to bid her good-bye."

"She's pretty," I agreed.

"I looked her up in the purser's office and found out that she's alone. I'm going down to see the steward in a few minutes. We'll have dinner with her tonight."

After awhile he left me and within an hour he was walking up and down the deck with her, talking to her in his strong, clear voice. Her red tam was a bright spot of color against the steel-green sea, and from time to time she looked up with a flashing bob of her head, and smiled with amusement and interest, and anticipation. At dinner we had champagne, and were very joyous—afterwards Anson ran the pool with infectious gusto, and several people who had seen me with him asked me his name. He and the girl were talking and laughing together on a lounge in the bar when I went to bed.

I saw less of him on the trip than I had hoped. He wanted to arrange a foursome, but there was no one available, so I saw him only at meals. Sometimes, though, he would have a cocktail in the bar, and he told me about the girl in the red tam, and his adventures with her, making them all bizarre and amusing, as he had a way of doing, and I was glad that he was himself again, or at least the self that I knew, and with which I felt at home. I don't think he was ever happy unless someone was in love with him, responding to him like filings to a magnet, helping him to explain himself, promising him something. What it was I do not know. Perhaps they promised that there would always be women in the world who would spend their brightest, freshest, rarest hours to nurse and protect that superiority he cherished in his heart.

WINTER DREAMS

Some of the caddies were poor as sin and lived in one-room houses with a neurasthenic cow in the front yard, but Dexter Green's father owned the second best grocery store in Black Bear—the best one was "The Hub," patronized by the wealthy people from Sherry Island—and Dexter caddied only for pocket-money.

In the fall when the days became crisp and grey and the long Minnesota winter shut down like the white lid of a box, Dexter's skis moved over the snow that hid the fairways of the golf course. At these times the country gave him a feeling of profound melancholy—it offended him that the links should lie in enforced fallowness, haunted by ragged sparrows for the long season. It was dreary, too, that on the tees where the gay colors fluttered in summer there were now only the desolate sand boxes knee-deep in crusted ice. When he crossed the hills the wind blew cold as misery, and if the sun was out he tramped with his eyes squinted up against the hard dimensionless glare.

In April the winter ceased abruptly. The snow ran down into Black Bear Lake scarcely tarrying for the early golfers to brave the season with red and black balls. Without elation, without an interval of moist glory, the cold was gone.

Dexter knew that there was something dismal about this northern spring, just as he knew there was something gorgeous about the fall. Fall made him clench his hands and tremble and repeat idiotic sentences to himself and make brisk abrupt gestures of command to imaginary audiences and armies. October filled him with hope which November raised to a sort of ecstatic triumph, and in this mood the fleeting brilliant impressions of the summer at Sherry Island were ready grist to his mill. He became a golf champion and defeated Mr. T. A. Hedrick in a marvelous match played a hundred times over the fairways of his imagination, a match each detail of which he changed about untiringly—sometimes he won with almost laughable ease, sometimes he came up magnificently from behind. Again, stepping from a Pierce-Arrow automobile, like Mr. Mortimer Jones, he strolled frigidly into the lounge of the Sherry Island Golf Club—or perhaps, surrounded by an admiring crowd, he gave an exhibition of fancy diving from the springboard of the club raft. . . . Among those who watched him in open-mouthed wonder was Mr. Mortimer Jones.

And one day it came to pass that Mr. Jones—himself and not his ghost—came up to Dexter with tears in his eyes and said that Dexter was the — — best caddy in the club and wouldn't he decide not to quit if Mr. Jones made it worth his while, because every other — — caddy in the club lost one ball a hole for him—regularly.

"No, sir," said Dexter decisively, "I don't want to caddy any-more." Then, after a pause: "I'm too old."

"You're not more than fourteen. Why the devil did you decide just this morning that you wanted to quit? You promised that next week you'd go over to the state tournament with me."

"I decided I was too old."

Dexter handed in his "A Class" badge, collected what money was due him from the caddy-master and walked home to Black Bear Village.

"The best — — caddy I ever saw," shouted Mr. Mortimer Jones over a drink that afternoon. "Never lost a ball! Willing! Intelligent! Quiet! Honest! Grateful!—"

The little girl who had done this was eleven—beautifully ugly as little girls are apt to be who are destined after a few years to be inexpressibly lovely and bring no end of misery to a great number of men. The spark, however, was perceptible. There was a general ungodliness in the way her lips twisted down at the corners when she smiled and in the—Heaven help us!—in the almost passionate quality of her eyes. Vitality is born early in such women. It was utterly in evidence now, shining through her thin frame in a sort of glow.

She had come eagerly out onto the course at nine o'clock with a white linen nurse and five small new golf clubs in a white can-vas bag which the nurse was carrying. When Dexter first saw her she was standing by the caddy house, rather ill at ease and trying to conceal the fact by engaging her nurse in an obviously unnatural conversation graced by startling and irrelevant grimaces from herself.

"Well, it's certainly a nice day, Hilda," Dexter heard her say. She drew down the corners of her mouth, smiled and glanced furtively around, her eyes in transit falling for an instant on Dexter.

Then to the nurse:

"Well, I guess there aren't very many people out here this morning, are there?"

The smile again—radiant, blatantly artificial—convincing.

"I don't know what we're supposed to do now," said the nurse, looking nowhere in particular.

"Oh, that's all right. I'll fix it up."

Dexter stood perfectly still, his mouth slightly ajar. He knew that if he moved forward a step his stare would be in her line of vision—if he moved backward he would lose his full view of her face. For a moment he had not realized how young she was. Now he remembered having seen her several times the year before—in bloomers.

Suddenly, involuntarily, he laughed, a short abrupt laugh—then, startled by himself, he turned and began to walk quickly away.

"Boy!"

Dexter stopped.

"Boy—"

Beyond question he was addressed. Not only that, but he was treated to that absurd smile, that preposterous smile—the memory of which at least a dozen men were to carry into middle age.

"Boy, do you know where the golf teacher is?"

"He's giving a lesson."

"Well, do you know where the caddy-master is?"

"He isn't here yet this morning."

"Oh." For a moment this baffled her. She stood alternately on her right and left foot.

"We'd like to get a caddy," said the nurse. "Mrs. Mortimer Jones sent us out to play golf and we don't know how without we get a caddy."

Here she was stopped by an ominous glance from Miss Jones, followed immediately by the smile.

"There aren't any caddies here except me," said Dexter to the nurse, "and I got to stay here in charge until the caddy-master gets here."

"Oh."

Miss Jones and her retinue now withdrew and at a proper distance from Dexter became involved in a heated conversation, which was concluded by Miss Jones taking one of the clubs and hitting it on the ground with violence. For further emphasis she raised it again and was about to bring it down smartly upon the nurse's bosom, when the nurse seized the club and twisted it from her hands.

"You damn little mean old *thing!*" cried Miss Jones wildly.

Another argument ensued. Realizing that the elements of the comedy were implied in the scene, Dexter several times began to laugh, but each time restrained the laugh before it reached audibility. He could not resist the monstrous conviction that the little girl was justified in beating the nurse.

The situation was resolved by the fortuitous appearance of the caddy-master, who was appealed to immediately by the nurse.

"Miss Jones is to have a little caddy and this one says he can't go."

"Mr. McKenna said I was to wait here till you came," said Dexter quickly.

"Well, he's here now." Miss Jones smiled cheerfully at the caddy-master. Then she dropped her bag and set off at a haughty mince toward the first tee.

"Well?" The caddy-master turned to Dexter. "What you standing there like a dummy for? Go pick up the young lady's clubs."

"I don't think I'll go out today," said Dexter.

"You don't—"

"I think I'll quit."

The enormity of his decision frightened him. He was a favorite caddy and the thirty dollars a month he earned through the summer were not to be made elsewhere around the lake. But he had received a strong emotional shock and his perturbation required a violent and immediate outlet.

It is not so simple as that, either. As so frequently would be the case in the future, Dexter was unconsciously dictated to by his winter dreams.

II

Now, of course, the quality and the seasonability of these winter dreams varied, but the stuff of them remained. They persuaded Dexter several years later to pass up a business course at the state university—his father, prospering now, would have paid his way— for the precarious advantage of attending an older and more famous university in the East, where he was bothered by his scanty funds. But do not get the impression, because his winter dreams happened to be concerned at first with musings on the rich, that there was anything merely snobbish in the boy. He wanted not association with glittering things and glittering people—he wanted the glittering things themselves. Often he reached out for the best without knowing why he wanted it—and sometimes he ran up against the mysterious denials and prohibitions in which life indulges. It is with one of those denials and not with his career as a whole that this story deals.

He made money. It was rather amazing. After college he went to the city from which Black Bear Lake draws its wealthy patrons. When he was only twenty-three and had been there not quite two years, there were already people who liked to say: "Now *there's* a boy—" All about him rich men's sons were peddling bonds precariously, or investing patrimonies precariously, or plodding through the two dozen volumes of the "George Washington Commercial Course," but Dexter borrowed a thousand dollars on his college degree and his confident mouth, and bought a partnership in a laundry.

It was a small laundry when he went into it but Dexter made a specialty of learning how the English washed fine woolen golf-stockings without shrinking them, and within a year he was catering to the trade that wore knickerbockers. Men were insisting that their Shetland hose and sweaters go to his laundry just as they had insisted on a caddy who could find golf balls. A little later he was doing their wives' lingerie as well—and running five branches in different parts of the city. Before he was twenty-seven he owned the largest string of laundries in his section of the country. It was then that he sold out and went to New York. But the part of his story that concerns us goes back to the days when he was making his first big success.

When he was twenty-three Mr. Hart—one of the grey-haired men who liked to say "Now there's a boy"—gave him a guest card to the Sherry Island Golf Club for a week-end. So he signed his name one day on the register, and that afternoon played golf in a foursome with Mr. Hart and Mr. Sandwood and Mr. T. A. Hedrick. He did not consider it necessary to remark that he had once carried Mr. Hart's bag over these same links and that he knew every trap and gully with his eyes shut—but he found himself glancing at the four caddies who trailed them, trying to catch a gleam or gesture that would remind him of himself, that would lessen the gap which lay between his present and his past.

It was a curious day, slashed abruptly with fleeting, familiar impressions. One minute he had the sense of being a trespasser—in the next he was impressed by the tremendous superiority he felt toward Mr. T. A. Hedrick, who was a bore and not even a good golfer anymore.

Then, because of a ball Mr. Hart lost near the fifteenth green, an enormous thing happened. While they were searching the stiff grasses of the rough there was a clear call of "Fore!" from behind a hill in their rear. And as they all turned abruptly from their search a bright new ball sliced abruptly over the hill and caught Mr. T. A. Hedrick in the abdomen.

"By Gad!" cried Mr. T. A. Hedrick, "they ought to put some of these crazy women off the course. It's getting to be outrageous."

A head and a voice came up together over the hill:

"Do you mind if we go through?"

"You hit me in the stomach!" declared Mr. Hedrick wildly.

"Did I?" The girl approached the group of men. "I'm sorry. I yelled 'Fore!'"

Her glance fell casually on each of the men—then scanned the fairway for her ball.

"Did I bounce into the rough?"

It was impossible to determine whether this question was ingenuous or malicious. In a moment, however, she left no doubt, for as her partner came up over the hill she called cheerfully:

"Here I am! I'd have gone on the green except that I hit something."

As she took her stance for a short mashie shot, Dexter looked at her closely. She wore a blue gingham dress, rimmed at throat and shoulders with a white edging that accentuated her tan. The quality of exaggeration, of thinness, which had made her passionate eyes and down-turning mouth absurd at eleven, was gone now. She was arrestingly beautiful. The color in her cheeks was centered like the color in a picture—it was not a "high" color, but a sort of fluctuating and feverish warmth, so shaded that it seemed at any moment it would recede and disappear. This color and the mobility of her mouth gave a continual impression of flux, of intense life, of passionate vitality—balanced only partially by the sad luxury of her eyes.

She swung her mashie impatiently and without interest, pitching the ball into a sandpit on the other side of the green. With a quick insincere smile and a careless "Thank you!" she went on after it.

"That Judy Jones!" remarked Mr. Hedrick on the next tee, as they waited—some moments—for her to play on ahead. "All she needs is to be turned up and spanked for six months and then to be married off to an old-fashioned cavalry captain."

"My God, she's good-looking!" said Mr. Sandwood, who was just over thirty.

"Good-looking!" cried Mr. Hedrick contemptuously. "She always looks as if she wanted to be kissed! Turning those big cow-eyes on every calf in town!"

It was doubtful if Mr. Hedrick intended a reference to the maternal instinct.

"She'd play pretty good golf if she'd try," said Mr. Sandwood.

"She has no form," said Mr. Hedrick solemnly.

"She has a nice figure," said Mr. Sandwood.

"Better thank the Lord she doesn't drive a swifter ball," said Mr. Hart, winking at Dexter.

Later in the afternoon the sun went down with a riotous swirl of gold and varying blues and scarlets, and left the dry rustling night of western summer. Dexter watched from the verandah of the golf club, watched the even overlap of the waters in the little wind, silver molasses under the harvest moon. Then the moon held a finger to her lips and the lake became a clear pool, pale and quiet. Dexter put on his bathing suit and swam out to the farthest raft, where he stretched dripping on the wet canvas of the springboard.

There was a fish jumping and a star shining and the lights around the lake were gleaming. Over on a dark peninsula a piano was playing the songs of last summer and of summers before that—songs from "Chin-Chin" and "The Count of Luxembourg" and "The Chocolate Soldier"—and because the sound of a piano over a stretch of water had always seemed beautiful to Dexter he lay perfectly quiet and listened.

The tune the piano was playing at that moment had been gay and new five years before when Dexter was a sophomore at college. They had played it at a prom once when he could not afford the luxury of proms, and he had stood outside the gymnasium and listened. The sound of the tune precipitated in him a sort of ecstasy and it was with that ecstasy he viewed what happened to him now. It was a mood of intense appreciation, a sense that, for once, he was magnificently attuned to life and that everything about him was radiating a brightness and a glamour he might never know again.

A low pale oblong detached itself suddenly from the darkness of the island, spitting forth the reverberate sound of a racing motor-boat. Two white streamers of cleft water rolled themselves out behind it and almost immediately the boat was beside him, drowning out the hot tinkle of the piano in the drone of its spray. Dexter, raising himself on his arms, was aware of a figure standing at the wheel, of two dark eyes regarding him over the lengthening space of water—then the boat had gone by and was sweeping in an immense and purposeless circle of spray round and round in the middle of the lake. With equal eccentricity one of the circles flattened out and headed back toward the raft.

"Who's that?" she called, shutting off her motor. She was so near now that Dexter could see her bathing suit, which consisted apparently of pink rompers.

The nose of the boat bumped the raft, and as the latter tilted rakishly he was precipitated toward her. With different degrees of interest they recognized each other.

"Aren't you one of those men we played through this afternoon?" she demanded.

He was.

"Well, do you know how to drive a motorboat? Because if you do I wish you'd drive this one so I can ride on the surf-board behind. My name is Judy Jones"—she favored him with an absurd smirk—rather, what tried to be a smirk, for, twist her mouth as she might, it was not grotesque, it was merely beautiful—"and I live in a house over there on the island, and in that house there is a man waiting for me. When he drove up at the door I drove out of the dock because he says I'm his ideal."

There was a fish jumping and a star shining and the lights around the lake were gleaming. Dexter sat beside Judy Jones and she explained how her boat was driven. Then she was in the water, swimming to the floating surf-board with a sinuous crawl. Watching her was without effort to the eye, watching a branch waving or a sea-gull flying. Her arms, burned to butternut, moved sinuously among the dull platinum ripples, elbow appearing first, casting the forearm back with a cadence of falling water, then reaching out and down, stabbing a path ahead.

They moved out into the lake; turning, Dexter saw that she was kneeling on the low rear of the now up-tilted surf-board.

"Go faster," she called, "fast as it'll go."

Obediently he jammed the lever forward and the white spray mounted at the bow. When he looked around again the girl was standing up on the rushing board, her arms spread wide, her eyes lifted toward the moon.

"It's awful cold," she shouted. "What's your name?"

He told her.

"Well, why don't you come to dinner tomorrow night?"

His heart turned over like the fly-wheel of the boat, and, for the second time, her casual whim gave a new direction to his life.

III

Next evening while he waited for her to come downstairs, Dexter peopled the soft deep summer room and the sun-porch that opened from it with the men who had already loved Judy Jones. He knew the sort of men they were—the men who when he first went to college had entered from the great prep schools with graceful clothes and the deep tan of healthy summers. He had seen that, in one sense, he was better than these men. He was newer and stronger. Yet in acknowledging to himself that he wished his children to be like them he was admitting that he was but the rough, strong stuff from which they eternally sprang.

When the time had come for him to wear good clothes, he had known who were the best tailors in America, and the best tailors in America had made him the suit he wore this evening. He had acquired that particular reserve peculiar to his university, that set it off from other universities. He recognized the value to him of such a mannerism and he had adopted it; he knew that to be careless in dress and manner required more confidence than to be careful. But carelessness was for his children. His mother's name had been Krimslich. She was a Bohemian of the peasant class and she had talked broken English to the end of her days. Her son must keep to the set patterns.

At a little after seven Judy Jones came downstairs. She wore a blue silk afternoon dress, and he was disappointed at first that she had not put on something more elaborate. This feeling was accentuated when, after a brief greeting, she went to the door of a butler's pantry and pushing it open called: "You can serve dinner, Martha." He had rather expected that a butler would announce dinner, that there would be a cocktail. Then he put these thoughts behind him as they sat down side by side on a lounge and looked at each other.

"Father and Mother won't be here," she said thoughtfully.

He remembered the last time he had seen her father, and he was glad the parents were not to be here tonight—they might wonder who he was. He had been born in Keeble, a Minnesota village fifty miles farther north, and he always gave Keeble as his home instead of Black Bear Village. Country towns were well enough to come from if they weren't inconveniently in sight and used as foot-stools by fashionable lakes.

They talked of his university, which she had visited frequently during the past two years, and of the nearby city which supplied Sherry Island with its patrons, and whither Dexter would return next day to his prospering laundries.

During dinner she slipped into a moody depression which gave Dexter a feeling of uneasiness. Whatever petulance she uttered in her throaty voice worried him. Whatever she smiled at—at him, at a chicken liver, at nothing—it disturbed him that her smile could have no root in mirth, or even in amusement. When the scarlet corners of her lips curved down, it was less a smile than an invitation to a kiss.

Then, after dinner, she led him out on the dark sun-porch and deliberately changed the atmosphere.

"Do you mind if I weep a little?" she said.

"I'm afraid I'm boring you," he responded quickly.

"You're not. I like you. But I've just had a terrible afternoon. There was a man I cared about, and this afternoon he told me out of a clear sky that he was poor as a church-mouse. He'd never even hinted it before. Does this sound horribly mundane?"

"Perhaps he was afraid to tell you."

"Suppose he was," she answered. "He didn't start right. You see, if I'd thought of him as poor—well, I've been mad about loads of poor men, and fully intended to marry them all. But in this case, I hadn't thought of him that way and my interest in him wasn't strong enough to survive the shock. As if a girl calmly informed her fiancé that she was a widow. He might not object to widows, but—

"Let's start right," she interrupted herself suddenly. "Who are you, anyhow?"

For a moment Dexter hesitated. Then:

"I'm nobody," he announced. "My career is largely a matter of futures."

"Are you poor?"

"No," he said frankly, "I'm probably making more money than any man my age in the Northwest. I know that's an obnoxious remark, but you advised me to start right."

There was a pause. Then she smiled and the corners of her mouth drooped and an almost imperceptible sway brought her closer to him, looking up into his eyes. A lump rose in Dexter's throat, and he waited breathless for the experiment, facing the unpredictable compound that would form mysteriously from the elements of their lips. Then he saw—she communicated her excitement to him, lavishly, deeply, with kisses that were not a promise but a fulfilment. They aroused in him not hunger demanding renewal but surfeit that would demand more surfeit . . . kisses that were like charity, creating want by holding back nothing at all.

It did not take him many hours to decide that he had wanted Judy Jones ever since he was a proud, desirous little boy.

IV

It began like that—and continued, with varying shades of intensity, on such a note right up to the dénouement. Dexter surrendered a part of himself to the most direct and unprincipled personality with which he had ever come in contact. Whatever Judy wanted, she went after with the full pressure of her charm. There was no divergence of method, no jockeying for position or premeditation of effects—there was a very little mental side to any of her affairs. She simply made men conscious to the highest degree of her physical loveliness. Dexter had no desire to change her. Her deficiencies were knit up with a passionate energy that transcended and justified them.

When, as Judy's head lay against his shoulder that first night, she whispered, "I don't know what's the matter with me. Last night I thought I was in love with a man and tonight I think I'm in love with you—" —it seemed to him a beautiful and romantic thing to say. It was the exquisite excitability that for the moment he controlled and owned. But a week later he was compelled to view this same quality in a different light. She took him in her roadster to a picnic supper and after supper she disappeared, likewise in her roadster, with another man. Dexter became enormously upset and was scarcely able to be decently civil to the other people present. When she assured him that she had not kissed the other man, he knew she was lying—yet he was glad that she had taken the trouble to lie to him.

He was, as he found before the summer ended, one of a varying dozen who circulated about her. Each of them had at one time been favored above all others—about half of them still basked in the solace of occasional sentimental revivals. Whenever one showed signs of dropping out through long neglect, she granted him a brief honeyed hour, which encouraged him to tag along for a year or so longer. Judy made these forays upon the helpless and defeated without malice, indeed half unconscious that there was anything mischievous in what she did.

When a new man came to town everyone dropped out—dates were automatically cancelled.

The helpless part of trying to do anything about it was that she did it all herself. She was not a girl who could be "won" in the kinetic sense—she was proof against cleverness, she was proof against charm; if any of these assailed her too strongly she would immediately resolve the affair to a physical basis, and under the magic of her physical splendor the strong as well as the brilliant played her game and not their own. She was entertained only by the gratification of her desires and by the direct exercise of her own charm. Perhaps from so much youthful love, so many youthful lovers, she had come, in self-defense, to nourish herself wholly from within.

Succeeding Dexter's first exhilaration came restlessness and dissatisfaction. The helpless ecstasy of losing himself in her was opiate rather than tonic. It was fortunate for his work during the winter that those moments of ecstasy came infrequently. Early in their acquaintance it had seemed for awhile that there was a deep and spontaneous mutual attraction—that first August, for example—three days of long evenings on her dusky verandah, of strange wan kisses through the late afternoon, in shadowy alcoves or behind the protecting trellises of the garden arbors, of mornings when she was fresh as a dream and almost shy at meeting him in the clarity of the rising day. There was all the ecstasy of an engagement about it, sharpened by his realization that there was no engagement. It was during those three days that, for the first time, he had asked her to marry him. She said "maybe someday," she said "kiss me," she said "I'd like to marry you," she said "I love you"—she said—nothing.

The three days were interrupted by the arrival of a New York man who visited at her house for half September. To Dexter's agony, rumor engaged them. The man was the son of the president of a great trust company. But at the end of a month it was reported that Judy was yawning. At a dance one night she sat all evening in a motorboat with a local beau, while the New Yorker searched the club for her frantically. She told the local beau that she was bored with her visitor and two days later he left. She was seen with him at the station and it was reported that he looked very mournful indeed.

On this note the summer ended. Dexter was twenty-four and he found himself increasingly in a position to do as he wished. He joined two clubs in the city and lived at one of them. Though he was by no means an integral part of the stag-lines at these clubs, he managed to be on hand at dances where Judy Jones was likely to appear. He could have gone out socially as much as he liked— he was an eligible young man, now, and popular with downtown fathers. His confessed devotion to Judy Jones had rather solidified his position. But he had no social aspirations and rather despised the dancing men who were always on tap for the Thursday or Saturday parties and who filled in at dinners with the younger married set. Already he was playing with the idea of going east to New York. He wanted to take Judy Jones with him. No disillusion as to the world in which she had grown up could cure his illusion as to her desirability.

Remember that—for only in the light of it can what he did for her be understood.

Eighteen months after he first met Judy Jones he became engaged to another girl. Her name was Irene Scheerer, and her father was one of the men who had always believed in Dexter. Irene was light-haired and sweet and honorable, and a little stout, and she had two suitors whom she pleasantly relinquished when Dexter formally asked her to marry him.

Summer, fall, winter, spring, another summer, another fall—so much he had given of his active life to the incorrigible lips of Judy Jones. She had treated him with interest, with encouragement, with malice, with indifference, with contempt. She had inflicted on him the innumerable little slights and indignities possible in such a case—as if in revenge for having ever cared for him at all. She had beckoned him and yawned at him and beckoned him again and he had responded often with bitterness and narrowed eyes. She had brought him ecstatic happiness and intolerable agony of spirit. She had caused him untold inconvenience and not a little trouble. She had insulted him and she had ridden over him and she had played his interest in her against his interest in his work—for fun. She had done everything to him except to criticize him—this she had not done—it seemed to him only because it might have sullied the utter indifference she manifested and sincerely felt toward him.

When autumn had come and gone again it occurred to him that he could not have Judy Jones. He had to beat this into his mind but he convinced himself at last. He lay awake at night for awhile and argued it over. He told himself the trouble and the pain she had caused him, he enumerated her glaring deficiencies as a wife. Then he said to himself that he loved her, and after awhile he fell asleep. For a week, lest he imagined her husky voice over the telephone or her eyes opposite him at lunch, he worked hard and late and at night he went to his office and plotted out his years.

At the end of a week he went to a dance and cut in on her once. For almost the first time since they had met he did not ask her to sit out with him or tell her that she was lovely. It hurt him that she did not miss these things—that was all. He was not jealous when he saw that there was a new man tonight. He had been hardened against jealousy long before.

He stayed late at the dance. He sat for an hour with Irene Scheerer and talked about books and about music. He knew very little about either. But he was beginning to be master of his own time now, and he had a rather priggish notion that he—the young and already fabulously successful Dexter Green—should know more about such things.

That was in October when he was twenty-five. In January, Dexter and Irene became engaged. It was to be announced in June and they were to be married three months later.

The Minnesota winter prolonged itself interminably, and it was almost May when the winds came soft and the snow ran down into Black Bear Lake at last. For the first time in over a year Dexter was enjoying a certain tranquillity of spirit. Judy Jones had been in Florida and afterwards in Hot Springs and somewhere she had been engaged and somewhere she had broken it off. At first, when Dexter had definitely given her up, it had made him sad that people still linked them together and asked for news of her, but when he began to be placed at dinner next to Irene Scheerer people didn't ask him about her anymore—they told him about her. He ceased to be an authority on her.

May at last. Dexter walked the streets at night when the darkness was damp as rain, wondering that so soon, with so little done, so much of ecstasy had gone from him. May one year back had been marked by Judy's poignant, unforgivable, yet forgiven turbulence— it had been one of those rare times when he fancied she had grown to care for him. That old penny's worth of happiness he had spent for this bushel of content. He knew that Irene would be no more than a curtain spread behind him, a hand moving among gleaming tea cups, a voice calling to children . . . fire and loveliness were gone, the magic of nights and the wonder of the varying hours and seasons . . . slender lips, down-turning, dropping to his lips and bearing him up into a heaven of eyes. . . . The thing was deep in him. He was too strong and alive for it to die lightly.

In the middle of May when the weather balanced for a few days on the thin bridge that led to deep summer he turned in one night at Irene's house. Their engagement was to be announced in a week now—no one would be surprised at it. And tonight they would sit together on the lounge at the University Club and look on for an hour at the dancers. It gave him a sense of solidity to go with her— she was so sturdily popular, so intensely "great."

He mounted the steps of the brownstone house and stepped inside.

"Irene," he called.

Mrs. Scheerer came out of the living room to meet him.

"Dexter," she said, "Irene's gone upstairs with a splitting headache. She wanted to go with you but I made her go to bed."

"Nothing serious, I—"

"Oh, no. She's going to play golf with you in the morning. You can spare her for just one night, can't you, Dexter?"

Her smile was kind. She and Dexter liked each other. In the living room he talked for a moment before he said good-night.

Returning to the University Club, where he had rooms, he stood in the doorway for a moment and watched the dancers. He leaned against the doorpost, nodded at a man or two—yawned.

"Hello, darling."

The familiar voice at his elbow startled him. Judy Jones had left a man and crossed the room to him—Judy Jones, a slender enamelled doll in cloth of gold: gold in a band at her head, gold in two slipper points at her dress's hem. The fragile glow of her face seemed to blossom as she smiled at him. A breeze of warmth and light blew through the room. His hands in the pockets of his dinner jacket tightened spasmodically. He was filled with a sudden excitement.

"When did you get back?" he asked casually.

"Come here and I'll tell you about it."

She turned and he followed her. She had been away—he could have wept at the wonder of her return. She had passed through enchanted streets, doing things that were like provocative music. All mysterious happenings, all fresh and quickening hopes, had gone away with her, come back with her now.

She turned in the doorway.

"Have you a car here? If you haven't, I have."

"I have a coupé."

In then, with a rustle of golden cloth. He slammed the door. Into so many cars she had stepped—like this—like that—her back against the leather, so—her elbow resting on the door—waiting. She would have been soiled long since had there been anything to soil her—except herself—but this was her own self outpouring.

With an effort he forced himself to start the car and back into the street. This was nothing, he must remember. She had done this before and he had put her behind him, as he would have crossed a bad account from his books.

He drove slowly downtown and, affecting abstraction, traversed the deserted streets of the business section, peopled here and there where a movie was giving out its crowd or where consumptive or pugilistic youth lounged in front of pool halls. The clink of glasses and the slap of hands on the bars issued from saloons, cloisters of glazed glass and dirty yellow light.

She was watching him closely and the silence was embarrassing, yet in this crisis he could find no casual word with which to profane the hour. At a convenient turning he began to zig-zag back toward the University Club.

"Have you missed me?" she asked suddenly.

"Everybody missed you."

He wondered if she knew of Irene Scheerer. She had been back only a day—her absence had been almost contemporaneous with his engagement.

"What a remark!" Judy laughed sadly—without sadness. She looked at him searchingly. He became absorbed in the dashboard.

"You're handsomer than you used to be," she said thoughtfully. "Dexter, you have the most rememberable eyes."

He could have laughed at this, but he did not laugh. It was the sort of thing that was said to sophomores. Yet it stabbed at him.

"I'm awfully tired of everything, darling." She called everyone darling, endowing the endearment with careless, individual camaraderie. "I wish you'd marry me."

The directness of this confused him. He should have told her now that he was going to marry another girl, but he could not tell her. He could as easily have sworn that he had never loved her.

"I think we'd get along," she continued, on the same note, "unless probably you've forgotten me and fallen in love with another girl."

Her confidence was obviously enormous. She had said, in effect, that she found such a thing impossible to believe, that if it were true he had merely committed a childish indiscretion—and probably to show off. She would forgive him, because it was not a matter of any moment but rather something to be brushed aside lightly.

"Of course you could never love anybody but me," she continued. "I like the way you love me. Oh, Dexter, have you forgotten last year?"

"No, I haven't forgotten."

"Neither have I!"

Was she sincerely moved—or was she carried along by the wave of her own acting?

"I wish we could be like that again," she said, and he forced himself to answer:

"I don't think we can."

"I suppose not. . . . I hear you're giving Irene Scheerer a violent rush."

There was not the faintest emphasis on the name, yet Dexter was suddenly ashamed.

"Oh, take me home," cried Judy suddenly; "I don't want to go back to that idiotic dance—with those children."

Then, as he turned up the street that led to the residence district, Judy began to cry quietly to herself. He had never seen her cry before.

The dark street lightened, the dwellings of the rich loomed up around them, he stopped his coupé in front of the great white bulk of the Mortimer Jones house, somnolent, gorgeous, drenched with the splendor of the damp moonlight. Its solidity startled him. The strong walls, the steel of the girders, the breadth and beam and pomp of it were there only to bring out the contrast with the young beauty beside him. It was sturdy to accentuate her slightness—as if to show what a breeze could be generated by a butterfly's wing.

He sat perfectly quiet, his nerves in wild clamor, afraid that if he moved he would find her irresistibly in his arms. Two tears had rolled down her wet face and trembled on her upper lip.

"I'm more beautiful than anybody else," she said brokenly. "Why can't I be happy?" Her moist eyes tore at his stability—her mouth turned slowly downward with an exquisite sadness: "I'd like to marry you if you'll have me, Dexter. I suppose you think I'm not worth having, but I'll be so beautiful for you, Dexter."

A million phrases of anger, pride, passion, hatred, tenderness fought on his lips. Then a perfect wave of emotion washed over him, carrying off with it a sediment of wisdom, of convention, of doubt, of honor. This was his girl who was speaking, his own, his beautiful, his pride.

"Won't you come in?" He heard her draw in her breath sharply. Waiting.

"All right," his voice was trembling, "I'll come in."

V

It was strange that neither when it was over nor a long time afterward did he regret that night. Looking at it from the perspective of ten years, the fact that Judy's flare for him endured just one month seemed of little importance. Nor did it matter that by his yielding he subjected himself to a deeper agony in the end and gave serious hurt to Irene Scheerer and to Irene's parents, who had befriended him. There was nothing sufficiently pictorial about Irene's grief to stamp itself on his mind.

Dexter was at bottom hard-minded. The attitude of the city on his action was of no importance to him, not because he was going to leave the city, but because any outside attitude on the situation seemed superficial. He was completely indifferent to popular opinion. Nor, when he had seen that it was no use, that he did not possess in himself the power to move fundamentally or to hold Judy Jones, did he bear any malice toward her. He loved her and he would love her until the day he was too old for loving—but he could not have her. So he tasted the deep pain that is reserved only for the strong, just as he had tasted for a little while the deep happiness.

Even the ultimate falsity of the grounds upon which Judy terminated the engagement, that she did not want to "take him away" from Irene—Judy, who had wanted nothing else—did not revolt him. He was beyond any revulsion or any amusement.

He went east in February with the intention of selling out his laundries and settling in New York—but the war came to America in March and changed his plans. He returned to the West, handed over the management of the business to his partner, and went into the first officers' training-camp in late April. He was one of those young thousands who greeted the war with a certain amount of relief, welcoming the liberation from webs of tangled emotion.

VI

This story is not his biography, remember, although things creep into it which have nothing to do with those dreams he had when he was young. We are almost done with them and with him now. There is only one more incident to be related here, and it happens seven years farther on.

It took place in New York, where he had done well—so well that there were no barriers too high for him. He was thirty-two years old, and, except for one flying trip immediately after the war, he had not been west in seven years. A man named Devlin from Detroit came into his office to see him in a business way, and then and there this incident occurred, and closed out, so to speak, this particular side of his life.

"So you're from the Middle West," said the man Devlin with careless curiosity. "That's funny—I thought men like you were probably born and raised on Wall Street. You know—wife of one of my best friends in Detroit came from your city. I was an usher at the wedding."

Dexter waited with no apprehension of what was coming.

"Judy Simms," said Devlin with no particular interest; "Judy Jones she was once."

"Yes, I knew her." A dull impatience spread over him. He had heard, of course, that she was married—perhaps deliberately he had heard no more.

"Awfully nice girl," brooded Devlin meaninglessly. "I'm sort of sorry for her."

"Why?" Something in Dexter was alert, receptive, at once.

"Oh, Lud Simms has gone to pieces in a way. I don't mean he ill-uses her, but he drinks and runs around—"

"Doesn't she run around?"

"No. Stays at home with her kids."

"Oh."

"She's a little too old for him," said Devlin.

"Too old!" cried Dexter. "Why, man, she's only twenty-seven."

He was possessed with a wild notion of rushing out into the streets and taking a train to Detroit. He rose to his feet spasmodically.

"I guess you're busy," Devlin apologized quickly. "I didn't realize—"

"No, I'm not busy," said Dexter, steadying his voice. "I'm not busy at all. Not busy at all. Did you say she was—twenty-seven? No, I said she was twenty-seven."

"Yes, you did," agreed Devlin dryly.

"Go on, then. Go on."

"What do you mean?"

"About Judy Jones."

Devlin looked at him helplessly.

"Well, that's—I told you all there is to it. He treats her like the devil. Oh, they're not going to get divorced or anything. When he's particularly outrageous she forgives him. In fact, I'm inclined to think she loves him. She was a pretty girl when she first came to Detroit."

A pretty girl! The phrase struck Dexter as ludicrous.

"Isn't she—a pretty girl, anymore?"

"Oh, she's all right."

"Look here," said Dexter, sitting down suddenly, "I don't understand. You say she was a 'pretty girl' and now you say she's 'all right.' I don't understand what you mean—Judy Jones wasn't a pretty girl, at all. She was a great beauty. Why, I knew her, I knew her. She was—"

Devlin laughed pleasantly.

"I'm not trying to start a row," he said. "I think Judy's a nice girl and I like her. I can't understand how a man like Lud Simms could fall madly in love with her, but he did." Then he added: "Most of the women like her."

Dexter looked closely at Devlin, thinking wildly that there must be a reason for this, some insensitivity in the man or some private malice.

"Lots of women fade just like *that*," Devlin snapped his fingers. "You must have seen it happen. Perhaps I've forgotten how pretty she was at her wedding. I've seen her so much since then, you see. She has nice eyes."

A sort of dullness settled down upon Dexter. For the first time in his life he felt like getting very drunk. He knew that he was laughing loudly at something Devlin had said, but he did not know what it was or why it was funny. When, in a few minutes, Devlin went he lay down on his lounge and looked out the window at the New York skyline into which the sun was sinking in dull lovely shades of pink and gold.

He had thought that having nothing else to lose he was invulnerable at last—but he knew that he had just lost something more, as surely as if he had married Judy Jones and seen her fade away before his eyes.

The dream was gone. Something had been taken from him. In a sort of panic he pushed the palms of his hands into his eyes and tried to bring up a picture of the waters lapping on Sherry Island and the moonlit verandah, and gingham on the golf links and the dry sun and the gold color of her neck's soft down. And her mouth damp to his kisses and her eyes plaintive with melancholy and her freshness like new fine linen in the morning. Why, these things were no longer in the world! They had existed and they existed no longer.

For the first time in years the tears were streaming down his face. But they were for himself now. He did not care about mouth and eyes and moving hands. He wanted to care and he could not care. For he had gone away and he could never go back anymore. The gates were closed, the sun was gone down and there was no beauty but the grey beauty of steel that withstands all time. Even the grief he could have borne was left behind in the country of illusion, of youth, of the richness of life, where his winter dreams had flourished.

"Long ago," he said, "long ago, there was something in me, but now that thing is gone. Now that thing is gone, that thing is gone. I cannot cry. I cannot care. That thing will come back no more."

THE BABY PARTY

When John Andros felt old he found solace in the thought of life continuing through his child. The dark trumpets of oblivion were less loud at the patter of his child's feet or at the sound of his child's voice babbling mad non sequiturs to him over the telephone. The latter incident occurred every afternoon at three when his wife called the office from the country, and he came to look forward to it as one of the vivid minutes of his day.

He was not physically old, but his life had been a series of struggles up a series of rugged hills, and here at thirty-eight having won his battles against ill health and poverty he cherished less than the usual number of illusions. Even his feeling about his little girl was qualified. She had interrupted his rather intense love affair with his wife, and she was the reason for their living in a suburban town, where they paid for country air with endless servant troubles and the weary merry-go-round of the commuting train.

It was little Ede as a definite piece of youth that chiefly interested him. He liked to take her on his lap and examine minutely her fragrant, downy scalp and her eyes with their irises of morning blue. Having paid this homage John was content that the nurse should take her away. After ten minutes the very vitality of the child irritated him; he was inclined to lose his temper when things were broken, and one Sunday afternoon when she had disrupted a bridge game by permanently hiding the ace of spades, he had made a scene that had reduced his wife to tears.

This was absurd and John was ashamed of himself. It was inevitable that such things would happen, and it was impossible that little Ede should spend all her indoor hours in the nursery upstairs when she was becoming, as her mother said, more nearly a "real person" every day.

She was two and a half and this afternoon, for instance, she was going to a baby party. Grown-up Edith, her mother, had telephoned the information to the office, and little Ede had confirmed the business by shouting "I yam going to a *pantry!*" into John's unsuspecting left ear.

"Drop in at the Markeys' when you get home, won't you, dear?" resumed her mother. "It'll be funny. Ede's going to be all dressed up in her new pink dress—"

The conversation terminated abruptly with a squawk which indicated that the telephone had been pulled violently to the floor. John laughed and decided to get an early train out; the prospect of a baby party in someone else's house amused him.

"What a peach of a mess!" he thought humorously. "A dozen mothers and each one looking at nothing but her own child. All the babies breaking things and grabbing at the cake, and each mama going home thinking about the subtle superiority of her own child to every other child there."

He was in a good humor today—all the things in his life were going better than they had ever gone before. When he got off the train at his station he shook his head at an importunate taxi-man and began to walk up the long hill toward his house through the crisp December twilight. It was only six o'clock but the moon was out, shining with proud brilliance on the thin sugary snow that lay over the lawns.

As he walked along drawing his lungs full of cold air his happiness increased, and the idea of a baby party appealed to him more and more. He began to wonder how Ede compared to other children of her own age and if the pink dress she was to wear was something radical and mature. Increasing his gait he came in sight of his own house, where the lights of a defunct Christmas tree still blossomed in the window, but he continued on past the walk. The party was at the Markeys' next door.

As he mounted the brick step and rang the bell he became aware of voices inside, and he was glad he was not too late. Then he raised his head and listened—the voices were not children's voices, but they were loud and pitched high with anger; there were at least three of them and one, which rose as he listened to a hysterical sob, he recognized immediately as his wife's.

"There's been some trouble," he thought quickly.
Trying the door he found it unlocked and pushed it open.

The baby party began at half past four, but Edith Andros, calculating
shrewdly that the new dress would stand out more sensationally
against vestments already rumpled, planned the arrival of herself and
little Ede for five. When they appeared it was already a flourishing
affair. Four baby girls and nine baby boys, each one curled and
washed and dressed with all the care of a proud and jealous heart,
were dancing to the music of a phonograph. Never more than two
or three were dancing at once, but as all were continually in motion
running to and from their mothers for encouragement, the general
effect was the same.

As Edith and her daughter entered, the music was temporarily
drowned out by a sustained chorus, consisting largely of the word
cute and directed toward little Ede, who stood looking timidly about
and fingering the edges of her pink dress. She was not kissed—this
is the sanitary age—but she was passed along a row of mamas each
one of whom said "cu-u-ute" to her and held her pink little hand
before passing her on to the next. After some encouragement and
a few mild pushes she was absorbed into the dance and became an
active member of the party.

Edith stood near the door talking to Mrs. Markey and keeping
one eye on the tiny figure in the pink dress. She did not care for Mrs.
Markey; she considered her both snippy and common, but John and
Joe Markey were congenial and went in together on the commuting
train every morning, so the two women kept up an elaborate pretense of warm amity. They were always reproaching each other for
"not coming to see me," and they were always planning the kind
of parties that began with "You'll have to come to dinner with us
soon, and we'll go in to the theatre," but never matured further.

"Little Ede looks perfectly darling," said Mrs. Markey, smiling and moistening her lips in a way that Edith found particularly
repulsive. "So *grown-up*—I can't *believe* it!"

Edith wondered if "little Ede" referred to the fact that Billy
Markey, though several months younger, weighed almost five
pounds more. Accepting a cup of tea she took a seat with two other

ladies on a divan and launched into the real business of the afternoon, which of course lay in relating the recent accomplishments and insouciances of her child.

An hour passed. Dancing palled and the babies took to sterner sport. They ran into the dining room, rounded the big table and essayed the kitchen door, from which they were rescued by an expeditionary force of mothers. Having been rounded up they immediately broke loose, and rushing back to the dining room tried the familiar swinging door again. The word "overheated" began to be used, and small white brows were dried with small white handkerchiefs. A general attempt to make the babies sit down began, but the babies squirmed off laps with peremptory cries of "Down! Down!" and the rush into the fascinating dining room began anew.

This phase of the party came to an end with the arrival of refreshments, a large cake with two candles, and saucers of vanilla ice cream. Billy Markey, a stout laughing baby with red hair and legs somewhat bowed, blew out the candles and placed an experimental thumb on the white frosting. The refreshments were distributed, and the children ate greedily but without confusion—they had behaved remarkably well all afternoon. They were modern babies who ate and slept at regular hours, so their dispositions were good and their faces healthy and pink—such a peaceful party would not have been possible thirty years ago.

After the refreshments a gradual exodus began. Edith glanced anxiously at her watch—it was almost six and John had not arrived. She wanted him to see Ede with the other children—to see how dignified and polite and intelligent she was and how the only ice-cream spot on her dress was some that had dropped from her chin when she was joggled from behind.

"You're a darling," she whispered to her child, drawing her suddenly against her knee. "Do you know you're a darling? Do you *know* you're a darling?"

Ede laughed. "Bow-wow," she said suddenly.

"Bow-wow?" Edith looked around. "There isn't any bow-wow."

"Bow-wow," repeated Ede. "I want a bow-wow."

Edith followed the small pointing finger.

"That isn't a bow-wow, dearest, that's a teddy-bear."

"Bear?"

"Yes, that's a teddy-bear, and it belongs to Billy Markey. You don't want Billy Markey's teddy-bear, do you?"

Ede did want it.

She broke away from her mother and approached Billy Markey, who held the toy closely in his arms. Ede stood regarding him with inscrutable eyes and Billy laughed.

Grown-up Edith looked at her watch again, this time impatiently.

The party had dwindled until, besides Ede and Billy, there were only two babies remaining—and one of the two remained only by virtue of having hidden himself under the dining-room table. It was selfish of John not to come. It showed so little pride in the child. Other fathers had come, half a dozen of them, to call for their wives, and they had stayed for awhile and looked on.

There was a sudden wail. Ede had obtained Billy's teddy-bear by pulling it forcibly from his arms, and on Billy's attempt to recover it, she had pushed him casually to the floor.

"Why, Ede!" cried her mother, repressing an inclination to laugh.

Joe Markey, a handsome, broad-shouldered man of thirty-five, picked up his son and set him on his feet. "You're a fine fellow," he said jovially. "Let a girl knock you over! You're a fine fellow."

"Did he bump his head?" Mrs. Markey returned anxiously from bowing the next to last remaining mother out the door.

"No-o-o-o," exclaimed Markey. "He bumped something else, didn't you, Billy? He bumped something else."

Billy had so far forgotten the bump that he was already making an attempt to recover his property. He seized a leg of the bear which projected from Ede's enveloping arms and tugged at it but without success.

"No," said Ede emphatically.

Suddenly, encouraged by the success of her former half accidental maneuver, Ede dropped the teddy-bear, placed her hands on Billy's shoulders and pushed him backward off his feet.

This time he landed less harmlessly; his head hit the bare floor just off the rug with a dull hollow sound, whereupon he drew in his breath and delivered an agonized yell.

Immediately the room was in confusion. With an exclamation Markey hurried to his son, but his wife was first to reach the injured baby and catch him up into her arms.

"Oh, *Billy*," she cried, "what a terrible bump! She ought to be spanked."

Edith, who had rushed immediately to her daughter, heard this remark and her lips came sharply together.

"Why, Ede," she whispered perfunctorily, "you bad girl!"

Ede put back her little head suddenly and laughed. It was a loud laugh, a triumphant laugh with victory in it and challenge and contempt. Unfortunately it was also an infectious laugh. Before her mother realized the delicacy of the situation, she too had laughed, an audible, distinct laugh not unlike the baby's and partaking of the same overtones.

Then, as suddenly, she stopped.

Mrs. Markey's face had grown red with anger and Markey, who had been feeling the back of the baby's head with one finger, looked at her, frowning.

"It's swollen already," he said with a note of reproof in his voice. "I'll get some witch-hazel."

But Mrs. Markey had lost her temper. "I don't see anything funny about a child being hurt!" she said in a trembling voice.

Little Ede meanwhile had been looking at her mother curiously. She noted that her own laugh had produced her mother's, and she wondered if the same cause would always produce the same effect. So she chose this moment to throw back her head and laugh again.

To her mother the additional mirth added the final touch of hysteria to the situation. Pressing her handkerchief to her mouth she giggled irrepressibly. It was more than nervousness—she felt that in a peculiar way she was laughing with her child—they were laughing together.

It was in a way a defiance—those two against the world.

While Markey rushed upstairs to the bathroom for ointment, his wife was walking up and down rocking the yelling boy in her arms.

"Please go home!" she broke out suddenly. "The child's badly hurt, and if you haven't the decency to be quiet, you'd better go home."

"Very well," said Edith, her own temper rising. "I've never seen anyone make such a mountain out of—"

"Get out!" cried Mrs. Markey frantically. "There's the door, get out—I never want to see you in our house again. You or your brat either!"

Edith had taken her daughter's hand and was moving quickly toward the door, but at this remark she stopped and turned around, her face contracting with indignation.

"Don't you dare call her that!"

Mrs. Markey did not answer but continued walking up and down, muttering to herself and to Billy in an inaudible voice.

Edith began to cry.

"I will get out!" she sobbed. "I've never heard anybody so rude and c-common in my life. I'm glad your baby did get pushed down—he's nothing but a f-fat little fool anyhow."

Joe Markey reached the foot of the stairs just in time to hear this remark.

"Why, Mrs. Andros," he said sharply, "can't you see the child's hurt? You really ought to control yourself."

"Control m-myself!" exclaimed Edith brokenly. "You better ask her to c-control herself. I've never heard anybody so c-common in my life."

"She's insulting me!" Mrs. Markey was now livid with rage. "Did you hear what she said, Joe? I wish you'd put her out. If she won't go, just take her by the shoulders and put her out!"

"Don't you dare touch me!" cried Edith. "I'm going just as quick as I can find my c-coat!"

Blind with tears she took a step toward the hall. It was just at this moment that the door opened and John Andros walked anxiously in.

"John!" cried Edith and fled to him wildly.

"What's the matter? Why, what's the matter?"

"They're—they're putting me out!" she wailed, collapsing against him. "He'd just started to take me by the shoulders and put me out. I want my coat!"

"That's not true," objected Markey hurriedly. "Nobody's going to put you out." He turned to John. "Nobody's going to put her out," he repeated. "She's—"

"What do you mean 'put her out'?" demanded John abruptly. "What's all this talk, anyhow?"

"Oh, let's go!" cried Edith. "I want to go. They're so *common*, John!"

"Look here!" Markey's face darkened. "You've said that about enough. You're acting sort of crazy."

"They called Ede a brat!"

For the second time that afternoon little Ede expressed emotion at an inopportune moment. Confused and frightened at the shouting voices, she began to cry, and her tears had the effect of conveying that she felt the insult in her heart.

"What's the idea of this?" broke out John. "Do you insult your guests in your own house?"

"It seems to me it's your wife that's done the insulting!" answered Markey crisply. "In fact, your baby there started all the trouble."

John gave a contemptuous snort. "Are you calling names at a little baby?" he inquired. "That's a fine manly business!"

"Don't talk to him, John," insisted Edith. "Find my coat!"

"You must be in a bad way," went on John angrily, "if you have to take out your temper on a helpless little baby."

"I never heard anything so damn twisted in my life," shouted Markey. "If that wife of yours would shut her mouth for a minute—"

"Wait a minute! You're not talking to a woman and child now—"

There was an incidental interruption. Edith had been fumbling on a chair for her coat, and Mrs. Markey had been watching her with hot angry eyes. Suddenly she laid Billy down on the sofa, where he immediately stopped crying and pulled himself upright, and coming into the hall she quickly found Edith's coat and handed it to her without a word. Then she went back to the sofa, picked up Billy, and rocking him in her arms looked again at Edith with hot angry eyes. The interruption had taken less than half a minute.

"Your wife comes in here and begins shouting around about how common we are!" burst out Markey violently. "Well, if we're so damn common you'd better stay away! And what's more you'd better get out now!"

Again John gave a short, contemptuous laugh.

"You're not only common," he returned. "You're evidently an awful bully—when there's any helpless women and children around." He felt for the knob and swung the door open. "Come on, Edith."

Taking up her daughter in her arms, his wife stepped outside and John, still looking contemptuously at Markey, started to follow.

"Wait a minute!" Markey took a step forward; he was trembling slightly, and two large veins on his temple were suddenly full of blood. "You don't think you can get away with that, do you? With me?"

Without a word John walked out the door, leaving it open.

Edith, still weeping, had started for home. After following her with his eyes until she reached her own walk, John turned back toward the lighted doorway where Markey was slowly coming down the slippery steps. He took off his overcoat and hat, tossed them off the path onto the snow. Then, sliding a little on the iced walk, he took a step forward.

At the first blow, they both slipped and fell heavily to the sidewalk, half rising then, and again pulling each other to the ground. They found a better foothold in the thin snow to the side of the walk and rushed at each other, both swinging wildly and pressing out the snow into a pasty mud underfoot.

The street was deserted, and except for their short tired gasps and the padded sound as one or the other slipped down into the slushy mud, they fought in silence, clearly defined to each other by the full moonlight as well as by the amber glow that shone out of the open door. Several times they both slipped down together, and then for awhile the conflict threshed about wildly on the lawn.

For ten, fifteen, twenty minutes they fought there senselessly in the moonlight. They had both taken off coats and vests at some silently agreed upon interval and now their shirts dripped from their backs in wet pulpy shreds. Both were torn and bleeding and so exhausted that they could stand only when by their position they mutually supported each other—the impact, the mere effort of a blow, would send them both to their hands and knees.

But it was not weariness that ended the business, and the very meaninglessness of the fight was a reason for not stopping. They stopped because once when they were straining at each other on the ground, they heard a man's footsteps coming along the sidewalk.

They had rolled somehow into the shadow, and when they heard these footsteps they stopped fighting, stopped moving, stopped breathing, lay huddled together like two boys playing Indian until the footsteps had passed. Then, staggering to their feet, they looked at each other like two drunken men.

"I'll be damned if I'm going on with this thing anymore," cried Markey thickly.

"I'm not going on anymore either," said John Andros. "I've had enough of this thing."

Again they looked at each other, sulkily this time, as if each suspected the other of urging him to a renewal of the fight. Markey spat out a mouthful of blood from a cut lip; then he cursed softly, and picking up his coat and vest, shook off the snow from them in a surprised way, as if their comparative dampness was his only worry in the world.

"Want to come in and wash up?" he asked suddenly.

"No thanks," said John. "I ought to be going home—my wife'll be worried."

He too picked up his coat and vest and then his overcoat and hat. Soaking wet and dripping with perspiration, it seemed absurd that less than half an hour ago he had been wearing all these clothes.

"Well—good-night," he said hesitantly.

Suddenly they both walked toward each other and shook hands. It was no perfunctory hand-shake: John Andros's arm went around Markey's shoulder, and he patted him softly on the back for a little while.

"No harm done," he said brokenly.

"No—you?"

"No, no harm done."

"Well," said John Andros after a minute, "I guess I'll say good-night."

"Good-night."

Limping slightly and with his clothes over his arm, John Andros turned away. The moonlight was still bright as he left the dark patch of trampled ground and walked over the intervening lawn. Down at the station, half a mile away, he could hear the rumble of the seven o'clock train.

"But you must have been crazy," cried Edith brokenly. "I thought you were going to fix it all up there and shake hands. That's why I went away."

"Did you want us to fix it up?"

"Of course not, I never want to see them again. But I thought of course that was what you were going to do." She was touching the bruises on his neck and back with iodine as he sat placidly in a hot bath. "I'm going to get the doctor," she said insistently. "You may be hurt internally."

He shook his head. "Not a chance," he answered. " I don't want this to get all over town."

"I don't understand yet how it all happened."

"Neither do I." He smiled grimly. "I guess these baby parties are pretty rough affairs."

"Well, one thing—" suggested Edith hopefully, "I'm certainly glad we have beefsteak in the house for tomorrow's dinner."

"Why?"

"For your eye, of course. Do you know I came within an ace of ordering veal? Wasn't that the luckiest thing?"

Half an hour later, dressed except that his neck would accommodate no collar, John moved his limbs experimentally before the glass. "I believe I'll get myself in better shape," he said thoughtfully. "I must be getting old."

"You mean so that next time you can beat him?"

"I did beat him," he announced. "At least, I beat him as much as he beat me. And there isn't going to be any next time. Don't you go calling people common anymore. If you get in any trouble, you just take your coat and go home. Understand?"

"Yes, dear," she said meekly. "I was very foolish and now I understand."

Out in the hall, he paused abruptly by the baby's door.

"Is she asleep?"

"Sound asleep. But you can go in and peek at her—just to say good-night."

They tiptoed in and bent together over the bed. Little Ede, her cheeks flushed with health, her pink hands clasped tight together, was sleeping soundly in the cool dark room. John reached over the railing of the bed and passed his hand lightly over the silken hair.

"She's asleep," he murmured in a puzzled way.

"Naturally, after such an afternoon."

"Miz Andros," the colored maid's stage whisper floated in from the hall, "Mr. and Miz Markey downstairs an' want to see you. Mr. Markey he's all cut up in pieces, mam'n. His face look like a roast beef. An' Miz Markey she 'pear mighty mad."

"Why, what incomparable nerve!" exclaimed Edith. "Just tell them we're not home. I wouldn't go down for anything in the world."

"You most certainly will." John's voice was hard and set.

"What?"

"You'll go down right now, and what's more, whatever that other woman does, you'll apologize for what you said this afternoon. After that you don't ever have to see her again."

"Why—John, I can't."

"You've got to. And just remember that she probably hated to come over here just twice as much as you hate to go downstairs."

"Aren't you coming? Do I have to go alone?"

"I'll be down—in just a minute."

John Andros waited until she had closed the door behind her; then he reached over into the bed, and picking up his daughter, blankets and all, sat down in the rocking-chair holding her tightly in his arms. She moved a little and he held his breath, but she was sleeping soundly and in a moment she was resting quietly in the hollow of his elbow. Slowly he bent his head until his cheek was against her bright hair. "Dear little girl," he whispered. "Dear little girl, dear little girl."

John Andros knew at length what it was he had fought for so savagely that evening. He had it now, he possessed it forever, and for some time he sat there rocking very slowly to and fro in the darkness.

ABSOLUTION

There was once a priest with cold, watery eyes, who, in the still of the night, wept cold tears. He wept because the afternoons were warm and long, and he was unable to attain a complete mystical union with our Lord. Sometimes, near four o'clock, there was a rustle of Swede girls along the path by his window, and in their shrill laughter he found a terrible dissonance that made him pray aloud for the twilight to come. At twilight the laughter and the voices were quieter, but several times he had walked past Romberg's Drug Store when it was dusk and the yellow lights shone inside and the nickel taps of the soda-fountain were gleaming, and he had found the scent of cheap toilet soap desperately sweet upon the air. He passed that way when he returned from hearing confessions on Saturday nights, and he grew careful to walk on the other side of the street so that the smell of the soap would float upward before it reached his nostrils as it drifted, rather like incense, toward the summer moon.

But there was no escape from the hot madness of four o'clock. From his window, as far as he could see, the Dakota wheat thronged the valley of the Red River. The wheat was terrible to look upon and the carpet pattern to which in agony he bent his eyes sent his thoughts brooding through grotesque labyrinths, open always to the unavoidable sun.

One afternoon when he had reached the point where the mind runs down like an old clock, his housekeeper brought into his study a beautiful, intense little boy of eleven named Rudolph Miller. The little boy sat down in a patch of sunshine and the priest, at his walnut desk, pretended to be very busy. This was to conceal his relief that someone had come into his haunted room.

Presently he turned around and found himself staring into two enormous, staccato eyes, lit with gleaming points of cobalt light.

For a moment their expression startled him—then he saw that his visitor was in a state of abject fear.

"Your mouth is trembling," said Father Schwartz, in a haggard voice.

The little boy covered his quivering mouth with his hand.

"Are you in trouble?" asked Father Schwartz, sharply. "Take your hand away from your mouth and tell me what's the matter."

The boy—Father Schwartz recognized him now as the son of a parishioner, Mr. Miller, the freight agent—moved his hand reluctantly off his mouth and became articulate in a despairing whisper.

"Father Schwartz—I've committed a terrible sin."

"A sin against purity?"

"No, Father . . . worse."

Father Schwartz's body jerked sharply.

"Have you killed somebody?"

"No—but I'm afraid—" the voice rose to a shrill whimper.

"Do you want to go to confession?"

The little boy shook his head miserably. Father Schwartz cleared his throat so that he could make his voice soft and say some quiet, kind thing. In this moment he should forget his own agony and try to act like God. He repeated to himself a devotional phrase, hoping that in return God would help him to act correctly.

"Tell me what you've done," said his new soft voice.

The little boy looked at him through his tears and was reassured by the impression of moral resiliency which the distraught priest had created. Abandoning as much of himself as he was able to this man, Rudolph Miller began to tell his story.

"On Saturday, three days ago, my father he said I had to go to confession, because I hadn't been for a month, and the family they go every week, and I hadn't been. So I just as leave go, I didn't care. So I put it off till after supper because I was playing with a bunch of kids and Father asked me if I went and I said 'no,' and he took me by the neck and he said 'You go now,' so I said 'All right,' so I went over to church. And he yelled after me: 'Don't come back till you go.' . . ."

II

"On Saturday, Three Days Ago"

The plush curtain of the confessional rearranged its dismal creases, leaving exposed only the bottom of an old man's old shoe. Behind the curtain an immortal soul was alone with God and the Reverend Adolphus Schwartz, priest of the parish. Sound began, a labored whispering, sibilant and discreet, broken at intervals by the voice of the priest in audible question.

Rudolph Miller knelt in the pew beside the confessional and waited, straining nervously to hear and yet not to hear what was being said within. The fact that the priest was audible alarmed him. His own turn came next, and the three or four others who waited might listen unscrupulously while he admitted his violations of the Sixth and Ninth Commandments.

Rudolph had never committed adultery, nor even coveted his neighbor's wife—but it was the confession of the associate sins that was particularly hard to contemplate. In comparison he relished the less shameful fallings away—they formed a greyish background which relieved the ebony mark of sexual offenses upon his soul.

He had been covering his ears with his hands, hoping that his refusal to hear would be noticed, and a like courtesy rendered to him in turn, when a sharp movement of the penitent in the confessional made him sink his face precipitately into the crook of his elbow. Fear assumed solid form and pressed out a lodging between his heart and his lungs. He must try now with all his might to be sorry for his sins—not because he was afraid, but because he had offended God. He must convince God that he was sorry and to do so he must first convince himself. After a tense emotional struggle he achieved a tremulous self-pity, and decided that he was now ready. If, by allowing no other thought to enter his head, he could preserve this state of emotion unimpaired until he went into that large coffin set on end, he would have survived another crisis in his religious life.

For some time, however, a demoniac notion had partially possessed him. He could go home now, before his turn came, and tell his mother that he had arrived too late and found the priest gone. This, unfortunately, involved the risk of being caught in a lie. As an alternative he could say that he *had* gone to confession, but this meant that he must avoid communion next day, for communion taken upon an uncleansed soul would turn to poison in his mouth, and he would crumple limp and damned from the altar rail.

Again Father Schwartz's voice became audible.

"And for your—"

The words blurred to a husky mumble and Rudolph got excitedly to his feet. He felt that it was impossible for him to go to confession this afternoon. He hesitated tensely. Then from the confessional came a tap, a creak and a sustained rustle. The slide had fallen and the plush curtain trembled. Temptation had come to him too late. . . .

"Bless me, Father, for I have sinned. . . . I confess to Almighty God and to you, Father, that I have sinned. . . . Since my last confession it has been one month and three days. . . . I accuse myself of—taking the Name of the Lord in vain. . . ."

This was an easy sin. His curses had been but bravado—telling of them was little less than a brag.

". . . of being mean to an old lady."

The wan shadow moved a little on the latticed slat.

"How, my child?"

"Old lady Swenson," Rudolph's murmur soared jubilantly. "She got our baseball that we knocked in her window, and she wouldn't give it back, so we yelled 'Twenty-three Skidoo' at her all afternoon. Then about five o'clock she had a fit and they had to have the doctor."

"Go on, my child."

"Of—of not believing I was the son of my parents."

"What?" The interrogator was distinctly startled.

"Of not believing that I was the son of my parents."

"Why not?"

"Oh, just pride," answered the penitent airily.

"You mean you thought you were too good to be the son of your parents?"

"Yes, Father." On a less jubilant note.

"Go on."

"Of being disobedient and calling my mother names. Of slandering people behind my back. Of smoking—"

Rudolph had now exhausted the minor offenses and was approaching the sins it was agony to tell. He held his fingers against his face like bars as if to press out between them the shame in his heart.

"Of dirty words and immodest thoughts and desires," he whispered very low.

"How often?"

"I don't know."

"Once a week? Twice a week?"

"Twice a week."

"Did you yield to these desires?"

"No, Father."

"Were you alone when you had them?"

"No, Father. I was with two boys and a girl."

"Don't you know, my child, that you should avoid the occasions of sin as well as the sin itself? Evil companionship leads to evil desires and evil desires to evil actions. Where were you when this happened?"

"In a barn in back of—"

"I don't want to hear any names," interrupted the priest sharply.

"Well, it was up in the loft of this barn and this girl and— a fella, they were saying things—saying immodest things, and I stayed."

"You should have gone—you should have told the girl to go."

He should have gone! He could not tell Father Schwartz how his pulse had bumped in his wrist, how a strange, romantic excitement had possessed him when those curious things had been said. Perhaps in the houses of delinquency among the dull and hard-eyed incorrigible girls can be found those for whom has burned the whitest fire.

"Have you anything else to tell me?"

"I don't think so, Father."

Rudolph felt a great relief. Perspiration had broken out under his tight-pressed fingers.

"Have you told any lies?"

The question startled him. Like all those who habitually and instinctively lie, he had an enormous respect and awe for the truth. Something almost exterior to himself dictated a quick, hurt answer.

"Oh, no, Father, I never tell lies."

For a moment, like the commoner in the king's chair, he tasted the pride of the situation. Then as the priest began to murmur conventional admonitions he realized that in heroically denying he had told lies, he had committed a terrible sin—he had told a lie in confession.

In automatic response to Father Schwartz's "Make an act of contrition," he began to repeat aloud meaninglessly:

"Oh, my God, I am heartily sorry for having offended Thee. . . ."

He must fix this now—it was a bad mistake—but as his teeth shut on the last words of his prayer there was a sharp sound, and the slat was closed.

A minute later when he emerged into the twilight the relief in coming from the muggy church into an open world of wheat and sky postponed the full realization of what he had done. Instead of worrying he took a deep breath of the crisp air and began to say over and over to himself the words "Blatchford Sarnemington, Blatchford Sarnemington!"

Blatchford Sarnemington was himself, and these words were in effect a lyric. When he became Blatchford Sarnemington a suave nobility flowed from him. Blatchford Sarnemington lived in great sweeping triumphs. When Rudolph half closed his eyes it meant that Blatchford had established dominance over him and, as he went by, there were envious mutters in the air: "Blatchford Sarnemington! There goes Blatchford Sarnemington."

He was Blatchford now for awhile as he strutted homeward along the staggering road, but when the road braced itself in macadam in order to become the main street of Ludwig, Rudolph's exhilaration faded out and his mind cooled and he felt the horror of his lie. God, of course, already knew of it—but Rudolph reserved a corner of his mind where he was safe from God, where he prepared the subterfuges with which he often tricked God. Hiding now in this corner he considered how he could best avoid the consequences of his misstatement.

At all costs he must avoid communion next day. The risk of anger-
ing God to such an extent was too great. He would have to drink
water "by accident" in the morning and thus, in accordance with
a church law, render himself unfit to receive communion that day.
In spite of its flimsiness this subterfuge was the most feasible that
occurred to him. He accepted its risks and was concentrating on
how best to put it into effect, as he turned the corner by Romberg's
Drug Store and came in sight of his father's house.

III

Rudolph's father, the local freight agent, had floated with the second
wave of German and Irish stock to the Minnesota-Dakota country. Theoretically, great opportunities lay ahead of a young man of
energy in that day and place, but Carl Miller had been incapable of
establishing either with his superiors or his subordinates the reputation for approximate immutability which is essential to success in
a hierarchic industry. Somewhat gross, he was, nevertheless, insuf-
ficiently hard-headed and unable to take fundamental relationships
for granted, and this inability made him suspicious, unrestful and
continually dismayed.

His two bonds with the colorful life were his faith in the Roman
Catholic Church and his mystical worship of the Empire Builder,
James J. Hill. Hill was the apotheosis of that quality in which Miller
himself was deficient—the sense of things, the feel of things, the hint
of rain in the wind on the cheek. Miller's mind worked late on the old
decisions of other men, and he had never in his life felt the balance
of any single thing in his hands. His weary, sprightly, undersized
body was growing old in Hill's gigantic shadow. For twenty years
he had lived alone with Hill's name and God.

On Sunday morning Carl Miller awoke in the dustless quiet of six
o'clock. Kneeling by the side of the bed he bent his yellow-grey hair
and the full dapple bangs of his mustache into the pillow, and prayed
for several minutes. Then he drew off his night-shirt—like the rest
of his generation he had never been able to endure pajamas—and
clothed his thin, white, hairless body in woollen underwear.

He shaved. Silence in the other bedroom where his wife lay nervously asleep. Silence from the screened-off corner of the hall where

his son's cot stood, and his son slept among his Alger books, his collection of cigar-bands, his mothy pennants—"Cornell," "Hamline," and "Greetings from Pueblo, New Mexico"—and the other possessions of his private life. From outside Miller could hear the shrill birds and the whirring movement of the poultry and, as an undertone, the low, swelling click-a-tick of the six-fifteen through-train for Montana and the green coast beyond. Then as the cold water dripped from the washrag in his hand he raised his head suddenly—he had heard a furtive sound from the kitchen below.

He dried his razor hastily, slipped his dangling suspenders to his shoulders, and listened. Someone was walking in the kitchen, and he knew by the light foot-fall that it was not his wife. With his mouth faintly ajar he ran quickly down the stairs and opened the kitchen door.

Standing by the sink, with one hand on the still dripping faucet and the other clutching a full glass of water, stood his son. The boy's eyes, still heavy with sleep, met his father's with a frightened, reproachful beauty. He was barefooted and his pajamas were rolled up at the knees and sleeves.

For a moment they both remained motionless—Carl Miller's brow went down and his son's went up, as though they were striking a balance between the extremes of emotion which filled them. Then the bangs of the parent's mustache descended portentously until they obscured his mouth, and he gave a short glance around to see if anything had been disturbed.

The kitchen was garnished with sunlight which beat on the pans and made the smooth boards of the floor and table yellow and clean as wheat. It was the center of the house where the fire burned and the tins fitted into tins like toys, and the steam whistled all day on a thin pastel note. Nothing was moved, nothing touched—except the faucet where beads of water still formed and dripped with a white flash into the sink below.

"What are you doing?"

"I got awful thirsty, so I thought I'd just come down and get—"

"I thought you were going to communion."

A look of vehement astonishment spread over his son's face.

"I forgot all about it."

"Have you drunk any water?"

"No—"

As the word left his mouth Rudolph knew it was the wrong answer, but the faded indignant eyes facing him had signalled up the truth before the boy's will could act. He realized, too, that he should never have come downstairs; some vague necessity for verisimilitude had made him want to leave a wet glass as evidence by the sink; the honesty of his imagination had betrayed him.

"Pour it out," commanded his father, "that water!"

Rudolph despairingly inverted the tumbler.

"What's the matter with you, anyways?" demanded Miller angrily.

"Nothing."

"Did you go to confession yesterday?"

"Yes."

"Then why were you going to drink water?"

"I don't know—I forgot."

"Maybe you care more about being a little bit thirsty than you do about your religion."

"I forgot." Rudolph could feel the tears straining in his eyes.

"That's no answer."

"Well, I did."

"You better look out!" His father held to a high, persistent, inquisitory note: "If you're so forgetful that you can't remember your religion something better be done about it."

Rudolph filled a sharp pause with:

"I can remember it all right."

"First you begin to neglect your religion," cried his father, fanning his own fierceness, "the next thing you'll begin to lie and steal, and the *next* thing is the *reform* school!"

Not even this familiar threat could deepen the abyss that Rudolph saw before him. He must either tell all now, offering his body for what he knew would be a ferocious beating, or else tempt the thunderbolts by receiving the Body and Blood of Christ with sacrilege upon his soul. And of the two the former seemed more terrible—it was not so much the beating he dreaded as the savage ferocity, outlet of the ineffectual man, which would lie behind it.

"Put down that glass and go upstairs and dress!" his father ordered. "And when we get to church, before you go to communion, you better kneel down and ask God to forgive you for your carelessness."

Some accidental emphasis in the phrasing of this command acted like a catalytic agent on the confusion and terror of Rudolph's mind. A wild, proud anger rose in him, and he dashed the tumbler passionately into the sink.

His father uttered a strained, husky sound, and sprang for him. Rudolph dodged to the side, tipped over a chair, and tried to get beyond the kitchen table. He cried out sharply when a hand grasped his pajama shoulder, then he felt the dull impact of a fist against the side of his head and glancing blows on the upper part of his body. As he slipped here and there in his father's grasp, dragged or lifted when he clung instinctively to an arm, aware of sharp smarts and strains, he made no sound except that he laughed hysterically several times. Then in less than a minute the blows abruptly ceased. After a lull during which Rudolph was tightly held and during which they both trembled violently and uttered strange, truncated words, Carl Miller half dragged, half threatened his son upstairs.

"Put on your clothes!"

Rudolph was now both hysterical and cold. His head hurt him, and there was a long, shallow scratch on his neck from his father's fingernail, and he sobbed and trembled as he dressed. He was aware of his mother standing at the doorway in a wrapper, her wrinkled face compressing and squeezing and opening out into a new series of wrinkles which floated and eddied from neck to brow. Despising her nervous ineffectuality and avoiding her rudely when she tried to touch his neck with witch-hazel, he made a hasty, choking toilet. Then he followed his father out of the house and along the road toward the Catholic church.

IV

They walked without speaking except when Carl Miller acknowledged automatically the existence of passers-by. Rudolph's uneven breathing alone ruffled the hot Sunday silence.

His father stopped decisively at the door of the church.

"I've decided you'd better go to confession again. Go in and tell Father Schwartz what you did and ask God's pardon."

"You lost your temper, too!" said Rudolph quickly.

Carl Miller took a step toward his son, who moved cautiously backward.

"All right, I'll go."

"Are you going to do what I say?" cried his father in a hoarse whisper.

"All right."

Rudolph walked into the church and for the second time in two days entered the confessional and knelt down. The slat went up almost at once.

"I accuse myself of missing my morning prayers."

"Is that all?"

"That's all."

A maudlin exultation filled him. Not easily ever again would he be able to put an abstraction before the necessities of his ease and pride. An invisible line had been crossed and he had become aware of his isolation—aware that it applied not only to those moments when he was Blatchford Sarnemington but that it applied to all his inner life. Hitherto such phenomena as "crazy" ambitions and petty shames and fears had been but private reservations, unacknowledged before the throne of his official soul. Now he realized unconsciously that his private reservations were himself—and all the rest a garnished front and a conventional flag. The pressure of his environment had driven him into the lonely secret road of adolescence.

He knelt in the pew beside his father. Mass began. Rudolph knelt up—when he was alone he slumped his posterior back against the seat—and tasted the consciousness of a sharp, subtle revenge. Beside him his father prayed that God would forgive Rudolph, and asked also that his own outbreak of temper would be pardoned. He glanced sidewise at this son and was relieved to see that the strained, wild look had gone from his face and that he had ceased sobbing. The Grace of God, inherent in the Sacrament, would do the rest, and perhaps after Mass everything would be better. He was proud of Rudolph in his heart and beginning to be truly as well as formally sorry for what he had done.

Usually, the passing of the collection box was a significant point for Rudolph in the services. If, as was often the case, he had no money to drop in he would be furiously ashamed and bow his head and pretend not to see the box, lest Jeanne Brady in the pew behind should take notice and suspect an acute family poverty. But today he glanced coldly into it as it skimmed under his eyes, noting with casual interest the large number of pennies it contained.

When the bell rang for communion, however, he quivered. There was no reason why God should not stop his heart. During the past twelve hours he had committed a series of mortal sins increasing in gravity, and he was now to crown them all with a blasphemous sacrilege.

"*Dómini, non sum dignus, ut intres sub tectum meum: sed tantum dic verbo, et sănábitur ánima mea. . . .*"

There was a rustle in the pews and the communicants worked their ways into the aisle with downcast eyes and joined hands. Those of larger piety pressed together their fingertips to form steeples. Among these latter was Carl Miller. Rudolph followed him toward the altar rail and knelt down, automatically taking up the napkin under his chin. The bell rang sharply, and the priest turned from the altar with the white Host held above the chalice:

"*Corpus Dómini nostri Jesu Christi custódiat ánimam meam in vitam ætérnam.*"

A cold sweat broke out on Rudolph's forehead as the communion began. Along the line Father Schwartz moved, and with gathering nausea Rudolph felt his heart-valves weakening at the will of God. It seemed to him that the church was darker and that a great quiet had fallen, broken only by the inarticulate mumble which announced the approach of the Creator of Heaven and Earth. He dropped his head down between his shoulders and waited for the blow.

Then he felt a sharp nudge in his side. His father was poking him to sit up, not to slump against the rail; the priest was only two places away.

"*Corpus Dómini nostri Jesu Christi custódiat ánimam tuam in vitam ætérnam.*"

Rudolph opened his mouth. He felt the sticky wax taste of the wafer on his tongue. He remained motionless for what seemed an interminable period of time, his head still raised, the wafer undissolved in his mouth. Then again he started at the pressure of his father's elbow, and saw that the people were falling away from the altar like leaves and turning with blind downcast eyes to their pews, alone with God.

Rudolph was alone with himself, drenched with perspiration and deep in mortal sin. As he walked back to his pew the sharp taps of his cloven hoofs were loud upon the floor, and he knew that it was a dark poison he carried in his heart.

v

"Sagitta Volante in Die"

The beautiful little boy with eyes like blue stones, and lashes that sprayed open from them like flower-petals, had finished telling his sin to Father Schwartz—and the square of sunshine in which he sat had moved forward half an hour into the room. Rudolph had become less frightened now; once eased of the story a reaction had set in. He knew that as long as he was in the room with this priest God would not stop his heart, so he sighed and sat quietly, waiting for the priest to speak.

Father Schwartz's cold watery eyes were fixed upon the carpet pattern on which the sun had brought out the swastikas and the flat bloomless vines and the pale echoes of flowers. The hall clock ticked insistently toward sunset, and from the ugly room and from the afternoon outside the window arose a stiff monotony, shattered now and then by the reverberate clapping of a far-away hammer on the dry air. The priest's nerves were strung thin and the beads of his rosary were crawling and squirming like snakes upon the green felt of his table top. He could not remember now what it was he should say.

Of all the things in this lost Swede town he was most aware of this little boy's eyes—the beautiful eyes, with lashes that left them reluctantly and curved back as though to meet them once more.

For a moment longer the silence persisted while Rudolph waited, and the priest struggled to remember something that was slipping farther and farther away from him, and the clock ticked in the broken house. Then Father Schwartz stared hard at the little boy and remarked in a peculiar voice—

"When a lot of people get together in the best places things go glimmering."

Rudolph started and looked quickly at Father Schwartz's face.

"I said—" began the priest, and paused, listening. "Do you hear the hammer and the clock ticking and the bees? Well, that's no good. The thing is to have a lot of people in the center of the world, wherever that happens to be. Then"—his watery eyes widened knowingly—"things go glimmering."

"Yes, Father," agreed Rudolph, feeling a little frightened.

"What are you going to be when you grow up?"

"Well, I was going to be a baseball player for awhile," answered Rudolph nervously, "but I don't think that's a very good ambition, so I think I'll be an actor or a navy officer."

Again the priest stared at him.

"I see *exactly* what you mean," he said, with a fierce air.

Rudolph had not meant anything in particular, and at the implication that he had, he became more uneasy.

"This man is crazy," he thought, "and I'm scared of him. He wants me to help him out some way, and I don't want to."

"You look as if things went glimmering," cried Father Schwartz wildly. "Did you ever go to a party?"

"Yes, Father."

"And did you notice that everybody was properly dressed? That's what I mean. Just as you went into the party there was a moment when everybody was properly dressed. Maybe two little girls were standing by the door and some boys were leaning over the banisters, and there were bowls around full of flowers."

"I've been to a lot of parties," said Rudolph, rather relieved that the conversation had taken this turn.

"Of course," continued Father Schwartz triumphantly, "I knew you'd agree with me. But my theory is that when a whole lot of people get together in the best places things go glimmering all the time."

Rudolph found himself thinking of Blatchford Sarnemington.

"Please listen to me!" commanded the priest impatiently. "Stop worrying about last Saturday. Apostasy implies an absolute damnation only on the supposition of a previous perfect faith. Does that fix it?"

Rudolph had not the faintest idea what Father Schwartz was talking about, but he nodded and the priest nodded back at him and returned to his mysterious preoccupation.

"Why," he cried, "they have lights now as big as stars—do you realize that? I heard of one light they had in Paris or somewhere that was as big as a star. A lot of people had it—a lot of gay people. They have all sorts of things now that you never dreamed of.

"Look here—" He came nearer to Rudolph, but the boy drew away, so Father Schwartz went back and sat down in his chair, his eyes dried out and hot.

"Did you ever see an amusement park?"

"No, Father."

"Well, go and see an amusement park." The priest waved his hand vaguely. "It's a thing like a fair, only much more glittering. Go to one at night and stand a little way off from it in a dark place—under dark trees. You'll see a big wheel made of lights turning in the air and a long slide shooting boats down into the water. A band playing somewhere and a smell of peanuts—and everything will twinkle. But it won't remind you of anything, you see. It will all just hang out there in the night like a colored balloon—like a big yellow lantern on a pole."

Father Schwartz frowned as he suddenly thought of something.

"But don't get up close," he warned Rudolph, "because if you do you'll only feel the heat and the sweat and the life."

All this talking seemed particularly strange and awful to Rudolph, because this man was a priest. He sat there, half terrified, his beautiful eyes open wide and staring at Father Schwartz. But underneath his terror he felt that his own inner convictions were confirmed. There was something ineffably gorgeous somewhere that had nothing to do with God. He no longer thought that God was angry at him about the original lie, because He must have understood that Rudolph had done it to make things finer in the confessional, brightening up the dinginess of his admissions by saying a thing radiant and proud. At the moment when he had affirmed immaculate honor a silver pennon had flapped out into the breeze somewhere and there had been the crunch of leather and the shine of silver spurs and a troop of horsemen waiting for dawn on a low green hill. The sun had made stars of light on their breastplates like the picture at home of the German cuirassiers at Sedan.

But now the priest was muttering inarticulate and heart-broken words, and the boy became wildly afraid. Horror entered suddenly in at the open window, and the atmosphere of the room changed. Father Schwartz collapsed precipitously down on his knees and let his body settle back against a chair.

"Oh, my God!" he cried out, in a strange voice, and wilted to the floor.

Then a human oppression rose from the priest's worn clothes and mingled with the faint smell of old food in the corners. Rudolph gave a sharp cry and ran in a panic from the house—while the collapsed man lay there quite still, filling his room, filling it with voices and faces until it was crowded with echolalia, and rang loud with a steady, shrill note of laughter.

Outside the window the blue sirocco trembled over the wheat, and girls with yellow hair walked sensuously along roads that bounded the fields, calling innocent, exciting things to the young men who were working in the lines between the grain. Legs were shaped under starchless gingham, and rims of the necks of dresses were warm and damp. For five hours now hot fertile life had burned in the afternoon. It would be night in three hours, and all along the land there would be these blonde northern girls and the tall young men from the farms lying out beside the wheat, under the moon.

RAGS MARTIN-JONES AND
THE PR-NCE OF W-LES

The *Majestic* came gliding into New York harbor on an April morning. She sniffed at the tug-boats and turtle-gaited ferries, winked at a gaudy young yacht, and ordered a cattle-boat out of her way with a snarling whistle of steam. Then she parked at her private dock with all the fuss of a stout lady sitting down, and announced complacently that she had just come from Cherbourg and Southampton with a cargo of the very best people in the world.

The very best people in the world stood on the deck and waved idiotically to their poor relations who were waiting on the dock for gloves from Paris. Before long a great toboggan had connected the *Majestic* with the North American continent and the ship began to disgorge these very best people in the world—who turned out to be Gloria Swanson, two buyers from Lord & Taylor, the financial minister from Graustark with a proposal for funding the debt, and an African king who had been trying to land somewhere all winter and was feeling violently seasick.

The photographers worked passionately as the stream of passengers flowed onto the dock. There was a burst of cheering at the appearance of a pair of stretchers laden with two middle-westerners who had drunk themselves delirious on the last night out.

The deck gradually emptied but when the last bottle of Benedictine had reached shore the photographers still remained at their posts. And the officer in charge of debarkation still stood at the foot of the gang-way, glancing first at his watch and then at the deck as if some important part of the cargo was still on board. At last from the watchers on the pier there arose a long-drawn "Ah-h-h!" as a final entourage began to stream down from deck B.

First came two French maids, carrying small, purple dogs, and followed by a squad of porters, blind and invisible under innumerable bunches and bouquets of fresh flowers. Another maid followed, leading a sad-eyed orphan child of a French flavor, and close upon its heels walked the second officer pulling along three neurasthenic wolfhounds, much to their reluctance and his own.

A pause. Then the captain, Sir Howard George Witchcraft, appeared at the rail, with something that might have been a pile of gorgeous silver fox fur standing by his side—

Rags Martin-Jones, after five years in the capitals of Europe, was returning to her native land!

Rags Martin-Jones was not a dog. She was half a girl and half a flower and as she shook hands with Captain Sir Howard George Witchcraft she smiled as if someone had told her the newest, freshest joke in the world. All the people who had not already left the pier felt that smile trembling on the April air and turned around to see.

She came slowly down the gang-way. Her hat, an expensive, inscrutable experiment, was crushed under her arm so that her scant boy's hair, convict's hair, tried unsuccessfully to toss and flop a little in the harbor wind. Her face was like seven o'clock on a wedding morning save where she had slipped a preposterous monocle into an eye of clear childish blue. At every few steps her long lashes would tilt out the monocle and she would laugh, a bored, happy laugh, and replace the supercilious spectacle in the other eye.

Tap! Her one hundred and five pounds reached the pier and it seemed to sway and bend from the shock of her beauty. A few porters fainted. A large, sentimental shark which had followed the ship across made a despairing leap to see her once more, and then dove, broken-hearted, back into the deep sea. Rags Martin-Jones had come home.

There was no member of her family there to meet her for the simple reason that she was the only member of her family left alive. In 1912 her parents had gone down on the *Titanic* together rather than be separated in this world, and so the Martin-Jones fortune of seventy-five millions had been inherited by a very little girl on her tenth birthday. It was what the consumer always refers to as a "shame."

Rags Martin-Jones (everybody had forgotten her real name long ago) was now photographed from all sides. The monocle persistently fell out and she kept laughing and yawning and replacing it, so no very clear picture of her was taken—except by the motion-picture camera. All the photographs, however, included a flustered handsome young man, with an almost ferocious love-light burning in his eyes, who had met her on the dock. His name was John M. Chestnut, he had already written the story of his success for the "American Magazine" and he had been hopelessly in love with Rags ever since the time when she, like the tides, had come under the influence of the summer moon.

When Rags became really aware of his presence they were walking down the pier, and she looked at him blankly as though she had never seen him before in this world.

"Rags," he began, "Rags—"

"John M. Chestnut?" she inquired, inspecting him with great interest.

"Of course!" he exclaimed angrily. "Are you trying to pretend you don't know me? That you didn't write me to meet you here?"

She laughed. A chauffeur appeared at her elbow and she twisted out of her coat, revealing a dress made in great splashy checks of sea-blue and grey. She shook herself like a wet bird.

"I've got a lot of junk to declare," she remarked absently.

"So have I," said Chestnut anxiously, "and the first thing I want to declare is that I've loved you, Rags, every minute since you've been away."

She stopped him with a groan.

"Please! There were some young Americans on the boat. The subject has become a bore."

"My God!" cried Chestnut. "Do you mean to say that you class *my* love with what was said to you on a *boat?*"

His voice had risen and several people in the vicinity turned to hear.

"Sh!" she warned him. "I'm not giving a circus. If you want me to even see you while I'm here you'll have to be less violent."

But John M. Chestnut seemed unable to control his voice.

"Do you mean to say"—it trembled to a carrying pitch—"that you've forgotten what you said on this very pier five years ago last Thursday?"

Half the passengers from the ship were now watching the scene on the dock and another little eddy drifted out of the customs house to see.

"John"—her displeasure was increasing—"if you raise your voice again I'll arrange it so you'll have plenty of chance to cool off. I'm going to the Ritz. Come and see me there this afternoon."

"But, Rags—!" he protested hoarsely. "Listen to me. Five years ago—"

Then the watchers on the dock were treated to a curious sight. A beautiful lady in a checkered dress of sea-blue and grey took a brisk step forward so that her hands came into contact with an excited young man by her side. The young man retreating instinctively reached back with his foot, but, finding nothing, relapsed gently off the thirty-foot dock and plopped, after a not ungraceful revolution, into the Hudson River.

A shout of alarm went up and there was a rush to the edge just as his head appeared above water. He was swimming easily and, perceiving this, the young lady who had apparently been the cause of the accident leaned over the pier and made a megaphone of her hands.

"I'll be in at half past four," she cried.

And with a cheerful wave of her hand, which the engulfed gentleman was unable to return, she adjusted her monocle, threw one haughty glance at the gathered crowd and walked leisurely from the scene.

II

The five dogs, the three maids and the French orphan were installed in the largest suite at the Ritz and Rags tumbled lazily into a steaming bath, fragrant with herbs, where she dozed for the greater part of an hour. At the end of that time she received business calls from a masseuse, a manicure and finally a Parisian hair-dresser, who restored her hair-cut to criminal's length. When John M. Chestnut arrived at four he found half a dozen lawyers and bankers, the administrators of the Martin-Jones trust fund, waiting in the hall.

They had been there since half past one and were now in a state of considerable agitation.

After one of the maids had subjected him to a severe scrutiny, possibly to be sure that he was thoroughly dry, John was conducted immediately into the presence of M'selle. M'selle was in her bedroom reclining on the chaise longue among two dozen silk pillows that had accompanied her from the other side. John came into the room somewhat stiffly and greeted her with a formal bow.

"You look better," she said, raising herself from her pillows and staring at him appraisingly. "It gave you a color."

He thanked her coldly for the compliment.

"You ought to go in every morning." And then she added irrelevantly, "I'm going back to Paris tomorrow."

John Chestnut gasped.

"I wrote you that I didn't intend to stay more than a week anyhow," she added.

"But, Rags—"

"Why should I? There isn't an amusing man in New York."

"But listen, Rags, won't you give me a chance? Won't you stay for, say, ten days and get to know me a little?"

"Know you!" Her tone implied that he was already a far too open book. "I want a man who's capable of a gallant gesture."

"Do you mean you want me to express myself entirely in pantomime?"

Rags uttered a disgusted sigh.

"I mean you haven't any imagination," she explained patiently. "No Americans have any imagination. Paris is the only large city where a civilized woman can breathe."

"Don't you care for me at all anymore?"

"I wouldn't have crossed the Atlantic to see you if I didn't. But as soon as I looked over the Americans on the boat I knew I couldn't marry one. I'd just hate you, John, and the only fun I'd have out of it would be the fun of breaking your heart."

She began to twist herself down among the cushions until she almost disappeared from view.

"I've lost my monocle," she explained.

After an unsuccessful search in the silken depths she discovered the elusive glass hanging down the back of her neck.

"I'd love to be in love," she went on, replacing the monocle in her childish eye. "Last spring in Sorrento I almost eloped with an Indian rajah, but he was half a shade too dark, and I took an intense dislike to one of his other wives."

"Don't talk that rubbish!" cried John, sinking his face into his hands.

"Well, I didn't marry him," she protested. "But in one way he had a lot to offer. He was the third richest subject of the British Empire. That's another thing—are you rich?"

"Not as rich as you."

"There you are. What have you to offer me?"

"Love."

"Love!" She disappeared again among the cushions. "Listen, John. Life to me is a series of glistening bazaars with a merchant in front of each one rubbing his hands together and saying 'Patronize this place here. Best bazaar in the world.' So I go in with my purse full of beauty and money and youth, all prepared to buy. 'What have you got for sale?' I ask him, and he rubs his hands together and says: 'Well, Mademoiselle, today we have some perfectly be-*oo*-tiful love.' Sometimes he hasn't even got that in stock but he sends out for it when he finds I have so much money to spend. Oh, he always gives me love before I go—and for nothing. That's the one revenge I have."

John Chestnut rose despairingly to his feet and took a step toward the window.

"Don't throw yourself out," Rags exclaimed quickly.

"All right." He tossed his cigarette down into Madison Avenue.

"It isn't just you," she said in a softer voice. "Dull and uninspired as you are, I care for you more than I can say. But life's so endless here. Nothing ever comes off."

"Loads of things come off," he insisted. "Why, today there was an intellectual murder in Hoboken and a suicide by proxy in Maine. A bill to sterilize agnostics is before Congress—"

"I have no interest in humor," she objected, "but I have an almost archaic predilection for romance. Why, John, last month I sat at a dinner table while two men flipped a coin for the kingdom of Schwartzberg-Rhineminster. In Paris I knew a man named Blutchdak who really started the war, and has a new one planned for year after next."

"Well, just for a rest you come out with me tonight," he said doggedly.

"Where to?" demanded Rags with scorn. "Do you think I still thrill at a night-club and a bottle of sugary mousseux? I prefer my own gaudy dreams."

"I'll take you to the most highly strung place in the city."

"What'll happen? You've got to tell me what'll happen."

John Chestnut suddenly drew a long breath and looked cautiously around as if he were afraid of being overheard.

"Well, to tell you the truth," he said in a low worried tone, "if everything was known, something pretty awful would be liable to happen to *me*."

She sat upright and the pillows tumbled about her like leaves.

"Do you mean to imply that there's anything shady in your life?" she cried, with laughter in her voice. "Do you expect me to believe that? No, John, you'll have your fun by plugging ahead on the beaten path—just plugging ahead."

Her mouth, a small insolent rose, dropped the words on him like thorns. John took his hat and coat from the chair and picked up his cane.

"For the last time—will you come along with me tonight and see what you will see?"

"See what? See who? Is there anything in this country worth seeing?"

"Well," he said, in a matter-of-fact tone, "for one thing you'll see the Prince of Wales."

"What?" She left the chaise longue at a bound. "Is he back in New York?"

"He will be tonight. Would you care to see him?"

"Would I? I've never seen him. I've missed him everywhere. I'd give a year of my life to see him for an hour." Her voice trembled with excitement.

"He's been in Canada. He's down here incognito for the big prize fight this afternoon. And I happen to know where he's going to be tonight."

Rags gave a sharp ecstatic cry:

"Dominic! Louise! Germaine!"

The three maids came running. The room filled suddenly with vibrations of wild, startled light.

"Dominic, the car!" cried Rags in French. "St. Raphael, my gold dress and the slippers with the real gold heels. The big pearls too—all the pearls, and the egg diamond and the stockings with the sapphire clocks. Germaine—send for a beauty-parlor on the run. My bath again—ice cold and half full of almond cream. Dominic—Tiffany's, like lightning, before they close! Find me a brooch, a pendant, a tiara, anything—it doesn't matter—with the arms of the House of Windsor."

She was fumbling at the buttons of her dress—and as John turned quickly to go it was already sliding from her shoulders.

"Orchids!" she called after him, "orchids, for the love of heaven! Four dozen, so I can choose four."

And then maids flew here and there about the room like frightened birds. "Perfume, St. Raphael, open the perfume trunk, and my rose-colored sables, and my diamond garters, and the sweet-oil for my hands! Here, take these things! This too—and this—Ouch!—and this!"

With becoming modesty John Chestnut closed the outside door. The six trustees in various postures of fatigue, of ennui, of resignation, of despair, were still cluttering up the outer hall.

"Gentlemen," announced John Chestnut, "I fear that Miss Martin-Jones is much too weary from her trip to talk to you this afternoon."

III

"This place, for no particular reason, is called the Hole in the Sky."

Rags looked around her. They were on a roof garden wide open to the April night. Overhead the true stars winked cold and there was a lunar sliver of ice in the dark west. But where they stood it was warm as June, and the couples dining or dancing on the opaque glass floor were unconcerned with the forbidding sky.

"What makes it so warm?" she whispered as they moved toward a table.

"It's some new invention that keeps the warm air from rising. I don't know the principle of the thing, but I know that they can keep it open like this even in the middle of winter—"

"Where's the Prince of Wales?" she demanded tensely.

John looked around.

"He hasn't arrived yet. He won't be here for about half an hour." She sighed profoundly.

"It's the first time I've been excited in four years."

Four years—one year less than he had loved her. He wondered if when she was sixteen, a wild lovely child, sitting up all night in restaurants with officers who were to leave for Brest next day, losing the glamour of life too soon in the old, sad, poignant days of the war, she had ever been so lovely as under these amber lights and this dark sky. From her excited eyes to her tiny slipper heels, which were striped with layers of real silver and gold, she was like one of those amazing ships that are carved complete in a bottle. She was finished with that delicacy, with that care, as though the long lifetime of some worker in fragility had been used to make her so. John Chestnut wanted to take her up in his hands, turn her this way and that, examine the tip of a slipper or the tip of an ear or squint closely at the fairy stuff from which her lashes were made.

"Who's that?" She pointed suddenly to a handsome Latin at a table over the way.

"That's Roderigo Minerlino, the movie and face-cream star. Perhaps he'll dance after while."

Rags became suddenly aware of the sound of violins and drums but the music seemed to come from far away, seemed to float over the crisp night and on to the floor with the added remoteness of a dream.

"The orchestra's on another roof," explained John. "It's a new idea— Look, the entertainment's beginning."

A negro girl, thin as a reed, emerged suddenly from a masked entrance into a circle of harsh barbaric light, startled the music to a wild minor and commenced to sing a rhythmic, tragic song. The pipe of her body broke abruptly and she began a slow incessant step, without progress and without hope, like the failure of a savage insufficient dream. She had lost Papa Jack, she cried over and over with a hysterical monotony at once despairing and unreconciled. One by one the loud horns tried to force her from the steady beat of madness but she listened only to the mutter of the drums which were isolating her in some lost place in time, among many thousand forgotten years. After the failure of the piccolo, she made herself again into a thin brown line, wailed once with a sharp and terrible intensity, then vanished into sudden darkness.

"If you lived in New York you wouldn't need to be told who she is," said John when the amber light flashed on. "The next fella is Sheik B. Smith, a comedian of the fatuous, garrulous sort—"

He broke off. Just as the lights went down for the second number Rags had given a long sigh and leaned forward tensely in her chair. Her eyes were rigid like the eyes of a pointer dog, and John saw that they were fixed on a party that had come through a side entrance and were arranging themselves around a table in the half darkness.

The table was shielded with palms and Rags at first made out only three dim forms. Then she distinguished a fourth who seemed to be placed well behind the other three—a pale oval of a face topped with a glimmer of dark yellow hair.

"Hello!" ejaculated John. "There's his majesty now."

Her breath seemed to die murmurously in her throat. She was dimly aware that the comedian was now standing in a glow of white light on the dancing floor, that he had been talking for some moments, and that there was a constant ripple of laughter in the air. But her eyes remained motionless, enchanted. She saw one of the party bend and whisper to another, and, after the low glitter of a match, the bright button of a cigarette end gleamed in the background. How long it was before she moved she did not know. Then something seemed to happen to her eyes, something white, something terribly urgent, and she wrenched about sharply to find herself full in the center of a baby spotlight from above. She became aware

that words were being said to her from somewhere and that a quick
trail of laughter was circling the roof, but the light blinded her and
instinctively she made a half movement from her chair.

"Sit still!" John was whispering across the table. "He picks somebody out for this every night."

Then she realized—it was the comedian, Sheik B. Smith. He
was talking to her, arguing with her—about something that seemed
incredibly funny to everyone else, but came to her ears only as a blur
of muddled sound. Instinctively she had composed her face at the
first shock of the light and now she smiled. It was a gesture of rare
self-possession. Into this smile she insinuated a vast impersonality,
as if she were unconscious of the light, unconscious of his attempt
to play upon her loveliness—but amused at an infinitely removed
him, whose darts might have been thrown just as successfully at
the moon. She was no longer a "lady"—a lady would have been
harsh or pitiful or absurd; Rags stripped her attitude to a sheer consciousness of her own impervious beauty, sat there glittering until
the comedian began to feel alone as he had never felt alone before.
At a signal from him the spotlight was switched suddenly out. The
moment was over.

The moment was over, the comedian left the floor and the faraway
music began. John leaned toward her.

"I'm sorry. There really wasn't anything to do. You were
wonderful."

She dismissed the incident with a casual laugh—then she started,
there were now only two men sitting at the table across the floor.

"He's gone!" she exclaimed in quick distress.

"Don't worry—he'll be back. He's got to be awfully careful, you
see, so he's probably waiting outside with one of his aides until it
gets dark again."

"Why has he got to be careful?"

"Because he's not supposed to be in New York. He's even under
one of his second-string names."

The lights dimmed again and almost immediately a tall man
appeared out of the darkness and approached their table.

"May I introduce myself?" he said rapidly to John in a supercilious British voice. "Lord Charles Este, of Baron Marchbanks'

party." He glanced at John closely as if to be sure that he appreciated the significance of the name.

John nodded.

"That is between ourselves, you understand."

"Of course."

Rags groped on the table for her untouched champagne and tipped the glassful down her throat.

"Baron Marchbanks requests that your companion will join his party during this number."

Both men looked at Rags. There was a moment's pause.

"Very well," she said, and glanced back again interrogatively at John. Again he nodded. She rose and with her heart beating wildly threaded the tables, making the half circuit of the room; then melted, a slim figure in shimmering gold, into the table set in half darkness.

IV

The number drew to a close and John Chestnut sat alone at his table, stirring auxiliary bubbles in his glass of champagne. Just before the lights went on there was a soft rasp of gold cloth and Rags, flushed and breathing quickly, sank into her chair. Her eyes were shining with tears.

John looked at her moodily.

"Well, what did he say?"

"He was very quiet."

"Didn't he say a word?"

Her hand trembled as she took up her glass of champagne.

"He just looked at me while it was dark. And he said a few conventional things. He was like his pictures, only he looks very bored and tired. He didn't even ask my name."

"Is he leaving New York tonight?"

"In half an hour. He and his aides have a car outside, and they expect to be over the border before dawn."

"Did you find him—fascinating?"

She hesitated and then slowly nodded her head.

"That's what everybody says," admitted John glumly. "Do they expect you back there?"

"I don't know." She looked uncertainly across the floor but the celebrated personage had again withdrawn from his table to some retreat outside. As she turned back an utterly strange young man who had been standing for a moment in the main entrance came toward them hurriedly. He was a deathly pale person in a dishevelled and inappropriate business suit, and he laid a trembling hand on John Chestnut's shoulder.

"Monte!" exclaimed John, starting up so suddenly that he upset his champagne. "What is it? What's the matter?"

"They've picked up the trail!" said the young man in a shaken whisper. He looked around. "I've got to speak to you alone."

John Chestnut jumped to his feet, and Rags noticed that his face too had become white as the napkin in his hand. He excused himself and they retreated to an unoccupied table a few feet away. Rags watched them curiously for a moment, then she resumed her scrutiny of the table across the floor. Would she be asked to come back? The prince had simply risen and bowed and gone outside. Perhaps she should have waited until he returned, but though she was still tense with excitement she had, to some extent, become Rags Martin-Jones again. Her curiosity was satisfied—any new urge must come from him. She wondered if she had really felt an intrinsic charm—she wondered especially if he had in any marked way responded to her beauty.

The pale person called Monte disappeared and John returned to the table. Rags was startled to find that a tremendous change had come over him. He lurched into his chair like a drunken man.

"John! What's the matter?"

Instead of answering he reached for the champagne bottle, but his fingers were trembling so that the splattered wine made a wet yellow ring around his glass.

"Are you sick?"

"Rags," he said unsteadily, "I'm all through."

"What do you mean?"

"I'm all through, I tell you." He managed a sickly smile. "There's been a warrant out for me for over an hour."

"What have you done?" she demanded in a frightened voice. "What's the warrant for?"

The lights went out for the next number and he collapsed suddenly over the table.

"What is it?" she insisted, with rising apprehension. She leaned forward—his answer was barely audible.

"Murder?" She could feel her body grow cold as ice.

He nodded. She took hold of both arms and tried to shake him upright, as one shakes a coat into place. His eyes were rolling in his head.

"Is it true? Have they got proof?"

Again he nodded drunkenly.

"Then you've got to get out of the country now! Do you understand, John? You've got to get out *now*, before they come looking for you here!"

He loosed a wild glance of terror toward the entrance.

"Oh, God!" cried Rags, "why don't you do something?" Her eyes strayed here and there in desperation, became suddenly fixed. She drew in her breath sharply, hesitated and then whispered fiercely into his ear.

"If I arrange it, will you go to Canada tonight?"

"How?"

"I'll arrange it—if you'll pull yourself together a little. This is Rags talking to you, don't you understand, John? I want you to sit here and not move until I come back!"

A minute later she had crossed the room under cover of the darkness.

"Baron Marchbanks," she whispered softly, standing just behind his chair.

He motioned her to sit down.

"Have you room in your car for two more passengers tonight?"

One of the aides turned around abruptly.

"His lordship's car is full," he said shortly.

"It's terribly urgent." Her voice was trembling.

"Well," said the prince hesitantly, "I don't know."

Lord Charles Este looked at the prince and shook his head.

"I don't think it's advisable. This is a ticklish business anyhow with contrary orders from home. You know we agreed there'd be no complications."

The prince frowned.

"This isn't a complication," he objected.

Este turned frankly to Rags.

"Why is it urgent?"

Rags hesitated.

"Why"—she flushed suddenly—"it's a runaway marriage."

The prince laughed.

"Good!" he exclaimed. "That settles it. Este is just being official. Bring him over right away. We're leaving shortly, what?"

Este looked at his watch.

"Right now!"

Rags rushed away. She wanted to move the whole party from the roof while the lights were still down.

"Hurry!" she cried in John's ear. "We're going over the border— with the Prince of Wales. You'll be safe by morning."

He looked up at her with dazed eyes. She hurriedly paid the check, and seizing his arm piloted him as inconspicuously as possible to the other table, where she introduced him with a word. The prince acknowledged his presence by shaking hands—the aides nodded, only faintly concealing their displeasure.

"We'd better start," said Este, looking impatiently at his watch.

They were on their feet when suddenly an exclamation broke from all of them—two policemen and a redhaired man in plain clothes had come in at the main door.

"Out we go," breathed Este, impelling the party toward the side entrance. "There's going to be some kind of riot here." He swore— two more bluecoats barred the exit there. They paused uncertainly. The plain-clothes man was beginning a careful inspection of the people at the tables.

Este looked sharply at Rags and then at John, who shrank back behind the palms.

"Is that one of your revenue fellas out there?" demanded Este.

"No," whispered Rags. "There's going to be trouble. Can't we get out this entrance?"

The prince with rising impatience sat down again in his chair.

"Let me know when you chaps are ready to go." He smiled at Rags. "Now just suppose we all get in trouble just for that jolly face of yours."

Then suddenly the lights went up. The plain-clothes man whirled around quickly and sprang to the middle of the cabaret floor.

"Nobody try to leave this room!" he shouted. "Sit down, that party behind the palms! Is John M. Chestnut in this room?"

Rags gave a short involuntary cry.

"Here!" cried the detective to the policeman behind him. "Take a look at that funny bunch over there. Hands up, you men!"

"My God!" whispered Este, "we've got to get out of here!" He turned to the prince. "This won't do, Ted. You can't be seen here. I'll stall them off while you get down to the car."

He took a step toward the side entrance.

"Hands up, there!" shouted the plain-clothes man. "And when I say hands up I mean it! Which one of you's Chestnut?"

"You're mad!" cried Este. "We're British subjects. We're not involved in this affair in any way!"

A woman screamed somewhere and there was a general movement toward the elevator, a movement which stopped short before the muzzles of two automatic pistols. A girl next to Rags collapsed in a dead faint to the floor, and at the same moment the music on the other roof began to play.

"Stop that music!" bellowed the plain-clothes man. "And get some earrings on that whole bunch—quick!"

Two policemen advanced toward the party, and simultaneously Este and the other aides drew their revolvers, and, shielding the prince as they best could, began to edge toward the side. A shot rang out and then another, followed by a crash of silver and china as half a dozen diners overturned their tables and dropped quickly behind.

The panic became general. There were three shots in quick succession and then a fusillade. Rags saw Este firing coolly at the eight amber lights above, and a thick fume of grey smoke began to fill the air. As a strange undertone to the shouting and screaming came the incessant clamor of the distant jazz band.

Then in a moment it was all over. A shrill whistle rang out over the roof, and through the smoke Rags saw John Chestnut advancing toward the plain-clothes man, his hands held out in a gesture of surrender. There was a last nervous cry, a chill clatter as someone inadvertently stepped into a pile of dishes, and then a heavy silence fell on the roof—even the band seemed to have died away.

"It's all over!" John Chestnut's voice rang out wildly on the night air. "The party's over. Everybody who wants to can go home!"

Still there was silence—Rags knew it was the silence of awe—the strain of guilt had driven John Chestnut insane.

"It was a great performance," he was shouting. "I want to thank you one and all. If you can find any tables still standing, champagne will be served as long as you care to stay."

It seemed to Rags that the roof and the high stars suddenly began to swim round and round. She saw John take the detective's hand and shake it heartily, and she watched the detective grin and pocket his gun. The music had recommenced, and the girl who had fainted was suddenly dancing with Lord Charles Este in the corner. John was running here and there patting people on the back, and laughing and shaking hands. Then he was coming toward her, fresh and innocent as a child.

"Wasn't it wonderful?" he cried.

Rags felt a faintness stealing over her. She groped backward with her hand toward a chair.

"What was it?" she cried dazedly. "Am I dreaming?"

"Of course not! You're wide awake. I made it up, Rags, don't you see? I made up the whole thing for you. I had it invented! The only thing real about it was my name!"

She collapsed suddenly against his coat, clung to his lapels and would have wilted to the floor if he had not caught her quickly in his arms.

"Some champagne—quick!" he called, and then he shouted at the Prince of Wales, who stood nearby. "Order my car quick, you! Miss Martin-Jones has fainted from excitement."

V

The skyscraper rose bulkily through thirty tiers of windows before it attenuated itself to a graceful sugar-loaf of shining white. Then it darted up again another hundred feet, thinned to a mere oblong tower in its last fragile aspiration toward the sky. At the highest of its high windows Rags Martin-Jones stood full in the stiff breeze, gazing down at the city.

"Mr. Chestnut wants to know if you'll come right in to his private office."

Obediently her slim feet moved along the carpet into a high cool chamber overlooking the harbor and the wide sea.

John Chestnut sat at his desk, waiting, and Rags walked to him and put her arms around his shoulder.

"Are you sure *you*'re real?" she asked anxiously. "Are you absolutely *sure?*"

"You only wrote me a week before you came," he protested modestly, "or I could have arranged a revolution."

"Was the whole thing just *mine?*" she demanded. "Was it a perfectly useless, gorgeous thing, just for me?"

"Useless?" He considered. "Well, it started out to be. At the last minute I invited a big restaurant man to be there, and while you were at the other table I sold him the whole idea of the night-club."

He looked at his watch.

"I've got one more thing to do—and then we've got just time to be married before lunch." He picked up his telephone. "Jackson? . . . Send a triplicated cable to Paris, Berlin and Budapest and have those two bogus dukes who tossed up for Schwartzberg-Rhineminster chased over the Polish border. If the Duchy won't act, lower the rate of exchange to point triple zero naught two. Also, that idiot Blutchdak is in the Balkans again, trying to start a new war. Put him on the first boat for New York or else throw him in a Greek jail."

He rang off, turned to the startled cosmopolite with a laugh.

"The next stop is the City Hall. Then if you like we'll run over to Paris."

"John," she asked him intently, "who was the Prince of Wales?"

He waited till they were in the elevator, dropping twenty floors at a swoop. Then he leaned forward and tapped the lift boy on the shoulder.

"Not so fast, Cedric. This lady isn't used to falls from high places."

The elevator boy turned around, smiled. His face was pale, oval, framed in yellow hair. Rags blushed like fire.

"Cedric's from Wessex," explained John. "The resemblance is, to say the least, amazing. Princes are not particularly discreet, and I suspect Cedric of being a Guelph in some left-handed way."

Rags took the monocle from around her neck and threw the ribbon over Cedric's head.

"Thank you," she said simply, "for the second greatest thrill of my life."

John Chestnut began rubbing his hands together in a commercial gesture.

"Patronize this place, lady," he besought her. "Best bazaar in the city!"

"What have you got for sale?"

"Well, M'selle, today we have some perfectly bee-*oo*-tiful love."

"Wrap it up, Mr. Merchant," cried Rags Martin-Jones. "It looks like a bargain to me."

THE ADJUSTER

At five o'clock the somber egg-shaped room at the Ritz ripens to a subtle melody—the light *clat-clat* of one lump, two lumps, into the cup and the *ding* of the shining teapots and cream pots as they kiss elegantly in transit upon a silver tray. There are those who cherish that amber hour above all other hours, for now the pale pleasant toil of the lilies who inhabit the Ritz is over—the singing decorative part of the day remains.

Moving your eyes around the slightly raised horseshoe balcony you might, one spring afternoon, have seen young Mrs. Alphonse Karr and young Mrs. Charles Hemple at a table for two. The one in the dress was Mrs. Hemple—when I say "the dress" I refer to that black immaculate affair with the big buttons and the red ghost of a cape at the shoulders, a gown suggesting with faint and fashionable irreverence the garb of a French cardinal, as it was meant to do when it was invented in the Rue de la Paix. Mrs. Karr and Mrs. Hemple were twenty-three years old and their enemies said that they had done very well for themselves. Either might have had her limousine waiting at the hotel door, but both of them much preferred to walk home (up Park Avenue) through the April twilight.

Luella Hemple was tall with the sort of flaxen hair that English country girls should have, but seldom do. Her skin was radiant and there was no need of putting anything on it at all, but in deference to an antiquated fashion—this was the year 1920—she had powdered out its high roses and drawn on it a new mouth and new eyebrows—which were no more successful than such meddling deserves. This, of course, is said from the vantage-point of 1925. In those days the effect she gave was exactly right.

"I've been married three years," she was saying as she squashed out a cigarette in an exhausted lemon. "The baby will be two years old tomorrow. I must remember to get—"

She took a gold pencil from her case and wrote "Candles" and "Things you pull, with paper caps" on an ivory date pad. Then, raising her eyes, she looked at Mrs. Karr and hesitated.

"Shall I tell you something outrageous?"

"Try," said Mrs. Karr cheerfully.

"Even my baby bores me. That sounds unnatural, Ede, but it's true. He doesn't *begin* to fill my life. I love him with all my heart, but when I have him to take care of for an afternoon I get so nervous that I want to scream. After two hours I begin praying for the moment the nurse'll walk in the door."

When she had made this confession Luella breathed quickly and looked closely at her friend. She didn't really feel unnatural at all. This was the truth. There couldn't be anything vicious in the truth.

"It may be because you don't love Charles," ventured Mrs. Karr, unmoved.

"But I do! I hope I haven't given you that impression with all this talk." She decided that Ede Karr was stupid. "It's the very fact that I do love Charles that complicates matters. I cried myself to sleep last night because I know we're drifting slowly but surely toward a divorce. It's the baby that keeps us together."

Ede Karr, who had been married five years, looked at her critically to see if this was a pose, but Luella's lovely eyes were grave and sad.

"And what is the trouble?" Ede inquired.

"It's plural," said Luella, frowning. "First there's food. I'm a vile housekeeper and I have no intention of turning into a good one. I hate to order groceries, and I hate to go into the kitchen and poke around to see if the ice box is clean, and I hate to pretend to the servants that I'm interested in their work, when really I never want to hear about food until it comes on the table. You see, I never learned to cook, and consequently a kitchen is about as interesting to me as a—as a boiler room. It's simply a machine that I don't understand. It's easy to say, 'Go to cooking school,' the way people do in books—but, Ede, in real life does anybody ever change into a model *Hausfrau*—unless they have to?"

"Go on," said Ede noncommittally. "Tell me more."

"Well, as a result the house is always in a riot. The servants leave every week. If they're young and incompetent I can't train them, so we have to let them go. If they're experienced, they hate a house where a woman doesn't take an intense interest in the price of asparagus. So they leave—and half the time we eat at restaurants and hotels."

"I don't suppose Charles likes that."

"Hates it. In fact he hates about everything that I like. He's luke-warm about the theatre, hates the opera, hates dancing, hates cock-tail parties—sometimes I think he hates everything pleasant in the world. I sat home for a year or so. While Chuck was on the way, and while I was nursing him, I didn't mind. But this year I told Charles frankly that I was still young enough to want some fun. And since then we've been going out whether he wants to or not." She paused, brooding. "I'm so sorry for him I don't know what to do, Ede—but if we sat home I'd just be sorry for myself. And to tell you another true thing, I'd rather that he'd be unhappy than me."

Luella was not so much stating a case as thinking aloud. She considered that she was being very fair. Before her marriage men had always told her that she was "a good sport" and she had tried to carry this fairness into her married life. So she always saw Charley's point of view as clearly as she saw her own.

If she had been a pioneer wife she would probably have fought the fight side by side with her husband. But here in New York there wasn't any fight. They weren't struggling together to obtain a far-off peace and leisure—she had more of either than she could use. Luella, like several thousand other young wives in New York, hon-estly wanted something to do. If she had had a little more money and a little less love, she could have gone in for horses or for vagari-ous amour. Or if they had had a little less money, her surplus energy would have been absorbed by hope and even by effort. But the Charles Hemples were in between. They were of that enormous American class who wander over Europe every summer, sneering rather pathetically and wistfully at the customs and traditions and pastimes of other countries, because they have no customs or tradi-tions or pastimes of their own. It is a class sprung yesterday from fathers and mothers who might just as well have lived two hundred years ago.

The tea-hour had turned abruptly into the before-dinner hour. Most of the tables had emptied until the room was dotted rather than crowded with shrill isolated voices and remote, surprising laughter—in one corner the waiters were already covering the tables with white for dinner.

"Charles and I are on each other's nerves." In the new silence Luella's voice rang out with startling clearness, and she lowered it precipitately. "Little things. He keeps rubbing his face with his hand—all the time, at table, at the theatre—even when he's in bed. It drives me wild, and when things like that begin to irritate you, it's nearly over." She broke off and, reaching backward, drew up a light fur around her neck. "I hope I haven't bored you, Ede. It's on my mind because tonight tells the story. I made an engagement for tonight—an interesting engagement, a supper after the theatre to meet some Russians, singers or dancers or something, and Charles says he won't go. If he doesn't—then I'm going alone. And that's the end."

She put her elbows on the table suddenly and, bending her eyes down into her smooth gloves, began to cry, stubbornly and quietly. There was no one near to see, but Ede Karr wished that she had taken her gloves off. She would have reached out consolingly and touched her bare hand. But the gloves were a symbol of the difficulty of sympathizing with a woman to whom life had given so much. Ede wanted to say that it would "come out all right," that it wasn't "so bad as it seemed," but she said nothing. Her only reaction was impatience and distaste.

A waiter stepped near and laid a folded paper on the table, and Mrs. Karr reached for it.

"No, you mustn't," murmured Luella brokenly. "No, I invited *you!* I've got the money right here."

II

The Hemples' apartment—they owned it—was in one of those impersonal white palaces that are known by number instead of name. They had furnished it on their honeymoon, gone to England for the big pieces, to Florence for the bric-à-brac and to Venice for the lace and sheer linen of the curtains and for the glass of many colors which littered the table when they entertained. Luella enjoyed choosing things on her honeymoon. It gave a purposeful air to the trip and saved it from ever turning into the rather dismal wandering among big hotels and desolate ruins which European honeymoons are apt to be.

They returned and life began. On the grand scale. Luella found herself a lady of substance. It amazed her sometimes that the specially created apartment and the specially created limousine were hers, just as indisputably as the mortgaged suburban bungalow out of the "Ladies' Home Journal" and the last year's car that fate might have given her instead. She was even more amazed when it all began to bore her. But it did. . . .

The evening was at seven when she turned out of the April dusk, let herself into the hall and saw her husband waiting in the living room before an open fire. She came in without a sound, closed the door noiselessly behind her and stood watching him for a moment through the pleasant effective vista of the small salon which intervened. Charles Hemple was in the middle thirties, with a young serious face and distinguished iron-grey hair which would be white in ten years more. That and his deep-set, dark-grey eyes were his most noticeable features—women always thought his hair was romantic; most of the time Luella thought so too.

At this moment she found herself hating him a little, for she saw that he had raised his hand to his face and was rubbing it nervously over his chin and mouth. It gave him an air of unflattering abstraction and sometimes even obscured his words so that she was continually saying "What?" She had spoken about it several times, and he had apologized in a surprised way. But obviously he didn't realize how noticeable and how irritating it was, for he continued to do it. Things had now reached such a precarious state that Luella dreaded speaking of such matters anymore—a certain sort of word might precipitate the imminent scene.

Luella tossed her gloves and purse abruptly on the table. Hearing the faint sound her husband looked out toward the hall.

"Is that you, dear?"

"Yes, dear."

She went into the living room, and walked into his arms and kissed him tensely. Charles Hemple responded with unusual formality and then turned her slowly around so that she faced across the room.

"I've brought someone home to dinner."

She saw then that they were not alone, and her first feeling was of strong relief; the rigid expression on her face softened into a shy charming smile as she held out her hand.

"This is Doctor Moon—this is my wife."

A man a little older than her husband, with a round, pale, slightly lined face, came forward to meet her.

"Good evening, Mrs. Hemple," he said. "I hope I'm not interfering with any arrangement of yours."

"Oh, no," Luella cried quickly. "I'm delighted that you're coming to dinner. We're quite alone."

Simultaneously she thought of her engagement tonight and wondered if this could be a clumsy trap of Charles' to keep her at home. If it were, he had chosen his bait badly. This man—a tired placidity radiated from him, from his face, from his heavy, leisurely voice, even from the three-year-old shine of his clothes.

Nevertheless she excused herself and went into the kitchen to see what was planned for dinner. As usual they were trying a new pair of servants, the luncheon had been ill-cooked and ill-served—she would let them go tomorrow. She hoped Charles would talk to them—she hated to get rid of servants. Sometimes they wept and sometimes they were insolent, but Charles had a way with them. And they were always afraid of a man.

The cooking on the stove, however, had a soothing savor. Luella gave instructions about "which china" and unlocked a bottle of precious chianti from the buffet. Then she went in to kiss young Chuck good night.

"Has he been good?" she demanded as he crawled enthusiastically into her arms.

"Very good," said the governess. "We went for a long walk over by Central Park."

"Well aren't you a smart boy!" She kissed him ecstatically.

"And he put his foot into the fountain so we had to come home in a taxi right away and change his little shoe and stocking."

"That's right. Here, wait a minute, *Chuck!*" Luella unclasped the great yellow beads from around her neck and handed them to him. "You mustn't break Mamma's beads." She turned to the nurse. "Put them on my dresser, will you, after he's asleep?"

She felt a certain compassion for her son as she went away—the small enclosed life he led, that all children led, except in big families. He was a dear little rose, except on the days when she took care of him. His face was the same shape as hers; she was thrilled sometimes and formed new resolves about life when his heart beat against her own.

In her own pink and lovely bedroom she confined her attentions to her face, which she washed and restored. Doctor Moon didn't deserve a change of dress, and Luella found herself oddly tired, though she had done very little all day. She returned to the living room and they went in to dinner.

"Such a nice house, Mrs. Hemple," said Doctor Moon impersonally; "and let me congratulate you on your fine little boy."

"Thanks. Coming from a doctor, that's a nice compliment." She hesitated. "Do you specialize in children?"

"I'm not a specialist at all," he said. "I'm about the last of my kind—a general practitioner."

"The last in New York anyhow," remarked Charles. He had begun rubbing his face nervously and Luella fixed her eyes on Doctor Moon so that she wouldn't see. But at Charles's next words she looked back at him sharply.

"In fact," he said unexpectedly, "I've invited Doctor Moon here because I wanted you to have a talk with him tonight."

Luella sat up straight in her chair.

"A talk with *me?*"

"Doctor Moon's an old friend of mine and I think he can tell you a few things, Luella, that you ought to know."

"Why—" She tried to laugh but she was surprised and annoyed. "I don't see exactly what you mean. There's nothing the matter with me. I don't believe I've ever felt better in my life."

Doctor Moon looked at Charles, asking permission to speak. Charles nodded and his hand went up automatically to his face.

"Your husband has told me a great deal about your unsatisfactory life together," said Doctor Moon, still impersonally. "He wonders if I can be of any help in smoothing things out."

Luella's face was burning.

"I have no particular faith in psychoanalysis," she said coldly, "and I scarcely consider myself a subject for it."

"Neither have I," answered Doctor Moon, apparently unconscious of the snub; "I have no particular faith in anything but myself. I told you I am not a specialist, nor, I may add, a faddist of any sort. I promise nothing."

For a moment Luella considered leaving the room. But the effrontery of the suggestion aroused her curiosity too.

"I can't imagine what Charles has told you," she said, controlling herself with difficulty, "much less why. But I assure you that our affairs are a matter entirely between my husband and me. If you have no objections, Doctor Moon, I'd much prefer to discuss something— less personal."

Doctor Moon nodded heavily and politely. He made no further attempt to open the subject, and dinner proceeded in what was little more than a defeated silence. Luella determined that whatever happened she would adhere to her plans for tonight. An hour ago her independence had demanded it, but now some gesture of defiance had become necessary to her self-respect. She would stay in the living room for a short moment after dinner; then when the coffee came she would excuse herself and dress to go out.

But when they did leave the dining room, it was Charles who, in a quick, unarguable way, vanished.

"I have a letter to write," he said; "I'll be back in a moment." Before Luella could make a diplomatic objection he went quickly down the corridor to his room and she heard him shut his door.

Angry and confused, Luella poured the coffee and sank into a corner of the couch, looking intently at the fire.

"Don't be afraid, Mrs. Hemple," said Doctor Moon suddenly. "This was forced upon me. I do not act as a free agent—"

"I'm not afraid of you," she interrupted. But she knew that she was lying. She was a little afraid of him, if only for his dull insensitiveness to her distaste.

"Tell me about your trouble," he said very naturally, as though she were not a free agent either. He wasn't even looking at her, and except that they were alone in the room, he scarcely seemed to be addressing her at all.

The words that were in Luella's mind, her will, on her lips, were: "I'll do no such thing." What she actually said amazed her. It came out of her spontaneously, with apparently no cooperation of her own.

"Didn't you see him rubbing his face at dinner?" she said despairingly. "Are you blind? He's become so irritating to me that I think I'll go mad."

"I see." Doctor Moon's round face nodded.

"Don't you see I've had enough of home?" Her breasts seemed to struggle for air under her dress. "Don't you see how bored I am with keeping house, with the baby—everything seems as if it's going on forever and ever? I want excitement, and I don't care what form it takes or what I pay for it, so long as it makes my heart beat."

"I see."

It infuriated Luella that he claimed to understand. Her feeling of defiance had reached such a pitch that she preferred that no one should understand. She was content to be justified by the impassioned sincerity of her desires.

"I've tried to be good, and I'm not going to try anymore. If I'm one of those women who wreck their lives for nothing, then I'll do it now. You can call me selfish, or silly, and be quite right; but in five minutes I'm going out of this house and begin to be alive."

This time Doctor Moon didn't answer, but he raised his head as if he were listening to something that was taking place a little distance away.

"You're not going out," he said after a moment; "I'm quite sure you're not going out."

Luella laughed.

"I *am* going out."

He disregarded this.

"You see, Mrs. Hemple, your husband isn't well. He's been trying to live your kind of life and the strain of it has been too much for him. When he rubs his mouth—"

Light steps came down the corridor and the maid, with a frightened expression on her face, tiptoed into the room.

"Mrs. Hemple—"

Startled at the interruption Luella turned quickly.

"Yes?"

"Can I speak to—?" Her fear broke precipitately through her slight training. "Mr. Hemple, he's sick! He came into the kitchen awhile ago and began throwing all the food out of the ice box, and now he's in his room, crying and singing—"

Suddenly Luella heard his voice.

III

Charles Hemple had had a nervous collapse. There were twenty years of almost uninterrupted toil upon his shoulders, and the recent pressure at home had been too much for him to bear. His attitude toward his wife was the weak point in what had otherwise been a strong-minded and well-organized career—he was aware of her intense selfishness, but it is one of the many flaws in the scheme of human relationships that selfishness in women has an irresistible appeal to many men. Luella's selfishness existed side by side with a childish beauty and, in consequence, Charles Hemple had begun to take the blame upon himself for situations which she had obviously brought about. It was an unhealthy attitude and his mind had sickened, at length, with his attempts to put himself in the wrong.

After the first shock and the momentary flush of pity that followed it, Luella looked at the situation with impatience. She was "a good sport"—she couldn't take advantage of Charles when he was sick. The question of her liberties had to be postponed until he was on his feet. Just when she had determined to be a wife no longer, Luella was compelled to be a nurse as well. She sat beside his bed while he talked about her in his delirium—about the days of their engagement, and how some friend had told him then that he was making a mistake, and about his happiness in the early months of their marriage, and his growing disquiet as the gap appeared. Evidently he had been more aware of it than she had thought—more than he ever said.

"Luella!" He would lurch up in bed. "Luella! Where *are* you?"

"I'm right here, Charles, beside you." She tried to make her voice cheerful and warm.

"If you want to go, Luella, you'd better go. I don't seem to be enough for you anymore."

She denied this soothingly.

"I've thought it over, Luella, and I can't ruin my health on account of you—" Then quickly, and passionately: "Don't go, Luella, for God's sake, don't go away and leave me! Promise me you won't! I'll do anything you say if you won't go."

His humility annoyed her most; he was a reserved man, and she had never guessed at the extent of his devotion before.

"I'm only going for a minute. It's Doctor Moon, your friend, Charles. He came today to see how you were, don't you remember? And he wants to talk to me before he goes."

"You'll come back?" he persisted.

"In just a little while. There—lie quiet."

She raised his head and plumped his pillow into freshness. A new trained nurse would arrive tomorrow.

In the living room Doctor Moon was waiting—his suit more worn and shabby in the afternoon light. She disliked him inordinately, with an illogical conviction that he was in some way to blame for her misfortune, but he was so deeply interested that she couldn't refuse to see him. She hadn't asked him to consult with the specialists, though—a doctor who was so down at the heel. . . .

"Mrs. Hemple." He came forward, holding out his hand, and Luella touched it, lightly and uneasily.

"You seem well," he said.

"I am well, thank you."

"I congratulate you on the way you've taken hold of things."

"But I haven't taken hold of things at all," she said coldly. "I do what I have to—"

"That's just it."

Her impatience mounted rapidly.

"I do what I have to, and nothing more," she continued. "And with no particular good-will."

Suddenly she opened up to him again, as she had the night of the catastrophe—realizing that she was putting herself on a footing of intimacy with him, yet unable to restrain her words.

"The house isn't going," she broke out bitterly. "I had to discharge the servants, and now I've got a woman in by the day. And the baby has a cold, and I've found out that his nurse doesn't know her business, and everything's just as messy and terrible as it can be!"

"Would you mind telling me how you found out the nurse didn't know her business?"

"You find out various unpleasant things when you're forced to stay around the house."

He nodded, his weary face turning here and there about the room.

"I feel somewhat encouraged," he said slowly. "As I told you, I promise nothing. I only do the best I can."

Luella looked up at him, startled.

"What do you mean?" she protested. "You've done nothing for me—nothing at all!"

"Nothing much—yet," he said heavily. "It takes time, Mrs. Hemple."

The words were said in a dry monotone that was somehow without offense, but Luella felt that he had gone too far. She got to her feet.

"I've met your type before," she said coldly. "For some reason you seem to think that you have a standing here as 'the old friend of the family.' But I don't make friends quickly, and I haven't given you the privilege of being so"—she wanted to say "insolent," but the word eluded her—"so personal with me."

When the front door had closed behind him, Luella went into the kitchen to see if the woman understood about the three different dinners—one for Charles, one for the baby and one for herself. It was hard to do with only a single servant when things were so complicated. She must try another employment agency—this one had begun to sound bored.

To her surprise, she found the cook with hat and coat on, reading a newspaper at the kitchen table.

"Why"—Luella tried to think of the name—"why, what's the matter, Mrs.—"

"Mrs. Danski is my name."

"What's the matter?"

"I'm afraid I won't be able to accommodate you," said Mrs. Danski. "You see, I'm only a plain cook, and I'm not used to preparing invalid's food."

"But I've counted on you."

"I'm very sorry." She shook her head stubbornly. "I've got my own health to think of. I'm sure they didn't tell me what kind of a job it was when I came. And when you asked me to clean out your husband's room, I knew it was way beyond my powers."

"I won't ask you to clean anything," said Luella desperately. "If you'll just stay until tomorrow. I can't possibly get anybody else tonight."

Mrs. Danski smiled politely.

"I got my own children to think of, just like you."

It was on Luella's tongue to offer her more money, but suddenly her temper gave way.

"I've never heard of anything so selfish in my life!" she broke out. "To leave me at a time like this! You're an old fool!"

"If you'd pay me for my time, I'd go," said Mrs. Danski calmly.

"I won't pay you a cent unless you'll stay!"

She was immediately sorry she had said this, but she was too proud to withdraw the threat.

"You will so pay me!"

"You go out that door!"

"I'll go when I get my money," asserted Mrs. Danski indignantly. "I got my children to think of."

Luella drew in her breath sharply and took a step forward. Intimidated by her intensity, Mrs. Danski turned and flounced, muttering, out of the door.

Luella went to the phone and, calling up the agency, explained that the woman had left.

"Can you send me someone right away? My husband is sick and the baby's sick—"

"I'm sorry, Mrs. Hemple. There's no one in the office now. It's after four o'clock."

Luella argued for awhile. Finally she obtained a promise that they would telephone to an emergency woman they knew. That was the best they could do until tomorrow.

She called several other agencies, but the servant industry had apparently ceased to function for the day. After giving Charles his medicine she tiptoed softly into the nursery.

"How's baby?" she asked abstractedly.

"Ninety-nine one," whispered the nurse, holding the thermometer to the light. "I just took it."

"Is that much?" asked Luella, frowning.

"It's just three-fifths of a degree. That isn't so much for the afternoon. They often run up a little with a cold."

Luella went over to the cot and laid her hand on her son's flushed cheek, thinking, in the midst of her anxiety, how much he resembled the incredible cherub of the "Lux" advertisement in the bus.

She turned to the nurse.

"Do you know how to cook?"

"Why—I'm not a good cook."

"Well, can you do the baby's food tonight? That old fool has left and I can't get anyone and I don't know what to do."

"Oh yes, I can do the baby's food."

"That's all right, then. I'll try to fix something for Mr. Hemple. Please have your door open so you can hear the bell when the doctor comes. And let me know."

So many doctors! There had scarcely been an hour all day when there wasn't a doctor in the house. The specialist and their family physician every morning, then the baby doctor—and this afternoon there had been Doctor Moon, placid, persistent, unwelcome, in the parlor. Luella went into the kitchen. She could cook bacon and eggs for herself—she had often done that after the theatre. But the vegetables for Charles were a different matter—they must be left to boil or stew or something, and the stove had so many doors and ovens that she couldn't decide which to use. She chose a blue pan that looked new, sliced carrots into it and covered them with a little water. As she put it on the stove and tried to remember what to do next, the phone rang. It was the agency.

"Yes, this is Mrs. Hemple speaking."

"Why, the woman we sent to you has returned here with the claim that you refused to pay her for her time."

"I explained to you that she refused to stay," said Luella hotly. "She didn't keep her agreement and I didn't feel I was under any obligation—"

"We have to see that our people are paid," the agency informed her. "Otherwise we wouldn't be helping them at all, would we? I'm sorry, Mrs. Hemple, but we won't be able to furnish you with anyone else until this little matter is arranged."

"Oh, I'll pay, I'll pay!" she cried.

"Of course we like to keep on good terms with our clients—"

"Yes—yes!"

"So if you'll send her money around tomorrow? It's seventy-five cents an hour."

"But how about tonight?" she exclaimed. "I've got to have someone tonight."

"Why—it's pretty late now. I was just going home myself."

"But I'm Mrs. Charles Hemple! Don't you understand? I'm perfectly good for what I say I'll do. I'm the wife of Charles Hemple, of 14 Broadway—"

Simultaneously she realized that Charles Hemple of 14 Broadway was a helpless invalid—he was neither a reference nor a refuge anymore. In despair at the sudden callousness of the world, she hung up the receiver.

After another ten minutes of frantic muddling in the kitchen she went to the baby's nurse, whom she disliked, and confessed that she was unable to cook her husband's dinner. The nurse announced that she had a splitting headache, and that with a sick child her hands were full already, but she consented, without enthusiasm, to show Luella what to do.

Swallowing her humiliation, Luella obeyed orders while the nurse experimented, grumbling, with the unfamiliar stove. Dinner was started after a fashion. Then it was time for the nurse to bathe

Chuck, and Luella sat down alone at the kitchen table, and listened to the bubbling perfume that escaped from the pans.

"And women do this every day," she thought. "Thousands of women. Cook and take care of sick people—and go out to work too."

But she didn't think of those women as being like her, except in the superficial aspect of having two feet and two hands. She said it as she might have said "South Sea Islanders wear nose-rings." She was merely slumming today in her own home and she wasn't enjoying it. For her, it was merely a ridiculous exception.

Suddenly she became aware of slow approaching steps in the dining room and then in the butler's pantry. Half afraid that it was Doctor Moon coming to pay another call, she looked up—and saw the nurse coming through the pantry door. It flashed through Luella's mind that the nurse was going to be sick too. And she was right— the nurse had hardly reached the kitchen door when she lurched and clutched at the handle as a winged bird clings to a branch. Then she receded wordlessly to the floor. Simultaneously, the doorbell rang and Luella, getting to her feet, gasped with relief that the baby doctor had come.

"Fainted, that's all," he said, taking the girl's head into his lap. The eyes fluttered. "Yep, she fainted, that's all."

"Everybody's sick!" cried Luella with a sort of despairing humor. "Everybody's sick but me, doctor."

"This one's not sick," he said after a moment. "Her heart is normal already. She just fainted."

When she had helped the doctor raise the quickening body to a chair, Luella hurried into the nursery and bent over the baby's bed. She let down one of the iron sides quietly. The fever seemed to be gone now—the flush had faded away. She bent over to touch the small cheek.

Suddenly Luella began to scream.

IV

Even after her baby's funeral, Luella still couldn't believe that she had lost him. She came back to the apartment and walked around the nursery in a circle, saying his name. Then, frightened by grief, she sat down and stared at his white rocker with the red chicken painted on the side.

"What will become of me now?" she whispered to herself. "Something awful is going to happen to me when I realize that I'll never see Chuck anymore!"

She wasn't sure yet. If she waited here till twilight, the nurse might still bring him in from his walk. She remembered a tragic confusion in the midst of which someone had told her that Chuck was dead, but if that was so, then why was his room waiting, with his small brush and comb still on the bureau, and why was she here at all?

"Mrs. Hemple."

She looked up. The weary, shabby figure of Doctor Moon stood in the door.

"You go away," Luella said dully.

"Your husband needs you."

"I don't care."

Doctor Moon came a little way into the room.

"I don't think you understand, Mrs. Hemple. He's been calling for you. You haven't anyone now except him."

"I hate you," she said suddenly.

"If you like. I promised nothing, you know. I do the best I can. You'll be better when you realize that your baby is gone, that you're not going to see him anymore."

Luella sprang to her feet.

"My baby isn't dead!" she cried. "You lie! You always lie!" Her flashing eyes looked into his and caught something there, at once brutal and kind, that awed her and made her impotent and acquiescent. She lowered her own eyes in tired despair.

"All right," she said wearily. "My baby is gone. What shall I do now?"

"Your husband is much better. All he needs is rest and kindness. But you must go to him and tell him what's happened."

"I suppose you think you made him better," said Luella bitterly.

"Perhaps. He's nearly well."

Nearly well—then the last link that held her to her home was broken. This part of her life was over—she could cut it off here, with its grief and oppression, and be off now, free as the wind.

"I'll go to him in a minute," Luella said in a far-away voice. "Please leave me alone."

Doctor Moon's unwelcome shadow melted into the darkness of the hall.

"I can go away," Luella whispered to herself. "Life has given me back freedom, in place of what it took away from me."

But she mustn't linger even a minute, or Life would bind her again and make her suffer once more. She called the apartment porter and asked that her trunk be brought up from the storeroom. Then she began taking things from the bureau and wardrobe, trying to approximate as nearly as possible the possessions that she had brought to her married life. She even found two old dresses that had formed part of her trousseau—out of style now, and a little tight in the hips—which she threw in with the rest. A new life. Charles was well again, and her baby, whom she had worshipped, and who had bored her a little, was dead.

When she had packed her trunk, she went into the kitchen automatically, to see about the preparations for dinner. She spoke to the cook about the special things for Charles and said that she herself was dining out. The sight of one of the small pans that had been used to cook Chuck's food caught her attention for a moment—but she stared at it unmoved. She looked into the ice box and saw it was clean and fresh inside. Then she went into Charles's room. He was sitting up in bed and the nurse was reading to him. His hair was almost white now, silvery white, and underneath it his eyes were huge and dark in his thin young face.

"The baby is sick?" he asked in his own natural voice.

She nodded.

He hesitated, closing his eyes for a moment. Then he asked: "The baby is dead?"

"Yes."

For a long time he didn't speak. The nurse came over and put her hand on his forehead. Two large, strange tears welled from his eyes.

"I knew the baby was dead."

After another long wait, the nurse spoke.

"The doctor said he could be taken out for a drive today while there was still sunshine. He needs a little change."

"Yes."

"I thought"—the nurse hesitated. "I thought perhaps it would do you both good, Mrs. Hemple, if you took him instead of me."

Luella shook her head hastily.

"Oh no," she said. "I don't feel able to, today."

The nurse looked at her oddly. With a sudden feeling of pity for Charles, Luella bent down gently and kissed his cheek. Then, without a word, she went to her own room, put on her hat and coat, and with her suitcase started for the front door.

Immediately she saw that there was a shadow in the hall. If she could get past that shadow, she was free. If she could go to the right or left of it, or order it out of her way! But stubbornly, it refused to move, and with a little cry she sank down into a hall chair.

"I thought you'd gone," she wailed. "I told you to go away."

"I'm going soon," said Doctor Moon, "but I don't want you to make an old mistake."

"I'm not making a mistake—I'm leaving my mistakes behind."

"You're trying to leave yourself behind but you can't. The more you try to run away from yourself, the more you'll have yourself with you."

"But I've got to go away," she insisted wildly. "Out of this house of death and failure!"

"You haven't failed yet. You've only begun."

She stood up.

"Let me pass."

"No."

Abruptly she gave way, as she always did when he talked to her. She covered her face with her hands and burst into tears.

"Go back into that room and tell the nurse you'll take your husband for a drive," he suggested.

"I can't."

"Oh, yes."

Once more Luella looked at him and knew that she would obey. With the conviction that her spirit was broken at last, she took up her suitcase and walked back through the hall.

V

The nature of the curious influence that Doctor Moon exerted upon her Luella could not guess. But as the days passed, she found herself doing many things that had been repugnant to her before. She stayed at home with Charles, and when he grew better she went out with him sometimes to dinner, or the theatre, but only when he expressed a wish. She visited the kitchen every day, and kept an unwilling eye on the house, at first with a horror that it would go wrong again, then from habit. And she felt that it was all somehow mixed up with Doctor Moon—it was something he kept telling her about life, or almost telling her, and yet concealing from her as though he were afraid to have her know.

With the resumption of their normal life, she found that Charles was less nervous. His habit of rubbing his face had left him, and if the world seemed less gay and happy to her than it had before she experienced a certain peace, sometimes, that she had never known.

Then, one afternoon, Doctor Moon told her suddenly that he was going away.

"Do you mean for good?" she demanded with a touch of panic.

"For good."

For a strange moment she wasn't sure whether she was glad or sorry.

"You don't need me anymore," he said quietly. "You don't realize it, but you've grown up."

He came over and, sitting on the couch beside her, took her hand. Luella sat silent and tense—listening.

"We make an agreement with children that they can sit in the audience without helping to make the play," he said, "but if they still sit in the audience after they're grown, somebody's got to work double time for them, so that they can enjoy the light and glitter of the world."

"But I want the light and glitter," she protested. "That's all there is in life. There can't be anything wrong in wanting to have things warm."

"Things will still be warm."

"How?"

"Things will warm themselves from you."

Luella looked at him, startled.

"It's your turn to be the center, to give others what was given to you for so long. You've got to give security to young people and peace to your husband, and a sort of charity to the old. You've got to let the people who work for you depend on you. You've got to cover up a few more troubles than you show, and be a little more patient than the average person, and do a little more instead of a little less than your share. The light and glitter of the world is in your hands."

He broke off suddenly.

"Get up," he said, "and go to that mirror and tell me what you see."

Obediently Luella got up and went close to a purchase of her honeymoon, a Venetian pier-glass on the wall.

"I see new lines in my face here," she said, raising her finger and placing it between her eyes, "and a few shadows at the sides that might be—that are little wrinkles."

"Do you care?"

She turned quickly. "No," she said.

"Do you realize that Chuck is gone? That you'll never see him anymore?"

"Yes." She passed her hands slowly over her eyes. "But that all seems so vague and far away."

"Vague and far away," he repeated; and then: "And are you afraid of me now?"

"Not any longer," she said, and she added frankly, "now that you're going away."

He moved toward the door. He seemed particularly weary tonight, as though he could hardly move about at all.

"The household here is in your keeping," he said in a tired whisper. "If there is any light and warmth in it, it will be your light and warmth; if it is happy, it will be because you've made it so. Happy things may come to you in life, but you must never go seeking them anymore. It is your turn to make the fire."

"Won't you sit down a moment longer?" Luella ventured.

"There isn't time." His voice was so low now that she could scarcely hear the words. "But remember that whatever suffering comes to you, I can always help you—if it is something that can be helped. I promise nothing."

He opened the door. She must find out now what she most wanted to know, before it was too late.

"What have you done to me?" she cried. "Why have I no sorrow left for Chuck—for anything at all? Tell me; I almost see, yet I can't see. Before you go—tell me who you are!"

"Who am I?—" His worn suit paused in the doorway. His round, pale face seemed to dissolve into two faces, a dozen faces, a score, each one different yet the same—sad, happy, tragic, indifferent, resigned—until threescore Doctor Moons were ranged like an infinite series of reflections, like months stretching into the vista of the past.

"Who am I?" he repeated. "I am five years."

The door closed.

At six o'clock Charles Hemple came home, and as usual Luella met him in the hall. Except that now his hair was dead white, his long illness of two years had left no mark upon him. Luella herself was more noticeably changed—she was a little stouter, and there were those lines around her eyes that had come when Chuck died one evening back in 1921. But she was still lovely, and there was a mature kindness about her face at twenty-eight, as if suffering had touched her only reluctantly and then hurried away.

"Ede and her husband are coming to dinner," she said. "I've got theatre tickets, but if you're tired, I don't care whether we go or not."

"I'd like to go."

She looked at him.

"You wouldn't."

"I really would."

"We'll see how you feel after dinner."

He put his arm around her waist. Together they walked into the nursery where the two children were waiting up to say good-night.

HOT AND COLD BLOOD

One day when the young Mathers had been married for about a year, Jaqueline walked into the rooms of the hardware brokerage which her husband carried on with more than average success. At the open door of the inner office she stopped and said: "Oh, excuse me—" She had interrupted an apparently trivial yet somehow intriguing scene. A young man named Bronson whom she knew slightly was standing with her husband; the latter had risen from his desk. Bronson seized her husband's hand and shook it earnestly—something more than earnestly. When they heard Jaqueline's step in the doorway both men turned and Jaqueline saw that Bronson's eyes were red.

A moment later he came out, passing her with a somewhat embarrassed "How do you do?" She walked into her husband's office.

"What was Ed Bronson doing here?" she demanded curiously, and at once.

Jim Mather smiled at her, half shutting his grey eyes, and drew her quietly to a sitting position on his desk.

"He just dropped in for a minute," he answered easily. "How's everything at home?"

"All right." She looked at him with curiosity. "What did he want?" she insisted.

"Oh, he just wanted to see me about something."

"What?"

"Oh, just something. Business."

"Why were his eyes red?"

"Were they?" He looked at her innocently—and then suddenly they both began to laugh. Jaqueline rose and walked around the desk and plumped down into his swivel chair.

"You might as well tell me," she announced cheerfully, "because I'm going to stay right here till you do."

"Well,—" he hesitated, frowning. "He wanted me to do him a little favor."

Then Jaqueline understood—or rather her mind leaped half accidentally to the truth.

"Oh." Her voice tightened a little. "You've been lending him some money."

"Only a little."

"How much?"

"Only three hundred."

"*Only* three hundred." The voice was of the texture of Bessemer cooled. "How much do we spend a month, Jim?"

"Why,—why, about five or six hundred, I guess." He shifted uneasily. "Listen, Jack. Bronson'll pay that back. He's in a little trouble. He's made a mistake about a girl out in Woodmere—"

"And he knows you're famous for being an easy mark, so he comes to you," interrupted Jaqueline.

"No." He denied this formally.

"Don't you suppose I could use that three hundred dollars?" she demanded. "How about that trip to New York we couldn't afford last November?"

The lingering smile faded from Mather's face. He went over and shut the door to the outer office.

"Listen, Jack," he began, "you don't understand this. Bronson's one of the men I eat lunch with almost every day. We used to play together when we were kids—we went to school together. Don't you see that I'm just the person he'd be right to come to in trouble? And that's just why I couldn't refuse."

Jaqueline gave her shoulders a twist as if to shake off this reasoning.

"Well," she answered decidedly, "all I know is that he's no good. He's always lit and if he doesn't choose to work he has no business living off the work you do."

They were sitting now on either side of the desk, each having adopted the attitude of one talking to a child. They began their sentences with "Listen!" and their faces wore expressions of rather tried patience.

"If you can't understand, I can't tell you," Mather concluded, at the end of fifteen minutes, on what was, for him, an irritated key. "Such obligations do happen to exist sometimes among men and they have to be met. It's more complicated than just refusing to lend money—especially in a business like mine where so much depends on the good will of men downtown."

Mather was putting on his coat as he said this. He was going home with her on the street car to lunch. They were between automobiles—they had sold their old one and were going to get a new one in the spring.

Now the street car, on this particular day, was distinctly unfortunate. The argument in the office might have been forgotten under other circumstances, but what followed irritated the scratch until it became a serious temperamental infection.

They found a seat near the front of the car. It was late February and an eager, unpunctilious sun was turning the scrawny street snow into dirty cheerful rivulets that echoed in the gutters. Because of this the car was less full than usual—there was no one standing. The motorman had even opened his window and a yellow breeze was blowing the late breath of winter from the car.

It occurred pleasurably to Jaqueline that her husband sitting beside her was handsome and kind above other men. It was silly to try to change him. Perhaps Bronson might return the money after all, and anyhow three hundred dollars wasn't a fortune. Of course he had no business doing it—but then—

Her musings were interrupted as an eddy of passengers pushed up the aisle. Jaqueline wished they'd put their hands over their mouths when they coughed, and she hoped that Jim would get a new machine pretty soon. You couldn't tell what disease you'd run into in these trolleys.

She turned to Jim to discuss the subject—but Jim had stood up and was offering his seat to a woman who had been standing beside him in the aisle. The woman, without so much as a grunt, sat down. Jaqueline frowned.

The woman was about fifty and enormous. When she first sat down she was content merely to fill the unoccupied part of the seat, but after a moment she began to expand and to spread her great rolls of fat over a larger and larger area until the process took on the aspect of violent trespassing. When the car rocked in Jaqueline's direction the woman slid with it, but when it rocked back she managed by some exercise of ingenuity to dig in and hold the ground won.

Jaqueline caught her husband's eye—he was swaying on a strap—and in an angry glance conveyed to him her entire disapproval of his action. He apologized mutely and became urgently engrossed in a row of car cards. The fat woman moved once more against Jaqueline—she was now practically overlapping her. Then she turned puffy, disagreeable eyes full on Mrs. James Mather, and coughed rousingly in her face.

With a smothered exclamation Jaqueline got to her feet, squeezed with brisk violence past the fleshy knees and made her way, pink with rage, toward the rear of the car. There she seized a strap, and there she was presently joined by her husband in a state of considerable alarm.

They exchanged no word but stood silently side by side for ten minutes while a row of men sitting in front of them crackled their newspapers and kept their eyes fixed virtuously upon the day's cartoons.

When they left the car at last Jaqueline exploded.

"You big *fool!*" she cried wildly. "Did you see that horrible woman you gave your seat to? Why don't you consider *me* occasionally instead of every fat selfish washwoman you meet?"

"How should I know——"

But Jaqueline was as angry at him as she had ever been—it was unusual for anyone to get angry at him.

"You didn't see any of those men getting up for *me*, did you? No wonder you were too tired to go out last Monday night. You'd probably given your seat to some—to some horrible, Polish *wash*woman that's strong as an ox and *likes* to stand up!"

They were walking along the slushy street stepping wildly into great pools of water. Confused and distressed, Mather could utter neither apology nor defense.

Jaqueline broke off and then turned to him with a curious light in her eyes. The words in which she couched her summary of the situation were probably the most disagreeable that had ever been addressed to him in his life.

"The trouble with you, Jim, the reason you're such an easy mark, is that you've got the ideas of a college freshman—you're a professional nice fellow."

II

The incident and the unpleasantness were forgotten. Mather's vast good nature had smoothed over the roughness within an hour. References to it fell with a dying cadence throughout several days—then ceased and tumbled into the limbo of oblivion. I say "limbo," for oblivion is, unfortunately, never quite oblivious. The subject was drowned out by the fact that Jaqueline with her customary spirit and coolness began the long, arduous, uphill business of bearing a child. Her natural traits and prejudices became intensified and she was less inclined to let things pass.

It was April now, and as yet they had not bought a car. Mather had discovered that he was saving practically nothing and that in another half-year he would have a family on his hands. It worried him. A wrinkle—small, tentative, undisturbing—appeared for the first time as a shadow around his honest, friendly eyes. He worked far into the spring twilight now and frequently brought home with him the overflow from his office day. The new car would have to be postponed for awhile.

April afternoon, and all the city shopping on Washington Street. Jaqueline walked slowly past the shops, brooding without fear or depression on the shape into which her life was now being arbitrarily forced. Dry summer dust was in the wind; the sun bounded cheerily from the plate-glass windows and made radiant gasoline rainbows where automobile drippings had formed pools on the street.

Jaqueline stopped. Not six feet from her a bright new sport roadster was parked at the curb. Beside it stood two men in conversation, and at the moment when she identified one of them as young Bronson she heard him say to the other in a casual tone:

"What do you think of it? Just got it this morning."

Jaqueline turned abruptly and walked with quick tapping steps to her husband's office. With her usual curt nod to the stenographer she strode by her to the inner room. Mather looked up from his desk in surprise at her brusque entry.

"Jim," she began breathlessly, "did Bronson ever pay you that three hundred?"

"Why—no," he answered hesitantly, "not yet. He was in here last week and he explained that he was a little bit hard up."

Her eyes gleamed with angry triumph.

"Oh, he did?" she snapped. "Well, he's just bought a new sport roadster that must have cost anyhow twenty-five hundred dollars."

He shook his head, unbelieving.

"I saw it," she insisted. "I heard him say he'd just bought it."

"He *told* me he was hard up," repeated Mather helplessly.

Jaqueline audibly gave up by heaving a profound noise, a sort of groanish sigh.

"He was *using* you! He knew you were easy and he was *using* you. Can't you see? He wanted *you* to buy him the car and you *did!*" She laughed bitterly. "He's probably roaring his sides out to think how easily he worked you."

"Oh, no," protested Mather with a shocked expression, "you must have mistaken somebody for him—"

"We walk—and he rides on our money," she interrupted excitedly. "Oh, it's rich—it's rich. If it wasn't so maddening, it'd be just absurd. Look here—!" Her voice grew sharper, more restrained—there was a touch of contempt in it now. "You spend half your time doing things for people who don't give a damn about you or what becomes of you. You give up your seat on the street car to *hogs*, and come home too dead tired to even *move*. You're on all sorts of committees that take at least an hour a day out of your business and you don't get a cent out of them. You're—eternally—being *used!* I won't stand it! I thought I married a man—not a professional samaritan who's going to fetch and carry for the world!"

As she finished her invective Jaqueline reeled suddenly and sank into a chair—nervously exhausted.

"Just at this time," she went on brokenly, "I need you. I need your strength and your health and your arms around me. And if you—if you just give it to *every*one, it's spread *so* thin when it reaches me—"

He knelt by her side, moving her tired young head until it lay against his shoulder.

"I'm sorry, Jaqueline," he said humbly. "I'll be more careful. I didn't realize what I was doing."

"You're the dearest person in the world," murmured Jaqueline huskily, "but I want all of you and the best of you for me."

He smoothed her hair over and over. For a few minutes they rested there silently, having attained a sort of Nirvana of peace and understanding. Then Jaqueline reluctantly raised her head as they were interrupted by the voice of Miss Clancy in the doorway.

"Oh, I beg your pardon."

"What is it?"

"A boy's here with some boxes. It's C.O.D."

Mather rose and followed Miss Clancy into the outer office.

"It's fifty dollars."

He searched his wallet—he had omitted to go to the bank that morning.

"Just a minute," he said abstractedly. His mind was on Jaqueline, Jaqueline who seemed forlorn in her trouble, waiting for him in the other room. He walked into the corridor, and opening the door of "Clayton and Drake, Brokers" across the way, swung wide a low gate and went up to a man seated at a desk.

"Morning, Fred," said Mather.

Drake, a little man of thirty with pince-nez and bald head, rose and shook hands.

"Morning, Jim. What can I do for you?"

"Why, a boy's in my office with some stuff C.O.D. and I haven't a cent. Can you let me have fifty till this afternoon?"

Drake looked closely at Mather. Then, slowly and startlingly, he shook his head—not up and down but from side to side.

"Sorry, Jim," he answered stiffly, "I've made a rule never to make a personal loan to anybody on any conditions. I've seen it break up too many friendships."

"What?"

Mather had come out of his abstraction now, and the monosyllable held an undisguised quality of shock. Then his natural tact acted automatically, springing to his aid and dictating his words though his brain was suddenly numb. His immediate instinct was to put Drake at ease in his refusal.

"Oh, I see." He nodded his head as if in full agreement, as if he himself had often considered adopting just such a rule. "Oh, I see how you feel. Well—I just—I wouldn't have you break a rule like that for anything. It's probably a good thing."

They talked for a minute longer. Drake justified his position easily; he had evidently rehearsed the part a great deal. He treated Mather to an exquisitely frank smile.

Mather went politely back to his office leaving Drake under the impression that the latter was the most tactful man in the city. Mather knew how to leave people with that impression. But when he entered his own office and saw his wife staring dismally out the window into the sunshine he clenched his hands, and his mouth moved in an unfamiliar shape.

"All right, Jack," he said slowly, "I guess you're right about most things, and I'm wrong as hell."

III

During the next three months Mather thought back through many years. He had had an unusually happy life. Those frictions between man and man, between man and society, which harden most of us into a rough and cynical quarrelling trim, had been conspicuous by their infrequency in his life. It had never occurred to him before that he had paid a price for this immunity, but now he perceived how here and there, and constantly, he had taken the rough side of the road to avoid enmity or argument, or even question.

There was, for instance, much money that he had lent privately, about thirteen hundred dollars in all, which he realized, in his new enlightenment, he would never see again. It had taken Jaqueline's harder, feminine intelligence to know this. It was only now when he owed it to Jaqueline to have money in the bank that he missed these loans at all.

He realized too the truth of her assertions that he was continually doing favors—a little something here, a little something there;

the sum total, in time and energy expended, was appalling. It had pleased him to do the favors. He reacted warmly to being thought well of, but he wondered now if he had not been merely indulging a selfish vanity of his own. In suspecting this, he was, as usual, not quite fair to himself. The truth was that Mather was essentially and enormously romantic.

He decided that these expenditures of himself made him tired at night, less efficient in his work and less of a prop to Jaqueline, who, as the months passed, grew more heavy and bored, and sat through the long summer afternoons on the screened verandah waiting for his step at the end of the walk.

Lest that step falter, Mather gave up many things—among them the presidency of his college alumni association. He let slip other labors less prized. When he was put on a committee, men had a habit of electing him chairman and retiring into a dim background, where they were inconveniently hard to find. He was done with such things now. Also he avoided those who were prone to ask favors— fleeing a certain eager look that would be turned on him from some group at his club.

The change in him came slowly. He was not exceptionally unworldly—under other circumstances Drake's refusal of money would not have surprised him. Had it come to him as a story he would scarcely have given it a thought. But it had broken in with harsh abruptness upon a situation existing in his own mind, and the shock had given it a powerful and literal significance.

It was mid-August now and the last of a baking week. The curtains of his wide-open office windows had scarcely rippled all the day, but lay like sails becalmed in warm juxtaposition with the smothering screens. Mather was worried—Jaqueline had overtired herself and was paying for it by violent sick headaches, and business seemed to have come to an apathetic standstill. That morning he had been so irritable with Miss Clancy that she had looked at him in surprise. He had immediately apologized, wishing afterwards that he hadn't. He was working at high speed through this heat—why shouldn't she?

She came to his door now, and he looked up faintly frowning.

"Mr. Edward Lacy."

"All right," he answered listlessly. Old man Lacy—he knew him slightly. A melancholy figure—a brilliant start back in the eighties, and now one of the city's failures. He couldn't imagine what Lacy wanted unless he were soliciting.

"Good afternoon, Mr. Mather."

A little, solemn, grey-haired man stood on the threshold. Mather rose and greeted him politely.

"Are you busy, Mr. Mather?"

"Well, not so *very*." He stressed the qualifying word slightly.

Mr. Lacy sat down, obviously ill at ease. He kept his hat in his hands and clung to it tightly as he began to speak.

"Mr. Mather, if you've got five minutes to spare, I'm going to tell you something that—that I find at present it's necessary for me to tell you."

Mather nodded. His instinct warned him that there was a favor to be asked, but he was tired, and with a sort of lassitude he let his chin sink into his hand, welcoming any distraction from his more immediate cares.

"You see," went on Mr. Lacy—Mather noticed that the hands which fingered at the hat were trembling—"back in eighty-four your father and I were very good friends. You've heard him speak of me no doubt."

Mather nodded.

"I was asked to be one of the pallbearers. Once we were—very close. It's because of that that I come to you now. Never before in my life have I ever had to come to anyone as I've come to you now, Mr. Mather—come to a stranger. But as you grow older your friends die or move away or some misunderstanding separates you. And your children die unless you're fortunate enough to go first—and pretty soon you get to be alone, so that you don't have any friends at all. You're isolated." He smiled faintly. His hands were trembling violently now.

"Once upon a time almost forty years ago your father came to me and asked me for a thousand dollars. I was a few years older than he was, and though I knew him only slightly, I had a high opinion of him. That was a lot of money in those days, and he had no security—he had nothing but a plan in his head—but I liked the way he had of looking out of his eyes—you'll pardon me if I say you look not unlike him—so I gave it to him without security."

Mr. Lacy paused.

"Without security," he repeated. "I could afford it then. I didn't lose by it. He paid it back with interest at six per-cent before the year was up."

Mather was looking down at his blotter, tapping out a series of triangles with his pencil. He knew what was coming now, and his muscles physically tightened as he mustered his forces for the refusal he would have to make.

"I'm now an old man, Mr. Mather," the cracked voice went on. "I've made a failure—I *am* a failure—only we needn't go into that now. I have a daughter, an unmarried daughter who lives with me. She does stenographic work and has been very kind to me. We live together, you know, on Selby Avenue—we have an apartment, quite a nice apartment."

The old man sighed quaveringly. He was trying—and at the same time was afraid—to get to his request. It was insurance, it seemed. He had a ten-thousand-dollar policy, he had borrowed on it up to the limit, and he stood to lose the whole amount unless he could raise four hundred and fifty dollars. He and his daughter had about seventy-five dollars between them. They had no friends—he had explained that—and they had found it impossible to raise the money. . . .

Mather could stand the miserable story no longer. He could not spare the money, but he could at least relieve the old man of the blistered agony of asking for it.

"I'm sorry, Mr. Lacy," he interrupted as gently as possible, "but I can't lend you that money."

"No?" The old man looked at him with faded, blinking eyes that were beyond all shock, almost, it seemed, beyond any human emotion except ceaseless care. The only change in his expression was that his mouth dropped slowly ajar.

Mather fixed his eyes determinately upon his blotter.

"We're going to have a baby in a few months, and I've been saving for that. It wouldn't be fair to my wife to take anything from her—or the child—right now."

His voice sank to a sort of mumble. He found himself saying platitudinously that business was bad—saying it with revolting facility.

Mr. Lacy made no argument. He rose without visible signs of disappointment. Only his hands were still trembling and they worried Mather. The old man was apologetic—he was sorry to have bothered him at a time like this. Perhaps something would turn up. He had thought that if Mr. Mather did happen to have a good deal extra—why, he might be the person to go to because he was the son of an old friend.

As he left the office he had trouble opening the outer door. Miss Clancy helped him. He went shabbily and unhappily down the corridor with his faded eyes blinking and his mouth still faintly ajar.

Jim Mather stood by his desk and put his hand over his face and shivered suddenly as if he were cold. But the five-o'clock air outside was hot as a tropic noon.

IV

The twilight was hotter still an hour later as he stood at the corner waiting for his car. The trolley-ride to his house was twenty-five minutes, and he bought a pink-jacketed newspaper to appetize his listless mind. Life had seemed less happy, less glamorous of late. Perhaps he had learned more of the world's ways—perhaps its glamor was evaporating little by little with the hurried years.

Nothing like this afternoon, for instance, had ever happened to him before. He could not dismiss the old man from his mind. He pictured him plodding home in the weary heat—on foot, probably, to save carfare—opening the door of a hot little flat, and confessing to his daughter that the son of his friend had not been able to help him out. All evening they would plan helplessly until they said good night to each other—father and daughter, isolated by chance in this world—and went to lie awake with a pathetic loneliness in their two beds.

Mather's street car came along, and he found a seat near the front, next to an old lady who looked at him grudgingly as she moved over. At the next block a crowd of girls from the department-store district flowed up the aisle, and Mather unfolded his paper. Of late he had not indulged his habit of giving up his seat. Jaqueline was right—the average young girl was able to stand as well as he was. Giving up his seat was silly, a mere gesture. Nowadays not one woman in a dozen even bothered to thank him.

It was stifling hot in the car, and he wiped the heavy damp from his forehead. The aisle was thickly packed now, and a woman standing beside his seat was thrown momentarily against his shoulder as the car turned a corner. Mather took a long breath of the hot foul air, which persistently refused to circulate, and tried to center his mind on a cartoon at the top of the sporting page.

"Move for'ard ina car, please!" The conductor's voice pierced the opaque column of humanity with raucous irritation. "Plen'y of room for'ard!"

The crowd made a feeble attempt to shove forward, but the unfortunate fact that there was no space into which to move precluded any marked success. The car turned another corner, and again the woman next to Mather swayed against his shoulder. Ordinarily he would have given up his seat if only to avoid this reminder that she was there. It made him feel unpleasantly cold-blooded. And the car was horrible—horrible. They ought to put more of them on the line these sweltering days.

For the fifth time he looked at the pictures in the comic strip. There was a beggar in the second picture, and the wavering image of Mr. Lacy persistently inserted itself in the beggar's place. God! Suppose the old man really did starve to death—suppose he threw himself into the river.

"Once," thought Mather, "he helped my father. Perhaps if he hadn't my own life would have been different than it has been. But Lacy could afford it then—and I can't."

To force out the picture of Mr. Lacy, Mather tried to think of Jaqueline. He said to himself over and over that he would have been sacrificing Jaqueline to a played-out man who had had his chance and failed. Jaqueline needed her chance now as never before.

Mather looked at his watch. He had been on the car ten minutes. Fifteen minutes still to ride, and the heat increasing with breathless intensity. The woman swayed against him once more, and looking out the window he saw that they were turning the last downtown corner.

It occurred to him that perhaps he ought, after all, to give the woman his seat—her last sway toward him had been a particularly tired sway. If he were sure she was an older woman—but the texture of her dress as it brushed his hand gave somehow the impression that she was a young girl. He did not dare look up to see. He was afraid of the appeal that might look out of her eyes if they were old eyes or the sharp contempt if they were young.

For the next five minutes his mind worked in a vague suffocated way on what now seemed to him the enormous problem of whether or not to give her the seat. He felt dimly that doing so would partially atone for his refusal to Mr. Lacy that afternoon. It would be rather terrible to have done those two cold-blooded things in succession—and on such a day.

He tried the cartoon again, but in vain. He must concentrate on Jaqueline. He was dead tired now, and if he stood up he would be more tired. Jaqueline would be waiting for him, needing him. She would be depressed and she would want him to hold her quietly in his arms for an hour after dinner. When he was tired this was rather a strain. And afterwards when they went to bed she would ask him from time to time to get her her medicine or a glass of ice-water. He hated to show any weariness in doing these things. She might notice and, needing something, refrain from asking for it.

The girl in the aisle swayed against him once more—this time it was more like a sag. She was tired, too. Well, it was weary to work. The ends of many proverbs that had to do with toil and the long day floated fragmentarily through his mind. Everybody in the world was tired—this woman, for instance, whose body was sagging so wearily, so strangely against his. But his home came first and his girl that he loved was waiting for him there. He must keep his strength for her, and he said to himself over and over that he would not give up his seat.

Then he heard a long sigh, followed by a sudden exclamation, and he realized that the girl was no longer leaning against him. The exclamation multiplied into a clatter of voices—then came a pause—then a renewed clatter that travelled down the car in calls and little staccato cries to the conductor. The bell clanged violently, and the hot car jolted to a sudden stop.

"Girl fainted up here!"

"Too hot for her!"

"Just keeled right over!"

"Get back there! Gangway, you!"

The crowd eddied apart. The passengers in front squeezed back and those on the rear platform temporarily disembarked. Curiosity and pity bubbled out of suddenly conversing groups. People tried to help, got in the way. Then the bell rang and voices rose stridently again.

"Get her out all right?"

"Say, did you see that?"

"This damn company ought to—"

"Did you see the man that carried her out? He was pale as a ghost, too."

"Yes, but did you hear—"

"What?"

"That fella. That pale fella that carried her out. He was sittin' beside her—he says she's his wife!"

The house was quiet. A breeze pressed back the dark vine leaves of the verandah, letting in thin yellow rods of moonlight on the wicker chairs. Jaqueline rested placidly on the long settee with her head in his arms. After awhile she stirred lazily; her hand reaching up patted his cheek.

"I think I'll go to bed now. I'm so tired. Will you help me up?"

He lifted her and then laid her back among the pillows.

"I'll be with you in a minute," he said gently. "Can you wait for just a minute?"

He passed into the lighted living room, and she heard him thumbing the pages of a telephone directory; then she listened as he called a number.

"Hello, is Mr. Lacy there? Why—yes, it *is* pretty important—if he hasn't gone to sleep."

A pause. Jaqueline could hear restless sparrows splattering through the leaves of the magnolia over the way. Then her husband at the telephone:

"Is this Mr. Lacy? Oh, this is Mather. Why—why, in regard to that matter we talked about this afternoon, I think I'll be able to fix that up after all." He raised his voice a little as though someone at the other end found it difficult to hear. "James Mather's son, I said— About that little matter this afternoon—"

"THE SENSIBLE THING"

At the Great American Lunch Hour young George O'Kelly straightened his desk deliberately and with an assumed air of interest. No one in the office must know that he was in a hurry, for success is a matter of atmosphere, and it is not well to advertise the fact that your mind is separated from your work by a distance of seven hundred miles.

But once out of the building he set his teeth and began to run, glancing now and then at the gay noon of early spring which filled Times Square and loitered less than twenty feet over the heads of the crowd. The crowd all looked slightly upward and took deep March breaths, and the sun dazzled their eyes so that scarcely anyone saw anyone else but only their own reflection on the sky.

George O'Kelly, whose mind was over seven hundred miles away, thought that all outdoors was horrible. He rushed into the subway and for ninety-five blocks bent a frenzied glance on a car-card which showed vividly how he had only one chance in five of keeping his teeth for ten years. At 137th Street he broke off his study of commercial art, left the subway and began to run again, a tireless, anxious run that brought him this time to his home—one room in a high, horrible apartment-house in the middle of nowhere.

There it was on the bureau, the letter—in sacred ink, on blessed paper—all over the city, people, if they listened, could hear the beating of George O'Kelly's heart. He read the commas, the blots, and the thumb-smudge on the margin—then he threw himself hopelessly upon his bed.

He was in a mess, one of those terrific messes which are ordinary incidents in the life of the poor, which follow poverty like birds of prey. The poor go under or go up or go wrong or even go on, somehow, in a way the poor have—but George O'Kelly was so new to poverty that had any one denied the uniqueness of his case he would have been astounded.

Less than two years ago he had been graduated with honors from the Massachusetts Institute of Technology and had taken a position with a firm of construction engineers in southern Tennessee. All his life he had thought in terms of tunnels and skyscrapers and great squat dams and tall, three-towered bridges that were like dancers holding hands in a row, with heads as tall as cities and skirts of cable strand. It had seemed romantic to George O'Kelly to change the sweep of rivers and the shape of mountains so that life could flourish in the old bad lands of the world where it had never taken root before. He loved steel, and there was always steel near him in his dreams, liquid steel, steel in bars and blocks and beams and formless plastic masses, waiting for him, as paint and canvas to his hand. Steel inexhaustible, to be made lovely and austere in his imaginative fire. . . .

At present he was an insurance clerk at forty dollars a week with his dream slipping fast behind him. The dark little girl who had made this mess, this terrible and intolerable mess, was waiting to be sent for in a town in Tennessee.

In fifteen minutes the woman from whom he sublet his room knocked and asked him with maddening kindness if, since he was home, he would have some lunch. He shook his head, but the interruption aroused him, and getting up from the bed he wrote a telegram.

"Letter depressed me have you lost your nerve you are foolish and just upset to think of breaking off why not marry me immediately sure we can make it all right—"

He hesitated for a wild minute and then added in a hand that could scarcely be recognized as his own: "In any case I will arrive tomorrow at six o'clock."

When he finished he ran out of the apartment and down to the telegraph office near the subway stop. He possessed in this world not quite one hundred dollars, but the letter showed that she was "nervous" and this left him no choice. He knew what "nervous" meant—that she was emotionally depressed, that the prospect of marrying into a life of poverty and struggle was putting too much strain upon her love.

George O'Kelly reached the insurance company at his usual run, the run that had become almost second nature to him, that seemed best to express the tension under which he lived. He went straight to the manager's office.

"I want to see you, Mr. Chambers," he announced breathlessly.

"Well?" Two eyes, eyes like winter windows, glared at him with ruthless impersonality.

"I want to get four days' vacation."

"Why, you had a vacation just two weeks ago!" said Mr. Chambers in surprise.

"That's true," admitted the distraught young man, "but now I've got to have another."

"Where'd you go last time? To your home?"

"No, I went to—a place in Tennessee."

"Well, where do you want to go this time?"

"Well, this time I want to go to—a place in Tennessee."

"You're consistent, anyhow," said the manager dryly. "But I didn't realize you were employed here as a traveling salesman."

"I'm not," cried George desperately, "but I've got to go."

"All right," agreed Mr. Chambers, "but you don't have to come back. So don't!"

"I won't." And to his own astonishment as well as Mr. Chambers' George's face grew pink with pleasure. He felt happy, exultant—for the first time in six months he was absolutely free. Tears of gratitude stood in his eyes, and he seized Mr. Chambers warmly by the hand.

"I want to thank you," he said with a rush of emotion. "I don't want to come back. I think I'd have gone crazy if you'd said that I could come back. Only I couldn't quit myself, you see, and I want to thank you for—for quitting for me."

He waved his hand magnanimously, shouted aloud, "You owe me three days' salary but you can keep it!" and rushed from the office. Mr. Chambers rang for his stenographer to ask if O'Kelly had seemed queer lately. He had fired many men in the course of his career, and they had taken it in many different ways, but none of them had thanked him—ever before.

II

Jonquil Cary was her name, and to George O'Kelly nothing had ever looked so fresh and pale as her face when she saw him and fled to him eagerly along the station platform. Her arms were raised to him, her mouth was half parted for his kiss, when she held him off suddenly and lightly and, with a touch of embarrassment, looked around. Two boys, somewhat younger than George, were standing in the background.

"This is Mr. Craddock and Mr. Holt," she announced cheerfully. "You met them when you were here before."

Disturbed by the transition of a kiss into an introduction and suspecting some hidden significance, George was more confused when he found that the automobile which was to carry them to Jonquil's house belonged to one of the two young men. It seemed to put him at a disadvantage. On the way Jonquil chattered between the front and back seats, and when he tried to slip his arm around her under cover of the twilight she compelled him with a quick movement to take her hand instead.

"Is this street on the way to your house?" he whispered. "I don't recognize it."

"It's the new boulevard. Jerry just got this car today, and he wants to show it to me before he takes us home."

When, after twenty minutes, they were deposited at Jonquil's house, George felt that the first happiness of the meeting, the joy he had recognized so surely in her eyes back in the station, had been dissipated by the intrusion of the ride. Something that he had looked forward to had been rather casually lost, and he was brooding on this as he said good-night stiffly to the two young men. Then his ill humor faded as Jonquil drew him into a familiar embrace under the dim light of the front hall and told him in a dozen ways, of which the best was without words, how she had missed him. Her emotion reassured him, promised his anxious heart that everything would be all right.

They sat together on the sofa, overcome by each other's presence, beyond all except fragmentary endearments. At the supper hour Jonquil's father and mother appeared and were glad to see George. They liked him, and had been interested in his engineering career when he had first come to Tennessee over a year before. They had been sorry when he had given it up and gone to New York to look for something more immediately profitable, but while they deplored the curtailment of his career they sympathized with him and were ready to recognize the engagement. During dinner they asked about his progress in New York.

"Everything's going fine," he told them with enthusiasm. "I've been promoted—better salary."

He was miserable as he said this—but they were all *so* glad.

"They must like you," said Mrs. Cary, "that's certain—or they wouldn't let you off twice in three weeks to come down here."

"I told them they had to," explained George hastily; "I told them if they didn't I wouldn't work for them anymore."

"But you ought to save your money," Mrs. Cary reproached him gently. "Not spend it all on this expensive trip."

Dinner was over—he and Jonquil were alone and she came back into his arms.

"So glad you're here," she sighed. "Wish you never were going away again, darling."

"Do you miss me?"

"Oh, so much, so much."

"Do you—do other men come to see you often? Like those two kids?"

The question surprised her. The dark velvet eyes stared at him.

"Why, of course they do. All the time. Why—I've told you in letters that they did, dearest."

This was true—when he had first come to the city there had been already a dozen boys around her, responding to her picturesque fragility with adolescent worship, and a few of them perceiving that her beautiful eyes were also sane and kind.

"Do you expect me never to go anywhere"—Jonquil demanded, leaning back against the sofa-pillows until she seemed to look at him from many miles away—"and just fold my hands and sit still—forever?"

"What do you mean?" he blurted out in a panic. "Do you mean you think I'll never have enough money to marry you?"

"Oh, don't jump at conclusions so, George."

"I'm not jumping at conclusions. That's what you said."

George decided suddenly that he was on dangerous ground. He had not intended to let anything spoil this night. He tried to take her again in his arms, but she resisted unexpectedly, saying:

"It's hot. I'm going to get the electric fan."

When the fan was adjusted they sat down again, but he was in a supersensitive mood and involuntarily he plunged into the specific world he had intended to avoid.

"When will you marry me?"

"Are you ready for me to marry you?"

All at once his nerves gave way, and he sprang to his feet.

"Let's shut off that damned fan," he cried. "It drives me wild. It's like a clock ticking away all the time I'll be with you. I came here to be happy and forget everything about New York and time—"

He sank down on the sofa as suddenly as he had risen. Jonquil turned off the fan, and drawing his head down into her lap began stroking his hair.

"Let's sit like this," she said softly. "Just sit quiet like this, and I'll put you to sleep. You're all tired and nervous and your sweetheart'll take care of you."

"But I don't want to sit like this," he complained, jerking up suddenly. "I don't want to sit like this at all. I want you to kiss me. That's the only thing that makes me rest. And anyway I'm not nervous—it's you that's nervous. I'm not nervous at all."

To prove that he wasn't nervous he left the couch and plumped himself into a rocking-chair across the room.

"Just when I'm ready to marry you you write me the most nervous letters, as if you're going to back out, and I have to come rushing down here—"

"You don't have to come if you don't want to."

"But I *do* want to!" insisted George.

It seemed to him that he was being very cool and logical and that she was putting him deliberately in the wrong. With every word they were drawing farther and farther apart—and he was unable to stop himself or to keep worry and pain out of his voice.

But in a minute Jonquil began to cry sorrowfully and he came back to the sofa and put his arm around her. He was the comforter now, drawing her head close to his shoulder, murmuring old familiar things until she grew calmer and only trembled a little, spasmodically, in his arms. For over an hour they sat there, while the evening pianos thumped their last cadences into the street outside. George did not move, or think, or hope, lulled into numbness by the premonition of disaster. The clock would tick on, past eleven, past twelve, and then Mrs. Cary would call down gently over the banister—beyond that he saw only tomorrow and despair.

III

In the heat of the next day the breaking-point came. They had each guessed the truth about the other, but of the two she was the more ready to admit the situation.

"There's no use going on," she said miserably. "You know you hate the insurance business, and you'll never do well in it."

"That's not it," he insisted stubbornly. "I hate going on alone. If you'll marry me and come with me and take a chance with me, I can make good at anything, but not while I'm worrying about you down here."

She was silent a long time before she answered, not thinking—for she had seen the end—but only waiting, because she knew that every word would seem more cruel than the last. Finally she spoke:

"George, I love you with all my heart, and I don't see how I can ever love anyone else but you. If you'd been ready for me two months ago I'd have married you—now I can't because it doesn't seem to be the sensible thing."

He made wild accusations—there was someone else—she was keeping something from him!

"No, there's no one else."

This was true. But reacting from the strain of this affair she had found relief in the company of young boys like Jerry Holt, who had the merit of meaning absolutely nothing in her life.

George didn't take the situation well, at all. He seized her in his arms and tried literally to kiss her into marrying him at once. When this failed he broke into a long monologue of self-pity and ceased only when he saw that he was making himself despicable in her sight. He threatened to leave when he had no intention of leaving, and refused to go when she told him that, after all, it was best that he should.

For awhile she was sorry, then for another while she was merely kind.

"You'd better go now!" she cried at last, so loud that Mrs. Cary came downstairs in alarm.

"Is something the matter?"

"I'm going away, Mrs. Cary," said George brokenly. Jonquil had left the room.

"Don't feel so badly, George." Mrs. Cary blinked at him in helpless sympathy—sorry and, in the same breath, glad that the little tragedy was almost done. "If I were you I'd go home to your mother for a week or so. Perhaps after all this is the sensible thing—"

"Please don't talk!" he cried. "Please don't say anything to me now!"

Jonquil came into the room again, her sorrow and her nervousness alike tucked under powder and rouge and hat.

"I've ordered a taxi-cab," she said impersonally. "We can drive around until your train leaves."

She walked out on the front porch. George put on his coat and hat and stood for a minute exhausted in the hall—he had eaten scarcely a bite since he had left New York. Mrs. Cary came over, drew his head down and kissed him on the cheek, and he felt very ridiculous and weak in his knowledge that the scene had been ridiculous and weak at the end. If he had only gone the night before—left her for the last time with a decent pride.

The taxi had come, and for an hour these two that had been lovers rode along the less-frequented streets. He held her hand and grew calmer in the sunshine, seeing too late that there had been nothing all along to do or say.

"I'll come back," he told her.

"I know you will," she answered, trying to put a cheery faith into her voice. "And we'll write each other—sometimes."

"No," he said, "we won't write. I couldn't stand that. Someday I'll come back."

"I'll never forget you, George."

They reached the station, and she went with him while he bought his ticket. . . .

"Why, George O'Kelly and Jonquil Cary!"

It was a man and a girl whom George had known when he had worked in town, and Jonquil seemed to greet their presence with relief. For an interminable five minutes they all stood there talking; then the train roared into the station, and with ill-concealed agony in his face George held out his arms toward Jonquil. She took an uncertain step toward him, faltered, and then pressed his hand quickly as if she were taking leave of a chance friend.

"Good-bye, George," she was saying, "I hope you have a pleasant trip."

"Good-bye, George. Come back and see us all again."

Dumb, almost blind with pain, he seized his suitcase, and in some dazed way got himself aboard the train.

Past clanging street-crossings, gathering speed through wide suburban spaces toward the sunset. Perhaps she too would see the sunset and pause for a moment, turning, remembering, before he faded with her sleep into the past. This night's dusk would cover up forever the sun and the trees and the flowers and laughter of his young world.

IV

On a damp afternoon in September of the following year a young man with his face burned to a deep copper glow got off a train at a city in Tennessee. He looked around anxiously, and seemed relieved when he found that there was no one in the station to meet him. He taxied to the best hotel in the city where he registered with some satisfaction as George O'Kelly, Cuzco, Peru.

Up in his room he sat for a few minutes at the window looking down into the familiar street below. Then with his hand trembling faintly he took off the telephone receiver and called a number.

"Is Miss Jonquil in?"

"This is she."

"Oh—" His voice after overcoming a faint tendency to waver went on with friendly formality.

"This is George O'Kelly. Did you get my letter?"

"Yes. I thought you'd be in today."

Her voice, cool and unmoved, disturbed him, but not as he had expected. This was the voice of a stranger, unexcited, pleasantly glad to see him—that was all. He wanted to put down the telephone and catch his breath.

"I haven't seen you for—a long time." He succeeded in making this sound offhand. "Over a year."

He knew how long it had been—to the day.

"It'll be awfully nice to talk to you again."

"I'll be there in about an hour."

He hung up. For four long seasons every minute of his leisure had been crowded with anticipation of this hour, and now this hour was here. He had thought of finding her married, engaged, in love—he had not thought she would be unstirred at his return.

There would never again in his life, he felt, be another ten months like these he had just gone through. He had made an admittedly remarkable showing for a young engineer—stumbled into two unusual opportunities, one in Peru, whence he had just returned, and another, consequent upon it, in New York, whither he was bound. In this short time he had risen from poverty into a position of unlimited opportunity.

He looked at himself in the dressing-table mirror. He was almost black with tan, but it was a romantic black, and in the last week, since he had had time to think about it, it had given him considerable pleasure. The hardiness of his frame, too, he appraised with a sort of fascination. He had lost part of an eyebrow somewhere, and he still wore an elastic bandage on his knee, but he was too young not to realize that on the steamer many women had looked at him with unusual tributary interest.

His clothes, of course, were frightful. They had been made for him by a Greek tailor in Lima—in two days. He was young enough, too, to have explained this sartorial deficiency to Jonquil in his otherwise laconic note. The only further detail it contained was a request that he should *not* be met at the station.

George O'Kelly, of Cuzco, Peru, waited an hour and a half in the hotel, until, to be exact, the sun had reached a midway position in the sky. Then, freshly shaven and talcum-powdered toward a somewhat more Caucasian hue, for vanity at the last minute had overcome romance, he engaged a taxi-cab and set out for the house he knew so well.

He was breathing hard—he noticed this but he told himself that it was excitement, not emotion. He was here; she was not married—that was enough. He was not even sure what he had to say to her. But this was the moment of his life that he felt he could least easily have dispensed with. There was no triumph, after all, without a girl concerned, and if he did not lay his spoils at her feet he could at least hold them for a passing moment before her eyes.

The house loomed up suddenly beside him, and his first thought was that it had assumed a strange unreality. There was nothing changed—only everything was changed. It was smaller and it seemed shabbier than before—there was no cloud of magic hovering over its roof and issuing from the windows of the upper floor. He rang the doorbell and an unfamiliar colored maid appeared. Miss Jonquil would be down in a moment. He wet his lips nervously and walked into the sitting room—and the feeling of unreality increased. After all, he saw, this was only a room, and not the enchanted chamber where he had passed those poignant hours. He sat in a chair, amazed to find it a chair, realizing that his imagination had distorted and colored all these simple familiar things.

Then the door opened and Jonquil came into the room—and it was as though everything in it suddenly blurred before his eyes. He had not remembered how beautiful she was, and he felt his face grow pale and his voice diminish to a poor sigh in his throat.

She was dressed in pale green, and a gold ribbon bound back her dark, straight hair like a crown. The familiar velvet eyes caught his as she came through the door, and a spasm of fright went through him at her beauty's power of inflicting pain.

He said "Hello," and they each took a few steps forward and shook hands. Then they sat in chairs quite far apart and gazed at each other across the room.

"You've come back," she said, and he answered just as tritely: "I wanted to stop in and see you as I came through."

He tried to neutralize the tremor in his voice by looking anywhere but at her face. The obligation to speak was on him, but, unless he immediately began to boast, it seemed that there was nothing to say. There had never been anything casual in their previous relations—it didn't seem possible that people in this position would talk about the weather.

"This is ridiculous," he broke out in sudden embarrassment. "I don't know exactly what to do. Does my being here bother you?"

"No." The answer was both reticent and impersonally sad. It depressed him.

"Are you engaged?" he demanded.

"No."

"Are you in love with someone?"

She shook her head.

"Oh." He leaned back in his chair. Another subject seemed exhausted—the interview was not taking the course he had intended.

"Jonquil," he began, this time on a softer key, "after all that's happened between us, I wanted to come back and see you. Whatever I do in the future I'll never love another girl as I've loved you."

This was one of the speeches he had rehearsed. On the steamer it had seemed to have just the right note—a reference to the tenderness he would always feel for her combined with a non-committal attitude toward his present state of mind. Here with the past around him, beside him, growing minute by minute more heavy on the air, it seemed theatrical and stale.

She made no comment, sat without moving, her eyes fixed on him with an expression that might have meant everything or nothing.

"You don't love me anymore, do you?" he asked her in a level voice.

"No."

When Mrs. Cary came in a minute later, and spoke to him about his success—there had been a half-column about him in the local paper—he was a mixture of emotions. He knew now that he still wanted this girl, and he knew that the past sometimes comes back— that was all. For the rest he must be strong and watchful and he would see.

"And now," Mrs. Cary was saying, "I want you two to go and see the lady who has the chrysanthemums. She particularly told me she wanted to see you because she'd read about you in the paper."

They went to see the lady with the chrysanthemums. They walked along the street, and he recognized with a sort of excitement just how her shorter footsteps always fell in between his own. The lady turned out to be nice, and the chrysanthemums were enormous and extraordinarily beautiful. The lady's gardens were full of them, white and pink and yellow, so that to be among them was a trip back into the heart of summer. There were two gardens full, and a gate between them; when they strolled toward the second garden the lady went first through the gate.

And then a curious thing happened. George stepped aside to let Jonquil pass, but instead of going through she stood still and stared at him for a minute. It was not so much the look, which was not a smile, as it was the moment of silence. They saw each other's eyes, and both took a short, faintly accelerated breath, and then they went on into the second garden. That was all.

The afternoon waned. They thanked the lady and walked home slowly, thoughtfully, side by side. Through dinner too they were silent. George told Mr. Cary something of what had happened in South America and managed to let it be known that everything would be plain sailing for him in the future.

Then dinner was over, and he and Jonquil were alone in the room which had seen the beginning of their love affair and the end. It seemed to him long ago and inexpressibly sad. On that sofa he had felt agony and grief such as he would never feel again. He would never be so weak or so tired and miserable and poor. Yet he knew that that boy of fifteen months before had had something, a trust, a warmth that was gone forever. The sensible thing—they had done the sensible thing. He had traded his first youth for strength and carved success out of despair. But with his youth, life had carried away the freshness of his love.

"You won't marry me, will you?" he said quietly.

Jonquil shook her dark head.

"I'm never going to marry," she answered.

He nodded.

"I'm going on to Washington in the morning," he said.

"Oh—"

"I have to go. I've got to be in New York by the first, and meanwhile I want to stop off in Washington."

"Business?"

"No-o," he said as if reluctantly. "There's someone there I must see who was very kind to me when I was so—down and out."

This was invented. There was no one in Washington for him to see—but he was watching Jonquil narrowly, and he was sure that she winced a little, that her eyes closed and then opened wide again.

"But before I go I want to tell you the things that happened to me since I saw you, and, as maybe we won't meet again, I wonder if—if just this once you'd sit in my lap like you used to. I wouldn't ask except since there's no one else—yet—perhaps it doesn't matter."

She nodded, and in a moment was sitting in his lap as she had sat so often in that vanished spring. The feel of her head against his shoulder, of her familiar body, sent a shock of emotion over him. His arms holding her had a tendency to tighten around her, so he leaned back and began to talk thoughtfully into the air.

He told her of a despairing two weeks in New York which had terminated with an attractive if not very profitable job in a construction plant in Jersey City. When the Peru business had first presented itself it had not seemed an extraordinary opportunity. He was to be third assistant engineer on the expedition, but only ten of the American party, including eight rodmen and surveyors, had ever reached Cuzco. Ten days later the chief of the expedition was dead of yellow fever. That had been his chance, a chance for anybody but a fool, a marvelous chance—

"A chance for anybody but a fool?" she interrupted innocently.

"Even for a fool," he continued. "It was wonderful. Well, I wired New York—"

"And so," she interrupted again, "they wired that you ought to take a chance?"

"Ought to!" he exclaimed, still leaning back. "That I *had* to. There was no time to lose—"

"Not a minute?"

"Not a minute."

"Not even time for—" she paused.

"For what?"

"Look."

He bent his head forward suddenly, and she drew herself to him in the same moment, her lips half open like a flower.

"Yes," he whispered into her lips. "There's all the time in the world. . . ."

All the time in the world—his life and hers. But for an instant as he kissed her he knew that though he search through eternity he could never recapture those lost April hours. He might press her close now till the muscles knotted on his arms—she was something desirable and rare that he had fought for and made his own—but never again an intangible whisper in the dusk or on the breeze of night. . . .

Well, let it pass, he thought; April is over, April is over. There are all kinds of love in the world, but never the same love twice.

GRETCHEN'S FORTY WINKS

The sidewalks were scratched with brittle leaves, and the bad little boy next door froze his tongue to the iron mail-box. Snow before night, sure. Autumn was over. This, of course, raised the coal question and the Christmas question; but Roger Halsey, standing on his own front porch, assured the dead suburban sky that he hadn't time for worrying about the weather. Then he let himself hurriedly into the house, and shut the subject out into the cold twilight.

The hall was dark but from above he heard the voices of his wife and the nursemaid and the baby in one of their interminable conversations—which consisted chiefly of "Don't!" and "Look out, Maxy!" and "Oh, there he *goes!*" punctuated by wild threats and vague bumpings and the recurrent sound of small, venturing feet.

Roger turned on the hall light and walked into the living room and turned on the red silk lamp. He put his bulging portfolio on the table, and sitting down rested his intense young face in his hand for a few minutes, shading his eyes carefully from the light. Then he lit a cigarette, squashed it out, and going to the foot of the stairs called for his wife.

"Gretchen!"

"Hello, dear." Her voice was full of laughter. "Come see baby."

He swore softly.

"I can't see baby now," he said aloud. "How long 'fore you'll be down?"

There was a mysterious pause and then a succession of "Don'ts" and "Look outs, Maxy" evidently meant to avert some threatened catastrophe.

"How long 'fore you'll be down?" repeated Roger, slightly irritated.

"Oh, I'll be right down."

"How soon?" he shouted.

He had trouble every day at this hour in adapting his voice from the urgent key of the city to the proper casualness for a model home. But tonight he was deliberately impatient. It almost disappointed him when Gretchen came running down the stairs, three at a time, crying "What is it?" in a rather surprised voice.

They kissed—lingered over it some moments. They had been married three years, and they were much more in love than that implies. It was seldom that they hated each other with that violent hate of which only young couples are capable, for Roger was still actively sensitive to her beauty.

"Come in here," he said abruptly. "I want to talk to you."

His wife, a bright-colored, Titian-haired girl, vivid as a French rag-doll, followed him into the living room.

"Listen, Gretchen"—he sat down at the end of the sofa— "beginning with tonight I'm going to— What's the matter?"

"Nothing. I'm just looking for a cigarette. Go on."

She tiptoed breathlessly back to the sofa and settled at the other end.

"Gretchen—" Again he broke off. Her hand, palm upward, was extended toward him. "Well, what is it?" he asked wildly.

"Matches."

"What?"

In his impatience it seemed incredible that she should ask for matches, but he fumbled automatically in his pocket.

"Thank you," she whispered. "I didn't mean to interrupt you. Go on."

"Gretch—"

Scratch! The match flared. They exchanged a tense look.

Her fawn's eyes apologized mutely this time and he laughed. After all she had done no more than light a cigarette; but when he was in this mood her slightest positive action irritated him beyond measure.

"When you've got time to listen," he said crossly, "you might be interested in discussing the poorhouse question with me."

"What poorhouse?" Her eyes were wide, startled; she sat quiet as a mouse.

"That was just to get your attention. But beginning tonight I start on what'll probably be the most important six weeks of my life—the six weeks that'll decide whether we're going on forever in this rotten little house in this rotten little suburban town."

Boredom replaced alarm in Gretchen's black eyes. She was a southern girl, and any question that had to do with getting ahead in the world always tended to give her a headache.

"Six months ago I left the New York Lithographic Company," announced Roger, "and went in the advertising business for myself."

"I know," interrupted Gretchen resentfully; "and now instead of getting six hundred a month sure, we're living on a risky five hundred."

"Gretchen," said Roger sharply, "if you'll just believe in me as hard as you can for six weeks more, we'll be rich. I've got a chance now to get some of the biggest accounts in the country." He hesitated. "And for these six weeks we won't go out at all, and we won't have anyone here. I'm going to bring home work every night, and we'll pull down all the blinds and if anyone rings the doorbell we won't answer."

He smiled airily as if it were a new game they were going to play. Then, as Gretchen was silent, his smile faded, and he looked at her uncertainly.

"Well, what's the matter?" she broke out finally. "Do you expect me to jump up and sing? You do enough work as it is. If you try to do any more you'll end up with a nervous breakdown. I read about a—"

"Don't worry about me," he interrupted; "I'm all right. But you're going to be bored to death sitting here every evening."

"No, I won't," she said without conviction—"except tonight."

"What about tonight?"

"George Tompkins asked us to dinner."

"Did you accept?"

"Of course I did," she said impatiently. "Why not? You're always talking about what a terrible neighborhood this is, and I thought maybe you'd like to go to a nicer one for a change."

"When I go to a nicer neighborhood I want to go for good," he said grimly.

"Well, can we go?"

"I suppose we'll have to if you've accepted."

Somewhat to his annoyance the conversation abruptly ended. Gretchen jumped up and kissed him sketchily and rushed into the kitchen to light the hot water for a bath. With a sigh he carefully deposited his portfolio behind the bookcase—it contained only sketches and layouts for display advertising, but it seemed to him the first thing a burglar would look for. Then he went abstractedly upstairs, dropped into the baby's room for a casual moist kiss and began dressing for dinner.

They had no automobile, so George Tompkins called for them at six-thirty. Tompkins was a successful interior decorator, a broad, rosy man with a handsome mustache and a strong odor of jasmine. He and Roger had once roomed side by side in a boarding house in New York, but they had met only intermittently in the past five years.

"We ought to see each other more," he told Roger tonight. "You ought to go out more often, old boy. Cocktail?"

"No thanks."

"No? Well, your fair wife will—won't you, Gretchen?"

"I love this house," she exclaimed, taking the glass and looking admiringly at ship models, Colonial whiskey bottles, and other fashionable débris of 1925.

"*I* like it," said Tompkins with satisfaction. "I did it to please myself, and I succeeded."

Roger stared moodily around the stiff, plain room, wondering if they could have blundered into the kitchen by mistake.

"You look like the devil, Roger," said his host. "Have a cocktail and cheer up."

"Have one," urged Gretchen.

"What?" Roger turned around absently. "Oh, no thanks. I've got to work after I get home."

"Work!" Tompkins smiled. "Listen, Roger, you'll kill yourself with work. Why don't you bring a little balance into your life— work a little, then play a little?"

"That's what I tell him," said Gretchen.

"Do you know an average business man's day?" demanded Tompkins as they went in to dinner. "Coffee in the morning, eight hours' work interrupted by a bolted luncheon, and then home again with dyspepsia and a bad temper to give the wife a pleasant evening."

Roger laughed shortly.

"You've been going to the movies too much," he said dryly.

"What?" Tompkins looked at him with some irritation. "Movies? I've hardly ever been to the movies in my life. I think the movies are atrocious. My opinions on life are drawn from my own observations. I believe in a balanced life."

"What's that?" demanded Roger.

"Well"—he hesitated—"probably the best way to tell you would be to describe my own day. Would that seem horribly egotistic?"

"Oh, no!" Gretchen looked at him with interest. "I'd love to hear about it."

"Well, in the morning I get up and go through a series of exercises. I've got one room fitted up as a little gymnasium, and I punch the bag and do shadow-boxing and weight-pulling for an hour. Then after a cold bath— There's a thing now! Do you take a daily cold bath?"

"No," admitted Roger, "I take a hot bath in the evening three or four times a week."

A horrified silence fell. Tompkins and Gretchen exchanged a glance as if something obscene had been said.

"What's the matter?" broke out Roger, glancing from one to the other in some irritation. "You know I don't take a bath every day—I haven't got the time."

Tompkins gave a prolonged sigh.

"After my bath," he continued, drawing a merciful veil of silence over the matter, "I have breakfast and drive to my office in New York, where I work until four. Then I lay off, and if it's summer I hurry out here for nine holes of golf, or if it's winter I play squash for an hour at my club. Then a good snappy game of bridge until dinner. Dinner is liable to have something to do with business— but in a pleasant way. Perhaps I've just finished a house for some customer, and he wants me to be on hand for his first party to see that the lighting is soft enough and all that sort of thing. Or maybe I sit down with a good book of poetry and spend the evening alone. At any rate I do something every night to get me out of myself."

"It must be wonderful," said Gretchen enthusiastically. "I wish we lived like that."

Tompkins bent forward earnestly over the table.

"You can," he said impressively. "There's no reason why you shouldn't. Look here, if Roger'll play nine holes of golf every day it'll do wonders for him. He won't know himself. He'll do his work better, never get that tired nervous feeling— What's the matter?"

He broke off. Roger had perceptibly yawned.

"Roger," cried Gretchen sharply, "there's no need to be so rude. If you did what George said, you'd be a lot better off." She turned indignantly to their host. "The latest is that he's going to work at *night* for the next six weeks. He says he's going to pull down the blinds and shut us up like hermits in a cave. He's been doing it every Sunday for the last year; now he's going to do it *every night* for *six weeks*."

Tompkins shook his head sadly.

"At the end of six weeks," he remarked, "he'll be starting for the sanitarium. Let me tell you, every private hospital in New York is full of cases like yours. You just strain the human nervous system a little too far, and *bang!*—you've broken something. And in order to save sixty hours you're laid up sixty weeks for repairs." He broke off, changed his tone and turned to Gretchen with a smile. "Not to mention what happens to you. It seems to me it's the wife rather than the husband who bears the brunt of these insane periods of overwork."

"I don't mind," protested Gretchen loyally.

"Yes, she does," said Roger grimly; "she minds like the devil. She's a shortsighted little egg, and she thinks it's going to be forever until I get started and she can have some new clothes. But it can't be helped. The saddest thing about women is that, after all, their best trick is to sit down and fold their hands."

"Your ideas on women are about twenty years out of date," said Tompkins pityingly. "Women won't sit down and wait anymore."

"Then they'd better marry men of forty," insisted Roger stubbornly. "If a girl marries a young man for love she ought to be willing to make any sacrifice within reason, so long as her husband keeps going ahead."

"Let's not talk about it," said Gretchen impatiently. "Please, Roger, let's have a good time just this once."

When Tompkins dropped them in front of their house at eleven Roger and Gretchen stood for a moment on the sidewalk looking at the winter moon. There was a fine damp dusty snow in the air, and Roger drew a long breath of it and put his arm around Gretchen exultantly.

"I can make more money than he can," he said tensely. "And I'll be doing it in just forty days."

"Forty days," she sighed. "It seems such a long time—when everybody else is always having fun. If I could only sleep for forty days."

"Why don't you, honey? Just take forty winks, and when you wake up everything'll be fine."

She was silent for a moment.

"Roger," she asked thoughtfully, "do you think George meant what he said about taking me horseback riding on Sunday?"

Roger frowned.

"I don't know. Probably not—I hope to Heaven he didn't." He hesitated. "As a matter of fact, he made me sort of sore tonight—all that junk about his cold bath."

With their arms about each other they started up the walk to the house.

"I'll bet he doesn't take a cold bath every morning," continued Roger ruminatively, "or three times a week either." He fumbled in his pocket for the key and inserted it in the lock with savage precision. Then he turned around defiantly. "I'll bet he hasn't had a bath for a month."

II

After a fortnight of intensive work, Roger Halsey's days blurred into each other and passed by in blocks of twos and threes and fours. From eight until five-thirty he was in his office. Then a half-hour on the commuting train, where he scrawled notes on the backs of envelopes under the dull yellow light. By seven-thirty his crayons, shears and sheets of white cardboard were spread over the living-room table, and he labored there with much grunting and sighing until midnight, while Gretchen lay on the sofa with a book, and the doorbell tinkled occasionally behind the drawn blinds. At twelve there was always an argument as to whether he would come to bed. He would agree to come after he had cleared up everything; but as he was invariably sidetracked by half a dozen new ideas, he usually found Gretchen sound asleep when he tiptoed upstairs.

Sometimes it was three o'clock before Roger squashed his last cigarette into the overloaded ash-tray, and he would undress in the darkness, disembodied with fatigue, but with a sense of triumph that he had lasted out another day.

Christmas came and went and he scarcely noticed that it was gone. He remembered it afterwards as the day he completed the window-cards for Garrod's shoes. This was one of the eight large accounts for which he was pointing in January—if he got half of them he was assured a quarter of a million dollars' worth of business during the year.

But the world outside his business became a chaotic dream. He was aware that on two cool December Sundays George Tompkins had taken Gretchen horseback riding, and that another time she had gone out with him in his automobile to spend the afternoon skiing on the country-club hill. A picture of Tompkins, in an expensive frame, had appeared one morning on their bedroom wall. And one night he was shocked into a startled protest when Gretchen went to the theatre with Tompkins in town.

But his work was almost done. Daily now his layouts arrived from the printers until seven of them were piled and docketed in his office safe. He knew how good they were. Money alone couldn't buy such work; more than he realized himself, it had been a labor of love.

December tumbled like a dead leaf from the calendar. There was an agonizing week when he had to give up coffee because it made his heart pound so. If he could hold on now for four days—three days—

On Thursday afternoon H. G. Garrod was to arrive in New York. On Wednesday evening Roger came home at seven to find Gretchen poring over the December bills with a strange expression in her eyes.

"What's the matter?"

She nodded at the bills. He ran through them, his brow wrinkling in a frown.

"Gosh!"

"I can't help it," she burst out suddenly. "They're terrible."

"Well, I didn't marry you because you were a wonderful housekeeper. I'll manage about the bills some way. Don't worry your little head over it."

She regarded him coldly.

"You talk as if I were a child."

"I have to," he said with sudden irritation.

"Well, at least I'm not a piece of bric-à-brac that you can just put somewhere and forget."

He knelt down by her quickly and took her arms in his hands.

"Gretchen, listen!" he said breathlessly. "For God's sake don't go to pieces now! We're both all stored up with malice and reproach, and if we had a quarrel it'd be terrible. I love you, Gretchen. Say you love me—quick!"

"You know I love you."

The quarrel was averted but there was an unnatural tenseness all through dinner. It came to a climax afterwards when he began to spread his working materials on the table.

"Oh, Roger," she protested, "I thought you didn't have to work tonight."

"I didn't think I'd have to, but something came up."

"I've invited George Tompkins over."

"Oh, gosh!" he exclaimed. "Well, I'm sorry, honey, but you'll have to phone him not to come."

"He's left," she said. "He's coming straight from town. He'll be here any minute now."

Roger groaned. It occurred to him to send them both to the movies, but somehow the suggestion stuck on his lips. He did not want her at the movies—he wanted her here, where he could look up and know she was by his side.

George Tompkins arrived breezily at eight o'clock.

"Aha!" he cried reprovingly, coming into the room. "Still at it."

Roger agreed coolly that he was.

"Better quit—better quit before you have to." He sat down with a long sigh of physical comfort and lit a cigarette. "Take it from a fellow who's looked into the question scientifically. We can stand so much, and then—Bang!"

"If you'll excuse me"—Roger made his voice as polite as possible—"I'm going upstairs and finish this work."

"Just as you like, Roger." George waved his hand carelessly. "It isn't that *I* mind. I'm the friend of the family and I'd just as soon see the Missus as the Mister." He smiled playfully. "But if I were you, old boy, I'd put away my work and get a good night's sleep."

When Roger had spread out his materials on the bed upstairs he found that he could still hear the rumble and murmur of their voices through the thin floor. He began wondering what they found to talk about. As he plunged deeper into his work his mind had a tendency to revert sharply to his question, and several times he arose and paced nervously up and down the room.

The bed was ill adapted to his work. Several times the paper slipped from the board on which it rested and the pencil punched through. Everything was wrong tonight. Letters and figures blurred before his eyes, and as an accompaniment to the beating of his temples came those persistent murmuring voices.

At ten he realized that he had done nothing for more than an hour, and with a sudden exclamation he gathered together his papers, replaced them in his portfolio and went downstairs. They were sitting together on the sofa when he came in.

"Oh, hello!" cried Gretchen, rather unnecessarily, he thought. "We were just discussing you."

"Thank you," he answered ironically. "What particular part of my anatomy was under the scalpel?"

"Your health," said Tompkins jovially.

"My health's all right," answered Roger shortly.

"But you look at it so selfishly, old fella," cried Tompkins. "You only consider yourself in the matter. Don't you think Gretchen has any rights? If you were working on a wonderful sonnet or a—a portrait of some madonna or something"—he glanced at Gretchen's Titian hair—"why, then I'd say go ahead. But you're not. It's just some silly advertisement about how to sell Nobald's hair tonic, and if all the hair tonic ever made was dumped into the ocean tomorrow the world wouldn't be one bit the worse for it."

"Wait a minute," said Roger angrily; "that's not quite fair. I'm not kidding myself about the importance of my work—it's just as useless as the stuff you do. But to Gretchen and me it's just about the most important thing in the world."

"Are you implying that *my* work is useless?" demanded Tompkins incredulously.

"No. Not if it brings happiness to some poor sucker of a pants manufacturer who doesn't know how to spend his money."

Tompkins and Gretchen exchanged a glance.

"Oh-h-h!" exclaimed Tompkins ironically. "I didn't realize that all these years I've just been wasting my time."

"You're a loafer," said Roger rudely.

"Me?" cried Tompkins angrily. "You call me a loafer because I have a little balance in my life and find time to do interesting things? Because I play hard as well as work hard and don't let myself get to be a dull, tiresome drudge?"

Both men were angry now and their voices had risen, though on Tompkins's face there still remained the semblance of a smile.

"What I object to," said Roger steadily, "is that for the last six weeks you seem to have done all your playing around here."

"Roger!" cried Gretchen. "What do you mean by talking like that?"

"Just what I said."

"You've just lost your temper." Tompkins lit a cigarette with ostentatious coolness. "You're so nervous from overwork you don't know what you're saying. You're on the verge of a nervous break—"

"You get out of here!" cried Roger fiercely. "You get out of here right now—before I throw you out!"

Tompkins got angrily to his feet.

"You—*you* throw me out?" he cried incredulously.

They were actually moving toward each other when Gretchen stepped between them, and grabbing Tompkins's arm urged him toward the door.

"He's acting like a fool, George, but you better get out," she cried, groping in the hall for his hat.

"He insulted me!" shouted Tompkins. "He threatened to throw me out!"

"Never mind, George," pleaded Gretchen. "He doesn't know what he's saying. Please go! I'll see you at ten o'clock tomorrow."

She opened the door.

"You won't see him at ten o'clock tomorrow," said Roger steadily. "He's not coming to this house anymore."

Tompkins turned to Gretchen.

"It's his house," he suggested. "Perhaps we'd better meet at mine."

Then he was gone and Gretchen had shut the door behind him. Her eyes were full of angry tears.

"See what you've done!" she sobbed. "The only friend I had, the only person in the world who liked me enough to treat me decently, is insulted by my husband in my own house."

She threw herself on the sofa and began to cry passionately into the pillows.

"He brought it on himself," said Roger stubbornly. "I've stood as much as my self-respect will allow. I don't want you going out with him anymore."

"I will go out with him!" cried Gretchen wildly. "I'll go out with him all I want! Do you think it's any fun living here with you?"

"Gretchen," he said coldly, "get up and put on your hat and coat and go out that door and never come back!"

Her mouth fell slightly ajar.

"But I don't want to get out," she said dazedly.

"Well then, behave yourself." And he added in a gentler voice: "I thought you were going to sleep for this forty days."

"Oh yes," she cried bitterly, "easy enough to say! But I'm tired of sleeping." She got up, faced him defiantly. "And what's more I'm going riding with George Tompkins tomorrow."

"You won't go out with him if I have to take you to New York and sit you down in my office until I get through."

She looked at him with rage in her eyes.

"I hate you," she said slowly. "And I'd like to take all the work you've done and tear it up and throw it in the fire. And just to give you something to worry about tomorrow, I probably won't be here when you get back."

She got up from the sofa and very deliberately looked at her flushed, tear-stained face in the mirror. Then she ran upstairs and slammed herself into the bedroom.

Automatically Roger spread out his work on the living-room table. The bright colors of the designs, the vivid ladies—Gretchen had posed for one of them—holding orange ginger ale or glistening silk hosiery, dazzled his mind into a sort of coma. His restless crayon moved here and there over the pictures, shifting a block of letters half an inch to the right, trying a dozen blues for a cool blue, and eliminating the word that made a phrase anaemic and pale. Half an hour passed—he was deep in the work now; there was no sound in the room but the velvety scratch of the crayon over the glossy board.

After a long while he looked at his watch—it was after three. The wind had come up outside and was rushing by the house corners in loud alarming swoops, like a heavy body falling through space. He stopped his work and listened. He was not tired now, but his head felt as if it was covered with bulging veins like those pictures that hang in doctors' offices showing a body stripped of decent skin. He put his hands to his head and felt it all over. It seemed to him that on his temple the veins were knotty and brittle around an old scar.

Suddenly he began to be afraid. A hundred warnings he had heard swept into his mind. People did wreck themselves with overwork, and his body and brain were of the same vulnerable and perishable stuff. For the first time he found himself envying George Tompkins' calm nerves and healthy routine. He arose and began pacing the room in a panic.

"I've got to sleep," he whispered to himself tensely. "Otherwise I'm going crazy."

He rubbed his hand over his eyes and returned to the table to put up his work, but his fingers were shaking so that he could scarcely grasp the board. The sway of a bare branch against the window made him start and cry out. He sat down on the sofa and tried to think.

"Stop! Stop! Stop!" the clock said: "Stop! Stop! Stop!"

"I can't stop," he answered aloud. "I can't afford to stop."

Listen! Why, there was the wolf at the door now! He could hear its sharp claws scrape along the varnished woodwork. He jumped up, and running to the front door flung it open—then started back with a ghastly cry. An enormous wolf was standing on the porch, glaring at him with red, malignant eyes. As he watched it the hair bristled on its neck; it gave a low growl and disappeared in the darkness. Then Roger realized with a silent, mirthless laugh that it was the police dog from over the way.

Dragging his limbs wearily into the kitchen, he brought the alarm-clock into the living room and set it for seven. Then he wrapped himself in his overcoat, lay down on the sofa and fell immediately into a heavy, dreamless sleep.

When he awoke the light was still shining feebly, but the room was the grey color of a winter morning. He got up, and looking anxiously at his hands found to his relief that they no longer trembled. He felt much better. Then he began to remember in detail the events of the night before, and his brow drew up again in three shallow wrinkles. There was work ahead of him, twenty-four hours of work; and Gretchen, whether she wanted to or not, must sleep for one more day.

Roger's mind glowed suddenly as if he had just thought of a new advertising idea. A few minutes later he was hurrying through the sharp morning air to Kingsley's drug store.

"Is Mr. Kingsley down yet?"

The druggist's head appeared around the corner of the prescription room.

"I wonder if I can talk to you alone."

At seven-thirty, back home again, Roger walked into his own kitchen. The general housework girl had just arrived and was taking off her hat.

"Bebé"—he was not on familiar terms with her; this was her name—"I want you to cook Mrs. Halsey's breakfast right away. I'll take it up myself."

It struck Bebé that this was an unusual service for so busy a man to render his wife, but if she had seen his conduct when he had carried the tray from the kitchen she would have been even more surprised. For he set it down on the dining-room table and put into the coffee half a teaspoonful of a white substance that was *not* powdered sugar. Then he mounted the stairs and opened the door of the bedroom.

Gretchen woke up with a start, glanced at the twin bed which had not been slept in and bent on Roger a glance of astonishment—which changed to contempt when she saw the breakfast in his hand. She thought he was bringing it as a capitulation.

"I don't want any breakfast," she said coldly, and his heart sank, "except some coffee."

"No breakfast?" Roger's voice expressed disappointment.

"I said I'd take some coffee."

Roger discreetly deposited the tray on a table beside the bed and returned quickly to the kitchen.

"We're going away until tomorrow afternoon," he told Bebé, "and I want to close up the house right now. So you just put on your hat and go home."

He looked at his watch. It was ten minutes to eight and he wanted to catch the eight-ten train. He waited five minutes and then tiptoed softly upstairs and into Gretchen's room. She was sound asleep. The coffee cup was empty save for black dregs and a film of thin brown paste on the bottom. He looked at her rather anxiously but her breathing was regular and clear.

From the closet he took a suitcase and very quickly began filling it with her shoes—street shoes, evening slippers, rubber-soled oxfords—he had not realized that she owned so many pairs. When he closed the suitcase it was bulging.

He hesitated a minute, took a pair of sewing scissors from a box and, following the telephone wire until it went out of sight behind the dresser, severed it in one neat clip. He jumped as there was a soft knock at the door. It was the nursemaid. He had forgotten her existence.

"Mrs. Halsey and I are going up to the city till tomorrow," he said glibly. "Take Maxy to the beach and have lunch there. Stay all day."

Back in the room, a wave of pity passed over him. Gretchen seemed suddenly lovely and helpless, sleeping there. It was somehow terrible to rob her young life of a day. He touched her hair with his fingers and as she murmured something in her dream he leaned over and kissed her bright cheek. Then he picked up the suitcase full of shoes, locked the door and ran briskly down the stairs.

III

By five o'clock that afternoon the last package of cards for Garrod's shoes had been sent by messenger to H. G. Garrod at the Biltmore Hotel. He was to give a decision next morning. At five-thirty Roger's stenographer tapped him on the shoulder.

"Mr. Golden, the superintendent of the building, to see you."

Roger turned around dazedly.

"Oh, how-do?"

Mr. Golden came directly to the point. If Mr. Halsey intended to keep the office any longer, the little oversight about the rent had better be remedied right away.

"Mr. Golden," said Roger wearily, "everything'll be all right tomorrow. If you worry me now maybe you'll never get your money. After tomorrow nothing'll matter."

Mr. Golden looked at the tenant uneasily. Young men sometimes did away with themselves when business went wrong. Then his eye fell unpleasantly on the initialled suitcase beside the desk.

"Going on a trip?" he asked pointedly.

"What? Oh, no. That's just some clothes."

"Clothes, eh? Well, Mr. Halsey, just to prove that you mean what you say, suppose you let me keep that suitcase until tomorrow noon."

"Help yourself."

Mr. Golden picked it up with a deprecatory gesture.

"Just a matter of form," he remarked.

"I understand," said Roger, swinging around to his desk. "Good afternoon."

Mr. Golden seemed to feel that the conversation should close on a softer key.

"And don't work too hard, Mr. Halsey. You don't want to have a nervous break—"

"No," shouted Roger, "I don't. But I will if you don't leave me alone!"

As the door closed behind Mr. Golden, Roger's stenographer turned sympathetically around.

"You shouldn't have let him get away with that," she said. "What's in there? Clothes?"

"No," answered Roger absently. "Just all my wife's shoes."

He slept in the office that night on a sofa beside his desk. At dawn he awoke with a nervous start, rushed out into the street for coffee and returned in ten minutes in a panic—afraid that he might have missed Mr. Garrod's telephone call. It was then six-thirty.

By eight o'clock his whole body seemed to be on fire. When his two artists arrived he was stretched on the couch in almost physical pain. The phone rang imperatively at nine-thirty, and he picked up the receiver with trembling hands.

"Hello."

"Is this the Halsey agency?"

"Yes, this is Mr. Halsey speaking."

"This is Mr. H. G. Garrod."

Roger's heart stopped beating.

"I called up, young fellow, to say that this is wonderful work you've given us here. We want all of it and as much more as your office can do."

"Oh God!" cried Roger into the transmitter.

"What?" Mr. H. G. Garrod was considerably startled. "Say, wait a minute there!"

But he was talking to nobody. The phone had clattered to the floor, and Roger, stretched full length on the couch, was sobbing as if his heart would break.

IV

Three hours later, his face somewhat pale but his eyes calm as a child's, Roger opened the door of his wife's bedroom with the morning paper under his arm. At the sound of his footsteps she started awake.

"What time is it?" she demanded.

He looked at his watch.

"Twelve o'clock."

Suddenly she began to cry.

"Roger," she said brokenly, "I'm sorry I was so bad last night."

He nodded coolly.

"Everything's all right now," he answered. Then, after a pause: "I've got the account—the biggest one."

She turned toward him quickly.

"You have?" Then, after a minute's silence: "Can I get a new dress?"

"Dress?" He laughed shortly. "You can get a dozen. This account alone will bring us in forty thousand a year. It's one of the biggest in the West."

She looked at him, startled.

"Forty thousand a year!"

"Yes."

"Gosh"—and then faintly—"I didn't know it'd really be anything like that." Again she thought a minute. "We can have a house like George Tompkins'."

"I don't want an interior-decoration shop."

"Forty thousand a year!" she repeated again, and then added softly: "Oh, Roger—"

"Yes?"

"I'm not going out with George Tompkins."

"I wouldn't let you, even if you wanted to," he said shortly.

She made a show of indignation.

"Why, I've had a date with him for this Thursday for weeks."

"It isn't Thursday."

"It is."

"It's Friday."

"Why, Roger, you must be crazy! Don't you think I know what day it is?"

"It isn't Thursday," he said stubbornly. "Look!" And he held out the morning paper.

"Friday!" she exclaimed. "Why, this is a mistake! This must be last week's paper. Today's Thursday."

She closed her eyes and thought for a moment.

"Yesterday was Wednesday," she said decisively. "The laundress came yesterday. I guess I *know*."

"Well," he said smugly, "look at the paper. There isn't any question about it."

With a bewildered look on her face she got out of bed and began searching for her clothes. Roger went into the bathroom to shave. A minute later he heard the springs creak again. Gretchen was getting back into bed.

"What's the matter?" he inquired, putting his head around the corner of the bathroom.

"I'm scared," she said in a trembling voice. "I think my nerves are giving away. I can't find any of my shoes."

"Your shoes? Why, the closet's full of them."

"I know, but I can't see one." Her face was pale with fear. "Oh, Roger!"

Roger came to her bedside and put his arm around her.

"Oh, Roger," she cried, "what's the matter with me? First that newspaper and now all my shoes. Take care of me, Roger."

"I'll get the doctor," he said.

He walked remorselessly to the telephone and took up the receiver.

"Phone seems to be out of order," he remarked after a minute; "I'll send Bebé."

The doctor arrived in ten minutes.

"I think I'm on the verge of a collapse," Gretchen told him in a strained voice.

Doctor Gregory sat down on the edge of the bed and took her wrist in his hand.

"It seems to be in the air this morning."

"I got up," said Gretchen in an awed voice, "and I found that I'd lost a whole day. I had an engagement to go riding with George Tompkins—"

"What?" exclaimed the doctor in surprise. Then he laughed.

"George Tompkins won't go riding with anyone for many days to come."

"Has he gone away?" asked Gretchen curiously.

"He's going west."

"Why?" demanded Roger. "Is he running away with somebody's wife?"

"No," said Doctor Gregory. "He's had a nervous breakdown."

"What?" they exclaimed in unison.

"He just collapsed like an opera-hat in his cold shower."

"But he was always talking about his—his balanced life," gasped Gretchen. "He had it on his mind."

"I know," said the doctor. "He's been babbling about it all morning. I think it's driven him a little mad. He worked pretty hard at it, you know."

"At what?" demanded Roger in bewilderment.

"At keeping his life balanced." He turned to Gretchen. "Now all I'll prescribe for this lady here is a good rest. If she'll just stay around the house for a few days and take forty winks of sleep she'll be as fit as ever. She's been under some strain."

"Doctor," exclaimed Roger hoarsely, "don't you think I'd better have a rest or something? I've been working pretty hard lately."

"You!" Doctor Gregory laughed, slapped him violently on the back. "My boy, I never saw you looking better in your life."

Roger turned away quickly to conceal his smile—winked forty times, or almost forty times, at the autographed picture of Mr. George Tompkins, which hung slightly askew on the bedroom wall.

ADDITIONAL STORIES
April 1925–April 1928

ONE OF MY OLDEST FRIENDS

All afternoon Marion had been happy. She wandered from room to room of their little apartment, strolling into the nursery to help the nurse-girl feed the children from dripping spoons, and then reading for awhile on their new sofa, the most extravagant thing they had bought in their five years of marriage.

When she heard Michael's step in the hall she turned her head and listened; she liked to hear him walk, carefully always as if there were children sleeping close by.

"Michael."

"Oh—hello." He came into the room, a tall, broad, thin man of thirty with a high forehead and kind black eyes.

"I've got some news for you," he said immediately. "Charley Hart's getting married."

"No!"

He nodded.

"Who's he marrying?"

"One of the little Lawrence girls from home." He hesitated. "She's arriving in New York tomorrow and I think we ought to do something for them while she's here. Charley's about my oldest friend."

"Let's have them up for dinner—"

"I'd like to do something more than that," he interrupted. "Maybe a theatre party. You see—" Again he hesitated. "It'd be a nice courtesy to Charley."

"All right," agreed Marion, "but we mustn't spend much—and I don't think we're under any obligation."

He looked at her in surprise.

"I mean," went on Marion, "we—we hardly see Charley anymore. We hardly ever see him at all."

"Well, you know how it is in New York," explained Michael apologetically. "He's just as busy as I am. He has made a big name for himself and I suppose he's pretty much in demand all the time."

189

They always spoke of Charley Hart as their oldest friend. Five years before, when Michael and Marion were first married, the three of them had come to New York from the same western city. For over a year they had seen Charley nearly every day and no domestic adventure, no uprush of their hopes and dreams, was too insignificant for his ear. His arrival in times of difficulty never failed to give a pleasant, humorous cast to the situation.

Of course Marion's babies had made a difference, and it was several years now since they had called up Charley at midnight to say that the pipes had broken or the ceiling was falling in on their heads; but so gradually had they drifted apart that Michael still spoke of Charley rather proudly as if he saw him every day. For awhile Charley dined with them once a month and all three found a great deal to say; but the meetings never broke up anymore with, "I'll give you a ring tomorrow." Instead it was, "You'll have to come to dinner more often," or even, after three or four years, "We'll see you soon."

"Oh, I'm perfectly willing to give a little party," said Marion now, looking speculatively about her. "Did you suggest a definite date?"

"Week from Saturday." His dark eyes roamed the floor vaguely. "We can take up the rugs or something."

"No." She shook her head. "We'll have a dinner, eight people, very formal and everything, and afterwards we'll play cards."

She was already speculating on whom to invite. Charley of course, being an artist, probably saw interesting people every day.

"We could have the Willoughbys," she suggested doubtfully. "She's on the stage or something—and he writes movies."

"No—that's not it," objected Michael. "He probably meets that crowd at lunch and dinner every day until he's sick of them. Besides, except for the Willoughbys, who else like that do we know? I've got a better idea. Let's collect a few people who've drifted down here from home. They've all followed Charley's career and they'd probably enjoy seeing him again. I'd like them to find out how natural and unspoiled he is after all."

After some discussion they agreed on this plan and within an hour Marion had her first guest on the telephone:

"It's to meet Charley Hart's fiancée," she explained. "Charley Hart, the artist. You see, he's one of our oldest friends."

As she began her preparations her enthusiasm grew. She rented a serving-maid to assure an impeccable service and persuaded the neighborhood florist to come in person and arrange the flowers. All the "people from home" had accepted eagerly and the number of guests had swollen to ten.

"What'll we talk about, Michael?" she demanded nervously on the eve of the party. "Suppose everything goes wrong and everybody gets mad and goes home?"

He laughed.

"Nothing will. You see, these people all know each other—"

The phone on the table asserted itself and Michael picked up the receiver.

"Hello . . . why, hello, Charley."

Marion sat up alertly in her chair.

"Is that so? Well, I'm very sorry. I'm very, very sorry. . . . I hope it's nothing serious."

"Can't he come?" broke out Marion.

"Sh!" Then into the phone, "Well, it certainly is too bad, Charley. No, it's no trouble for us at all. We're just sorry you're ill."

With a dismal gesture Michael replaced the receiver.

"The Lawrence girl had to go home last night and Charley's sick in bed with grippe."

"Do you mean he can't come?"

"He can't come."

Marion's face contracted suddenly and her eyes filled with tears.

"He says he's had the doctor all day," explained Michael dejectedly. "He's got fever and they didn't even want him to go to the telephone."

"I don't care," sobbed Marion. "I think it's terrible. After we've invited all these people to meet him."

"People can't help being sick."

"Yes they *can*," she wailed illogically. "They can help it some way. And if the Lawrence girl was going to leave last night why didn't he let us know *then*?"

"He said she left unexpectedly. Up to yesterday afternoon they both intended to come."

"I don't think he c-cares a bit. I'll bet he's glad he's sick. If he'd cared he'd have brought her to see us long ago."

She stood up suddenly.

"I'll tell you one thing," she assured him vehemently. "I'm just going to telephone everybody and call the whole thing off."

"Why, Marion—"

But in spite of his half-hearted protests she picked up the phone book and began looking for the first number.

They bought theatre tickets next day hoping to fill the hollowness which would invest the evening. Marion had wept when the unintercepted florist arrived at five with boxes of flowers and she felt that she must get out of the house to avoid the ghosts who would presently people it. In silence they ate an elaborate dinner composed of all the things that she had bought for the party.

"It's only eight," said Michael afterwards. "I think it'd be sort of nice if we dropped in on Charley for a minute, don't you?"

"Why, no," Marion answered, startled. "I wouldn't think of it."

"Why not? If he's seriously sick I'd like to see how well he's being taken care of."

She saw that he had made up his mind, so she fought down her instinct against the idea and they taxied to a tall pile of studio apartments on Madison Avenue.

"You go on in," urged Marion nervously. "I'd rather wait out here."

"Please come in."

"Why? He'll be in bed and he doesn't want any women around."

"But he'd like to see you—it'd cheer him up. And he'd know that we understood about tonight. He sounded awfully depressed over the phone."

He urged her from the cab.

"Let's only stay a minute," she whispered tensely as they went up in the elevator. "The show starts at half-past eight."

"Apartment on the right," said the elevator man.

They rang the bell and waited. The door opened and they walked directly into Charley Hart's great studio room.

It was crowded with people; from end to end ran a long lamp-lit dinner table strewn with ferns and young roses, from which a gay murmur of laughter and conversation arose into the faintly smoky air. Twenty women in evening dress sat on one side in a row chatting across the flowers at twenty men, with an elation born of the sparkling burgundy which dripped from many bottles into thin chilled glass. Up on the high narrow balcony which encircled the room a string quartet was playing something by Stravinski in a key that was pitched just below the women's voices and filled the air like an audible wine.

The door had been opened by one of the waiters, who stepped back deferentially from what he thought were two belated guests— and immediately a handsome man at the head of the table started to his feet, napkin in hand, and stood motionless, staring toward the newcomers. The conversation faded into half silence and all eyes followed Charley Hart's to the couple at the door. Then, as if the spell was broken, conversation resumed, gathering momentum word by word—the moment was over.

"Let's get out!" Marion's low, terrified whisper came to Michael out of a void and for a minute he thought he was possessed by an illusion, that there was no one but Charley in the room after all. Then his eyes cleared and he saw that there were many people here—he had never seen so many! The music swelled suddenly into the tumult of a great brass band and a wind from the loud horns seemed to blow against them; without turning he and Marion each made one blind step backward into the hall, pulling the door to after them.

"Marion—!"

She had run toward the elevator, stood with one finger pressed hard against the bell which rang through the hall like a last high note from the music inside. The door of the apartment opened suddenly and Charley Hart came out into the hall.

"Michael!" he cried, "Michael and Marion, I want to explain! Come inside. I want to *explain*, I tell you."

He talked excitedly—his face was flushed and his mouth formed a word or two that did not materialize into sound.

"Hurry up, Michael," came Marion's voice tensely from the elevator.

"Let me explain," cried Charley frantically. "I want—"

Michael moved away from him—the elevator came and the gate clanged open.

"You act as if I'd committed some crime." Charley was following Michael along the hall. "Can't you understand that this is all an accidental situation?"

"It's all right," Michael muttered, "I understand."

"No, you don't." Charley's voice rose with exasperation. He was working up anger against them so as to justify his own intolerable position. "You're going away mad and I asked you to come in and join the party. Why did you come up here if you won't come in? Did you—?"

Michael walked into the elevator.

"Down, please!" cried Marion. "Oh, I want to go down, *please!*"

The gate clanged shut.

They told the taxi-man to take them directly home—neither of them could have endured the theatre. Driving uptown to their apartment, Michael buried his face in his hands and tried to realize that the friendship which had meant so much to him was over. He saw now that it had been over for some time, that not once during the past year had Charley sought their company and the shock of the discovery far outweighed the affront he had received.

When they reached home, Marion, who had not said a word in the taxi, led the way into the living room and motioned for her husband to sit down.

"I'm going to tell you something that you ought to know," she said. "If it hadn't been for what happened tonight I'd probably never have told you—but now I think you ought to hear the whole story." She hesitated. "In the first place, Charley Hart wasn't a friend of yours at all."

"What?" He looked up at her dully.

"He wasn't your friend," she repeated. "He hasn't been for years. He was a friend of mine."

"Why, Charley Hart was—"

"I know what you're going to say—that Charley was a friend to both of us. But it isn't true. I don't know how he considered you at first but he stopped being your friend three or four years ago."

"Why—" Michael's eyes glowed with astonishment. "If that's true, why was he with us all the time?"

"On account of me," said Marion steadily. "He was in love with me."

"What?" Michael laughed incredulously. "You're imagining things. I know how he used to pretend in a kidding way—"

"It wasn't kidding," she interrupted, "not underneath. It began that way—and it ended by his asking to run away with him."

Michael frowned.

"Go on," he said quietly. "I suppose this is true or you wouldn't be telling me about it—but it simply doesn't seem real. Did he just suddenly begin to—to—"

He closed his mouth suddenly, unable to say the words.

"It began one night when we three were out dancing," Marion hesitated. "And at first I thoroughly enjoyed it. He had a faculty for noticing things—noticing dresses and hats and the new ways I'd do my hair. He was good company. He could always make me feel important, somehow, and attractive. Don't get the idea that I preferred his company to yours—I didn't. I knew how completely selfish he was, and what a will-o'-the-wisp. But I encouraged him, I suppose—I thought it was fine. It was a new angle on Charley, and he was amusing at it, just as he was at everything he did."

"Yes—" agreed Michael with an effort. "I suppose it was—hilariously amusing."

"At first he liked you just the same. It didn't occur to him that he was doing anything treacherous to you. He was just following a natural impulse—that was all. But after a few weeks he began to find you in the way. He wanted to take me to dinner without you along—and it couldn't be done. Well, that sort of thing went on for over a year."

"What happened then?"

"Nothing happened. That's why he stopped coming to see us anymore."

Michael rose slowly to his feet.

"Do you mean—"

"Wait a minute. If you'll think a little you'll see it was bound to turn out that way. When he saw that I was trying to let him down easily so that he'd be simply one of our oldest friends again, he broke away. He didn't want to be one of our oldest friends—that time was over."

"I see."

"Well—" Marion stood up and began biting nervously at her lip, "that's all. I thought this thing tonight would hurt you less if you understood the whole affair."

"Yes," Michael answered in a dull voice, "I suppose that's true."

Michael's business took a prosperous turn, and when summer came they went to the country, renting a little old farmhouse where the children played all day on a tangled half acre of grass and trees. The subject of Charley was never mentioned between them and as the months passed he receded to a shadowy background in their minds. Sometimes, just before dropping off to sleep, Michael found himself thinking of the happy times the three of them had had together five years before—then the reality would intrude upon the illusion and he would be repelled from the subject with almost physical distaste.

One warm evening in July he lay dozing on the porch in the twilight. He had had a hard day at his office and it was welcome to rest here while the summer light faded from the land.

At the sound of an automobile he raised his head lazily. At the end of the path a local taxi-cab had stopped and a young man was getting out. With an exclamation Michael sat up. Even in the dusk he recognized those shoulders, that impatient walk—

"Well, I'm damned," he said softly.

As Charley Hart came up the gravel path Michael noticed in a glance that he was unusually disheveled. His handsome face was drawn and tired, his clothes were out of press and he had the unmistakable look of needing a good night's sleep.

He came up on the porch, saw Michael and smiled in a wan, embarrassed way.

"Hello, Michael."

Neither of them made any move to shake hands but after a moment Charley collapsed abruptly into a chair.

"I'd like a glass of water," he said huskily. "It's hot as hell."

Without a word Michael went into the house—returned with a glass of water which Charley drank in great noisy gulps.

"Thanks," he said, gasping. "I thought I was going to pass away."

He looked about him with eyes that only pretended to take in his surroundings.

"Nice little place you've got here," he remarked; his eyes returned to Michael. "Do you want me to get out?"

"Why—no. Sit and rest if you want to. You look all in."

"I am. Do you want to hear about it?"

"Not in the least."

"Well, I'm going to tell you anyhow," said Charley defiantly. "That's what I came out here for. I'm in trouble, Michael, and I haven't got anybody to go to except you."

"Have you tried your friends?" asked Michael coolly.

"I've tried about everybody—everybody I've had time to go to. God!" He wiped his forehead with his hand. "I never realized how hard it was to raise a simple two thousand dollars."

"Have you come to me for two thousand dollars?"

"Wait a minute, Michael. Wait till you hear. It just shows you what a mess a man can get into without meaning any harm. You see, I'm the treasurer of a society called the Independent Artists' Benefit—a thing to help struggling students. There was a fund, thirty-five hundred dollars, and it's been lying in my bank for over a year. Well, as you know, I live pretty high—make a lot and spend a lot—and about a month ago I began speculating a little through a friend of mine—"

"I don't know why you're telling me all this," interrupted Michael impatiently. "I—"

"Wait a minute, won't you—I'm almost through." He looked at Michael with frightened eyes. "I used that money sometimes without even realizing that it wasn't mine. I've always had plenty of my own, you see. Till this week." He hesitated. "This week there was a meeting of this society and they asked me to turn over the money. Well, I went to a couple of men to try and borrow it and as soon as my back was turned one of them blabbed. There was a terrible blow-up last night. They told me unless I handed over the two thousand this morning they'd send me to jail—" His voice rose and he looked around wildly. "There's a warrant out for me now—and if I can't get the money I'll kill myself, Michael; I swear to God I will; I won't go to prison. I'm an artist—not a business man. I—"

He made an effort to control his voice.

"Michael," he whispered, "you're my oldest friend. I haven't got anyone in the world but you to turn to."

"You're a little late," said Michael uncomfortably. "You didn't think of me four years ago when you asked my wife to run away with you."

A look of sincere surprise passed over Charley's face.

"Are you mad at me about that?" he asked in a puzzled way. "I thought you were mad because I didn't come to your party."

Michael did not answer.

"I supposed she'd told you about that long ago," went on Charley. "I couldn't help it about Marion. I was lonesome and you two had each other. Every time I went to your house you'd tell me what a wonderful girl Marion was and finally I—I began to agree with you. How could I help falling in love with her, when for a year and a half she was the only decent girl I knew?" He looked defiantly at Michael. "Well, you've got her, haven't you. I didn't take her away. I never so much as kissed her—do you have to rub it in?"

"Look here," said Michael sharply, "just why should I lend you this money."

"Well—" Charley hesitated, laughed uneasily, "I don't know any exact reason. I just thought you would."

"Why should I?"

"No reason at all, I suppose, from your way of looking at it."

"That's the trouble. If I gave it to you it would just be because I was slushy and soft. I'd be doing something that I don't want to do."

"All right." Charley smiled unpleasantly. "That's logical. Now that I think, there's no reason why you should lend it to me. Well—" he shoved his hands into his coat pocket and throwing his head back slightly seemed to shake the subject off like a cap, "I won't go to prison—and maybe you'll feel differently about it tomorrow."

"Don't count on that."

"Oh, I don't mean I'll ask you again. I mean something—quite different."

He nodded his head, turned quickly and walking down the gravel path was swallowed up in the darkness. Where the path met the road Michael heard his footsteps cease as if he were hesitating. Then they turned down the road toward the station a mile away.

Michael sank into his chair, burying his face in his hands. He heard Marion come out of the door.

"I listened," she whispered. "I couldn't help it. I'm glad you didn't lend him anything."

She came close to him and would have sat down in his lap but an almost physical repulsion came over him and he got up quickly from his chair.

"I was afraid he'd work on your sentiment and make a fool of you," went on Marion. She hesitated. "He hated you, you know. He used to wish you'd die. I told him that if he ever said so to me again I'd never see him anymore."

Michael looked up at her darkly.

"In fact, you were very noble."

"Why, Michael—"

"You let him say things like that to you—and then when he comes here, down and out, without a friend in the world to turn to, you say you're glad I sent him away."

"It's because I love you, dear—"

"No it isn't!" he interrupted savagely. "It's because hate's cheap in this world. Everybody's got it for sale. My God! What do you suppose I think of myself now?"

"He's not worth feeling that way about."

"Please go away!" cried Michael passionately. "I want to be alone."

Obediently she left him and he sat down again in the darkness of the porch, a sort of terror creeping over him. Several times he made a motion to get up but each time he frowned and remained motionless. Then after another long while he jumped suddenly to his feet, cold sweat starting from his forehead. The last hour, the months just passed, were washed away and he was swept years back in time. Why, they were after Charley Hart, his old friend. Charley

Hart who had come to him because he had no other place to go. Michael began to run hastily about the porch in a daze, hunting for his hat and coat.

"Why Charley!" he cried aloud.

He found his coat finally and, struggling into it, ran wildly down the steps. It seemed to him that Charley had gone out only a few minutes before.

"Charley!" he called when he reached the road. "Charley, come back here. There's been a mistake!"

He paused, listening. There was no answer. Panting a little he began to run doggedly along the road through the hot night.

It was only half past eight o'clock but the country was very quiet and the frogs were loud in the strip of wet marsh that ran along beside the road. The sky was salted thinly with stars and after a while there would be a moon, but the road ran among dark trees and Michael could scarcely see ten feet in front of him. After awhile he slowed down to a walk, glancing at the phosphorous dial of his wrist watch—the New York train was not due for an hour. There was plenty of time.

In spite of this he broke into an uneasy run and covered the mile between his house and the station in fifteen minutes. It was a little station, crouched humbly beside the shining rails in the darkness. Beside it Michael saw the lights of a single taxi waiting for the next train.

The platform was deserted and Michael opened the door and peered into the dim waiting room. It was empty.

"That's funny," he muttered.

Rousing a sleepy taxi-driver, he asked if there had been anyone waiting for the train. The taxi-driver considered—yes, there had been a young man waiting, about twenty minutes ago. He had walked up and down for awhile, smoking a cigarette, and then gone away into the darkness.

"That's funny," repeated Michael. He made a megaphone of his hands and facing toward the woods across the track shouted aloud.

"Charley!"

There was no answer. He tried again. Then he turned back to the driver.

"Have you any idea what direction he went."

The man pointed vaguely down the New York road which ran along beside the railroad track.

"Down there somewhere."

With increasing uneasiness Michael thanked him and started swiftly along the road which was white now under the risen moon. He knew now as surely as he knew anything that Charley had gone off by himself to die. He remembered the expression on his face as he had turned away and the hand tucked down close in his coat pocket as if it clutched some menacing thing.

"Charley!" he called in a terrible voice.

The dark trees gave back no sound. He walked on past a dozen fields bright as silver under the moon, pausing every few minutes to shout and then waiting tensely for an answer.

It occurred to him that it was foolish to continue in this direction—Charley was probably back by the station in the woods somewhere. Perhaps it was all imagination; perhaps even now Charley was pacing the station platform waiting for the train from the city. But some impulse beyond logic made him continue. More than that—several times he had the sense that someone was in front of him, someone who just eluded him at every turning, out of sight and earshot, yet leaving always behind him a dim, tragic aura of having passed that way. Once he thought he heard steps among the leaves on the side of the road but it was only a piece of vagrant newspaper blown by the faint hot wind.

It was a stifling night—the moon seemed to be beating hot rays down upon the sweltering earth. Michael took off his coat and threw it over his arm as he walked. A little way ahead of him now was a stone bridge over the tracks and beyond that an interminable line of telephone poles which stretched in diminishing perspective toward an endless horizon. Well, he would walk to the bridge and then give up. He would have given up before except for this sense he had that someone was walking very lightly and swiftly just ahead.

Reaching the stone bridge he sat down on a rock, his heart beating in loud exhausted thumps under his dripping shirt. Well, it was hopeless—Charley was gone, perhaps out of range of his help forever. Far away beyond the station he heard the approaching siren of the nine-thirty train.

Michael found himself wondering suddenly why he was here. He despised himself for being here. On what weak chord in his nature had Charley played in those few minutes, forcing him into this senseless, frightened run through the night? They had discussed it all and Charley had been unable to give a reason why he should be helped.

He got to his feet with the idea of retracing his steps but before turning he stood for a minute in the moonlight looking down the road. Across the track stretched the line of telephone poles and, as his eyes followed them as far as he could see, he heard again, louder now and not far away, the siren of the New York train which rose and fell with musical sharpness on the still night. Suddenly his eyes, which had been traveling down the tracks, stopped and were focused suddenly upon one spot in the line of poles, perhaps a quarter of a mile away. It was a pole just like the others and yet it was different— there was something about it that was indescribably different.

And watching it as one might concentrate on some figure in the pattern of a carpet, something curious happened in his mind and instantly he saw everything in a completely different light. Something had come to him in a whisper of the breeze, something that changed the whole complexion of the situation. It was this: He remembered having read somewhere that at some point back in the dark ages a man named Gerbert had all by himself summed up the whole of European civilization. It became suddenly plain to Michael that he himself had just now been in a position like that. For one minute, one spot in time, all the mercy in the world had been vested in him.

He realized all this in the space of a second with a sense of shock and instantly he understood the reason why he should have helped Charley Hart. It was because it would be intolerable to exist in a world where there was no help—where any human being could be as alone as Charley had been alone this afternoon.

Why, that was it, of course—he had been trusted with that chance. Someone had come to him who had no other place to go—and he had failed.

All this time, this moment, he had been standing utterly motionless staring at the telephone pole down the track, the one that his eye had picked out as being different from the others. The moon was so bright now that near the top he could see a white bar set crosswise on the pole and as he looked the pole and the bar seemed to have become isolated as if the other poles had shrunk back and away.

Suddenly a mile down the track he heard the click and clamor of the electric train when it left the station, and as if the sound had startled him into life he gave a short cry and set off at a swaying run down the road, in the direction of the pole with the crossed bar.

The train whistled again. Click—click—click—it was nearer now, six hundred, five hundred yards away and as it came under the bridge he was running in the bright beam of its searchlight. There was no emotion in his mind but terror—he knew only that he must reach that pole before the train, and it was fifty yards away, struck out sharp as a star against the sky.

There was no path on the other side of the tracks under the poles but the train was so close now that he dared wait no longer or he would be unable to cross at all. He darted from the road, cleared the tracks in two strides and with the sound of the engine at his heels raced along the rough earth. Twenty feet, thirty feet—as the sound of the electric train swelled to a roar in his ears he reached the pole and threw himself bodily on a man who stood there close to the tracks, carrying him heavily to the ground with the impact of his body.

There was the thunder of steel in his ear, the heavy clump of the wheels on the rails, a swift roaring of air, and the nine-thirty train had gone past.

"Charley," he gasped incoherently, "Charley."

A white face looked up at him in a daze. Michael rolled over on his back and lay panting. The hot night was quiet now—there was no sound but the faraway murmur of the receding train.

"Oh, God!"

Michael opened his eyes to see that Charley was sitting up, his face in his hands.

"S'all right," gasped Michael, "s'all right, Charley. You can have the money. I don't know what I was thinking about. Why—why, you're one of my oldest friends."

Charley shook his head.

"I don't understand," he said brokenly. "Where did you come from—how did you get here?"

"I've been following you. I was just behind."

"I've been here for half an hour."

"Well, it's good you chose this pole to—to wait under. I've been looking at it from down by the bridge. I picked it out on account of the crossbar."

Charley had risen unsteadily to his feet and now he walked a few steps and looked up the pole in the full moonlight.

"What did you say?" he asked after a minute, in a puzzled voice. "Did you say this pole had a crossbar?"

"Why, yes. I was looking at it a long time. That's how—"

Charley looked up again and hesitated curiously before he spoke.

"There isn't any crossbar," he said.

A PENNY SPENT

The Ritz Grill in Paris is one of those places where things happen—like the first bench as you enter Central Park South, or Morris Gest's office, or Herrin, Illinois. I have seen marriages broken up there at an ill-considered word and blows struck between a professional dancer and a British baron, and I know personally of at least two murders that would have been committed on the spot but for the fact that it was July and there was no room. Even murders require a certain amount of space, and in July the Ritz Grill has no room at all.

Go in at six o'clock of a summer evening, planting your feet lightly lest you tear some college boy bag from bag, and see if you don't find the actor who owes you a hundred dollars or the stranger who gave you a match once in Red Wing, Minnesota, or the man who won your girl away from you with silver phrases just ten years ago. One thing is certain—that before you melt out into the green-and-cream Paris twilight you will have the feel of standing for a moment at one of the predestined centers of the world.

At seven-thirty, walk to the center of the room and stand with your eyes shut for half an hour—this is a merely hypothetical suggestion—and then open them. The grey and blue and brown and slate have faded out of the scene and the prevailing note, as the haberdashers say, has become black and white. Another half hour and there is no note at all—the room is nearly empty. Those with dinner engagements have gone to keep them and those without any have gone to pretend they have. Even the two Americans who opened up the bar that morning have been led off by kind friends. The clock makes one of those quick little electric jumps to nine. We will too.

It is nine o'clock by Ritz time, which is just the same as any other time. Mr. Julius Bushmill, manufacturer; b. Canton, Ohio, June 1, 1876; m. 1899, Jessie Pepper; Mason; Republican; Congregationalist; Delegate M. A. of A. 1908; pres. 1909–1912; director

Grimes, Hansen Co. since 1911; director Midland R. R. of Indiana—all that and more—walks in, moving a silk handkerchief over a hot scarlet brow. It is his own brow. He wears a handsome dinner coat but has no vest on because the hotel valet has sent both his vests to the dry-cleaners by mistake, a fact which has been volubly explained to Mr. Bushmill for half an hour. Needless to say the prominent manufacturer is prey to a natural embarrassment at this discrepancy in his attire. He has left his devoted wife and attractive daughter in the lounge while he seeks something to fortify his entrance into the exclusive and palatial dining room.

The only other man in the bar was a tall, dark, grimly handsome young American, who slouched in a leather corner and stared at Mr. Bushmill's patent-leather shoes. Self-consciously Mr. Bushmill looked down at his shoes, wondering if the valet had deprived him of them too. Such was his relief to find them in place that he grinned at the young man and his hand went automatically to the business card in his coat pocket.

"Couldn't locate my vests," he said cordially. "That blamed valet took both my vests. See?"

He exposed the shameful overexpanse of his starched shirt.

"I beg your pardon?" said the young man, looking up with a start.

"My vests," repeated Mr. Bushmill with less gusto—"lost my vests."

The young man considered.

"I haven't seen them," he said.

"Oh, not here!" exclaimed Bushmill. "Upstairs."

"Ask Jack," suggested the young man and waved his hand toward the bar.

Among our deficiencies as a race is the fact that we have no respect for the contemplative mood. Bushmill sat down, asked the young man to have a drink, obtained finally the grudging admission that he would have a milk shake; and after explaining the vest matter in detail, tossed his business card across the table. He was not the frock-coated-and-impressive type of millionaire which has become so frequent since the war. He was rather the 1910 model—a sort of cross between Henry VIII and "our Mr. Jones will be in Minneapolis on Friday." He was much louder and more provincial and warm-hearted than the new type.

He liked young men, and his own young man would have been about the age of this one, had it not been for the defiant stubbornness of the German machine-gunners in the last days of the war.

"Here with my wife and daughter," he volunteered. "What's your name?"

"Corcoran," answered the young man, pleasantly but without enthusiasm.

"You American—or English?"

"American."

"What business you in?"

"None."

"Been here long?" continued Bushmill stubbornly.

The young man hesitated.

"I was born here," he said.

Bushmill blinked and his eyes roved involuntarily around the bar.

"*Born* here!" he repeated.

Corcoran smiled.

"Up on the fifth floor."

The waiter set the two drinks and a dish of Saratoga chips on the table. Immediately Bushmill became aware of an interesting phenomenon—Corcoran's hand commenced to flash up and down between the dish and his mouth, each journey transporting a thick layer of potatoes to the eager aperture, until the dish was empty.

"Sorry," said Corcoran, looking rather regretfully at the dish. He took out a handkerchief and wiped his fingers. "I didn't think what I was doing. I'm sure you can get some more."

A series of details now began to impress themselves on Bushmill— that there were hollows in this young man's cheeks that were not intended by the bone structure, hollows of undernourishment or ill health; that the fine flannel of his unmistakably Bond Street suit was shiny from many pressings—the elbows were fairly gleaming—and that his whole frame had suddenly collapsed a little as if the digestion of the potatoes and milk shake had begun immediately instead of waiting for the correct half hour.

"Born here, eh?" he said thoughtfully. "Lived a lot abroad, I guess."

"Yes."

"How long since you've had a square meal?"

The young man started.

"Why, I had lunch," he said. "About one o'clock I had lunch."

"One o'clock last Friday," commented Bushmill skeptically.

There was a long pause.

"Yes," admitted Corcoran, "about one o'clock last Friday."

"Are you broke? Or are you waiting for money from home?"

"This is home." Corcoran looked around abstractedly. "I've spent most of my life in the Ritz hotels of one city or another. I don't think they'd believe me upstairs if I told them I was broke. But I've got just enough left to pay my bill when I move out tomorrow."

Bushmill frowned.

"You could have lived a week at a small hotel for what it costs you here by the day," he remarked.

"I don't know the names of any other hotels."

Corcoran smiled apologetically. It was a singularly charming and somehow entirely confident smile, and Julius Bushmill was filled with a mixture of pity and awe. There was something of the snob in him, as there is in all self-made men, and he realized that this young man was telling the defiant truth.

"Any plans?"

"No."

"Any abilities—or talents?"

Corcoran considered.

"I can speak most languages," he said. "But talents—I'm afraid the only one I have is for spending money."

"How do you know you've got that?"

"I can't very well help knowing it." Again he hesitated. "I've just finished running through a matter of half a million dollars."

Bushmill's exclamation died on its first syllable as a new voice, impatient, reproachful and cheerfully anxious, shattered the seclusion of the grill.

"Have you seen a man without a vest named Bushmill? A very old man about fifty? We've been waiting for him about two or three hours."

"Hallie," called Bushmill, with a groan of remorse, "here I am. I'd forgotten you were alive."

"Don't flatter yourself it's *you* we missed," said Hallie, coming up. "It's only your money. Mama and I want food—and we must look it: two nice French gentlemen wanted to take us to dinner while we were waiting in the hall!"

"This is Mr. Corcoran," said Bushmill. "My daughter."

Hallie Bushmill was young and vivid and light, with boy's hair and a brow that bulged just slightly, like a baby's brow, and under it small perfect features that danced up and down when she smiled. She was constantly repressing their tendency toward irresponsible gaiety, as if she feared that, once encouraged, they would never come back to kindergarten under that childish brow anymore.

"Mr. Corcoran was born here in the Ritz," announced her father. "I'm sorry I kept you and your mother waiting, but to tell the truth we've been fixing up a little surprise." He looked at Corcoran and winked perceptibly. "As you know, I've got to go to England day after tomorrow and do some business in those ugly industrial towns. My plan was that you and your mother should make a month's tour of Belgium and Holland and end up at Amsterdam, where Hallie's— where Mr. Nosby will meet you—"

"Yes, I know all that," said Hallie. "Go on. Let's have the surprise."

"I had planned to engage a courier," continued Mr. Bushmill, "but fortunately I ran into my friend Corcoran this evening and he's agreed to go instead."

"I haven't said a word—" interrupted Corcoran in amazement, but Bushmill continued with a decisive wave of his hand:

"Brought up in Europe, he knows it like a book; born in the Ritz, he understands hotels; taught by experience"—here he looked significantly at Corcoran—"taught by experience, he can prevent you and your mother from being extravagant and show you how to observe the happy mean."

"Great!" Hallie looked at Corcoran with interest. "We'll have a regular loop, Mr.—"

She broke off. During the last few minutes a strange expression had come into Corcoran's face. It spread suddenly now into a sort of frightened pallor.

"Mr. Bushmill," he said with an effort, "I've got to speak to you alone—at once. It's very important. I—"

Hallie jumped to her feet.

"I'll wait with Mother," she said with a curious glance. "Hurry—both of you."

As she left the bar, Bushmill turned to Corcoran anxiously.

"What is it?" he demanded. "What do you want to say?"

"I just wanted to tell you that I'm going to faint," said Corcoran. And with remarkable promptitude he did.

II

In spite of the immediate liking that Bushmill had taken to young Corcoran, a certain corroboratory investigation was, of course, necessary. The Paris branch of the New York bank that had handled the last of the half-million told him what he needed to know. Corcoran was not given to drink, heavy gambling or vice; he simply spent money—that was all. Various people, including certain officers of the bank who had known his family, had tried to argue with him at one time or another, but he was apparently an incurable spendthrift. A childhood and youth in Europe with a wildly indulgent mother had somehow robbed him of all sense of value or proportion.

Satisfied, Bushmill asked no more—no one knew what had become of the money and, even if they had, a certain delicacy would have prevented him from inquiring more deeply into Corcoran's short past. But he did take occasion to utter a few parting admonitions before the expedition boarded the train.

"I'm letting you hold the purse strings because I think you've learned your lesson," he said, "but just remember that this time the money isn't your own. All that belongs to you is the seventy-five dollars a week that I pay you in salary. Every other expenditure is to be entered in that little book and shown to me."

"I understand."

"The first thing is to watch what you spend—and prove to me that you've got the common sense to profit by your mistake. The second and most important thing is that my wife and daughter are to have a good time."

With the first of his salary Corcoran supplied himself with histories and guidebooks of Holland and Belgium, and on the night before their departure, as well as on the night of their arrival in Brussels, he sat up late absorbing a mass of information that he had never, in his travels with his mother, been aware of before. They had not gone in for sight-seeing. His mother had considered it something which only school-teachers and vulgar tourists did, but Mr. Bushmill had impressed upon him that Hallie was to have all the advantages of travel; he must make it interesting for her by keeping ahead of her every day.

In Brussels they were to remain five days. The first morning Corcoran took three seats in a touring bus, and they inspected the guild halls and the palaces and the monuments and the parks, while he corrected the guide's historical slips in stage whispers and congratulated himself on doing so well.

But during the afternoon it drizzled as they drove through the streets and he grew tired of his own voice, of Hallie's conventional "Oh, isn't that interesting," echoed by her mother, and he wondered if five days wasn't too long to stay here after all. Still he had impressed them, without doubt; he had made a good start as the serious and well-informed young man. Moreover he had done well with the money. Resisting his first impulse to take a private limousine for the day, which would certainly have cost twelve dollars, he had only three bus tickets at one dollar each to enter in the little book. Before he began his nightly reading he put it down for Mr. Bushmill to see. But first of all he took a steaming hot bath—he had never ridden in a rubber-neck wagon with ordinary sightseers before and he found the idea rather painful.

The next day the tour continued, but so did the drizzling rain, and that evening, to his dismay, Mrs. Bushmill came down with a cold. It was nothing serious, but it entailed two doctor's visits at American prices, together with the cost of the dozen remedies which European physicians order under any circumstances, and it was a discouraging note which he made in the back of his little book that night:

> One ruined hat (She claimed it was an old hat,
>   but it didn't look old to me) $10.00
> 3 bus tickets for Monday   3.00
> 3 bus   "   " Tuesday   2.00
> Tips to incompetent guide   1.50
> 2 doctor's visits   8.00
> Medicines   2.25
>   _____
> Total for two days sightseeing $26.75

And, to balance that, Corcoran thought of the entry he might have made had he followed his first instinct:

> One comfortable limousine for two days,
>   including tip to chauffeur $26.00

Next morning Mrs. Bushmill remained in bed while he and Hallie took the excursion train to Waterloo. He had diligently mastered the strategy of the battle, and as he began his explanations of Napoleon's maneuvers, prefacing it with a short account of the political situation, he was rather disappointed at Hallie's indifference. Luncheon increased his uneasiness. He wished he had brought along the cold-lobster luncheon, put up by the hotel, that he had extravagantly considered. The food at the local restaurant was execrable and Hallie stared desolately at the hard potatoes and vintage steak, and then out the window at the melancholy rain. Corcoran wasn't hungry either, but he forced himself to eat with an affectation of relish. Two more days in Brussels! And then Antwerp! And Rotterdam! And The Hague! Twenty-five more days of history to get up in the still hours of the night, and all for an unresponsive young person who did not seem to appreciate the advantages of travel.

They were coming out of the restaurant, and Hallie's voice, with a new note in it, broke in on his meditations.

"Get a taxi; I want to go home."

He turned to her in consternation.

"What? You want to go back without seeing the famous indoor panorama, with paintings of all the actions and the life-size figures of the casualties in the foreground—"

"There's a taxi," she interrupted. "Quick!"

"A taxi!" he groaned, running after it through the mud. "And these taxis are robbers—we might have had a limousine out and back for the same price."

In silence they returned to the hotel. As Hallie entered the elevator she looked at him with suddenly determined eyes.

"Please wear your dinner coat tonight. I want to go out somewhere and dance—and please send flowers."

Corcoran wondered if this form of diversion had been included in Mr. Bushmill's intentions—especially since he had gathered that Hallie was practically engaged to the Mr. Nosby who was to meet them in Amsterdam.

Distraught with doubt he went to a florist and priced orchids. But a corsage of three would come to twenty-four dollars, and this was not an item he cared to enter in the little book. Regretfully, he compromised on sweet peas and was relieved to find her wearing them when she stepped out of the elevator at seven in a pink-petaled dress.

Corcoran was astounded and not a little disturbed by her loveliness—he had never seen her in full evening dress before. Her perfect features were dancing up and down in delighted anticipation, and he felt that Mr. Bushmill might have afforded the orchids after all.

"Thanks for the pretty flowers," she cried eagerly. "Where are we going?"

"There's a nice orchestra here in the hotel."

Her face fell a little.

"Well, we can start here—"

They went down to the almost-deserted grill, where a few scattered groups of diners swooned in midsummer languor, and only half a dozen Americans arose with the music and stalked defiantly around the floor. Hallie and Corcoran danced. She was surprised to find how well he danced, as all tall, slender men should, with such a delicacy of suggestion that she felt as though she were being turned here and there as a bright bouquet or a piece of precious cloth before five hundred eyes.

But when they had finished dancing she realized that there were only a score of eyes—after dinner even these began to melt apathetically away.

"We'd better be moving on to some gayer place," she suggested.

He frowned.

"Isn't this gay enough?" he asked anxiously. "I rather like the happy mean."

"That sounds good. Let's go there!"

"It isn't a café—it's a principle I'm trying to learn. I don't know whether your father would want—"

She flushed angrily.

"Can't you be a little human?" she demanded. "I thought when father said you were born in the Ritz you'd know something about having a good time."

He had no answer ready. After all, why should a girl of her conspicuous loveliness be condemned to desolate hotel dances and public-bus excursions in the rain?

"Is this your idea of a riot?" she continued. "Do you ever think about anything except history and monuments? Don't you know anything about having fun?"

"Once I knew quite a lot."

"What?"

"In fact—once I used to be rather an expert at spending money."

"Spending money!" she broke out. "For these?"

She unpinned the corsage from her waist and flung it on the table. "Pay the check, please. I'm going upstairs to bed."

"All right," said Corcoran suddenly, "I've decided to give you a good time."

"How?" she demanded with frozen scorn. "Take me to the movies?"

"Miss Bushmill," said Corcoran grimly, "I've had good times beyond the wildest flights of your very provincial, Middle-Western imagination. I've entertained from New York to Constantinople—given affairs that have made Indian rajahs weep with envy. I've had prima donnas break ten-thousand-dollar engagements to come to my smallest dinners. When you were still playing who's-got-the-button back in Ohio I entertained on a cruising trip that was so much fun that I had to sink my yacht to make the guests go home."

"I don't believe it. I—" Hallie gasped.

"You're bored," he interrupted. "Very well. I'll do my stuff. I'll do what I know how to do. Between here and Amsterdam you're going to have the time of your life."

III

Corcoran worked quickly. That night, after taking Hallie to her room, he paid several calls—in fact he was extraordinarily busy up to eleven o'clock next morning. At that hour he tapped briskly at the Bushmills' door.

"You are lunching at the Brussels Country Club," he said to Hallie directly, "with Prince Abrisini, Countess Perimont and Major Sir Reynolds Fitz-Hugh, the British attaché. The Bolls-Ferrari landaulet will be ready at the door in half an hour."

"But I thought we were going to the culinary exhibit," objected Mrs. Bushmill in surprise. "We had planned—"

"*You* are going," said Corcoran politely, "with two nice ladies from Wisconsin. And afterwards you are going to an American tea room and have an American luncheon with American food. At twelve o'clock a dark conservative town car will be waiting downstairs for your use."

He turned to Hallie.

"Your new maid will arrive immediately to help you dress. She will oversee the removal of your things in your absence so that nothing will be mislaid. This afternoon you entertain at tea."

"Why, how can I entertain at tea?" cried Hallie. "I don't know a soul in the place—"

"The invitations are already issued," said Corcoran.

Without waiting for further protests he bowed slightly and retired through the door.

The next three hours passed in a whirl. There was the gorgeous landaulet with a silk-hatted, satin-breeched, plum-colored footman beside the chauffeur, and a wilderness of orchids flowering from the little jars inside. There were the impressive titles that she heard in a daze at the country club as she sat down at a rose-littered table; and out of nowhere a dozen other men appeared during luncheon and stopped to be introduced to her as they went by. Never in her two years as the belle of a small Ohio town had Hallie had such attention, so many compliments—her features danced up and down with delight. Returning to the hotel, she found that they had been moved dexterously to the royal suite, a huge high salon and two sunny bedrooms overlooking a garden. Her capped maid—exactly like the French maid she had once impersonated in a play—was in attendance, and there was a new deference in the manner of all the servants in the hotel. She was bowed up the steps—other guests were gently brushed aside for her—and bowed into the elevator, which clanged shut in the faces of two irate Englishwomen and whisked her straight to her floor.

Tea was a great success. Her mother, considerably encouraged by the pleasant two hours she had spent in congenial company, conversed with the clergyman of the American Church, while Hallie moved enraptured through a swarm of charming and attentive men. She was surprised to learn that she was giving a dinner dance that night at the fashionable Café Royal—and even the afternoon faded before the glories of the night. She was not aware that two specially hired entertainers had left Paris for Brussels on the noon train until they bounced hilariously in upon the shining floor. But she knew that there were a dozen partners for every dance, and chatter that had nothing to do with monuments or battlefields. Had she not been so thoroughly and cheerfully tired, she would have protested frantically at midnight when Corcoran approached her and told her he was taking her home.

Only then, half asleep in the luxurious depths of the town car, did she have time to wonder.

"How on earth—? How did you do it?"

"It was nothing—I had no time," said Corcoran disparagingly. "I knew a few young men around the embassies. Brussels isn't very gay, you know, and they're always glad to help stir things up. All the rest was—even simpler. Did you have a good time?"

No answer.

"Did you have a good time?" he repeated a little anxiously. "There's no use going on, you know, if you didn't have a—"

"The Battle of Wellington was won by Major Sir Corcoran Fitz-Hugh Abrisini," she muttered, decisively but indistinctly.

Hallie was asleep.

IV

After three more days Hallie finally consented to being torn away from Brussels, and the tour continued through Antwerp, Rotterdam and The Hague. But it was not the same sort of tour that had left Paris a short week before. It traveled in two limousines, for there were always at least one pair of attentive cavaliers in attendance—not to mention a quartet of hirelings who made the jumps by train. Corcoran's guidebooks and histories appeared no more. In Antwerp they did not stay at a mere hotel, but at a famous old shooting box on the outskirts of the city which Corcoran hired for six days, servants and all.

Before they left, Hallie's photograph appeared in the Antwerp papers over a paragraph which spoke of her as the beautiful American heiress who had taken Brabant Lodge and entertained so delightfully that a certain Royal Personage had been several times in evidence there.

In Rotterdam, Hallie saw neither the Boompjes nor the Groote Kerk—they were both obscured by a stream of pleasant young Dutchmen who looked at her with soft blue eyes. But when they reached The Hague and the tour neared its end, she was aware of a growing sadness—it had been such a good time and now it would be over and put away. Already Amsterdam and a certain Ohio gentleman, who didn't understand entertaining on the grand scale, were sweeping toward her—and though she tried to be glad she wasn't glad at all. It depressed her too that Corcoran seemed to be avoiding her—he had scarcely spoken to her or danced with her since they left Antwerp. She was thinking chiefly of that on the last afternoon as they rode through the twilight toward Amsterdam and her mother drowsed sleepily in a corner of the car.

"You've been so good to me," she said. "If you're still angry about that evening in Brussels, please try to forgive me now."

"I've forgiven you long ago."

They rode into the city in silence and Hallie looked out the window in a sort of panic. What would she do now with no one to take care of her, to take care of that part of her that wanted to be young and gay forever? Just before they drew up at the hotel, she turned again to Corcoran and their eyes met in a strange disquieting glance. Her hand reached out for his and pressed it gently, as if this was their real good-bye.

Mr. Claude Nosby was a stiff, dark, glossy man, leaning hard toward forty, whose eyes rested for a hostile moment upon Corcoran as he helped Hallie from the car.

"Your father arrives tomorrow," he said portentously. "His attention has been called to your picture in the Antwerp papers and he is hurrying over from London."

"Why shouldn't my picture be in the Antwerp papers, Claude?" inquired Hallie innocently.

"It seems a bit unusual."

Mr. Nosby had had a letter from Mr. Bushmill which told him of the arrangement. He looked upon it with profound disapproval. All through dinner he listened without enthusiasm to the account which Hallie, rather spiritedly assisted by her mother, gave of the adventure; and afterwards when Hallie and her mother went to bed he informed Corcoran that he would like to speak to him alone.

"Ah—Mr. Corcoran," he began, "would you be kind enough to let me see the little account book you are keeping for Mr. Bushmill?"

"I'd rather not," answered Corcoran pleasantly. "I think that's a matter between Mr. Bushmill and me."

"It's the same thing," said Nosby impatiently. "Perhaps you are not aware that Miss Bushmill and I are engaged."

"I had gathered as much."

"Perhaps you can gather too that I am not particularly pleased at the sort of good time you chose to give her."

"It was just an ordinary good time."

"That is a matter of opinion. Will you give me the notebook?"

"Tomorrow," said Corcoran, still pleasantly, "and only to Mr. Bushmill. Good-night."

Corcoran slept late. He was awakened at eleven by the telephone, through which Nosby's voice informed him coldly that Mr. Bushmill had arrived and would see him at once. When he rapped at his employer's door ten minutes later, he found Hallie and her mother also were there, sitting rather sulkily on a sofa. Mr. Bushmill nodded at him coolly but made no motion to shake hands.

"Let's see that account book," he said immediately.

Corcoran handed it to him, together with a bulky packet of vouchers and receipts.

"I hear you've all been out raising hell," said Bushmill.

"No," said Hallie, "only Mama and me."

"You wait outside, Corcoran. I'll let you know when I want you."

Corcoran descended to the lobby and found out from the porter that a train left for Paris at noon. Then he bought a "New York Herald" and stared at the headlines for half an hour. At the end of that time he was summoned upstairs.

Evidently a heated discussion had gone on in his absence. Mr. Nosby was staring out the window with a look of patient resignation. Mrs. Bushmill had been crying, and Hallie, with a triumphant frown on her childish brow, was making a camp stool out of her father's knee.

"Sit down," she said sternly.

Corcoran sat down.

"What do you mean by giving us such a good time?"

"Oh, drop it, Hallie!" said her father impatiently. He turned to Corcoran: "Did I give you any authority to lay out twelve thousand dollars in six weeks? Did I?"

"You're going to Italy with us," interrupted Hallie reassuringly. "We—"

"Will you be quiet?" exploded Bushmill. "It may be funny to you, but I don't like to make bad bets, and I'm pretty sore."

"What nonsense!" remarked Hallie cheerfully. "Why, you were laughing a minute ago!"

"Laughing! You mean at that idiotic account book? Who wouldn't laugh? Four titles at five hundred francs a head! One baptismal font to American Church for presence of clergyman at tea. It's like the log book of a lunatic asylum!"

"Never mind," said Hallie. "You can charge the baptismal font off your income tax."

"That's consoling," said her father grimly. "Nevertheless, this young man will spend no more of my money for me."

"But he's still a wonderful guide. He knows everything—don't you? All about the monuments and catacombs and the Battle of Waterloo."

"Will you please let me talk to Mr. Corcoran?" Hallie was silent. "Mrs. Bushmill and my daughter and Mr. Nosby are going to take a trip through Italy as far as Sicily, where Mr. Nosby has some business, and they want you—that is, Hallie and her mother think they would get more out of it if you went along. Understand—it isn't going to be any royal fandango this time. You'll get your salary and your expenses and that's all you'll get. Do you want to go?"

"No, thanks, Mr. Bushmill," said Corcoran quietly. "I'm going back to Paris at noon."

"You're not!" cried Hallie indignantly. "Why—why how am I going to know which is the Forum and the—the Acropolis and all that?" She rose from her father's knee. "Look here, Daddy, I can persuade him." Before they guessed her intentions she had seized Corcoran's arm, dragged him into the hall and closed the door behind her.

"You've got to come," she said intensely. "Don't you understand? I've seen Claude in a new light and I can't marry him and I don't dare tell Father, and I'll go mad if we have to go off with him alone."

The door opened and Mr. Nosby peered suspiciously out into the hall.

"It's all right," cried Hallie. "He'll come. It was just a question of more salary and he was too shy to say anything about it."

As they went back in Bushmill looked from one to the other.

"Why do you think you ought to get more salary?"

"So he can spend it, of course," explained Hallie triumphantly. "He's got to keep his hand in, hasn't he?"

This unanswerable argument closed the discussion. Corcoran was to go to Italy with them as courier and guide at three hundred and fifty dollars a month, an advance of some fifty dollars over what he had received before. From Sicily they were to proceed by boat to Marseilles, where Mr. Bushmill would meet them. After that Mr. Corcoran's services would be no longer required—the Bushmills and Mr. Nosby would sail immediately for home.

They left next morning. It was evident even before they reached Italy that Mr. Nosby had determined to run the expedition in his own way. He was aware that Hallie was less docile and less responsive than she had been before she came abroad, and when he spoke of the wedding a curious vagueness seemed to come over her, but he knew that she adored her father and that in the end she would do whatever her father liked. It was only a question of getting her back to America before any silly young men, such as this unbalanced spendthrift, had the opportunity of infecting her with any nonsense. Once in the factory town and in the little circle where she had grown up, she would slip gently back into the attitude she had held before.

So for the first four weeks of the tour he was never a foot from her side, and at the same time he managed to send Corcoran on a series of useless errands which occupied much of his time. He would get up early in the morning, arrange that Corcoran should take Mrs. Bushmill on a day's excursion and say nothing to Hallie until they were safely away. For the opera in Milan, the concerts in Rome, he bought tickets for three, and on all automobile trips he made it plain to Corcoran that he was to sit with the chauffeur outside.

In Naples they were to stop for a day and take the boat trip to the Island of Capri in order to visit the celebrated Blue Grotto. Then, returning to Naples, they would motor south and cross to Sicily. In Naples Mr. Nosby received a telegram from Mr. Bushmill, in Paris, which he did not read to the others, but folded up and put into his pocket. He told them, however, that on their way to the Capri steamer he must stop for a moment at an Italian bank.

Mrs. Bushmill had not come along that morning, and Hallie and Corcoran waited outside in the cab. It was the first time in four weeks that they had been together without Mr. Nosby's stiff, glossy presence hovering near.

"I've got to talk to you," said Hallie in a low voice. "I've tried so many times, but it's almost impossible. He got Father to say that if you molested me, or even were attentive to me, he could send you immediately home."

"I shouldn't have come," answered Corcoran despairingly. "It was a terrible mistake. But I want to see you alone just once—if only to say good-bye."

As Nosby hurried out of the bank, he broke off and bent his glance casually down the street, pretending to be absorbed in some interesting phenomenon that was taking place there. And suddenly, as if life were playing up to his subterfuge, an interesting phenomenon did immediately take place on the corner in front of the bank. A man in his shirt-sleeves rushed suddenly out of the side street, seized the shoulder of a small, swarthy hunchback standing there and, swinging him quickly around, pointed at their taxi-cab. The man in his shirt-sleeves had not even looked at them—it was as if he had known that they would be there.

The hunchback nodded and instantly both of them disappeared— the first man into the side street which had yielded him up, the hunchback into nowhere at all. The incident took place so quickly that it made only an odd visual impression upon Corcoran—he did not have occasion to think of it again until they returned from Capri eight hours later.

The Bay of Naples was rough as they set out that morning, and the little steamer staggered like a drunken man through the persistent waves. Before long Mr. Nosby's complexion was running through a gamut of yellows, pale creams and ghostly whites, but he insisted that he scarcely noticed the motion and forced Hallie to accompany him in an incessant promenade up and down the deck.

When the steamer reached the coast of the rocky, cheerful little island, dozens of boats put out from shore and swarmed about dizzily in the waves as they waited for passengers to the Blue Grotto. The constant Saint Vitus' dance which they performed in the surf turned Mr. Nosby from a respectable white to a bizarre and indecent blue and compelled him to a sudden decision.

"It's too rough," he announced. "We won't go."

Hallie, watching fascinated from the rail, paid no attention. Seductive cries were floating up from below:

"Theesa a good boat, lady an' ge'man!"

"I spik American—been America two year!"

"Fine, sunny day for go to see Blue Grotte!"

The first passengers had already floated off, two to a boat, and now Hallie was drifting with the next batch down the gangway.

"Where are you going, Hallie?" shouted Mr. Nosby. "It's too dangerous today. We're going to stay on board."

Hallie, half down the gangway, looked back over her shoulder.

"Of course I'm going!" she cried. "Do you think I'd come all the way to Capri and miss the Blue Grotto?"

Nosby took one more look at the sea—then he turned hurriedly away. Already Hallie, followed by Corcoran, had stepped into one of the small boats and was waving him a cheerful good-bye.

They approached the shore, heading for a small dark opening in the rocks. When they arrived, the boatman ordered them to sit on the floor of the boat to keep from being bumped against the low entrance. A momentary passage through darkness, then a vast space opened up around them and they were in a bright paradise of ultramarine, a cathedral cave where the water and air and the high-vaulted roof were of the most radiant and opalescent blue.

"Ver' pret'," sing-songed the boatman. He ran his oar through the water and they watched it turn to an incredible silver.

"I'm going to put my hand in!" said Hallie, enraptured. They were both kneeling now, and as she leaned forward to plunge her hand under the surface the strange light enveloped them like a spell and their lips touched—then all the world turned to blue and silver, or else this was not the world but a delightful enchantment in which they would dwell forever.

"Ver' beaut'ful," sang the boatman. "Come back see Blue Grotte tomorrow, next day. Ask for Frederico, fine man for Blue Grotte. Oh, chawming!"

Again their lips sought each other and blue and silver seemed to soar like rockets above them, burst and shower down about their shoulders in protective atoms of color, screening them from time, from sight. They kissed again. The voices of tourists were seeking echoes here and there about the cave. A brown naked boy dived from a high rock, cleaving the water like a silver fish, and starting a thousand platinum bubbles to churn up through the blue light.

"I love you with all my heart," she whispered. "What shall we do? Oh, my dear, if you only had a little common sense about money!"

The cavern was emptying, the small boats were feeling their way out, one by one, to the glittering restless sea.

"Good-bye, Blue Grotte!" sang the boatman. "Come again soo-oon!"

Blinded by the sunshine they sat back apart and looked at each other. But though the blue and silver was left behind, the radiance about her face remained.

"I love you," rang as true here under the blue sky.

Mr. Nosby was waiting on the deck, but he said not a word—only looked at them sharply and sat between them all the way back to Naples. But for all his tangible body, they were no longer apart. He had best be quick and interpose his four thousand miles.

It was not until they had docked and were walking from the pier that Corcoran was jerked sharply from his mood of rapture and despair by something that sharply recalled to him the incident of the morning. Directly in their path, as if waiting for them, stood the swarthy hunchback to whom the man in the shirt-sleeves had pointed out their taxi. No sooner did he see them, however, than he stepped quickly aside and melted into a crowd. When they had passed, Corcoran turned back, as if for a last look at the boat, and saw in the sweep of his eye that the hunchback was pointing them out in his turn to still another man.

As they got into a taxi Mr. Nosby broke the silence.

"You'd better pack immediately," he said. "We're leaving by motor for Palermo right after dinner."

"We can't make it tonight," objected Hallie.

"We'll stop at Cosenza. That's halfway."

It was plain that he wanted to bring the trip to an end at the first possible moment. After dinner he asked Corcoran to come to the hotel garage with him while he engaged an automobile for the trip, and Corcoran understood that this was because Hallie and he were not to be left together. Nosby, in an ill humor, insisted that the garage price was too high; finally he walked out and up to a dilapidated taxi in the street. The taxi agreed to make the trip to Palermo for twenty-five dollars.

"I don't believe this old thing will make the grade," ventured Corcoran. "Don't you think it would be wiser to pay the difference and take the other car?"

Nosby stared at him, his anger just under the surface.

"We're not all like you," he said dryly. "We can't all afford to throw it away."

Corcoran took the snub with a cool nod.

"Another thing," he said. "Did you get money from the bank this morning—or anything that would make you likely to be followed?"

"What do you mean?" demanded Nosby quickly.

"Somebody's been keeping pretty close track of our movements all day."

Nosby eyed him shrewdly.

"You'd like us to stay here in Naples a day or so more, wouldn't you?" he said. "Unfortunately you're not running this party. If you stay, you can stay alone."

"And you won't take the other car?"

"I'm getting a little weary of your suggestions."

At the hotel, as the porters piled the bags into the high old-fashioned car, Corcoran was again possessed by a feeling of being watched. With an effort he resisted the impulse to turn his head and look behind. If this was a product of his imagination, it was better to put it immediately from his mind.

It was already eight o'clock when they drove off into a windy twilight. The sun had gone behind Naples, leaving a sky of pigeon's-blood and gold, and as they rounded the bay and climbed slowly toward Torre Annunziata, the Mediterranean momentarily toasted the fading splendor in pink wine. Above them loomed Vesuvius and from its crater a small persistent fountain of smoke contributed darkness to the gathering night.

"We ought to reach Cosenza about twelve," said Nosby.

No one answered. The city had disappeared behind a rise of ground, and now they were alone, tracing down the hot mysterious shin of the Italian boot where the Maffia sprang out of rank human weeds and the Black Hand rose to throw its ominous shadow across two continents. There was something eerie in the sough of the wind over these grey mountains, crowned with the decayed castles. Hallie suddenly shivered.

"I'm glad I'm American," she said. "Here in Italy I feel that everybody's dead. So many people dead and all watching from up on those hills—Carthaginians and old Romans and Moorish pirates and medieval princes with poisoned rings—"

The solemn gloom of the countryside communicated itself to all of them. The wind had come up stronger and was groaning through the dark massed trees along the way. The engine labored painfully up the incessant slopes and then coasted down winding spiral roads until the brakes gave out a burning smell. In the dark little village of Eboli they stopped for gasoline, and while they waited for their change another car came quickly out of the darkness and drew up behind.

Corcoran looked at it closely, but the lights were in his face and he could distinguish only the pale blots of four faces which returned his insistent stare. When the taxi had driven off and toiled a mile uphill in the face of the sweeping wind, he saw the lamps of the other car emerge from the village and follow. In a low voice he called Nosby's attention to the fact—whereupon Nosby leaned forward nervously and tapped on the front glass.

"*Piu presto!*" he commanded. "*Il sera sono tropo tarde!*"

Corcoran translated the mutilated Italian and then fell into conversation with the chauffeur. Hallie had dozed off to sleep with her head on her mother's shoulder. It might have been twenty minutes later when she awoke with a start to find that the car had stopped. The chauffeur was peering into the engine with a lighted match, while Corcoran and Mr. Nosby were talking quickly in the road.

"What is it?" she cried.

"He's broken down," said Corcoran, "and he hasn't got the proper tools to make the repair. The best thing is for all of you to start out on foot for Agropoli. That's the next village—it's about two miles away."

"Look!" said Nosby uneasily. The lights of another car had breasted a rise less than a mile behind.

"Perhaps they'll pick us up?" asked Hallie.

"We're taking no such chances," answered Corcoran. "This is the special beat of one of the roughest gangs of holdup men in Southern Italy. What's more, we're being followed. When I asked the chauffeur if he knew that car that drove up behind us in Eboli, he shut right up. He's afraid to say."

As he spoke he was helping Hallie and her mother from the car. Now he turned authoritatively to Nosby.

"You better tell me what you got in that Naples bank."

"It was ten thousand dollars in English bank notes," admitted Nosby in a frightened voice.

"I thought so. Some clerk tipped them off. Hand over those notes to me!"

"Why should I?" demanded Nosby. "What are you going to do with them?"

"I'm going to throw them away," said Corcoran. His head went up alertly. The complaint of a motor car taking a hill in second speed was borne toward them clearly on the night. "Hallie, you and your mother start on with the chauffeur. Run as fast as you can for a hundred yards or so and then keep going. If I don't show up, notify the carabinieri in Agropoli." His voice sank lower. "Don't worry, I'm going to fix this thing. Good-bye."

As they started off he turned again to Nosby.

"Hand over that money," he said.

"You're going to—"

"I'm going to keep them here while you get Hallie away. Don't you see that if they got her up in these hills they could ask any amount of money they wanted?"

Nosby paused irresolute. Then he pulled out a thick packet of fifty-pound notes and began to peel half a dozen from the top.

"I want *all* of it," snapped Corcoran. With a quick movement he wrested the packet violently from Nosby's hand. "Now go on!"

Less than half a mile away, the lights of the car dipped into sight. With a broken cry Nosby turned and stumbled off down the road.

Corcoran took a pencil and an envelope from his pocket and worked quickly for a few minutes by the glow of the headlights. Then he wet one finger and held it up tentatively in the air as if he were making an experiment. The result seemed to satisfy him. He waited, ruffling the large thin notes—there were forty of them—in his hands.

The lights of the other car came nearer, slowed up, came to a stop twenty feet away.

Leaving the engine running idle, four men got out and walked toward him.

"*Buona séra!*" he called, and then continued in Italian, "We have broken down."

"Where are the rest of your people?" demanded one of the men quickly.

"They were picked up by another car. It turned around and took them back to Agropoli," Corcoran said politely. He was aware that he was covered by two revolvers, but he waited an instant longer, straining to hear the flurry in the trees which would announce a gust of wind. The men drew nearer.

"But I have something here that may interest you." Slowly, his heart thumping, he raised his hand, bringing the packet of notes into the glare of the headlight. Suddenly out of the valley swept the wind, louder and nearer—he waited a moment longer until he felt the first cold freshness on his face. "Here are two hundred thousand lire in English bank notes!" He raised the sheaf of paper higher as if to hand it to the nearest man. Then he released it with a light upward flick and immediately the wind seized upon it and whirled the notes in forty directions through the air.

The nearest man cursed and made a lunge for the closest piece. Then they were all scurrying here and there about the road while the frail bills sailed and flickered in the gale, pirouetting like elves along the grass, bouncing and skipping from side to side in mad perversity.

From one side to the other they ran, Corcoran with them—crumpling the captured money into their pockets, then scattering always farther and farther apart in wild pursuit of the elusive beckoning symbols of gold.

Suddenly Corcoran saw his opportunity. Bending low, as if he had spotted a stray bill beneath the car, he ran toward it, vaulted over the side and hitched into the driver's seat. As he plunged the lever into first, he heard a cursing cry and then a sharp report, but the warmed car had jumped forward safely and the shot went wide.

In a moment, his teeth locked and muscles tense against the fusillade, he had passed the stalled taxi and was racing along into the darkness. There was another report close at hand and he ducked wildly, afraid for an instant that one of them had clung to the running board—then he realized that one of their shots had blown out a tire.

After three-quarters of a mile he stopped, cut off his motor and listened. There wasn't a sound, only the drip from his radiator onto the road.

"Hallie!" he called. "Hallie!"

A figure emerged from the shadows not ten feet away, then another figure and another.

"Hallie!" he said.

She clambered into the front seat with him—her arms went about him.

"You're safe!" she sobbed. "We heard the shots and I wanted to go back."

Mr. Nosby, very cool now, stood in the road.

"I don't suppose you brought back any of that money," he said.

Corcoran took three crumpled bank notes from his pocket.

"That's all," he said. "But they're liable to be along here any minute and you can argue with them about the rest."

Mr. Nosby, followed by Mrs. Bushmill and the chauffeur, stepped quickly into the car.

"Nevertheless," he insisted shrilly, as they moved off, "this has been a pretty expensive business. You've flung away ten thousand dollars that was to have bought goods in Sicily."

"Those are English bank notes," said Corcoran. "Big notes too. Every bank in England and Italy will be watching for those numbers."

"But we don't know the numbers!"

"I took all the numbers," said Corcoran.

The rumor that Mr. Julius Bushmill's purchasing department keeps him awake nights is absolutely unfounded. There are those who say that a once conservative business is expanding in a way that is more sensational than sound, but they are probably small, malevolent rivals with a congenital disgust for the Grand Scale. To all gratuitous advice, Mr. Bushmill replies that even when his son-in-law seems to be throwing it away, it all comes back. His theory is that the young idiot really has a talent for spending money.

"NOT IN THE GUIDEBOOK"

This story began three days before it got into the papers. Like many other news-hungry Americans in Paris this spring, I opened the "Franco-American Star" one morning and having skimmed the hackneyed headlines (largely devoted to reporting the sempiternal "Lafayette-love-Washington" bombast of French and American orators) I came upon something of genuine interest.

"Look at that!" I exclaimed, passing it over to the twin bed. But the occupant of the twin bed immediately found an article about Leonora Hughes, the dancer, in another column, and began to read it. So of course I demanded the paper back.

"You don't realize—" I began.

"I wonder," interrupted the occupant of the twin bed, "if she's a real blonde."

However, when I issued from the domestic suite a little later I found other men in various cafés saying "Look at that!" as they pointed to the Item of Interest. And about noon I found another writer (whom I have since bribed with champagne to hold his peace) and together we went down into Franco-American officialdom to see. We discovered that the story began about three days before it got into the papers.

It began on a boat, and with a young woman who, though she wasn't even faintly uneasy, was leaning over the rail. She was watching the parallels of longitude as they swam beneath the keel, and trying to read the numbers on them, but of course the S. S. *Olympic* travels too fast for that, and all that the young woman could see was the agate-green, foliage-like spray, changing and complaining around the stern. Though there was little to look at except the spray and a dismal Scandinavian tramp in the distance and the admiring millionaire who was trying to catch her eye from the first-class deck above, Milly Cooley was perfectly happy. For she was beginning life over.

Hope is a usual cargo between Naples and Ellis Island, but on ships bound east for Cherbourg it is noticeably rare. The first-class passengers specialize in sophistication and the steerage passengers go in for disillusion (which is much the same thing) but the young woman by the rail was going in for hope raised to the ultimate power. It was not her own life she was beginning over, but someone else's, and this is a much more dangerous thing to do.

Milly was a frail, dark, appealing girl with the spiritual, haunted eyes that so frequently accompany South European beauty. By birth her mother and father had been respectively Czech and Roumanian, but Milly had missed the overshort upper lip and the pendulous, pointed nose that disfigure the type—her features were regular and her skin was young and olive-white and clear.

The good-looking, pimply young man with eyes of a bright marbly blue who was asleep on a dunnage bag a few feet away was her husband—it was his life that Milly was beginning over. Through the six months of their marriage he had shown himself to be shiftless and dissipated, but now they were getting off to a new start. Jim Cooley deserved a new start, for he had been a hero in the war. There was a thing called "shell shock" which justified anything unpleasant in a war hero's behavior—Jim Cooley had explained that to her on the second day of their honeymoon when he had gotten abominably drunk and knocked her down with his open hand.

"I get crazy," he said emphatically next morning, and his marbly eyes rolled back and forth realistically in his head. "I get started, thinkin' I'm fightin' the war, an' I take a poke at whatever's in front of me, see?"

He was a Brooklyn boy, and he had joined the marines. And on a June twilight he had crawled fifty yards out of his lines to search the body of a Bavarian captain that lay out in plain sight. He found a copy of German regimental orders, and in consequence his own brigade attacked much sooner than would otherwise have been possible, and perhaps the war was shortened by so much as a quarter of an hour. The fact was appreciated by the French and American races in the form of engraved slugs of precious metal which Jim showed around for four years before it occurred to him how nice it would be to have a permanent audience. Milly's mother was impressed with his martial achievement, and a marriage was arranged—Milly didn't realize her mistake until twenty-four hours after it was too late.

At the end of several months Milly's mother died and left her daughter two hundred and fifty dollars. The event had a marked effect on Jim. He sobered up and one night came home from work with a plan for turning over a new leaf, for beginning life over. By the aid of his war record he had obtained a job with a bureau that took care of American soldier graves in France. The pay was small but then, as everyone knew, living was dirt cheap over there. Hadn't the forty a month that he drew in the war looked good to the girls and the wine-sellers of Paris? Especially when you figured it in French money.

Milly listened to his tales of the land where grapes were full of champagne and then thought it all over carefully. Perhaps the best use for her money would be in giving Jim his chance, the chance that he had never had since the war. In a little cottage in the outskirts of Paris they could forget this last six months and find peace and happiness and perhaps even love as well.

"Are you going to try?" she asked simply.

"Of course I'm going to try, Milly."

"You're going to make me think I didn't make a mistake?"

"Sure I am, Milly. It'll make a different person out of me. Don't you believe it?"

She looked at him. His eyes were bright with enthusiasm, with determination. A warm glow had spread over him at the prospect— he had never really had his chance before.

"All right," she said finally. "We'll go."

They were there. The Cherbourg breakwater, a white stone snake, glittered along the sea at dawn—behind it red roofs and steeples and then small, neat hills traced with a warm, orderly pattern of toy farms. "Do you like this French arrangement?" it seemed to say. "It's considered very charming, but if you don't agree just shift it about—set this road here, this steeple there. It's been done before, and it always comes out lovely in the end!"

It was Sunday morning, and Cherbourg was in flaring collars and high lace hats. Donkey carts and diminutive automobiles moved to the sound of incessant bells. Jim and Milly went ashore on a tug-boat and were inspected by customs officials and immigration authorities. Then they were free with an hour before the Paris train, and they moved out into the bright thrilling world of French blue. At a point of vantage, a pleasant square that continually throbbed with soldiers and innumerable dogs and the clack of wooden shoes, they sat down at a café.

"Du vaah," said Jim to the waiter. He was a little disappointed when the answer came in English. After the man went for the wine he took out his two war medals and pinned them to his coat. The waiter returned with the wine, seemed not to notice the medals, made no remark. Milly wished Jim hadn't put them on—she felt vaguely ashamed.

After another glass of wine it was time for the train. They got into the strange little third-class carriage, an engine that was out of some boy's playroom began to puff and, in a pleasant informal way, jogged them leisurely south through the friendly lived-over land.

"What are we going to do first when we get there?" asked Milly.

"First?" Jim looked at her abstractedly and frowned. "Why, first I got to see about the job, see?" The exhilaration of the wine had passed and left him surly. "What do you want to ask so many questions for? Buy yourself a guidebook, why don't you?"

Milly felt a slight sinking of the heart—he hadn't grumbled at her like this since the trip was first proposed.

"It didn't cost as much as we thought, anyhow," she said cheerfully. "We must have over a hundred dollars left anyway."

He grunted. Outside the window Milly's eyes were caught by the sight of a dog drawing a legless man.

"Look!" she exclaimed. "How funny!"

"Aw, dry up. I've seen it all before."

An encouraging idea occurred to her: it was in France that Jim's nerves had gone to pieces; it was natural that he should be cross and uneasy for a few hours.

Westward through Caen, Lisieux and the rich green plains of Calvados. When they reached the third stop Jim got up and stretched himself.

"Going out on the platform," he said gloomily. "I need to get a breath of air; hot in here."

It was hot, but Milly didn't mind. Her eyes were excited with all she saw—a pair of little boys in black smocks began to stare at her curiously through the windows of the carriage.

"American?" cried one of them suddenly.

"Hello," said Milly. "What place is this?"

"Pardon?"

They came closer.

"What's the name of this place?"

Suddenly the two boys poked each other in the stomach and went off into roars of laughter. Milly didn't see that she had said anything funny.

There was an abrupt jerk as the train started. Milly jumped up in alarm and put her head out the carriage window.

"Jim!" she called.

She looked up and down the platform. He wasn't there. The boys, seeing her distraught face, ran along beside the train as it moved from the station. He must have jumped for one of the rear cars. But—

"Jim!" she cried wildly. The station slid past. "Jim!"

Trying desperately to control her fright, she sank back into her seat and tried to think. Her first supposition was that he had gone to a café for a drink and missed the train—in that case she should have got off too while there was still time, for otherwise there was no telling what would happen to him. If this were one of his spells he might just go on drinking, until he had spent every cent of their money. It was unbelievably awful to imagine—but it was possible.

She waited, gave him ten, fifteen minutes to work his way up to this car—then she admitted to herself that he wasn't on the train. A dull panic began—the sudden change in her relations to the world was so startling that she thought neither of his delinquency nor of what must be done, but only of the immediate fact that she was alone. Erratic as his protection had been, it was something. Now— why, she might sit in this strange train until it carried her to China and there was no one to care!

After a long while it occurred to her that he might have left part of the money in one of the suitcases. She took them down from the rack and went feverishly through all the clothes. In the bottom of an old pair of pants that Jim had worn on the boat she found two bright American dimes. The sight of them was somehow comforting and she clasped them tight in her hand. The bags yielded up nothing more.

An hour later, when it was dark outside, the train slid in under the yellow misty glow of the Gare du Nord. Strange, incomprehensible station cries fell on her ears, and her heart was beating loud as she wrenched at the handle of the door. She took her own bag with one hand and picked up Jim's suitcase in the other, but it was heavy and she couldn't get out the door with both, so in a rush of anger she left the suitcase in the carriage.

On the platform she looked left and right with the forlorn hope that he might appear, but she saw no one except a Swedish brother and sister from the boat whose tall bodies, straight and strong under the huge bundles they both carried, were hurrying out of sight. She took a quick step after them and then stopped, unable to tell them of the shameful thing that had happened to her. They had worries of their own.

With the two dimes in one hand and her suitcase in the other, Milly walked slowly along the platform. People hurried by her, baggage-smashers under forests of golf sticks, excited American girls full of the irrepressible thrill of arriving in Paris, obsequious porters from the big hotels. They were all walking and talking very fast, but Milly walked slowly because ahead of her she saw only the yellow arc of the waiting room and the door that led out of it and after that she did not know where she would go.

II

By 10 P.M. Mr. Bill Driscoll was usually weary, for by that time he had a full twelve-hour day behind him. After that he only went out with the most celebrated people. If someone had tipped off a multi-millionaire or a moving-picture director—at that time American directors were swarming over Europe looking for new locations—about Bill Driscoll, he would fortify himself with two cups of coffee, adorn his person with his new dinner coat and show them the most dangerous dives of Montmartre in the very safest way.

Bill Driscoll looked good in his new dinner coat, with his reddish brown hair soaked in water and slicked back from his attractive forehead. Often he regarded himself admiringly in the mirror, for it was the first dinner coat he had ever owned. He had earned it himself, with his wits, as he had earned the swelling packet of American bonds which awaited him in a New York bank. If you have been in Paris during the past two years you must have seen his large white auto-bus with the provoking legend on the side:

WILLIAM DRISCOLL
HE SHOWS YOU THINGS NOT IN THE GUIDEBOOK

When he found Milly Cooley it was after three o'clock and he had just left Director and Mrs. Claude Peebles at their hotel after escorting them to those celebrated apache dens, Zelli's and *Le Rat Mort* (which are about as dangerous, all things considered, as the Biltmore Hotel at noon), and he was walking homeward toward his pension on the Left Bank. His eye was caught by two disreputable-looking parties under the lamp post who were giving aid to what was apparently a drunken girl. Bill Driscoll decided to cross the street— he was aware of the tender affection which the French police bore toward embattled Americans, and he made a point of keeping out of trouble. Just at that moment Milly's subconscious self came to her aid and she called out "Let me go!" in an agonized moan.

The moan had a Brooklyn accent. It was a Brooklyn moan.

Driscoll altered his course uneasily and, approaching the group, asked politely what was the matter, whereat one of the disreputable parties desisted in his attempt to open Milly's tightly clasped left hand.

The man answered quickly that she had fainted. He and his friend were assisting her to the gendarmerie. They loosened their hold on her and she collapsed gently to the ground.

Bill came closer and bent over her, being careful to choose a position where neither man was behind him. He saw a young, frightened face that was drained now of the color it possessed by day.

"Where did you find her?" he inquired in French.

"Here. Just now. She looked to be so tired—"

Bill put his hand in his pocket and when he spoke he tried very hard to suggest by his voice that he had a revolver there.

"She is American," he said. "You leave her to me."

The man made a gesture of acquiescence and took a step backward, his hand going with a natural movement to his coat as if he intended buttoning it. He was watching Bill's right hand, the one in his coat-pocket, and Bill happened to be left-handed. There is nothing much faster than an untelegraphed left-hand blow—this one traveled less than eighteen inches and the recipient staggered back against a lamp post, embraced it transiently and regretfully and settled to the ground. Nevertheless Bill Driscoll's successful career might have ended there, ended with the strong shout of "*Voleurs!*" which he raised into the Paris night, had the other man had a gun. The other man indicated that he had no gun by retreating ten yards down the street. His prostrate companion moved slightly on the sidewalk and, taking a step toward him, Bill drew back his foot and kicked him full in the head as a football player kicks a goal from placement. It was not a pretty gesture, but he had remembered that he was wearing his new dinner coat and he didn't want to wrestle on the ground for the piece of poisonous hardware.

In a moment two gendarmes in a great hurry came running down the moonlit street.

III

Two days after this it came out in the papers—"*War hero deserts wife en route to Paris*," I think, or "*American Bride arrives penniless, Husbandless at Gare du Nord.*" The police were informed, of course, and word was sent out to the provincial departments to seek an American named James Cooley who was without *carte d'identité*. The newspapers learned the story at the American Aid Society and made a neat pathetic job of it, because Milly was young and pretty and curiously loyal to her husband. Almost her first words were to explain that it was all because his nerves had been shattered in the war.

Young Driscoll was somewhat disappointed to find that she was married. Not that he had fallen in love at first sight—on the contrary, he was unusually level-headed—but after the moonlight rescue, which rather pleased him, it didn't seem appropriate that she should have a heroic husband wandering over France. He had carried her to his own pension that night, and his landlady, an American widow named Mrs. Horton, had taken a fancy to Milly and wanted to look after her, but before eleven o'clock on the day the paper appeared, the office of the American Aid Society was literally jammed with Samaritans. They were mostly rich old ladies from America who were tired of the Louvre and the Tuileries and anxious for something to do. Several eager but sheepish Frenchmen, inspired by a mysterious and unfathomable gallantry, hung about outside the door.

The most insistent of the ladies was a Mrs. Coots, who considered that Providence had sent her Milly as a companion. If she had heard Milly's story in the street she wouldn't have listened to a word, but print makes things respectable. After it got into the "Franco-American Star," Mrs. Coots was sure Milly wouldn't make off with her jewels.

"I'll pay you well, my dear," she insisted shrilly. "Twenty-five a week. How's that?"

Milly cast an anxious glance at Mrs. Horton's faded, pleasant face.

"I don't know—" she said hesitantly.

"I can't pay you anything," said Mrs. Horton, who was confused by Mrs. Coots' affluent, positive manner. "You do as you like. I'd love to have you."

"You've certainly been kind," said Milly, "but I don't want to impose—"

Driscoll, who had been walking up and down with his hands in his pockets, stopped and turned toward her quickly.

"I'll take care of that," he said quickly. "You don't have to worry about that."

Mrs. Coots' eyes flashed at him indignantly.

"She's better with me," she insisted. "Much better." She turned to the secretary and remarked in a pained, disapproving stage whisper, "Who is this forward young man?"

Again Milly looked appealingly at Mrs. Horton.

"If it's not too much trouble I'd rather stay with you," she said. "I'll help you all I can—"

It took another half hour to get rid of Mrs. Coots, but finally it was arranged that Milly was to stay at Mrs. Horton's pension, until some trace of her husband was found. Later the same day they ascertained that the American Bureau of Military Graves had never heard of Jim Cooley—he had no job promised him in France.

However distressing her situation, Milly was young and she was in Paris in mid-June. She decided to enjoy herself. At Mr. Bill Driscoll's invitation she went on an excursion to Versailles next day in his rubberneck wagon. She had never been on such a trip before. She sat among garment buyers from Sioux City and school teachers from California and honeymoon couples from Japan and was whirled through fifteen centuries of Paris, while Bill stood up in front with the megaphone pressed to his voluble and original mouth.

"Building on our left is the Louvre, ladies and gentlemen. Excursion number twenty-three leaving tomorrow at ten sharp takes you inside. Sufficient to remark now that it contains fifteen thousand works of art of every description. The oil used in its oil paintings would lubricate all the cars in the state of Oregon over a period of two years. The frames alone if placed end to end—"

Milly watched him, believing every word. It was hard to remember that he had come to her rescue that night. Heroes weren't like that—she knew; she had lived with one. They brooded constantly on their achievements and retailed them to strangers at least once a day. When she had thanked this young man he told her gravely that Mr. Carnegie had been trying to get him on the ouija board all that day.

After a dramatic stop before the house in which Landru, the Bluebeard of France, had murdered his fourteen wives, the expedition proceeded on to Versailles. There, in the great hall of mirrors, Bill Driscoll delved into the forgotten scandal of the eighteenth century as he described the meeting between "Louie's girl and Louie's wife."

"Du Barry skipped in, wearing a creation of mauve georgette, held out by bronze hoops over a tablier of champagne lace. The gown had a ruched collarette of Swedish fox, lined with yellow satin fulgurante which matched the hansom that brought her to the party. She was nervous, ladies. She didn't know how the queen was going to take it. After awhile the queen walked in wearing an oxidized silver gown with collar, cuffs and flounces of Russian ermine and strappings of dentist's gold. The bodice was cut with a very long waistline and the skirt arranged full in front and falling in picot-edged points tipped with the crown jewels. When Du Barry saw her she leaned over to King Louie and whispered: 'Royal Honeyboy, who's that lady with all the laundry on that just came in the door?'

"'That isn't a lady,' said Louie. 'That's my wife.'

"Most of the Court almost broke their contracts laughing. The ones that didn't died in the Bastille."

That was the first of many trips that Milly took in the rubberneck wagon—to Malmaison, to Passy, to St-Cloud. The weeks passed, three of them, and still there was no word from Jim Cooley, who seemed to have stepped off the face of the earth when he vanished from the train.

In spite of a sort of dull worry that possessed her when she thought of her situation, Milly was happier than she had ever been. It was a relief to be rid of the incessant depression of living with a morbid and broken man. Moreover, it was thrilling to be in Paris when it seemed that all the world was there, when each arriving boat dumped a new thousand into the pleasure ground, when the streets were so clogged with sight-seers that Bill Driscoll's buses were reserved for days ahead. And it was pleasantest of all to stroll down to the corner and watch the blood-red sun sink like a slow penny into the Seine while she sipped coffee with Bill Driscoll at a café.

"How would you like to go to Château-Thierry with me tomorrow?" he asked her one evening.

The name struck a chord in Milly. It was at Château-Thierry that Jim Cooley, at the risk of his life, had made his daring expedition between the lines.

"My husband was there," she said proudly.

"So was I," he remarked. "And I didn't have any fun at all."

He thought for a moment.

"How old are you?" he asked suddenly.

"Eighteen."

"Why don't you go to a lawyer and get a divorce?"

The suggestion shocked Milly.

"I think you'd better," he continued, looking down at the pavement. "It's easier here than anywhere else. Then you'd be free."

"I couldn't," she said, frightened. "It wouldn't be fair. You see, he doesn't—"

"I know," he interrupted. "But I'm beginning to think that you're spoiling your life with this man. Is there anything except his war record to his credit?"

"Isn't that enough?" answered Milly gravely.

"Milly—" He raised his eyes. "Won't you think it over carefully?"

She got up uneasily. He looked very honest and safe and cool sitting there, and for a moment she was tempted to do what he said, to put the whole thing in his hands. But looking at him she saw now what she hadn't seen before, that the advice was not disinterested— there was more than an impersonal care for her future in his eyes. She turned away with a mixture of emotions.

Side by side, and in silence, they walked back towards the pension. From a high window the plaintive wail of a violin drifted down into the street, mingling with practice chords from an invisible piano and a shrill incomprehensible quarrel of French children over the way. The twilight was fast dissolving into a starry blue Parisian evening, but it was still light enough for them to make out the figure of Mrs. Horton standing in front of the pension. She came towards them swiftly, talking as she came.

"I've got some news for you," she said. "The secretary of the American Aid Society just telephoned. They've located your husband, and he'll be in Paris the day after tomorrow."

IV

When Jim Cooley, the war hero, left the train at the small town of Evreux, he walked very fast until he was several hundred yards from the station. Then, standing behind a tree, he watched until the train pulled out and the last puff of smoke burst up behind a little hill. He stood for several minutes, laughing and looking after the train, until abruptly his face resumed his normal injured expression and he turned to examine the place in which he had chosen to be free.

It was a sleepy provincial village with two high lines of silver sycamores along its principal street, at the end of which a fine fountain purred crystal water from a cat's mouth of cold stone. Around the fountain was a square and on the sidewalks of the square several groups of small iron tables indicated open-air cafés. A farm wagon drawn by a single white ox was toiling toward the fountain and several cheap French cars, together with a 1910 Ford, were parked at intervals along the street.

"It's a hick town," he said to himself with some disgust. "Reg'lar hick town."

But it was peaceful and green, and he caught sight of two stockingless ladies entering the door of a shop—and the little tables by the fountain were inviting. He walked up the street and at the first café sat down and ordered a large beer.

"I'm free," he said to himself. "Free, by God!"

His decision to desert Milly had been taken suddenly—in Cherbourg, as they got on the train. Just at that moment he had seen a little French girl who was the real thing, and he realized that he didn't want Milly "hanging on him" anymore. Even on the boat he had played with the idea, but until Cherbourg he had never quite made up his mind. He was rather sorry now that he hadn't thought to leave Milly a little money, enough for one night—but then somebody would be sure to help her when she got to Paris. Besides, what he didn't know didn't worry him, and he wasn't going ever to hear about her again.

"Cognac this time," he said to the waiter.

He needed something strong. He wanted to forget. Not to forget Milly, that was easy, she was already behind him; but to forget himself. He felt that he had been abused. He felt that it was Milly who had deserted him, or at least that her cold mistrust was responsible for driving him away. What good would it have done if he had gone on to Paris anyways? There wasn't enough money left to keep two people for very long—and he had invented the job on the strength of a vague rumor that the American Bureau of Military Graves gave jobs to veterans who were broke in France. He shouldn't have brought Milly, wouldn't have if he had had the money to get over. But, though he was not aware of it, there was another reason why he had brought Milly. Jim Cooley hated to be alone.

"Cognac," he said to the waiter. "A big one. *Très grand*."

He put his hand in his pocket and fingered the blue notes that had been given him in Cherbourg in exchange for his American money. He took them out and counted them. Crazy-looking kale. It was funny you could buy things with it just like you could do with the real mazuma.

He beckoned to the waiter.

"Hey!" he remarked conversationally. "This is funny money you got here, ain't it?"

But the waiter spoke no English and was unable to satisfy Jim Cooley's craving for companionship. Never mind. His nerves were at rest now—body was glowing triumphantly from top to toe.

"This is the life," he muttered to himself. "Only live once. Might as well enjoy it." And then aloud to the waiter, "'Nother one of those big cognacs. Two of them. I'm set to go."

He went—for several hours. He awoke at dawn in a bedroom of a small inn, with red streaks in his eyes and fever pounding in his head. He was afraid to look in his pockets until he had ordered and swallowed another cognac, and then he found that his worst fears were justified. Of the ninety-odd dollars with which he had got off the train only six were left.

"I must have been crazy," he whispered to himself.

There remained his watch. His watch was large and methodical, and on the outer case two hearts were picked out in diamonds from the dark solid gold. It had been part of the booty of Jim Cooley's heroism, for when he had located the paper in the German officer's pocket he had found it clasped tight in the dead hand. One of the diamond hearts probably stood for some human grief back in Friedland or Berlin, but when Jim married he told Milly that the diamond hearts stood for their hearts and would be a token of their everlasting love. Before Milly fully appreciated this sentimental suggestion their enduring love had been tarnished beyond repair and the watch went back into Jim's pocket where it confined itself to marking time instead of emotion.

But Jim Cooley had loved to show the watch, and he found that parting with it would be much more painful than parting with

Milly—so painful, in fact, that he got drunk in anticipation of his sorrow. Late that afternoon, already a reeling figure at which the town boys jeered along the streets, he found his way into the shop of a *bijoutier*, and when he issued forth into the street he was in possession of a ticket of redemption and a note for two thousand francs which, he figured dimly, was about one hundred and twenty dollars. Muttering to himself, he stumbled back to the square.

"One American can lick three Frenchmen!" he remarked to three small stout bourgeois drinking their beer at a table.

They paid no attention. He repeated his jeer.

"One American—" tapping his chest, "can beat up three dirty frogs, see?"

Still they didn't move. It infuriated him. Lurching forward, he seized the back of an unoccupied chair and pulled at it. In what seemed less than a minute there was a small crowd around him and the three Frenchmen were all talking at once in excited voices.

"Aw, go on, I meant what I said!" he cried savagely. "One American can wipe up the ground with three Frenchmen!"

And now there were two men in uniform before him—two men with revolver holsters on their hips, dressed in red and blue.

"You heard what I said," he shouted. "I'm a hero—I'm not afraid of the whole damn French army!"

A hand fell on his arm, but with blind passion he wrenched it free and struck at the black mustached face before him. Then there was a rushing, crashing noise in his ears as fists and then feet struck at him, and the world seemed to close like water over his head.

V

When they located him and, after a personal expedition by one of the American vice consuls, got him out of jail, Milly realized how much these weeks had meant to her. The holiday was over. But even though Jim would be in Paris tomorrow, even though the dreary round of her life with him was due to recommence, Milly decided to take the trip to Château-Thierry just the same. She wanted a last few hours of happiness that she could always remember. She supposed they would return to New York—what chance Jim might have had of obtaining a position had vanished now that he was marked by a fortnight in a French prison.

The bus, as usual, was crowded. As they approached the little village of Château-Thierry, Bill Driscoll stood up in front with his megaphone and began to tell his clients how it had looked to him when his division went up to the line five years before.

"It was nine o'clock at night," he said, "and we came out of a wood and there was the Western Front. I'd read about it for three years back in America, and here it was at last—it looked like the line of a forest fire at night except that fireworks were blazing up instead of grass. We relieved a French regiment in new trenches that weren't three feet deep. At that, most of us were too excited to be scared until the top sergeant was blown to pieces with shrapnel about two o'clock in the morning. That made us think. Two days later we went over and the only reason I didn't get hit was that I was shaking so much they couldn't aim at me."

The listeners laughed and Milly felt a faint thrill of pride. Jim hadn't been scared—she'd heard him say so, many times. All he'd thought about was doing a little more than his duty. When others were in the comparative safety of the trenches he had gone into no-man's land alone.

After lunch in the village the party walked over the battlefield, changed now into a peaceful undulating valley of graves. Milly was glad she had come—the sense of rest after a struggle soothed her. Perhaps after the bleak future, her life might be quiet as this peaceful land. Perhaps Jim would change someday. If he had risen once to such a height of courage there must be something deep inside him that was worth while, that would make him try once more.

Just before it was time to start home Driscoll, who had hardly spoken to her all day, suddenly beckoned her aside.

"I want to talk to you for the last time," he said.

The last time— Milly felt a flutter of unexpected pain. Was tomorrow so near?

"I'm going to say what's in my mind," he said, "and please don't be angry. I love you, and you know it; but what I'm going to say isn't because of that—it's because I want you to be happy."

Milly nodded. She was afraid she was going to cry.

"I don't think your husband's any good," he said.

She looked up.

"You don't know him," she exclaimed quickly. "You can't judge."

"I can judge from what he did to you. I think this shell-shock business is all a plain lie. And what does it matter what he did five years ago?"

"It matters to me," cried Milly. She felt herself growing a little angry. "You can't take that away from him. He acted brave."

Driscoll nodded.

"That's true. But other men were brave."

"You weren't," she said scornfully. "You just said you were scared to death—and when you said it all the people laughed. Well, nobody laughed at Jim—they gave him a medal because he wasn't afraid."

When Milly had said this she was sorry, but it was too late now. At his next words she leaned forward in surprise.

"That was a lie too," said Bill Driscoll slowly. "I told it because I wanted them to laugh. I wasn't even in the attack."

He stared silently down the hill.

"Well then," said Milly contemptuously, "how can you sit here and say things about my husband when—when you didn't even—"

"It was only a professional lie," he said impatiently. "I happened to be wounded the night before."

He stood up suddenly.

"There's no use," he said. "I seem to have made you hate me, and that's the end. There's no use saying any more."

He stared down the hill with haunted eyes.

"I shouldn't have talked to you here," he cried. "There's no luck here for me. Once before I lost something I wanted, not a hundred yards from this hill. And now I've lost you."

"What was it you lost," demanded Milly bitterly. "Another girl?"

"There's never been any other girl but you."

"What was it then?"

He hesitated.

"I told you I was wounded," he said. "I was. For two months I didn't know I was alive. But the worst of it was that some dirty sneak thief had been through my pockets, and I guess he got the credit for a copy of German orders that I'd just brought in. He took a gold watch too. I'd pinched them both off the body of a German officer out between the lines."

Mr. and Mrs. William Driscoll were married the following spring and started off on their honeymoon in a car that was much larger than the King of England's. There were two dozen vacant places in it, so they gave many rides to tired pedestrians along the white poplar-lined roads of France. The wayfarers, however, always sat in the back seat as the conversation in front was not for profane ears. The tour progressed through Lyons, Avignon, Bordeaux, and smaller places not in the guidebook.

PRESUMPTION

Sitting by the window and staring out into the early autumn dusk, San Juan Chandler remembered only that Noel was coming tomorrow; but when, with a romantic sound that was half gasp, half sigh, he turned from the window, snapped on the light and looked at himself in the mirror, his expression became more materially complicated. He leaned closer. Delicacy balked at the abominable word "pimple," but some such blemish had undoubtedly appeared on his cheek within the last hour, and now formed, with a pair from last week, a distressing constellation of three. Going into the bathroom adjoining his room—Juan had never possessed a bathroom to himself before—he opened a medicine closet, and after peering about, carefully extracted a promising-looking jar of black ointment and covered each slight protuberance with a black gluey mound. Then, strangely dotted, he returned to the bedroom, put out the light and resumed his vigil over the shadowy garden.

He waited. That roof among the trees on the hill belonged to Noel Garneau's house. She was coming back to it tomorrow; he would see her there. . . . A loud clock on the staircase inside struck seven. Juan went to the glass and removed the ointment with a handkerchief. To his chagrin, the spots were still there, even slightly irritated from the chemical sting of the remedy. That settled it—no more chocolate malted milks or eating between meals during his visit to Culpepper Bay. Taking the lid from the jar of talcum he had observed on the dressing table, he touched the laden puff to his cheek. Immediately his brows and lashes bloomed with snow and he coughed chokingly, observing that the triangle of humiliation was still observable upon his otherwise handsome face.

"Disgusting," he muttered to himself. "I never saw anything so disgusting." At twenty, such childish phenomena should be behind him.

Downstairs three gongs, melodious and metallic, hummed and sang. He listened for a moment, fascinated. Then he wiped the powder from his face, ran a comb through his yellow hair and went down to dinner.

Dinner at Cousin Cora's he had found embarrassing. She was so stiff and formal about things like that, and so familiar about Juan's private affairs. The first night of his visit he had tried politely to pull out her chair and bumped into the maid; the second night he remembered the experience—but so did the maid, and Cousin Cora seated herself unassisted. At home Juan was accustomed to behave as he liked; like all children of deferent and indulgent mothers, he lacked both confidence and good manners.

Tonight there were guests.

"This is San Juan Chandler, my cousin's son—Mrs. Holyoke—and Mr. Holyoke."

The phrase "my cousin's son" seemed to explain him away, seemed to account for his being in Miss Chandler's house: "You understand—we must have our poor relations with us occasionally." But a tone which implied that would be rude—and certainly Cousin Cora, with all her social position, couldn't be rude.

Mr. and Mrs. Holyoke acknowledged the introduction politely and coolly, and dinner was served. The conversation, dictated by Cousin Cora, bored Juan. It was about the garden and about her father, for whom she lived and who was dying slowly and unwillingly upstairs. Toward the salad Juan was wedged into the conversation by a question from Mr. Holyoke and a quick look from his cousin.

"I'm just staying for a week," he answered politely; "then I've got to go home, because college opens pretty soon."

"Where are you at college?"

Juan named his college, adding almost apologetically, "You see, my father went there."

He wished that he could have answered that he was at Yale or Princeton, where he had wanted to go. He was prominent at Henderson and belonged to a good fraternity, but it annoyed him when people occasionally failed to recognize his alma mater's name.

"I suppose you've met all the young people here," supposed Mrs. Holyoke—"my daughter?"

"Oh, yes"—her daughter was the dumpy, ugly girl with the thick spectacles—"oh, yes." And he added, "I knew some people who lived here before I came."

"The little Garneau girl," explained Cousin Cora.

"Oh, yes. Noel Garneau," agreed Mrs. Holyoke. "Her mother's a great beauty. How old is Noel now? She must be—"

"Seventeen," supplied Juan; "but she's old for her age."

"Juan met her on a ranch last summer. They were on a ranch together. What is it that they call those ranches, Juan?"

"Dude ranches."

"Dude ranches. Juan and another boy worked for their board." Juan saw no reason why Cousin Cora should have supplied this information; she continued on an even more annoying note: "Noel's mother sent her out there to keep her out of mischief, but Juan says the ranch was pretty gay itself."

Mr. Holyoke supplied a welcome change of subject.

"Your name is—" he inquired, smiling and curious.

"San Juan Chandler. My father was wounded in the battle of San Juan Hill and so they called me after it—like Kenesaw Mountain Landis."

He had explained this so many times that the sentences rolled off automatically—in school he had been called Santy, in college he was Don.

"You must come to dinner while you're here," said Mrs. Holyoke vaguely.

The conversation slipped away from him as he realized freshly, strongly, that Noel would arrive tomorrow. And she was coming because he was here. She had cut short a visit in the Adirondacks on receipt of his letter. Would she like him now—in this place that was so different from Montana? There was a spaciousness, an air of money and pleasure about Culpepper Bay for which San Juan Chandler—a shy, handsome, spoiled, brilliant, penniless boy from a small Ohio city—was unprepared. At home, where his father was a retired clergyman, Juan went with the nice people. He didn't realize until this visit to a fashionable New England resort that where there are enough rich families to form a self-sufficient and exclusive group, such a group is invariably formed. On the dude ranch they had all dressed alike; here his ready-made Prince of Wales suit seemed exaggerated in style, his hat correct only in theory—an imitation hat—his very ties only projections of the ineffable Platonic ties which were worn here at Culpepper Bay. Yet all the differences were so small that he was unable quite to discern them.

But from the morning three days ago when he had stepped off the train into a group of young people who were waiting at the station for some friend of their own, he had been uneasy; and Cousin Cora's introductions, which seemed to foist him horribly upon whomever he was introduced to, did not lessen his discomfort. He thought mechanically that she was being kind, and considered himself lucky that her invitation had coincided with his wild desire to see Noel Garneau again. He did not realize that in three days he had come to hate Cousin Cora's cold and snobbish patronage.

Noel's fresh, adventurous voice on the telephone next morning made his own voice quiver with nervous happiness. She would call for him at two and they would spend the afternoon together. All morning he lay in the garden, trying unsuccessfully to renew his summer tan in the mild lemon light of the September sun, sitting up quickly whenever he heard the sound of Cousin Cora's garden shears at the end of a neighboring border. He was back in his room, still meddling desperately with the white powder puff, when Noel's roadster stopped outside and she came up the front walk.

Noel's eyes were dark blue, almost violet, and her lips, Juan had often thought, were like very small, very soft, red cushions—only cushions sounded all wrong, for they were really the most delicate lips in the world. When she talked they parted to the shape of "Oo!" and her eyes opened wide as though she was torn between tears and laughter at the poignancy of what she was saying. Already, at seventeen, she knew that men hung on her words in a way that frightened her. To Juan, her most indifferent remarks assumed a highly ponderable significance and begot an intensity in him—a fact which Noel had several times found somewhat of a strain.

He ran downstairs, down the gravel path toward her.

"Noel, my dear," he wanted so much to say, "you are the loveliest thing—the loveliest thing. My heart turns over when I see your beautiful face and smell that sweet fresh smell you have around you."

That would have been the precious, the irreplaceable truth. Instead he faltered, "Why, hello, Noel! How are you? . . . Well, I certainly am glad. Well, is this your car? What kind is it? Well, you certainly look fine."

And he couldn't look at her, because when he did his face seemed to him to be working idiotically—like someone else's face. He got in, they drove off and he made a mighty effort to compose himself; but as her hand left the steering wheel to fall lightly on his, a perverse instinct made him jerk his hand away. Noel perceived the embarrassment and was puzzled and sorry.

They went to the tennis tournament at the Culpepper Club. He was so little aware of anything except Noel that later he told Cousin Cora they hadn't seen the tennis, and believed it himself.

Afterward they loitered about the grounds, stopped by innumerable people who welcomed Noel home. Two men made him uneasy—one a small handsome youth of his own age with shining brown eyes that were bright as the glass eyes of a stuffed owl, the other a tall, languid dandy of twenty-five who was introduced to her, Juan rightly deduced, at his own request.

When they were in a group of girls he was more comfortable. He was able to talk, because being with Noel gave him confidence before these others, and his confidence before others made him more confident with Noel. The situation improved.

There was one girl, a sharp, pretty blonde named Holly Morgan, with whom he had spent some facetiously sentimental hours the day before, and in order to show Noel that he had been able to take care of himself before her return he made a point of talking aside to Holly Morgan. Holly was not responsive. Juan was Noel's property, and though Holly liked him, she did not like him nearly well enough to annoy Noel.

"What time do you want me for dinner, Noel?" she asked.

"Eight o'clock," said Noel. "Billy Harper'll call for you."

Juan felt a twinge of disappointment. He had thought that he and Noel were to be alone for dinner; that afterward they would have a long talk on the dark verandah and he would kiss her lips as he had upon that never-to-be-forgotten Montana night, and give her his D.K.E. pin to wear. Perhaps the others would leave early—he had told Holly Morgan of his love for Noel; she should have sense enough to know.

At twilight Noel dropped him at Miss Chandler's gate, lingered for a moment with the engine cut off. The promise of the evening—the first lights in the houses along the bay, the sound of a remote piano, the little coolness in the wind—swung them both up suddenly into that paradise which Juan, drunk with ecstasy and terror, had been unable to evoke.

"Are you glad to see me?" she whispered.

"Am I glad?" The words trembled on his tongue. Miserably he struggled to bend his emotion into a phrase, a look, a gesture, but his mind chilled at the thought that nothing, nothing, nothing could express what he felt in his heart.

"You embarrass me," he said wretchedly. "I don't know what to say."

Noel waited, attuned to what she expected, sympathetic, but too young quite to see that behind that mask of egotism, of moody childishness, which the intensity of Juan's devotion compelled him to wear, there was a tremendous emotion.

"Don't be embarrassed," Noel said. She was listening to the music now, a tune they had danced to in the Adirondacks. The wings of a trance folded about her and the inscrutable someone who waited always in the middle distance loomed down over her with passionate words and dark romantic eyes. Almost mechanically, she started the engine and slipped the gear into first.

"At eight o'clock," she said, almost abstractedly. "Good-bye, Juan."

The car moved off down the road. At the corner she turned and waved her hand and Juan waved back, happier than he had ever been in his life, his soul dissolved to a sweet gas that buoyed up his body like a balloon. Then the roadster was out of sight and, all unaware, he had lost her.

II

Cousin Cora's chauffeur took him to Noel's door. The other male guest, Billy Harper, was, he discovered, the young man with the bright brown eyes whom he had met that afternoon. Juan was afraid of him; he was on such familiar, facetious terms with the two girls—toward Noel his attitude seemed almost irreverent—that Juan was slighted during the conversation at dinner. They talked of the Adirondacks and they all seemed to know the group who had been there. Noel and Holly spoke of boys at Cambridge and New Haven and of how wonderful it was that they were going to school in New York this winter. Juan meant to invite Noel to the autumn dance at his college, but he thought that he had better wait and do it in a letter, later on. He was glad when dinner was over.

The girls went upstairs. Juan and Billy Harper smoked.

"She certainly is attractive," broke out Juan suddenly, his repression bursting into words.

"Who? Noel?"

"Yes."

"She's a nice girl," agreed Harper gravely.

Juan fingered the D.K.E. pin in his pocket.

"She's wonderful," he said. "I like Holly Morgan pretty well— I was handing her a sort of line yesterday afternoon—but Noel's really the most attractive girl I ever knew."

Harper looked at him curiously, but Juan, released from the enforced and artificial smile of dinner, continued enthusiastically: "Of course it's silly to fool with two girls. I mean, you've got to be careful not to get in too deep."

Billy Harper didn't answer. Noel and Holly came downstairs. Holly suggested bridge, but Juan didn't play bridge, so they sat talking by the fire. In some fashion Noel and Billy Harper became involved in a conversation about dates and friends, and Juan began boasting to Holly Morgan, who sat beside him on the sofa.

"You must come to a prom at college," he said suddenly. "Why don't you? It's a small college, but we have the best bunch in our house and the proms are fun."

"I'd love it."

"You'd only have to meet the people in our house."

"What's that?"

"D.K.E." He drew the pin from his pocket. "See?"

Holly examined it, laughed and handed it back.

"I wanted to go to Yale," he went on, "but my family always go to the same place."

"I love Yale," said Holly.

"Yes," he agreed vaguely, half hearing her, his mind moving between himself and Noel. "You must come up. I'll write you about it."

Time passed. Holly played the piano, Noel took a ukulele from the top of the piano, strummed it and hummed. Billy Harper turned the pages of the music. Juan listened, restless, unamused. Then they sauntered out into the dark garden, and finding himself beside Noel at last, Juan walked her quickly ahead until they were alone.

"Noel," he whispered, "here's my Deke pin. I want you to have it."

She looked at him expressionlessly.

"I saw you offering it to Holly Morgan," she said.

"Noel," he cried in alarm, "I wasn't offering it to her. I just showed it to her. Why, Noel, do you think—"

"You invited her to the prom."

"I didn't. I was just being nice to her."

The others were close behind. She took the Deke pin quickly and put her finger to his lips in a facile gesture of caress.

He did not realize that she had not been really angry about the pin or the prom, and that his unfortunate egotism was forfeiting her interest.

At eleven o'clock Holly said she must go, and Billy Harper drove his car to the front door.

"I'm going to stay a few minutes if you don't mind," said Juan, standing in the door with Noel. "I can walk home."

Holly and Billy Harper drove away. Noel and Juan strolled back into the drawing room, where she avoided the couch and sat down in a chair.

"Let's go out on the verandah," suggested Juan uncertainly.

"Why?"

"Please, Noel."

Unwillingly she obeyed. They sat side by side on a canvas settee and he put his arm around her.

"Kiss me," he whispered. She had never seemed so desirable to him before.

"No."

"Why not?"

"I don't want to. I don't kiss people anymore."

"But—me?" he demanded incredulously.

"I've kissed too many people. I'll have nothing left if I keep on kissing people."

"But you'll kiss me, Noel?"

"Why?"

He could not even say, "Because I love you." But he could say it, he knew that he could say it, when she was in his arms.

"If I kiss you once, will you go home?"

"Why, do you want me to go home?"

"I'm tired. I was traveling last night and I can never sleep on a train. Can you? I can never—"

Her tendency to leave the subject willingly made him frantic.

"Then kiss me once," he insisted.

"You promise?"

"You kiss me first."

"No, Juan, you promise first."

"Don't you want to kiss me?"

"Oh-h-h!" she groaned.

With gathering anxiety Juan promised and took her in his arms. For one moment at the touch of her lips, the feeling of her, of Noel, close to him, he forgot the evening, forgot himself—rather became the inspired, romantic self that she had known. But it was too late. Her hands were on his shoulders, pushing him away.

"You promised."

"Noel—"

She got up. Confused and unsatisfied, he followed her to the door.

"Noel—"

"Good-night, Juan."

As they stood on the doorstep her eyes rose over the line of dark trees toward the ripe harvest moon. Some glowing thing would happen to her soon, she thought, her mind far away. Something that would dominate her, snatch her up out of life, helpless, ecstatic, exalted.

"Good-night, Noel. Noel, please—"

"Good-night, Juan. Remember we're going swimming tomorrow. It's wonderful to see you again. Good-night."

She closed the door.

III

Toward morning he awoke from a broken sleep, wondering if she had not kissed him because of the three spots on his cheek. He turned on the light and looked at them. Two were almost invisible. He went into the bathroom, doused all three with the black ointment and crept back into bed.

Cousin Cora greeted him stiffly at breakfast next morning.

"You kept your great-uncle awake last night," she said. "He heard you moving around in your room."

"I only moved twice," he said unhappily. "I'm terribly sorry."

"He has to have his sleep, you know. We all have to be more considerate when there's someone sick. Young people don't always think of that. And he was so unusually well when you came."

It was Sunday, and they were to go swimming at Holly Morgan's house, where a crowd always collected on the bright easy beach. Noel called for him, but they arrived before any of his half-humble remarks about the night before had managed to attract her attention. He spoke to those he knew and was introduced to others, made ill at ease again by their cheerful familiarity with one another, by the correct informality of their clothes. He was sure they noticed that he had worn only one suit during his visit to Culpepper Bay, varying it with white flannel trousers. Both pairs of trousers were out of press now, and after keeping his great-uncle awake, he had not felt like bothering Cousin Cora about it at breakfast.

Again he tried to talk to Holly, with the vague idea of making Noel jealous, but Holly was busy and she eluded him. It was ten minutes before he extricated himself from a conversation with the obnoxious Miss Holyoke. At the moment he managed this he perceived to his horror that Noel was gone.

When he last saw her she had been engaged in a light but somehow intent conversation with the tall well-dressed stranger she had met yesterday. Now she wasn't in sight. Miserable and horribly alone, he strolled up and down the beach, trying to look as if he were having a good time, seeming to watch the bathers, but keeping a sharp eye out for Noel. He felt that his self-conscious perambulations were attracting unbearable attention, and sat down unhappily on a sand dune beside Billy Harper. But Billy Harper was neither cordial nor communicative, and after a minute hailed a man across the beach and went to talk to him.

Juan was desperate. When, suddenly, he spied Noel coming down from the house with the tall man, he stood up with a jerk, convinced that his features were working wildly.

She waved at him.

"A buckle came off my shoe," she called. "I went to have it put on. I thought you'd gone in swimming."

He stood perfectly still, not trusting his voice to answer. He understood that she was through with him; there was someone else. Immediately he wanted above all things to be away. As they came nearer, the tall man glanced at him negligently and resumed his vivacious, intimate conversation with Noel. A group suddenly closed around them.

Keeping the group in the corner of his eye, Juan began to move carefully and steadily toward the gate that led to the road. He started when the casual voice of a man behind him said "Going?" and he answered "Got to" with what purported to be a reluctant nod. Once behind the shelter of the parked cars, he began to run, slowed down as several chauffeurs looked at him curiously. It was a mile and a half to the Chandler house and the day was broiling, but he walked fast lest Noel, leaving the party— "with that man," he thought bitterly— should overtake him trudging along the road. That would be more than he could bear.

There was the sound of a car behind him. Immediately Juan left the road and sought concealment behind a convenient hedge. It was no one from the party, but thereafter he kept an eye out for available cover, walking fast, or even running, over unpromising open spaces.

He was within sight of his cousin's house when it happened. Hot and disheveled, he had scarcely flattened himself against the back of a tree when Noel's roadster, with the tall man at the wheel, flashed by down the road. Juan stepped out and looked after them. Then, blind with sweat and misery, he continued on toward home.

IV

At luncheon, Cousin Cora looked at him closely.

"What's the trouble?" she inquired. "Did something go wrong at the beach this morning?"

"Why, no," he exclaimed in simulated astonishment. "What made you think that?"

"You have such a funny look. I thought perhaps you'd had some trouble with the little Garneau girl."

He hated her.

"No, not at all."

"You don't want to get any idea in your head about her," said Cousin Cora.

"What do you mean?" He knew with a start what she meant.

"Any ideas about Noel Garneau. You've got your own way to make." Juan's face burned. He was unable to answer. "I say that in all kindness. You're not in any position to think anything serious about Noel Garneau."

Her implications cut deeper than her words. Oh, he had seen well enough that he was not essentially of Noel's sort, that being nice in Akron wasn't enough at Culpepper Bay. He had that realization that comes to all boys in his position that for every advantage—that was what his mother called this visit to Cousin Cora's—he paid a harrowing price in self-esteem. But a world so hard as to admit such an intolerable state of affairs was beyond his comprehension. His mind rejected it all completely, as it had rejected the dictionary name for the three spots on his face. He wanted to let go, to vanish, to be home. He determined to go home tomorrow, but after this heart-rending conversation he decided to put off the announcement until tonight.

That afternoon he took a detective story from the library and retired upstairs to read on his bed. He finished the book by four o'clock and came down to change it for another. Cousin Cora was on the verandah arranging three tables for tea.

"I thought you were at the club," she exclaimed in surprise. "I thought you'd gone up to the club."

"I'm tired," he said. "I thought I'd read."

"Tired!" she exclaimed. "A boy your age! You ought to be out in the open air playing golf—that's why you have that spot on your cheek"—Juan winced; his experiments with the black salve had irritated it to a sharp redness—"instead of lying around reading on a day like this."

"I haven't any clubs," said Juan hurriedly.

"Mr. Holyoke told you you could use his brother's clubs. He spoke to the caddie master. Run on now. You'll find lots of young people up there who want to play. I'll begin to think you're not having a good time."

In agony Juan saw himself dubbing about the course alone— seeing Noel coming under his eye. He never wanted to see Noel again except out in Montana—some bright day, when she would come saying, "Juan, I never knew—never understood what your love was."

Suddenly he remembered that Noel had gone into Boston for the afternoon. She would not be there. The horror of playing alone suddenly vanished.

The caddie master looked at him disapprovingly as he displayed his guest card, and Juan nervously bought a half dozen balls at a dollar each in an effort to neutralize the imagined hostility. On the first tee he glanced around. It was after four and there was no one in sight except two old men practicing drives from the top of a little hill. As he addressed his ball he heard someone come up on the tee behind him, and he breathed easier at the sharp crack that sent his ball a hundred and fifty yards down the fairway.

"Playing alone?"

He looked around. A stout man of fifty, with a huge face, high forehead, long wide upper lip and great undershot jaw, was taking a driver from a bulging bag.

"Why—yes."

"Mind if I go 'round with you?"

"Not at all."

Juan greeted the suggestion with a certain gloomy relief. They were evenly matched, the older man's steady short shots keeping pace with Juan's occasional brilliancy. Not until the seventh hole did the conversation rise above the fragmentary boasting and formalized praise which forms the small talk of golf.

"Haven't seen you around before."

"I'm just visiting here," Juan explained, "staying with my cousin, Miss Chandler."

"Oh, yes—know Miss Chandler very well. Nice old snob."

"What?" inquired Juan.

"Nice old snob, I said. No offense. . . . Your honor, I think."

Not for several holes did Juan venture to comment on his partner's remark.

"What do you mean when you say she's a nice old snob?" he inquired with interest.

"Oh, it's an old quarrel between Miss Chandler and me," answered the older man brusquely. "She's an old friend of my wife's. When we were married and came out to Culpepper Bay for the summer, she tried to freeze us out. Said my wife had no business marrying me—I was an outsider."

"What did you do?"

"We just let her alone. She came 'round, but naturally I never had much love for her. She even tried to put her oar in before we were married." He laughed. "Cora Chandler of Boston—how she used to boss the girls around in those days! At twenty-five she had the sharpest tongue in Back Bay. They were old people there, you know—Emerson and Whittier to dinner and all that. My wife belonged to that crowd too. I was from the Middle West. . . . Oh, too bad. I should have stopped talking. That makes me two up again."

Suddenly Juan wanted to present his case to this man—not quite as it was, but adorned with a dignity and significance it did not so far possess. It began to round out in his mind as the sempiternal struggle of the poor young man against a snobbish, purse-proud world. This new aspect was comforting, and he put out of his mind the less pleasant realization that, superficially at least, money hadn't entered into it. He knew in his heart that it was his unfortunate egotism that had repelled Noel, his embarrassment, his absurd attempt to make her jealous with Holly. Only indirectly was his poverty concerned; under different circumstances it might have given a touch of romance.

"I know exactly how you must have felt," he broke out suddenly as they walked toward the tenth tee. "I haven't any money and I'm in love with a girl who has—and it just seems as if every busybody in the world is determined to keep us apart."

For a moment Juan believed this. His companion looked at him sharply.

"Does the girl care about you?" he inquired.

"Yes."

"Well, go after her, young man. All the money in this world hasn't been made by a long shot."

"I'm still in college," said Juan, suddenly taken aback.

"Won't she wait for you?"

"I don't know. You see, the pressure's pretty strong. Her family want her to marry a rich man"—his mind visualized the tall well-dressed stranger of this morning and invention soared—"an easterner that's visiting here, and I'm afraid they'll all sweep her off her feet. If it's not this man, it's the next."

His friend considered.

"You can't have everything, you know," he said presently. "I'm the last man to advise a young man to leave college, especially when I don't know anything about him or his abilities; but if it's going to break you up not to get her, you better think about getting to work."

"I've been considering that," said Juan, frowning. The idea was ten seconds old in his mind.

"All the girls are crazy now, anyhow," broke out the older man. "They begin to think of men at fifteen, and by the time they're seventeen they've run off with the chauffeur next door."

"That's true," agreed Juan absently. He was absorbed in the previous suggestion. "The trouble is that I don't live in Boston. If I left college I'd want to be near her, because it might be a few months before I'd be able to support her. And I don't know how I'd go about getting a position in Boston."

"If you're Cora Chandler's cousin, that oughtn't to be difficult. She knows everybody in town. And the girl's family will probably help you out, once you've got her—some of them are fools enough for anything in these crazy days."

"I wouldn't like that."

"Rich girls can't live on air," said the older man grimly.

They played for awhile in silence. Suddenly, as they approached a green, Juan's companion turned to him frowning.

"Look here, young man," he said. "I don't know whether you are really thinking of leaving college or whether I've just put the idea in your head. If I have, forget it. Go home and talk it over with your family. Do what they tell you to."

"My father's dead."

"Well, then ask your mother. She's got your best interest at heart."

His attitude had noticeably stiffened, as if he were sorry he had become even faintly involved in Juan's problem. He guessed that there was something solid in the boy, but he suspected his readiness to confide in strangers and his helplessness about getting a job. Something was lacking—not confidence, exactly—"It might be a few months before I was able to support her"—but something stronger, fiercer, more external. When they walked together into the caddie house he shook hands with him and was about to turn away, when impulse impelled him to add one word more.

"If you decide to try Boston come and see me," he said. He pressed a card into Juan's hand. "Good-bye. Good luck. Remember, a woman's like a street car—"

He walked into the locker room. After paying his caddie, Juan glanced down at the card which he still held in his hand.

"Harold Garneau," it read, "23–27 State Street."

A moment later Juan was walking nervously and hurriedly from the grounds of the Culpepper Club, casting no glance behind.

V

One month later San Juan Chandler arrived in Boston and took an inexpensive room in a small downtown hotel. In his pocket was two hundred dollars in cash and an envelope full of Liberty Bonds aggregating fifteen hundred dollars more—the whole being a fund which had been started by his father when he was born, to give him his chance in life. Not without argument had he come into possession of this—not without tears had his decision to abandon his last year at college been approved by his mother. He had not told her everything, simply that he had an advantageous offer of a position in Boston; the rest she guessed and was tactfully silent. As a matter of fact, he had neither a position nor a plan; but he was twenty-one now, with the blemishes of youth departed forever. One thing Juan knew—he was going to marry Noel Garneau. The sting and hurt and shame of that Sunday morning ran through his dreams, stronger than any doubts he might have felt, stronger even than the romantic boyish love for her that had blossomed one dry, still Montana night. That was still there, but locked apart; what had happened later overlay it, muffled it. It was necessary now to his pride, his self-respect, his very existence, that he have her, in order to wipe out his memory of the day on which he had grown three years.

He hadn't seen her since. The following morning he had left Culpepper Bay and gone home.

Yes, he had a wonderful time. Yes, Cousin Cora had been very nice.

Nor had he written, though a week later a surprised but somehow flippant and terrible note had come from her, saying how pleasant it was to have seen him again and how bad it was to leave without saying good-bye.

"Holly Morgan sends her best," it concluded, with kind, simulated reproach. "Perhaps she ought to be writing instead of me. I always thought you were fickle, and now I know it."

The poor effort which she had made to hide her indifference made him shiver. He did not add the letter to a certain cherished package tied with blue ribbon, but burned it up in an ash tray—a tragic gesture which almost set his mother's house on fire.

So he began his life in Boston, and the story of his first year there is a fairy tale too immoral to be told. It is the story of one of those mad, illogical successes upon whose substantial foundations ninety-nine failures are later reared. Though he worked hard, he deserved no special credit for it—no credit, that is, commensurate with the reward he received. He ran into a man who had a scheme, a preposterous scheme, for the cold storage of sea food which he had been trying to finance for several years. Juan's inexperience allowed him to be responsive and he invested twelve hundred dollars. In the first year this appalling indiscretion paid him 400 per-cent. His partner attempted to buy him out, but they reached a compromise and Juan kept his shares.

The inner sense of his own destiny which had never deserted him whispered that he was going to be a rich man. But at the end of that year an event took place which made him think that it didn't matter after all.

He had seen Noel Garneau twice—once entering a theatre and once riding through a Boston street in the back of her limousine, looking, he thought afterwards, bored and pale and tired. At the time he had thought nothing; an overwhelming emotion had seized his heart, held it helpless, suspended, as though it were in the grasp of material fingers. He had shrunk back hastily under the awning of a shop and waited trembling, horrified, ecstatic, until she went by. She did not know he was in Boston—he did not want her to know until he was ready. He followed her every move in the society columns of the papers. She was at school, at home for Christmas, at Hot Springs for Easter, coming out in the fall. Then she was a debutante, and every day he read of her at dinners and dances and assemblies and balls and charity functions and theatricals of the Junior League. A dozen blurred newspaper unlikenesses of her filled a drawer of his desk. And still he waited. Let Noel have her fling.

When he had been sixteen months in Boston, and when Noel's first season was dying away in the hum of the massed departure for Florida, Juan decided to wait no longer. So on a raw, damp February day, when children in rubber boots were building dams in the snow-filled gutters, a blond, handsome, well-dressed young man walked up the steps of the Garneaus' Boston house and handed his card to the maid. With his heart beating loud, he went into a drawing room and sat down.

A sound of a dress on the stairs, light feet in the hall, an exclamation—Noel!

"Why, Juan," she exclaimed, surprised, pleased, polite, "I didn't know you were in Boston. It's so good to see you. I thought you'd thrown me over forever."

In a moment he found voice—it was easier now than it had been. Whether or not she was aware of the change, he was a nobody no longer. There was something solid behind him that would prevent him ever again from behaving like a self-centered child.

He explained that he might settle in Boston, and allowed her to guess that he had done extremely well; and though it cost him a twinge of pain, he spoke humorously of their last meeting, implying that he had left the swimming party on an impulse of anger at her. He could not confess that the impulse had been one of shame. She laughed. Suddenly he grew curiously happy.

Half an hour passed. The fire glowed in the hearth. The day darkened outside and the room moved into that shadowy twilight, that weather of indoors, which is like a breathless starshine. He had been standing; now he sat down beside her on the couch.

"Noel—"

Footsteps sounded lightly through the hall as the maid went through to the front door. Noel reached up quickly and turned up the electric lamp on the table behind her head.

"I didn't realize how dark it was growing," she said, rather quickly, he thought. Then the maid stood in the doorway.

"Mr. Templeton," she announced.

"Oh, yes," agreed Noel.

Mr. Templeton, with a Harvard-Oxford drawl, mature, very much at home, looked at him with just a flicker of surprise, nodded, mumbled a bare politeness and took an easy position in front of the fire. He exchanged several remarks with Noel which indicated a certain familiarity with her movements. Then a short silence fell. Juan rose.

"I want to see you soon," he said. "I'll phone, shall I, and you tell me when I can call?"

She walked with him to the door.

"So good to talk to you again," she told him cordially. "Remember, I want to see a lot of you, Juan."

When he left he was happier than he had been for two years. He ate dinner alone at a restaurant, almost singing to himself; and then, wild with elation, walked along the waterfront till midnight. He awoke thinking of her, wanting to tell people that what had been lost was found again. There had been more between them than the mere words said—Noel's sitting with him in the half darkness, her slight but perceptible nervousness as she came with him to the door.

Two days later he opened the "Transcript" to the society page and read down to the third item. There his eyes stopped, became like china eyes:

Mr. and Mrs. Harold Garneau announce the engagement of their daughter Noel to Mr. Brooks Fish Templeton. Mr. Templeton graduated from Harvard in the class of 1912 and is a partner in—

VI

At three o'clock that afternoon Juan rang the Garneaus' doorbell and was shown into the hall. From somewhere upstairs he heard girls' voices, and another murmur came from the drawing room on the right, where he had talked to Noel only the week before.

"Can you show me into some room that isn't being used?" he demanded tensely of the maid. "I'm an old friend—it's very important—I've got to see Miss Noel alone."

He waited in a small den at the back of the hall. Ten minutes passed—ten minutes more; he began to be afraid she wasn't coming. At the end of half an hour the door bounced open and Noel came hurriedly in.

"Juan!" she cried happily. "This is wonderful! I might have known you'd be the first to come." Her expression changed as she saw his face, and she hesitated. "But why were you shown in here?" she went on quickly. "You must come and meet everyone. I'm rushing around today like a chicken without a head."

"Noel!" he said thickly.

"What?"

Her hand was on the door knob. She turned, startled.

"Noel, I haven't come to congratulate you," Juan said, his face white and firm, his voice harsh with his effort at self-control. "I've come to tell you you're making an awful mistake."

"Why—Juan!"

"And you know it," he went on. "You know no one loves you as I love you, Noel. I want you to marry me."

She laughed nervously.

"Why, Juan, that's silly! I don't understand your talking like that. I'm engaged to another man."

"Noel, will you come here and sit down?"

"I can't, Juan—there're a dozen people outside. I've got to see them. It wouldn't be polite. Another time, Juan. If you come another time I'd love to talk to you."

"Now!" The word was stark, unyielding, almost savage. She hesitated. "Ten minutes," he said.

"I've really got to go, Juan."

She sat down uncertainly, glancing at the door. Sitting beside her, Juan told her simply and directly everything that had happened to him since they had met, a year and a half before. He told her of his family, his Cousin Cora, of his inner humiliation at Culpepper Bay. Then he told her of coming to Boston and of his success, and how at last, having something to bring to her, he had come only to find he was too late. He kept back nothing. In his voice, as in his mind, there was no pretense now, no self-consciousness, but only a sincere and overmastering emotion. He had no defense for what he was doing, he said, save this—that he had somehow gained the right to present his case, to have her know how much his devotion had inspired him, to have her look once, if only in passing, upon the fact that for two years he had loved her faithfully and well.

When Juan finished, Noel was crying. It was terrible, she said, to tell her all this—just when she had decided about her life. It hadn't been easy, yet it was done now, and she was really going to marry this other man. But she had never heard anything like this before—it upset her. She was—oh, so terribly sorry, but there was no use. If he had cared so much he might have let her know before.

But how could he let her know? He had had nothing to offer her except the fact that one summer night out west they had been overwhelmingly drawn together.

"And you love me now," he said in a low voice. "You wouldn't cry, Noel, if you didn't love me. You wouldn't care."

"I'm—I'm sorry for you."

"It's more than that. You loved me the other day. You wanted me to sit beside you in the dark. Didn't I feel it—didn't I know? There's something between us, Noel—a sort of pull. Something you always do to me and I to you—except that one sad time. Oh, Noel, don't you know how it breaks my heart to see you sitting there two feet away from me, to want to put my arms around you and know you've made a senseless promise to another man?"

There was a knock outside the door.

"Noel!"

She raised her head, putting a handkerchief quickly to her eyes. "Yes?"

"It's Brooks. May I come in?" Without waiting for an answer, Templeton opened the door and stood looking at them curiously. "Excuse me," he said. He nodded brusquely at Juan. "Noel, there are lots of people here—"

"In a minute," she said lifelessly.

"Aren't you well?"

"Yes."

He came into the room, frowning.

"What's been upsetting you, dear?" He glanced quickly at Juan, who stood up, his eyes blurred with tears. A menacing note crept into Templeton's voice. "I hope no one's been upsetting you."

For answer, Noel flopped down over a hill of pillows and sobbed aloud.

"Noel"—Templeton sat beside her and put his arm on her shoulder—"Noel." He turned again to Juan. "I think it would be best if you left us alone, Mr. ——" The name escaped his memory. "Noel's a little tired."

"I won't go," said Juan.

"Please wait outside then. We'll see you later."

"I won't wait outside. I want to speak to Noel. It was you who interrupted."

"And I have a perfect right to interrupt." His face reddened angrily. "Just who the devil are you, anyhow?"

"My name is Chandler."

"Well, Mr. Chandler, you're in the way here—is that plain? Your presence here is an intrusion and a presumption."

"We look at it in different ways."

They glared at each other angrily. After a moment Templeton raised Noel to a sitting posture.

"I'm going to take you upstairs, dear," he said. "This has been a strain today. If you lie down till dinnertime—"

He helped her to her feet. Not looking at Juan, and still dabbing her face with her handkerchief, Noel suffered herself to be persuaded into the hall. Templeton turned in the doorway.

"The maid will give you your hat and coat, Mr. Chandler."

"I'll wait right here," said Juan.

VII

He was still there at half-past six, when, following a quick knock, a large broad bulk which Juan recognized as Mr. Harold Garneau came into the room.

"Good evening, sir," said Mr. Garneau, annoyed and peremptory. "Just what can I do for you?"

He came closer and a flicker of recognition passed over his face.

"Oh!" he muttered.

"Good evening, sir," said Juan.

"It's you, is it?" Mr. Garneau appeared to hesitate. "Brooks Templeton said that you were—that you insisted on seeing Noel"—he coughed—"that you refused to go home."

"I want to see Noel, if you don't mind."

"What for?"

"That's between Noel and me, Mr. Garneau."

"Mr. Templeton and I are quite entitled to represent Noel in this case," said Mr. Garneau patiently. "She has just made the statement before her mother and me that she doesn't want to see you again. Isn't that plain enough?"

"I don't believe it," said Juan stubbornly.

"I'm not in the habit of lying."

"I beg your pardon. I meant—"

"I don't want to discuss this unfortunate business with you," broke out Garneau contemptuously. "I just want you to leave right now—and not come back."

"Why do you call it an unfortunate business?" inquired Juan coolly.

"Good-night, Mr. Chandler."

"You call it an unfortunate business because Noel's broken her engagement."

"You are presumptuous, sir!" cried the older man. "Unbearably presumptuous."

"Mr. Garneau, you yourself were once kind enough to tell me—"

"I don't give a damn what I told you!" cried Garneau. "You get out of here now!"

"Very well, I have no choice. I wish you to be good enough to tell Noel that I'll be back tomorrow afternoon."

Juan nodded, went into the hall and took his hat and coat from a chair. Upstairs, he heard running footsteps and a door opened and closed—not before he had caught the sound of impassioned voices and a short broken sob. He hesitated. Then he continued on along the hall toward the front door. Through a portière of the dining room he caught sight of a manservant laying the service for dinner.

He rang the bell the next afternoon at the same hour. This time the butler, evidently instructed, answered the door.

Miss Noel was not at home. Could he leave a note? It was no use; Miss Noel was not in the city. Incredulous but anxious, Juan took a taxi-cab to Harold Garneau's office.

"Mr. Garneau can't see you. If you like, he will speak to you for a moment on the phone."

Juan nodded. The clerk touched a button on the waiting-room switchboard and handed an instrument to Juan.

"This is San Juan Chandler speaking. They told me at your residence that Noel had gone away. Is that true?"

"Yes." The monosyllable was short and cold. "She's gone away for a rest. Won't be back for several months. Anything else?"

"Did she leave any word for me?"

"No! She hates the sight of you."

"What's her address?"

"That doesn't happen to be your affair. Good-morning."

Juan went back to his apartment and mused over the situation. Noel had been spirited out of town—that was the only expression he knew for it. And undoubtedly her engagement to Templeton was at least temporarily broken. He had toppled it over within an hour. He must see her again—that was the immediate necessity. But where? She was certainly with friends, and probably with relatives. That latter was the first clue to follow—he must find out the names of the relatives she had most frequently visited before.

He phoned Holly Morgan. She was in the South and not expected back in Boston till May.

Then he called the society editor of the "Boston Transcript." After a short wait, a polite, attentive, feminine voice conversed with him on the wire.

"This is Mr. San Juan Chandler," he said, trying to intimate by his voice that he was a distinguished leader of cotillions in the Back Bay. "I want to get some information, if you please, about the family of Mr. Harold Garneau."

"Why don't you apply directly to Mr. Garneau?" advised the society editor, not without suspicion.

"I'm not on speaking terms with Mr. Garneau."

A pause; then—"Well, really, we can't be responsible for giving out information in such a peculiar way."

"But there can't be any secret about who Mr. and Mrs. Garneau's relations are!" protested Juan in exasperation.

"But how can we be sure that you—"

He hung up the receiver. Two other papers gave no better results, a third was willing, but ignorant. It seemed absurd, almost like a conspiracy, that in a city where the Garneaus were so well known he could not obtain the desired names. It was as if everything had tightened up against his arrival on the scene. After a day of fruitless and embarrassing inquiries in stores, where his questions were looked upon with the suspicion that he might be compiling a sucker list, and of poring through back numbers of the Social Register, he saw that there was but one resource—that was Cousin Cora. Next morning he took the three-hour ride to Culpepper Bay.

It was the first time he had seen her for a year and a half, since the disastrous termination of his summer visit. She was offended—that he knew—especially since she had heard from his mother of the unexpected success. She greeted him coldly and reproachfully; but she told him what he wanted to know, because Juan asked his questions while she was still startled and surprised by his visit. He left Culpepper Bay with the information that Mrs. Garneau had one sister, the famous Mrs. Morton Poindexter, with whom Noel was on terms of great intimacy. Juan took the midnight train for New York.

The Morton Poindexters' telephone number was not in the New York phone book, and Information refused to divulge it; but Juan procured it by another reference to the Social Register. He called the house from his hotel.

"Miss Noel Garneau—is she in the city?" he inquired, according to his plan. If the name was not immediately familiar, the servant would reply that he had the wrong number.

"Who wants to speak to her, please?"

That was a relief; his heart sank comfortably back into place.

"Oh—a friend."

"No name?"

"No name."

"I'll see."

The servant returned in a moment.

No, Miss Garneau was not there, was not in the city, was not expected. The phone clicked off suddenly.

Late that afternoon a taxi dropped him in front of the Morton Poindexters' house. It was the most elaborate house that he had ever seen, rising to five stories on a corner of Fifth Avenue and adorned even with that ghost of a garden which, however minute, is the proudest gesture of money in New York.

He handed no card to the butler, but it occurred to him that he must be expected, for he was shown immediately into the drawing room. When, after a short wait, Mrs. Poindexter entered he experienced for the first time in five days a touch of uncertainty.

Mrs. Poindexter was perhaps thirty-five, and of that immaculate fashion which the French describe as *bien soignée*. The inexpressible loveliness of her face was salted with another quality which for want of a better word might be called dignity. But it was more than dignity, for it wore no rigidity, but instead a softness so adaptable, so elastic, that it would withdraw from any attack which life might bring against it, only to spring back at the proper moment, taut, victorious and complete. San Juan saw that even though his guess was correct as to Noel's being in the house, he was up against a force with which he had had no contact before. This woman seemed to be not entirely of America, to possess resources which the American woman lacked or handled ineptly.

She received him with a graciousness which, though it was largely external, seemed to conceal no perturbation underneath. Indeed, her attitude appeared to be perfectly passive, just short of encouraging. It was with an effort that he resisted the inclination to lay his cards on the table.

"Good-evening." She sat down on a stiff chair in the center of the room and asked him to take an easy-chair nearby. She sat looking at him silently until he spoke.

"Mrs. Poindexter, I am very anxious to see Miss Garneau. I telephoned your house this morning and was told that she was not here." Mrs. Poindexter nodded. "However, I know she is here," he continued evenly. "And I'm determined to see her. The idea that her father and mother can prevent me from seeing her, as though I had disgraced myself in some way—or that you, Mrs. Poindexter, can prevent me from seeing her"—his voice rose a little— "is preposterous. This is not the year 1500—nor even the year 1910."

He paused. Mrs. Poindexter waited for a moment to see if he had finished. Then she said, quietly and unequivocally, "I quite agree with you."

Save for Noel, Juan thought he had never seen anyone so beautiful before.

"Mrs. Poindexter," he began again, in a more friendly tone, "I'm sorry to seem rude. I've been called presumptuous in this matter, and perhaps to some extent I am. Perhaps all poor boys who are in love with wealthy girls are presumptuous. But it happens that I am no longer a poor boy, and I have good reason to believe that Noel cares for me."

"I see," said Mrs. Poindexter attentively. "But of course I knew nothing about all that."

Juan hesitated, again disarmed by her complaisance. Then a surge of determination went over him.

"Will you let me see her?" he demanded. "Or will you insist on keeping up this farce a little longer?"

Mrs. Poindexter looked at him as through considering.

"Why should I let you see her?"

"Simply because I ask you. Just as, when someone says 'Excuse me,' you step aside for him in a doorway."

Mrs. Poindexter frowned.

"But Noel is concerned in this matter as much as you. And I'm not like a person in a crowd. I'm more like a bodyguard, with instructions to let no one pass, even if they say 'Excuse me' in a most appealing voice."

"You have instructions only from her father and mother," said Juan, with rising impatience. "She's the person concerned."

"I'm glad you begin to admit that."

"Of course I admit it," he broke out. "I want you to admit it."

"I do."

"Then what's the point of all this absurd discussion?" he demanded heatedly.

She stood up suddenly.

"I bid you good-evening, sir."

Taken aback, Juan stood up too.

"Why, what's the matter?"

"I will not be spoken to like that," said Mrs. Poindexter, still in a low cool voice. "Either you can conduct yourself quietly or you can leave this house at once."

Juan realized that he had taken the wrong tone. The words stung at him and for a moment he had nothing to say—as though he were a scolded boy at school.

"This is beside the question," he stammered finally. "I want to talk to Noel."

"Noel doesn't want to talk to you."

Suddenly Mrs. Poindexter held out a sheet of notepaper to him. He opened it. It said:

Aunt Jo: As to what we talked about this afternoon: If that intolerable bore calls, as he will probably do, and begins his presumptuous whining, please speak to him frankly. Tell him I never loved him, that I never at any time claimed to love him and that his persistence is revolting to me. Say that I am old enough to know my own mind and that my greatest wish is never to see him again in this world.

Juan stood there aghast. His universe was suddenly about him. Noel did not care, she had never cared. It was all a preposterous joke on him, played by those to whom the business of life had been such jokes from the beginning. He realized now that fundamentally they were all akin—Cousin Cora, Noel, her father, this cold, lovely woman here—affirming the prerogative of the rich to marry always within their caste, to erect artificial barriers and standards against those who could presume upon a summer's philandering. The scales fell from his eyes and he saw his year and a half of struggle and effort not as progress toward a goal but only as a little race he had run by himself, outside, with no one to beat except himself—no one who cared.

Blindly he looked about for his hat, scarcely realizing it was in the hall. Blindly he stepped back when Mrs. Poindexter's hand moved toward him half a foot through the mist and Mrs. Poindexter's voice said softly, "I'm sorry." Then he was in the hall, the note still clutched in the hand that struggled through the sleeve of his overcoat, the words which he felt he must somehow say choking through his lips.

"I didn't understand. I regret very much that I've bothered you. It wasn't clear to me how matters stood—between Noel and me—"

His hand was on the door knob.

"I'm sorry, too," said Mrs. Poindexter. "I didn't realize from what Noel said that what I had to do would be so hard—Mr. Templeton."

"Chandler," he corrected her dully. "My name's Chandler."

She stood dead still; suddenly her face went white.

"What?"

"My name—it's Chandler."

Like a flash she threw herself against the half-open door and it bumped shut. Then in a flash she was at the foot of the staircase.

"Noel!" she cried in a high, clear call. "Noel! Noel! Come down, Noel!" Her lovely voice floated up like a bell through the long high central hall. "Noel! Come down! It's Mr. Chandler! It's Chandler!"

THE ADOLESCENT MARRIAGE

Chauncey Garnett, the architect, once had a miniature city constructed, composed of all the buildings he had ever designed. It proved to be an expensive and somewhat depressing experiment, for the toy, instead of resulting in a harmonious whole, looked like a typical cross-section of Philadelphia. Garnett found it depressing to be reminded that he himself had often gone in for monstrosities, and even more depressing to realize that his architectural activities had extended over half a century. In disgust, he distributed the tiny houses to his friends and they ended up as the residences of undiscriminating dolls.

Garnett had never—at least not yet—been called a nice old man; yet he was both old and nice. He gave six hours a day to his offices in Philadelphia or to his branch in New York, and during the remaining time demanded only a proper peace in which to brood quietly over his crowded and colorful past. In several years no one had demanded a favor that could not be granted with pen and check book, and it seemed that he had reached an age safe from the intrusion of other people's affairs. This calm, however, was premature, and it was violently shattered one afternoon in the summer of 1925 by the shrill clamor of a telephone bell.

George Wharton was speaking. Could Chauncey come to his house at once on a matter of the greatest importance?

On the way to Chestnut Hill, Garnett dozed against the grey duvetyn cushions of his limousine, his sixty-eight-year-old body warmed by the June sunshine, his sixty-eight-year-old mind blank save for some vivid unsubstantial memory of a green branch overhanging green water. Reaching his friend's house, he awoke placidly and without a start. George Wharton, he thought, was probably troubled by some unexpected surplus of money. He would want Garnett to plan a church—one of these modern churches with a cabaret on the twentieth floor, car-cards in every pew and a soda-fountain in the sanctuary. He was of a younger generation than Garnett—a modern man.

Wharton and his wife were waiting in the gilt-and-morocco intimacy of the library.

"I couldn't come to your office," said Wharton immediately. "In a minute you'll understand why."

Garnett noticed that his friend's hands were slightly trembling.

"It's about Lucy," Wharton added.

It was a moment before Garnett placed Lucy as their daughter.

"What's happened to Lucy?"

"Lucy's married. She ran up to Connecticut about a month ago and got married."

A moment's silence.

"Lucy's only sixteen," continued Wharton. "The boy's twenty."

"That's very young," said Garnett considerately, "but then—my grandmother married at sixteen and no one thought much about it. Some girls develop much quicker than others—"

"We know all that, Chauncey." Wharton waved it aside impatiently. "The point is, these young marriages don't work nowadays. They're not normal. They end in a mess."

Again Garnett hesitated.

"Aren't you a little premature in looking ahead for trouble? Why don't you give Lucy a chance? Why not wait and see if it's going to turn out a mess?"

"It's a mess already," cried Wharton passionately. "And Lucy's life's a mess. The one thing her mother and I cared about—her happiness—that's a mess, and we don't know what to do—what to do."

His voice trembled and he turned away to the window—came back again impulsively.

"Look at us, Chauncey. Do we look like the kind of parents who would drive a child into a thing like this? She and her mother have been like sisters—just like sisters. She and I used to go on parties together—football games and all that sort of thing—ever since she was a little kid. She's all we've got, and we always said we'd try to steer a middle course with her—give her enough liberty for her self-respect and yet keep an eye on where she went and who she went with—at least till she was eighteen. Why, by God, Chauncey, if you'd told me six weeks ago that this thing could happen—" He shook his head helplessly. Then he continued in a quieter voice. "When she came and told us what she'd done it just about broke our hearts, but we tried to make the best of it. Do you know how long the marriage—if you can call it that—lasted? Three weeks. It lasted three weeks. She came home with a big bruise on her shoulder where he'd hit her."

"Oh, dear!" said Mrs. Wharton in a low tone. "Please—"

"We talked it over," continued her husband grimly, "and she decided to go back to this—this young"—again he bowed his head before the insufficiency of expletives—"and try to make a go of it. But last night she came home again, and now she says it's definitely over."

Garnett nodded. "Who's the man?" he inquired.

"Man!" cried Wharton. "It's a boy. His name's Llewellyn Clark."

"What's that?" exclaimed Garnett in surprise. "Llewellyn Clark? Jesse Clark's son? The young fellow in my office?"

"Yes."

"Why, he's a nice young fellow," Garnett declared. "I can't believe he'd—"

"Neither could I," interrupted Wharton quietly. "I thought he was a nice young fellow too. And what's more, I rather suspected that my daughter was a pretty decent young girl."

Garnett was astonished and annoyed. He had seen Llewellyn Clark not an hour before in the small drafting room he occupied in the Garnett & Linquist offices. He understood now why Clark wasn't going back to Boston Tech this fall. And in the light of this revelation he remembered that there had been a change in the boy during the past month—absences, late arrivals, a certain listlessness in his work.

Mrs. Wharton's voice broke in upon the ordering of his mind.

"Please do something, Chauncey," she said. "Talk to him. Talk to them both. She's only sixteen and we can't bear to see her life ruined by a divorce. It isn't that we care what people will say; it's only Lucy we care about, Chauncey."

"Why don't you send her abroad for a year?"

Wharton shook his head.

"That doesn't solve the problem. If they have an ounce of character between them they'll make an attempt to live together."

"But if you think so badly of him—"

"Lucy's made her choice. He's got some money—enough. And there doesn't seem to be anything vicious in his record so far."

"What's his side of it?"

Wharton waved his hands helplessly.

"I'm damned if I know. Something about a hat. Some bunch of rubbish. Elsie and I have no idea why they ran away, and now we can't get a clear idea why they won't stick together. Unfortunately his father and mother are dead." He paused. "Chauncey, if you could see your way clear—"

An unpleasant prospect began to take shape before Garnett's eyes. He was an old man with one foot, at least, in the chimney corner. From where he stood, this youngest generation was like something infinitely distant, and perceived through the large end of a telescope. "Oh, of course—" he heard himself saying vaguely. So hard to think back to that young time. Since his youth such a myriad of prejudices and conventions had passed through the fashion show and died away with clamour and acrimony and commotion. It would be difficult even to communicate with these children. How hollowly and fatuously his platitudes would echo on their ears. And how bored he would be with their selfishness and with their shallow confidence in opinions manufactured day before yesterday.

He sat up suddenly. Wharton and his wife were gone, and a slender dark-haired girl whose body hovered delicately on the last edge of childhood had come quietly into the room. She regarded him for a moment with a shadow of alarm in her intent brown eyes; then sat down on a stiff chair near him.

"I'm Lucy," she said. "They told me you wanted to talk to me."

She waited. It occurred to Garnett that he must say something, but the form his speech should take eluded him.

"I haven't seen you since you were ten years old," he began uneasily.

"Yes," she agreed, with a small, polite smile.

There was another silence. He must say something to the point before her young attention slipped utterly away.

"I'm sorry you and Llewellyn have quarreled," he broke out. "It's silly to quarrel like that. I'm very fond of Llewellyn, you know."

"Did he send you here?"

Garnett shook his head. "Are you—in love with him?" he inquired.

"Not anymore."

"Is he in love with you?"

"He says so, but I don't think he is—anymore."

"You're sorry you married him?"

"I'm never sorry for anything that's done."

"I see."

Again she waited.

"Your father tells me this is a permanent separation."

"Yes."

"May I ask why?"

"We just couldn't get along," she answered simply. "I thought he was terribly selfish and he thought the same about me. We fought all the time, from almost the first day."

"He hit you?"

"Oh, that!" She dismissed that as unimportant.

"How do you mean—selfish?"

"Just selfish," she answered childishly. "The most selfish thing I ever saw in my life. I never saw anything so selfish in my life."

"What did he do that was selfish?" persisted Garnett.

"Everything. He was so stingy—Gosh!" Her eyes were serious and sad. "I can't stand anybody to be so stingy. About money," she explained contemptuously. "Then he'd lose his temper and swear at me and say he was going to leave me if I didn't do what he wanted me to." And she added, still very gravely, "Gosh!"

"How did he happen to hit you?"

"Oh, he didn't mean to hit me. I was trying to hit him on account of something he did, and he was trying to hold me and so I bumped into a still."

"A still!" exclaimed Garnett, startled.

"The woman had a still in our room because she had no other place to keep it. Down on Beckton Street, where we lived."

"Why did Llewellyn take you to such a place?"

"Oh, it was a perfectly good place except that the woman had this still. We looked around two or three days and it was the only apartment we could afford." She paused reminiscently and then added, "It was very nice and quiet."

"H'm. You never really got along at all?"

"No." She hesitated. "He spoiled it all. He was always worrying about whether we'd done the right thing. He'd get out of bed at night and walk up and down worrying about it. I wasn't complaining. I was perfectly willing to be poor if we could get along and be happy. I wanted to go to cooking school, for instance, and he wouldn't let me. He wanted me to sit in the room all day and wait for him."

"Why?"

"He was afraid that I wanted to go home. For three weeks it was one long quarrel from morning till night. I couldn't stand it."

"It seems to me that a lot of this quarreling was over nothing," ventured Garnett.

"I haven't explained it very well, I guess," she said with sudden weariness. "I knew a lot of it was silly and so did Llewellyn. Sometimes we'd apologize to each other, and be in love like we were before we were married. That's why I went back to him. But it wasn't any use." She stood up. "What's the good of talking about it any more? You wouldn't understand."

Garnett wondered if he could get back to his office before Llewellyn Clark went home. He could talk to Clark, while the girl only confused him as she teetered disconcertingly between adolescence and disillusion. But when Clark reported to him just as the five o'clock bell rang, the same sensation of impotence stole over Garnett, and he stared at his apprentice blankly for a moment, as if he had never seen him before.

Llewellyn Clark looked older than his twenty years—a tall, almost thin young man with dark red hair of a fine, shiny texture, and auburn eyes. He was of a somewhat nervous type, talented and impatient, but Garnett could find little of the egotist in his reserved, attentive face.

"I hear you've been getting married," Garnett began abruptly.
Clark's cheeks deepened to the color of his hair.

"Who told you that?" he demanded.

"Lucy Wharton. She told me the whole story."

"Then you know it, sir," said Clark almost rudely. "You know all there is to know."

"What do you intend to do?"

"I don't know." Clark stood up, breathing quickly. "I can't talk about it. It's my affair, you see. I—"

"Sit down, Llewellyn."

The young man sat down, his face working—suddenly it crinkled uncontrollably and two great tears, stained faintly with the dust of the day's toil, gushed from his eyes.

"Oh, hell!" he said brokenly, wiping his eyes with the back of his hand.

"I've been wondering why you two can't make a go of it after all." Garnett looked down at his desk. "I like you, Llewellyn, and I like Lucy. Why not fool everybody and—"

Llewellyn shook his head emphatically.

"Not me," he said. "I don't care a snap of my finger about her. She can go jump in the lake for all I care."

"Why did you take her away?"

"I don't know. We'd been in love for almost a year and marriage seemed a long way off. It came over us all of a sudden—"

"Why couldn't you get along?"

"Didn't she tell you?"

"I want your version."

"Well, it started one afternoon when she took all our money and threw it away."

"Threw it away?"

"She took it and bought a new hat. It was only thirty-five dollars, but it was all we had. If I hadn't found forty-five cents in an old suit we wouldn't have had any dinner."

"I see," said Garnett dryly.

"Then—oh, one thing happened after another. She didn't trust me, she didn't think I could take care of her, she kept saying she was going home to her mother. And finally we began to hate each other.

It was a great mistake, that's all, and I'll probably spend a good part of my life paying for it. Wait till it leaks out!" He laughed bitterly. "I'll be the Leopold and Loeb of Philadelphia—you'll see."

"Aren't you thinking about yourself a little too much?" suggested Garnett coldly.

Llewellyn looked at him in unfeigned surprise.

"About myself?" he repeated. "Mr. Garnett, I'll give you my word of honor, this is the first time I've ever thought about that side of it. Right now I'd do anything in the world to save Lucy any pain—except live with her. She's got great things in her, Mr. Garnett." His eyes filled again with tears. "She's just as brave and honest, and sweet sometimes—I'll never marry anybody else, you can bet your life on that, but—we were just poison to each other. I never want to see her anymore."

After all, thought Garnett, it was only the old human attempt to get something for nothing—neither of them had brought to the marriage any trace of tolerance or moral experience. However trivial the reasons for their incompatibility, it was firmly established now in both their hearts, and perhaps they were wise in realizing that the wretched voyage, too hastily embarked upon, was over.

That night Garnett had a long and somewhat painful talk with George Wharton, and on the following morning he went to New York, where he spent several days. When he returned to Philadelphia, it was with the information that the marriage of Lucy and Llewellyn Clark had been annulled by the state of Connecticut on the ground of their minority. They were free.

II

Almost everyone who knew Lucy Wharton liked her, and her friends rose rather valiantly to the occasion. There was a certain element, of course, who looked at her with averted eyes; there were slights, there were the stares of the curious; but since it was wisely given out, upon Chauncey Garnett's recommendation, that the Whartons themselves had insisted upon the annulment, the burden of the affair fell less heavily upon Lucy than upon Llewellyn. He became not exactly a pariah—cities live too quickly to linger long over any single scandal—but he was cut off entirely from the crowd in which he had grown up, and much bitter and unpleasant comment reached his ears.

He was a boy who felt things deeply, and in the first moment of depression he contemplated leaving Philadelphia. But gradually a mood of defiant indifference took possession of him—try as he might he wasn't able to feel in his heart that he had done anything morally wrong. He hadn't thought of Lucy as being sixteen, but only as the girl whom he loved beyond understanding. What did age matter? Hadn't people married as children, almost, one hundred—two hundred years ago? The day of his elopement with Lucy had been like an ecstatic dream—he the young knight, scorned by her father, the baron, as a mere youth, bearing her away, and all willing, on his charger, in the dead of the night.

And then the realization, almost before his eyes had opened from their romantic vision, that marriage meant the complicated adjustment of two lives to each other, and that love is a small part only of the long, long marriage day. Lucy was a devoted child whom he had contracted to amuse—an adorable and somewhat frightened child, that was all.

As suddenly as it had begun it was over. Doggedly Llewellyn went his way, alone with his mistake. And so quickly had his romance bloomed and turned to dust that after a month a merciful unreality began to clothe it as if it were something vaguely sad that had happened long ago.

One day in July he was summoned to Chauncey Garnett's private office. Few words had passed between them since their conversation the month before, but Llewellyn saw that there was no hostility in the older man's attitude. He was glad of that, for now that he felt himself utterly alone, cut off from the world in which he had grown up, his work had come to be the most important thing in his life.

"What are you doing, Llewellyn?" asked Garnett, picking up a yellow pamphlet from the litter of his desk.

"Helping Mr. Carson with the Municipal Country Club."

"Take a look at this." He handed the pamphlet to Llewellyn. "There isn't a gold mine in it—but there's a good deal of this gilt-edge hot air they call publicity. It's a syndicate of twenty papers,

you see. The best plans for—what is it?—a neighborhood store—
you know, a small drug store or grocery store that could fit into a nice
street without being an eye-sore. Or else for a suburban cottage—
that'll be the regular thing. Or thirdly for a small factory recreation
house."

Llewellyn read over the specifications.

"The last two aren't so interesting," he said. "Suburban cottage—
that'll be the usual thing, as you say—recreation house, no. But I'd
like to have a shot at the first, sir—the store."

Garnett nodded. "The best part is that the plan which wins each
competition materializes as a building right away. And therein lies
the prize. The building is yours. You design it, it's put up for you,
then you sell it and the money goes into your own pocket. Matter
of six or seven thousand dollars—and there won't be more than six
or seven hundred other young architects trying."

Llewellyn read it over again carefully.

"I like it," he said. "I'd like to try the store."

"Well, you've got a month. I wouldn't mind it a bit, Llewellyn, if
that prize came into this office."

"I can't promise you that." Again Llewellyn ran his eyes over the
conditions, while Garnett watched him with quiet interest.

"By the way," he asked suddenly, "what do you do with yourself
all the time, Llewellyn?"

"How do you mean, sir?"

"At night. Over the week-ends. Do you ever go out?"

Llewellyn hesitated. "Well, not so much—now."

"You mustn't let yourself brood over this business, you know."

"I'm not brooding."

Mr. Garnett put his glasses carefully away in their case.

"Lucy isn't brooding," he said suddenly. "Her father told me that
she's trying to live just as normal a life as possible."

Silence for a moment.

"I'm glad," said Llewellyn in an expressionless voice.

"You must remember that you're free as air now," said Garnett.
"You don't want to let yourself dry up and get bitter. Lucy's father
and mother are encouraging her to have callers and go to dances—
behave just as she did before—"

"Before Rudolph Rassendale came along," said Llewellyn grimly. He held up the pamphlet. "May I keep this, Mr. Garnett?"

"Oh, yes." His employer's hand gave him permission to retire. "Tell Mr. Carson that I've taken you off the country club for the present."

"I can finish that too," said Llewellyn promptly. "In fact—"

His lips shut. He had been about to remark that he was doing practically the whole thing himself anyhow.

"Well—?"

"Nothing, sir. Thank you very much."

Llewellyn withdrew, excited by his opportunity and relieved by the news of Lucy. She was herself again, so Mr. Garnett had implied; perhaps her life wasn't so irrevocably wrecked after all. If there were men to come and see her, to take her out to dances, then there were men to care for her. He found himself vaguely pitying them—if they knew what a handful she was, the absolute impossibility of dealing with her, even of talking to her. At the thought of those desolate weeks he shivered, as though recalling a nightmare.

Back in his room that night, he experimented with a few tentative sketches. He worked late, his imagination warming to the set task, but next day the result seemed "arty" and pretentious—like a design for a tea shop. He scrawled "Ye Olde-Fashioned Butcher Shoppe. Veree Unsanitaree" across the face of it and tore it into pieces, which he tossed into the wastebasket.

During the first weeks in August he continued his work on the plans for the country club, trusting that for the more personal venture some burst of inspiration would come to him toward the end of the allotted time. And then one day occurred an incident which he had long dreaded in the secret corners of his mind—walking home along Chestnut Street he ran unexpectedly into Lucy.

It was about five o'clock, when the crowds were thickest. Suddenly they found themselves in an eddy facing each other and then borne along side by side as if fate had pressed into service all these swarming hundreds to throw them together.

"Why, Lucy!" he exclaimed, raising his hat automatically. She stared at him with startled eyes. A woman laden with bundles collided with her and a purse slipped from Lucy's hand.

"Thank you very much," she said as he retrieved it. Her voice was tense, breathless. "That's all right. Give it to me. I have a car right here."

Their eyes joined for a moment, cool, impersonal, and he had a vivid memory of their last meeting—of how they had stood, like this, hating each other with a cold fury.

"Are you sure I can't help you?"

"Quite sure. Our car's at the curb."

She nodded quickly. Llewellyn caught a glimpse of an unfamiliar limousine and a short smiling man of forty who helped her inside.

He walked home—for the first time in weeks he was angry, excited, confused. He must get away tomorrow. It was all too recent for any such casual encounter as this—the wounds she had left on him were raw and they opened easily.

"The little fool!" he said to himself bitterly. "The selfish little fool! She thought I wanted to walk along the street with her as if nothing had ever happened. She dares to imagine that I'm made of the same flimsy stuff as herself!"

He wanted passionately to spank her, to punish her in some way like an insolent child. Until dinnertime he paced up and down in his room, going over in his mind the forlorn and useless arguments, reproaches, imprecations, furies, that had made up their short married life. He rehearsed every quarrel from its trivial genesis down to the time when a merciful exhaustion intervened and brought them, almost hysterical, into each other's arms. A brief moment of peace—then again the senseless, miserable human battle.

"Lucy," he heard himself saying, "listen to me. It isn't that I want you to sit here waiting for me. It's your hands, Lucy—suppose you went to cooking school and burned your pretty hands. I don't want your hands coarsened and roughened, and if you'll just have patience till next week when my money comes in—I won't stand it! Do you hear? I'm not going to have my wife doing that! No use of being *stubborn*—"

Wearily, just as he had been made weary by those arguments in reality, he dropped into a chair and reached listlessly for his drawing materials. Laying them out, he began to sketch, crumpling each one into a ball before a dozen lines marred the paper. It was her fault, he whispered to himself, it was all her fault. "If I'd been fifty years old I couldn't have changed her."

Yet he could not rid himself of her dark young face set sharp and cool against the August gloaming, against the hot hurrying crowds of that afternoon.

"Quite sure. Our car's at the curb."

Llewellyn nodded to himself and tried to smile grimly.

"Well, I've got one thing to be thankful for," he told himself. "My responsibility will be over before long."

He had been sitting for a long while looking at a blank sheet of drawing paper, but presently his pencil began to move in light strokes at the corner. He watched it idly, impersonally, as though it were a motion of his fingers imposed on him from outside. Finally he looked at the result with disapproval, scratched it out and then blocked it in again in exactly the same way.

Suddenly he chose a new pencil, picked up his ruler and made a measurement on the paper, and then another. An hour passed. The sketch took shape and outline, varied itself slightly, yielded in part to an eraser and appeared in an improved form. After two hours he raised his head, and catching sight of his tense, absorbed face he started with surprise. There were a dozen half-smoked cigarettes in the tray beside him.

When he turned out his light at last it was half-past five. The milk wagons were rumbling through the twilit streets outside, and the first sunshine streaming pink over the roofs of the houses across the way fell upon the board which bore his night's work. It was the plan of a suburban bungalow.

III

As the August days passed, Llewellyn continued to think of Lucy with a certain anger and contempt. If she could accept so lightly what had happened just two months ago, he had wasted his emotion upon a girl who was essentially shallow. It cheapened his conception of her, of himself, of the whole affair. Again the idea came to him of leaving Philadelphia and making a new start farther west, but his interest in the outcome of the competition decided him to postpone his departure for a few weeks more.

The blueprints of his design were made and dispatched. Mr. Garnett cautiously refused to make any prophecies, but Llewellyn knew that everyone in the office who had seen the drawing felt a vague excitement about it. Almost literally he had drawn a bungalow in the air—a bungalow that had never been lived in before. It was neither Italian, Elizabethan, New England or California Spanish, nor a mongrel form with features from each one. Someone dubbed it "the tree house," and there was a certain happiness in the label, but its charm proceeded less from any bizarre quality than from the virtuosity of the conception as a whole—an unusual length here and there, an odd, tantalizingly familiar slope of the roof, a door that was like the door to the secret places of a dream. Chauncey Garnett remarked that it was the first skyscraper he had ever seen built with one story—but he recognized that Llewellyn's unquestionable talent had matured overnight. Except that the organizers of the competition were probably seeking something more adapted to standardization, it might have had a chance for the award.

Only Llewellyn was sure. When he was reminded that he was only twenty-one, he kept silent, knowing that, whatever his years, he would never again be twenty-one at heart. Life had betrayed him. He had squandered himself on a worthless girl and the world had punished him for it—as ruthlessly as though he had spent spiritual coin other than his own. Meeting Lucy on the street again, he passed her without a flicker of his eye—and returned to his room, his day spoiled by the sight of that young distant face, the insincere reproach of those dark haunting eyes.

Early in September arrived a letter from New York informing him that from four hundred plans submitted the judges of the competition had chosen his for the prize. Llewellyn walked into Mr. Garnett's office without excitement, but with a strong sense of elation, and laid the letter on his employer's desk.

"I'm especially glad," he said, "because before I go away I wanted to do something to justify your belief in me."

Mr. Garnett's face assumed an expression of concern.

"It's this business of Lucy Wharton, isn't it?" he demanded. "It's still on your mind?"

"I can't stand meeting her," said Llewellyn. "It always makes me feel—like the devil."

"But you ought to stay till they put up your house for you."

"I'll come back for that, perhaps. I want to leave tonight."

Garnett looked at him thoughtfully.

"I don't like to see you go away," he said. "I'm going to tell you something I didn't intend to tell you. Lucy needn't worry you a bit anymore—your responsibility is absolutely over."

"Why's that?" Llewellyn felt his heart quicken.

"She's going to marry another man."

"Going to marry another man!" repeated Llewellyn mechanically.

"She's going to marry George Hemmick, who represents her father's business in Chicago. They're going out there to live."

"I see."

"The Whartons are delighted," continued Garnett. "I think they've felt this thing pretty deeply—perhaps more deeply than it deserves. And I've been sorry all along that the brunt of it fell on you. But you'll find the girl you really want one of these days, Llewellyn, and meanwhile the sensible thing for everyone concerned is to forget that it happened at all."

"But I can't forget," said Llewellyn in a strained voice. "I don't understand what you mean by all that—you people—you and Lucy, and her father and mother. First it was such a tragedy, and now it's something to forget! First I was this vicious young man and now I'm to go ahead and 'find the girl I want.' Lucy's going to marry somebody and live in Chicago. Her father and mother feel fine because our elopement didn't get in the newspapers and hurt their social position. It came out 'all right'!"

Llewellyn stood there speechless, aghast and defeated by this manifestation of the world's indifference. It was all about nothing—his very self-reproaches had been pointless and in vain.

"So that's that," he said finally in a new, hard voice. "I realize now that from beginning to end I was the only one who had any conscience in this affair after all."

IV

The little house, fragile yet arresting, all aglitter like a toy in its fresh coat of robin's-egg blue, stood out delicately against the clear sky. Set upon new-laid sod between two other bungalows, it swung your eye sharply toward itself, held your glance for a moment, then turned up the corners of your lips with the sort of smile reserved for children. Something went on in it, you imagined; something charming and not quite real. Perhaps the whole front opened up like the front of a doll's house; you were tempted to hunt for the catch because you felt an irresistible inclination to peer inside.

Long before the arrival of Llewellyn Clark and Mr. Garnett a small crowd had gathered—the constant efforts of two policemen were required to keep people from breaking through the strong fence and trampling the tiny garden. When Llewellyn's eye first fell upon it, as their car rounded a corner, a lump rose in his throat. That was his own—something that had come alive out of his mind. Suddenly he realized that it was not for sale, that he wanted it more than anything in the world. It could mean to him what love might have meant, something always bright and warm where he could rest from whatever disappointments life might have in store. And unlike love it would set no traps for him. His career opened up before him in a shining path and for the first time in half a year he was radiantly happy.

The speeches, the congratulations, passed in a daze. When he got up to make a stumbling but grateful acknowledgment, even the sight of Lucy standing close to another man on the edge of the crowd failed to send a pang through him as it would have a month before. That was the past and only the future counted. He hoped with all his heart, without reservations now, or bitterness, that she would be happy.

Afterwards when the crowd melted away he felt the necessity of being alone. Still in a sort of trance he went inside the house again and wandered from room to room, touching the walls, the furniture, the window casements, with almost a caress. He pulled aside curtains and gazed out; he stood for awhile in the kitchen and seemed to see the fresh bread and butter on the white boards of the table and hear the kettle, murmurous on the stove. Then back through the dining room—the remembered planning that the summer evening light should fall through the window just so— and into the bedroom, where he watched a breeze ruffle the edge of a curtain faintly, as if someone already lived here. He would sleep in this room tonight, he thought. He would buy things for a cold supper from a corner store. He was sorry for everyone who was not an architect, who could not make their own houses—he wished he could have set up every stick and stone with his own hands.

The September dusk fell. Returning from the store he set out his purchases on the dining-room table—cold roast chicken, bread and jam, and a bottle of milk. He ate lingeringly—then he sat back in his chair and smoked a cigarette, his eyes wandering about the walls. This was home. Llewellyn, brought up by a series of aunts, scarcely remembered ever having had a home before. Except of course where he had lived with Lucy. Those barren rooms in which they were so miserable together had been, nevertheless, a sort of home. Poor children—he looked back on them both, himself as well as her, from a great distance. Little wonder their love had made a faint, frail effort, a gesture, and then, unprepared for the oppression of those stifling walls, starved quickly to death.

Half an hour passed. Outside the silence was heavy except for the complaint of some indignant dog far down the street. Llewellyn's mind, detached by the unfamiliar, almost mystical surroundings, drifted away from the immediate past; he was thinking of the day when he had first met Lucy a year before. Little Lucy Wharton— how touched he had been by her trust in him, by her confidence that, at twenty, he was experienced in the ways of the world.

He got to his feet and began to walk slowly up and down the room—starting suddenly as the front doorbell pealed through the house for the first time. He opened the door and Mr. Garnett stepped inside.

"Good evening, Llewellyn," he said. "I came back to see if the king was happy in his castle."

"Sit down," said Llewellyn tensely. "I've got to ask you something. Why is Lucy marrying this man? I want to know."

"Why, I think I told you that he's a good deal older," answered Garnett quietly. "She feels that he understands."

"I want to see her!" Llewellyn cried. He leaned miserably against the mantelpiece. "Oh God—I don't know what to do. Mr. Garnett, we're in love with each other, don't you realize that? Can you stay in this house and not realize it? It's her house and mine—why, every room in it is haunted with Lucy! She came in when I was at dinner and sat with me—just now I saw her in front of the mirror in the bedroom brushing her hair—"

"She's out on the porch," interrupted Garnett quietly. "I think she wants to talk to you. In a few months she's going to have a child."

For a few minutes Chauncey Garnett moved about the empty room, looking at this feature or that, here and there, until the walls seemed to fade out and melt into the walls of the little house where he had brought his own wife over forty years ago. It was long gone, that house—the gift of his father-in-law, it would have seemed an atrocity to this generation. Yet on many a forgotten late afternoon when he had turned in at its gate and the gas had flamed out at him cheerfully from its windows he had got from it a moment of utter peace that no other house had given him since—

—until this house. The same quiet secret thing was here. Was it that his old mind was confusing the two, or that love had built this out of the tragedy in Llewellyn's heart? Leaving the question unanswered he found his hat and walked out on the dark porch, scarcely glanced at the single shadow on the porch chair a few yards away.

"You see, I never bothered to get that annulment after all," he said, as if he were talking to himself. "I thought it over carefully and I saw that you two were good people. And I had an idea that eventually you'd do the right thing. Good people—so often do."

When he reached the curb he looked back at the house. Again his mind, or his eyes, blurred and it seemed to him that it was that other house of forty years ago. Then, feeling vaguely ineffectual and a little guilty because he had meddled in other people's affairs, he turned and walked off hastily down the street.

THE DANCE
[IN A LITTLE TOWN]

All my life I have had a rather curious horror of small towns: not suburbs—they are quite a different matter—but the little lost cities of New Hampshire and Georgia and Kansas, and upper New York. I was born in New York City, and even as a little girl I never had any fear of the streets or the strange foreign faces—but on the occasions when I've been in the sort of place I'm referring to, I've been oppressed with the consciousness that there was a whole hidden life, a whole series of secret implications, significances and terrors, just below the surface, of which I knew nothing. In the cities everything good or bad eventually comes out, comes out of people's hearts, I mean. Life moves about, moves on, vanishes. In the small towns—those of between five and twenty-five thousand people—old hatreds, old and unforgotten affairs, ghostly scandals and tragedies, seem unable to die, but live on all tangled up with the natural ebb and flow of outward life.

Nowhere has this sensation come over me more insistently than in the South. Once out of Atlanta and Birmingham and New Orleans, I often have the feeling that I can no longer communicate with the people around me. The men and the girls speak a language wherein courtesy is combined with violence, fanatic morality with corn-drinking recklessness, in a fashion which I can't understand. In "Huckleberry Finn" Mark Twain described some of those towns perched along the Mississippi River, with their fierce feuds and their equally fierce revivals—and some of them haven't fundamentally changed beneath their new surface of flivvers and radios. They are deeply uncivilized to this day.

I speak of the South because it was in a small southern city of this type that I once saw the surface crack for a minute and something savage, uncanny and frightening rear its head. Then the surface closed again—and when I have gone back there since, I've been surprised to find myself as charmed as ever by the magnolia trees and the singing darkies in the street and the sensuous warm nights. I have been charmed too by the bountiful hospitality and the languorous easy-going outdoor life and the almost universal good manners. But all too frequently I am the prey of a vivid nightmare that recalls what I experienced in that town five years ago.

Davis—that is not its real name—has a population of about twenty thousand people, one-third of them colored. It is a cotton-mill town and the workers of that trade, several thousand gaunt and ignorant "poor whites," live together in an ill-reputed section known as "Cotton Hollow." The population of Davis has varied in its seventy-five years. Once it was under consideration for the capital of the state, and so the older families and their kin form a proud little aristocracy, even when individually they have sunk to destitution.

That winter I'd made the usual round in New York until about April, when I decided I never wanted to see another invitation again. I was tired and I wanted to go to Europe for a rest, but the Baby Panic of 1921 hit Father's business, and so it was suggested that I go South and visit Aunt Musidora Hale instead.

Vaguely I imagined that I was going to the country, but on the day I arrived, the Davis "Courier" published an hilarious old picture of me on its society page, and I found I was in for another season. On a small scale, of course: there were Saturday-night dances at the little country club with its nine-hole golf course and some informal dinner parties and several attractive and attentive boys. I didn't have a dull time at all and when after three weeks I wanted to go home, it wasn't because I was bored. On the contrary I wanted to go home because I'd allowed myself to get rather interested in a good-looking young man named Charley Kincaid, without realizing that he was engaged to another girl.

We'd been drawn together from the first because he was almost the only boy in town who'd gone north to college, and I was still young enough to think that America revolved around Harvard and Princeton and Yale. He liked me too—I could see that—but when I heard that his engagement to a girl named Marie Bannerman had been announced six months before, there was nothing for me except to go away. The town was too small to avoid people, and though so far there hadn't been any talk, I was sure that—well, that if we kept meeting the emotion we were beginning to feel would somehow get into words. I'm not mean enough to take a man away from another girl.

Marie Bannerman was almost a beauty. Perhaps she would have been a beauty if she'd had any clothes, and if she hadn't used bright pink rouge in two high spots on her cheeks and powdered her nose and chin to a funereal white. Her hair was shining black, her features were lovely, and an affliction of one eye kept it always half-closed and gave an air of humorous mischief to her face.

I was leaving on a Monday, and on Saturday night a crowd of us dined at the country club as usual before the dance. There was Joe Cable, the son of a former governor, a handsome, dissipated and yet somehow charming young man; Catherine Jones, a pretty, sharp-eyed girl with an exquisite figure, who under her rouge might have been any age from eighteen to twenty-five; Marie Bannerman; Charley Kincaid; myself and two or three others.

I loved to listen to the genial flow of bizarre neighborhood anecdote at this kind of party. For instance one of the girls, together with her entire family, had that afternoon been evicted from her house for non-payment of rent. She told the story wholly without self-consciousness, merely as something troublesome but amusing. And I loved the banter which presumed every girl to be infinitely beautiful and attractive, and every man to have been secretly and hopelessly in love with every girl present from their respective cradles.

"—we liked to die laughin'". . . "—said he was fixin' to shoot him without he stayed away." The girls "'clared to heaven"; the men "took oath" on inconsequential statements. "How come you nearly about forgot to come by for me—" and the incessant Honey, Honey, Honey, Honey until the word seemed to roll like a genial liquid from heart to heart.

Outside, the May night was hot, a still night, velvet, soft-pawed, splattered thick with stars. It drifted heavy and sweet into the large room where we sat and where we would later dance, with no sound in it except the occasional long crunch of an arriving car on the drive. Just at that moment I hated to leave Davis as I never had hated to leave a town before—I felt that I wanted to spend my life in this town, drifting and dancing forever through these long, hot, romantic nights.

Yet horror was already hanging over that little party, was waiting tensely among us, an uninvited guest, and telling off the hours until it could show its pale and blinding face. Beneath the chatter and laughter something was going on, something secret and obscure that I didn't know.

Presently the colored orchestra arrived, followed by the first trickle of the dance crowd. An enormous red-faced man in muddy knee boots, and with a revolver strapped around his waist, clumped in and paused for a moment at our table before going upstairs to the locker room. It was Bill Abercrombie, the sheriff, the son of Congressman Abercrombie. Some of the boys asked him half-whispered questions, and he replied in an attempt at an undertone.

"Yes. . . . He's in the swamp all right; farmer saw him near the crossroads store. . . . Like to have a shot at him myself."

I asked the boy next to me what was the matter.

"Nigger case," he said, "over in Kisco, about two miles from here. He's hiding in the swamp and they're going in after him tomorrow."

"What'll they do to him?"

"Hang him, I guess."

The notion of the forlorn darky crouching dismally in a desolate bog waiting for dawn and death depressed me for a moment. Then the feeling passed and was forgotten.

After dinner Charley Kincaid and I walked out on the verandah—he had just heard that I was going away. I kept as close to the others as I could, answering his words but not his eyes—something inside me was protesting against leaving him on such a casual note. The temptation was strong to let something flicker up between us here at the end. I wanted him to kiss me—my heart promised that if he kissed me, just once, it would accept with equanimity the idea of never seeing him anymore; but my mind knew it wasn't so.

The other girls began to drift inside and upstairs to the dressing room to improve their complexions, and with Charley still beside me, I followed. Just at that moment I wanted to cry—perhaps my eyes were already blurred, or perhaps it was my haste lest they should be, but I opened the door of a small card room by mistake, and with my error the tragic machinery of the night began to function. In the card room, not five feet from us, stood Marie Bannerman, Charley's fiancée, and Joe Cable. They were in each other's arms, absorbed in a passionate and oblivious kiss.

I closed the door quickly, and without glancing at Charley opened the right door and ran upstairs.

II

A few minutes later Marie Bannerman entered the crowded dressing room. She saw me and came over, smiling in a sort of mock despair, but she breathed quickly and the smile trembled a little on her mouth.

"You won't say a word, Honey, will you?" she whispered.

"Of course not." I wondered how that could matter, now that Charley Kincaid knew.

"Who else was it that saw us?"

"Only Charley Kincaid and me."

"Oh!" She looked a little puzzled. Then she added: "He didn't wait to say anything, honey. When we came out he was just going out the door. I thought he was going to wait and romp all over Joe."

"How about his romping all over you?" I couldn't help asking.

"Oh, he'll do that." She laughed wryly. "But honey, I know how to handle him. It's just when he's first mad that I'm scared of him—he's got an awful temper." She whistled reminiscently. "I know, because this happened once before."

I wanted to slap her. Turning my back, I walked away on the pretext of borrowing a pin from Katie, the negro maid. Catherine Jones was claiming the latter's attention with a short gingham garment which needed repair.

"What's that?" I asked.

"Dancing-dress," she answered shortly, her mouth full of pins. When she took them out, she added, "It's all come to pieces, I've used it so much."

"Are you going to dance here tonight?"

"Going to try."

Somebody had told me that she wanted to be a dancer—that she had taken lessons in New York.

"Can I help you fix anything?"

"No, thanks—unless—can you sew? Katie gets so excited Saturday night that she's no good for anything except fetching pins. I'd be everlasting grateful to you, honey."

I had reasons for not wanting to go downstairs just yet, and so I sat down and worked on her dress for half an hour. I wondered if Charley had gone home, if I would ever see him again—I scarcely dared to wonder if what he had seen would set him free, ethically. When I went down finally he was not in sight.

The room was now crowded; the tables had been removed and dancing was general. At that time, just after the war, all Southern boys had a way of agitating their heels from side to side, pivoting on the ball of the foot as they danced, and to acquiring this accomplishment I had devoted many hours. There were plenty of stags, almost all of them cheerful with corn-liquor; I refused on an average at least two drinks a dance. Even when it is mixed with a soft drink, as is the custom, rather than gulped from the neck of a warm bottle, it is a formidable proposition. Only a few girls like Catherine Jones took an occasional sip from some boy's flask down at the dark end of the verandah.

I liked Catherine Jones—she seemed to have more energy than these other girls, though Aunt Musidora sniffed rather contemptuously whenever Catherine stopped for me in her car to go to the movies, remarking that she guessed "the bottom rail had gotten to be the top rail now." Her family were "new and common," but it seemed to me that perhaps her very commonness was an asset. Almost every girl in Davis confided in me at one time or another that her ambition was to "get away and come to New York," but only Catherine Jones had actually taken the step of studying stage dancing with that end in view.

She was often asked to dance at these Saturday night affairs, something "classic" or perhaps an acrobatic clog—on one memorable occasion she had annoyed the governing board by a "shimmy" (then the scapegrace of jazz), and the novel and somewhat startling excuse made for her was that she was "so tight she didn't know what she was doing anyhow." She impressed me as a curious personality, and I was eager to see what she would produce tonight.

At twelve o'clock the music always ceased, as dancing was forbidden on Sunday morning. So at eleven-thirty a vast fanfaronade of drum and cornet beckoned the dancers and the couples on the verandahs, and the ones in the cars outside, and the stragglers from the bar, into the ballroom. Chairs were brought in and galloped up *en masse* and with a great racket to the slightly raised platform. The orchestra had evacuated this and taken a place beside. Then, as the rearward lights were lowered, they began to play a tune accompanied by a curious drum-beat that I had never heard before, and simultaneously Catherine Jones appeared upon the platform. She wore the short, country girl's dress upon which I had lately labored, and a wide sunbonnet under which her face, stained yellow with powder, looked out at us with rolling eyes and a vacant negroid leer. She began to dance.

I had never seen anything like it before, and until five years later I wasn't to see it again. It was the Charleston—it must have been the Charleston. I remember the double drum-beat like a shouted *"Hey! Hey!"* and the unfamiliar swing of the arms and the odd knock-kneed effect. She had picked it up, heaven knows where.

Her audience, familiar with negro rhythms, leaned forward eagerly—even to them it was something new, but it is stamped on my mind as clearly and indelibly as though I had seen it yesterday. The figure on the platform swinging and stamping, the excited orchestra, the waiters grinning in the doorway of the bar, and all around through many windows the soft languorous southern night seeping in from swamp and cottonfield and lush foliage and brown, warm streams. At what point a feeling of tense uneasiness began to steal over me I don't know. The dance could scarcely have taken ten minutes; perhaps the first beats of the barbaric music disquieted me—long before it was over I was sitting rigid in my seat, and my eyes were wandering here and there around the hall, passing along the rows of shadowy faces as if seeking some security that was no longer there.

I'm not a nervous type, nor am I given to panic, but for a moment I was afraid that if the music and the dance didn't stop I'd be hysterical. Something was happening all about me. I knew it as well as if I could see into these unknown souls. Things were happening, but one thing especially was leaning over so close that it almost touched us, that it did touch us. . . . I almost screamed as a hand brushed accidentally against my back.

The music stopped. There was applause and protracted cries of encore, but Catherine Jones shook her head definitely at the orchestra leader and made as though to leave the platform. The appeals for more continued—again she shook her head, and it seemed to me that her expression was rather angry. Then a strange incident occurred. At the protracted pleading of someone in the front row, the colored orchestra leader began the vamp of the tune, as if to lure Catherine Jones into changing her mind. Instead she turned toward him, snapped out, "Didn't you hear me say no?" and then, surprisingly, slapped his face. The music stopped and an amused murmur terminated abruptly as a muffled but clearly audible shot rang out.

Immediately we were on our feet, for the sound indicated that it had been fired within or near the house. One of the chaperones gave a little scream, but when some wag called out "Caesar's in that henhouse again," the momentary alarm dissolved into laughter. The club manager, followed by several curious couples, went out to have a look around, but the rest were already moving around the floor to the strains of "Good Night, Ladies," which traditionally ended the dance.

I was glad it was over. The man with whom I had come went to get his car. I called a waiter and sent him for my golf clubs, which were in the stack upstairs. I strolled out on the porch and waited, wondering again if Charley Kincaid had gone home.

Suddenly I was aware, in that curious way in which you become aware of something that has been going on for several minutes, that there was a tumult inside. Women were shrieking; there was a cry of "Oh, my God!" then the sounds of a stampede on the inside stairs and footsteps running back and forth across the ballroom. A girl appeared from somewhere and pitched forward in a dead faint—almost immediately another girl did the same, and I heard a frantic male voice shouting into a telephone. Then, hatless and pale, a young man rushed out on the porch, and with hands that were cold as ice, seized my arm.

"What is it?" I cried. "A fire? What's happened?"

"Marie Bannerman's dead upstairs in the women's dressing room. Shot through the throat!"

III

The rest of that night is a series of visions that seem to have no connection with one another, that follow each other with the sharp instantaneous transitions of scenes in the movies. There was a group who stood arguing on the porch, in voices now raised, now hushed, about what should be done and how every waiter in the club, "even old Moses," ought to be given the third degree tonight. That a "nigger" had shot and killed Marie Bannerman was the instant and unquestioned assumption—in the first unreasoning instant, anyone who doubted it would have been under suspicion. The guilty one was said to be Katie Golstien, the colored maid, who had discovered the body and fainted. It was said to be "that nigger they were looking for over near Kisco." It was any darky at all.

Within half an hour people began to drift out, each with his little contribution of new discoveries. The crime had been committed with Sheriff Abercrombie's gun—he had hung it, belt and all, in full view on the wall before coming down to dance. It was missing—they were hunting for it now. Instantly killed, the doctor said—bullet had been fired from only a few feet away.

Then a few minutes later another young man came out and made an announcement in a loud, grave voice:

"They've arrested Charley Kincaid."

My head reeled. Upon the group gathered on the verandah fell an awed, stricken silence.

"—arrested Charley Kincaid!"

"Charley *Kincaid?*"

Why, he was one of the best, one of themselves.

"That's the craziest thing I ever heard of!"

The young man nodded, shocked like the rest but self-important with his information.

"He wasn't downstairs when Catherine Jones was dancing—he says he was in the men's locker room. And Marie Bannerman told a lot of girls that they'd had a row, and she was scared of what he'd do."

Again an awed silence.

"That's the craziest thing I ever heard!" someone said again.

"Charley *Kincaid!*"

The narrator waited a moment. Then he added:

"He caught her kissing Joe Cable—"

I couldn't keep silence a minute longer.

"What about it?" I cried out. "I was with him at the time. He wasn't—he wasn't angry at all."

They looked at me, their faces startled, confused, unhappy. Suddenly the footsteps of several men sounded loud through the ballroom and a moment later Charley Kincaid, his face dead white, came out the front door between the sheriff and another man. Crossing the porch quickly they descended the steps and disappeared in the darkness. A moment later there was the sound of a starting car.

When an instant later far away down the road I heard the eerie scream of an ambulance, I got up desperately and called to my escort, who formed part of the whispering group.

"I've got to go," I said. "I can't stand this. Either take me home or I'll find a place in another car." Reluctantly he shouldered my clubs—the sight of them made me realize that I now couldn't leave on Monday after all—and followed me down the steps just as the black body of the ambulance curved in at the gate—a ghastly shadow on the bright, starry night.

IV

The situation, after the first wild surmises, the first burst of unreasoning loyalty to Charley Kincaid, had died away, was outlined by the Davis "Courier" and by most of the state newspapers in this fashion: Marie Bannerman died in the women's dressing room of the Davis Country Club from the effects of a shot fired at close quarters from a revolver just after eleven forty-five o'clock on

Saturday night. Many persons had heard the shot; moreover it had undoubtedly been fired from the revolver of Sheriff Abercrombie, which had been hanging in full sight on the wall of the next room. Abercrombie himself was down in the ballroom when the murder took place, as many witnesses could testify. The revolver was not found.

So far as was known, the only man who had been upstairs at the time the shot was fired was Charles Kincaid. He was engaged to Miss Bannerman, but according to several witnesses they had quarreled seriously that evening. Miss Bannerman herself had mentioned the quarrel, adding that she was afraid and wanted to keep away from him until he cooled off.

Charles Kincaid asserted that at the time the shot was fired he was in the men's locker room—where, indeed, he was found, immediately after the discovery of Miss Bannerman's body. He denied having had any words with Miss Bannerman at all. He had heard the shot but it had had no significance for him—if he thought anything of it, he thought that "someone was potting cats outdoors."

Why had he chosen to remain in the locker room during the dance?

No reason at all. He was tired. He was waiting until Miss Bannerman wanted to go home.

The body was discovered by Katie Golstien, the colored maid, who herself was found in a faint when the crowd of girls surged upstairs for their coats. Returning from the kitchen, where she had been getting a bite to eat, Katie had found Miss Bannerman, her dress wet with blood, already dead on the floor.

Both the police and the newspapers attached importance to the geography of the country club's second story. It consisted of a row of three rooms—the women's dressing room and the men's locker room at either end, and in the middle a room which was used as a cloak-room and for the storage of golf clubs. The women's and men's rooms had no outlet except into this chamber, which was connected by one stairs with the ballroom below, and by another with the kitchen. According to the testimony of three negro cooks and the white caddy master, no one but Katie Golstien had gone up the kitchen stairs that night.

As I remember it after five years, the foregoing is a pretty accurate summary of the situation when Charley Kincaid was accused of first-degree murder and committed for trial. Other people, chiefly negroes, were suspected (at the loyal instigation of Charley Kincaid's friends), and several arrests were made, but nothing ever came of them, and upon what grounds they were based I have long forgotten. One group, in spite of the disappearance of the pistol, claimed persistently that it was a suicide and suggested some ingenious reasons to account for the absence of the weapon.

Now when it is known how Marie Bannerman happened to die so savagely and so violently, it would be easy for me, of all people, to say that I believed in Charley Kincaid all the time. But I didn't. I thought that he had killed her, and at the same time I knew that I loved him with all my heart. That it was I who first happened upon the evidence which set him free was due not to any faith in his innocence but to a strange vividness with which, in moods of excitement, certain scenes stamp themselves on my memory, so that I can remember every detail and how that detail struck me at the time.

It was one afternoon early in July, when the case against Charley Kincaid seemed to be at its strongest, that the horror of the actual murder slipped away from me for a moment and I began to think about other incidents of that same haunted night. Something Marie Bannerman had said to me in the dressing room persistently eluded me, bothered me—not because I believed it to be important, but simply because I couldn't remember. It was gone from me, as if it had been a part of the fantastic undercurrent of small-town life which I had felt so strongly that evening, the sense that things were in the air, old secrets, old loves and feuds and unresolved situations that I, an outsider, could never fully understand. Just for a minute it seemed to me that Marie Bannerman had pushed aside the curtain; then it had dropped into place again—the house into which I might have looked was dark now forever.

Another incident, perhaps less important, also haunted me. The tragic events of a few minutes after had driven it from everyone's mind, but I had a strong impression that for a brief space of time I wasn't the only one to be surprised. When the audience had demanded an encore from Catherine Jones, her unwillingness to dance again had been so acute that she had been driven to the point of slapping the orchestra leader's face. The discrepancy between his offense and the venom of the rebuff recurred to me again and again. It wasn't natural—or, more important, it hadn't *seemed* natural. In view of the fact that Catherine Jones had been drinking, it was explicable; but it worried me now as it had worried me then. Rather to lay its ghost than to do any investigating, I pressed an obliging young man into service and called on the leader of the band.

His name was Thomas, a very dark, very simple-hearted virtuoso of the traps, and it took less than ten minutes to find out that Catherine Jones' gesture had surprised him as much as it had me. He had known her a long time, seen her at dances since she was a little girl—why, the very dance she did that night was one she had rehearsed with his orchestra a week before. And a few days later she had come to him and said she was sorry.

"I knew she would," he concluded. "She's a right good-hearted girl. My sister Katie was her nurse from when she was born up to the time she went to school."

"Your sister—?"

"Katie. She's the maid out the country club. Katie Golstien. You been reading 'bout her in the papers in 'at Charley Kincaid case. She's the maid. Katie Golstien. She's the maid at the country club what found the body of Miss Bannerman."

"So Katie was Miss Catherine Jones' nurse?"

"Yes ma'am."

Going home, stimulated but unsatisfied, I asked my companion a quick question.

"Were Catherine and Marie good friends?"

"Oh, yes," he answered without hesitation. "All the girls are good friends here, except when two of them are tryin' to get hold of the same man. Then they warm each other up a little."

"Why do you suppose Catherine hasn't married? Hasn't she got lots of beaux?"

"Off and on. She only likes people for a day or so at a time. That is—all except Joe Cable.

Now a scene burst upon me, broke over me like a dissolving wave. And suddenly, my mind shivering from the impact, I remembered what Marie Bannerman had said to me in the dressing room: "Who else was it that saw?" She had caught a glimpse of someone else, a figure passing so quickly that she could not identify it, out of the corner of her eye.

And suddenly, simultaneously, I seemed to see that figure, as if I too had been vaguely conscious of it at the time, just as one is aware of a familiar gait or outline on the street long before there is any flicker of recognition. On the corner of my own eye was stamped a hurrying figure—that might have been Catherine Jones.

But when the shot was fired Catherine Jones was in full view of over fifty people. Was it credible that Katie Golstien, a woman of fifty, who as a nurse had been known and trusted by three generations of Davis people, would shoot down a young girl in cold blood at Catherine Jones' command?

"*But when the shot was fired Catherine Jones was in full view of over fifty people.*"

That sentence beat in my head all night, taking on fantastic variations, dividing itself into phrases, segments, individual words.

"*But when the shot was fired* . . . Catherine Jones was in full view . . . of over fifty people.*"

When the shot was fired! What shot? The shot we heard. When the shot was fired. . . . When the shot was fired. . . .

The next morning at nine o'clock, with the pallor of sleeplessness buried under a quantity of paint such as I had never worn before or have since, I walked up a rickety flight of stairs to the sheriff's office.

Abercrombie, engrossed in his morning's mail, looked up curiously as I came in the door.

"Catherine Jones did it," I cried, struggling to keep the hysteria out of my voice. "She killed Marie Bannerman with a shot we didn't hear because the orchestra was playing and everybody was pushing up the chairs. The shot we heard was when Katie fired the pistol out the window after the music was stopped. To give Catherine an alibi!"

V

I was right—as everyone now knows—but for a week, until Katie Golstien broke down under a fierce and ruthless inquisition, nobody believed me. Even Charley Kincaid, as he afterward confessed, didn't dare to think it could be true.

What had been the relations between Catherine and Joe Cable no one ever knew, but evidently she had determined that his clandestine affair with Marie Bannerman had gone too far.

Then Marie chanced to come into the women's room while Catherine was dressing for her dance—and there again there is a certain obscurity, for Catherine always claimed that Marie got the revolver, threatened her with it and that in the ensuing struggle the trigger was pulled. In spite of everything I always rather liked Catherine Jones, but in justice it must be said that only a simple-minded and very exceptional jury would have let her off with five years. And in just about five years from her commitment my husband and I are going to make a round of the New York musical shows and look hard at all the members of the chorus from the very front row.

After the shooting she must have thought quickly. Katie was told to wait until the music stopped, fire the revolver out the window and then hide it—Catherine Jones neglected to specify where. Katie, on the verge of collapse, obeyed instructions but she was never able to specify where she had hid the revolver. And no one ever knew until a year later when Charley and I were on our honeymoon and Sheriff Abercrombie's ugly weapon dropped out of my golf bag onto a Hot Springs golf links. The bag must have been standing just outside the dressing room door; Katie's trembling hand had dropped the revolver into the first aperture she could see.

We live in New York. Small towns make us both uncomfortable. Every day we read about the crime waves in the big cities, but at least a wave is something tangible that you can provide against. What I dread above all things is the unknown depths, the incalculable ebb and flow, the secret shapes of things that drift through opaque darkness under the surface of the sea.

YOUR WAY AND MINE

One spring afternoon in the first year of the present century a young man was experimenting with a new typewriter in a brokerage office on lower Broadway. At his elbow lay an eight-line letter and he was endeavoring to make a copy on the machine, but each attempt was marred by a monstrous capital rising unexpectedly in the middle of a word or by the disconcerting intrusion of some symbol such as $ or % into an alphabet whose membership was set at twenty-six many years ago. Whenever he detected a mistake he made a new beginning with a fresh sheet, but after the fifteenth try he was aware of a ferocious instinct to cast the machine from the window.

The young man's short blunt fingers were too big for the keys. He was big all over; indeed his bulky body seemed to be in the very process of growth for it had ripped his coat at the back seam, while his trousers clung to thigh and calf like skin tights. His hair was yellow and tousled—you could see the paths of his broad fingers in it—and his eyes were of a hard brilliant blue, but the lids drooping a little over them reinforced an impression of lethargy that the clumsy body conveyed. His age was twenty-one.

"What do you think the eraser's for, McComas?"

The young man looked around.

"What's that?" he demanded brusquely.

"The eraser," repeated the short alert human fox who had come in the outer door and paused behind him. "That there's a good copy except for one word. Use your head or you'll be sitting there until tomorrow."

The human fox moved on into his private office. The young man sat for a moment, motionless, sluggish. Suddenly he grunted, picked up the eraser referred to and flung it savagely out of the window.

Twenty minutes later he opened the door of his employer's office. In his hand was the letter, immaculately typed, and the addressed envelope.

"Here it is, sir," he said, frowning a little from his late concentration.

The human fox took it, glanced at it and then looked at McComas with a peculiar smile.

"You didn't use the eraser?"

"No, I didn't, Mr. Woodley."

"You're one of those thorough young men, aren't you?" said the fox sarcastically.

"What?"

"I said 'thorough' but since you weren't listening I'll change it to 'pig-headed.' Whose time did you waste just to avoid a little erasure that the best typists aren't too proud to make? Did you waste your time or mine?"

"I wanted to make one good copy," answered McComas steadily. "You see I never worked a typewriter before."

"Answer my question," snapped Mr. Woodley. "When you sat there making two dozen copies of that letter were you wasting your time or mine?"

"It was mostly my lunch time," McComas replied, his big face flushing to an angry pink. "I've got to do things my own way or not at all."

For answer Mr. Woodley picked up the letter and envelope, folded them, tore them once and again and dropped the pieces into the wastepaper basket with a toothy little smile.

"That's my way," he announced. "What do you think of that?"

Young McComas had taken a step forward as if to snatch the fragments from the fox's hand.

"By Golly," he cried. "By Golly. Why, for two cents I'd take down your pants and spank you!"

With an angry snarl Mr. Woodley sprang to his feet, fumbled in his pocket and threw a handful of change upon his desk.

Ten minutes later the outside man coming in to report perceived that neither young McComas nor his hat were in their usual places.

But in the private office he found Mr. Woodley, his face crimson and foam bubbling between his teeth, shouting frantically into the telephone. The outside man noticed to his surprise that Mr. Woodley was in daring dishabille and that there were six suspender buttons scattered upon the office floor.

II

In 1902 Henry McComas weighed 196 pounds. In 1905 when he journeyed back to his home town, Elmira, to marry the love of his boyhood he tipped accurate beams at 210. His weight remained constant for two years but after the Panic of 1907 it bounded to 220, about which comfortable figure it was apparently to hover for the rest of his life.

He looked mature beyond his years—under certain illuminations his yellow hair became a dignified white—and his bulk added to the impression of authority that he gave. During his first five years off the farm there was never a time when he wasn't scheming to get into business for himself.

For a temperament like Henry McComas', which insisted on running at a pace of its own, independence was an utter necessity. He must make his own rules, willy-nilly, even though he join the ranks of those many abject failures who have also tried. Just one week after he had achieved his emancipation from other people's hierarchies he was moved to expound his point to Theodore Drinkwater, his partner—this because Drinkwater had wondered aloud if he intended never to come downtown before eleven.

"I doubt it," said McComas.

"What's the idea?" demanded Drinkwater indignantly. "What do you think the effect's going to be on our office force?"

"Does Miss Johnston show any sign of being demoralized?"

"I mean after we get more people. It isn't as if you were an old man, Mac, with your work behind you. You're only twenty-eight, not a day older than me. What'll you do at forty?"

"I'll be downtown at eleven o'clock," said McComas, "every working day of my life."

Later in the week one of their first clients invited them to lunch at a celebrated business club; the club's least member was a rajah of the swelling, expanding empire.

"Look around, Ted," whispered McComas as they left the dining room. "There's a man looks like a prize fighter, and there's one who looks like a ham actor. That's a plumber there behind you; there's a coal heaver and a couple of cowboys—do you see? There's a chronic invalid and a confidence man, a pawnbroker—that one on the right. By Golly, where are all the big business men we came to see?"

The route back to their office took them by a small restaurant where the clerks of the district flocked to lunch.

"Take a look at them, Ted, and you'll find the men who know the rules—and think and act and look like just what they are."

"I suppose if they put on a pink mustache and came to work at five in the afternoon they'd get to be great men," scoffed Drinkwater.

"Posing is exactly what I don't mean. Just accept yourself. We're brought up on fairy stories about the new leaf, but who goes on believing them except those who have to believe, and have to hope or else go crazy. I think America will be a happier country when the individual begins to look his personal limitations in the face. Anything that's in your character at twenty-one is usually there to stay."

In any case what was in Henry McComas' was there to stay. Henry McComas wouldn't dine with a client in a bad restaurant for a proposition of three figures, wouldn't hurry his luncheon for a proposition of four, wouldn't go without it for a proposition of five. And in spite of these peculiarities the exporting firm in which he owned forty-nine per-cent of the stock began to pepper South America with locomotives, dynamos, barb wire, hydraulic engines, cranes, mining machinery, and other appurtenances of civilization. In 1913 when Henry McComas was thirty-four he owned a house on 92nd Street and calculated that his income for the next year would come to thirty thousand dollars. And because of a sudden and unexpected demand from Europe which was not for pink lemonade, it came to twice that. The buying agent for the British Government arrived, followed by the buying agents for the French, Belgian, Russian and Serbian Governments, and a share of the commodities required were assembled under the stewardship of Drinkwater and McComas. There was a chance that they would be rich men. Then suddenly this eventuality began to turn on the woman Henry McComas had married.

Stella McComas was the daughter of a small hay and grain dealer of upper New York. Her father was unlucky and always on the verge of failure, so she grew up in the shadow of worry. Later, while Henry McComas got his start in New York, she earned her living by teaching physical culture in the public schools of Utica. In consequence she brought to her marriage a belief in certain stringent rules for the care of the body and an exaggerated fear of adversity.

For the first years she was so impressed with her husband's rapid rise and so absorbed in her babies that she accepted Henry as something infallible and protective, outside the scope of her provincial wisdom. But as her little girl grew into short dresses and hair ribbons, and her little boy into the custody of an English nurse she had more time to look closely at her husband. His leisurely ways, his corpulency, his sometimes maddening deliberateness, ceased to be the privileged idiosyncrasies of success, and became only facts.

For a while he paid no great attention to her little suggestions as to his diet, her occasional crankiness as to his hours, her invidious comparisons between his habits and the fancied habits of other men. Then one morning a peculiar lack of taste in his coffee precipitated the matter into the light.

"I can't drink the stuff—it hasn't had any taste for a week," he complained. "And why is it brought in a cup from the kitchen? I like to put the cream and sugar in myself."

Stella avoided an answer but later he reverted to the matter.

"About my coffee. You'll remember—won't you?—to tell Rose."

Suddenly she smiled at him innocently.

"Don't you feel better, Henry?" she asked eagerly.

"What?"

"Less tired, less worried?"

"Who said I was tired and worried? I never felt better in my life."

"There you are." She looked at him triumphantly. "You laugh at my theories but this time you'll have to admit there's something in them. You feel better because you haven't had sugar in your coffee for over a week."

He looked at her incredulously.

"What have I had?"

"Saccharine."

He got up indignantly and threw his newspaper on the table.

"I might have known it," he broke out. "All that bringing it out from the kitchen. What the devil is saccharine?"

"It's a substitute, for people who have a tendency to run to fat."

For a moment he hovered on the edge of anger—then he sat down shaking with laughter.

"It's done you good," she said reproachfully.

"Well, it won't do me good any more," he said grimly. "I'm thirty-four years old and I haven't been sick a day in ten years. I've forgotten more about my constitution than you'll ever know."

"You don't live a healthy life, Henry. It's after forty that things begin to tell."

"Saccharine!" he exclaimed, again breaking into laughter. "Saccharine! I thought perhaps it was something to keep me from drink. You know they have these—"

Suddenly she grew angry.

"Well why not? You ought to be ashamed to be so fat at your age. You wouldn't be if you took a little exercise and didn't lie around in bed all morning."

Words utterly failed her.

"If I wanted to be a farmer," said her husband quietly, "I wouldn't have left home. This saccharine business is over today—do you see?"

Their financial situation rapidly improved. By the second year of the war they were keeping a limousine and chauffeur and began to talk vaguely of a nice summer house on Long Island Sound. Month by month a swelling stream of materials flowed through the ledgers of Drinkwater and McComas to be dumped on the insatiable bonfire across the ocean. Their staff of clerks tripled and the atmosphere of the office was so charged with energy and achievement that Stella herself often liked to wander in on some pretext during the afternoon.

One day early in 1916 she called to learn that Mr. McComas was out and was on the point of leaving when she ran into Ted Drinkwater coming out of the elevator.

"Why, Stella," he exclaimed, "I was thinking about you only this morning."

The Drinkwaters and the McComases were close if not particularly spontaneous friends. Nothing but their husbands' intimate association would have thrown the two women together, yet they were "Henry, Ted, Mollie and Stella" to each other and in ten years scarcely a month had passed without their partaking in a superficially cordial family dinner. The dinner being over, each couple indulged in an unsparing post-mortem over the other without, however, any sense of disloyalty. They were used to each other—so Stella was somewhat surprised by Ted Drinkwater's personal eagerness at meeting her this afternoon.

"I want to see you," he said in his intent direct way. "Have you got a minute, Stella? Could you come into my office?"

"Why, yes."

As they walked between rows of typists toward the glassed privacy of THEODORE DRINKWATER, PRESIDENT, Stella could not help thinking that he made a more appropriate business figure than her husband. He was lean, terse, quick. His eye glanced keenly from right to left as if taking the exact measure of every clerk and stenographer in sight.

"Sit down, Stella."

She waited, a feeling of vague apprehension stealing over her. Drinkwater frowned.

"It's about Henry," he said.

"Is he sick?" she demanded quickly.

"No. Nothing like that." He hesitated. "Stella, I've always thought you were a woman with a lot of common sense."

She waited.

"This is a thing that's been on my mind for over a year," he continued. "He and I have battled it out so often that—that a certain coldness has grown up between us."

"Yes?" Stella's eyes blinked nervously.

"It's about the business," said Drinkwater abruptly. "A coldness with a business partner is a mighty unpleasant thing."

"What's the matter?"

"The old story, Stella. These are big years for us and he thinks business is going to wait while he carries on in the old country-store way. Down at eleven, hour and a half for lunch, won't be nice to a man he doesn't like for love or money. In the last six months he's lost us about three sizable orders by things like that."

Instinctively she sprang to her husband's defense.

"But hasn't he saved money too by going slow? On that thing about the copper, you wanted to sign right away and Henry—"

"Oh that—" He waved it aside a little hurriedly. "I'm the last man to deny that Henry has a wonderful instinct in certain ways—"

"But it was a great big thing," she interrupted. "It would have practically ruined you if he hadn't put his foot down. He said—"

She pulled herself up short.

"Oh, I don't know," said Drinkwater with an expression of annoyance. "Perhaps not as bad as that. Anyway, we all make mistakes and that's aside from the question. We have the opportunity right now of jumping into Class A. I mean it. Another two years of this kind of business and we can each put away our first million dollars. And, Stella, whatever happens, I am determined to put away mine. Even—" He considered his words for a moment. "Even if it comes to breaking with Henry."

"Oh!" Stella exclaimed. "I hope—"

"I hope not too. That's why I wanted to talk to you. Can't you do something, Stella? You're about the only person he'll listen to. He's so darn pig-headed he can't understand how he disorganizes the office. Get him up in the morning. No man ought to lie in bed till eleven."

"He gets up at half past nine."

"He's down here at eleven. That's what counts. Stir him up. Tell him you want more money. Orders are more money and there are lots of orders around for anyone who goes after them."

"I'll see what I can do," she said anxiously. "But I don't know—Henry's difficult—very set in his ways."

"You'll think of something. You might—" He smiled grimly. "You might give him a few more bills to pay. Sometimes I think an extravagant wife's the best inspiration a man can have. We need more pep down here. I've got to be the pep for two. I mean it, Stella, I can't carry this thing alone."

Stella left the office with her mind in a panic. All the fears and uncertainties of her childhood had been brought suddenly to the surface. She saw Henry cast off by Ted Drinkwater and trying unsuccessfully to run a business of his own. With his easygoing ways! They would slide downhill, giving up the servants one by one, the car, the house. Before she reached home her imagination had envisaged poverty, her children at work—starvation. Hadn't Ted Drinkwater just told her that he himself was the life of the concern—that he kept things moving? What would Henry do alone?

For a week she brooded over the matter, guarding her secret but looking with a mixture of annoyance and compassion at Henry over the dinner table. Then she mustered up her resolution. She went to a real estate agent and handed over her entire bank account of nine thousand dollars as the first payment on a house they had fearfully coveted on Long Island. . . . That night she told Henry.

"Why, Stella, you must have gone crazy," he cried aghast. "You must have gone crazy. Why didn't you ask me?"

He wanted to take her by the shoulders and shake her.

"I was afraid, Henry," she answered truthfully.

He thrust his hands despairingly through his yellow hair.

"Just at this time, Stella. I've just taken out an insurance policy that's more than I can really afford—we haven't paid for the new car—we've had a new front put on this house—last week your sable coat. I was going to devote tonight to figuring just how close we were running on money."

"But can't you—can't you take something out of the business until things get better?" she demanded in alarm.

"That's just what I can't do. It's impossible. I can't explain because you don't understand the situation down there. You see Ted and I— can't agree on certain things—"

Suddenly a new light dawned on her and she felt her body flinch. Supposing that by bringing about this situation she had put her husband into his partner's hands. Yet wasn't that what she wanted— wasn't it necessary for the present that Henry should conform to Drinkwater's methods?

"Sixty thousand dollars," repeated Henry in a frightened voice that made her want to cry. "I don't know where I am going to get enough to buy it on mortgage." He sank into a chair. "I might go and see the people you dealt with tomorrow and make a compromise— let some of your nine thousand go."

"I don't think they would," she said, her face set. "They were awfully anxious to sell—the owner's going away."

She had acted on impulse, she said, thinking that in their increasing prosperity the money would be available. He had been so generous about the new car—she supposed that now at last they could afford what they wanted.

It was typical of McComas that after the first moment of surprise he wasted no energy in reproaches. But two days later he came home from work with such a heavy and dispirited look on his face that she could not help but guess that he and Ted Drinkwater had had it out—and that what she wanted had come true. That night in shame and pity she cried herself to sleep.

III

A new routine was inaugurated in Henry McComas' life. Each morning Stella woke him at eight and he lay for fifteen minutes in an unwilling trance, as if his body were surprised at this departure from the custom of a decade. He reached the office at nine-thirty as promptly as he had once reached it at eleven—on the first morning his appearance caused a flutter of astonishment among the older employees—and he limited his lunch time to a conscientious hour. No longer could he be found asleep on his office couch between two and three o'clock on summer afternoons—the couch itself vanished into that limbo which held his leisurely periods of digestion and his cherished surfeit of sleep. These were his concessions to Drinkwater in exchange for the withdrawal of sufficient money to cover his immediate needs.

Drinkwater of course could have bought him out, but for various reasons the senior partner did not consider this advisable. One of them, though he didn't admit it to himself, was his absolute reliance on McComas in all matters of initiative and decision. Another reason was the tumultuous condition of the market, for as 1916 boomed on with the tragic battle of the Somme the allied agents sailed once more to the city of plenty for the wherewithal of another year. Coincidently Drinkwater and McComas moved into a suite that was like a floor in a country club, and there they sat all day while anxious and gesticulating strangers explained what they must have, helplessly pledging their peoples to thirty years of economic depression. Drinkwater and McComas farmed out a dozen contracts a week and started the movement of countless tons toward Europe. Their names were known up and down the Street now—they had forgotten what it was to be kept waiting on a telephone.

But though profits increased and Stella, settled in the Long Island house, seemed for the first time in years perfectly satisfied, Henry McComas found himself growing irritable and nervous. What he missed most was the sleep for which his body hungered and which seemed to descend upon him at its richest just as he was shocked back into the living world each morning. And in spite of all material gains he was always aware that he was walking in his own paths no longer.

Their interests broadened and Drinkwater was frequently away on trips to the industrial towns of New England or the South. In consequence the detail of the office fell upon McComas—and he took it hard. A man capable of enormous concentration, he had previously harvested his power for hours of importance. Now he was inclined to fritter it away upon things that in perspective often proved to be inessentials. Sometimes he was engaged in office routine until six, then at home working until midnight when he tumbled, worn out but often still wide-eyed, into his beleaguered bed.

The firm's policy was to slight their smaller accounts in Cuba and the West Indies and concentrate upon the tempting business of the war, and all through the summer they were hurrying to clear the scenes for the arrival of a new purchasing commission in September. When it arrived it unexpectedly found Drinkwater in Pennsylvania, temporarily out of reach. Time was short and the orders were to be placed in bulk. After much anxious parley over the telephone McComas persuaded four members of the commission to meet him for an hour at his own house that night.

Thanks to his own foresight everything was in order. If he hadn't been able to be specific over the phone the coup toward which he had been working would have ended in failure. When it was brought off he was due for a rest and he knew it acutely. He'd had sharp fierce headaches in the past few weeks—he had never known a headache before.

The commissioners had been indefinite as to what time he could expect them that night. They were engaged for dinner and would be free somewhere between nine and eleven. McComas reached home at six, rested for a half hour in a steaming bath and then stretched himself gratefully on his bed. Tomorrow he would join Stella and the children in the country. His week-ends had been too infrequent in this long summer of living alone in the 92nd Street house with a deaf housekeeper. Ted Drinkwater would have nothing to say now, for this deal, the most ambitious of all, was his own. He had originated and engineered it—it seemed as if fate had arranged Drinkwater's absence in order to give him the opportunity of concluding it himself.

He was hungry. He considered whether to take cold chicken and buttered toast at the hands of the housekeeper or to dress and go out to the little restaurant on the corner. Idly he reached his hand toward the bell, abandoned the attempt in the air, overcome by a pleasing languor which dispelled the headache that had bothered him all day.

That reminded him to take some aspirin and as he got up to go toward the bureau he was surprised at the weakened condition in which the hot bath had left him. After a step or two he turned about suddenly and plunged rather than fell back upon the bed. A faint feeling of worry passed over him and then an iron belt seemed to wind itself around his head and tighten, sending a spasm of pain through his body. He would ring for Mrs. Corcoran, who would call a doctor to fix him up. In a moment he would reach up his hand to the bell beside his bed. In a minute—he wondered at his indecision—then he cried out sharply as he realized the cause of it. His will had already given his brain the order and his brain had signaled it to his hand. It was his hand that would not obey.

He looked at the hand. Rather white, relaxed, motionless, it lay upon the counterpane. Again he gave it a command, felt his neck cords tighten with the effort. It did not move.

"It's asleep," he thought, but with rising alarm. "It'll pass off in a minute."

Then he tried to reach his other hand across his body to massage away the numbness but the other hand remained with a sort of crazy indifference on its own side of the bed. He tried to lift his foot—his knees. . . .

After a few seconds he gave a snort of nervous laughter. There was something ridiculous about not being able to move your own foot. It was like someone else's foot, a foot in a dream. For a moment he had the fantastic notion that he must be asleep. But no—the unmistakable sense of reality was in the room.

"This is the end," he thought, without fear, almost without emotion. "This thing, whatever it is, is creeping over me. In a minute I shall be dead."

But the minute passed and another minute, and nothing happened, nothing moved except the hand of the little leather clock on his dresser which crept slowly over the point of seven minutes to seven. He turned his head quickly from side to side, shaking it as a runner kicks his legs to warm up. But there was no answering response from the rest of his body, only a slight rise and fall between belly and chest as he breathed out and in and a faint tremble of his helpless limbs from the faint tremble of the bed.

"Help!" he called out, "Mrs. Corcoran. Mrs. Cor-ker-an, help! Mrs. Corker—"

There was no answer. She was in the kitchen probably. No way of calling her except by the bell, two feet over his head. Nothing to do but lie there until this passed off, or until he died, or until someone inquired for him at the front door.

Through the open window of the connecting bathroom he could hear the grind and clang of the street cars on Madison Avenue, the incessant auto horns and even the clump-clump of the elevated on Lexington, two blocks away. It seemed strange that life was continuing just as usual, while he lay there, no longer a part of it, stricken from the roll, most of him dead. Just at this hour Stella in the country would be up in the nursery while young Henry was put to bed.

"No, Father isn't coming tonight," she would say. "Father's very busy."

No. At that moment Father had nothing to do at all. He was even considering dissolving partnership and retiring permanently from human affairs. . . .

The clock ticked past nine o'clock. In a house two blocks away the four members of the commission finished dinner, looked at their watches and issued forth into the September night with briefcases in their hands. Outside a private detective nodded and took his place beside the chauffeur in the waiting limousine. One of the men gave an address on 92nd Street.

Ten minutes later Henry McComas heard the doorbell ring through the house. If Mrs. Corcoran was in the kitchen she would hear it too. On the contrary if she was in her room with the door shut she would hear nothing.

He waited, listening intently for the sound of foot-steps. A minute passed. Two minutes. The doorbell rang again.

"Mrs. Corcoran!" he cried desperately.

Sweat began to roll from his forehead and down the folds of his neck. Again he shook his head desperately from side to side, and his will made a last mighty effort to kick his limbs into life. Not a movement, not a sound, except a third peal of the bell, impatient and sustained this time, and singing like a trumpet of doom in his ear.

Suddenly he began to swear at the top of his voice calling in turn upon Mrs. Corcoran, upon the men in the street, asking them to break down the door, reassuring, imprecating, explaining. When he finished, the bell had stopped ringing; there was silence once more within the house.

A few minutes later the four men outside reentered their limousine and drove south and west toward the docks. They were to sleep on board ship that night. They worked late for there were papers to go ashore but long after the last of them was asleep Henry McComas lay awake and felt the sweat rolling from his neck and forehead. Perhaps all his body was sweating. He couldn't tell.

IV

For a year and a half Henry McComas lay silent in hushed and darkened rooms and fought his way back to life. Stella listened while a famous specialist explained that certain nervous systems were so constituted that only the individual could judge what was, or wasn't, a strain. The specialist realized that a host of hypochondriacs imposed upon this fact to nurse and pamper themselves through life when in reality they were as hardy and phlegmatic as the policeman on the corner, but it was nevertheless a fact. Henry McComas' large, lazy body had been the protection and insulation of a nervous intensity as fine and taut as a hair wire. With proper rest it functioned brilliantly for three or four hours a day—fatigued ever so slightly over the danger line it snapped like a straw.

Stella listened, her face wan and white. Then a few weeks later she went to Ted Drinkwater's office and told him what the specialist had said. Drinkwater frowned uncomfortably—he remarked that specialists were paid to invent consoling nonsense. He was sorry but business must go on, and he thought it best for everyone, including Henry, that the partnership be dissolved. He didn't blame Henry but he couldn't forget that just because his partner didn't see fit to keep in good condition they had missed the opportunity of a lifetime.

After a year Henry McComas found one day that he could move his arms down to the wrists; from that hour onward he grew rapidly well. In 1919 he went into business for himself with very little except his abilities and his good name and by the time this story ends, in 1926, his name alone was good for several million dollars.

What follows is another story. There are different people in it and it takes place when Henry McComas' personal problems are more or less satisfactorily solved; yet it belongs to what has gone before. It concerns Henry McComas' daughter.

Honoria was nineteen, with her father's yellow hair (and, in the current fashion, not much more of it), her mother's small pointed chin and eyes that she might have invented herself, deep-set yellow eyes with short stiff eyelashes that sprang from them like the emanations from a star in a picture. Her figure was slight and childish and when she smiled you were afraid that she might expose the loss of some baby teeth, but the teeth were there, a complete set, little and white. Many men had looked upon Honoria in flower. She expected to be married in the fall.

Who to marry was another matter. There was a young man who traveled incessantly back and forth between London and Chicago playing in golf tournaments. If she married him she would at least be sure of seeing her husband every time he passed through New York. There was Max Van Camp who was unreliable, she thought, but good-looking in a brisk sketchy way. There was a dark man named Strangler who played polo and would probably beat her with a riding crop like the heroes of Ethel M. Dell. And there was Russel Codman, her father's right-hand man, who had a future and whom she liked best of all.

He was not unlike her father in many ways—slow in thought, leisurely and inclined to stoutness—and perhaps these qualities had first brought him to Henry McComas' favor. He had a genial manner and a hearty confident smile, and he had made up his mind about Honoria when he first saw her stroll into her father's office one day three years before. But so far he hadn't asked her to marry him, and though this annoyed Honoria, she liked him for it too—he wanted to be secure and successful before he asked her to share his life. Max Van Camp, on the other hand, had asked her a dozen times. He was a quick-witted "alive" young man of the new school, continually bubbling over with schemes that never got beyond McComas' wastepaper basket—one of those curious vagabonds of business who drift from position to position like strolling minstrels and yet manage to keep moving in an upward direction all their lives. He had appeared in McComas' office the year before bearing an introductory letter from a friend.

"And how long did you work for Mr. Heinsohn?" inquired McComas, after perusing the letter.

"I didn't exactly work for him."

"Oh. Well, how long have you known him?"

"As a matter of fact I haven't the pleasure of his acquaintance," admitted Van Camp. "A man named Horace O'Sullivan obtained that letter for me. I worked for O'Sullivan, and Mr. Heinsohn was a great friend of O'Sullivan's brother and I'd heard that Mr. Heinsohn knew you."

"And you call that a recommendation?" said McComas, amused.

"Well, sir,—money's still money, no matter how many hands it's passed through. If *somebody* hadn't believed in me I wouldn't have got the letter at all."

He got the position. For a long while neither he nor his employer, nor anyone in the office, was quite sure what the position was. McComas at that time was interested in exporting, in real estate developments and, as a venture, in the possibilities of carrying the chain store idea into new fields.

Van Camp wrote advertising, investigated properties and accomplished such vague duties as might come under the phrase, "We'll get Van Camp to do that." He gave the effect always of putting much more clamor and energy into a thing than it required, and there were those who, because he was somewhat flashy and often wasted himself like an unemployed dynamo, called him a bluff and pronounced that he was usually wrong.

"What's the matter with you young fellows?" Henry McComas said to him one day. "You seem to think business is some sort of trick game, discovered about 1910, that nobody ever heard of before. You can't even look at a proposition unless you put it into this new language of your own. What do you mean you want to 'sell' me this proposition? Do you want to suggest it—or are you asking money for it?"

"Just a figure of speech, Mr. McComas."

"Well, don't fool yourself that it's anything else. Business sense is just common sense with your personal resources behind it—nothing more."

"I've heard Mr. Codman say that," agreed Max Van Camp meekly.

"He's probably right. See here—" he looked keenly at Van Camp; "how would you like a little competition with that same gentleman? I'll put up a bonus of five hundred dollars on who comes in ahead."

"I'd like nothing better, Mr. McComas."

"All right. Now listen. We've got retail hardware stores in every city of over a thousand population in Ohio and Indiana. Some fellow named McTeague is horning in on the idea—he's taken the towns of twenty thousand and now he's got a chain as long as mine. I want to fight him in the towns of that size. Codman's gone to Ohio. Suppose you take Indiana. Stay six weeks. Go to every town of over twenty thousand in the state and buy up the best hardware stores in sight."

"Suppose I can only get the second-best?"

"Do what you can. There isn't any time to waste, because McTeague's got a good start on us. Think you can leave tonight?"

He gave some further instructions while Van Camp fidgeted impatiently. His mind had grasped what was required of him and he wanted to get away. He wanted to ask Honoria McComas one more question, the same one, before it was time to go.

He received the same answer because Honoria knew she was going to marry Russel Codman, just as soon as he asked her to. Sometimes when she was alone with Codman she would shiver with excitement, feeling that now surely the time had come at last—in a moment the words would flow romantically from his lips. What the words would be she didn't know, couldn't imagine, but they would be thrilling and extraordinary, not like the spontaneous appeals of Max Van Camp which she knew by heart.

She waited excitedly for Russel Codman's return from the West. This time, unless he spoke, she would speak herself. Perhaps he didn't want her after all, perhaps there was someone else. In that case she would marry Max Van Camp and make him miserable by letting him see that he was getting only the remnants of a blighted life.

Then before she knew it the six weeks were up and Russel Codman came back to New York. He reported to her father that he was coming to see her that night. In her excitement Honoria found excuses for being near the front door. The bell rang finally and a maid stepped by her and admitted a visitor into the hall.

"Max," she cried.

He came toward her and she saw that his face was tired and white.

"Will you marry me?" he demanded without preliminaries.

She sighed.

"How many times, Max?"

"I've lost count," he said cheerfully. "But I haven't even begun. Do I understand that you refuse?"

"Yes, I'm sorry."

"Waiting for Codman?"

She grew annoyed.

"That's not your affair."

"Where's your father?"

She pointed, not deigning to reply.

Max entered the library where McComas rose to meet him.

"Well?" inquired the older man. "How did you make out?"

"How did Codman make out?" demanded Van Camp.

"Codman did well. He bought about eighteen stores—in several cases the very stores McTeague was after."

"I knew he would," said Van Camp.

"I hope you did the same."

"No," said Van Camp unhappily. "I failed."

"What happened?" McComas slouched his big body reflectively back in his chair and waited.

"I saw it was no use," said Van Camp after a moment. "I don't know what sort of places Codman picked up in Ohio but if it was anything like Indiana they weren't worth buying. These towns of twenty thousand haven't got three good hardware stores. They've got one man who won't sell out on account of the local wholesaler; then there's one man that McTeague's got, and after that only little places on the corner. Anything else you'll have to build up yourself. I saw right away that it wasn't worth while." He broke off. "How many places did Codman buy?"

"Eighteen or nineteen."

"I bought three."

McComas looked at him impatiently.

"How did you spend your time?" he asked. "Take you two weeks apiece to get them?"

"Took me two days," said Van Camp gloomily. "Then I had an idea."

"What was that?" McComas' voice was ironical.

"Well—McTeague had all the good stores."

"Yes."

"So I thought the best thing was to buy McTeague's company over his head."

"What?"

"Buy his company over his head." And Van Camp added with seeming irrelevance, "you see I heard that he'd had a big quarrel with his uncle who owned fifteen per-cent of the stock."

"Yes," McComas was leaning forward now—the sarcasm gone from his face.

"McTeague only owned twenty-five per-cent, and the storekeepers themselves owned forty. So if I could bring round the uncle we'd have a majority. First I convinced the uncle that his money would be safer with McTeague as a branch manager in our organization—"

"Wait a minute—wait a minute," said McComas. "You go too fast for me. You say the uncle had fifteen per-cent—how'd you get the other forty?"

"From the owners. I told them the uncle had lost faith in McTeague and I offered them better terms. I had all their proxies on condition that they would be voted in a majority only."

"Yes," said McComas eagerly. Then he hesitated. "But it didn't work, you say. What was the matter with it? Not sound?"

"Oh, it was a sound scheme all right."

"Sound schemes always work."

"This one didn't."

"Why not?"

"The uncle died."

McComas laughed. Then he stopped suddenly and considered. "So you tried to buy McTeague's company over his head?"

"Yes," said Max with a shamed look. "And I failed."

The door flew open suddenly and Honoria rushed into the room.

"Father," she cried. At the sight of Max she stopped, hesitated, and then carried away by her excitement continued:

"Father—did you ever tell Russel how you proposed to Mother?"

"Why, let me see—yes, I think I did."

Honoria groaned.

"Well, he tried to use it again on me."

"What do you mean?"

"All these months I've been waiting—" she was almost in tears, "waiting to hear what he'd say. And then—when it came—it sounded *familiar*—as if I'd heard it before."

"It's probably one of my proposals," suggested Van Camp. "I've used so many."

She turned on him quickly.

"Do you mean to say you've ever proposed to any other girl but me?"

"Honoria—would you mind?"

"Mind. Of course I wouldn't mind. I'd never speak to you again as long as I lived."

"You say Codman proposed to you in the words I used to your mother?" demanded McComas.

"Exactly," she wailed. "He knew them by heart."

"That's the trouble with him," said McComas thoughtfully. "He always was my man and not his own. You'd better marry Max here."

"Why—" she looked from one to the other, "why—I never knew you liked Max, Father. You never showed it."

"Well, that's just the difference," said her father, "between your way and mine."

JACOB'S LADDER

It was a particularly sordid and degraded murder trial and Jacob Booth, writhing quietly on a spectators' bench, felt that he had childishly gobbled something without being hungry, simply because it was there. The newspapers had "humanized" the case, made a cheap, neat problem play out of an affair of the jungle, so passes that actually admitted one to the courtroom were hard to get. Such a pass had been tendered him the evening before.

Jacob looked around at the doors where a hundred people, inhaling and exhaling with difficulty, generated excitement by their eagerness, their breathless escape from their own private lives. The day was hot and there was sweat upon the crowd—obvious sweat in large dewy beads that would shake off on Jacob if he fought his way through to the doors. Someone behind him guessed that the jury wouldn't be out half an hour.

With the inevitability of a compass needle, his head swung toward the prisoner's table and he stared once more at the murderess' huge blank face garnished with red button eyes. She was Mrs. Choynski, *née* Delehanty, and fate had ordained that she should one day seize a meat ax and divide her sailor lover. The puffy hands that had swung the weapon turned an ink bottle about endlessly; several times she glanced at the crowd with a nervous smile.

Jacob frowned and looked around quickly; he had found a pretty face and lost it again. The face had edged sideways into his consciousness when he was absorbed in a mental picture of Mrs. Choynski in action—now it was faded back into the anonymity of the crowd. It was the face of a dark saint with tender luminous eyes and a skin pale and fair. Twice he searched the room, then he forgot and sat stiffly and uncomfortably, waiting.

The jury brought in a verdict of murder in the first degree; Mrs. Choynski squeaked "Oh, my God!" The sentence was postponed until next day. With a slow rhythmic roll the crowd pushed out into the August afternoon.

Jacob saw the face again, realizing why he hadn't seen it before. It belonged to a young girl beside the prisoner's table and it had been hidden by the full moon of Mrs. Choynski's head. Now the clear luminous eyes were bright with tears, and an impatient young man with a squashed nose was trying to attract the attention of the shoulder.

"Oh, get out!" said the girl, shaking the hand off impatiently. "Lee me alone, will you? Lee me alone. Geeze!"

The man sighed profoundly and stepped back. The girl embraced the dazed Mrs. Choynski and another lingerer remarked to Jacob that they were sisters. Then Mrs. Choynski was taken off the scene— her expression absurdly implied an important appointment—and the girl sat down at the desk and began to powder her face. Jacob waited; so did the young man with the squashed nose. The sergeant came up brusquely and Jacob gave him five dollars.

"Geeze!" cried the girl to the young man. "Can't you lee me alone?"

She stood up. Her presence, the obscure vibrations of her impatience, filled the courtroom. "Every day itsa same!"

Jacob moved nearer. The other man spoke to her rapidly.

"Miss Delehanty, we've been more than liberal with you and your sister and I'm only asking you to carry out your share of the contract. Our paper goes to press at—"

Miss Delehanty turned despairingly to Jacob.

"Can you beat it?" she demanded. "Now he wants a pitcher of my sister when she was a baby. And it's got my mother in it too."

"We'll take your mother out."

"I want my mother though. It's the only one I got of her."

"I'll promise to give you the picture back tomorrow."

"Oh, I'm sicka the whole thing." Again she was speaking to Jacob but without seeing him except as some element of the vague omnipresent public. "It gives me a pain in the eye." She made a clicking sound in her teeth that comprised the essence of all human scorn.

"I have a car outside, Miss Delehanty," said Jacob suddenly. "Don't you want me to run you home?"

"All right," she answered indifferently.

The newspaper man assumed a previous acquaintance between them; he began to argue in a low voice as the three moved toward the door.

"Every day it's like this," said Miss Delehanty bitterly. "These newspaper guys!"

Outside Jacob signaled for his car and as it drove up, large, open and bright, and the chauffeur jumped out and opened the door, the reporter, on the verge of tears, saw the picture slipping away and launched into a peroration of pleading.

"Go jump in the river!" said Miss Delehanty, sitting in Jacob's car. "Go—jump—in—the—river!"

The extraordinary force of her advice was such that Jacob regretted the limitations of her vocabulary. Not only did it evoke an image of the unhappy journalist hurling himself into the Hudson but it convinced Jacob that it was the only fitting and adequate way of disposing of the man. Leaving him to face his watery destiny, the car moved off down the street.

"You dealt with him pretty well," Jacob said.

"Sure," she admitted. "I get sore after awhile and then I can deal with anybody no matter who. How old would you think I was?"

"How old are you?"

"Sixteen."

She looked at him gravely, inviting him to wonder. Her face, the face of a saint, an intense little madonna, was lifted fragilely out of the mortal dust of the afternoon. On the pure parting of her lips no breath hovered; he had never seen a texture pale and immaculate as her skin, lustrous and garish as her eyes. His own well-ordered person seemed for the first time in his life gross and well-worn to him as he knelt suddenly at the heart of freshness.

"Where do you live?" he asked. The Bronx perhaps, Yonkers, Albany—Baffin's Bay. They could curve over the top of the world, drive on forever.

Then she spoke and, as the toad words vibrated with life in her voice, the moment passed. "Fifty-six Eas' Hunerd thuyty-thuyd. Stayin with a girl friend there."

They were waiting for a traffic light to change and she exchanged a haughty glance with a flushed man peering from a flanking taxi. The man took off his hat hilariously.

"Somebody's stenog," he cried. "And oh, *what* a stenog!"

An arm and hand appeared in the taxi window and pulled him back into the darkness of the cab.

Miss Delehanty turned to Jacob, a frown, the shadow of a hair in breadth, appearing between her eyes.

"A lot of em know me," she said. "We got a lot of publicity and pictures in the paper."

"I'm sorry it turned out badly."

She remembered the event of the afternoon, apparently for the first time in half an hour.

"She had it comin' to her, Mister. She never had a chance. But they'll never hang no woman in New York State."

"No. That's sure."

"She'll get life." Surely, it was not she who had spoken. The tranquillity of her face made her words separate themselves from her as soon as they were uttered and take on a corporate existence of their own.

"Did you use to live with her?"

"Me? Say, read the papers! I didn't even know she was my sister till they come and told me. I hadn't seen her since I was a baby." She pointed suddenly at one of the world's largest department stores. "There's where I work. Back to the old pick and shovel day after tomorrow."

"It's going to be a hot night," said Jacob. "Why don't we ride out into the country and have dinner."

She looked at him. His eyes were polite and kind. "All right," she said.

Jacob was thirty-three. Once he had possessed a tenor voice with destiny in it, but laryngitis had despoiled him of it in one feverish week ten years before. In despair that concealed not a little relief he bought a plantation in Florida and spent five years turning it into a golf course. When the land boom came in 1924 he sold his real estate for eight hundred thousand dollars.

Like so many Americans he valued things rather than cared about them. His apathy was neither fear of life nor was it an affectation— it was the racial violence grown tired. It was a humorous apathy: with no need for money, he had tried, tried hard, for a year and a half to marry the second richest woman in America. If he had loved her or pretended to he could have had her—but he had never been able to work himself up to more than the formal lie.

In person he was short, trim and handsome. Except when he was overcome by a desperate attack of apathy he was unusually charming; he went with a crowd of men who were sure that they were the best of New York and had by far the best time. During a desperate attack of apathy he was like a gruff white bird, ruffled and annoyed, and disliking mankind with all his heart.

He liked mankind that night under the summer moonshine of the "Borghese Gardens." The moon was a radiant egg, smooth and bright as Jenny Delehanty's face across the table; a salt wind blew in over the big estates collecting flower scents from their gardens and bearing them to the road-house lawn. The waiters hopped here and there like pixies through the hot night, their black backs disappearing into the gloom, their white shirt fronts gleaming startlingly out of an unfamiliar patch of darkness.

They drank a bottle of champagne and he told Jenny Delehanty a story.

"You are the most beautiful thing I have ever seen," he said, "but as it happens you are not my type and I have no designs on you at all. Nevertheless you can't go back to that store. Tomorrow I'm going to arrange a meeting between you and Billy Farrelly, who's directing a picture at the Famous Players on Long Island. Whether he'll see how beautiful you are I don't know, because I've never introduced anybody to him before."

There was no shadow, no ripple of a change in her expression, but there was irony in her eyes. Things like that had been said to her before, but the movie director was never available next day. Or else she had been tactful enough not to remind men of what they had promised last night.

"Not only are you beautiful," continued Jacob, "but you are somehow on the grand scale. Everything you do—yes, like reaching for that glass—or pretending to be self-conscious—or pretending to despair of me—gets across. If somebody's smart enough to see it, you might be something of an actress."

"I like Norma Shearer the best. Do you?"

Driving homeward through the soft night, she put up her face quietly to be kissed. Holding her in the hollow of his arm Jacob rubbed his cheek against her cheek's softness and then looked down at her for a long moment.

"Such a lovely child," he said gravely.

She smiled back at him; her hands played conventionally with the lapels of his coat.

"I had a wonderful time," she whispered. "Geeze! I hope I never have to go to court again."

"I hope you don't."

"Aren't you going to kiss me good-night?"

"This is Great Neck," he said, "that we're passing through. A lot of moving-picture stars live here."

"You're a card, handsome."

"Why?"

She shook her head from side to side and smiled.

"You're a card."

She saw then that he was a type with which she was not acquainted. He was surprised, not flattered, that she thought him droll. She saw that whatever his eventual purpose he wanted nothing of her now. Jenny Delehanty learned quickly; she let herself become grave and sweet and quiet as the night, and as they rolled over Queensboro Bridge into the city she was half asleep against his shoulder.

II

He called up Billy Farrelly next day.

"I want to see you," he said. "I found a girl I wish you'd take a look at."

"My gosh!" said Farrelly. "You're the third today."

"Not the third of this kind."

"All right. If she's white, she can have the lead in a picture I'm starting Friday."

"Joking aside, will you give her a test?"

"I'm not joking. She can have the lead, I tell you. I'm sick of these lousy actresses. I'm going out to the Coast next month. I'd rather be Constance Talmadge's water boy than own most of these young—" His voice was bitter with Irish disgust. "Sure, bring her over, Jake. I'll take a look at her."

Four days later when Mrs. Choynski, accompanied by two deputy sheriffs, had gone to Auburn to pass the remainder of her life, Jacob drove Jenny over the bridge to Astoria, Long Island.

"You've got to have a new name," he said, "and remember, you never had a sister."

"I thought of that," she answered. "I thought of a name too—Tootsie Defoe."

"That's rotten," he laughed; "just rotten."

"Well, you think of one if you're so smart."

"How about Jenny—Jenny—oh, anything—Jenny Prince."

"All right, handsome."

Jenny Prince walked up the steps of the Famous Players Studio and Billy Farrelly, in a bitter Irish humor, in contempt for himself and his profession, engaged her for one of the three leads in his picture.

"They're all the same," he said to Jacob. "Shucks! Pick 'em up out of the gutter today and they want gold plates tomorrow. I'd rather be Constance Talmadge's water boy than own a harem full of them."

"Do you like this girl?"

"She's all right. She's got a good side face. But they're all the same."

Jacob bought Jenny Prince an evening dress for a hundred and eighty dollars and took her to the Lido that night. He was pleased with himself and excited. They both laughed a lot and were happy.

"Can you believe you're in the movies?" he demanded.

"They'll probably kick me out tomorrow. It was too easy."

"No it wasn't. It was very good—psychologically. Billy Farrelly was in just the one mood—"

"I liked him."

"He's fine," agreed Jacob. But he was reminded that already another man was helping to open doors for her success. "He's a wild Irishman—look out for him."

"I know. You can tell when a guy wants to make you."

"What?"

"I don't mean he wanted to make me, handsome. But he's got that look about him, if you know what I mean." She distorted her lovely face with a wise smile. "He likes 'em; you could tell that this afternoon."

They drank a bottle of charged and very alcoholic grape juice; the head-waiter came over to their table.

"This is Miss Jenny Prince," said Jacob. "You'll see a lot of her, Lorenzo, because she's just signed a big contract with Famous Players. Always treat her with the greatest possible respect."

When Lorenzo had withdrawn, Jenny said: "You got the nicest eyes I ever seen."

It was her effort, the best she could do. Her face was serious and sad. "Honest," she repeated herself, "the nicest eyes I ever seen. Any girl would be glad to have eyes like yours."

He laughed but he was touched. His hand covered her arm lightly.

"Be good," he said. "Work hard and I'll be so proud of you—and we'll have some good times together."

"I always have a good time with you." Her eyes were full on his, in his, held there like hands. Her voice was clear and dry. "Honest, I'm not kidding about your eyes. You always think I'm kidding. I want to thank you for all you've done for me."

"I haven't done anything, you lunatic. I saw your face and I was— I was beholden to it—everybody ought to be beholden to it—"

Entertainers appeared and her eyes wandered hungrily away from him. She was so young—Jacob had never been so conscious of youth before. He had always considered himself on the young side, until tonight.

Afterwards in the dark cave of the taxi-cab, fragrant with the perfume he had bought for her that day, Jenny came close to him, clung to him. He kissed her, without enjoying it—there was no shadow of passion in her eyes or on her mouth, there was a faint spray of champagne on her breath. She clung nearer, desperately. He took her hands and put them in her lap. Her childish intention of giving herself to him shocked him.

"You're young enough to be my daughter," he said.

"You're not so old."

She leaned away from him resentfully.

"What's the matter? Don't you like me?"

"I shouldn't have let you have so much champagne."

"Why not? I've had a drink before. I was tight once."

"Well, you ought to be ashamed of yourself. And if I hear of your taking any more drinks, you'll hear from me."

"You got your nerve, haven't you?"

"What do you do? Let all the corner soda-jerkers maul you around whenever they want?"

"Oh, shut up."

For a moment they rode in silence. Then her hand crept across to his.

"I like you better than any guy I ever met, and I can't help that, can I?"

"Dear little Jenny." He put his arm around her again. Hesitating tentatively, he kissed her and again he was chilled by the innocence of her kiss, the eyes that at the moment of contact looked beyond him out into the darkness of the night, the darkness of the world. She did not know yet that splendor was something in the heart—at the moment when she should realize that and melt into the passion of the universe he could take her without question or regret.

"I like you enormously," he said. "Better than almost anyone I know. I mean that about drinking, though. You mustn't drink."

"I'll do anything you want," she said, and she repeated, looking at him directly, "Anything."

It was her last effort. The car drew up in front of her flat and he kissed her good-night.

He rode away in a mood of exultation, living more deeply in her youth and future than he had lived in himself for years. Thus, leaning forward a little on his cane, rich, young and happy, he was borne along dark streets and light toward a future of his own which he could not foretell.

III

A month later, climbing into a taxi-cab with Farrelly one night, he gave the latter's address to the driver.

"So you're in love with this baby," said Farrelly, pleasantly. "Very well, I'll get out of your way."

Jacob experienced a vast displeasure.

"I'm not in love with her," he said slowly. "Billy, I want you to leave her alone."

"Sure. I'll leave her alone," agreed Farrelly readily. "I didn't know you were interested—she told me she couldn't make you."

"The point is you're not interested either," said Jacob. "If I thought that you two really cared about each other, do you think I'd be fool enough to try and stand in the way? But you don't give a darn about her, and she's impressed and a little fascinated—"

"Sure," agreed Farrelly, bored. "I wouldn't touch her for anything."

Jacob laughed.

"Yes you would. Just for something to do. That's what I object to: anything—anything casual happening to her."

"I see what you mean. I'll let her alone, Jake."

Jacob was forced to be content with that. He had no faith in Billy Farrelly but he guessed that Farrelly liked him and wouldn't offend him unless stronger feelings were involved. But the holding hands under the table tonight had annoyed him. Jenny lied about it when he reproached her; she offered to let him take her home immediately, offered not to speak to Farrelly again all evening. Then he had seemed silly and pointless to himself. It would have been easier, when Farrelly said "So you're in love with this baby," to have been able to answer simply, "I am."

But he wasn't. He valued her now, more than he had ever thought possible. He watched in her the awakening of a sharply individual temperament. She liked quiet and simple things. She was developing the capacity to discriminate and shut the trivial and the inessential out of her life. He tried giving her books; then wisely he gave up that and brought her into contact with a variety of men. He made situations and then explained them to her, and he was pleased, as appreciation and politeness began to blossom before his eyes. He valued, too, her utter trust in him and the fact that she used him as a standard for judgments on other men.

Before the Farrelly picture was released, she was offered a two-year contract on the strength of her work in it—four hundred a week for six months and an increase on a sliding scale. But she would have to go to the Coast.

"Wouldn't you rather have me wait?" she said, as they drove in from the country one afternoon. "Wouldn't you rather have me stay here in New York—near you?"

"You've got to go where your work takes you. You ought to be able to look out for yourself. You're seventeen."

Seventeen—she was as old as he; she was ageless. Her dark eyes under a yellow straw hat were as full of destiny as though she had not just offered to toss destiny away.

"I wonder if you hadn't come along, someone else would of," she said—"to make me do things, I mean."

"You'd have done them yourself. Get it out of your head that you're dependent on me."

"I am. Everything is thanks to you."

"It isn't, though," he said emphatically, but he brought no reasons; he liked her to think that.

"I don't know what I'll do without you. You're my only friend"— and she added—"that I care about. You see? You understand what I mean?"

He laughed at her, enjoying the birth of her egotism implied in her right to be understood. She was lovelier that afternoon than he had ever seen her, delicate, resonant and, for him, undesirable. But sometimes he wondered if that sexlessness wasn't for him alone, wasn't a side that, perhaps purposely, she turned toward him. She was happiest of all with younger men, though she pretended to despise them. Billy Farrelly, obligingly and somewhat to her mild chagrin, had left her alone.

"When will you come out to Hollywood?"

"Soon," he promised. "And you'll be coming back to New York."

She began to cry.

"Oh, I'll miss you so much. I'll miss you so much!" Large tears of distress ran down her warm ivory cheeks.

"Oh, Geeze," she cried softly. "Oh, my God, you been good to me. Where's your hand? Where's your hand? You been the best friend anybody ever had. Where am I ever going to find a friend like you?"

She was acting now, but a lump arose in his throat and for a moment a wild idea ran back and forth in his mind like a blind man, knocking over its solid furniture: to marry her. He had only to make the suggestion, he knew, and she would come close to him and know no one else, because he would "understand" her forever.

Next day in the station she was pleased with her flowers, her compartment, with the prospect of a longer trip than she had ever taken before. When she kissed him good-bye her deep holy eyes came close to his again and she pressed against him as if in protest against the separation. Again she cried, but he knew that behind her tears lay the happiness of adventure in new fields. As he walked out of the station, New York was curiously empty. Through her eyes he had seen old colors once more—now they had faded back into the grey tapestry of the past. The next day he went to an office high in a building on Park Avenue and talked to a famous specialist he had not visited for a decade.

"I want you to examine the larynx again," he said. "There's not much hope, but something might have changed the situation."

He swallowed a complicated system of mirrors. He breathed in and out, made high and low sounds, coughed at a word of command. The specialist fussed and touched. Then he sat back and took out his eye-glass.

"There's no change," he said. "The cords are not diseased—they're simply worn out. It isn't anything that can be treated."

"I thought so," said Jacob, humbly, as if he had been guilty of an impertinence. "That's practically what you told me before. I wasn't sure how permanent it was."

He had lost something when he came out of the building on Park Avenue—a half hope, the love child of a wish, that someday—

"New York desolate," he wired her. "The night clubs all closed. Black wreaths on the Statue of Civic Virtue. Please work hard and be remarkably happy."

"Dear Jacob," she wired back, "miss you so. You are the nicest man that ever lived and I mean it, dear. Please don't forget me. Love from Jenny."

Winter came. The picture Jenny had made in the East was released, together with preliminary interviews and articles in the fan magazines. Jacob sat in his apartment, playing the "Kreutzer Sonata" over and over on his new phonograph and read her meagre and stilted but affectionate letters and the articles which said she was a discovery of Billy Farrelly's. In February he became engaged to an old friend, now a widow. They went to Florida and were suddenly snarling at each other in hotel corridors and over bridge games, so they decided not to go through with it after all. In the spring he took a stateroom on the *Paris*, but three days before sailing he disposed of it and went to California.

IV

Jenny met him at the station, kissed him and clung to his arm in the car all the way to the Ambassador Hotel.

"Well, the man came," she cried. "I never thought I'd get him to come. I never did."

Her accent betrayed an effort at control. The emphatic "Geeze!" with all the wonder, horror, disgust or admiration she could put in it was gone, but there was no mild substitute, no "swell" or "grand." If her mood required expletives outside her repertoire, she kept silent.

But at seventeen, months are years and Jacob perceived a change in her—in no sense was she a child any longer. There were fixed things in her mind—not distractions, for she was instinctively too polite for that, but simply things there. No longer was the studio a lark and a wonder and a divine accident; no longer "for a nickel I wouldn't turn up tomorrow." It was part of her life. Circumstances were stiffening into a career which went on independently of her casual hours.

"If this picture is as good as the other—I mean if I make a personal hit again, Hecksher'll break the contract. Everybody that's seen the rushes says it's the first one I've had sex appeal in."

"What are the rushes?"

"When they run off what they took the day before. They say it's the first time I've had sex appeal."

"I don't notice it," he teased her.

"You wouldn't. But I have."

"I know you have," he said and moved by an ill-considered impulse, he took her hand.

She glanced quickly at him. He smiled—half a second too late. Then she smiled and her glowing warmth veiled his mistake.

"Jake!" she cried. "I could bawl, I'm so glad you're here. I got you a room at the Ambassador. They were full but they kicked out somebody because I said I had to have a room. I'll send my car back for you in half an hour—it's good you came on Sunday because I got all day free."

They had luncheon in the furnished apartment she had leased for the winter. It was 1920 Moorish, taken over complete from a favorite of yesterday. Someone had told her it was horrible, for she joked about it; but when he pursued the matter he found that she didn't know why.

"I wish they had more nice men out here," she said once during lunch. "Of course there's a lot of nice ones, but I mean—oh, you know, like in New York. Men that know even more than a girl does, like you."

After lunch he learned that they were going to tea.

"Not today," he objected. "I want to see you alone."

"All right," she agreed doubtfully. "I suppose I could telephone. I thought—it's a lady that writes for a lot of newspapers and I've never been asked there before. Still if you don't want to—"

Her face had fallen a little and Jacob assured her that he couldn't be more willing. Gradually he found that they were going not to one party but to three.

"In my position, it's sort of the thing to do," she explained. "Otherwise you don't see anybody except the people on your own lot. And that's narrow—" He smiled. "Well anyhow," she finished, "anyhow, you smart alec, that's what everybody does on Sunday afternoon."

At the first tea Jacob noticed that there was an enormous preponderance of women over men, and of supernumeraries—lady journalists, cameramen's daughters, cutters' wives—over "people of importance." A young Latin named Raffino appeared for a brief moment, spoke to Jenny and departed; several stars passed through, asking about children's health with a domesticity that was somewhat overpowering. Another group of celebrities posed immobile, statue-like, in a corner. There was a somewhat inebriated and very much excited author apparently trying to make private engagements with one girl after another. As the afternoon waned, more people were suddenly a little tight; the communal voice was higher in pitch and greater in volume as Jacob and Jenny went out the door.

At the second tea, young Raffino—he was an actor, one of innumerable hopeful Valentinos—appeared again for a minute, talked to Jenny a little longer, a little more attentively this time, and went out. Jacob gathered that this party was not considered to have quite the swagger of the other. There was a bigger crowd around the cocktail table. There was more sitting down.

Jenny, he saw, drank only lemonade. He was surprised and pleased at her distinction and good manners. She talked to one person, never to everyone within hearing; then she listened, without finding it necessary to shift her eyes about. Deliberate or not on her part, he noticed that at both teas she was sooner or later talking to the guest of most consequence. Her seriousness, her air of saying, "This is my opportunity of learning something," beckoned their egotism imperatively near.

When they left to drive to the last party, a buffet supper, it was dark and the electric legends of hopeful realtors were gleaming to some vague purpose on Beverly Hills. Outside Grauman's Theatre a crowd was already gathered in the thin, warm rain.

"Look! Look!" she cried. It was the picture she had finished a month before.

They slid out of the thin rialto of Hollywood Boulevard and into the deep gloom of a side street; he put his arm about her and kissed her.

"Dear Jake." She smiled up at him.

"Jenny, you're so lovely; I didn't know you were so lovely."

She looked straight ahead, her face mild and quiet. A wave of annoyance passed over him and he pulled her toward him urgently— just as the car stopped at a lighted door.

They went into a bungalow crowded with people and smoke. The impetus of the formality which had begun the afternoon was long exhausted; everything had become at once vague and strident.

"This is Hollywood," explained an alert talkative lady who had been in his vicinity all day. "No airs on Sunday afternoon." She indicated the hostess. "Just a plain, simple, sweet girl." She raised her voice: "Isn't that so, darling—just a plain, simple, sweet girl?"

The hostess said, "Yeah. Who is?" And Jacob's informant lowered her voice again. "But that little girl of yours is the wisest one of the lot."

The totality of the cocktails Jacob had swallowed was affecting him pleasantly, but try as he might, the "plot" of the party—the key on which he could find ease and tranquillity—eluded him. There was something tense in the air—something competitive and insecure. Conversations with the men had a way of becoming empty and over-jovial or else melting off into a sort of suspicion. The women were nicer. At eleven o'clock, in the pantry, he suddenly realized that he hadn't seen Jenny for an hour. Returning to the living room he saw her come in, evidently from outside, for she tossed a raincoat from her shoulders. She was with Raffino. When she came up, Jacob saw that she was out of breath and her eyes were very bright. Raffino smiled at Jacob pleasantly and negligently; a few moments later, as he turned to go, he bent and whispered in Jenny's ear and she looked at him without smiling as she said good-night.

"I got to be on the lot at eight o'clock," she told Jacob presently. "I'll look like an old umbrella unless I go home. Do you mind, dear?"

"Heavens no!"

Their car drove over one of the interminable distances of the thin, stretched city.

"Jenny," he said, "you've never looked like you were tonight. Put your head on my shoulder."

"I'd like to. I'm tired."

"I can't tell you how radiant you've gotten to be."

"I'm just the same."

"No, you're not." His voice suddenly became a whisper, trembling with emotion. "Jenny, I'm in love with you."

"Jacob, don't be silly."

"I'm in love with you. Isn't it strange, Jenny? It happened just like that."

"You're not in love with me."

"You mean the fact doesn't interest you." He was conscious of a faint twinge of fear.

She sat up out of the circle of his arm. "Of course it interests me; you know I care more about you than anything in the world."

"More than about Mr. Raffino?"

"Oh—my—gosh!" she protested scornfully. "Raffino's nothing but a baby."

"I love you, Jenny."

"No, you don't."

He tightened his arm. Was it his imagination or was there a small instinctive resistance in her body? But she came close to him and he kissed her.

"You know that's crazy about Raffino."

"I suppose I'm jealous." Feeling insistent and unattractive, he released her. But the twinge of fear had become an ache. Though he knew that she was tired and that she felt strange at this new mood in him, he was unable to let the matter alone.

"I didn't realize how much a part of my life you were. I didn't know what it was I missed—but I know now. I wanted you near."

"Well, here I am."

He took her words as an invitation, but this time she relaxed wearily in his arms. He held her thus for the rest of the way, her eyes closed, her short hair falling straight back, like a girl drowned.

"The car'll take you to the hotel," she said when they reached the apartment. "Remember, you're having lunch with me at the studio tomorrow."

Suddenly they were in a discussion that was almost an argument, as to whether it was too late for him to come in. Neither could yet appreciate the change that his declaration had made in the other. Abruptly they had become like different people as Jacob tried desperately to turn back the clock to that night in New York six months before, and Jenny watched this mood, which was more than jealousy and less than love, snow under, one by one, the qualities of consideration and understanding which she knew in him and with which she felt at home.

"But I don't love you like that," she cried. "How can you come to me all at once and ask me to love you like that?"

"You love Raffino like that!"

"I swear I don't! I never even kissed him—not really!"

"H'm!" He was a gruff white bird now. He could scarcely credit his own unpleasantness, but something illogical as love itself urged him on. "An *act*or!"

"Oh, Jake," she cried, "please lemme go. I never felt so terrible and mixed up in my life."

"I'll go," he said suddenly. "I don't know what's the matter, except that I'm so mad about you that I don't know what I'm saying. I love you and you don't love me. Once you did, or thought you did—but that's evidently over."

"But I do love you." She thought for a moment; the red-and-green glow of a filling station on the corner lit up the struggle in her face.

"If you love me that much, I'll marry you tomorrow."

"Marry me!" he exclaimed. She was so absorbed in what she had just said that she did not notice.

"I'll marry you tomorrow," she repeated. "I like you better than anybody in the world and I guess I'll get to love you the way you want me to." She uttered a single half-broken sob. "But— I didn't know this was going to happen. Please let me alone tonight."

Jacob didn't sleep. There was music from the Ambassador Grill till late and a fringe of working girls hung about the carriage entrance waiting for their favorites to come out. Then a long, protracted quarrel between a man and a woman began in the hall outside, moved into the next room and continued as a low two-toned mumble through the intervening door. He went to the window sometime toward three o'clock and stared out into the clear splendor of the California night. Her beauty rested outside on the grass, on the damp, gleaming roofs of the bungalows, all around him, borne up like music on the night. It was in the room, on the white pillow, it rustled ghostlike in the curtains. His desire recreated her until she lost all vestiges of the old Jenny, even of the girl who had met him at the train that morning. Silently, as the night hours went by, he molded her over into an image of love—an image that would endure as long as love itself, or even longer—not to perish till he could say "I never really loved her." Slowly he created it with this and that illusion from his youth, this and that sad old yearning, until she stood before him identical with her old self only by name. Later, when he drifted off into a few hours' sleep, the image he had made stood near him, lingering in the room, joined in mystic marriage to his heart.

V

"I won't marry you unless you love me," he said, driving back from the studio.

She waited, her hands folded tranquilly in her lap.

"Do you think I'd want you if you were unhappy and unresponsive, Jenny? Knowing all the time you didn't love me?"

"I do love you. But not that way."

"What's 'that way'?"

She hesitated, her eyes were far off. "You don't—thrill me, Jake. I don't know—there been some men that sort of thrilled me when they touched me, dancing or anything. I know it's crazy, but—"

"Does Raffino thrill you?"

"Sort of—but not so much."

"And I don't at all?"

"I just feel comfortable and happy with you."

He should have urged her that that was best, but he couldn't say it, whether it was an old truth or an old lie.

"Anyhow, I told you I'll marry you; perhaps you might thrill me later."

He laughed, stopped suddenly.

"If I didn't thrill you, as you call it, why were you so ready to make me a present of yourself last summer?"

"I don't know. I guess I was young. You never know how you once felt, do you?"

She had become elusive to him, with that elusiveness that gives a hidden significance to the least significant remarks. And with the clumsy tools of jealousy and desire, he was trying to create the spell that is ethereal and delicate as the dust on a moth's wing.

"Listen, Jake," she said suddenly. "That lawyer my sister had, that Scharnhorst, called up the studio this afternoon."

"Your sister's all right," he said absently, and he added: "So a lot of men—thrill you."

"Well, if I've felt it with a lot of men, it couldn't have anything to do with real love, could it?" she said hopefully.

"But your theory is that love couldn't come without it."

"I haven't got any theories or anything. I just told you how I felt. You know more than me."

"I don't know anything at all."

There was a man waiting in the lower hall of the apartment house. Jenny went up and spoke to him; then, turning back to Jake, said in a low voice: "It's Scharnhorst. Would you mind waiting downstairs while he talks to me? He says it won't take half an hour."

He waited, smoking innumerable cigarettes. Ten minutes passed. Then the telephone operator beckoned him.

"Quick!" she said. "Miss Prince wants you on the telephone."

Jenny's voice was tense and frightened.

"Don't let Scharnhorst get out," she said. "He's on the stairs, maybe in the elevator. Make him come back here—"

Jacob put down the receiver just as the elevator clicked. He stood in front of the elevator door, barring the man inside.

"Mr. Scharnhorst?"

"Yeah." The face was keen and suspicious.

"Will you come up to Miss Prince's apartment again? There's something she forgot to say."

"I can see her later." He attempted to push past Jacob. Seizing him by the shoulders, Jacob shoved him back into the cage, slammed the door and pressed the button for the eighth floor.

"I'll have you arrested for this," Scharnhorst remarked. "Put into jail for assault!"

Jacob held him firmly by the arms. Upstairs, Jenny, with panic in her eyes, was holding open her door. After a slight struggle the lawyer went inside.

"What is it?" demanded Jacob.

"Tell him, you," she said. "Oh, Jake, he wants twenty thousand dollars!"

"What for?"

"To get my sister a new trial."

"But she hasn't a chance!" exclaimed Jacob. He turned to Scharnhorst. "You ought to know she hasn't a chance."

"There are some technicalities," said the lawyer uneasily—"things that nobody but an attorney would understand. She's very unhappy there, and her sister so rich and successful—Mrs. Choynski thought she ought to get another chance."

"You've been up there working on her, heh?"

"She sent for me."

"But the blackmail idea was your own. I suppose if Miss Prince doesn't feel like supplying twenty thousand to retain your firm, it'll come out that she's the sister of the notorious murderess."

Jenny nodded. "That's what he said."

"Just a minute." Jacob walked to the phone. "Western Union, please. Western Union? Please take a telegram." He gave the name and address of a man high in the political world of New York. "Here's the message:

"The convict Choynski threatening her sister, who is a picture actress, with exposure of relationship stop   Can you arrange it with warden that she be cut off from visitors until I can get east and explain the situation stop   Also wire me if two witnesses to an attempted blackmailing scheme are enough to disbar a lawyer in New York if charges proceed from such a quarter as Read, Van Tyne, Biggs & Company, or my uncle the surrogate stop Answer Ambassador Hotel, Los Angeles.   JACOB C. K. BOOTH."

He waited until the clerk had repeated the message.

"Now, Mr. Scharnhorst," he said, "the pursuit of art should not be interrupted by such alarms and excursions. Miss Prince, as you see, is considerably upset. It will show in her work tomorrow and a million people will be just a little disappointed. So we won't ask her for any decisions. In fact you and I will leave Los Angeles on the same train tonight."

VI

The summer passed. Jacob went about his useless life, sustained by the knowledge that Jenny was coming east in the fall. By fall there would have been many Raffinos, he supposed, and she would find that the thrill of their hands and eyes—and lips—was much the same. They were the equivalent, in a different world, of the affairs at a college house party, the undergraduates of a casual summer. And if it was still true that her feeling for him was less than romantic, then he would take her anyway, letting romance come after marriage as—so he had always heard—it had come to many wives before.

Her letters fascinated and baffled him. Through the ineptitude of expression he caught gleams of emotion—an ever-present gratitude, a longing to talk to him, and a quick, almost frightened reaction toward him, from—he could only imagine—some other man. In August she went on location; there were only post cards from some lost desert in Arizona, then for awhile nothing at all. He was glad of the break. He had thought over all the things that might have repelled her—of his portentousness, his jealousy, his manifest misery. This time it would be different. He would keep control of the situation. She would at least admire him once more, see in him the incomparably dignified and well-adjusted life.

Two nights before her arrival Jacob went to see her latest picture in a huge night-bound vault on Broadway. It was a college story. She walked into it with her hair knotted on the crown of her head—a familiar symbol for dowdiness—inspired the hero to a feat of athletic success and faded out of it, always subsidiary to him, in the shadow of the cheering stands. But there was something new in her performance: for the first time the arresting quality he had noticed in her voice a year before had begun to "get over" on the screen. Every move she made, every gesture, was poignant and important. Others in the audience saw it too. He fancied he could tell this by some change in the quality of their breathing, by a reflection of her clear, precise expression in their casual and indifferent faces. Reviewers, too, were aware of it though for the most part they were incapable of any precise definition of a personality.

But his first real consciousness of her public existence came from the attitude of her fellow passengers disembarking from the train. Busy as they were with friends or baggage, they found time to stare at her, to call their friends' attention, to repeat her name.

She was radiant. A communicative joy flowed from her and around her, as though her perfumer had managed to imprison ecstasy in a bottle. Once again there was a mystical transfusion, and blood began to course again through the hard veins of

New York—there was the pleasure of Jacob's chauffeur when she remembered him, the respectful frisking of the bell boys at the Plaza, the nervous collapse of the head-waiter at the restaurant where they dined. As for Jacob, he had control of himself now. He was gentle, considerate and polite, as it was natural for him to be—but as, in this case, he had found it necessary to plan. His manner promised and outlined an ability to take care of her, a will to be leaned on.

After dinner, their corner of the Colony restaurant cleared gradually of the theatre crowd and the sense of being alone settled over them. Their faces became grave, their voices very quiet.

"It's been five months since I saw you." He looked down at his hands thoughtfully. "Nothing has changed with me, Jenny. I love you with all my heart. I love your face and your faults and your mind and everything about you. The one thing I want in this world is to make you happy."

"I know," she whispered. "Gosh, I know!"

"Whether there's still only affection in your feeling toward me I don't know. If you'll marry me I think you'll find that the other things will come, will be there before you know it—and what you called a thrill will seem a joke to you, because life isn't for boys and girls, Jenny, but for men and women."

"Jacob," she whispered, "you don't have to tell me. I know."

He raised his eyes for the first time.

"What do you mean—you know?"

"I get what you mean. Oh, this is terrible! Jacob, listen! I want to tell you. Listen, dear, don't say anything. Don't look at me. Listen, Jacob, I fell in love with a man."

"What?" he asked blankly.

"I fell in love with somebody. That's what I mean about understanding about a silly thrill."

"You mean you're in love with me?"

"No."

The appalling monosyllable floated between them, danced and vibrated over the table. "No—No—No—*No—No!*"

"Oh, this is awful!" she cried. "I fell in love with a man I met on location this summer. I didn't mean to—I tried not to, but first thing I knew there I was in love and all the wishing in the world couldn't help it. I wrote you and asked you to come, but I didn't send the letter, and there I was, crazy about this man and not daring to speak to him, and bawling myself to sleep every night."

"An actor?" he heard himself saying in a dead voice. "Raffino?"

"Oh, no, no no! Wait a minute, let me tell you. It went on for three weeks and I honestly wanted to kill myself, Jake. Life wasn't worth while unless I could have him. And one night we got in a car by accident alone and he just caught me and made me tell him I loved him. He knew—he couldn't help knowing."

"It just—swept over you," said Jacob steadily. "I see."

"Oh, I knew you'd understand, Jake! You understand everything. You're the best person in the world, Jake, and don't I know it?"

"You're going to marry him?"

Slowly she nodded her head. "I said I'd have to come east first and see you." As her fear lessened, the extent of his grief became more apparent to her, and her eyes filled with tears.

"It only comes once, Jake, like that. That's what kept in my mind all those weeks I didn't hardly speak to him—if you lose it once, it'll never come like that again and then what do you want to live for? He was directing the picture—he was the same about me."

"I see."

As once before, her eyes held his like hands.

"Oh Ja-a-ake!" In that sudden croon of compassion, all-comprehending and deep as a song, the first force of the shock passed off. Jacob's teeth came together again and he struggled to conceal his misery. Mustering his features into an expression of irony, he called for the check. It seemed an hour later they were in a taxi going toward the Plaza Hotel.

She clung to him.

"Oh Jake, say it's all right. Say you understand. Darling Jake, my best friend, my only friend, say you understand!"

"Of course I do, Jenny." His hand patted her back automatically.

"Oh-h-h, Jake. You feel just awful, don't you?"

"I'll survive."

"Oh-h-h Jake!"

They reached the hotel. Before they got out Jenny glanced at her face in her vanity mirror and turned up the collar of her fur cape. In the lobby Jacob ran into several people and said, "Oh, I'm so sorry," in a strained, unconvincing voice. The elevator waited. Jenny, her face distraught and tearful, stepped in and held out her hand toward him with the fist clenched helplessly.

"Jake," she said once more.

"Good-night, Jenny."

She turned her face to the wire wall of the cage. The gate clanged.

"Hold on!" he almost said. "Do you realize what you're doing, starting that car like that?"

He turned and went out the door blindly.

"I've lost her," he whispered to himself, awed and frightened. "By God, I've lost her!"

He walked over 59th Street to Columbus Circle and then down Broadway. There were no cigarettes in his pocket—he had left them at the restaurant—so he went into a tobacco store. There was some confusion about the change and someone in the store laughed. When he came out he stood for a moment puzzled. Then the heavy tide of realization swept over him and beyond him, leaving him stunned and exhausted. It swept back upon him and over him again. As one re-reads a tragic story with the defiant hope that it will end differently, so he went back to the morning, to the beginning, to the previous year. But the tide came thundering back with the certainty that she was cut off from him forever in a high room at the Plaza Hotel.

He walked down Broadway. In great block letters over the porte-cochère of the Capitol Theatre five words glittered out into the night: "Carl Barbour and Jenny Prince."

The name startled him, as if a passer-by had spoken it. He stopped and stared. Other eyes rose to that sign, people hurried by him and turned in.

Jenny Prince.

Now that she no longer belonged to him, the name assumed a significance entirely its own. It hung there, cool and impervious on the night, a challenge, a defiance.

Jenny Prince.

"Come and rest upon my loveliness," it said. "Fulfill your secret dreams in wedding me for an hour."

JENNY PRINCE.

It was untrue—she was back at the Plaza Hotel, in love with somebody. But the name, with its bright insistence, rode high upon the night.

"I love my dear public. They are all so sweet to me."

The wave appeared far off, sent up white-caps, rolled toward him with the might of pain, washed over him. Never any more. Never any more. Beautiful child who tried so hard one night to give herself to me. Never any more. Never any more. The wave beat upon him, drove him down, pounding with hammers of agony on his ears. Proud and impervious, the name on high challenged the night.

JENNY PRINCE

She was there! All of her, the best of her—the effort, the power, the triumph, the beauty. Jacob moved forward with a group and bought a ticket at the window. Confused, he stared around the great lobby. Then he saw an entrance and, walking in, found himself a place in the vast throbbing darkness.

THE LOVE BOAT

The boat floated down the river through the summer night like a Fourth of July balloon, foot-loose in the heavens. The decks were brightly lit and restless with dancers, but bow and stern were in darkness so the boat had no more outline than an accidental cluster of stars. Between the black banks it floated, softly parting the mild dark tide from the sea and leaving in its wake small excited gusts of music—"Babes in the Wood" over and over, and "Moonlight Bay." Past the scattered lights of Pokus Landing, where a poet in an attic window saw yellow hair gleam in the turn of a dance. Past Ulm, where the moon came up out of a boiler works, and West Esther, where it slid, unregretted, behind a cloud.

The radiance of the boat itself was enough for, among others, the three young Harvard graduates; they were weary and a little depressed and they gave themselves up promptly to its enchantment. Their own boat was casually drifting and a collision was highly possible, but no one made a movement to start the engine and get out of the way.

"It makes me very sad," one of them said. "It is so beautiful that it makes me want to cry."

"Go on and cry, Bill."

"Will you cry too?"

"We'll all cry."

His loud, facetious "Boo-hoo!" echoed across the night, reached the steamer and brought a small lively crowd to the rail.

"Look! It's a launch."

"Some guys in a launch."

Bill got to his feet. The two crafts were scarcely ten feet apart.

"Throw us a hempen rope," he pleaded eloquently. "Come on— be impulsive. Please do."

Once in a hundred years there would have been a rope at hand. It was there that night. With a thud the coil struck the wooden bottom and in an instant the motorboat was darting along behind the steamer, as if in the wake of a harpooned whale.

Fifty high-school couples left the dance and scrambled for a place around the suddenly interesting stern rail. Fifty girls gave forth immemorial small cries of excitement and sham fright. Fifty young men forgot the mild exhibitionism which had characterized their manner of the evening and looked grudgingly at the more effectual show-off of three others. Mae Purley, without the involuntary quiver of an eye-lash, fitted the young man standing in the boat into her current dream, where he displaced Al Fitzpatrick with laughable ease. She put her hand on Al Fitzpatrick's arm and squeezed it a little because she had stopped thinking about him entirely and felt that he must be aware of it. Al, who had been standing with his eyes squinted up, watching the towed boat, looked tenderly at Mae and tried to put his arm about her shoulder. But Mae Purley and Bill Frothington, handsome and full of all the passionate promise in the world, had locked eyes across the intervening space.

They made love. For a moment they made love as no one ever dares to do—after. Their glance was closer than an embrace, more urgent than a call. There were no words for it. Had there been, and had Mae heard them, she would have fled to the darkest corner of the ladies' washroom and hid her face in a paper towel.

"We want to come on board!" Bill called. "We're life-preserver salesmen! How about pulling us around to the side?"

Mr. McVitty, the principal, arrived on the scene too late to interfere. The three young Harvard graduates—Ellsworth Ames soaking wet, unconsciously Byronic with his dark curls plastered damply to his forehead, Hamilton Abbot and Bill Frothington surer-footed and dry—climbed and were hoisted over the side. The motorboat bobbed on behind.

With a sort of instinctive reverence for the moment, Mae Purley hung back in the shadow, not through lack of confidence but through excess of it. She knew that he would come straight to her. That was never the trouble and never had been—the trouble was in keeping up her own interest after she had satisfied the deep but casual curiosity of her lips. But tonight was going to be different. She knew this

when she saw that he was in no hurry; he was leaning against the
rail making a couple of high-school seniors—who suddenly seemed
very embryonic to themselves—feel at ease.

He looked at her once.

"It's all right," his eyes said, without a movement of his face, "I
understand as well as you. I'll be there in just a minute."

Life burned high in them both; the steamer and its people were
at a distance and in darkness. It was one of those times.

"I'm a Harvard man," Mr. McVitty was saying, "class of 1907."
The three young men nodded with polite indifference. "I'm glad
to know we won the race," continued the principal, simulating a
reborn enthusiasm which had never existed. "I haven't been to New
London in fifteen years."

"Bill here rowed Number Two," said Ames. "That's a coaching
launch we've got."

"Oh. You were on the crew?"

"Crew's over now," said Bill impatiently. "Everything's over."

"Well, let me congratulate you—"

Shortly they froze him into silence. They were not his sort of
Harvard man—they wouldn't have known his name in four years
there together. But they would have been much more gracious and
polite about it had it not been this particular night. They hadn't
broken away from the hilarious mobs of classmates and relatives at
New London to exchange discomfort with the master of a mill-town
high school.

"Can we dance?" they demanded.

A few minutes later Bill and Mae Purley were walking down the
deck side by side. Life had met over the body of Al Fitzpatrick,
engulfing him. The two clear voices:

"Perhaps you'll dance with me," with the soft assurance of the
moonlight itself—and—"I'd love to," were nothing that could be
argued about, not by twice what Al Fitzpatrick pretended to be.
The most consoling thought in Al's head was that they might be
fought over.

What was it they said? Did you hear it? Can you remember?
Later that night she remembered only his pale wavy hair and the
long limbs that she followed around the dancing floor.

She was thin, a thin burning flame, colorless yet fresh. Her smile came first slowly, then with a rush, pouring out of her heart, shy and bold, as if all the life of that little body had gathered for a moment around her mouth and the rest of her was a wisp that the least wind would blow away. She was a changeling whose lips alone had escaped metamorphosis, whose lips were the only point of contact with reality.

"Then you live near?"

"Only about twenty-five miles from you," Bill said. "Isn't it funny?"

"Isn't it funny?"

They looked at each other, a trifle awed in the face of such manifest destiny. They stood between two lifeboats on the top deck. Mae's hand lay on his arm, playing with a loose ravel of his tweed coat. They had not kissed yet—that was coming in a minute. That was coming any time now, as soon as every cup of emotional moonlight had been drained of its possibilities and cast aside. She was seventeen.

"Are you glad I live near?"

She might have said "I'm delighted" or "Of course I am." But she whispered, "Yes; are you?"

"Mae—with an *e*," he said, and laughed in a husky whisper. Already they had a joke together. "You look so damn beautiful."

She accepted the compliment in silence, meeting his eyes. He pressed her to him by her merest elbow in a way that would have been impossible had she not been eager too. He never expected to see her after tonight.

"Mae—" His whisper was urgent. Mae's eyes came nearer, grew larger, dissolved against his face, like eyes on a screen. Her frail body breathed imperceptibly in his arms.

A dance stopped. There was clapping for an encore. Then clapping for another encore with what had seemed only a poor bar of music in between. There was another dance, scarcely longer than a kiss. They were heavily endowed for love, these two, and both of them had played with it before.

Down below, Al Fitzpatrick's awareness of time and space had reached a pitch that would have been invaluable to an investigator of the new mathematics. Bit by bit the boat presented itself to him as it really was, a wooden hulk garish with forty-watt bulbs, peopled by the commonplace young people of a commonplace town. The river was water, the moon was a flat meaningless symbol in the sky. He was in agony—which is to speak tritely. Rather, he was in deadly fear; his throat was dry, his mouth drooped into a hurt half-moon as he tried to talk to some of the other boys—shy, unhappy boys, who loitered around the stern.

Al was older than the rest—he was twenty-two, and out in the world for seven years. He worked in the Hammacker Mills and attended special high-school classes at night. Another year might see him assistant manager of the shops, and Mae Purley, with about as much eagerness as was to be expected in a girl who was having everything her own way, had half promised to marry him when she was eighteen.

His wasn't a temperament to go to pieces. When he had brooded up to the limit of his nature he felt a necessity for action. Miserably and desperately he climbed up to the top deck to make trouble.

Bill and Mae were standing close together by the lifeboat, quiet, absorbed and happy. They moved a little apart as he came near.

"Is that you, Mae?" called Al in a hard voice. "Aren't you going to come down and dance?"

"We were just coming."

They walked toward him in a trance.

"What's the idea?" Al said hoarsely. "You've been up here over two hours."

At their indifference he felt pain swelling and spreading inside him, constricting his breath.

"Have you met Mr. Frothington?" She laughed shyly at the unfamiliar name.

"Yeah," said Al rudely. "I don't see the idea of his keeping you up here."

"I'm sorry," said Bill. "We didn't realize."

"Oh, you didn't? Well, I *did*." His jealousy cut through their absorption. They acknowledged it by an effort to hurry, to be impersonal, to defer to his wishes. Ungraciously he followed and the three of them came in a twinkling upon a scene that had suddenly materialized on the deck below.

Ellsworth Ames, smiling but a little flushed, was leaning against the rail while Ham Abbot attempted to argue with a distraught young husky who kept trying to brush past him and get at Ames. Near them stood an indignant girl with another girl's soothing arm around her waist.

"What is it?" demanded Bill quickly.

The distraught young man glared at him. "Just a couple of snobs that come here and try to spoil everybody else's good time!" he cried wildly.

"He doesn't like me," said Ellsworth lightly. "I invited his girl to dance."

"She didn't want to dance with *you!*" shouted the other. "You think you're so damn smart—ask her if she wanted to dance with you."

The girl murmured indistinguishable words and disclaimed all responsibility by beginning to cry.

"You're too fresh, that's the trouble!" continued her defender. "I know what you said to her when you danced with her before. What do you think these girls are? They're just as good as anybody, see?"

Al Fitzpatrick moved in closer.

"Let's put 'em all off the boat," he suggested, stubborn and ashamed. "They haven't got any business butting in here."

A mild protest went up from the crowd, especially from the girls, and Abbot put his hand conciliatingly on the husky's shoulder. But it was too late.

"You'll put me off?" Ellsworth was saying coldly. "If you try to lay your hands on me I'll rearrange your whole face."

"Shut up, Ellie!" snapped Bill. "No use getting disagreeable. They don't want us, we'd better go." He stepped close to Mae, and whispered, "Good-night. Don't forget what I said. I'll drive over and see you Sunday afternoon."

As he pressed her hand quickly and turned away he saw the argumentative boy swing suddenly at Ames, who caught the blow with his left arm. In a moment they were slugging and panting, knee to knee in the small space left by the gathering crowd. Simultaneously

Bill felt a hand pluck at his sleeve and he turned to face Al Fitzpatrick. Then the deck was in an uproar. Abbot's attempt to separate Ames and his antagonist was misinterpreted; instantly he was involved in a battle of his own, cannonading against the other pairs, slipping on the smooth deck, bumping against noncombatants and scurrying girls who sent up shrill cries. He saw Al Fitzpatrick slap the deck suddenly with his whole body, not to rise again. He heard calls of "Get Mr. McVitty!" and then his own opponent was dropped by a blow he did not strike, and Bill's voice said: "Come on to the boat!"

The next few minutes streaked by in wild confusion. Avoiding Bill, whose hammer-like arms had felled their two champions, the high-school boys tried to pull down Ham and Ellie, and the harassed group edged and revolved toward the stern rail.

"Hidden-ball stuff!" Bill panted. "Save it for Haughton. I'm G-Gardner, you're Bradlee and Mahan—Hip!"

Mr. McVitty's alarmed face appeared above the combat, and his high voice, ineffectual at first, finally pierced the heat of battle.

"Aren't you ashamed of yourselves! Bob—Cecil—George Roberg! Let go, I say!"

Abruptly the battle was over and the combatants, breathing hard, eyed one another impassively in the moonlight.

Ellie laughed and held out a pack of cigarettes. Bill untied the motorboat and walked forward with the painter to bring it alongside.

"They claim you insulted one of the girls," said Mr. McVitty uncertainly. "Now that's no way to behave after we took you aboard."

"That's nonsense," snapped Ellie, between gasps. "I only told her I'd like to bite her neck."

"Do you think that was a very gentlemanly thing to say?" demanded Mr. McVitty heatedly.

"Come on, Ellie!" Bill cried. "Good-bye, everybody! Sorry there was such a row!"

They were already shadows of the past as they slipped one by one over the rail. The girls were turning cautiously back to their own men, and not one of them answered, and not one of them waved farewell.

"A bunch of meanies," remarked Ellie ironically. "I wish all you ladies had one neck so I could bite it all at once. I'm a glutton for ladies' necks."

Feeble retorts went up here and there like muffled pistol shots.

"*Good night, ladies,*" Ham sang, as Bill shoved away from the side:

> "*Good night, ladies,*
> *Good night, ladies,*
> *We're going to leave you*
> *now-ow-ow.*"

The boat moved up the river through the summer night while the launch, touched by its swell, rocked to and fro gently in the wide path of the moon.

II

On the following Sunday afternoon Bill Frothington drove over from Truro to the isolated rural slum known as Wheatly Village. He had stolen away from a house full of guests, assembled for his sister's wedding, to pursue what his mother would have called an "unworthy affair." But behind him lay an extremely successful career at Harvard and a youth somewhat more austere than the average, and this fall he would disappear for life into the banking house of Read, Hoppe and Co. in Boston. He felt that the summer was his own. And had the purity of his intentions toward Mae Purley been questioned he would have defended himself with righteous anger. He had been thinking of her for five days. She attracted him violently, and he was following the attraction with eyes that did not ask to see.

Mae lived in the less offensive quarter of town on the third floor of its only apartment house, an unsuccessful relic of those more prosperous days of New England textile weaving that ended twenty years ago. Her father was a time-keeper who had fallen out of the white-collar class; Mae's two older brothers were working at the loom, and Bill's only impression as he entered the dingy flat was one of hopeless decay. The mountainous, soiled mother, at once suspicious and deferential, and the anaemic, beaten Anglo-Saxon asleep on the couch after his Sunday dinner were no more than shadows against the poor walls. But Mae was clean and fresh. No breath of squalor touched her. The pale pure youth of her cheeks, and her thin childish body shining through a new organdy dress, measured up full to the summer day.

"Where you going to take my little girl?" Mrs. Purley asked anxiously.

"I'm going to run away with her," he said, laughing.

"Not with my little girl."

"Oh, yes I am. I don't see why she hasn't been run away with before."

"Not my little girl."

They held hands going downstairs, but not for an hour did the feeling of being intimate strangers pass. When the first promise of evening blew into the air at five o'clock and the light changed from white to yellow, their eyes met once in a certain way and Bill knew that it was time. They turned up a side road and down a wagon track, and in a moment the spell was around them again—the equal and opposite urge that drew them together. They talked about each other and then their voices grew quiet and they kissed, while chestnut blossoms slid in white diagonals through the air and fell across the car. After a long while, an instinct told her that they had stayed long enough. He drove her home.

It went on like that for two months. He would come for her in the late afternoon and they would go for dinner to the shore; afterwards they would drive around until they found the center of the summer night and park there while the enchanted silence spread over them like leaves over the babes in the woods. Someday, naturally, they were going to marry. For the present it was impossible—he must go to work in the fall. Vaguely and with more than a touch of sadness both of them realized that this wasn't true—that if Mae had been of another class an engagement would have been arranged at once. She knew that he lived in a great country house with a park and a caretaker's lodge, that there were stables full of cars and horses, and that house-parties and dances took place there all summer. Once they had driven past the gate and Mae's heart was leaden in her breast as she saw that those wide acres would lie between them all her life.

On his part Bill knew that it was impossible to marry Mae Purley. He was an only son and he wore one of those New England names that are carried with one always. Eventually he broached the subject to his mother.

"It isn't her poverty and ignorance," his mother said, among other things. "It's her lack of any standards—common women are common for life. You'd see her impressed by cheap and shallow people, by cheap and shallow things."

"But, Mother, this isn't 1850—it isn't as if she were marrying into the royal family."

"If it were, it wouldn't matter. But you have a name that for many generations has stood for leadership and self-control. People who have given up less and taken fewer responsibilities have had nothing to say aloud when men like your father and your Uncle George and your Great-grandfather Frothington held their heads high. Toss your pride away and see what you've left at thirty-five to take you through the rest of your life."

"But you can only live once," he protested—knowing nevertheless that what she said was, for him, right. His youth had been pointed to make him understand that exposition of superiority. He knew what it was to be the best, at home, at school, at Harvard. In his senior year he had known men to dodge behind a building and wait in order to walk with him across the Harvard Yard, not to be seen with him out of mere poor snobbishness, but to get something intangible, something he carried within him of the less obvious, less articulate experience of the race.

Several days later he went to see Mae and met her coming out of the flat. They sat on the stairs in the half darkness.

"Just think of these stairs," he said huskily. "Think how many times you've kissed me on these stairs. At night when I've brought you home. On every landing. Last month when we walked up and down together five times before we could say good-night."

"I hate these stairs. I wish I never had to go up them anymore."

"Oh, Mae, what are we going to do?"

She didn't answer for a moment.

"I've been thinking a lot these last three days," she said. "I don't think it's fair to myself to go on like this—or to Al."

"To Al," he said, startled. "Have you been seeing Al?"

"We had a long talk last night."

"*Al!*" he repeated incredulously.

"He wants to get married. He isn't mad anymore."

Bill tried suddenly to face the situation he had been dodging for two months, but the situation, with practiced facility, slid around the corner. He moved up a step till he was beside Mae and put his arm around her.

"Oh, let's get married!" she cried desperately. "You can. If you want to, you can."

"I do want to."

"Then why can't we?"

"We can—but not yet."

"Oh God—you've said that before."

For a tragic week they quarreled and came together over the bodies of unresolved arguments and irreconcilable facts. They parted finally on a trivial question as to whether he had once kept her waiting half an hour.

Bill went to Europe on the first possible boat and enlisted in an ambulance unit. When America went into the war he transferred to the aviation and Mae's pale face and burning lips faded off, faded out, against the wild dark background of the war.

III

In 1919 Bill fell romantically in love with a girl of "his own set." He met her on the Lido and wooed her on golf courses and in fashionable speakeasies and in cars parked at night, loving her much more from the first than he had ever loved Mae. She was a better person, prettier and more intelligent and with a kindlier heart. She loved him; they had much the same tastes and more than ample money.

There was a child, after awhile there were four children, then only three again. Bill grew a little stout after thirty, as athletes will. He was always going to take up something strenuous and get into real condition. He worked hard and drank a little too freely every week-end. Later he inherited the country house and lived there in the summer.

When he and Stella had been married eight years they felt safe for each other, safe from the catastrophes that had overtaken the majority of their friends. To Stella this brought relief; Bill, once he had accepted the idea of their safety, was conscious of a certain discontent, a sort of chemical restlessness. With a feeling of disloyalty to Stella, he shyly sounded his friends on the subject and found that in men of his age the symptoms were almost universal. Some blamed it on the war: "There'll never be anything like the war."

It was not variety of women that he wanted. The mere idea appalled him. There were always women "around." If he took a fancy to someone Stella invited her for a week-end, and men who liked Stella fraternally, or even somewhat sentimentally, were as often in the house. But the feeling persisted and grew stronger. Sometimes it would steal over him at dinner, a vast nostalgia, and the people at table would fade out and odd memories of his youth would come back to him. Sometimes a familiar taste or a smell would give him this sensation. Chiefly it had to do with the summer night.

One evening, walking down the lawn with Stella after dinner, the feeling seemed so close that he could almost grasp it. It was in the rustle of the pines, in the wind, in the gardener's radio down behind the tennis court.

"Tomorrow," Stella said, "there'll be a full moon."

She had stopped in a broad path of moonlight and was looking at him. Her hair was pale and lovely in the gentle light. She regarded him for a moment oddly, and he took a step forward as if to put his arms around her; then he stopped, unresponsive and dissatisfied. Stella's expression changed slightly and they walked on.

"That's too bad," he said suddenly. "Because tomorrow I've got to go away."

"Where?"

"To New York. Meeting of the trustees of school. Now that the kids are entered I feel I should."

"You'll be back Sunday?"

"Unless something comes up and I telephone."

"Ad Haughton's coming Sunday—and maybe the Ameses."

"I'm glad you won't be alone."

Suddenly Bill had remembered the boat floating down the river and Mae Purley on the deck under the summer moon. The image became a symbol of his youth, his introduction to life. Not only did he remember the deep excitement of that night but felt it again, her face against his, the rush of air about them as they stood by the lifeboat and the feel of its canvas cover to his hand.

When his car dropped him at Wheatly Village next afternoon he experienced a sensation of fright. Eleven years—she might be dead; quite possibly she had moved away. Any moment he might pass her on the street, a tired, already faded woman pushing a baby carriage and leading an extra child.

"I'm looking for a Miss Mae Purley," he said to a taxi driver. "It might be Fitzpatrick now."

"Fitzpatrick up at the works?"

Inquiries within the station established the fact that Mae Purley was indeed Mrs. Fitzpatrick. They lived just outside of town.

Ten minutes later the taxi stopped before a white Colonial house.

"They made it over from a barn," volunteered the taxi man. "There was a picture of it in one of them magazines."

Bill saw that someone was regarding him from behind the screen door. It was Mae. The door opened slowly and she stood in the hall, unchanged, slender as of old. Instinctively he raised his arms and then, as he took another step forward, instinctively he lowered them.

"Mae—"

"Bill—"

She was there. For a moment he possessed her, her frailty, her thin smoldering beauty—then he had lost her again. He could no more have embraced her than he could have embraced a stranger.

On the sun-porch they stared at each other.

"You haven't changed—" they said together.

It was gone from her. Words—casual, trivial, and insincere, poured from her mouth as if to fill the sudden vacancy in his heart.

"—imagine seeing you—know you anywhere—thought you'd forgotten me—talking about you only the other night—"

Suddenly he was without any inspiration. His mind became an utter blank, and try as he might he could summon up no attitude to fill it.

"It's a nice place you have here," he said stupidly.

"We like it. You'd never guess it but we made it out of an old barn."

"The taxi driver told me."

"—stood here for a hundred years empty—got it for almost nothing—pictures of it before and after in 'Home and Country Side—'"

Without warning his mind went blank again. What was the matter? Was he sick? He had even forgotten why he was here. He knew only that he was smiling benevolently and that he must hang on to that smile, for if it passed he could never recreate it. What did it mean when one's mind went blank. He must see a doctor tomorrow.

"—since Al's done so well. Of course Mr. Kohlsatt leans on him, so he don't get away much. I get away to New York sometimes. Sometimes we both get away together."

"Well you certainly have a nice place here," he said desperately. He must see a doctor in the morning. Dr. Flynn or Dr. Keyes or Dr. Given who was at Harvard with him. Or perhaps that specialist who was recommended to him by that woman at the Ameses'. Or Dr. Gross or Dr. Studeford or Dr. de Martel—

"—I never touch it, but Al always keeps something in the house. Al's gone to Boston, but I think I can find the key."

—or Dr. Ramsay or old Dr. Ogden who had brought him into the world. He hadn't realized that he knew so many doctors. He must make a list.

"—you're just exactly the same."

Suddenly Bill put both hands on his stomach, gave a short coarse laugh and said "Not here." His own act startled and surprised him, but it dissipated the blankness for a moment and he began to gather up the pieces of his afternoon. From her chatter he discovered her to be under the impression that in some vague and sentimental past she had thrown him over. Perhaps she was right. Who was she anyhow—this hard, commonplace article wearing Mae's body for a mask of life? Defiance rose in him.

"Mae, I've been thinking about that boat," he said desperately.

"What boat?"

"The steamboat on the Thames, Mae. I don't think we should let ourselves get old. Get your hat, Mae—let's go for a boat ride tonight."

"But I don't see the point," she protested. "Do you think just riding on a boat keeps people young? Maybe if it was salt water—"

"Don't you remember that night on the boat?" he said, as if he were talking to a child. "That's how we met. Two months later you threw me over and married Al Fitzpatrick."

"But I didn't marry Al then," she said. "It wasn't till two years later when he got a job as superintendent. There was a Harvard man I used to go around with that I almost married. He knew you. His name was Abbot—Ham Abbot."

"Ham Abbot—you saw *him* again?"

"We went around for almost a year. I remember Al was wild. He said if I had any more Harvard men around he'd shoot them. But there wasn't anything wrong with it. Ham was just cuckoo about me and I used to let him rave."

Bill had read somewhere that every seven years a change is completed in the individual that makes him different from his self of seven years ago. He clung to the idea desperately. Dimly he saw this person pouring him an enormous glass of applejack, dimly he gulped it down and, through a description of the house, fought his way to the front door.

"Notice the original beams. The beams were what we liked best—" She broke off suddenly. "I remember now about the boat. You were in a launch and you got on board with Ham Abbot that night."

The applejack was strong. Evidently it was fragrant also, for as they started off, the taxi-driver volunteered to show him where the gentleman could get some more. He would give him a personal introduction in a place down by the wharf.

Bill sat at a dingy table behind swinging doors and, while the sun went down behind the Thames, disposed of four more applejacks. Then he remembered that he was keeping the taxi waiting. Outside a boy told him that the driver had gone home to supper and would be back in half an hour.

He sauntered over to a bale of goods and sat down, watching the mild activity of the docks. It was dusk presently—stevedores appeared momentarily against the lighted hold of a barge and jerked quickly out of sight down an invisible incline. Next to the barge lay a steamer and people were going aboard—first a few people and then an increasing crowd. There was a breeze in the air and the moon came up rosy gold with a haze around.

Someone ran into him precipitately in the darkness, tripped, swore and staggered to his feet.

"I'm sorry," said Bill cheerfully. "Hurt yourself?"

"Pardon me," stuttered the young man. "Did I hurt *you?*"

"Not at all. Here, have a light."

They touched cigarettes.

"Where's the boat going?"

"Just down the river. It's the high-school picnic tonight."

"What?"

"The Wheatly High School picnic. The boat goes down to Groton—then it turns around and comes back."

Bill thought quickly.

"Who's the principal of the high school?"

"Mr. McVitty." The young man fidgeted impatiently. "So long, bud. I got to go aboard."

"Me too," whispered Bill to himself. "Me too."

Still he sat there lazily for a moment, listening to the sounds clear and distinct now from the open deck: the high echolalia of the girls, the boys calling significant but obscure jokes to one another across the night. He was feeling fine. The air seemed to have distributed the applejack to all the rusty and unused corners of his body. He bought another pint, stowed it in his hip pocket and walked on board with all the satisfaction, the insouciance of a transatlantic traveler.

A girl standing in a group near the gangplank raised her eyes to him as he went past. She was slight and fair. Her mouth curved down and then broke upward as she smiled, half at him, half at the man beside her. Someone made a remark and the group laughed; once again her glance slipped sideways and met his for an instant as he passed by.

Mr. McVitty was on the top deck with half a dozen other teachers, who moved aside at Bill's breezy approach.

"Good evening, Mr. McVitty. You don't remember me."

"I'm afraid I don't, sir." The principal regarded him with tentative noncommittal eyes.

"Yet I took a trip with you on this same boat, exactly eleven years ago tonight."

"This boat, sir, was only built last year."

"Well, a boat like it," said Bill. "I wouldn't have known the difference myself."

Mr. McVitty made no reply. After a moment Bill continued confidently, "We found that night that we were both sons of John Harvard."

"Yes?"

"In fact on that very day I had been pulling an oar against what I might refer to as dear old Yale."

Mr. McVitty's eyes narrowed. He came closer to Bill and his nose wrinkled slightly.

"Old Eli," said Bill. "In fact, Eli Yale."

"I see," said Mr. McVitty dryly. "And what can I do for you tonight?"

Someone came up with a question and in the enforced silence it occurred to Bill that he was present on the slightest of all pretexts—a previous and unacknowledged acquaintance. He was relieved when a dull rumble and a quiver of the deck indicated that they had left the shore.

Mr. McVitty, disengaged, turned toward him with a slight frown. "I seem to remember you now," he said. "We took three of you aboard from a motorboat and we let you dance. Unfortunately the evening ended in a fight."

Bill hesitated. In eleven years his relation to Mr. McVitty had somehow changed. He recalled Mr. McVitty as a more negligible, more easily dealt with person. There had been no such painful difficulties before.

"Perhaps you wonder how I happen to be here?" he suggested mildly.

"To be frank, I do, Mr.——"

"Frothington," supplied Bill. And he added brazenly, "It's rather a sentimental excursion for me. My greatest romance began on the evening you speak of. That was when I first met—my wife."

Mr. McVitty's attention was caught at last.

"You married one of our girls?"

Bill nodded.

"That's why I wanted to take this trip tonight."

"Your wife's with you?"

"No."

"I don't understand——" He broke off, and suggested gently, "Or maybe I do. Your wife is dead?"

After a moment Bill nodded. Somewhat to his surprise two great tears rolled suddenly down his face.

Mr. McVitty put his hand on Bill's shoulder.

"I'm sorry," he said. "I understand your feeling, Mr. Frothington, and I respect it. Please make yourself at home."

After a nibble at his bottle Bill stood in the door of the salon watching the dance. It might have been eleven years ago. There were the high-school characters that he and Ham and Ellie had laughed at afterwards—the fat boy who surely played center on the football team and the adolescent hero with the pompadour and the blatant good manners, president of his class. The pretty girl who had looked at him by the gangplank danced past him, and with a quick lift of his heart he placed her too, her confidence and the wide but careful distribution of her favors—she was the popular girl, as Mae had been eleven years before.

Next time she went past he touched the shoulder of the boy she was dancing with. "May I have some of this?" he said.

"What?" her partner gasped.

"May I have some of this dance?"

The boy stared at him without relinquishing his hold.

"Oh, it's all right, Red," she said impatiently. "That's the way they do now."

Red stepped sulkily aside. Bill bent his arm as nearly as he could into the tortuous clasp that they were all using—and started.

"I saw you talking to Mr. McVitty," said the girl, looking up into his face with a bright smile. "I don't know you, but I guess it's all right."

"I saw you before that."

"When?"

"Getting on the boat."

"I don't remember."

"What's your name?" he asked.

"May Schaffer. What's the matter?"

"Do you spell it with an *e?*"

"No—why?"

A quartet of boys had edged toward them. One of its members suddenly shot out as if propelled from inside the group and bumped awkwardly against Bill.

"Can I have part of this dance?" asked the boy with a sort of giggle.

Without enthusiasm Bill let go. When the next dance began he cut in again. She was lovely. Her happiness in her self, in the evening, would have transfigured a less pretty girl. He wanted to talk to her alone and was about to suggest that they go outside when there was a repetition of what had happened before—a young man was apparently shot by force from a group to Bill's side.

"Can I have a part of this dance?"

Bill joined Mr. McVitty by the rail.

"Pleasant evening," he remarked. "Don't you dance?"

"I enjoy dancing," said Mr. McVitty. And he added pointedly, "In my position it doesn't seem quite the thing to dance with young girls."

"That's nonsense," said Bill pleasantly. "Have a drink?"

Mr. McVitty walked suddenly away.

When he danced with May again he was cut in on almost immediately. People were cutting in all over the floor now—evidently he had started something. He cut back, and again he started to suggest that they go outside, but he saw that her attention was held by some horseplay going on across the room.

"I'm Daddy Browning," somebody was saying. "I got a swell love-nest up in the Bronx, Peaches."

"Won't you come outside?" said Bill. "There's the most wonderful moon."

"I'd rather dance."

"We could dance out there."

She leaned away from him and looked up with innocent scorn into his eyes.

"Where'd you get it?" she said.

"Get what?"

"All the happiness."

Before he could answer, someone cut in. For a moment he imagined that the boy had said "Part of this dance, Daddy?" but his annoyance at May's indifference drove the idea from his mind. Next time he went to the point at once.

"I live near here," he said. "I'd be awfully pleased if I could call and drive you over for a week-end sometime."

"What?" she asked vaguely. Again she was listening to a miniature farce being staged in the corner.

"My wife would like so much to have you," went on Bill. Great dreams of what he could do for this girl for old times' sake rose in his mind.

Her head swung toward him curiously.

"Why, Mr. McVitty told somebody your wife was dead."

"She isn't," said Bill.

Out of the corner of his eye he saw the inevitable catapult coming and danced quickly away from it.

A voice rang out: "Just look at old Daddy Browning step."

"Hey, Peaches."

"Peaches, ask him if I can have some of this dance."

Afterwards Bill only remembered the evening up to that point. A crowd swirled around him and someone kept demanding persistently who was a young boiler maker.

He decided, naturally enough, to teach them a lesson, as he had done before—and he told them so. Then there was a long discussion as to whether he could swim. After that the confusion deepened; there were blows and a short sharp struggle. He picked up the story himself in what must have been several minutes later when his head emerged from the cool waters of the Thames River.

The river was white with the moon, which had changed from rosy gold to a wafer of shining cheese on high. It was some time before he could locate the direction of the shore, but he moved around unworried in the water. The boat was a mere speck now, far down the river, and he laughed to think how little it all mattered, how little anything mattered. Then, feeling sure that he had his wind and wondering if the taxi was still waiting at Wheatly Village, he struck out for the dark shore.

IV

He was worried as he drew near home next afternoon—possessed of a dark unfounded fear. It was based, of course, on his own silly transgression. Stella would somehow hear of it. In his reaction from the debonair confidence of last night, it seemed inevitable that Stella would hear of it.

"Who's here?" he asked the butler immediately.

"No one, sir. The Ameses came about an hour ago, but there was no word so they went on. They said—"

"Isn't my wife here?"

"Mrs. Frothington left yesterday just after you."

The whips of panic descended upon him.

"How long after me?"

"Almost immediately, sir. The telephone rang and she answered it, and almost immediately she had her bag packed and left the house."

"Mr. Ad Haughton didn't come?"

"I haven't seen Mr. Haughton."

It had happened. The spirit of adventure had seized Stella too. He knew that her life had been not without a certain pressure from sentimental men, but that she would ever go anywhere without telling him—

He threw himself face downward on a couch. What had happened? He had never meant things to happen. Was that what she had meant when she had looked at him in that peculiar way the other night?

He went upstairs. Almost as soon as he entered the big bedroom he saw the note—written on blue stationery lest he miss it against the white pillow. In his misery an old counsel of his mother's came back to him: "The more terrible things seem the more you've got to keep yourself in shape."

Trembling, he divested himself of his clothes, turned on a bath and lathered his face. Then he poured himself a drink and shaved. It was like a dream, this change in his life. She was no longer his—even if she came back she was no longer his. Everything was different—this room, himself, everything that had existed yesterday. Suddenly he wanted it back. He got out of the bath tub and knelt down on the bath mat beside it and prayed. He prayed for Stella and himself and Ad Haughton—he prayed crazily for the restoration of his life, the life that he had just as crazily cut in two. When he came out of the bathroom with a towel around him, Ad Haughton was sitting on the bed.

"Hello Bill. Where's your wife?"

"Just a minute," Bill answered. He went back into the bathroom and swallowed a draught of rubbing alcohol guaranteed to produce violent gastric disturbances. Then he stuck his head out the door casually.

"Mouth full of gargle," he explained. "How are you, Ad? Open that envelope on the pillow and we'll see where she is."

"—She's gone to Europe with a dentist. Or rather her dentist is going to Europe, so she had to dash to New York—"

He hardly heard. His mind, released from worry, had drifted off again. There would be a full moon tonight—or almost a full moon. Something had happened under a full moon once. What it was he was unable for the moment to remember.

His long, lanky body, his little lost soul in the universe, sat there on the bathroom window seat.

"I'm probably the world's worst guy," he said, shaking his head at himself in the mirror, "probably the world's worst guy. But I can't help it. At my age you can't fight against what you know you are."

Trying his best to be better, he sat there faithfully for an hour. Then it was twilight and there were voices downstairs, and suddenly there it was, in the sky over his lawn, all the restless longing after fleeing youth in all the world—the bright uncapturable moon.

THE BOWL

There was a man in my class at Princeton who never went to football games. He spent his Saturday afternoons delving for minutiæ about Greek athletics and the somewhat fixed battles between Christians and wild beasts under the Antonines. Lately—several years out of college—he has discovered football players and is making etchings of them in the manner of the late George Bellows. But he was once unresponsive to the very spectacle at his door, and I suspect the originality of his judgments on what is beautiful, what is remarkable and what is fun.

I reveled in football, as audience, amateur statistician and foiled participant—for I had played in prep school, and once there was a headline in the school newspaper: "Deering and Mullins Star Against Taft in Stiff Game Saturday." When I came in to lunch after the battle the school stood up and clapped and the visiting coach shook hands with me and prophesied—incorrectly—that I was going to be heard from. The episode is laid away in the most pleasant lavender of my past. That year I grew very tall and thin, and when at Princeton the following fall I looked anxiously over the freshman candidates and saw the polite disregard with which they looked back at me, I realized that that particular dream was over. Keene said he might make me into a very fair pole vaulter—and he did—but it was a poor substitute; and my terrible disappointment that I wasn't going to be a great football player was probably the foundation of my friendship with Dolly Harlan. I want to begin this story about Dolly with a little rehashing of the Yale game up at New Haven, sophomore year.

Dolly was started at halfback; this was his first big game. I roomed with him and I had scented something peculiar about his state of mind, so I didn't let him out of the corner of my eye during the whole first half. With field glasses I could see the expression on his face—it was strained and incredulous, as it had been the day of his father's

381

death, and it remained so, long after any nervousness had had time
to wear off. I thought he was sick and wondered why Keene didn't
see and take him out; it wasn't until later that I learned what was
the matter.

It was the Yale Bowl. The size of it or the enclosed shape of it
or the height of the sides had begun to get on Dolly's nerves when
the team practiced there the day before. In that practice he dropped
one or two punts, for almost the first time in his life, and he began
thinking it was because of the Bowl.

There is a new disease called agoraphobia—afraid of crowds—
and another called siderodromophobia—afraid of railroad traveling—and my friend Doctor Glock, the psychoanalyst, would probably account easily for Dolly's state of mind. But here's what Dolly
told me afterwards:

"Yale would punt and I'd look up. The minute I looked up, the
sides of that damn pan would seem to go shooting up too. Then when
the ball started to come down, the sides began leaning forward and
bending over me until I could see all the people on the top seats
screaming at me and shaking their fists. At the last minute I couldn't
see the ball at all, but only the Bowl; every time it was just luck that
I was under it and every time I juggled it in my hands."

To go back to the game. I was in the cheering section with a good
seat on the forty-yard line—good, that is, except when a very vague
graduate, who had lost his friends and his hat, stood up in front of
me at intervals and faltered, "Stob Ted Coy!" under the impression
that we were watching a game played a dozen years before. When
he realized finally that he was funny he began performing for the
gallery and aroused a chorus of whistles and boos until he was
dragged unwillingly under the stand.

It was a good game—what is known in college publications as
a historic game. A picture of the team that played it now hangs in
every barber shop in Princeton, with Captain Gottlieb in the middle
wearing a white sweater, to show that they won a championship.
Yale had had a poor season, but they had the breaks in the first
quarter, which ended 3 to 0 in their favor.

Between quarters I watched Dolly. He walked around panting
and sucking a water bottle and still wearing that strained stunned

expression. Afterwards he told me he was saying over and over to himself: "I'll speak to Roper. I'll tell him between halves. I'll tell him I can't go through this anymore." Several times already he had felt an almost irresistible impulse to shrug his shoulders and trot off the field, for it was not only this unexpected complex about the Bowl—the truth was that Dolly fiercely and bitterly hated the game.

He hated the long, dull period of training, the element of personal conflict, the demand on his time, the monotony of the routine and the nervous apprehension of disaster just before the end. Sometimes he imagined that all the others detested it as much as he did, and fought down their aversion as he did and carried it around inside them like a cancer that they were afraid to recognize. Sometimes he imagined that a man here and there was about to tear off the mask and say, "Dolly, do you hate this lousy business as much as I do?"

His feeling had begun back at St. Regis' School and he had come up to Princeton with the idea that he was through with football forever. But upperclassmen from St. Regis kept stopping him on the campus and asking him how much he weighed, and he was nominated for vice president of our class on the strength of his athletic reputation—and it was autumn, with achievement in the air. He wandered down to freshman practice one afternoon, feeling oddly lost and dissatisfied, and smelled the turf and smelled the thrilling season. In half an hour he was lacing on a pair of borrowed shoes and two weeks later he was captain of the freshman team.

Once committed he saw that he had made a mistake; he even considered leaving college. For with his decision to play Dolly assumed a moral responsibility, personal to him, besides. To lose or to let down, or to be let down, was simply intolerable to him. It offended his Scotch sense of waste: why sweat blood for an hour with only defeat at the end?

Perhaps the worst of it was that he wasn't really a star player. No team in the country could have spared using him, but he could do no spectacular thing superlatively well, neither run, pass nor kick. He was five-feet-eleven and weighed a little more than a hundred and sixty; he was a first-rate defensive man, sure in interference, a fair line plunger and a fair punter. He never fumbled and he was never inadequate; his presence, his constant cold sure aggression, had a strong effect on other men. Morally he captained any team he played on and that was why Roper had spent so much time trying to get length in his kicks all season—he wanted him in the game.

In the second quarter Yale began to crack. It was a mediocre team composed of flashy material, but uncoordinated because of injuries and impending changes in the Yale coaching system. The quarterback, Josh Logan, had been a wonder at Exeter—I could testify to that—where games can be won by the sheer confidence and spirit of a single man. But college teams are too highly organized to respond so simply and boyishly, and they recover less easily from fumbles and errors of judgment behind the line.

So with nothing to spare, with much grunting and straining, Princeton moved steadily down the field. On the Yale twenty-yard line things suddenly happened. A Princeton pass was intercepted; the Yale man, excited by his own opportunity, dropped the ball and it bobbed leisurely in the general direction of the Yale goal. Jack Devlin and Dolly Harlan of Princeton and somebody—I forget who—from Yale were all about the same distance from it. What Dolly did in that split second was all instinct; it presented no problem to him. He was a natural athlete and in a crisis his nervous system thought for him. He might have raced the two others for the ball; instead, he took out the Yale man with savage precision while Devlin scooped up the ball and ran ten yards for a touchdown.

This was when the sports writers still saw games through the eyes of Ralph Henry Barbour. The press box was right behind me, and as Princeton lined up to kick goal I heard the radio man ask:

"Who's Number 22?"

"Harlan."

"Harlan is going to kick goal. Devlin, who made the touchdown, comes from Lawrenceville School. He is twenty years old. The ball went true between the bars."

Between the halves, as Dolly sat shaking with fatigue in the locker room, Little, the back-field coach, came and sat beside him.

"When the ends are right on you, don't be afraid to make a fair catch," Little said. "That big Havemeyer is liable to jar the ball right out of your hands."

Now was the time to say it: "I wish you'd tell Bill—" But the words twisted themselves into a trivial question about the wind. His feeling would have to be explained, gone into, and there wasn't time. His own self seemed less important in this room, redolent with the tired breath, the ultimate effort, the exhaustion of ten other men. He was shamed by a harsh sudden quarrel that broke out between an end and tackle; he resented the former players in the room— especially the graduate captain of two years before, who was a little tight and over-vehement about the referee's favoritism. It seemed terrible to add one more jot to all this strain and annoyance. But he might have come out with it all the same if Little hadn't kept saying in a low voice: "What a take-out, Dolly! What a beautiful take-out!" and if Little's hand hadn't rested there, patting his shoulder.

II

In the third quarter Joe Dougherty kicked an easy field goal from the twenty-yard line and we felt safe, until toward twilight a series of desperate forward passes brought Yale close to a score. But Josh Logan had exhausted his personality in sheer bravado and he was outguessed by the defense at the last. As the substitutes came running in, Princeton began a last march down the field. Then abruptly it was over and the crowd poured from the stands, and Gottlieb, grabbing the ball, leaped up in the air. For awhile everything was confused and crazy and happy; I saw some freshmen try to carry Dolly, but they were shy and he got away.

We all felt a great personal elation. We hadn't beaten Yale for three years and now everything was going to be all right. It meant a good winter at college, something pleasant and slick to think back upon in the damp cold days after Christmas, when a bleak futility settles over a university town. Down on the field an improvised and uproarious team ran through plays with a derby, until the snake dance rolled over them and blotted them out. Outside the Bowl, I saw two abysmally gloomy and disgusted Yale men get into a waiting taxi and in a tone of final abnegation tell the driver "New York." You couldn't find Yale men—in the manner of the vanquished they had absolutely melted away.

I begin Dolly's story with my memories of this game because that evening the girl walked into it. She was a friend of Josephine Pickman's and the four of us were going to drive up to the Midnight Frolic in New York. When I suggested to him that he'd be too tired he laughed dryly—he'd have gone anywhere that night to get the feel and rhythm of football out of his head. He walked into the hall of Josephine's house at half-past six, looking as if he'd spent the day in the barber shop save for a small and fetching strip of court plaster over one eye. He was one of the handsomest men I ever knew, anyhow; he appeared tall and slender in street clothes, his hair was dark, his eyes big and sensitive and dark, his nose aquiline and, like all his features, somehow romantic. It didn't occur to me then, but I suppose he was pretty vain—not conceited, but vain—for he always dressed in brown or soft light grey, with black ties, and people don't match themselves so successfully by accident.

He was smiling a little to himself as he came in. He shook my hand buoyantly and said, "Why, what a surprise to meet *you* here, Mr. Deering," in a kidding way. Then he saw the two girls through the long hall, one dark and shining, like himself, and one with gold hair that was foaming and frothing in the firelight, and said in the happiest voice I've ever heard, "Which one is mine?"

"Either you want, I guess."

"Seriously, which is Pickman?"

"She's light."

"Then the other one belongs to me. Isn't that the idea?"

"I think I'd better warn them about the state you're in."

Miss Thorne, small, flushed and lovely, stood beside the fire. Dolly went right up to her.

"You're mine," he said. "You belong to me."

She looked at him coolly, making up her mind; suddenly she liked him and smiled. But Dolly wasn't satisfied. He wanted to do something incredibly silly or startling to express his untold jubilation that he was free.

"I love you," he said. He took her hand, his brown velvet eyes regarding her tenderly, unseeingly, convincingly. "I love you."

For a moment the corners of her lips fell as if in dismay that she had met someone stronger, more confident, more challenging than herself. Then as she drew herself together visibly, he dropped her hand and the little scene in which he had expended the tension of the afternoon was over.

It was a bright cold November night and the rush of air past the open car brought a vague excitement, a sense that we were hurrying at top speed toward a brilliant destiny. The roads were packed with cars that came to long inexplicable halts while police, blinded by the lights, walked up and down the line giving obscure commands. Before we had been gone an hour New York began to be a distant hazy glow against the sky.

Miss Thorne, Josephine told me, was from Washington, and had just come down from a visit in Boston.

"For the game?" I said.

"No. She didn't go to the game."

"That's too bad. If you'd let me know I could have picked up a seat—"

"She wouldn't have gone. Vienna never goes to games."

I remembered now that she hadn't even murmured the conventional congratulations to Dolly.

"She hates football. Her brother was killed in a prep-school game last year. I wouldn't have brought her tonight, but when we got home from the game I saw she'd been sitting there holding a book open at the same page all afternoon. You see, he was this wonderful kid and her family saw it happen and naturally never got over it."

"But does she mind being with Dolly?"

"Of course not. She just ignores football. If anyone mentions it she simply changes the subject."

I was glad that it was Dolly and not, say, Jack Devlin who was sitting back there with her. And I felt rather sorry for Dolly. However strongly he felt about the game, he must have waited for some acknowledgment that his effort had existed.

He was probably giving her credit for a subtle consideration, yet, as the images of the afternoon flashed into his mind, he might have welcomed a compliment to which he could respond "What nonsense!" Neglected entirely, the images would become insistent and obtrusive.

I turned around and was somewhat startled to find that Miss Thorne was in Dolly's arms; I turned quickly back and decided to let them take care of themselves.

As we waited for a traffic light on upper Broadway, I saw a sporting extra headlined with the score of the game. The green sheet was more real than the afternoon itself—succinct, condensed and clear:

PRINCETON CONQUERS YALE 10–3
SEVENTY THOUSAND WATCH TIGER TRIM
BULLDOG
DEVLIN SCORES ON YALE FUMBLE

There it was—not like the afternoon, muddled, uncertain, patchy and scrappy to the end, but nicely mounted now in the setting of the past:

PRINCETON 10–YALE 3.

Achievement was a curious thing, I thought. Dolly was largely responsible for that. I wondered if all things that screamed in the headlines were simply arbitrary accents. As if people should ask, "What does it look like?"

"It looks most like a cat."

"Well then, let's call it a cat."

My mind, brightened by the lights and the cheerful tumult, suddenly grasped the fact that all achievement was a placing of emphasis—a molding of the confusion of life into form.

Josephine stopped in front of the New Amsterdam Theatre, where her chauffeur met us and took the car. We were early, but a small buzz of excitement went up from the undergraduates waiting in the lobby—"There's Dolly Harlan!"—and as we moved toward the elevator several acquaintances came up to shake his hand. Apparently oblivious to these ceremonies, Miss Thorne caught my eye and smiled. I looked at her with curiosity; Josephine had imparted the rather surprising information that she was just sixteen years old. I suppose my return smile was rather patronizing, but instantly I realized that the fact could not be imposed on. In spite of all the warmth and delicacy of her face, the figure that somehow reminded me of an exquisite, romanticized little ballerina, there was a quality in her that was as hard as steel. She had been brought up in Rome, Vienna and Madrid, with flashes of Washington—her father was one of those charming American diplomats who, with fine obstinacy, try to recreate the Old World in their children by making their education rather more royal than that of princes. Miss Thorne was sophisticated. In spite of all the abandon of American young people, sophistication is still a continental monopoly.

We walked in upon a number in which a dozen chorus girls in orange and black were racing wooden horses against another dozen dressed in Yale blue. When the lights went on, Dolly was recognized and some Princeton students set up a clatter of approval with the little wooden hammers given out for applause; he moved his chair unostentatiously into a shadow.

Almost immediately a flushed and very miserable young man appeared beside our table. In better form he would have been extremely prepossessing; indeed he flashed a charming and dazzling smile at Dolly, as if requesting his permission to speak to Miss Thorne.

Then he said, "I thought you weren't coming to New York tonight."

"Hello, Carl." She looked up at him coolly.

"Hello, Vienna. That's just it? 'Hello Vienna—Hello Carl.' But why? I thought you weren't coming to New York tonight."

Miss Thorne made no move to introduce the man, but we were conscious of his somewhat raised voice.

"I thought you promised me you weren't coming."

"I didn't expect to, child. I just left Boston this morning."

"And who did you meet in Boston—the fascinating Tunti?" he demanded.

"I didn't meet anyone, child."

"Oh, yes, you did! You met the fascinating Tunti and you discussed living on the Riviera." She didn't answer. "Why are you so dishonest, Vienna?" he went on. "Why did you tell me on the phone—"

"I am not going to be lectured," she said, her tone changing suddenly. "I told you if you took another drink I was through with you. I'm a person of my word and I'd be enormously happy if you went away."

"Vienna!" he cried in a sinking, trembling voice.

At this point I got up and danced with Josephine. When we came back there were people at the table—the men to whom we were to hand over Josephine and Miss Thorne, for I had allowed for Dolly being tired, and several others. One of them was Al Ratoni, the composer, who, it appeared, had been entertained at the embassy in Madrid. Dolly Harlan had drawn his chair aside and was watching the dancers. Just as the lights went down for a new number a man came up out of the darkness and leaning over Miss Thorne whispered in her ear. She started and made a motion to rise, but he put his hand on her shoulder and forced her down. They began to talk together in low excited voices.

The tables were packed close at the old Frolic. There was a man rejoining the party next to us and I couldn't help hearing what he said:

"A young fellow just tried to kill himself down in the washroom. He shot himself through the shoulder but they got the pistol away before—" A minute later his voice again: "—Carl Sanderson, they said."

When the number was over I looked around. Vienna Thorne was staring very rigidly at Miss Lillian Lorraine, who was rising toward the ceiling as an enormous telephone doll. The man who had leaned over Vienna was gone and the others were obliviously unaware that anything had happened. I turned to Dolly and suggested that he and I had better go, and after a glance at Vienna in which reluctance, weariness and then resignation were mingled, he consented. On the way to the hotel I told Dolly what had happened.

"Just some souse," he remarked after a moment's fatigued consideration. "He probably tried to miss himself and get a little sympathy. I suppose those are the sort of things a really attractive girl is up against all the time."

This wasn't my attitude. I could see that mussed white shirt front with very young blood pumping over it, but I didn't argue, and after awhile Dolly said, "I suppose that sounds brutal, but it seems a little soft and weak, doesn't it? Perhaps that's just the way I feel tonight."

When Dolly undressed I saw that he was a mass of bruises, but he assured me that none of them would keep him awake. Then I told him why Miss Thorne hadn't mentioned the game and he woke up suddenly—the familiar glitter came back into his eyes.

"So that was it! I wondered. I thought maybe you'd told her not to say anything about it."

Later, when the lights had been out half an hour, he suddenly said "I see" in a loud clear voice. I don't know whether he was awake or asleep.

III

I've put down as well as I can everything I can remember about the first meeting between Dolly and Miss Vienna Thorne. Reading it over, it sounds casual and insignificant, but the evening lay in the shadow of the game and all that happened seemed like that. Vienna went back to Europe almost immediately and for fifteen months passed out of Dolly's life.

It was a good year—it still rings true in my memory as a good year. Sophomore year is the most dramatic at Princeton, just as junior year is at Yale. It's not only the elections to the upperclass clubs but also everyone's destiny begins to work itself out. You can tell pretty well who's going to come through, not only by their immediate success but by the way they survive failure. Life was very full for me. I made the board of the "Princetonian," and our house burned down out in Dayton, and I had a silly half-hour fist-fight in the gymnasium with a man who later became one of my closest friends, and in March Dolly and I joined the upperclass club we'd always wanted to be in. I fell in love, too, but it would be an irrelevancy to tell about that here.

April came and the first real Princeton weather, the lazy green-and-gold afternoons and the bright thrilling nights haunted with the hour of senior singing. I was happy, and Dolly would have been happy except for the approach of another football season. He was playing baseball, which excused him from spring practice, but the bands were beginning to play faintly in the distance. They rose to concert pitch during the summer, when he had to answer the question "Are you going back early for football?" a dozen times a day. On the fifteenth of September he was down in the dust and heat of late-summer Princeton, crawling over the ground on all fours, trotting through the old routine and turning himself into just the sort of specimen that I'd have given ten years of my life to be.

From first to last he hated it—and never let down for a minute. He went into the Yale game that fall weighing a hundred and fifty-three pounds, though that wasn't the weight printed in the paper, and he and Joe McDonald were the only men who played all through that disastrous game. He could have been captain by lifting his finger—but that involves some stuff that I know confidentially and can't tell. His only horror was that by some chance he'd have to accept it. Two seasons! He didn't even talk about it now. He left the room or the club when the conversation veered around to football. He stopped announcing to me that he "wasn't going through that business anymore." This time it took the Christmas holidays to drive that unhappy look from his eyes.

Then at the New Year, Miss Vienna Thorne came home from Madrid and in February a man named Case brought her down to the Senior Prom.

IV

She was even prettier than she had been before, softer, externally at least, and a tremendous success. People passing her on the street jerked their heads quickly to look at her—a frightened look, as if they realized that they had almost missed something. She was temporarily tired of European men, she told me, letting me gather that there had been some sort of unfortunate love affair. She was coming out in Washington next fall.

Vienna and Dolly. She disappeared with him for two hours the night of the club dances, and Harold Case was in despair. When they walked in again at midnight I thought they were the handsomest pair I saw. They were both shining with that peculiar luminosity that dark people sometimes have. Harold Case took one look at them and went proudly home.

Vienna came back a week later, solely to see Dolly. Late that evening I had occasion to go up to the deserted club for a book and they called me from the rear terrace, which opens out to the ghostly stadium and to an unpeopled sweep of night. It was an hour of thaw, with spring voices in the warm wind, and wherever there was light enough you could see drops glistening and falling. You could feel the cold melting out of the stars and the bare trees and shrubbery toward Stony Brook turning lush in the darkness.

They were sitting together on a wicker bench, full of themselves and romantic and happy.

"We had to tell someone about it," they said.

"Now can I go?"

"No, Jeff," they insisted. "Stay here and envy us. We're in the stage where we want someone to envy us. Do you think we're a good match?"

What could I say?

"Dolly's going to finish at Princeton next year," Vienna went on, "but we're going to announce it after the season in Washington in the autumn."

I was vaguely relieved to find that it was going to be a long engagement.

"I approve of you, Jeff," Vienna said. "I want Dolly to have more friends like you. You're stimulating for him—you have ideas. I told Dolly he could probably find others like you if he looked around his class."

Dolly and I both felt a little uncomfortable.

"She doesn't want me to be a Babbitt," he said lightly.

"Dolly's perfect," asserted Vienna. "He's the most beautiful thing that ever lived, and you'll find I'm very good for him, Jeff. Already I've helped him make up his mind about one important thing." I guessed what was coming. "He's going to speak a little piece if they bother him about playing football next autumn, aren't you, child?"

"Oh, they won't *bother* me," said Dolly uncomfortably. "It isn't like that—"

"Well, they'll try to bully you into it, morally."

"Oh, no," he objected. "It isn't like that. Don't let's talk about it now, Vienna. It's such a swell night."

Such a swell night! When I think of my own love passages at Princeton, I always summon up that night of Dolly's, as if it had been I and not he who sat there with youth and hope and beauty in his arms.

Dolly's mother took a place on Ram's Point, Long Island, for the summer, and late in August I went east to visit him. Vienna had been there a week when I arrived, and my impressions were: first, that he was very much in love; and, second, that it was Vienna's party. All sorts of curious people used to drop in to see Vienna. I wouldn't mind them now—I'm more sophisticated—but then they seemed rather a blot on the summer. They were all slightly famous in one way or another, and it was up to you to find out how. There was a lot of talk and especially there was much discussion of Vienna's personality. Whenever I was alone with any of the other guests we discussed Vienna's sparkling personality. They thought I was dull, and most of them thought Dolly was dull. He was better in his line than any of them were in theirs, but his was the only specialty that wasn't mentioned. Still I felt vaguely that I was being improved and I boasted about knowing most of those people in the ensuing year, and was annoyed when people failed to recognize their names.

The day before I left, Dolly turned his ankle playing tennis, and afterwards he joked about it to me rather somberly.

"If I'd only broken it things would be so much easier. Just a quarter of an inch more bend and one of the bones would have snapped. By the way, look here."

He tossed me a letter. It was a request that he report at Princeton for practice on September fifteenth and that meanwhile he begin getting himself in good condition.

"You're not going to play this fall?"

He shook his head.

"No. I'm not a child anymore. I've played for two years and I want this year free. If I went through it again it'd be a piece of moral cowardice."

"I'm not arguing, but—would you have taken this stand if it hadn't been for Vienna?"

"Of course I would. If I let myself be bullied into it I'd never be able to look myself in the face again."

Two weeks later I got the following letter:

Dear Jeff: When you read this you'll be somewhat surprised. I have, actually this time, broken my ankle playing tennis. I can't even walk with crutches at present; it's on a chair in front of me swollen up and wrapped up as big as a house as I write. No one, not even Vienna, knows about our conversation on the same subject last summer and so let us both absolutely forget it. One thing, though—an ankle is a darn hard thing to break, though I never knew it before.

I feel happier than I have for years—no early-season practice, no sweat and suffer, a little discomfort and inconvenience, but free. I feel as if I've outwitted a whole lot of people, and it's nobody's business but that of your

Machiavellian (sic) Friend,

DOLLY.

P. S. You might as well tear up this letter.

It didn't sound like Dolly at all.

V

Once down at Princeton, I asked Frank Kane—who sells sporting goods on Nassau Street and can tell you offhand the name of the scrub quarterback in 1901—what was the matter with Bob Tatnall's team senior year.

"Injuries and tough luck," he said. "They wouldn't sweat after the hard games. Take Joe McDonald, for instance, All-American tackle the year before—he was slow and stale, and he knew it and didn't care. It's a wonder Bill got that outfit through the season at all."

I sat in the stands with Dolly and watched them beat Lehigh 3–0 and tie Bucknell by a fluke. The next week we were trimmed 14–0 by Notre Dame. On the day of the Notre Dame game Dolly was in Washington with Vienna, but he was awfully curious about it when he came back next day. He had all the sporting pages of all the papers and he sat reading them and shaking his head. Then he stuffed them suddenly into the wastepaper basket.

"This college is football crazy," he announced. "Do you know that English teams don't even train for sports?"

I didn't enjoy Dolly so much in those days. It was curious to see him with nothing to do. For the first time in his life he hung around— around the room, around the club, around casual groups—he who had always been going somewhere with dynamic indolence. His passage along a walk had once created groups—groups of classmates who wanted to walk with him, of underclassmen who followed with their eyes a moving shrine. He became democratic, he mixed around, and it was somehow not appropriate. He explained that he wanted to know more men in his class.

But people want their idols a little above them, and Dolly had been a sort of private and special idol. He began to hate to be alone, and that, of course, was most apparent to me. If I got up to go out and he didn't happen to be writing a letter to Vienna, he'd ask "Where are you going?" in a rather alarmed way and make an excuse to limp along with me.

"Are you glad you did it, Dolly?" I asked him suddenly one day.

He looked at me with reproach behind the defiance in his eyes.

"Of course I'm glad."

"I wish you were in that backfield, all the same."

"It wouldn't matter a bit. This year's game's in the Bowl. I'd probably be dropping kicks for them."

The week of the Navy game he suddenly began going to all the practices. He worried; that terrible sense of responsibility was at work. Once he had hated the mention of football—now he thought and talked of nothing else. The night before the Navy game I woke up several times to find the lights burning brightly in his room.

We lost 7–3 on Navy's last-minute forward pass over Devlin's head. After the first half Dolly left the stands and sat down with the players on the field. When he joined me afterwards his face was smudgy and dirty as if he had been crying.

The game was in Baltimore that year. Dolly and I were going to spend the night in Washington with Vienna, who was giving a dance. We rode over there in an atmosphere of sullen gloom and it was all I could do to keep him from snapping out at two naval officers who were holding an exultant post-mortem in the seat behind.

The dance was what Vienna called her second coming-out party. She was having only the people she liked this time, and these turned out to be chiefly importations from New York. The musicians, the playwrights, the vague supernumeraries of the arts, who had dropped in at Dolly's house on Ram's Point, were here in force. But Dolly, relieved of his obligations as host, made no clumsy attempt to talk their language that night. He stood moodily against the wall with some of that old air of superiority that had first made me want to know him. Afterwards on my way to bed I passed Vienna's sitting room and she called me to come in. She and Dolly, both a little white, were sitting across the room from each other and there was tensity in the air.

"Sit down, Jeff," said Vienna wearily. "I want you to witness the collapse of a man into a schoolboy." I sat down reluctantly. "Dolly's changed his mind," she said. "He prefers football to me."

"That's not it," said Dolly stubbornly.

"I don't see the point," I objected. "Dolly can't possibly play."

"But he thinks he can. Jeff, just in case you imagine I'm being pig-headed about it, I want to tell you a story. Three years ago, when we first came back to the United States, Father put my young brother in school. One afternoon we all went out to see him play football. Just after the game started he was hurt, but Father said, 'It's all right. He'll be up in a minute. It happens all the time.' But, Jeff, he never got up. He lay there and finally they carried him off the field and put a blanket over him. Just as we got to him he died."

She looked from one to the other of us and began to sob convulsively. Dolly went over, frowning, and put his arm around her shoulder.

"Oh, Dolly," she cried, "won't you do this for me—just this one little thing for me?"

He shook his head miserably. "I tried but I can't," he said. "It's my stuff, don't you understand, Vienna? People have got to do their stuff."

Vienna had risen and was powdering her tears at a mirror—now she flashed around angrily.

"Then I've been laboring under a misapprehension when I supposed you felt about it much as I did."

"Let's not go over all that. I'm tired of talking, Vienna. I'm tired of my own voice. It seems to me that no one I know does anything but talk anymore."

"Thanks. I suppose that's meant for me."

"It seems to me your friends talk a great deal. I've never heard so much jabber as I've listened to tonight. Is the idea of actually doing anything repulsive to you, Vienna?"

"It depends upon whether it's worth doing."

"Well, this is worth doing—to me."

"I know your trouble, Dolly," she said bitterly. "You're weak and you want to be admired. This year you haven't had a lot of little boys following you around as if you were Jack Dempsey, and it almost breaks your heart. You want to get out in front of them all and make a show of yourself and hear the applause."

He laughed shortly. "If that's your idea of how a football player feels—"

"Have you made up your mind to play?" she interrupted.

"If I'm any use to them—yes."

"Then I think we're both wasting our time."

Her expression was ruthless, but Dolly refused to see that she was in earnest. When I got away he was still trying to make her "be rational," and next day on the train he said that Vienna had been "a little nervous." He was deeply in love with her, and he didn't dare think of losing her; but he was still in the grip of the sudden emotion that had decided him to play, and his confusion and exhaustion of mind made him believe vainly that everything was going to be all right. But I had seen that look on Vienna's face the night she talked with Mr. Carl Sanderson at the Frolic two years before.

Dolly didn't get off the train at Princeton Junction, but continued on to New York. He went to two orthopedic specialists and one of them arranged a bandage braced with a whole little fence of whalebones that he was to wear day and night. The probabilities were that it would snap at the first brisk encounter, but he could run on it and stand on it when he kicked. He was out on University Field in uniform the following afternoon.

His appearance was a small sensation. I was sitting in the stands watching practice with Harold Case and young Daisy Cary. She was just beginning to be famous then, and I don't know whether she or Dolly attracted the most attention. In those times it was still rather daring to bring down a moving-picture actress—if that same young lady went to Princeton today she would probably be met at the station with a band.

Dolly limped around and everyone said, "He's limping!" He got under a punt and everyone said, "He did *that* pretty well!" The first team were laid off after the hard Navy game and everyone watched Dolly all afternoon. After practice I caught his eye and he came over and shook hands. Daisy asked him if he'd like to be in a football picture she was going to make. It was only conversation, but he looked at me with a dry smile.

When he came back to the room his ankle was swollen up as big as a stove pipe, and next day he and Keene fixed up an arrangement by which the bandage would be loosened and tightened to fit its varying size. We called it the balloon. The bone was nearly healed, but the little bruised sinews were stretched out of place again every day. He watched the Swarthmore game from the sidelines and the following Monday he was in scrimmage with the second team against the scrubs.

In the afternoons sometimes he wrote to Vienna. His theory was that they were still engaged, but he tried not to worry about it, and I think the very pain that kept him awake at night was good for that. When the season was over he would go and see.

We played Harvard and lost 7 to 3. Jack Devlin's collarbone was broken and he was out for the season, which made it almost sure that Dolly would play. Amid the rumors and the fears of mid-November the news aroused a spark of hope in an otherwise morbid undergraduate body—hope all out of proportion to Dolly's condition. He came back to the room the Thursday before the game with his face drawn and tired.

"They're going to start me," he said, "and I'm going to be back for punts. If they only knew—"

"Couldn't you tell Bill how you feel about that?"

He shook his head and I had a sudden suspicion that he was punishing himself for his "accident" last August. He lay silently on the couch while I packed his suitcase for the team train.

The actual day of the game was, as usual, like a dream—unreal with its crowds of friends and relatives and the inessential trappings of a gigantic show. The eleven little men who ran out on the field at last were like bewitched figures in another world, strange and infinitely romantic, blurred by a throbbing mist of people and sound. One aches with them intolerably, trembles with their excitement, but they have no traffic with us now. They are beyond help, consecrated and unreachable—vaguely holy.

The field is rich and green, the preliminaries are over and the teams trickle out into position. Head guards are put on; each man claps his hands and breaks into a lonely little dance. People are still talking around you, arranging themselves, but you have fallen silent and your eye wanders from man to man. There's Jack Whitehead, a senior, at end; Joe McDonald, large and reassuring, at tackle; Toole, a sophomore, at guard; Red Hopman, center; someone you can't identify at the other guard—Bunker probably—he turns and you see his number—Bunker; Bean Gile, looking unnaturally dignified and significant at the other tackle; Poore, another sophomore, at end. Back of them is Wash Sampson at quarter—imagine how he feels! But he runs here and there on light feet, speaking to this man and that, trying to communicate his alertness and his confidence of success. Dolly Harlan stands motionless, his hands on his hips, watching the Yale kicker tee up the ball; near him is Captain Bob Tatnall—

There's the whistle! The line of the Yale team sways ponderously forward from its balance, and a split second afterwards comes the sound of the ball. The field streams with running figures and the whole Bowl strains forward as if thrown by the current of an electric chair.

Suppose we fumbled right away.

Tatnall catches it, goes back ten yards, is surrounded and blotted out of sight. Spears goes through center for three. A short pass, Sampson to Tatnall, is completed, but for no gain. Harlan punts to Devereaux, who is downed in his tracks on the Yale forty-yard line.

Now we'll see what they've got.

It developed immediately that they had a great deal. Using an effective crisscross and a short pass over center, they carried the ball fifty-four yards to the Princeton six-yard line, where they lost it on a fumble, recovered by Red Hopman. After a trade of punts, they began another push, this time to the fifteen-yard line, where, after four hair-raising forward passes, two of them batted down by Dolly, we got the ball on downs. But Yale was still fresh and strong, and with a third onslaught the weaker Princeton line began to give way.

Just after the second quarter began Devereaux took the ball over for a touchdown and the half ended with Yale in possession of the ball on our ten-yard line. Score, Yale 7–Princeton 0.

We hadn't a chance. The team was playing above itself, better than it had played all year, but it wasn't enough. Save that it was the Yale game, when anything could happen, anything *had* happened, the atmosphere of gloom would have been deeper than it was, and in the cheering section you could cut it with a knife.

Early in the game Dolly Harlan had fumbled Devereaux's high punt, but recovered without gain; toward the end of the half another kick slipped through his fingers, but he scooped it up and, slipping past the end, went back twelve yards. Between halves he told Roper he couldn't seem to get under the ball, but they kept him there. His own kicks were carrying well and he was essential in the only backfield combination that could hope to score.

After the first play of the game he limped slightly, moving around as little as possible to conceal the fact. But I knew enough about football to see that he was in every play, starting at that rather slow pace of his and finishing with a quick side lunge that almost always took out his man. Not a single Yale forward pass was finished in his territory, but toward the end of the third quarter he dropped another kick—backed around in a confused little circle under it, lost it and recovered on the five-yard line just in time to avert a certain score. That made the third time, and I saw Ed Kimball throw off his blanket and begin to warm up on the sidelines.

Just at that point our luck began to change.

From a kick formation, with Dolly set to punt from behind our goal, Howard Bement, who had gone in for Wash Sampson at quarter, took the ball through the center of the line, got by the secondary defense and ran twenty-six yards before he was pulled down. Captain Tasker, of Yale, had gone out with a twisted knee, and Princeton began to pile plays through his substitute, between Bean Gile and Hopman, with George Spears and sometimes Bob Tatnall carrying the ball. We went up to the Yale forty-yard line, lost the ball on a fumble and recovered it on another as the third quarter ended. A wild ripple of enthusiasm ran through the Princeton stands. For the first time we had the ball in their territory with first down and the possibility of tying the score. You could hear the tenseness growing all around you in the intermission; it was reflected in the excited movements of the cheer leaders and the uncontrollable patches of sound that leaped out of the crowd, catching up voices here and there and swelling to an undisciplined roar.

I saw Kimball dash out on the field and report to the referee and I thought Dolly was through at last, and was glad, but it was Bob Tatnall who came out, sobbing, and brought the Princeton side cheering to its feet.

With the first play pandemonium broke loose and continued to the end of the game. At intervals it would swoon away to a plaintive humming; then it would rise to the intensity of wind and rain and thunder, and beat across the twilight from one side of the Bowl to the other like the agony of lost souls swinging across a gap in space.

The teams lined up on Yale's forty-one-yard line and Spears immediately dashed off tackle for six yards. Again he carried the ball—he was a wild unpopular Southerner with inspired moments—going through the same hole for five more and a first down. Dolly made two on a cross-buck and Spears was held at center. It was third down, with the ball on Yale's twenty-nine-yard line and eight to go.

There was some confusion immediately behind me, some pushing and some voices; a man was sick or had fainted—I never discovered which. Then my view was blocked out for a minute by rising bodies—and then everything went definitely crazy. Substitutes were jumping around down on the field, waving their blankets, the air was full of hats, cushions, coats and a deafening roar. Dolly Harlan, who had scarcely carried the ball a dozen times in his Princeton career, had picked a long pass from Kimball out of the air and, dragging a tackler, struggled five yards to the Yale goal.

VI

Some time later the game was over. There was a bad moment when Yale began another attack, but there was no scoring and Bob Tatnall's eleven had redeemed a mediocre season by tying a better Yale team. For us there was the feel of victory about it, the exaltation if not the jubilance, and the Yale faces issuing from out the Bowl wore the look of defeat. It would be a good year after all—a good fight at the last, a tradition for next year's team. Our class—those of us who cared—would go out from Princeton without the taste of final defeat. The symbol stood—such as it was; the banners blew proudly in the wind. All that is childish? Find us something to fill the niche of victory.

I waited for Dolly outside the dressing rooms until almost everyone had come out; then, as he still lingered, I went in. Someone had given him a little brandy, and since he never drank much, it was swimming in his head.

"Have a chair, Jeff." He smiled, broadly and happily. "Rubber! Tony! Get the distinguished guest a chair. He's an intellectual and he wants to interview one of the bone-headed athletes. Tony, this is Mr. Deering. They've got everything in this funny Bowl but armchairs. I love this Bowl. I'm going to build here."

He fell silent, thinking about all things happily. He was content. I persuaded him to dress—there were people waiting for us. Then he insisted on walking out upon the field, dark now, and feeling the crumbled turf with his shoe.

He picked up a divot from a cleat and let it drop, laughed, looked distracted for a minute, and turned away.

With Tad Davis, Daisy Cary and another girl, we drove to New York. He sat beside Daisy and was silly, charming and attractive. For the first time since I'd known him he talked about the game naturally, even with a touch of vanity.

"For two years I was pretty good and I was always mentioned at the bottom of the column as being among those who played. This year I dropped three punts and slowed up every play till Bob Tatnall kept yelling at me, 'I don't see why they won't take you out!' But a pass not even aimed at me fell in my arms and I'll be in the headlines tomorrow."

He laughed. Somebody touched his foot; he winced and turned white.

"How did you hurt it?" Daisy asked. "In football?"

"I hurt it last summer," he said shortly.

"It must have been terrible to play on it."

"It was."

All the Sad Young Men

"I suppose you had to."

"That's the way sometimes."

They understood each other. They were both workers—sick or well, there were things that Daisy also had to do. She spoke of how, with a vile cold, she had had to fall into an open-air lagoon out in Hollywood the winter before.

"Six times—with a fever of a hundred and two. But the production was costing ten thousand dollars a day."

"Couldn't they use a double?"

"They did whenever they could—I only fell in when it had to be done."

She was eighteen and I compared her background of courage and independence and achievement, of politeness based upon realities of cooperation, with that of most society girls I had known. There was no way in which she wasn't inestimably their superior—if she had looked for a moment my way—but it was Dolly's shining velvet eyes that signaled to her own.

"Can't you go out with me tonight?" I heard her ask him.

He was sorry, but he had to refuse. Vienna was in New York—she was going to see him. I didn't know, and Dolly didn't know, whether there was to be a reconciliation or a good-bye.

When she dropped Dolly and me at the Ritz there was real regret, that lingering form of it, in both their eyes.

"There's a marvelous girl," Dolly said. I agreed. "I'm going up to see Vienna. Will you get a room for us at the Biltmore?"

So I left him. What happened between him and Vienna I don't know; he has never spoken about it to this day. But what happened later in the evening was brought to my attention by several surprised and even indignant witnesses to the event.

Dolly walked into the Ambassador Hotel about ten o'clock and went to the desk to ask for Miss Cary's room. There was a crowd around the desk, among them some Yale or Princeton undergraduates from the game. Several of them had been celebrating and evidently one of them knew Daisy and had tried to get her room by phone. Dolly was abstracted and he must have made his way through them in a somewhat brusque way and asked to be connected with Miss Cary.

One young man stepped back, looked at him unpleasantly and said, "You seem to be in an awful hurry. Just who are you?"

There was one of those slight silent pauses and the people near the desk all turned to look. Something happened inside Dolly; he felt as if life had arranged his role to make possible this particular question—a question that now he had no choice but to answer. Still, there was silence. The small crowd waited.

"Why, I'm Dolly Harlan," he said deliberately. "What do you think of that?"

It was quite outrageous. There was a pause and then a sudden little flurry and chorus: "Dolly Harlan! What? What did he say?"

The clerk had heard the name—he gave it as the phone was answered from Miss Cary's room.

"Mr. Harlan's to go right up, please."

Dolly turned away, alone with his achievement, taking it for once to his breast. He found suddenly that he would not have it long so intimately—the memory would outlive the triumph and even the triumph would outlive the glow in his heart that was best of all. Tall and straight, an image of victory and pride, he moved across the lobby, oblivious alike to the fate ahead of him or the small chatter behind.

MAGNETISM

The pleasant ostentatious boulevard was lined at prosperous intervals with New England Colonial houses—without ship models in
the hall. When the inhabitants moved out here the ship models had
at last been given to the children. The next street was a complete
exhibit of the Spanish bungalow phase of West Coast architecture,
while two streets over the cylindrical windows and round tow-
ers of 1897—melancholy antiques which sheltered swamis, yogis,
fortune tellers, dressmakers, dancing teachers, art academies and
chiropractors—looked down now upon brisk buses and trolley cars.
A little walk around the block could, if you were feeling old that
day, be a discouraging affair.

On the green flanks of the modern boulevard, children, with their
knees marked by the red stains of the mercurochrome era, played
with Toys with a Purpose—beams that taught engineering, soldiers
that taught manliness, and dolls that taught motherhood. When the
dolls were so banged up that they stopped looking like real babies
and began to look like dolls, the children developed affection for
them. Everything in the vicinity, even the March sunlight, was new,
fresh, hopeful and thin, as you would expect in a city that had tripled
its population in fifteen years.

Among the very few domestics in sight that morning was a handsome young maid sweeping the steps of the biggest house on the
street. She was a large, simple Mexican girl with the large, simple
ambitions of the time and the locality, and she was already conscious of being a luxury—she received one hundred dollars a month
in return for her personal liberty. Sweeping, Dolores kept an eye
on the stairs inside, for Mr. Hannaford's car was waiting and he
would soon be coming down to breakfast. The Problem came first
this morning however, the Problem as to whether it was a duty or
a favor when she helped the English nurse down the steps with the

perambulator. The English nurse always said "Please," and "Thanks very much," but Dolores hated her and would have liked, without any special excitement, to beat her insensible. Like most Latins under the stimulus of American life she had irresistible impulses toward violence.

The nurse escaped, however. Her blue cape faded haughtily into the distance just as Mr. Hannaford, who had come quietly downstairs, stepped into the space of the front door.

"Good morning." He smiled at Dolores; he was young and extraordinarily handsome. Dolores tripped on the broom and fell off the stoop. George Hannaford hurried down the steps, reached her as she was getting to her feet cursing volubly in Mexican, just touched her arm with a helpful gesture and said, "I hope you didn't hurt yourself."

"Oh, no."

"I'm afraid it was my fault; I'm afraid I startled you, coming out like that."

His voice had real regret in it; his brow was knit with solicitude.

"Are you *sure* you're all right?"

"Aw, sure."

"Didn't turn your ankle?"

"Aw, no."

"I'm terribly sorry about it."

"Aw, it was not your fault."

He was still frowning as she went inside, and Dolores, who was not hurt and thought quickly, suddenly contemplated having a love affair with him. She looked at herself several times in the pantry mirror and stood close to him as she poured his coffee, but he read the paper and she saw that that was all for the morning.

Hannaford entered his car and drove to Jules Rennard's house. Jules was a French Canadian by birth and George Hannaford's best friend; they were fond of each other and spent much time together. Both of them were simple and dignified in their tastes and in their way of thinking, instinctively gentle, and in a world of the volatile and the bizarre found in each other a certain quiet solidity.

He found Jules at breakfast.

"I want to fish for barracuda," said George abruptly. "When will you be free? I want to take the boat and go down to lower California."

Jules had dark circles under his eyes. Yesterday he had closed out the greatest problem of his life by settling with his ex-wife for two hundred thousand dollars. He had married too young and the former slavey from the Quebec slums had taken to drugs upon her failure to rise with him. Yesterday in the presence of lawyers her final gesture had been to smash his finger with the base of a telephone. He was tired of women for awhile and welcomed the suggestion of a fishing trip.

"How's the baby?" he asked.

"The baby's fine."

"And Kay?"

"Kay's not herself—but I don't pay any attention. What did you do to your hand?"

"I'll tell you another time. What's the matter with Kay, George?"

"Jealous."

"Of who?"

"Helen Avery. It's nothing. She's not herself, that's all."

He got up.

"I'm late," he said. "Let me know as soon as you're free. Any time after Monday will suit me."

George left and drove out an interminable boulevard which narrowed into a long, winding concrete road and rose into the hilly country behind. Somewhere in the vast emptiness a group of buildings appeared, a barn-like structure, a row of offices, a large but quick restaurant and half a dozen small bungalows. The chauffeur dropped Hannaford at the main entrance. He went in and passed through various enclosures, each marked off by swinging gates and inhabited by a stenographer.

"Is anybody with Mr. Schroeder?" he asked, in front of a door lettered with that name.

"No, Mr. Hannaford."

Simultaneously his eye fell on a young lady who was writing at a desk aside and he lingered a moment.

"Hello, Margaret," he said. "How are you, darling?"

A delicate, pale beauty looked up, frowning a little, still abstracted in her work. It was Miss Donovan the script girl, a friend of many years.

"Hello. Oh, George, I didn't see you come in. Mr. Douglas wants to work on the brook sequence this afternoon."

"All right."

"These are the changes we decided on Thursday night." She smiled up at him and George wondered for the thousandth time why she had never gone into pictures.

"All right," he said. "Will initials do?"

"Your initials look like George Harris's."

"Very well, darling."

As he finished, Pete Schroeder opened his door and beckoned him.

"George, come here!" he said with an air of excitement. "I want you to listen to someone on the phone."

Hannaford went in.

"Pick up the phone and say 'Hello'," directed Schroeder. "Don't say who you are."

"Hello," said Hannaford obediently.

"Who is this?" asked a girl's voice.

Hannaford put his hand over the mouthpiece.

"What am I supposed to do?"

Schroeder snickered and Hannaford hesitated, smiling and suspicious.

"Who do you want to speak to?" he temporized into the phone.

"To George Hannaford, I want to speak to. Is this him?"

"Yes."

"Oh George—it's me."

"Who?"

"Me, Gwen. I had an awful time finding you. They told me—"

"Gwen who?"

"Gwen—can't you hear? From San Francisco—last Thursday night."

"I'm sorry," objected George. "Must be some mistake."

"Is this George Hannaford?"

"Yes."

The voice grew slightly tart.

"Well, this is Gwen Becker you spent last Thursday evening with in San Francisco. There's no use pretending you don't know who I am, because you do."

Schroeder took the apparatus from George and hung up the receiver.

"Somebody has been doubling for me up in Frisco," said Hannaford.

"So that's where you were Thursday night!"

"Those things aren't funny to me—not since that crazy Zeller girl. You can never convince them they've been sold because the man always looks something like you. What's new, Pete?"

"Let's go over to the stage and see."

Together they walked out a back entrance, along a muddy walk and, opening a little door in the big blank wall of the studio building, entered into its half darkness.

Here and there figures spotted the dim twilight, figures that turned up white faces to George Hannaford, like souls in purgatory watching the passage of a half-god through. Here and there were whispers and soft voices and, apparently from afar, the gentle tremolo of a small organ. Turning the corner made by some flats they came upon the white crackling glow of a stage with two people motionless upon it.

An actor in evening clothes, his shirt front, collar and cuffs tinted a brilliant pink, made as though to get chairs for them but they shook their heads and stood watching. For a long while nothing happened on the stage—no one moved. A row of lights went off with a savage hiss, went on again. The plaintive tap of a hammer begged admission to nowhere in the distance; a blue face appeared among the blinding lights above and called something unintelligible into the upper blackness. Then the silence was broken by a low clear voice from the stage.

"If you want to know why I haven't got stockings on, look in my dressing room. I spoiled four pairs yesterday and two already this morning. . . . This dress weighs six pounds."

A man stepped out of the group of observers and regarded the girl's brown legs; their lack of covering was scarcely distinguishable, but in any event her expression implied that she would do nothing about it. The lady was annoyed, and so intense was her personality that it had taken only a fractional flexing of her eyes to indicate the fact. She was a dark pretty girl with a figure that would be full-blown sooner than she wished. She was just eighteen.

Had this been the week before, George Hannaford's heart would have stood still. Their relationship had been in just that stage. He hadn't said a word to Helen Avery that Kay could have objected to, but something had begun between them on the second day of this picture that Kay had felt in the air. Perhaps it had begun even earlier, for he had determined when he saw Helen Avery's first release that she should play opposite him. Helen Avery's voice and the dropping of her eyes when she finished speaking, like a sort of exercise in control—that fascinated him. He had felt that they both tolerated something, that each knew half of some secret about people and life, and that if they rushed toward each other there would be a romantic communion of almost unbelievable intensity. It was this element of promise and possibility that had haunted him for a fortnight and was now dying away.

Hannaford was thirty, and he was a moving-picture actor only through a series of accidents. After a year in a small technical college he had taken a summer job with an electric company, and his first appearance in a studio was in the role of repairing a bank of Klieg lights. In an emergency he played a small part and made good, but for fully a year after that he thought of it as a purely transitory episode in his life. At first much of it had offended him—the almost hysterical egotism and excitability hidden under an extremely thin veil of elaborate good-fellowship. It was only recently with the advent of such men as Jules Rennard into pictures that he began to see the possibilities of a decent and secure private life, much as his would have been as a successful engineer. At last his success felt solid beneath his feet.

He met Kay Tompkins at the old Griffith Studios at Mamaroneck, and their marriage was a fresh personal affair, removed from most stage marriages. Afterwards they had possessed each other completely, had been pointed to: "Look, there's one couple in pictures who manage to stay together." It would have taken something out of many people's lives, people who enjoyed a vicarious security in the contemplation of their marriage, if they hadn't stayed together, and their love was fortified by a certain effort to live up to that.

He held women off by a polite simplicity that underneath was hard and watchful—when he felt a certain current being turned on he became emotionally stupid. Kay expected and took much more from men, but she too had a careful thermometer against her heart. Until the other night when she reproached him for being interested in Helen Avery, there had been an absolute minimum of jealousy between them.

George Hannaford was still absorbed in the thought of Helen Avery as he left the studio and walked toward his bungalow over the way. There was in his mind, first, a horror that anyone should come between him and Kay, and, second, a regret that he no longer carried that possibility in the forefront of his mind. It had given him a tremendous pleasure, like the things that had happened to him during his first big success, before he was so "made" that there was scarcely anything better ahead—it was something to take out and look at, a new and still mysterious joy. It hadn't been love, for he was critical of Helen Avery as he had never been critical of Kay. But his feeling of last week had been sharply significant and memorable, and he was restless now that it had passed.

Working that afternoon they were seldom together, but he was conscious of her, and he knew that she was conscious of him. She stood a long time with her back to him at one point, and when she turned at length their eyes swept past each other's, brushing like bird wings—simultaneously he saw they had gone far, in their way; it was well that he had drawn back. He was glad that someone came for her when the work was almost over.

Dressed he returned to the office wing, stopping in for a moment to see Schroeder. No one answered his knock, and turning the knob he went in—Helen Avery was there alone.

Hannaford shut the door and they stared at each other. Her face was young, frightened. In a moment in which neither of them spoke, it was decided that they would have some of this out now. Almost thankfully he felt the warm sap of emotion flow out of his heart and course through his body.

"Helen!"

She murmured, "What?" in an awed voice.

"I feel terribly about this." His voice was shaking.

Suddenly she began to cry; painful, audible sobs shook her.

"Have you got a handkerchief?" she said.

He gave her a handkerchief. At that moment there were steps outside. George opened the door halfway just in time to keep Schroeder from entering on the spectacle of her tears.

"Nobody's in," he said facetiously. For a moment longer he kept his shoulder against the door. Then he let it open slowly.

Outside in his limousine he wondered how soon Jules would be ready to go fishing.

II

From the age of twelve Kay Tompkins had worn men like rings on every finger. Her face was round, young, pretty and strong, a strength accentuated by the responsive play of brows and lashes around her clear, glossy, hazel eyes. She was the daughter of the senator from a western state, and she hunted unsuccessfully for glamour through a small western city until she was seventeen—when she ran away from home and went on the stage. She was one of those people who are famous far beyond their actual achievement. There was that excitement about her that seemed to reflect the excitement of the world. While she was playing small parts in Ziegfeld shows she attended proms at Yale, and during a temporary venture into pictures she met George Hannaford, already a star of the new "natural" type then just coming into vogue. In him she found what she had been seeking.

She was at present in what is known as a "dangerous state." For six months she had been helpless and dependent entirely upon George, and now that her son was the property of a strict and possessive English nurse, Kay, free again, suddenly felt the need of proving herself attractive. She wanted things to be as they had been before the baby was thought of. Also she felt that lately George had taken her too much for granted—she had a strong instinct that he was interested in Helen Avery.

When George Hannaford came home that night he had minimized to himself their quarrel of the previous evening and was surprised at her perfunctory greeting.

"What's the matter, Kay?" he asked after a minute. "Is this going to be another night like last night?"

"Do you know we're going out tonight?" she said, avoiding an answer.

"Where?"

"To Katherine Davis's. I didn't know whether you'd want to go—"

"I'd like to go."

"I didn't know whether you'd want to go. Arthur Busch said he'd stop for me."

They dined in silence. Without any secret thoughts to dip into like a child into a jam jar, George felt restless, and at the same time was aware that the atmosphere was full of jealousy, suspicion and anger. Until recently they had preserved between them something precious that made their house one of the pleasantest in Hollywood to enter. Now suddenly it might be any house—he felt common and he felt unstable. He had come near to making something bright and precious into something cheap and unkind. With a sudden surge of emotion he crossed the room and was about to put his arm around her when the doorbell rang. A moment later Dolores announced Mr. Arthur Busch.

Busch was an ugly, popular little man, a continuity writer and lately a director. A few years ago they had been hero and heroine to him and—even now, when he was a person of some consequence in the picture world, he accepted with equanimity Kay's use of him for such purposes as tonight's. He had been in love with her for years, but because his love seemed hopeless it had never caused him much distress.

They went on to the party. It was a housewarming, with Hawaiian musicians in attendance, and the guests were largely "of the old crowd." People who had been in the early Griffith pictures, even though they were scarcely thirty, were considered to be of "the old crowd"—they were different from those coming along now and they were conscious of it. They had a dignity and straightforwardness about them, from the fact that they had worked in pictures before pictures were bathed in a golden haze of success. They were still rather humble before their amazing triumph, and thus, unlike the new generation, who took it all for granted, they were constantly in touch with reality. Half a dozen or so of the women were especially aware of being unique. No one had come along to fill their places— here and there a pretty face had caught the public imagination for a year, but those of the old crowd were already legends, ageless and disembodied. With all this they were still young enough to believe that they would go on forever.

George and Kay were greeted affectionately; people moved over and made places for them. The Hawaiians performed and the Duncan sisters sang at the piano. From the moment George saw who was here, he guessed that Helen Avery would be here too and the fact annoyed him—it was not appropriate that she should be part of this gathering through which he and Kay had moved familiarly and tranquilly for years.

He saw her first when someone opened the swinging door to the kitchen, and when a little later she came out and their eyes met he knew absolutely that he didn't love her. He went up to speak to her, and at her first words he saw something had happened to her, too, that had dissipated the mood of the afternoon. She had got a big part.

"And I'm in a daze," she cried happily. "I didn't think there was a chance and I've thought of nothing else since I read the book a year ago."

"It's wonderful, I'm awfully glad."

He had the feeling, though, that he should look at her with a certain regret—one couldn't jump from such a scene as this afternoon to a plane of casual friendly interest. Suddenly she began to laugh.

"Oh, we're such actors, George—you and I."

"What do you mean?"

"You know what I mean."

"I don't."

"Oh yes, you do. You did this afternoon. It was a pity we didn't have a camera."

Short of declaring then and there that he loved her, there was absolutely nothing more to say. He grinned acquiescently. A group formed around them and absorbed them, and George, feeling that the evening had settled something, began to think about going home. An excited and sentimental elderly lady, someone's mother, came up and began telling him how much she believed in him, and he was polite and charming to her, as only he could be, for half an hour. Then he went to Kay, who had been sitting with Arthur Busch all evening, and suggested that they go.

She looked up unwillingly. She had had several highballs and the fact was mildly apparent. She did not want to go, but she got up after a mild argument, and George went upstairs for his coat. When he came down Katherine Davis told him that Kay had already gone out to the car.

The crowd had increased; to avoid a general good-night he went out through the sun-parlor door to the lawn; less than twenty feet away from him he saw the figures of Kay and Arthur Busch against a bright street lamp—they were standing close together and staring into each other's eyes. He saw that they were holding hands.

After the first start of surprise George instinctively turned about, retraced his steps, hurried through the room he had just left and came noisily out the front door. But Kay and Arthur Busch were still standing close together, and it was lingeringly and with abstracted eyes that they turned around finally and saw him. Then both of them seemed to make effort; they drew apart as if it was a physical ordeal. George said good-bye to Arthur Busch with special cordiality, and in a moment he and Kay were driving homeward through the clear California night.

He said nothing, Kay said nothing. He was incredulous. He suspected that Kay had kissed a man here and there, but he had never seen it happen or given it any thought; this was different. There had been an element of tenderness in it, and there was something veiled and remote in Kay's eyes that he had never seen there before.

Without having spoken they entered the house; Kay stopped by the library door and looked in.

"There's someone there," she said, and she added without interest: "I'm going upstairs. Please don't come in my room tonight."

As she ran up the stairs, the person in the library stepped out into the hall.

"Mr. Hannaford—"

He was a pale and hard young man; his face was vaguely familiar, but George didn't remember where he had seen it before.

"Mr. Hannaford?" said the young man. "I recognize you from your pictures." He looked at George obviously a little awed.

"What can I do for you?"

"Well—will you come in here?"

"What is it? I don't know who you are."

"My name is Donovan. I'm Margaret Donovan's brother." His face toughened a little.

"Is anything the matter?"

Donovan made a motion toward the door.

"Come in here." His voice was confident now, almost threatening.

George hesitated, then he walked into the library. Donovan followed and stood across the table from him, his legs apart, his hands in his pockets.

"Hannaford," he said, in the tone of a man trying to whip himself up to anger. "Margaret wants fifty thousand dollars."

"What the devil are you talking about?" exclaimed George incredulously.

"Margaret wants fifty thousand dollars," repeated Donovan.

"You're Margaret Donovan's brother?"

"I am."

"I don't believe it." But he saw the resemblance now. "Does Margaret know you're here?"

"She sent me here. She'll hand over those two letters for fifty grand, and no questions asked."

"What letters?" George chuckled irresistibly. "This is some joke of Schroeder's, isn't it?"

"This ain't a joke, Hannaford. I mean the letters you signed your name to this afternoon."

III

An hour later George went upstairs in a daze. The clumsiness of the affair was at once outrageous and astounding. That a friend of seven years should suddenly request his signature on papers that were not what they were purported to be made all his surroundings seem diaphanous and insecure. Even now the design engrossed him more than a defense against it, and he tried to recreate the steps by which Margaret had arrived at this act of recklessness or despair.

She had served as script girl in various studios and for various directors for ten years—earning first twenty, now a hundred dollars a week. She was lovely looking and she was intelligent—at any moment in those years she might have asked for a screen test, but some quality of initiative or ambition had been lacking. Not a few times had her opinion made or broken incipient careers—still she waited at directors' elbows, increasingly aware that the years were slipping away.

That she had picked George as a victim amazed him most of all. Once, during the year before his marriage, there had been a momentary warmth; he had taken her to a Mayfair Ball, and he remembered that he had kissed her going home that night in the car. The flirtation trailed along hesitatingly for a week—before it could develop into anything serious he had gone east and met Kay.

Young Donovan had shown him a carbon of the letters he had signed. They were written on the typewriter that he kept in his bungalow at the studio, and they were carefully and convincingly worded. They purported to be love-letters asserting that he was Margaret Donovan's lover, that he wanted to marry her and that for that reason he was about to arrange a divorce. It was incredible. Someone must have seen him sign them that morning—someone must have heard her say: "Your initials are like Mr. Harris's."

George was tired. He was training for a screen football game to be played next week, with the Southern California varsity as extras, and he was used to regular hours. In the middle of a confused and despairing sequence of thought about Margaret Donovan and Kay, he suddenly yawned. Mechanically he went upstairs, undressed and got into bed.

Just before dawn Kay came to him in the garden. There was a river that flowed past it now, and boats faintly lit with green and yellow lights moved slowly, remotely by. A gentle starlight fell like rain upon the dark sleeping face of the world—upon the black mysterious bosoms of the trees, the tranquil gleaming water and the farther shore.

The grass was damp and Kay came to him on hurried feet—her thin slippers were drenched with dew. She stood upon his shoes, nestling close to him, and held up her face as one shows a book open at a page.

"Think how you love me," she whispered. "I don't ask you to love me always like this, but I ask you to remember."

"You'll always be like this to me."

"Oh no, but promise me you'll remember." Her tears were falling. "I'll be different, but somewhere lost inside of me there'll always be the person I am tonight."

The scene dissolved slowly and George struggled into consciousness. He sat up in bed—it was morning. In the yard outside he heard the nurse instructing his son in the niceties of behavior for two-month-old babies. From the yard next door a small boy shouted mysteriously: "Who let that barrier through on me?"

Still in his pajamas George went to the phone and called his lawyer. Then he rang for his man and, while he was being shaved, a certain order evolved from the chaos of the night before: first, he must deal with Margaret Donovan; second, he must keep the matter from Kay, who in her present state might believe anything; and, third, he must fix things up with Kay. The last seemed the most important of all.

As he finished dressing he heard the phone ring downstairs and with an instinct of danger picked up the receiver.

"Hello. Oh, yes." Looking up he saw that both his doors were closed. "Good morning, Helen. . . . It's all right, Dolores. I'm taking it up here." He waited till he heard the receiver click downstairs. "How are you this morning, Helen?"

"George, I called up about last night. I can't tell you how sorry I am."

"Sorry? Why are you sorry?"

"For treating you like that. I don't know what was in me, George. I didn't sleep all night thinking how terrible I'd been."

A new disorder established itself in George's already littered mind.

"Don't be silly," he said. To his despair he heard his own voice run on: "For a minute I didn't understand, Helen. Then I thought it was better so."

"Oh, George," came her voice after a moment, very low.

Another silence. He began to put in a cuff-button.

"I had to call up," she said, after a moment. "I couldn't leave things like that."

The cuff-button dropped to the floor; he stooped to pick it up and then said "Helen!" urgently into the mouthpiece to cover the fact that he had momentarily been away.

"What George?"

At this moment the hall door opened and Kay, radiating a faint distaste, came into the room. She hesitated.

"Are you busy?"

"It's all right." He stared into the mouthpiece for a moment. "Well, good-bye," he muttered abruptly and hung up the receiver. He turned to Kay. "Good morning."

"I didn't mean to disturb you," she said distantly.

"You didn't disturb me." He hesitated. "That was Helen Avery."

"It doesn't concern me who it was. I came to ask you if we're going to the Cocoanut Grove tonight."

"Sit down, Kay?"

"I don't want to talk."

"Sit down a minute," he said impatiently.

She sat down.

"How long are you going to keep this up?" he demanded.

"I'm not keeping up anything. We're simply through, George, and you know it as well as I do."

"That's absurd," he said. "Why, a week ago—"

"It doesn't matter. We've been getting nearer to this for months, and now it's over."

"You mean you don't love me?" He was not particularly alarmed. They had been through scenes like this before.

"I don't know. I suppose I'll always love you in a way." Suddenly she began to sob, "Oh, it's all so sad. He's cared for me so long."

George stared at her. Face to face with what was apparently a real emotion he had no words of any kind. She was not angry, not threatening or pretending, not thinking about him at all, but concerned entirely with her emotions toward another man.

"What is it?" he cried. "Are you trying to tell me you're in love with this man?"

"I don't know," she said helplessly.

He took a step toward her—then went to the bed and lay down on it, staring in misery at the ceiling. After awhile a maid knocked to say that Mr. Busch and Mr. Castle, George's lawyer, were below. The fact carried no meaning to him. Kay went into her room, and he got up and followed her.

"Let's send word we're out," he said. "We can go away somewhere and talk this over."

"I don't want to go away."

She was already away, growing more mysterious and remote with every minute. The things on her dressing table were the property of a stranger.

He began to speak in a dry, hurried voice.

"If you're still thinking about Helen Avery—it's nonsense—I've never given a damn for anybody but you."

They went downstairs and into the living room. It was nearly noon—another bright emotionless California day. George saw that Arthur Busch's ugly face in the sunshine was wan and white; he took a step toward George and then stopped as if he were waiting for something, a challenge, a reproach, a blow.

In a flash the scene that would presently take place ran itself off in George's mind. He saw himself moving through the scene, saw his part, an infinite choice of parts, but in every one of them Kay would be against him and with Arthur Busch. And suddenly he rejected them all.

"I hope you'll excuse me," he said quickly to Mr. Castle. "I called you up because a script girl named Margaret Donovan wants fifty thousand dollars for some letters she claims I wrote her. Of course the whole thing is—" He broke off. It didn't matter. "I'll come to see you tomorrow." He walked up to Kay and Arthur, so that only they could hear.

"I don't know about you two—what you want to do. But leave me out of it; you haven't any right to inflict any of it on me, for after all it's not my fault. I'm not going to be mixed up in your emotions."

He turned and went out. His car was before the door and he said "Go to Santa Monica" because it was the first name that popped into his head. The car drove off into the everlasting hazeless sunlight.

He rode for three hours, past Santa Monica and then along toward Long Beach by another road. As if it were something he saw out of the corner of his eye and with but a fragment of his attention, he imagined Kay and Arthur Busch progressing through the afternoon. Kay would cry a great deal and the situation would seem harsh and unexpected to them at first—but the tender closing of the day would draw them together; they would turn inevitably toward each other, and he would slip more and more into the position of the enemy outside.

Kay had wanted him to get down in the dirt and dust of a scene—and scramble for her. Not him—he hated scenes. Once he stooped to compete with Arthur Busch in pulling at Kay's heart, he would never be the same to himself. He would always be a little like Arthur Busch—they would always have that in common like a shameful secret. There was little of the theatre about George—the millions before whose eyes the moods and changes of his face had flickered during ten years had not been deceived about that. From the moment when as a boy of twenty, his handsome eyes had gazed off into the imaginary distance of a Griffith Western, his audience had been really watching the progress of a straightforward, slow-thinking romantic man through an accidentally glamorous life.

His fault was that he had felt safe too soon. He realized suddenly that the Fairbankses in sitting side by side at table were not keeping up a pose. They were giving hostages to fate. This was perhaps the most bizarre community in the rich, wild, bored empire, and for a marriage to succeed here you must expect nothing—or you must be always together. For a moment his glance had wavered from Kay, and he stumbled blindly into disaster.

As he was thinking this and wondering where he would go and what he should do, he passed an apartment house that jolted his memory. It was on the outskirts of town, a pink horror built to represent something, somewhere, so cheaply and sketchily that whatever it copied the architect must have long since forgotten. And suddenly George remembered that he had once called for Margaret Donovan here the night of a Mayfair dance.

"Stop at this apartment!" he called through the speaking tube.

He went in. The negro elevator boy stared open-mouthed at him as they rose in the cage. Margaret Donovan herself opened the door.

When she saw him she shrank away with a little cry. As he entered and closed the door she retreated before him into the front room. George followed.

It was twilight outside and the apartment was dusky and sad. The last light fell softly on the standardized furniture and the great gallery of signed photographs of moving picture people that covered one wall. Her face was white, and as she stared at him she began nervously wringing her hands.

"What's this nonsense, Margaret?" George said, trying to keep any reproach out of his voice. "Do you need money that bad?"

She shook her head vaguely. Her eyes were still fixed on him with a sort of terror; George looked at the floor.

"I suppose this was your brother's idea—at least I can't believe you'd be so stupid." He looked up, trying to preserve the brusque masterly attitude of one talking to a naughty child, but at the sight of her face every emotion except pity left him. "I'm a little tired. Do you mind if I sit down?"

"No."

"I'm a little confused today," said George after a minute. "People seem to have it in for me today."

"Why, I thought —" Her voice became ironic in mid-sentence, "I thought everybody loved you, George."

"They don't."

"Only me?"

"Yes," he said abstractedly.

"I wish it had been only me. But then, of course, you wouldn't have been you."

Suddenly he realized that she meant what she was saying.

"That's just nonsense."

"At least you're here," Margaret went on. "I suppose I ought to be glad of that. And I am. I most decidedly am. I've often thought of you sitting in that chair, just at this time when it was almost dark. I used to make up little one-act plays about what would happen then. Would you like to hear one of them? I'll have to begin by coming over and sitting on the floor at your feet."

Annoyed and yet spellbound George kept trying desperately to seize upon a word or mood that would turn the subject.

"I've seen you sitting there so often that you don't look a bit more real than your ghost. Except that your hat has squashed your beautiful hair down on one side and you've got dark circles, or dirt, under your eyes. You look white, too, George. Probably you were on a party last night."

"I was. And I found your brother waiting for me when I got home."

"He's a good waiter, George. He's just out of San Quentin prison where he's been waiting the last six years."

"Then it was his idea?"

"We cooked it up together. I was going to China on my share."

"Why was I the victim?"

"That seemed to make it realer. Once I thought you were going to fall in love with me five years ago." The bravado suddenly melted out of her voice and it was still light enough to see that her mouth was quivering.

"I've loved you for years," she said. "Since the first day you came west and walked into the old Realart Studio. You were so brave about people, George. Whoever it was, you walked right up to them and tore something aside as if it was in your way and began to know them. I tried to make love to you, just like the rest, but it was difficult. You drew people right up close to you and held them there, not able to move either way."

"This is all entirely imaginary," said George, frowning uncomfortably. "And I can't control—"

"No, I know. You can't control charm. It's simply got to be used. You've got to keep your hand in if you have it, and go through life attaching people to you that you don't want. I don't blame you. If you only hadn't kissed me the night of the Mayfair dance. I suppose it was the champagne."

George felt as if a band which had been playing for a long time in the distance had suddenly moved up and taken a station beneath his window. He had always been conscious that things like this were going on around him—now that he thought of it he had always been conscious that Margaret loved him, but the faint music of these emotions in his ear had seemed to bear no relation to actual life. They were phantoms that he had conjured up out of nothing— he had never imagined their incarnations. At his wish they should die inconsequently away.

"You can't imagine what it's been like," Margaret continued, after a minute. "Things you've just said and forgotten I've put myself asleep night after night remembering—trying to squeeze something more out of them. After that night you took me to the Mayfair other men didn't exist for me anymore. And there were others, you know—lots of them. But I'd see you walking along somewhere about the lot, looking at the ground and smiling a little, as if something very amusing had just happened to you, the way you do. And I'd pass you and you'd look up and really smile: 'Hello, darling!' 'Hello, darling' and my heart would turn over. That would happen four times a day."

George stood up and she too jumped up quickly.

"Oh, I've bored you," she cried softly. "I might have known I'd bore you. You want to go home. Let's see—is there anything else— oh, yes, you might as well have those letters."

Taking them out of a desk, she took them to a window and identified them by a rift of lamp light.

"They're really beautiful letters. They'd do you credit. I suppose it was pretty stupid, as you say, but it ought to teach you a lesson about—about signing things, or something."

She tore the letters small and threw them in the wastebasket.

"Now go on," she said.

"Why must I go now?"

For the third time in twenty-four hours, sad and uncontrollable tears confronted him.

"Please go," she cried angrily. "Or stay if you like. I'm yours for the asking. You know it. You can have any woman you want in the world by just raising your hand. Would I amuse you?"

"Margaret—"

"Oh, go on then." She sat down and turned her face away. "After all you'll begin to look silly in a minute. You wouldn't like that, would you? So get out."

George stood there helpless, trying to put himself in her place and say something that wouldn't be priggish, but nothing came. He tried to force down his personal distress, his discomfort, his vague feeling of scorn—ignorant of the fact that she was watching him and understanding it all and loving the struggle in his face. Suddenly his own nerves gave way under the strain of the past twenty-four hours, and he felt his eyes grow dim and his throat tighten. He shook his head helplessly. Then he turned away—still not knowing that she was watching him and loving him until she thought her heart would burst with it—and went out to the door.

IV

The car stopped before his house, dark save for small lights in the nursery and the lower hall. He heard the telephone ringing, but when he answered it inside there was no one on the line. For a few minutes he wandered about in the darkness, moving from chair to chair and going to the window to stare out into the apposite emptiness of the night.

It was strange to be alone, to feel alone. In his overwrought condition the fact was not unpleasant. As the trouble of last night had made Helen Avery infinitely remote, so his talk with Margaret had acted as a katharsis to his own personal misery. It would swing back upon him presently he knew, but for a moment his mind was too tired to remember, to imagine or to care.

Half an hour passed. He saw Dolores issue from the kitchen, take the paper from the front steps and carry it back to the kitchen for a preliminary inspection. With a vague idea of packing his grip he went upstairs. He opened the door of Kay's room—and found her sitting up in bed in her nightgown.

For a moment he didn't speak but moved around in the bathroom between. Then he went into her room and switched on the lights.

"What's the matter?" he asked casually. "Aren't you feeling well?"

"I've been trying to get some sleep," she said. "George, do you think that girl's gone crazy?"

"What girl?"

"Margaret Donovan. I've never heard of anything so terrible in my life."

For a moment he thought that there had been some new development.

"Fifty thousand dollars!" she cried indignantly. "Why I wouldn't give it to her even if it was true. She ought to be sent to jail."

"Oh, it's not so terrible as that," he said. "She has a brother who's a pretty bad egg and it was his idea."

Kay sat forward in the bed.

"She's capable of anything," Kay said solemnly. "And you're just a fool if you don't see it. I've never liked her. She has dirty hair."

"Well, what of it?" he demanded impatiently, and added: "Where's Arthur Busch?"

"He went home right after lunch. Or rather I sent him home."

"You decided you were not in love with him?"

She looked up almost in surprise.

"In love with him? Oh, you mean this morning. I was just mad at you, you ought to have known that. I was a little sorry for him last night, but I guess it was the highballs."

"Well, what did you mean when you—" He broke off. Wherever he turned he found a muddle, and he resolutely determined not to think.

"My heavens!" exclaimed Kay. "Fifty thousand dollars."

"Oh, drop it. She tore up the letters—she wrote them herself—and everything's all right."

"George."

"Yes."

"Of course Schroeder will fire her right away."

"Of course he won't. He won't know anything about it."

"You mean to say you're not going to let her go? After this?"

He jumped up.

"My God!" he cried. "Do you suppose she thought that?"

"Thought what?"

"That I'd have them let her go?"

"You certainly ought to."

He looked hastily through the phone book for her name.

"Oxford 3313," he called. After an unusually long time the switchboard operator answered.

"Bourbon Apartments."

"Miss Margaret Donovan, please."

"Why—" The operator's voice broke off. "If you'll just wait a minute, please."

He held the line—the minute passed, then another. Then the operator's voice:

"I couldn't talk to you then. Miss Donovan has had an accident. She's shot herself."

"My God!"

"When you called they were taking her through the lobby to St. Catherine's hospital."

"Is she—is it serious?" George demanded frantically.

"They thought so at first, but now they think she'll be all right. They're going to probe for the bullet."

"Thank you."

He got up and turned to Kay.

"She's tried to kill herself," he said, in a strained voice. "I'll have to go around to the hospital. I was pretty clumsy this afternoon and I think I'm partly responsible for this."

"George," said Kay suddenly.

"What?"

"Don't you think it's sort of unwise to get mixed up in this. People might say—"

"I don't give a damn what they say," he answered roughly.

He went to his room and automatically began to prepare for going out. Catching sight of his face in the mirror he closed his eyes with a sudden exclamation of distaste, and abandoned the intention of brushing his hair.

"George," Kay called from the next room, "I love you."

"I love you too."

"Jules Rennard called up. Something about barracuda fishing. Don't you think it would be fun to get up a party? Men and girls both."

"Somehow the idea doesn't appeal to me. The whole idea of barracuda fishing—"

The phone rang below and he started. Dolores was answering it. It was a lady who had already called twice today.

"Is Mr. Hannaford in?"

"No," said Dolores promptly. She stuck out her tongue and hung up the phone just as George Hannaford came downstairs. She helped him into his coat, standing as close as she could to him, opened the door and followed a little way out on the porch.

"Meester Hannaford," she said suddenly. "That Miss Avery she call up five six times today. I tell her you out and say nothing to Missus."

"What?" He stared at her, wondering how much she knew about his affairs.

"She call up just now and I say you out."

"All right," he said absently.

"Meester Hannaford."

"Yes, Dolores."

"I deedn't hurt myself thees morning when I fell off the porch."

"That's fine. Good-night, Dolores."

"Good-night, Meester Hannaford."

George smiled at her, faintly, fleetingly, tearing a veil from between them, unconsciously promising her a possible admission to the thousand delights and wonders that only he knew and could command. Then he went to his waiting car and Dolores, sitting down on the stoop, rubbed her hands together in a gesture that might have expressed either ecstasy or strangulation, and watched the rising of the thin, pale California moon.

RECORD OF VARIANTS

The lists that follow record the emendations adopted from the surviving textual witnesses. Independent editorial emendations are also recorded. A headnote precedes the list of emendations for each story; this note describes the surviving evidence and explains the editorial strategy for the story. The sources of the readings, accepted and rejected, are given in the headnotes; sigla are employed sparingly. The following symbols are used:

~	the same word
¶	new paragraph
∧	space or the absence of punctuation or paragraphing
FSF	Fitzgerald
FSF/MSS	*F. Scott Fitzgerald Manuscripts* (New York: Garland, 1991)
MS/MSS	authorial manuscript/s
TS/TSS	typescript/s
ser	serial text
stet	refusal to emend, followed by explanation
ASYM	*All the Sad Young Men* (New York: Scribners, 1925)

"The Rich Boy"

For an account of the compositional history of "The Rich Boy" and a discussion of cruxes in its text, see the introduction, pp. xviii–xxiii. A ribbon TS from the Ober files, bearing Fitzgerald's final revisions for the serial text, survives at Princeton. This TS has been facsimiled in FSF/MSS, VI, 1: 173–233.

One or more additional TSS, deriving from the carbon of the ribbon TS in the Ober files, were revised by FSF in order to arrive at a version of the story for ASYM. None of these later TSS is known to be extant. The Cambridge text follows the ASYM text in substantives. The TS at Princeton has been useful as a source for accidentals. Substantive and accidental readings from the Princeton TS that have been adopted for the Cambridge text are given below. The rejected readings are from ASYM.

Substantive emendations

9.18	bridesmaids] bridesmaid		23.37	that] they
23.33	out] on			

Accidental emendations

5.1	individual∧] ~,	17.2	thinking∧] ~,
5.6	fellow∧"] ~,"	17.2	moment∧] ~,
5.21	hard∧] ~,	17.9	Thayer∧] ~,
6.35	freely∧]~,	18.11	New York"] ~ ~∧
7.4	thick-set∧]~,	19.14	dark-haired∧] ~,
7.10	Nevertheless∧]~,	19.15	high∧] ~,
7.34	Sorry, Dear∧"] sorry, dear,"	19.15	color∧] ~,
8.2	or∧] ~,	19.18	pockets,] ~∧
8.2	frequently∧] ~,	20.12	mothers∧] ~,
8.22	again—solemn] ~, ~	20.28	Moreover∧] ~,
8.27	on∧] ~,	20.32	her∧] ~,
8.30	enough∧] ~,	21.4	vacation∧] ~,
8.31	that,] ~∧	21.12	there∧] ~,
8.32	side,] ~∧	21.36	time∧] ~,
8.32	insincere∧] ~,	22.5	compromises∧] ~,
8.32	and,] ~∧	23.1	stop∧] ~,
8.32	hers,] ~∧	23.1	and,] ~∧
8.34	blossomed∧] ~,	23.2	him,] ~∧
9.1	women∧]~,	23.8	vest. ¶ "This] ~. ∧~
9.2	marry∧]~,	23.26	it∧] ~,
9.10	April∧]~,	23.36	still∧] ~,
9.30	severe∧]~,	24.9	excitement∧] ~,
10.22	bedroom∧] ~,	25.6	broke∧] ~,
10.33	English∧] ~,	25.20	funny∧] ~,
11.7	succeeded∧] ~,	25.30	and∧] ~,
11.12	French∧] ~,	25.30	increased∧] ~,
11.26	spoiled∧] ~,	25.32	year∧] ~,
11.29	minutes∧] ~,	26.18	marriages∧] ~,
13.6	her∧] ~,	27.3	Nevertheless∧] ~,
13.11	strong∧] ~,	27.5	stock exchange] Stock
13.20	abroad∧] ~,		Exchange
13.34	letters∧] ~,	27.25	judge,] ~∧
14.13	day∧] ~,	28.4	strong∧] ~,
14.15	me∧] ~,	28.14	Yes∧] ~,
15.1	house∧] ~,	29.13	Hunter∧] ~,
15.8	now∧] ~,	30.19	restaurant∧] ~,
15.12	her∧] ~,	30.22	up∧] ~,
15.21	sand∧] ~,	30.25	collapsed∧] ~,
15.22	Chance∧] ~,	31.9	four:] ~;
15.25	wheeled∧] ~,	32.3	house∧] ~,
15.31	kind∧] ~,	33.34	Homeric] *Homeric*
15.32	five∧] ~,	34.11	sentiment∧] ~,
16.29	Oh,] oh,	34.26	moment∧] ~,
16.31	hands∧] ~,	35.7	drink∧] ~,
16.31	Anson∧] ~,	35.15	"Oh∧] ~,
16.32	tremble∧] ~,	36.5	Save] save

36.37	reckonings,] ~∧		38.20	dark∧] ~,
36.37	leisure,] ~∧		40.8	world,] ~;
37.21	hands∧] ~,		41.6	partners∧] ~,
37.37	chairs∧] ~,		41.12	martinis] Martinis
38.19	beach club] Beach Club		41.23	me∧] ~,

Editorial emendations

8.14	Soto] Sota			runs parallel to Vanderbilt,
14.4	long, sustained] ~-~			one block west. Fitzgerald,
21.25	Vanderbilt] Madison			writing in Capri and Paris,
	(The Yale Club is at 50			was relying on memory.)
	Vanderbilt Avenue; since its	23.19		imminent] eminent
	opening in 1915, it has	26.1		in] of
	never had an entrance on	34.9		much more] much, more
	Madison Avenue, which			

"Winter Dreams"

For an account of FSF's revision of the serial text of "Winter Dreams" for its appearance in ASYM, see the introduction, pp. xxiii–xxv. No prepublication form of this story appears to survive. The differences between the serial and ASYM texts are so extensive as to constitute two separate versions. No substantive emendations have been adopted from the serial text. Accidental emendations, listed in the first table, derive from the serial text. Editorial emendations appear in the second table. Rejected readings in both tables are from ASYM unless otherwise indicated.

Accidental emendations

43.24	himself ∧] ~,		50.12	Luxembourg] Luxemburg
44.4	Club∧] ~,		50.26	low∧] ~,
44.18	state] State		53.29	way∧] ~,
44.21	master∧] ~,		54.34	supper∧] ~,
44.25	Grateful!—"] ~!∧"		56.12	visitor∧] ~,
44.31	smiled∧] ~,		56.13	station∧] ~,
45.6	smiled∧] ~,		56.14	twenty-four∧] ~,
45.36	golf∧] ~,		57.11	him∧] ~,
46.7	withdrew∧] ~,		57.11	him∧] ~,
46.21	caddy∧] ~,		57.23	late∧] ~,
46.34	caddy∧] ~,		58.1	October∧] ~,
46.36	shock∧] ~,		58.2	June∧] ~,
47.7	state] State		58.8	Florida∧] ~,
48.13	links∧] ~,		58.8	Springs∧] ~,
49.20	quick∧] ~,		58.9	engaged∧] ~,
50.2	dry∧] ~,		60.1	before∧] ~,

61.21	Jones] Joneses	65.20	care∧] ~,
62.21	her∧] ~,	65.22	down∧] ~,

Editorial emendations

45.3	irrelevant] irrevelant	60.26	camaraderie] comraderie
48.13	these] this		ASYM, comradie ser
50.23	attuned] attune	61.21	Jones] Joneses ASYM,
50.30	Dexter,] ~∧		Jones' ser
50.31	arms,] ~∧	62.26	engagement,] ~
		63.25	meaninglessly.] ~,

"The Baby Party"

No prepublication form of "The Baby Party" appears to survive. FSF revised the story between the serial and ASYM; the substantive variants in the later version have been accepted for the Cambridge text and appear in the first table below. In that table, the first reading is from ASYM (and the Cambridge text); the second is from the serial. This first table is followed by tables of accidental and editorial emendations. The accidental readings are taken from the serial text; rejected readings in both tables are from ASYM.

ASYM] *serial variants*

66.4	mad non sequiturs] grave inanities	67.21	sugary] blanket of
		67.22	lawns] town
66.7	vivid] sunny	67.29	he . . . walk] instead of turning in at the walk he continued on past it
66.8	physically] very		
66.9	rugged] rather rugged		
66.15	weary] dreary	68.6	they appeared] she arrived
66.18	fragrant, downy scalp] delicate yellow hair		
		68.8	jealous] anxious
66.18	morning] sea-shell	68.24	considered her] thought Mrs. Markey was
66.23	permanently hiding] tearing		
		68.25	Joe] Bill
66.25	was . . . himself] felt ashamed about it	68.31	further] any further
		68.34	repulsive] annoying
66.28	her mother] John's wife	69.8	tried] essayed
67.2	business] fact	70.1	"Bear?"] "Ted'-bear?"
67.2	"I . . . *pantry!*"] "Baby going to a party!"	70.19	Joe] Charley
		73.25	fumbling] jumbling
67.7	abruptly] abruptly there	73.32	than half a] than a
67.11	peach of a] beautiful	74.34	business, and the] ~. The
67.11	humorously] sardonically	76.1	crazy] mad
67.14	subtle] immeasurable	76.23	be] have been

77.7	His face look] Look	77.18	just remember] bear in
77.12	set] quiet		mind
		77.27	elbow] arm

Accidental emendations

66.30	half∧] ~,	70.33	maneuver] manuvre
67.12	mothers∧]~,	71.7	remark∧] ~,
67.18	man∧] ~,	71.13	baby's∧] ~,
67.26	age∧] ~,	71.16	anger∧] ~,
67.30	door.] ~,	72.31	Edith∧] ~,
68.20	dance∧] ~,	73.27	hot∧] ~,
68.22	Markey∧] ~,	73.31	hot∧] ~,
69.5	table∧] ~,	73.34	common∧] ~,
69.17	candles∧] ~,	73.35	And∧] ~,
69.19	ate∧] ~,	73.35	more∧] ~,
69.21	good∧] ~,	75.17	No∧] ~,
69.25	six∧] ~,	77.1	cool∧] ~,
69.27	was∧] ~,	77.14	and∧] ~,
70.6	arms.] ~:	77.25	little∧] ~,
70.7	eyes∧] ~,	77.26	soundly∧] ~,

Editorial emendation

66.23	hiding the] hiding up the

"Absolution"

No prepublication form of "Absolution" appears to be extant. The substantive variants between the serial and ASYM texts indicate a relatively light revision by FSF. These variants are recorded in the first table below. The ASYM readings (which appear first in each entry of this table) have been accepted for the Cambridge text; the rejected readings (which appear to the right of the bracket) are from the serial version. Accidental and editorial emendations are given in the second and third tables. The source for the accidental emendations is the serial text; rejected readings in both the second and third tables are from ASYM.

ASYM] *serial variants*

78.14	before it reached] somewhere between its counter and	84.16	gross] gross and utterly deficient in curiosity
78.30	enormous,] enormous and	84.16	was . . . unable] was unable
		84.20	Roman] Holy Roman
		85.27	pans] panes

85.30	toys] glittering toys	90.11	he] that he
86.36	outlet] typical	90.15	flower-petals] flowers
87.3	you better kneel] kneel	92.11	as big] a big
87.5	in] after	92.25	smell] hard smell
89.19	larger] exceptional	93.10	heart-broken words] dim
90.10	upon the floor,] on the		and terrible words
	floor.	93.21	echolalia] shadowy
90.10	and he knew that it] It		movements

Accidental emendations

78.26	sunshine∧] ~,	85.5	poultry∧] ~,
79.21	agony∧] ~,	85.19	barefooted∧] ~,
79.25	tears∧] ~,	87.13	head∧] ~,
79.33	went∧] ~,	87.18	held∧] ~,
80.2	Ago∧"] ~."	88.11	church∧] ~,
80.10	hear∧ and] ~, ~	88.19	crossed∧] ~,
80.24	form∧] ~,	88.34	son∧] ~,
80.35	late∧] ~,	89.1	heart∧] ~,
81.8	mumble∧] ~,	89.17	pews∧] ~,
81.11	creak∧] ~,	91.5	voice—] ~:
81.25	Skidoo∧'] ~,'	91.18	navy] Navy
81.26	fit∧]~,	91.20	air.] ~,
82.3	offenses∧] ~,	92.12	somewhere∧] ~,
83.32	cooled∧] ~,	93.13	knees∧] ~,
83.3	morning∧] ~,	93.17	clothes∧] ~,
84.18	unrestful∧] ~,		

Editorial emendations

78.21	thoughts] thought	89.15	*meum:*] ~;
81.30	interrogator] interrogation	89.16	*ánima*] *anima*
84.2	Hamline] Hamlin	90.13	*Die*] *Dei*
85.12	shoulders] shoulder		(See the explanatory note
89.15	*Dómini*] *Domini*		for this reading.)
89.15	*intres*] *interes*	92.14	of∧] of"

"Rags Martin-Jones and the Pr-nce of W-les"

The holograph of this story is extant in the Fitzgerald Papers at Princeton. It has been facsimiled in FSF/MSS, VI, 1: 77–130. This holograph has been useful in resolving questions of pointing and word division, but its text is so different from the ASYM text that they constitute two separate versions. Substantive, accidental, and editorial emendations are given below. The substantive and accidental variants adopted for the Cambridge text are from the holograph; rejected readings in all three tables are from ASYM.

Substantive emendations

102.31	after while] after a while	109.7	bunch over there] bunch
103.12	with a sharp] with sharp		across over there
106.6	he laid] he had laid		

Accidental emendations

94.11	continent∧] ~,	101.13	close!] ~.
94.19	middle-westerners]	101.14	House] house
	Middle-Westerners	101.17	go∧] ~,
94.21	emptied∧] ~,	101.23	Ouch] ouch
95.5	side—] ~.	101.35	cold∧] ~,
95.9	flower∧] ~,	102.32	drums∧] ~,
95.15	arm∧] ~,	103.3	minor∧] ~,
95.18	monocle∧] ~,	103.18	sigh∧] ~,
95.28	her∧ for] ~,~	103.20	entrance∧] ~,
95.37	out∧] ~,	103.22	palms∧] ~,
96.2	flustered∧] ~,	104.1	somewhere∧] ~,
96.17	elbow∧] ~,	104.2	her∧] ~,
96.29	risen∧] ~,	104.21	floor∧] ~,
96.32	here∧] ~,	105.6	champagne∧] ~,
97.2	dock∧] ~,	105.16	close∧] ~,
97.7	Rags—!] ~∧!	105.18	on∧] ~,
97.16	up∧] ~,	105.18	cloth∧] ~,
97.17	easily∧] ~,	106.28	answering∧] ~,
97.24	crowd∧] ~,	107.1	number∧] ~,
97.27	maids∧] ~,	107.17	hesitated∧] ~,
97.28	Ritz∧] ~,	109.16	somewhere∧] ~,
97.31	manicure∧] ~,	109.30	succession∧] ~,
98.1	one∧] ~,	110.25	lapels∧] ~,
98.5	M'selle.] m'selle.	111.9	*you*'re] *you're*
98.14	irrelevantly,] ~:	111.21	Berlin∧] ~,
98.32	boat∧] ~,	111.28	Then∧] ~,
99.22	stock∧] ~,	111.28	like∧] ~,
100.14	low∧] ~,	112.13	M'selle] m'selle

Editorial emendations

95.30	1912] 1913	102.22	care,] ~;
	(The *Titanic* sank on the	103.32	and, . . . match,] ~∧ . . .
	night of 14–15 April 1912.)		~∧
99.2	elusive] illusive	111.23	Duchy] Dutchy
100.8	mousseux] mousseaux		

"The Adjuster"

The TS of an early text of "The Adjuster" is extant in the Fitzgerald Papers at Princeton; it bears heavy revisions in FSF's hand. This TS differs significantly from the serial text, suggesting that one or more revised TSS intervened between the two. The serial text, in turn, varies so heavily from the ASYM text that they constitute two separate versions. The Cambridge text follows the substantives of ASYM; no editorial emendations have been made. Accidental emendations below are taken from the Princeton TS; rejected readings are from the ASYM version.

Accidental emendations

113.3	cup∧] ~,		119.13	bedroom∧] ~,
113.5	pale∧] ~,		119.17	room∧] ~,
113.16	old∧] ~,		119.24	York∧] ~,
113.20	tall∧] ~,		119.25	nervously∧] ~,
113.21	radiant∧] ~,		119.32	mine∧] ~,
114.2	caps∧] ~,		119.34	laugh∧] ~,
114.8	afternoon∧] ~,		119.35	see∧ exactly∧] ~, ~,
114.11	confession∧] ~,		120.2	nodded∧] ~,
114.24	First∧] ~,		120.22	that∧ . . . happened∧]
114.25	housekeeper∧] ~,			~, . . . ~,
114.36	result∧] ~,		120.26	then∧ . . . came∧] ~, . . . ~,
114.37	incompetent∧] ~,		120.31	objection∧ . . . room∧]
115.6	fact∧] ~,			~, . . . ~,
115.9	home∧] ~,		121.19	excitement,] ~;
115.19	sport∧] ~,		122.2	life∧] ~,
115.22	wife∧] ~,		122.4	corridor∧] ~,
116.13	mind∧] ~,		122.7	interruption∧] ~,
116.35	brac∧] ~,		122.23	beauty∧] ~,
117.4	trip∧] ~,		122.25	attitude∧] ~,
117.7	returned∧] ~,		124.17	nothing.] ~;
117.15	hall∧] ~,		124.33	baby∧] ~,
117.27	abstraction∧ . . . words∧]		125.32	sharply∧] ~,
	~, . . . ~,		126.3	Hemple. There's] Hemple;
117.35	sound∧] ~,			there's
118.3	formality∧] ~,		126.10	medicine∧] ~,
118.7	shy∧] ~,		126.23	left∧ . . . anyone∧] ~, . . .
118.16	tonight∧] ~,			~,
118.21	Nevertheless∧] ~,		126.25	Oh∧] ~,
118.25	wept∧] ~,		127.1	into it∧] ~ ~,
118.29	china∧] ~,		127.8	agreement∧] ~,
118.36	Well∧] ~,		127.11	her. "Otherwise] her;
119.1	fountain∧] ~,			"otherwise
119.5	Mamma's] mama's		127.29	kitchen∧] ~,
119.10	sometimes∧] ~,		128.9	home∧] ~,

128.18	Simultaneously, . . . rang∧]	131.14	But∧] ∼,
	∼∧ . . . ∼;	131.19	behind.] ∼,
130.17	again,] ∼;	131.35	him∧] ∼,
130.26	bed∧] ∼,	132.5	Charles,] ∼;
130.37	spoke.] ∼:	132.5	better∧] ∼,
131.4	hesitated.] ∼—	132.11	from her∧] ∼ ∼,
131.7	Oh∧] ∼,	132.15	before∧] ∼,

"Hot and Cold Blood"

Fitzgerald's grandchildren possess a carbon TS of the serial setting copy. Variant patterns between this carbon and the serial text suggest that FSF introduced a final round of light revision on the ribbon copy or in proof. He then revised "Hot and Cold Blood" heavily for its appearance in ASYM, cutting six paragraphs from the beginning of the story and four from the end, and polishing the style throughout. These cuts and revisions, listed in the first table below, are accepted for the Cambridge text. The first reading in each entry below is from ASYM (and the Cambridge text); the second reading is from the serial version.

ASYM] *serial variants*

135.1   One . . . average success.] ¶ Take the expression "cold-blooded" for instance— little shining pieces of ice circulating in the arteries, passing the heart every half hour and giving it a chill, flying through the brain like an express train through a prairie village and making warm decisions into cool ones. An unpleasant thought! ¶ But there was nothing cold-blooded about young Coatesworth. He liked people—and that's much rarer than it sounds. Some are impelled to seek company by an inexhaustible curiosity, some are driven to it by sheer boredom with themselves and others congregate for no more reason than that the pithecanthropus erectus hunted in groups a hundred thousand years ago. But young Coatesworth liked people. He had an almost blind eye for their imperfections, he knew how to keep his mouth shut and his blood was warm. He is what is often known among men as a "hell of a nice fellow." This was no casual compliment. As niceness goes in this somewhat unpleasant world, he *was*. ¶ So in college he had been enormously popular— vice-president of his class and manager of some athletic team. Afterwards, in the army, his company were wildly sentimental about him, and when the

war was over had a way of
writing him from Kokomo,
Indiana or Muscatine,
Iowa, about their successes
and their failures and the
births of their male
children. Coatesworth
always answered their
letters even when he was
very busy—because he
himself was somewhat
sentimental. Besides, he was
nice. ¶ When he was
twenty-seven he fell in love
with Jaqueline James, who
likewise lived in
Indianapolis, and married
her. She married him, of
course, because he was such
a nice fellow. Why he
married her is a little harder
to guess, because of all the
young girls in the city she
seemed the most completely
selfish and the most
exquisitely spoiled. People
went around talking about
the attraction of opposites
for each other—and meant
nothing complimentary to
Jaqueline James. ¶ After the
Coatesworths had been
married a year they came to
themselves and began to
look each other over with
discerning eyes. There was
a great deal of affection
between them and neither
found anything particularly
alarming in the other, for a
selfish person and an
unselfish person usually get
on together very well
indeed. He liked her for
being cool and clean and
jaunty, for wearing her
hardiness like a suit of

armor against the world
and being tender and warm
for him only. She was like a
silver cup. She was a plant
from the high places
sheathed with cool dew. ¶
She was like that when she
came one day into his office
where he carried on a
wholesale grocery
brokerage with more than
average success. Miss
Clancy, the stenographer,
nodded to her admiringly,
as she passed breezily
through the outer room.

135.4 she] Jacqueline
135.7 the latter] who
135.7 seized] had seized
135.8 and shook] was shaking
135.9 both men] they
135.10 Jaqueline] she
135.13 Ed Bronson] Bronson
135.15 Mather] Coatesworth
       (This name change is
       consistent throughout.)
136.8 was] was now
136.11 He's . . . mistake]
       He's—he's made a sort of
       mistake
136.29 lit] tight
137.2 where] where there's
137.28 discuss] broach
137.28 but Jim] but emitted a gasp
       instead. Jim
137.34 to spread] spread
137.37 woman] hog
138.33 curious] steely
138.35 were] had been
139.7 several days] the day
139.10 drowned] rather drowned
139.16 would] was going to
139.18 friendly] gray
139.20 car would] car, he decided,
       would
139.32 "What do you . . .
       morning."] "Isn't it a

beauty? I just bought it
today."

140.2 surprise . . . entry] surprise

140.8 snapped] snapped out
briskly

140.13 noise, a] noise that may
best be described as a

140.34 brokenly] brokenly now

141.16 he had omitted]
remembered that he had
forgotten

141.24 thirty] perhaps thirty

141.27 Why, a] Just this. A

142.6 It's] It's—it's

142.11 the latter] he himself

142.12 knew how to leave] had a
way of leaving

142.15 moved in an unfamiliar
shape] set in a hard,
straight line

142.17 and I'm] and I'm wrong.
I'm

142.22 quarrelling] fighting

143.1 appalling] somewhat
appalling

143.33 wishing afterwards]
wishing immediately
afterward

143.4 he was] it was

144.8 busy, Mr. Mather?"]
busy?"

145.9 refusal] refusal he knew

145.19 policy, he] policy and he

145.20 and] and to make a long
story short

145.22 them] them—that was all

146.1 saying platitudinously that]
saying something about

146.2 was] being

146.7 him] Mr. Coatesworth

146.8 to have] to—to have

146.21 listless] tired

147.2 Jaqueline] He supposed
Jaqueline

147.4 gesture] gesture, a sort of
showing off

148.8 appeal] piteous appeal

149.5 her!" ¶ "Just] her!" ¶ "Get
back there! Get back
there!" ¶ "Just

149.7 you!" ¶ The] you!" ¶ "Pale
as a ghost." ¶ The

149.21 her—he] her—an' he didn't
know—he

149.24 Jaqueline] The doctor was
gone now and Jaqueline

149.27 now. I'm] now. I'm tired.
I'm

149.28 back] down

149.29 minute?" ¶ He] minute?" ¶
I can wait forever—for
you." ¶ He

149.32 directory . . . as] directory.
She listened idly as

150.2 husband] husband's voice
again

150.4 Mather] Coatesworth, Mr.
Lacy.

150.5 I think I'll] I think—I guess
I'll

150.6 after] somehow or other
after

150.7 I said . . . afternoon—"]
I said—Coatesworth!"

150.8 The following sentences
were cut from the end of
the story: ¶ When he came
back to the verandah she
said hesitantly, "You're
tired too. Perhaps you'd
better not try to carry me."
¶ But he picked her up and,
still holding her in his arms,
he locked the door behind
them and turned out the
lights on the first floor and
started up the stairs. ¶ "Put
me down," she whispered.
"You're—you're carrying a
whole family now." ¶ But
he only laughed and told
her that he wasn't tired at
all. And she believed him
because what he said was
true.

The following emendations in accidentals are taken from the surviving carbon TS; in each case the reading following the bracket is from ASYM:

135.25	innocently—] ~,		140.30	samaritan] Samaritan
135.30	Well,—] ~∧—		143.8	work∧] ~,
136.1	understood—] ~,		143.17	now.] ~,
136.10	Why,—] ~∧—		143.30	herself∧] ~,
136.23	kids—] ~,		144.11	hands∧] ~,
137.2	money—] ~,		146.14	desk∧] ~,
137.14	dirty∧] ~,		147.28	Perhaps∧ . . . hadn't∧]
138.11	knees∧] ~,			~, . . . ~,
138.15	word∧] ~,		149.15	damn∧] ~'

" 'The Sensible Thing' "

No prepublication version appears to survive. FSF cut and revised so heavily between the serial and ASYM texts that the two constitute separate versions. The emendations below are taken from the serial text; in each case the reading following the bracket is from ASYM.

Substantive emendations

155.36	ground] grounds		156.21	anyway] anyways

Accidental emendations

151.14	subway∧] ~,		157.33	failed∧] ~,
152.2	the] The		157.33	self-pity∧] ~,
152.5	bridges∧] ~,		158.5	now!] ~,
152.11	bars∧] ~,		158.15	talk!] ~,
152.27	minute∧] ~,		163.22	America∧] ~,
153.24	emotion.] ~,		164.5	Business?] ~!
156.20	suddenly.] ~,		165.13	dusk∧] ~,
157.14	stubbornly.] ~;			

Editorial emendations

159.12	trip."] ~.∧		160.1	O'Kelly] Rollins
				(The character was named
				Rollins in the serial text.)

"Gretchen's Forty Winks"

A typescript of this story in the Fitzgerald Additional Papers at Princeton bears Fitzgerald's handwritten revisions; this typescript is the source of the emendations in accidentals listed in the second table below (with all rejected readings from ASYM). No substantive emendations have been taken from the typescript; no substantive or accidental emendations have been taken from the serial text. Substantive variants between the serial and ASYM texts are recorded in the first table; these variants are accepted for the Cambridge text.

ASYM] *serial variants*

166.5	assured] announced to	176.28	break—" ¶ "You]
166.7	shut] left		break——" ¶ "Shut up!"
167.9	was] was only		cried Roger fiercely. ¶
169.10	decorator,] decorator and		"Calm down, yourself! If
	his own house was a sort of		you took a cold bath every
	intensification of all the		morning you wouldn't be so
	houses he had ever		excitable." ¶ "You
	designed. He was	178.3	sofa and] sofa
169.11	strong odor of jasmine]	178.27	routine] body
	faint odor of imported	179.26	room. ¶ "I wonder . . .
	perfume		alone." ¶ At] room. ¶
169.16	Cocktail?] Here, have a		"Here I am." ¶ "Oh, I
	cocktail.		wonder . . . alone." ¶
169.18	fair] beautiful		"Come right back here, Mr.
169.20	admiringly . . . 1925.]		Halsey." ¶ At
	admiringly at the Chinese	179.28	back home again, Roger]
	tapestry that took up one		Roger, back home again,
	whole wall of the living	180.32	glibly. "Take . . . day."]
	room.		glibly.
169.24	the stiff, plain room . . .	181.6	a decision next] some sort
	mistake.] the room.		of decision by nine o'clock
170.27	continued . . . matter]		next
	continued	181.8	"Mr.] "Here's Mr.
173.10	disembodied with fatigue]	183.5	biggest] first
	hollow as a ghost	183.18	I don't want] I want a
173.19	two cool] three cool		home—not
173.21	afternoon] day	183.23	"I . . . shortly.] "I wouldn't
174.7	little head over] pretty		let you," he said shortly,
	head about		"even if you wanted to."
175.10	old boy] Roger	185.5	Gretchen. "He] Gretchen.
175.37	Nobald's] Peptow's		"He was always warning
176.17	don't] do not		Roger about overstrain. He

Accidental emendations

166.8	dark∧] ~,	167.36	tonight∧] ~,
166.10	conversations—] ~,	168.12	more,] ~∧
166.24	pause∧] ~,	169.7	kiss∧] ~,
167.13	rag-doll] ~∧~	169.17	No∧] ~,
167.29	time∧] ~,	169.22	*I*] I
167.30	all∧] ~,	169.29	no∧] ~,
167.36	But∧] ~,	170.32	business—] ~,

170.37	rate∧] ∼,		177.11	gone∧] ∼,
171.7	tired∧] ∼,		177.28	Well∧] ∼,
171.12	*night*] night		177.30	Oh∧] ∼,
171.14	*every night . . . six weeks*]		177.31	more∧] ∼,
	every night . . . six weeks		178.3	sofa∧] ∼,
171.20	*bang!*] bang!		178.17	loud∧] ∼,
171.22	tone∧] ∼,		178.31	eyes∧] ∼,
172.5	fine∧ damp∧] ∼, ∼,		178.36	said:] ∼;
172.22	other∧] ∼,		179.3	open—] ∼;
172.25	week∧] ∼,		180.1	*not*] not
172.35	shears∧] ∼,		180.4	in∧] ∼,
174.14	quickly∧] ∼,		180.4	astonishment—] ∼,
174.15	sake∧] ∼,		180.16	eight∧] ∼,
174.20	averted∧] ∼,		180.20	anxiously∧] ∼,
174.32	movies,] ∼;		180.26	box∧ and,] ∼, ∼∧
175.4	Bang] bang		180.37	fingers∧] ∼,
175.8	*I*] I		181.2	door∧] ∼,
175.9	Missus . . . Mister]		181.10	how-do] ∼, ∼
	missus . . . mister		181.35	alone!] ∼.
175.18	rested∧] ∼,		182.7	coffee∧] ∼,
175.24	portfolio∧] ∼,		182.22	Oh∧] ∼,
176.7	*my*] my		182.29	pale∧] ∼,
176.9	No. Not] No; not		183.37	*know*] know
176.19	now∧] ∼,		184.16	newspaper∧] ∼,
176.32	*you*] you			

"One of My Oldest Friends"

Only the serial text appears to survive. The following emendations, all editorial, have been introduced:

Substantive emendations

199.8	out of] out	200.34	woods] wood

Accidental emendations

191.25	grippe] grip	200.6	steps.] ∼,
193.6	burgundy] Burgundy	201.17	imagination;] ∼,
195.22	at it,] ∼ ∼∧		

"A Penny Spent"

Two TSS survive in the Fitzgerald Papers at Princeton. The first and more authoritative of the two is a 41-page document bearing extensive revisions in FSF's hand;

this TS has been facsimiled in FSF/MSS vi, 1: 131–71. The second TS at Princeton, 35 pages in length, is the carbon of the TS that was made from the 41-page document. Restorations and emendations below are taken from the 41-page TS. Rejected readings are from the serial text.

Substantive emendations

205.1	Ritz] Brix	220.27	off] away
	(The same emendation,	224.31	at Cosenza. That's halfway.
	from FSF's TS, is made		] halfway.
	throughout the story.)	225.1	trip to Palermo] trip
205.2	or Morris Gest's office, or	225.29	Torre Annunziata] Torre
	Herrin] or Herrin		dell' Annunziata
213.34	half a dozen] a half dozen	225.33	Cosenza] our destination
220.7	he's still] still he's		

Accidental emendations

206.3	coat∧] ~,	215.20	*You*] You
206.6	say∧] ~,	215.23	o'clock∧] ~,
206.28	man∧] ~,	215.30	place—] ~.
207.8	man, pleasantly∧] ~∧~,	215.32	protests∧] ~,
207.18	*Born*] Born	216.7	compliments—] ~;
209.6	*you*] you	216.22	Royal—] ~,
209.7	Mama] Mamma	216.33	earth—? How] earth—how
209.8	it:] ~;	217.8	days∧] ~,
209.9	hall!] ~.	217.21	Royal Personage] royal
209.15	gaiety] gaiety		personage
209.24	you—] ~.	217.30	her—] ~,
211.1	spend—] ~,	217.31	her∧ too∧] ~, ~,
211.8	never,] ~∧	217.33	afternoon∧] ~,
211.9	mother,] ~∧	218.4	silence∧] ~,
211.23	Still∧] ~,	218.8	strange∧] ~,
211.25	Moreover∧] ~,	218.34	gather∧ too∧] ~, ~,
212.3	(She] —she	219.8	coolly∧] ~,
212.4	me)] ~∧	219.13	Mama] mamma
212.6	" "] tickets for	219.16	"New York Herald"] ∧~ ~
212.13	days] ~'		~∧
212.17	explanations] explanation	222.16	disappeared—] ~,
212.25	hungry∧] ~,	223.3	Fine,] ~∧
213.3	foreground—] ~?	223.11	sea—] ~,
213.16	doubt∧] ~,	223.26	world∧] ~,
213.20	seven∧] ~,	223.32	other∧] ~,
214.4	eyes—] ~;	224.9	sunshine∧] ~,
214.36	envy. I've] ~. ¶ "~	225.1	street. The] ~. ¶ ~
215.6	well.] ~,	225.17	Unfortunately∧] ~,
215.11	fact∧] ~,	225.23	effort∧] ~,

226.21	fact—] ~,	228.31	them—] ~,
227.6	spoke∧] ~,	229.7	board—] ~;
227.19	so∧] ~,	229.16	him—] ~;
227.30	*all*] all	230.3	Grand Scale] grand scale
228.20	nearer—] ~;		

Editorial emendations

216.19	Church] church	221.36	a low] low

" 'Not in the Guidebook' "

A lightly revised TS (the revisions in FSF's hand) survives in the Fitzgerald Papers at Princeton. The title on the TS is enclosed within quotation marks; these are not present in the serial text but are restored here. The substantive and accidental emendations in the tables below are taken from this TS. In each entry, the first reading is adopted from the TS; the reading that follows the bracket is from the serial text.

The two cuts recorded in the substantives table were made at *Woman's Home Companion*. Ober included the following note in his files: "Mr. Aley [an editor at the magazine] called up and said that he had to cut out about two hundred words in Scott Fitzgerald's story. They changed the type of the magazine to larger type and they cut all their stories" (*As Ever, Scott Fitz—*, 80).

Substantive emendations

231.19	We discovered . . . papers.] *Cut for the serial text.*	242.1	down at the pavement] down
236.8	loud] loudly	243.7	a 1910 Ford] an ancient American one
240.29	proceeded on] proceeded		
241.8	"Most . . . Bastille."] *Cut for the serial text.*	243.7	parked at intervals] parked
		244.24	whispered to himself] whispered
241.36	you go to a lawyer and] you		

Accidental emendations

231.3	morning∧] ~,	234.16	pleasant∧] ~,
231.15	saying∧] ~,	234.24	heart—] ~;
232.12	type—] ~;	235.30	began—the] ~. The
233.2	arranged—] ~.	237.24	out∧] ~,
233.30	dawn—] ~;	237.27	matter,] ~;

237.31	gendarmerie] gendarmery	243.12	shop—] ~;
238.26	*Bride . . . Husbandless*]	243.33	long—] ~,
	bride . . . husbandless	244.12	English∧] ~,
238.30	Society∧ . . . neat∧] ~,	245.30	jail,] ~∧
	. . . ~,	246.8	Western Front] western
239.9	Tuileries∧] ~,		front
240.11	Japan∧] ~,	246.32	time—] ~!
240.37	walked in∧] ~ ~,	248.3	lines." [*space break*]] No
241.11	St-Cloud] St. Cloud		*space break.*
241.21	buses] busses	248.6	King] king
242.16	side, . . . silence,] ~∧ . . .		
	~∧		

Editorial emendations

233.23	Milly. It'll] Milly; it'll	240.12	Bill] their guide
237.3	good] well	243.18	thing,] ~∧
237.18	Left Bank] left bank	245.4	*bijoutier*] *bijouterie*
239.23	anything," said Mrs.	246.25	future,] ~∧
	Horton, who] anything."		
	Mrs. Horton		

"Presumption"

Only the serial text appears to survive. The single emendation below is editorial. No emendations in accidentals have been made.

251.3   lived] live

"The Adolescent Marriage"

Fitzgerald's grandchildren possess an unmarked carbon TS of this story. The ribbon copy of this TS (not extant) appears to have served as setting copy for the serial text. The following restorations and emendations, from the carbon TS, have been adopted for the Cambridge text. Rejected readings in these tables are from the serial.

Substantive emendations

279.4	toy . . . Philadelphia] toy	287.22	alone] along
	did not result in a	292.30	Early in September] A
	harmonious whole		week or so later
279.30	plan . . . sanctuary] plan	294.22	half a year] months
	one of these modern	295.2	summer evening] evening
	churches, perhaps	296.2	Oh God—I] I
281.1	Why, by God,] Why,	296.14	over] more than
286.2	bitterly . . . see."] bitterly.∧		

Accidental emendations

279.3	experiment,] ~;		290.34	*stubborn—"] stubborn."*
279.26	vivid∧] ~,		291.11	while∧] ~,
280.12	married." ¶ A] ~." ~		291.12	paper,] ~;
280.13	silence. ¶ "Lucy's] ~." ~		291.20	hours∧] ~,
280.15	considerately,] ~;		292.10	"the tree house,"] ∧~ ~
280.15	then—] ~∧			~, ∧
280.17	others—] ~.		292.11	label,] ~;
281.1	with—] ~,		292.16	story—] ~,
282.11	Unfortunately∧] ~,		292.25	it—] ~,
282.18	course—] ~,		293.25	Lucy,] ~∧
282.27	slender∧] ~,		293.28	'find . . . want.'] ∧~ . . . ~.∧
283.27	Gosh] gosh		294.18	love∧] ~,
283.28	stingy. About] stingy–about		294.21	before him∧] ~ ~,
284.2	it. Down] it—down		294.28	past∧] ~,
284.8	H'm. You] H'm—you		294.31	away∧] ~,
284.34	dark red] dark-red		294.32	trance∧] ~,
285.11	working—suddenly]		294.37	table∧] ~,
	working. Suddenly		295.7	houses—] ~;
285.16	it∧] ~,		295.10	store∧] ~,
285.24	sudden—"] ~."		295.12	lingeringly—] ~,
286.12	sometimes—] ~.		295.15	before. Except∧ of course∧]
287.6	him—] ~;			~—except, ~ ~,
287.7	might∧] ~,		295.22	Outside∧] ~,
287.12	dream—] ~;		295.26	Lucy∧] ~,
287.21	begun∧] ~,		296.4	mine—why] ~. Why
287.29	attitude. He] ~. ¶ He		296.7	bedroom∧] ~,
287.36	it—] ~,		296.15	father-in-law,] ~;
288.11	away. And] away, and		296.17	gate∧] ~,
288.25	night. Over] night—over		296.18	windows∧] ~,
288.37	before—"] ~."		296.19	since—] ~.
289.9	Well—?"] ~∧?"		296.20	∧until] —until
289.22	Shoppe. Veree		296.26	annulment∧] ~,
	Unsanitaree∧"] ~—~ ~,"		296.27	said,] ~∧
289.32	other∧] ~,		296.31	mind,] ~—
290.14	this—] ~;		296.31	eyes,] ~—
290.29	Lucy—suppose] Lucy.			
	Suppose			

Editorial emendation

294.4	your] the

"The Dance" ["In a Little Town"]

An early TS of this story, heavily revised by FSF, is among the Fitzgerald Papers at Princeton. Collation of this TS with the *Red Book* text indicates that FSF executed at least one more round of revising, either on a fresh TS or in proof. The first table below records the substantive variants between TS and serial; they are accepted for the Cambridge text as revisions by FSF.

In a letter to Harold Ober of 17 February 1926, Fitzgerald wrote: "Did you get my wire asking that the title *The Dance* be changed into *In a Little Town*? Of course its up to the Red Book" (*As Ever, Scott Fitz—*, 86). The magazine retained "The Dance" as the title. "In a Little Town" has been treated in this edition as an alternate title.

Serial] TS variants

298.4	all too frequently] once a month without fail	303.29	warm] humid
298.10	has varied in its] varied in	306.6	heard!" someone said again.] heard."
298.12	and so] so	306.21	ambulance] omnibus
299.5	beauty. Perhaps she] beauty—Perhaps	307.3	had been hanging] was hanging
299.18	bizarre neighborhood] bizarre	307.28	importance] some importance
299.22	but amusing] and amusing	308.33	Another] But another
299.36	had hated to leave a town] had	309.3	the rebuff] her rebuff
300.14	questions, . . . undertone.] questions.	309.25	ma'am] sah
		309.36	Now a] A
300.18	Nigger case] Nigger insulted a white girl	310.25	have since] since
		310.25	flight of stairs] stairs
302.7	and so] so	311.5	far. ¶ Then . . . come into]
302.10	free, ethically] morally free		far. Marie happened into
303.4	fanfaronade] fanarade	311.13	from her commitment my]
303.6	stragglers from the bar] couples on the verandas		my
		311.23	out of] out
303.19	a shouted] the shouted	311.24	The bag] It

The substantive and accidental emendations that follow derive from the Princeton TS; rejected readings are from the serial text.

Substantive emendations

298.21	an hilarious] a hilarious	305.25	made an] made the
301.9	me] I	309.20	out] out at
304.23	around] about		

Accidental emendations

298.2	charmed∧ too∧] ~, ~,	298.24	course∧] ~,
298.5	town∧] ~,	298.26	all∧] ~,
298.17	rest,] ~;	298.34	that—] ~;

299.2	meeting∧] ~,	304.19	chaperones] chaperons
299.8	black, . . . lovely,] ~; . . . ~;	304.20	out∧] ~,
299.19	instance∧] ~,	304.34	stairs∧] ~,
299.26	"—we] "We	305.30	"—arrested] "Arrested
299.27	heaven";] ~;"	305.34	rest∧] ~,
299.30	Honey∧] ~,	306.15	ballroom∧] ~,
300.19	swamp∧] ~,	306.16	sheriff] Sheriff
301.10	quickly∧] ~,	306.17	quickly∧] ~,
301.17	puzzled. Then] ~; then	308.28	feuds∧ . . . situations∧]
301.18	out∧] ~,		~, . . . ~,
301.22	But∧] ~,	309.19	sister—?] ~∧?
301.32	added,] ~:	310.10	fired∧] ~,
301.32	pieces,] ~—	310.15	*fired*∧] ~,
303.1	doing∧] ~,	310.19	*fired* . . .] ~—
303.27	around∧ . . . windows∧]	310.20	view . . .] ~—
	~, . . . ~,	310.25	sheriff's] Sheriff's
303.32	over∧] ~,	310.35	knows—] ~;
303.37	stop∧] ~,	311.20	instructions∧] ~,
304.15	stopped∧] ~,	311.22	later∧] ~,

Editorial emendations

Rejected readings, unless otherwise indicated, are from the serial text.

297.2	suburbs—] ~;	304.27	car. I called a waiter and
299.9	affliction] affection ser;		sent] car, and calling a
	affiction TS		waiter, I sent
300.10	boots,] ~∧	309.6	explicable;] ~,
303.36	type, . . . panic,] ~; . . . ~;		

"Your Way and Mine"

A lightly revised TS, with the revisions in FSF's hand, is extant in the Fitzgerald Papers at Princeton. This TS was sent to Ober, who had a ribbon and two carbon TSS made from it. The ribbon copy was sold to *Woman's Home Companion*. The two carbons are in the possession of Fitzgerald's grandchildren. All emendations in the first two tables below are taken from the Princeton TS. Rejected readings in these tables are from the serial text. Two long passages, apparently cut by the magazine editors to conserve space, are restored at 324.36 and 327.34.

Substantive emendations

313.31	I'd take . . . and spank] I'd spank	315.15	a pink mustache] pink mustaches
314.32	than me] than I	319.19	not as] not so

324.36	Through . . . affairs. . . .] *Cut for serial text.*		327.34	"And how . . . at all."] *Cut for serial text.*
327.8	Who] Whom		329.32	coming] going
			329.34	by] past

Accidental emendations

312.4	machine,] ~∧		322.11	club,] ~∧
312.9	sheet,] ~∧		324.30	Cor-ker-an, . . . Corker—"
312.17	blue,] ~∧			] Cor-cor-an, . . . Corcor—"
313.31	Golly . . . Golly] golly . . . golly		325.28	time,] ~∧
			327.24	Honoria,] ~∧
315.9	Golly] golly		328.18	required,] ~∧
315.20	believe,] ~∧		329.10	waste,] ~∧
317.13	anger—] ~,		331.12	per-cent,] per∧cent∧
319.13	Oh∧] ~,		332.18	Max∧] ~,

Editorial emendations

314.10	Panic] panic	327.34	Heinsohn] Hiensohn
325.1	horns∧] ~,		(The same emendation is made throughout the story.)
		328.3	O'Sullivan,] ~∧

"Jacob's Ladder"

A lightly revised TS of "Jacob's Ladder," with the revisions in FSF's hand, survives in the Fitzgerald Papers at Princeton. Collation of this TS against the serial text indicates that the story was copy-edited and expurgated by the *Post* editors (see the introduction, xxvi–xxx). The bowdlerized passages have been restored to the Cambridge text; instances of apparent editorial interference have been reversed, with all emendations recorded below. The *Post* editors also cut all mention of Famous Players Studio and of the Lido, a restaurant/cabaret in New York. These readings too have been restored. In each entry the first reading (that of the Cambridge text) derives from the surviving TS; the second reading is from the serial.

Substantive emendations

335.34	Fifty-six Eas'] Eas'	337.24	picture at the Famous Players] picture
336.12	hang no woman] send no woman to the chair	339.3	deputy sheriffs] stet
337.1	the second richest woman] one of the richest women		(The TS reads "United States marshals," but the prison at Auburn, New

York, was a state
institution. This correction
was likely made by the *Post*
editors and is accepted for
the Cambridge text.)

339.14 Famous Players Studio]
motion-picture studio
340.5 juice; the] juice. ¶ Presently
the
340.8 Famous Players] the
pictures
340.33 lap. Her . . . so old."] *Cut
for serial text.*
341.6 You got] You sure have got
341.25 It was her last effort. The]
The
342.8 try and] try to
342.15 alone, Jake] alone
342.28 inessential] unessential
343.32 "Oh, my God, you] "You

344.6 holy eyes] eyes
346.14 lunch] luncheon
346.17 lunch] luncheon
347.1 private engagements]
engagements
347.20 realtors] real estate brokers
348.28 gotten] got
351.13 there been] there have been
351.24 why were . . . summer?]
why did you seem to care so
much last summer?
354.14 once more] again
354.28 for the most part they]
most of them
357.12 By God, I've] I've
357.33 on] in
358.8 Beautiful child . . . any
more. The] The
358.17 vast throbbing]
fast-throbbing

Accidental emendations

333.1 trial∧] ~,
333.4 "humanized"] ∧~∧
333.8 doors∧] ~,
333.25 action—] ~;
333.26 tender∧] ~,
333.30 squeaked∧] ~,
334.1 roll∧] ~,
334.6 clear∧] ~,
334.10 Lee . . . Lee] Le' . . . Le'
334.18 lee] le'
334.19 alone?" ¶ She] ~?" ~
334.22 rapidly.] ~:
334.26 Jacob. ¶ "Can] ~. "~
334.28 baby. And] baby, and
334.33 Jacob∧] ~,
334.33 vague∧] ~,
335.5 guys!" ¶ Outside∧] ~!" ~,
335.24 madonna] Madonna
335.30 Bronx∧ perhaps,] ~, ~∧
335.33 spoke∧ and,] ~, ~∧
335.34 passed.] ~:
335.34 Hunerd] Hun'erd
335.35 Stayin∧] ~'

335.38 hilariously. ¶ "Somebody's]
~. "~
336.1 *what*] what
336.5 eyes. ¶ "A] ~. "~
336.6 ∧em] '~
336.10 hour. ¶ "She] ~. "~
336.11 Mister] mister
336.13 No. That's] No; that's
336.14 Surely,] ~∧
336.25 dinner."] ~?"
336.30 relief∧] ~,
336.34 Americans∧] ~,
336.35 affectation—] ~;
336.36 apathy: with] apathy. With
336.37 tried, tried hard,] ~—~
~—
337.2 her∧ . . . to∧] ~, . . . ~,
337.2 her—] ~;
337.4 person∧] ~,
337.5 apathy∧] ~,
337.11 "Borghese Gardens."] ∧~
~.∧
337.19 story. ¶ "You] ~. "~

337.22	Nevertheless∧] ~,		344.5	day∧ . . . station∧] ~, . . . ~,
337.34	glass—] ~,		344.12	more—] ~;
337.34	self-conscious—] ~,		344.21	eye-glass. ¶ "There's] ~. "~
338.2	arm∧] ~,		345.1	phonograph∧] ~,
338.7	coat. ¶ "I] ~. "~		345.4	widow. They] ~. ¶ ~
338.25	day. ¶ "I] ~. "~		345.7	*Paris*] Paris
339.3	later∧] ~,		345.11	Hotel. ¶ "Well,] ~. "~,
339.6	said,] ~;		345.19	her—] ~;
339.12	Prince."] ~?"		345.34	said∧ and∧] ~, ~,
339.15	himself∧] ~,		346.3	Jake!] ~,
339.30	No∧] ~,		346.3	here.] ~!
340.10	said:] ~,		346.4	full∧] ~,
340.11	seen." ¶ It] ~." ~		346.6	hour—it's] hour. It's
340.15	laughed∧] ~,		346.6	Sunday∧] ~,
340.15	lightly. ¶ "Be] ~. "~		346.14	oh,] Oh,
340.23	it—"] ~."		346.15	York. Men] York—men
340.25	him. She] ~. ¶ ~		346.17	tea. ¶ "Not] ~. "~
340.26	side,] ~∧		346.20	it's] It's
340.30	it—there] it. There		346.21	Still∧] ~,
340.31	mouth,] ~;		346.27	lot. And . . . narrow—"]
341.6	soda-jerkers] ~∧~			lot, and . . . narrow."
341.8	up.] ~!		346.27	Well∧] ~,
341.10	his. ¶ "I] ~. "~		346.27	finished,] ~—
341.13	again. Hesitating] ~. ¶ ~		346.28	alec,] Aleck,
341.17	heart—] ~;		346.30	tea∧] ~,
341.20	said. "Better] ~; "better		346.32	"people of importance."]
341.21	drinking,] ~∧			∧~ ~ ~.∧
341.22	said,] ~;		347.21	Grauman's] Graumans'
341.33	driver. ¶ "So] ~. "~		347.25	rialto] Rialto
341.34	Farrelly,] ~∧		347.31	urgently—] ~,
341.36	displeasure. ¶ "I'm] ~. "~		347.36	alert∧] ~,
342.3	Sure.] ~!		348.4	again.] ~:
342.8	fascinated—"] ~."		348.7	"plot"] ∧~∧
342.11	laughed. ¶ "Yes∧] ~. "~,		348.13	room∧] ~,
342.13	to:] ~—		348.22	Heavens∧] ~,
342.16	Farrelly∧] ~,		349.15	alone. ¶ "I] ~. "~
342.24	now,] ~∧		349.28	people∧] ~,
343.13	is∧] ~,		350.3	*act*or] actor
343.29	cry. ¶ "Oh,] ~. "~,		350.9	did—] ~,
343.30	much.] ~!		350.11	face. ¶ "If] ~. "~
343.31	cheeks. ¶ "Oh, Geeze,"]		350.20	Grill] grill
	cheeks. "Oh, geeze!"		350.22	long, protracted]
343.33	me.] ~!			long-protracted
343.37	mind∧] ~,		350.37	name. Later] ~. ¶ ~
344.1	furniture:] ~—		351.6	studio. ¶ She] ~. ~
344.3	"understand"] ∧~∧		351.7	lap. ¶ "Do] ~. "~

351.9	Jenny? Knowing]	356.1	it.] ~?
	Jenny—knowing	356.16	her,] ~∧
351.16	of—] ~,	356.16	tears. ¶ "It] ~. "~
351.23	suddenly. ¶ "If] ~. "~	356.22	hands. ¶ "Oh∧] ~. "~,
351.32	had, that Scharnhorst,]	356.29	him. ¶ "Oh∧] ~. "~,
	~—~ ~—	356.30	right.] ~!
351.35	men—] ~∧	356.30	understand.] ~!
352.14	frightened. ¶ "Don't] ~. "~	356.33	Jake. You] Jake, you
352.16	here—"] ~."	356.35	Oh-h-h∧] ~,
352.18	inside. ¶ "Mr.] ~. "~	357.1	lobby∧] ~,
352.26	this,"] ~!"	357.10	blindly. ¶ "I've] ~. "~
352.29	struggle∧] ~,	357.16	laughed. When] ~. ¶ ~
353.3	successful—] ~.	357.33	own. It] ~. ¶ ~
353.11	minute."] ~!"	357.33	impervious∧] ~,
353.23	message. ¶ "Now,] ~. "~,	357.35	*Jenny Prince*] Jenny Prince
354.22	performance:] ~;	358.1	JENNY PRINCE] Jenny
354.23	"get over"] ∧~ ~∧		Prince
354.25	it∧] ~,	358.12	JENNY PRINCE]
355.16	know!] ~.		Jenny Prince
355.17	me∧] ~,	358.14	beauty. Jacob] ~. ¶ ~
355.23	time. ¶ "What] ~. "~	358.15	window. Confused] ~ ¶ ~
355.34	table. "No—No—No— No—No!"] table: "No—no—no—no—no!"	358.16	and,] ~∧

Editorial emendations

353.18	scheme] scene TS, ser	355.8	the Colony restaurant] the restaurant ser, the Colony Restaurant TS

"The Love Boat"

Two TSS survive. The earlier of the two, heavily revised in FSF's hand, and with the final twenty-five leaves entirely in holograph draft, is in the Fitzgerald Papers at Princeton; it has been facsimiled in FSF/MSS, VI, 1: 247–94. A fresh TS was made from this heavily revised TS; the ribbon copy, which would have served as setting copy at the *Post*, does not survive. A carbon of this second typescript, however, is among the papers held by Fitzgerald's grandchildren. Collations among these TSS and the serial text indicate that FSF made one more light revision of "The Love Boat," either on the lost ribbon setting copy or on proofs.

The following substantive and accidental emendations, including the restoration of Daddy Browning and Peaches to the text (see the introduction, pp. xxx–xxxiii),

have as their source the earlier of the two TSS. Rejected readings in the tables below
are from the serial text.

Substantive emendations

362.23	damn] darn	378.22	old Daddy Browning] old
377.32	"I'm Daddy Browning . . .		daddy
	Peaches."] "I got a swell	378.23	¶ "Hey, Peaches."
	love nest up in the Bronx,"		¶ "Peaches, ask] ¶ "Ask
	somebody was saying.		

Accidental emendations

359.2	balloon,] ~∧	370.17	dinner, . . . nostalgia,]
359.4	darkness∧] ~;		~— . . . ~—
360.20	do—] ~∧	371.1	Sunday—] ~,
361.18	you—"] ~."	371.27	Mae—"] ~."
361.20	man—] ~;	371.28	Bill—"] ~."
361.31	itself—and—] ~, ~:	371.30	beauty—] ~;
362.28	Mae—"] ~."	371.32	other. ¶ "You] ~. "~
363.7	shy,] ~∧	371.33	changed—"] ~,"
363.15	eighteen. ¶ His] ~. ~	371.34	Words—] ~,
363.21	near. ¶ "Is] ~. "~	371.36	"—imagine] "Imagine
363.35	*did.*"] did."	371.37	night—"] ~."
364.3	smiling∧] ~,	372.2	might∧] ~,
364.14	*you!*"] you!"	372.9	'Home . . . Side—'"]
364.31	us,] ~;		∧~ . . . ~.∧"
365.15	Hip!"] hip!"	372.12	here. He] ~. ¶ ~
366.11	night∧] ~,	372.19	Well∧] ~,
366.22	Co.] Company	372.20	Dr. Flynn] Doctor ~
367.5	organdy] organdie	372.20	Dr. Keyes] Doctor ~
367.11	yes∧] ~,	372.21	Dr. Given] Doctor ~
367.23	while,] ~∧	372.22	Ameses'. Or] ~'; or
367.26	shore; afterwards] shore.	372.23	Dr. Gross] Doctor ~
	Afterward	372.23	Dr. Studeford] Doctor ~
367.29	woods.] wood.	372.23	Dr. de Martel] Doctor ~ ~
368.11	1850—it] 1850. It	372.26	Ogden∧] ~,
368.20	knowing∧ nevertheless∧]	372.31	own∧] ~'
	~, ~,	373.4	Mae—let's] Mae. Let's
368.37	moment. ¶ "I've] ~. "~	373.15	*him*] him
369.5	*Al!*"] Al!"	374.2	presently—stevedores]
369.9	Mae∧] ~,		presently. Stevedores
369.15	can—] ~,	374.5	aboard—] ~;
369.16	Oh∧ God—] ~, ~,	374.11	*you?*"] you?"
369.26	"his own set."] ∧~ ~ ~.∧	374.18	Groton—] ~,
370.13	"around."] ∧~.∧	374.34	laughed; once] ~. Once

375.25	Mr.] ~∧		378.32	later∧] ~,
375.36	Bill. And] Bill, and		379.6	afternoon—] ~,
376.1	last. ¶ "You] ~. "~		379.7	dark∧] ~,
376.3	nodded. ¶ "That's] ~. "~		379.13	word∧] ~,
376.11	shoulder. ¶ "I'm] ~. "~		379.32	note—] ~,
376.21	her∧ too,] ~, ~;		380.3	his—] ~;
376.32	using—] ~,		380.8	Haughton—] ~;
377.7	No—] ~;		380.8	life,] ~—
377.20	rail. ¶ "Pleasant] ~. "~		380.12	Hello∧] ~,
377.22	McVitty. And] McVitty; and		380.19	"—She's] "∧~
			380.22	tonight—] ~,
378.17	curiously. ¶ "Why,] ~. "~,		380.28	mirror,] ~—
378.29	before—] ~,			

Editorial emendation

359.7	Wood] Woods

"The Bowl"

A revised TS, with the revisions in FSF's hand, is among the Fitzgerald Papers at Princeton. Collation of this TS with the serial text indicates that FSF revised the story once more, lightly, before it saw print—either on the final copy submitted to the *Post* or in proofs. The emendations below are taken from the TS; rejected readings are from the serial text.

Substantive emendation

404.25	Biltmore] Madison

Accidental emendations

381.30	face—] ~;		387.14	No. She] No; she
382.5	enclosed] inclosed		387.34	mind,] ~∧
383.6	Bowl—] ~;		388.15	PRINCETON 10–YALE 3]
383.25	committed∧] ~,			PRINCETON, 10; YALE, 3
383.26	For∧ . . . play∧] ~, . . . ~,		388.21	Well∧] ~,
383.29	waste: why] waste. Why		388.28	Harlan!"] ~∧"
384.1	Morally∧] ~,		389.2	Washington—] ~;
384.13	So∧] ~,		389.7	continental] Continental
385.29	field∧] ~,		389.16	indeed∧] ~,
385.34	men—] ~;		390.17	shoulder∧] ~,
385.34	vanquished∧] ~,		390.18	"—Carl] "∧~
386.17	*you*] you		391.2	suddenly—] ~;
387.1	Then∧] ~,		391.21	"Princetonian,"] ∧~,∧

392.4	last∧ . . . it—] ∼, . . . ∼,		399.2	*that*] that
393.31	*bother*] bother		399.19	over∧] ∼,
394.11	talk∧] ∼,		400.20	balance,] ∼∧
394.16	Still∧] ∼,		401.3	Yale 7–Princeton 0] Yale,
395.2	actually∧] ∼,			7; Princeton, 0
395.11	Friend] friend		401.26	change. ¶ From] ∼. ∼
395.22	before—] ∼;		402.24	bodies—] ∼∧
396.21	football—] ∼;		403.1	year∧] ∼,
396.25	7–3] 7 to 3		404.3	workers—] ∼;
397.5	bed∧] ∼,		404.14	cooperation] coöperation
397.20	there∧] ∼,		404.19	York—] ∼;
397.27	tried∧] ∼,		405.5	role] rôle
397.30	mirror—] ∼;		405.12	name—] ∼;
397.34	Vienna.] ∼;		405.17	intimately—] ∼;
398.36	actress—] ∼;			

"Magnetism"

The ribbon setting copy of this story survives at the Albert and Shirley Small Special Collections Library, University of Virginia. This ribbon TS bears copy-editing and bowdlerization by editors at the *Post* (see the introduction, pp. xxxiii–xxxv). Collation of this setting copy with the serial text reveals further textual bleaching, likely carried out by the *Post* editors in proof. This same collation has brought to light a further round of authorial revision; these revisions are also listed below. An unmarked carbon of the setting copy is in the possession of Fitzgerald's grandchildren.

Substantive restorations, all deriving from the setting copy, are given below. In each case the reading following the bracket is from the *Post* text.

417.4	Please don't come in my room tonight.] Goodnight.	428.9	Oxford 3313] Oxford —
428.4	"My God!" he cried. "Do . . . that?"] "Do . . . that?" he cried.	428.18	herself." ¶"My God!" ¶"When you] herself. When you

The following readings were cut or revised in proof, likely by the *Post* editors. The original readings, which appear first in the entries below, have been restored. Rejected readings are from the serial text.

417.34	grand] thousand	427.18	Kay sat forward in the bed.] *Cut for serial text.*
427.2	her sitting up in bed in her nightgown] lying down		

The following readings are accepted from the *Post* text as likely proof revisions by FSF, or as necessary corrections. Rejected readings are from the setting-copy TS:

407.3	beat] have beaten	416.5	grinned acquiescently]
407.18	solicitude] solicitation		smiled
409.35	George] George politely	417.8	pale and hard] pale
411.12	dropping] quick dropping		somewhat tough
413.7	her] her as if she were an	417.16	toughened] hardened
	injured child	419.22	son] daughter
414.5	minimized to himself]	420.15	the mouthpiece] it
	forgotten	421.17	said] said in a strained
414.7	asked] said		voice
414.19	was aware that] that	422.28	ten] seven
414.21	their house] the house	422.30	his audience] they
414.26	announced] entered and	422.34	were not] were much more
	announced		than
415.1	scarcely] still under	426.10	helpless] helplessly
415.19	Kay] Helen	427.19	Kay said] she said
415.37	mean." ¶ "I don't."]	428.34	roughly] almost roughly
	mean."		

Accidental emendations

These emendations in accidentals derive from the *Post* text; rejected readings are from the setting-copy TS.

406.5	Coast] coast	412.25	her,] ~∧
406.12	boulevard,] ~∧	412.26	point,] ~∧
406.15	manliness,] ~∧	412.28	way;] ~,
406.17	dolls,] ~∧	412.32	knock,] ~∧
406.24	locality,] ~∧	413.8	handkerchief?"] ~,"
408.1	barracuda] Barracuda	413.18	round, young,] ~∧ ~∧
409.4	Oh,] ~∧	413.20	clear, glossy,] ~∧ ~∧
409.13	finished,] ~∧	413.21	state,] ~∧
410.19	half-god] half-God	413.22	seventeen—] ~∧
410.20	tremolo] tremulo	413.27	Yale,] ~∧
410.37	distinguishable,] ~∧	413.31	state."] ~".
411.2	annoyed,] ~∧	414.7	Kay?"] ~,"
411.10	earlier,] ~∧	414.32	years,] ~∧
411.14	control—] ~,	415.6	thus, . . . generation,]
411.22	company,] ~∧		~∧ . . . ~∧
411.33	Mamaroneck,] ~∧	415.17	here,] ~∧
411.36	to:] ~—	415.22	kitchen,] ~∧
412.8	men,] ~∧	415.23	her,] ~∧
412.10	Avery,] ~∧	415.24	her,] ~∧
412.15	Kay, and,] ~∧ ~∧	416.4	her,] ~∧
412.22	memorable,] ~∧	416.6	them, and George,] ~∧ ~
412.24	together,] ~∧		~∧

416.7	something,] ~∧		420.14	floor;] ~,
416.15	argument,] ~∧		420.15	said∧] ~,
416.28	effort;] ~,		421.15	room,] ~∧
416.29	cordiality,] ~∧		421.16	up∧] ~,
416.33	there,] ~∧		422.6	it;] ~,
416.35	it,] ~∧		422.9	said∧] ~,
417.4	interest:] ~,		422.9	Monica"] ~."
417.5	stairs,] ~∧		422.15	attention,] ~∧
417.8	familiar,] ~∧		422.19	other,] ~∧
418.6	years∧] ~;		422.23	heart,] ~∧
418.7	be∧] ~,		422.34	Fairbankses] Fairbanks
418.12	twenty,] ~∧		423.1	Kay,] ~∧
418.14	test,] ~∧		424.16	George. Probably] George,
418.18	away.] ~ . . .			probably
418.32	Harris's."] Harris'".		424.31	was,] ~∧
419.1	Kay,] ~∧		425.30	desk,] ~∧
419.11	shoes,] ~∧		426.1	hours,] ~∧
419.12	him,] ~∧		426.15	hours,] ~∧
419.22	two-month-old] two		426.22	ringing,] ~∧
	months old		427.5	matter?"] ~,"
419.26	and,] ~∧		427.21	added:] ~,
419.26	shaved,] ~∧		427.31	think.∧] ~."
419.34	yes] Yes		428.11	Apartments] apartments
419.35	Helen. . . .] ~ . . .		429.5	barracuda] Barracuda
420.4	George.] ~,		429.9	barracuda] Barracuda
420.8	on:] ~,			

Editorial emendations

415.15	places] place		424.20	San Quentin] St. ~
417.23	pockets] pocket		427.3	around in] around
422.22	him] he		427.37	Schroeder] Douglas
422.30	into the] into			

Hyphenated compounds

The compound words in the table below are hyphenated at the ends of lines in the Cambridge text. The hyphens should be preserved when quoting these words. All other compound words hyphenated at the ends of lines in this edition should be quoted as a single word.

33.5	cuff-buttons		85.6	through-train
46.25	caddy-master		99.21	be-*oo*-tiful
47.31	golf-stockings		115.24	far-off
49.29	cow-eyes		179.9	alarm-clock
69.27	ice-cream		193.1	lamp-lit
75.30	good-night		207.1	warm-hearted

EXPLANATORY NOTES

Annotated below are references to persons, places, literary and dramatic works, public figures, sports heroes, movie and cabaret stars, popular songs, and restaurants and hotels in the US and Europe.

"The Rich Boy"

7.3   he went to New Haven
The narrator means that Anson entered Yale University in New Haven, Connecticut.

7.20   gallant girls . . . from the fifth row
Chorus girls from Broadway shows and revues were regarded as fair game by wealthy young men, who attempted to secure favors from them with mash notes, flowers, and expensive gifts.

7.33   Pensacola
Site of the US Naval Air Station during the First World War; aviators were trained there to fly seaplanes, dirigibles, and free kite balloons. By the time the Armistice was signed in November 1918, some 438 officers and 5,538 enlisted men had passed through Pensacola or were still in training there.

7.34   "I'm Sorry, Dear"
A popular war song, with music by N. J. Clesi and lyrics by Harry Tobias, made famous by Fats Waller in a 1918 recording: "I'm sorry dear, so sorry dear, / I'm sorry I made you cry. / Won't you forget, won't you forgive, / Don't let us say goodbye."

9.29   the Ritz
The Ritz-Carlton Hotel, mentioned frequently in Fitzgerald's fiction, was then at Madison and 46th. It was famous for its elegantly appointed Palm Room.

9.35   the Yale Club

In 1915, while Fitzgerald was a student at Princeton, the Yale Club (for alumni, students, and faculty of the university) moved to a new building at 50 Vanderbilt Avenue, at the corner of Vanderbilt and East 44th. Some alumni kept rooms there, as Anson does in the story. Fitzgerald was familiar with the Yale Club: while he was living in Manhattan just after the war, he and his fellow Princeton alumni were allowed to share the facilities of the Yale Club until the new Princeton Club at Park and 39th could be completed. The narrator of "The Rich Boy" does likewise—see p. 210000 of the text.

10.17   Hempstead
14.3   Southampton

Many wealthy families maintained residences in Hempstead, a community in east central Long Island. Southampton was a vacation spot on the south shore of Long Island east of Shinnecock Bay—an area then known for its beautiful scenery and its isolation.

12.16   the Links

An exclusive club in Manhattan on East 62nd Street, about a block from Central Park.

13.27   the armistice was signed

The armistice that ended the First World War began at 11:00 a.m. on 11 November 1918: the eleventh hour of the eleventh day of the eleventh month (Matthew 20:1–16). In some sectors, fighting continued until the hour of the cease-fire.

14.3   Hot Springs, and Tuxedo Park

The Homestead, a resort at Hot Springs in the Virginia mountains, was known for its mineral baths, golf courses, and well-to-do clientele. Tuxedo Park was a gated residential enclave located some forty miles outside New York in Orange County, close to the New Jersey border. Pierre Lorrilard, of the tobacco family, created Tuxedo Park in 1886. The residents were quite wealthy; some maintained strings of polo ponies. The black dinner jacket known as a tuxedo takes its name from the community, where it first became an item of fashionable attire.

14.33   as 1920 . . . twelve thousand dollars

Anson is doing very well. The purchasing power of $12,000 in 1920 would be approximately equal to that of $116,800 in 2005, relative to the US Consumer Price Index and adjusted for inflation and other factors. (To compare monetary values elsewhere in this volume, see Samuel H. Williamson, "What Is the Relative Value?" *Economic History Services*, at http://eh.net/hmit/compare/.) Jenny Prince's movie contract in "Jacob's Ladder" (p. 342) pays her $400 per week in 1927—or about the equivalent of $5,000 per week in 2005. And the $50,000 demanded of George Hannaford by the blackmailer in "Magnetism" (p. 417) is equal to $570,000 in the current economy.

15.17   Palm Beach . . . Lake Worth . . . Breakers and the Royal Poinciana . . . Everglades Club

Palm Beach, where Jordan Baker plays golf in *The Great Gatsby*, is a fashionable resort in Florida. The Breakers and the Royal Poinciana were posh hotels built at nearby Lake Worth, Florida, by Henry Morrison Flagler, a Standard Oil magnate and real-estate developer. Anson and his friends would have patronized the second incarnation of the Breakers, erected in the fall and winter of 1903–4 after the original hotel burned down in June 1903. These two hotels were frequented by members of the Rockefeller, Vanderbilt, Astor, Carnegie, and Morgan families, as was the elegant Everglades Club, where wealthy newlyweds often honeymooned.

15.26   the double-shuffle

A popular three-step dance (a variation on the polka) with extra steps interpolated for syncopation in the music. Dancers moved counter-clockwise around the floor.

16.5   "*Rose of Washington Square*"

A popular song of the period with music by the vaudeville accompanist James F. Hanley and words by Ballard MacDonald, an alumnus of Princeton who later wrote lyrics for Broadway productions. The song exists in both serious and comic versions. Fitzgerald is quoting, approximately, from the chorus of the comic rendition: "Rose of Washington Square, she's withering there; / In basement air she's fading . . . / She's got those Broadway vampires lashed to the mast; / She's got no future, but oh! What a past; / She's Rose of Washington Square."

17.8   Bar Harbor

Bar Harbor, Maine, a resort town facing Frenchman Bay, was a popular vacation spot for the rich and socially prominent during the Gilded Age. According to the second sentence of *This Side of Paradise*, Amory Blaine's parents met at Bar Harbor.

17.34   a cutaway coat

A coat with the front of the skirt cut back to curve toward the tails; worn by men (usually with striped trousers, vest, winged collar, and ascot) for formal daytime occasions, such as weddings—and, among members of Anson's set, for Sunday morning churchgoing.

18.6   Wheatley Hills

An area of Long Island, a little east of Great Neck and Manhasset, where many wealthy New Yorkers (Vanderbilts, Chryslers, Woolworths, Guggenheims) maintained large estates.

19.10   Junior League . . . Plaza . . . the Assembly

The Junior League and the Assembly were organizations for wealthy women who wished to help the poor and indigent, to do civic good works, and to socialize with one another. Dolly, at the age of seventeen or eighteen, would have "come out" as a debutante at the Plaza Hotel.

31.11   St. Thomas's church

Many members of this Protestant Episcopal church at Fifth Avenue and 53rd Street were wealthy and socially prominent. One of the carved stone ornaments above its "marriage door," to the left of the main entrance, resembles a dollar sign—a matter for joking among the parishioners.

31.24   Queensboro Bridge

A handsome double-decker bridge connecting midtown Manhattan, at 59th Street, with Astoria in Long Island City, in the borough of Queens. The Queensboro Bridge is mentioned in *The Great Gatsby* and, later in this volume, in "Jacob's Ladder."

32.22   Westchester County

This county, lying on the east bank of the Hudson River north of New York City, was the location of many private estates for the well-to-do.

33.17   continuities for pictures

A continuity in the motion-picture business is a written plan, set down in advance of filming, which gives in detail the order and connection of scenes.

35.29 non-alcoholic champagne

"The Rich Boy" is set during Prohibition, which went into effect in January 1919. No alcoholic drinks would have been served at the Plaza; guests who wanted whiskey would have brought it in flasks or private bottles.

36.30 Central told him . . . the exchange

In the 1920s, one placed a telephone call by giving the number to a "Central" operator and waiting for the connection to be made. Telephone numbers of the time were preceded by lettered prefixes standing for exchanges—Rhinelander or Plaza, for example, in New York City. It was possible to tell the approximate location of a residence or business in a city if one knew the telephone exchange. A few paragraphs later in the story, Anson pays a desk attendant for his telephone calls; this was before the invention of coin-operated telephones.

37.26 Rye

Rye, northeast of New York City, near the Connecticut border, is a few miles east of Scarsdale.

41.7 the *Paris* moved off

The *Paris*, launched in 1921, aimed for the top tier of the transatlantic trade. (Jacob Booth, the protagonist of "Jacob's Ladder," later in this volume, books a stateroom on the *Paris*.) The ship was decorated in a combination of Art Nouveau, Art Deco, and Moorish styles and was the most elegant vessel in the Compagnie Générale Transatlantique (the French Line). The Fitzgeralds traveled to France on the *Paris* in April 1928.

"Winter Dreams"

43.18 Black Bear Lake

This fictional body of water is a lightly disguised version of White Bear Lake, near Fitzgerald's hometown of St. Paul, Minnesota. He attended dances at the White Bear Yacht Club as a youth; after marriage, he and Zelda lived at the lake twice—once in August 1921 and again during the summer of 1922.

44.2 Pierce-Arrow

This huge, richly appointed automobile, with a thirteen-liter engine, was the most elegant luxury car of the period.

49.7 a short mashie shot
A mashie, during the 1920s, was one of the standard irons in a golfer's bag, used for medium-length shots, with about the loft of a five-iron.

50.12 "Chin-Chin" and "The Count of Luxembourg" and "The Chocolate Soldier"
This scene occurs before high-quality phonographs and record discs were generally available. Popular songs from Broadway musicals were mostly circulated in sheet music; young people played the songs on pianos or guitars while their friends sang along. As Fitzgerald notes, the three songs mentioned in this scene (which is set in 1915) were "songs of last summer and of summers before that." "Chin-Chin Chinaman" was a comic song from Act 2 of the popular 1896 musical *The Geisha*, by Sidney Jones; Fitzgerald might have seen the revival on Broadway in 1913. *The Count of Luxembourg*, with music by Franz Lehár and lyrics by Adrian Ross and Basil Hood, opened on Broadway in September 1912 and ran for 120 performances. *The Chocolate Soldier* (based on Shaw's *Arms and the Man*), with music by Oscar Straus, book and lyrics by Stanislaus Stange, had its New York opening in September 1909 and lasted for 296 nights.

58.1 when he was twenty-five
The chronology of "Winter Dreams" is slightly off. No attempt has been made to repair it by emendation. In working out the time scheme of the story, Fitzgerald seems to have lost track of 1906–7. The only definite date in the narrative is February 1917, at the end of section V, just before Dexter enters the army for the First World War. He should therefore be twenty-six in the reading glossed here, not twenty-five. If Fitzgerald's chronology is followed, the final scene in "Winter Dreams" occurs in 1924, though the story was first published in *Metropolitan Magazine* in December 1922.

59.30 a coupé
A closed, two-door automobile; most coupés seated only two people and provided privacy for the occupants.

62.30 the war came to America in March
The US did not formally declare war on Germany and its allies until 6 April 1917, but diplomatic relations ceased in February, and war seemed certain by March.

"The Baby Party"

76.16   beefsteak . . . your eye
A home remedy for a black eye was to apply a piece of beefsteak, in order to reduce swelling.

"Absolution"

78.10   nickel taps of the soda-fountain
Drug stores of the time often had soda fountains, where soda-jerks concocted drinks with ice, soda-water, flavored syrup, and ice cream. Soda water was dispensed through shiny swan-necked taps, some of them nickel-plated. For a gloss on "soda-jerks," see the annotations for "Jacob's Ladder."

80.13   the Sixth and Ninth Commandments
As numbered by the Catholic Church, these are the commandments against adultery and coveting one's neighbor's wife.

81.25   'Twenty-three Skidoo'
A slang term from the early 1920s, mildly disrespectful and of uncertain origin. An approximate equivalent would be "Beat it!" or "Scram!"

83.30   the road braced itself in macadam
A "macadamized" road was covered with crushed stone bound together with tar or asphalt. The Scottish engineer John L. MacAdam (b. 1756) invented the process.

84.21   the Empire Builder, James J. Hill
St. Paul native James J. Hill (1838–1916) built railroads throughout the upper midwestern and western states. His Great Northern System was independently financed, making its way without federal aid or land grants. Hill's mansion, erected in the late 1880s, was familiar to Fitzgerald during his boyhood; it still stands at 240 Summit Avenue and boasts thirty-two rooms, a ballroom, and a two-story art gallery.

85.1   his Alger books
The boys' novels of Horatio Alger, Jr. (1832–99), follow a predictable formula. A young man of modest means overcomes the odds and, through pluck and luck, achieves high fortune and sterling repute. In the first chapter

of *This Side of Paradise*, Fitzgerald mentions one of the most popular of the Alger books—*Do and Dare; or, a Brave Boy's Fight for a Fortune* (1884).

85.2   "Cornell," "Hamline"

Fitzgerald means Cornell University in Ithaca, New York, a member (with Princeton, Harvard, Yale, and other colleges) of the prestigious Ivy League, and Hamline University, a small Methodist institution in his native St. Paul.

89.15 and ff.   *Dómini, non sum dignus . . .*
Corpus Dómini nostri . . .

Latin from the Ordinary of the Roman Catholic Mass, ca. 1910. The priest administers the sacrament first to himself (*meam*), then to each communicant (*tuam*). The initial passage can be translated as follows: "Lord, I am not worthy that Thou shouldst come under my roof; but only say the word, and my soul will be healed." The second and third passages: "May the Body of our Lord Jesus Christ preserve (my/your) soul unto life everlasting."

90.13   *"Sagitta Volante in Die"*

Psalms 90:6. "Fear not the arrow that flieth in the day . . . ." See J. I. Morse, "Fitzgerald's *Sagitta Volante in Dei*: An Emendation and a Possible Source," *Fitzgerald/Hemingway Annual 1972*: 321–22. *Dei*, an error in transcription, has been editorially emended to *Die* for the Cambridge text. This passage from Psalm 90 seems to have had special meaning for Fitzgerald; later he used verses 5–6, in Latin, in his meditation on insomnia "Sleeping and Waking" (1934). See the Cambridge edition of *My Lost City*, p. 163. The entire passage can be translated as follows: "His truth shall compass thee with a shield: thou shalt not be afraid of the terror of the night. / Of the arrow that flieth in the day, of the business that walketh about in the dark: of invasion, or of the noonday devil" (Douay version, 1914).

93.9   the German cuirassiers at Sedan

Fitzgerald has in mind the 1870 battle, during the Franco-Prussian War, which occurred at Sedan, a city on the Meuse River in northeastern France. The French were defeated in the engagement; the Prussian cuirassiers were a unit of heavy cavalry equipped with breastplates and plumed or spiked helmets.

"Rags Martin-Jones and the Pr-nce of W-les"

94.1   The *Majestic*

The luxurious *Majestic*, a liner in the White Star fleet, began life as the partly built German liner *Bismarck* (construction was halted by the advent of the First World War). The ship was awarded to the British under the reparations agreements in the Treaty of Versailles as compensation for the *Britannic*, which was sunk by a German mine in 1916. The *Majestic* was completed in 1921 and thereafter worked the transatlantic service between Southampton and New York.

94.13   Gloria Swanson . . . Lord & Taylor . . . Graustark

Fitzgerald is progressing from the sublime to the upmarket to the fictional. Gloria Swanson (1899–1983), famous for her great beauty, her acting ability, and her upturned nose, starred in Paramount films during the 1920s. Lord & Taylor, then a department store for the carriage trade, had moved in 1914 from its spot on the "Ladies' Mile" downtown to a new building at Fifth Avenue and 38th Street. The American novelist George Barr McCutcheon created the fictional Balkan kingdom of Graustark; he wrote a series of novels set there, including *Graustark* (1901), *Beverly of Graustark* (1904), and *The Prince of Graustark* (1914).

100.31   the Prince of Wales

Edward, Prince of Wales (1894–1972), made a tour of the US and Canada in the summer and fall of 1919. He was regarded as the world's most eligible bachelor at the time; many young American women threw themselves at him. During his visit he attended the Ziegfeld *Follies* in New York and was given a ticker-tape parade by the city.

109.22   earrings

Police slang for handcuffs.

112.1   Wessex . . . a Guelph

The elevator boy might be the natural son of one of the members of the British royal family. The Guelphs were a European (primarily German) royal dynasty from which the British House of Hanover was descended; the first Hanover king, George I, took the throne of England in 1714. To downplay these German origins, and for other reasons, George V (the father of the Prince of Wales of this story) changed the family name to Windsor in

1917. Wessex is a former Anglo-Saxon kingdom in southernmost England, famous as the setting for many of Thomas Hardy's novels.

"The Adjuster"

113.15   Rue de la Paix

This Paris street, on the Right Bank, 2nd arrondissement, near the Place de l'Opéra, was famous for its women's clothing stores and its jewelers.

117.11   the "Ladies' Home Journal"

A mass-circulation magazine aimed at middle-class women. Fitzgerald's admonitory essay "Imagination—and a Few Mothers" appeared there in June 1923 and is reprinted in the Cambridge edition of *My Lost City*, pp. 58–65.

126.19   the "Lux" advertisement in the bus

Lux was a bath soap that featured sudsy babies in its advertisements; "car-cards" (also mentioned in the third paragraph of "'The Sensible Thing,'" two stories further on in this volume) were advertisements posted above the windows in buses and subway cars. In the spring of 1919, as an apprentice at the Barron Collier agency in New York City, Fitzgerald wrote copy for car-cards.

"Hot and Cold Blood"

136.8   the texture of Bessemer cooled

Bessemer, a high-grade steel, was made by forcing air through molten iron to remove carbon and other impurities. Several of the steel mills in Birmingham, Alabama (not far from Zelda's home town of Montgomery), used this process.

"'The Sensible Thing'"

152.2   Massachusetts Institute of Technology

This prestigious engineering and technical college in Cambridge, Massachusetts, was descended from Boston Tech, near Copley Square in the city. Boston Tech is mentioned later in this volume in "The Adolescent Marriage."

157.2 the evening pianos
A favorite after-dinner activity in middle-class homes of the period was to play popular songs on the piano. See the gloss for "Winter Dreams" at 50.12.

159.28 Cuzco, Peru
A city in southern Peru, famous for its Incan ruins, predominantly Indian in population, and a trading center for textiles and agricultural produce.

"Gretchen's Forty Winks"

181.5 Biltmore Hotel
The Fitzgeralds honeymooned at the Biltmore in 1920—until they were asked to leave because they were disturbing the other guests. The hotel stood at Madison and 43rd, across from Grand Central Station. Its main restaurant, called The Cascades, featured a 28-foot waterfall; the Biltmore was also reputed to have the finest Turkish baths in the city.

"One of My Oldest Friends"

202.25 Gerbert
This Frenchman, born ca. 945, became archbishop of Rheims and then pope in 999 (as Sylvester II). Gerbert was learned in mathematics and astronomy and wrote on theology and the natural sciences. He died in 1003 and was succeeded by John XVII.

"A Penny Spent"

205.2 Morris Gest
Gest (1881–1942), a Jewish immigrant from Lithuania, began as a prop boy in the Boston theatre district; eventually he became a famous New York producer, best known for bringing plays from the Moscow Art Theatre to the US. His productions of *Aphrodite* and *Mecca*, which featured scantily clad exotic dancers, were considered risqué and drew heavy criticism from the plain folk.

205.3   Herrin, Illinois

This city, in a coal-mining region of southern Illinois, was the site in 1922 of the Herrin Massacre, a clash between strikers and imported scabs that resulted in over twenty deaths.

205.10   tear some college boy bag from bag

In college slang of the time, "bags" were trousers; to "debag" a boy was to remove his pants.

207.21   Saratoga chips

An early name for potato chips, or crisps, first served by a cook named George Crum at Moon Lake Lodge in Saratoga Springs, New York, during the early 1850s.

207.33   Bond Street suit

A garment purchased on Bond Street in Westminster, London, the location of the best men's clothing stores in the city.

211.15   Brussels . . . the guild halls

Large guild houses in the Italian Baroque style were erected in the Grand Place at the center of Brussels between 1695 and 1700; they remain popular tourist attractions today. Among the guilds represented are those for haberdashers, boatmen, bakers, and archers.

215.16   Bolls-Ferrari landaulet

Fitzgerald is playing with the names Rolls-Royce and Ferrari, two manufacturers of luxury automobiles. A landaulet was a small car, usually equipped with a folding top.

216.19   the American Church

Fitzgerald means the American Church in Paris, an interdenominational fellowship for US expatriates and visitors to the city, officially chartered in 1857.

216.22   Café Royal

Probably the café of Le Royal, a well-known hotel at 119 Boulevard M. Lemonnier, in Old Brussels.

217.15   shooting box

A British term meaning a small lodge or house, usually inhabited only during the hunting season.

217.20   Brabant Lodge

Apparently fictitious, but Brabant is the Belgian province in which Brussels is located; its name derives from the Duchy of Brabant, which flourished as a center of art, religion, and trade during the sixteenth century.

217.23   Boompjes . . . Groote Kerk

Boompjes was a large sea dyke in south central Rotterdam along the Nieuwe Maas; Groote Kerk is the name given to the plaza where St. Laurenskerk, a fifteenth-century church, is located.

221.24   sit with the chauffeur outside

Some touring cars of the period were equipped with closed compartments for the passengers; chauffeurs sat in open seats in front, exposed to the elements. Ordering Corcoran to sit outside with the chauffeur would remind him that he was a hired guide, not a family companion, and certainly not a proper suitor for Hallie.

221.26   Blue Grotto

La Grotta Azzura, on Capri, is a sea-cave wide enough for a small boat to enter; it remains one of the chief tourist attractions on the island. The Fitzgeralds visited the Blue Grotto while they were on the island in 1926.

225.29   Torre Annunziata

This seaport in the province of Naples lies on the east side of the bay and at the south foot of Mount Vesuvius. In the 1920s it was known for its ironworks, an arms factory, and mineral springs.

225.37   the Black Hand

Fitzgerald probably has in mind the Italian *Mano Nera*, a collective term applied to several extortion rackets operated by Sicilian immigrant gangsters in New York, Chicago, New Orleans, and Kansas City from about 1890 to 1920. The Black Hand was also the byname of the secret Serbian terrorist group that was instrumental in planning the assassination of Archduke Francis Ferdinand in 1914.

226.13   Eboli . . . Agropoli

Eboli is a town in the Cilento region of Italy, very near the famous Grotta di Pertosa. Agropoli, mentioned several paragraphs along in the story, is one of the highest towns on the Cilento coast; it looks out over the Tyrrhenian Sea. Agropoli is more than two miles from Eboli; Fitzgerald has moved them closer together for the purposes of his plot.

226.24   the mutilated Italian

Nosby is saying, approximately, "More sooner! The evening is too late!" (He's urging the driver to go faster because it's getting dark.)

"'Not in the Guidebook'"

231.9   Leonora Hughes

This blonde American dancer enjoyed her greatest success in London and Paris in 1919 and 1920. She and her partner, who was known by the single name Maurice, were dancing rivals of Vernon and Irene Castle in Paris and New York. Hughes made headlines in the autumn of 1920 when she returned to New York aboard the liner *Olympic* and neglected to declare her furs and jewels to customs officers. These valuables were impounded during her visit, but she was found innocent of wrongdoing. See "Dancer's $100,000 Gems and Furs Held," *New York Times*, 25 November 1920.

231.24   *S. S. Olympic*

Mentioned in the gloss just above, the *Olympic* was the sister ship of the *Titanic* in the White Star Line. Her collision with the Royal Navy cruiser *Hawke* in September 1911 caused the *Titanic*, then under construction, to be completed more rapidly. The luxurious *Olympic* was popular with wealthy and famous travelers, including Charlie Chaplin and the Prince of Wales. Fitzgerald traveled to Europe on the *Olympic* in February 1931, after having returned to the US in January for his father's funeral.

234.8   "Du vaah"

Jim is attempting to order *"Du vin"* — some wine.

237.15   apache dens, Zelli's and *Le Rat Mort*

In French slang of the period, an *apache* was a Parisian gangster or petty criminal. Apache dancers were popular in Paris clubs of the 1920s, where (dressed as street ruffians) they performed violent, kinetic, erotic dances for the patrons. Maurice and Leonora Hughes, mentioned above, were among the first apache dancers. Zelli's and *Le Rat Mort* were two chic dinner restaurants in Montmartre, near the Place Pigalle.

238.13 *"Voleurs!"*
French for "Thieves!" or "Stop, thief!"

240.27 Landru, the Bluebeard of France
Henri-Désiré Landru, a French serial killer who murdered at least ten wives between 1915 and 1919, preyed upon middle-aged widows with financial assets. He was accused of disposing of the bodies by dismembering them and burning the parts in a stove.

240.32 Du Barry skipped in . . .
Jeanne Bécu, Comtesse Du Barry, a courtesan of illegitimate birth, was the mistress of Louis XV from 1768 until his death in 1774. His queen was Marie Leszcynska of Poland.

241.11 Malmaison . . . Passy . . . St-Cloud
All places of interest in Paris: Malmaison was the residence of the Empress Josephine from her divorce in 1809 until her death in 1814; Passy, a residential district with a large English colony, was favored by artists and writers; several events of importance took place in St-Cloud, including the assassination of Henri III in 1589 and the marriage of Bonaparte to Marie Louise in 1810.

241.26 Château-Thierry
In a battle beginning in late May 1918, advance troops of the US Third Division met and defeated German forces near the French village of Château-Thierry. This was the opening engagement of the Aisne Offensive: a subsequent attempt by the Germans to move toward Vaux and Belleau Wood was halted, also by US troops, on 4 June. These victories, among the first for American forces in the war, were greeted with much exuberance by the home press.

244.6 Crazy-looking kale . . . the real mazuma
Slang words for paper money. Kale is a leafy green vegetable; *mazuma* is a derivative of *mezuma/mezumen*, Yiddish for "cash."

"Presumption"

251.18   San Juan Hill

During the spring and summer of 1898, the US and Spain fought a brief war over influence in Cuba. On 1 July the Rough Riders, under the command of Leonard Wood and Theodore Roosevelt, made a famous and widely publicized charge against the Spanish at San Juan Hill. The war ended on 12 August.

251.19   Kenesaw Mountain Landis

This American judge (1866–1944) was appointed commissioner of baseball following the "Black Sox" scandal in the 1919 World Series. Known for his aversion to socialism, Landis had earlier sentenced William D. "Big Bill" Haywood to a twenty-year prison term for labor agitation—a sentence that was later reversed by the US Supreme Court. Landis was named for Kennesaw [sic] Mountain in Georgia, the site of a Civil War battle in which his father lost a leg.

252.1   Prince of Wales suit

Edward, Prince of Wales, made various articles of men's clothing popular during the 1920s. He believed in "soft dressing" and often appeared in wide, side-creased trousers and unlined double-breasted jackets. He favored belts rather than braces and was frequently seen in woolly pullovers.

253.37   his D.K.E. pin

Members of Delta Kappa Epsilon, a men's social fraternity at many American colleges, are known as Dekes. To ask a young woman to wear one's fraternity pin was a step toward engagement for marriage.

262.27   Back Bay . . . Emerson and Whittier

The Back Bay section of Boston, with its broad avenues and handsome houses, was the most fashionable residential area of the city. Ralph Waldo Emerson (1803–82) and John Greenleaf Whittier (1807–92) were respected literary figures in Cambridge and Boston.

264.35   Liberty Bonds

These US government bonds, issued to help finance American participation in the First World War, paid 3.5 percent interest. They were authorized by the First Liberty Loan Act, passed by Congress in April 1917, and were sometimes sold door-to-door during bond drives.

268.11   the "Transcript"

The *Boston Transcript*, founded 1830, was the most traditional and conservative of the city's newspapers; important social news was reported in the society section. See T. S. Eliot's poem "The *Boston Evening Transcript*."

272.25   portière

A curtain that hangs over a door or passageway to prevent draughts or to serve as a screen.

"The Adolescent Marriage"

279.23   Chestnut Hill

This community for wealthy and socially prominent Bostonians was developed by such North Shore families as the Cabots, Lowells, Saltonstalls, and Lawrences between 1880 and 1910. Chestnut Hill was connected to the city by the Beacon Street extension railway.

281.28   Boston Tech

From 1861 until 1916, Boston Tech (located near Copley Square) was the major college of engineering and technical studies in the city. In 1916 the college changed its name to the Massachusetts Institute of Technology (MIT) and moved to nearby Cambridge. The name "Boston Tech" continued to be used during the next decade or so. See the gloss for MIT in " 'The Sensible Thing.' "

289.1   Rudolf Rassendale

Llewellyn means Rudolf Rassendyll, the hero of *The Prisoner of Zenda* (1894), Anthony Hope's most popular novel, later transformed into a successful play by Edward Rose. Rudolf, a young English gentleman, bears a marked resemblance to the king of Ruritania (a fictional land). Through a series of accidents and coincidences, he impersonates the king and becomes romantically involved with Flavia, the king's betrothed—hence the reference in this story.

"The Dance" ["In a Little Town"]

297.20   corn-drinking recklessness

These Southern men drink corn liquor, also called "moonshine" or "white lightning" or "bust head," a potent concoction distilled from corn mash and sold by bootleggers.

298.17 Baby Panic of 1921

A short, severe post-war recession caused by industrial overproduction and defense cuts. This panic was marked by widespread wage cuts; in August 1921 unemployment reached 5.7 million in the US.

304.12 began the vamp

In music, a vamp is a simple accompaniment improvised to fit a song—not to be confused with the same word (a shortened form of "vampire") used in Fitzgerald's day to refer to a fast, flirtatious girl.

304.24 "Good Night, Ladies"

A traditional tune, of uncertain authorship and adjustable lyrics, played by a band or orchestra at the end of the evening. The song is mentioned also in "The Love Boat," later in this volume.

"Your Way and Mine"

314.8 Elmira . . . Utica

Elmira, the home town of Henry McComas, was a small, quiet city in the Chemung Valley south of the Finger Lakes district in New York. Mark Twain's wife, Olivia Landon, was from Elmira; they were married there in 1870 and summered in a family home in Elmira for twenty years. Utica, New York (several paragraphs along), where Stella McComas teaches physical culture in the public schools, was a less attractive place—a rough industrial town located along the Mohawk River in the center of the state. Many of its inhabitants were working-class Irish and Italians; the primary industries in the town were textiles and firearms. The novelist Harold Frederic, author of *The Damnation of Theron Ware* (1896), was born in Utica in 1856 and began his writing career as a newspaperman in the city.

314.10 Panic of 1907

The last major US bank panic before the crash in 1929 occurred in the autumn of 1907, during the presidency of Theodore Roosevelt. The Knickerbocker Trust and the Westinghouse Electric Company both failed in October, causing stock market prices to plummet and depositors to make runs on their banks. J. P. Morgan and other financiers restored order by moving money from strong institutions to weak ones. In the wake of this panic, the US Congress passed the Aldrich-Vreeland Act of 1908, a stop-gap measure that eased credit and put additional money into circulation.

322.8   battle of the Somme

This battle in July 1916, near the Somme River in northern France, was one of the most costly in the First World War. It was a joint British and French assault on German forces; the attack failed and resulted in the loss of some 58,000 allied troops. The use of barbed wire by the Germans was particularly effective at the Somme.

327.15   the heroes of Ethel M. Dell

Ethel M. Dell was the nom de plume of Ethel Mary Savage (1881–1939), a reclusive English writer of best-selling romances. Dell's novels, usually set in India or in other British colonial possessions, were racy for the time. To amuse themselves, her cousins took copies of her novels and marked the multitudinous occurrences of the words *passion*, *tremble*, *pant*, and *thrill*.

"Jacob's Ladder"

333.–   "Jacob's Ladder"

In Genesis 28:10–22, Jacob (son of Isaac and Rebecca, brother of Esau) dreams of a great ladder, stretching from heaven to earth, with angels ascending and descending upon it. Fitzgerald seems to have intended only a general connection between this scriptural passage and his story. He might have wanted to call attention to Jacob Booth's idealized dreams about Jenny Prince; he might have wanted to emphasize Jacob's wish to marry Jenny, since the biblical Jacob was a great patriarch, fathering eleven children and living to the age of 147 (Genesis 46:29–48). Fitzgerald might also have known the hymn "We Are Climbing Jacob's Ladder"—likely of African American origin but frequently sung in Protestant churches.

335.31   Baffin's Bay

Probably Baffin Bay, the body of water lying between the Northwest Territories of Canada and Greenland, though possibly Fitzgerald had in mind Baffin's Bay on the Gulf Coast of Texas. Or he might have been familiar with "Hurrah for Baffin's Bay," a song of nautical nonsense from the 1903 musical version of *The Wizard of Oz*, a production often staged by traveling theatre companies of the time.

335.34   "Eas' Hunerd thuyty-thuyd . . . ."

Jenny is living with a girl friend near the southern edge of Harlem, then a mixed-race neighborhood. Because rents were low in Harlem, many clerks, shop-girls, and office workers lived there. Jenny's accent betrays her low social origins; as the story progresses her diction becomes neutral, and her accent disappears—except at moments when she becomes upset or emotional. Professionally a shift in accent would have been important to Jenny, since the "talkies" (motion pictures with sound tracks) were making their debut in 1927, the year in which "Jacob's Ladder" was set and published. Some Hollywood stars of the silent era—Douglas Fairbanks and Clara Bow, for example—saw their popularity fade when their voices did not translate well to the talkies.

336.31   Florida . . . land boom

Jacob sold his golf course at the right moment. Beginning in early 1924, frenzied optimism about the potential for tourism in Florida caused land prices there to skyrocket. (In 1925, beach property was selling for over 3,000 dollars a front foot.) Prices remained inflated until September 1926, when the bubble broke and left many investors bankrupt. The decline was brought about in part by a hurricane that damaged Miami heavily; economic analysts later saw the bursting of the Florida land bubble as a forecast of the stock-market crash of 1929.

337.24   Famous Players

Astoria Studios, on 36th Street in the Astoria section of Queens, was opened in September 1920 as the East Coast center for Famous Players-Lasky (later Paramount), one of the major movie studios in American cinema history. D. W. Griffith, mentioned later in the story, shot three of his films there; parts of Rudolph Valentino's *The Sheik* were filmed on its sound stages; the Marx Brothers made *The Cocoanuts* and *Animal Crackers* on the Astoria lot. Its great advantage was easy access to Broadway talent. Several young actors broke into the movies there, including Buddy Rogers and Thelma Todd. Famous Players acquired the screen rights to *This Side of Paradise* in 1923 but did not make a movie from the novel. The studio did produce a film of *The Great Gatsby* in 1926, starring Warner Baxter as Gatsby and Lois Wilson as Daisy. All references to Famous Players were removed from the text before it was published in the *Post*.

337.37   Norma Shearer

Fitzgerald knew Norma Shearer (1900–83), a popular movie actress during the 1920s and 1930s and the wife of the MGM producer Irving Thalberg, the original for Monroe Stahr in *The Last Tycoon*. Shearer, who played chic, sophisticated women on-screen, won an Oscar for her role in *The Divorcée* (1930). Stella Calman in Fitzgerald's 1932 short story "Crazy Sunday" is based on Shearer. Her career took a turn upward after she married Thalberg, whose influence in Hollywood was strong.

338.12 Great Neck

A town on the north shore of Long Island in which the Fitzgeralds lived from October 1922 until April 1924. Many celebrities lived in or near Great Neck, including Oscar Hammerstein, Groucho Marx, W. C. Fields, and Fanny Brice. Fitzgerald based West Egg in *The Great Gatsby* on Great Neck.

338.22 Queensboro Bridge

Astoria, a residential section in the northwestern part of Queens, is part of Long Island City. Both are reached via the Queensboro Bridge, a two-decked, cantilevered span that opened in 1907. The bridge passes over Blackwell's Island in the East River (today called Roosevelt Island), then the site of several prisons and reformatories—appropriate to the story, since mention will be made several paragraphs along of the women's prison at Auburn. Heading back over the bridge into Manhattan after dinner, Jacob and Jenny would have been treated to a spectacular view of the city, including the East Side docks and some of the early skyscrapers, though not the Chrysler Building or the Empire State Building, neither of which had yet been erected.

338.35 Constance Talmadge

Constance Talmadge (1900–73) was a teenager when she broke into the movies—as Jenny will be in this story. D. W. Griffith gave her the role of the Mountain Girl in his 1916 movie *Intolerance*; she played opposite Douglas Fairbanks in *The Matrimaniac* later that same year. During the mid-1920s, at the height of her popularity, she was paid almost $100,000 for each film in which she appeared. Fitzgerald was hired by United Artists in January 1927 to write a flapper movie for Talmadge; he moved to Hollywood and produced a treatment entitled "Lipstick," in which a young woman acquires a magic lipstick that makes men want to kiss her. The film was never produced; the treatment was published in the *Fitzgerald/Hemingway Annual 1978*. Talmadge, like Norma Shearer, glossed above, was married to a wealthy movie producer. Her husband, Joe Schenck, produced movies in both New York and Hollywood and was also a part owner of the Coney Island amusement park.

339.4 Auburn

Until 1933, the New York State Prison for Women was located at Auburn, in the Finger Lakes region of the state. The "Auburn System," famous in its day, called for heavy regimentation, silence at all times, and isolation of inmates at night in single cells.

339.26 the Lido

Fitzgerald probably has in mind the Club Lido, a swank establishment at Seventh Avenue and 52nd Street, where the dancers Bill Reardon and Edythe Baker demonstrated the latest steps, and where the torch singer Libby Holman held forth. Another possibility is the Lido-Venice, a fashionable restaurant at 35 East 53rd Street, patronised by Vanderbilts, Nasts, Dukes, Thaws, Whitneys, and Stuyvesants. The Lido-Venice opened in April 1924 but was closed twice in 1925 for serving liquor in violation of the Volstead Act.

341.6 corner soda-jerkers

Soda-jerkers (or soda-jerks) were young men, usually dressed in white jackets and caps, who made fizzy drinks and sundaes for customers at drug-store soda fountains. The work involved jerking a handle to release a stream of soda water into a glass—hence the name. The job carried no status but made it easy for the soda-jerk to meet young girls. Jacob, already jealous, is implying that Jenny's first boyfriends were low-class Lotharios who "mauled" her, i.e., subjected her to heavy sexual handling.

344.30 Statue of Civic Virtue

During the 1920s and 1930s this statue, designed by Frederick William MacMonnies, stood in front of City Hall in lower Manhattan. It was sculpted by the Piccirilli brothers, master marble carvers who emigrated to the US from Tuscany and maintained studios in the Bronx. (Attilio and Furio Piccirilli sculpted the two lions that flank the front steps of the New York Public Library.) The Statue of Civic Virtue, which depicted an unclad hero surrounded by writhing mermaids, was considered a scandalous work. Today it stands in Kew Gardens in Queens. Jacob's wire to Jenny ("New York desolate . . . The night clubs all closed. Black wreaths on the Statue of Civic Virtue . . .") recalls Nick's similar remarks to Daisy in *The Great Gatsby* (p. 12 of the 1925 Scribner's first edition).

344.37 "Kreutzer Sonata"

Jacob is listening to one of Beethoven's greatest violin sonatas, a work composed in 1803 and first performed in that year by the celebrated violinist George Bridgetower (1779–1860), with Beethoven as the accompanist. In 1890, relatively late in his career, Leo Tolstoy borrowed Beethoven's title for his novella *Kreitserova sonata*. Fitzgerald might have wanted readers to think of both the sonata and the novella. He knew the Tolstoy story in translation and made it part of Amory Blaine's reading in *This Side of Paradise* (p. 118 of the Cambridge edition). The novella, still thought to be controversial during the 1920s, addresses issues that are important in "Jacob's Ladder": whether marriage is necessary; whether sexual allure is inherently deceitful; whether homosexuality is acceptable; and whether art can function as a substitute for sexual involvement.

345.11 Ambassador Hotel

The Ambassador on Wilshire Boulevard was the most celebrated hotel in Hollywood during the 1920s and 1930s. The building had an Alhambra-like interior, with Moorish arches, ornate stone fireplaces, colorful tile floors, and a semi-tropical courtyard. The Fitzgeralds stayed there in 1927 while he was writing "Lipstick," the screen treatment mentioned above in the note on Constance Talmadge. They shared a four-apartment bungalow with the screen stars Carmel Myers and John Barrymore and the writer Carl Van Vechten.

347.21 Grauman's Theatre

The showman Sid Grauman (1879–1950) operated several motion-picture theatres in downtown Los Angeles, including the Rialto, the Metropolitan, and the Million Dollar; but Fitzgerald has in mind here one of the two theatres that Grauman built on Hollywood Boulevard (see the reference three sentences along in the story). The first of these was the Egyptian Theatre, decorated with hieroglyphics and paintings of Egyptian figures, all inspired by the discovery of King Tut's tomb. The Egyptian Theatre opened on 18 October 1922 with the first-ever Hollywood movie première—of *Robin Hood*, starring Douglas Fairbanks. Grauman's Chinese Theatre, also on Hollywood Boulevard, opened on 18 May 1927, three months before "Jacob's Ladder" appeared in the *Post*. Fitzgerald would not have seen the Chinese Theatre in its finished state—by the time it opened he had returned to Europe—but the theatre was under construction while he was living in Hollywood in January 1927, and he might later have seen photographs of the finished building. The Chinese Theatre was designed to resemble a large red pagoda; beginning in the 1930s, many popular Hollywood stars put their signatures, handprints, and footprints in wet concrete in the forecourt of the theatre.

347.25   the thin rialto of Hollywood Boulevard
A rialto is a theatre district or marketplace. The name derives from Rialto, an island and district in Venice; a popular marketplace is located in the vicinity of the Rialto bridge.

355.8   the Colony
The Colony, at 667 Madison Avenue, was known for its upstairs gambling club. Customers included prominent gangsters and gamblers, among them Arnold Rothstein, the original for Wolfsheim in *The Great Gatsby*. During the early 1920s the restaurant was used as a rendezvous by adulterous couples: gangsters would bring their molls, and members of the upper crust would arrive with their demi-mondaines. Because Prohibition was in effect, alcohol was served in demitasse cups; the liquor supply was kept in a service elevator so that it could be whisked upstairs whenever the city inspectors arrived. By 1926 (now having shifted its entrance to 61st Street) the Colony had lost most of its shady clientele and had become a favorite restaurant for the socially elite, including members of the Vanderbilt, Widener, McCormick, Whitney, and Astor families. Jacob takes Jenny to the Colony shortly after it has shed its unsavory image, though memories of its former reputation might linger. The reference to the restaurant was excised between the surviving typescript and publication of the story in the *Post*.

356.28   Plaza Hotel . . . 59th Street to Columbus
Circle . . . Broadway . . . Capitol Theatre
Jake says goodbye to Jenny in the lobby of the Plaza, then leaves the hotel and walks west along 59th Street to Columbus Circle. He turns left and walks down Broadway to 51st Street, where he enters the enormous Capitol Theatre, a 4,000-seat auditorium built in 1919 by a group of investors headed by Major Edward J. Bowes. The Capitol was opulent and showy: it had a huge wood-paneled lobby with a marble staircase, and its foyer was illuminated by three rock-crystal chandeliers salvaged from the old Sherry's restaurant on Fifth Avenue. Its manager, the showman Samuel "Roxy" Rothapfel, later built the huge, ornate Roxy Theatre further down Broadway, just north of Times Square.

"The Love Boat"

359.7 "Babes in the Wood" . . . "Moonlight Bay"
Two romantic songs from Fitzgerald's teenage years. "Babes in the Wood" was a brother–sister duet (music by Jerome Kern, lyrics by Schuyler Greene) from the 1915 Broadway musical *Very Good Eddie*. Fitzgerald used lyrics from the song and appropriated its title, slightly altered, for his short story "Babes in the Woods," first published in the *Nassau Literary Magazine* (May 1917), then revised for the *Smart Set* (September 1919), and finally incorporated into *This Side of Paradise* (1920). Fitzgerald alludes to the song later in the story, at 367.29: "while the enchanted silence spread over them like leaves over the babes in the woods." *Very Good Eddie* is based on the story of Hansel and Gretel; the two children in the musical fall asleep in the forest, after singing "Babes in the Wood," and in most stagings are then covered by leaves falling from above. "Moonlight Bay," with music by Percy Weinrich and words by Edward Madden, was a romantic tune popular in 1912. Madden also wrote the lyrics for the 1909 sing-along hit "By the Light of the Silvery Moon," with music by Gus Edwards.

365.14 "Hidden-ball stuff! . . . Save it for Haughton. I'm
G-Gardner, you're Bradlee and Mahan—Hip!"
Bill and his inebriated friends are organizing themselves to make a rush on the high-school boys. They are Harvard men: the references are to the famous Harvard football teams of 1912–15, which won thirty-three games in a row. Percy Haughton was the coach; Ned Mahan, Frederick Bradlee, and Henry Gardner were members of the backfield. "Hidden-ball stuff" would be a deceptive play, designed to conceal which back was carrying the football. The word "hip!" would be the last call in the snap count, signaling to the center to hike the ball and begin the play.

369.27 met her on the Lido and wooed her on golf courses
Fitzgerald means the Lido Golf Club, an establishment for wealthy sportsmen built between 1914 and 1917 on Long Beach Island by a group of investors that included Otto Kahn and Cornelius Vanderbilt. The club, which borders Lido Beach, became a top-flight venue for golf, ranking with Shinnecock Hills and the Garden City Golf Club. A restaurant and a dance club in New York City, both also called the Lido, are identified in the annotations for "Jacob's Ladder."

373.3   steamboat on the Thames

The Thames River, in southern Connecticut, empties into Long Island Sound. Groton, Connecticut, mentioned several paragraphs along, is a ship-building and port city near the mouth of the Thames.

375.10   John Harvard . . . Eli Yale

The founding benefactors of Harvard University and Yale University. John Harvard was a clergyman in Charlestown, Massachusetts; Elihu Yale was a merchant who grew wealthy through trade with the Far East. Yale men, and their sports teams, are called Elis.

376.25   "May I have some of this?" he said.

Bill is "cutting in"—interrupting a dance between two partners to take the boy's place. This was common practice at the pre-war dances of his youth; pretty girls expected boys from the stag line to cut in. Now, eleven years after his graduation from college, Bill's behavior is old-fashioned and laughable to the teenagers.

377.32   Daddy Browning . . . Peaches

The teenagers are suggesting that Bill has a sexual itch for May. Edward "Daddy" Browning was a 51-year-old millionaire who made headlines in April 1926 by marrying Frances "Peaches" Heenan, a plump 15-year-old whom he met at a high-school dance. Browning had earlier helped Peaches to land a spot in Earl Carroll's *Vanities*, a girlie show on West 49th Street, but Peaches had gained twenty pounds and lost her position. The marriage did not endure: Peaches left Daddy in October 1926 and sued for divorce, alleging mental cruelty and sexual perversion. (Her most sensational charge was that he kept a honking gander in their bedroom.) The divorce trial was fare for the tabloids. Peaches was found not credible by the judge; she was granted a divorce but received little money or property. Four days after the decision, she signed a $100,000 contract to go on the vaudeville stage. She appeared (in a scanty outfit, and with a pet gander) and told of her adventures; vendors at her performances sold printed copies of the divorce-trial transcript for 15 cents. The references to Daddy Browning and Peaches appear in the holograph draft of this scene and in the carbon of the setting copy, but they were cut before the story appeared in the *Post*. See the introduction, pp. xxx–xxxiii. See also Gregg Baptista, "Restoring a Scandal to 'The Love Boat': Daddy, Peaches, and *Tender Is the Night*," *F. Scott Fitzgerald Review*, 4 (2005).

"The Bowl"

381.4   Antonines

A collective name for a group of Roman emperors of the second century: Antoninus Pius, Marcus Aurelius, Verus, and Commodus.

381.6   George Bellows

George Wesley Bellows (1882–1925), a pupil of Robert Henri, was a second-generation member of the Ashcan School of American artists. His realistic paintings and lithographs of urban scenes and sporting events (including early football games) have remained famous; his best-known painting is "A Stag at Sharkey's," which depicts a bloody boxing match.

381.13   Taft

Taft, founded in 1890 in Watertown, Connecticut, is a boys' preparatory school. In the passage that follows, Fitzgerald is remembering his one moment of glory as a prep football player, in October 1912, when he starred in the victory of his own school, Newman, over Kingsley. Other prep schools mentioned in this story include Exeter, Lawrenceville, and St. Regis (a fictional school attended by Amory Blaine in *This Side of Paradise*). Bucknell, Lehigh, Swarthmore, and Notre Dame (also later in the story) are American colleges whose teams played Princeton at football.

381.21   Keene . . . pole vaulter

Fitzgerald might be playing with names here. The track coach at Princeton during his years at the university was Keene Fitzpatrick, whose team was the first to beat Yale in a dual meet.

382.5   Yale Bowl

This elliptical football stadium, modeled on the amphitheater at Pompeii, opened on 21 November 1914 for the Yale–Harvard game. With a seating capacity of over 70,000, the Yale Bowl was then one of the largest venues for football in the country. Its walls were thirty feet high; its seats, placed end-to-end, would have stretched for thirty miles. Ivy League colleges were major football powers in the US before the First World War; the only games that truly mattered for Yale, Harvard, and Princeton, however, were those played against each other.

382.25   "Stob Ted Coy!"

The drunken spectator is lost in the past. Edward H. "Ted" Coy, one of Fitzgerald's boyhood heroes, played football at Yale from 1906 to 1909, well before the years in which this story is set. Ted Fay, a character in Fitzgerald's 1928 story "The Freshest Boy," is loosely based on Coy.

383.2 "I'll speak to Roper . . . ."

Bill Roper coached the Princeton football team in 1906–8, 1910–11, and 1919–30.

384.26 Ralph Henry Barbour

Barbour (1870–1944) was a prolific writer of sports stories for boys. He emphasized school spirit and character-building in his narratives, many of which were set at exclusive boys' prep schools or at Ivy-League colleges. His novels include *The Half-Back* (1899), *Behind the Line* (1902), *The Crimson Sweater* (1906), and *Forward Pass* (1908). Amory Blaine, in *This Side of Paradise*, reads Barbour's *For the Honor of the School* (1900).

384.27 kick goal . . . fair catch . . . field goal

In American football, a touchdown is worth six points; in Fitzgerald's day, a player would "kick goal" after the touchdown for an additional point. (This kick, which must pass through the uprights of the goal in order to count, is now called the "extra point.") Today the ball is snapped by the center to the holder, who positions the ball for the kicker. In the early years of football, however, the kick was often executed by a single player who "drop-kicked" the ball through the uprights—i.e., dropped it on the ground and kicked it on the up-bounce. Then, as now, a player signaled for a "fair catch" of a punt by holding up his arm. If he caught the ball before it hit the ground, players from the opposing squad were not allowed to tackle him. Once he caught the ball he could not advance it. If he missed the catch he was fair game, and an opponent could recover possession of the ball for his team—an important point in this story. A successful "field goal" is a three-point kick, from any spot on the field, which goes through the uprights. Field goals were often drop-kicked in Fitzgerald's day: in 1913 Hobey Baker, a football star at Princeton, salvaged a 3–3 tie with Yale by drop-kicking a field goal from forty-three yards out. Football, as Fitzgerald describes it in "The Bowl," was primarily a running game; the forward pass had only been made legal in 1906. Few substitutions were allowed, and most players performed on both offense and defense.

385.30 snake dance

After football games, fans of the winning team would form a long line, and each fan would place his hands on the waist or shoulders of the fan in front of him. The aggregation, thus linked, would execute a joyous, sinuous "snake dance."

386.3 Midnight Frolic

Lightly clad showgirls from Florenz Ziegfeld's *Follies* were featured in the floor shows at the Midnight Frolic, a glitzy supper club on the roof of the New Amsterdam Theatre, 214 West 42nd Street. (The theatre is mentioned several paragraphs along.) Fitzgerald invokes the Midnight Frolic in some of his other writings, including the 1920 stories "Myra Meets His Family" and "The Offshore Pirate," and in the 1934 reminiscence "'Show Mr. and Mrs. F. to Number—'", written with his wife, Zelda. Fitzgerald's most memorable evening at the Midnight Frolic occurred on 8 June 1915, when he escorted his teenaged sweetheart Ginevra King to the club—chaperoned, alas, by her mother.

386.8 strip of court plaster

An adhesive bandage, or "band-aid," or "sticking plaster." The term "court plaster" originates with the small, round, black adhesive patches (which mimicked beauty spots) worn by members of the royal court in London in the late eighteenth century. The term "court plaster" was slightly archaic by the time Fitzgerald published "The Bowl"; perhaps he meant to suggest a connection between Dolly's "small and fetching" bandage and the beauty marks worn by the courtiers.

387.20 Her brother was killed . . .

In the early years of the twentieth century, football players often wore no helmets and used few pads. Serious injuries were common, and deaths were not unknown. Eighteen college players died from football injuries in 1905, causing US President Theodore Roosevelt to call a meeting of representatives from Harvard, Yale, and Princeton and to urge them to reform the game—or he would have it declared illegal. A few changes were made to the rules for 1906 (the most important being to outlaw the "flying wedge" formation), but football remained a dangerous sport.

388.5 sporting extra . . . green sheet
TIGER . . . BULLDOG

Metropolitan newspapers, sold by news vendors on the city streets, produced sporting "extras" (single or double sheets folded, usually printed on colored paper) immediately after important athletic contests. The Tiger and Bulldog in the headline are the school mascots—the tiger for Princeton and the bulldog for Yale. The chorus girls at the New Amsterdam Theatre, several paragraphs along, are dressed in orange and black (the Princeton school colors) or in "Yale blue."

390.3   the men to whom we were to hand over Josephine and Miss Thorne

It would have been accepted practice for Dolly and the narrator to "hand over" their dates, by prearrangement, to other men midway through the evening—if Dolly were fatigued from the game, for example. These substitutes would be friends (often underclassmen from their eating club or social set) who would escort the women home.

390.21   Miss Lillian Lorraine

Eulallen De Jacques (1892–1955), a beauty of tempestuous disposition, took the stage name Miss Lillian Lorraine when she began performing in the Ziegfeld *Follies*. She was a headliner at the Midnight Frolic, a popular actress in vaudeville, and a star in stage shows for other producers. For several years she was Florenz Ziegfeld's mistress, but she turned down his marriage proposals, once marrying her chauffeur simply to spite Ziegfeld. Her heavy drinking and violent temper wrecked her career.

391.16   Sophomore year is the most dramatic at Princeton . . .

Princeton has no social fraternities; the eating clubs, for juniors and seniors, are an approximate equivalent. In the spring of each year (during Fitzgerald's time at the university) the clubs conducted rushes and, during Bicker Week in March, offered membership bids to sophomores. The clubs were ranked variously by seniority and prestige; it mattered greatly to many sophomores which bids they received—if they received any at all. Most of the clubs were, and are still, housed in handsome buildings on Prospect Avenue. Fitzgerald belonged to University Cottage Club. Other honors for sophomores were announced each spring: the narrator's selection a few lines below to the board of the *Princetonian* (the student newspaper) would have put him in the running for the editorship during his senior year.

391.31   spring practice

College football teams conduct practices in the spring to condition the players and to install new offensive and defensive schemes for the fall season.

392.25   She was coming out in Washington next fall.
Young women of high social class "came out" (were formally introduced to society) at elaborate debutante balls in the fall and spring of each year. A girl usually came out shortly after she turned eighteen; she was then considered eligible for marriage.

393.5   Stony Brook
A Quaker community to the west of Princeton, named for a nearby stream.

393.24   Babbitt
An allusion to *Babbitt* (1922), the bestselling satirical novel by Sinclair Lewis in which the eponymous protagonist is a caricature of the conventional American businessman.

394.3   Ram's Point, Long Island
Fitzgerald probably has in mind Ram Head on Ram Island, across Coecles Harbor from Shelter Island near the tip of Long Island.

395.17   Nassau Street
The major thoroughfare in the town of Princeton. The university faces Nassau Street; the side opposite the university is lined with restaurants, shops, and bookstores, many of which cater to the college students.

396.19   the Navy game
This would be the football game with the United States Naval Academy at Annapolis, Maryland, then a regular opponent for Princeton and other Ivy-League schools.

398.8   Jack Dempsey
Jack Dempsey (1895–1983), nicknamed the "Manassa Mauler," held the world heavyweight boxing title from 1919 to 1926. He was a popular sports figure, much idolized by boys and young men during the 1920s.

398.25   Princeton Junction
To reach Princeton by rail, one leaves the train at Princeton Junction and takes a spur line into town. The train on this spur line was then (and is still) known as the "Dinky."

398.30   University Field

In Fitzgerald's time, this was a large field used for sports practices, rallies, and other college events.

398.33   Daisy Cary

Daisy is based on Lois Moran (1909–90), a beautiful young movie actress whom Fitzgerald met and admired in Hollywood in 1927. Jenny Prince in "Jacob's Ladder" and Rosemary Hoyt in *Tender Is the Night* are also versions of Lois Moran. (In early drafts of *Tender Is the Night*, Rosemary is called "Jenny Prince.") The incident, later in the story, in which Daisy must dive repeatedly into a lagoon on a movie set appears again in *Tender Is the Night*.

404.22   Ritz . . . Biltmore . . . Ambassador Hotel

Three luxury hotels. The Ritz and the Biltmore have been glossed earlier; the Ambassador, where Daisy is staying, was a new caravansary on the east side of Park Avenue, occupying the entire block between 51st and 52nd Streets. Queen Marie of Rumania was one of its first guests.

"Magnetism"

406.13   the red stains of the mercurochrome era

The scratches and scrapes of these children have been treated with what was then a relatively new medicine—tincture of mercurochrome, a topical antiseptic discovered in 1919 by Hugh Young, a doctor at Johns Hopkins University. Mercurochrome leaves a red-orange stain on the skin.

411.23   Klieg lights

Hot, bright, carbon-arc lights invented in 1911 by John and Anton Kliegl, German-born brothers who also created scenic effects for theatre productions. Klieg lights were used on nearly all movie sets; lengthy exposure to the lights could cause a form of conjunctivitis called "Klieg eye."

411.33   the old Griffith Studios at Mamaroneck

In 1919, in an effort to escape industry control over his productions, the director D. W. Griffith joined with Mary Pickford, Douglas Fairbanks, and Charlie Chaplin to form United Artists. He moved his company from Hollywood to a new studio located in Mamaroneck, on the north shore of Long Island Sound. Among the films made there was *Way Down East* (1920), starring Lillian Gish and Richard Barthelmess.

413.26   Ziegfeld shows . . . proms at Yale
Like many aspiring actresses, Kay has performed in the productions of
Florenz Ziegfeld, whose Midnight Frolic floor show is glossed in the annotations for "The Bowl." Pretty young actresses were sometimes escorted to
prom weekends by boys at Yale, Princeton, and other comparable schools,
as Daisy Cary is in "The Bowl."

415.15–16   the Duncan sisters
In 1923 the Vaudeville stars Rosetta and Vivian Duncan began performing
in *Topsy and Eva*, a musical based on *Uncle Tom's Cabin*. The production ran for forty-seven weeks in Chicago and lasted for four months on
Broadway, then went on a national road tour. The Duncan sisters were in
Hollywood in 1927 (the year in which "Magnetism" was published) to con-
vert their stage show into an eighty-minute movie; parts of this film were
directed by D. W. Griffith. They also appeared in the movie *It's a Great Life*
(1929), directed by Sam Wood.

418.34   the Southern California varsity as extras
Fitzgerald means the varsity football team at the University of Southern
California in Los Angeles. Howard Jones, who coached the team, sometimes
secured summer jobs for his players in the movie industry. The film star John
Wayne (1907–79) was a lineman at Southern Cal during his college years;
he got his start in the industry in a job arranged by Jones—as an assistant
prop man on a movie directed by John Ford.

420.27   the Cocoanut Grove
A dancing and dining club in the Ambassador Hotel in Hollywood, popular with movie people and famous for its indoor waterfall and its papier-
mâché palm trees and cocoanuts. These props, saved from the set of
Rudolph Valentino's film *The Sheik*, had been installed amongst the tables.
Stuffed monkeys with electrified amber eyes swung from the palm trees; the
southernmost wall of the club was painted with a moonwashed Hawaiian
landscape.

422.34   the Fairbankses . . . were not keeping up a pose
The film stars Douglas Fairbanks (1883–1939) and Mary Pickford (1893–
1979), wed in 1920, were known to have one of the strongest marriages in
Hollywood—though it eventually ended in 1935. They lived at "Pickfair,"
a refurbished hunting lodge in Beverly Hills that boasted an artificial beach,

riding stables, and a boating lagoon. The Fitzgeralds were guests there in 1927.

424.20   San Quentin prison
Originally built in 1852, San Quentin (located north of San Francisco) was reserved for especially violent criminals. Between 1893 and 1942 some 215 inmates were executed there by hanging.

424.30   the old Realart Studio
A movie studio in downtown Hollywood where many early silent classics were filmed. Realart became a subsidiary of Paramount in the early 1920s.

ILLUSTRATIONS

Plate 1 Front panel of the dust jacket for the Scribners 1926 first edition. The designer, Cleonike Damianakes, who signed his work "Cleon," also supplied the jacket art for three Hemingway titles published by Scribners: *In Our Time*, *The Sun Also Rises*, and *A Farewell to Arms*. Fitzgerald Papers, Princeton University Libraries.

Plate 2 Publicity photograph of the movie actress Lois Moran, the original for Jenny Prince in "Jacob's Ladder" and for Rosemary Hoyt in *Tender Is the Night*. Courtesy Tim Young and Richard Buller.

Plate 3 Cover of the testimony transcript in the Daddy Browning–Peaches Heenan divorce trial, showing Peaches in her stage outfit and the gander in hat and bow tie. These transcripts were sold at Peaches' vaudeville performances. The divorce case is mentioned in "The Love Boat." Reproduced from the copy in the University of Minnesota Law Library.

Plate 4 Advertising poster for the Midnight Frolic, a Florenz Ziegfeld extravaganza presented on the rooftop of the New Amsterdam Theatre at 214 West 42nd Street. Dolly Harlan and his friends take their dates to the Midnight Frolic in "The Bowl."

APPENDIX 1

PASSAGES CUT FROM "THE RICH BOY"

The three passages below were cut between the surviving typescript of "The Rich Boy" (which Fitzgerald mailed to Harold Ober in early August 1925 from Paris, and which bears his final revisions for the *Red Book* version) and the version prepared for *All the Sad Young Men*. The first passage, about the social ostracism of "a Jew named Hirsh," appears in neither the serial version nor the collected text.

The second and third passages were removed by Fitzgerald at the request of his friend Ludlow Fowler, who was the model for Anson Hunter. Fowler asked that the excisions be made before the text was published in *Red Book*; but Fitzgerald, in Europe, was unable to have the passages removed, and they appear in the serial text. Fowler worried that the passages might identify him as the original for Anson. Fitzgerald did cut these two passages in galleys before publishing the story in *All the Sad Young Men*. See the introduction, xxii–xxiii.

1. In the typescript, this passage (about Anson's uncle, Robert Hunter) follows "Wheatley Hills" at 18.6 of the Cambridge text:

His favorite stories had to do with the menace of socialism and how a Jew named Hirsh had tried to get into a certain fashionable Club on Long Island.

"First he went to a riding school and taught himself to ride and by God the fool wasn't scared of anything. I went out with him one afternoon and his horse threw him about three times to the mile, and, by God, the fool got up and mounted and tried it again. I got to like the man. I took him aside afterwards and I said 'Look here, Hirsh, these people are making a fool of you. You'll never get into that club if you stay down here twenty years. I'm telling it to you because I like you.' I said 'You're a man!'"

2. In the typescript, this passage follows "restless dissatisfaction" at 17.7 of the Cambridge text:

There was a pretty debutante he knew in his car and for two days they took their meals together. At first he told her a little about Paula and invented an esoteric incompatibility that was keeping them apart. The girl was of a wild impulsive nature and she was flattered by Anson's confidences. Like Kipling's soldier he might have possessed himself of most of her before he reached New York, but, luckily he was sober and kept control.

3. In the typescript, these two sentences follow "wild night before" at 17.35 of the Cambridge text:

Once, by some mutual instinct several children got up from the front row and moved to the last. He told this story frequently and it was usually greeted with hilarious laughter.

APPENDIX 2

COMPOSITION, PUBLICATION, AND EARNINGS

Dates of publication and amounts earned for the stories are taken from Fitzgerald's correspondence (especially that with Harold Ober, his literary agent) and from his professional ledger. Publication and price are for first US serial appearances only; the fees are those paid before Ober's commission was deducted.

Fitzgerald sold "Absolution" directly to H. L. Mencken, the editor of the *American Mercury*, and did not use Harold Ober as an intermediary. Fitzgerald did not record a price paid to him for the story in his ledger, but Mencken was unable to pay rates comparable to those offered by such mass-circulation magazines as the *Post* and *Red Book*. In 1932, for example, Mencken could pay Fitzgerald only $200 for "Crazy Sunday."

Much of the information in this appendix appeared first in Bryant Mangum's *A Fortune Yet: Money in the Art of F. Scott Fitzgerald's Short Stories* (New York: Garland, 1991). Abbreviations of magazine titles are as follows: *Saturday Evening Post* (*Post*), *Metropolitan* (*Metro*), *Woman's Home Companion* (*WHC*), *Hearst's International* (*Hearst's*), and *American Mercury* (*AmMerc*).

ALL THE SAD YOUNG MEN (1926)

Title	Composed	Published	Price
"The Rich Boy"	Mar.–Aug. 1925	*Red Book* 46 (Jan.–Feb. 1926)	$3,500
"Winter Dreams"	Sept. 1922	*Metro* 56 (Dec. 1922)	$900
"The Baby Party"	Feb. 1924	*Hearst's* 47 (Feb. 1925)	$1,500
"Absolution"	June 1923	*AmMerc* 2 (June 1924)	
"Rags Martin-Jones"	Dec. 1923	*McCall's* 51 (July 1924)	$1,750

"The Adjuster"	Dec. 1924	*Red Book* 45 (Sept. 1925)	$2,000
"Hot and Cold Blood"	April 1923	*Hearst's* 44 (Aug. 1923)	$1,500
"'The Sensible Thing"	Nov. 1923	*Liberty* 1 (5 July 1924)	$1,750
"Gretchen's Forty Winks"	Jan. 1924	*Post* 196 (15 March 1924)	$1,200

ADDITIONAL STORIES

Title	*Composed*	*Published*	*Price*
"One of My Oldest Friends"	Mar. 1924	*WHC* 52 (Sept. 1925)	$1,750
"A Penny Spent"	July 1925	*Post* 198 (10 Oct. 1925)	$2,000
"'Not in the Guidebook'"	Feb. 1925	*WHC* 52 (Nov. 1925)	$1,750
"Presumption"	Nov. 1925	*Post* 198 (9 Jan. 1926)	$2,500
"The Adolescent Marriage"	Dec. 1925	*Post* 198 (6 Mar. 1926)	$2,500
"The Dance"	Jan. 1926	*Red Book* 47 (June 1926)	$2,000
"Your Way and Mine"	Feb. 1926	*WHC* 54 (May 1927)	$1,750
"Jacob's Ladder"	June 1927	*Post* 200 (20 Aug. 1927)	$3,000
"The Love Boat"	Aug. 1927	*Post* 200 (8 Oct. 1927)	$3,500
"The Bowl"	Nov. 1927	*Post* 200 (21 Jan. 1928)	$3,500
"Magnetism"	Dec. 1927	*Post* 200 (3 Mar. 1928)	$3,500